o/7
c P

Oct 07

OCT   2002

FIC
SHIRLEY Shirley, John

Spider moon

DUE DATE

THIS DELUXE SIGNED EDITION OF

SPIDER MOON

IS LIMITED TO **1500** SIGNED COPIES

SPIDER MOON

SPIDER MOON

JOHN SHIRLEY

CEMETERY DANCE PUBLICATIONS

Baltimore
❖ 2002 ❖

Cemetery Dance Publications 2002
ISBN 1-58767-054-2

Dust Jacket Art: © 2002 by Paul Maurides
Dust Jacket Design: Gail Cross
Typesetting and Design: Bill Walker
Printed in the United States of America

Cemetery Dance Publications
P.O. Box 943
Abingdon, MD 21009
http://www.cemeterydance.com

10 9 8 7 6 5 4 3 2 1

FIRST EDITION

For Philo Drummond
and his arch rival,
Steve Wilcox

"I mixed myself up in everything that came along. It was the only way I could forget myself."
Doc Holliday to Bat Masterson in:
—*The Sunset Trail* (1905)

THE FIRST PART

Open the box, just open the box

1

That morning, like any morning, I brushed my teeth, gargled, showered, ate some Raisin Bran, drank some coffee while reading the lead paragraphs on the front page, and took the Muni to work in downtown San Francisco. A little later that day, I was going to the emergency room to see my son; a little later yet, I was getting drunk at the edge of a pool of blood.

The meeting with Maceburger, the Vice President of Publishing, took place right before I was notified that my son was dying. Thinking back on it, as I tell you this, it was like that information about Frankie was right there in the air, just hanging there like a headline suspended in space—barely out of view—as if I could almost see it from the corners of my eyes.

That's probably because Frankie had been headed that way for a while, in some kind of way, and I could *feel* him going down, despite all the reassurance from his counselor, and his Mom, and the soccer coach, and his English teacher—and from him.

Maybe that feeling was why, even though I hadn't got the news, the meeting went the way it did. But then, I was a book editor, sitting in an office with my superior, who was laying down the law, and that was always about me holding myself back. Reining myself in, tension on the leash.

I hadn't had that feeling of having to constantly hold myself back so much with old Ledbetter, though. Ledbetter, you see, had sold the company to these weasels not so long before. Old Ledbetter and I didn't agree half the time, but we understood each other.

"As you know, Slim," Maceburger was saying to me, "book publishing is changing—has already changed." He snapped his lower lip with his rabbity front teeth and slowly turned an empty Pepsi One can under his right hand, as if trying to screw it into the desk top.

For this meeting, he sat behind his leathertopped desk—a cue that was not lost on me—and Peter Eickoff from Marketing sat to Maceburger's right, on the leather sofa of the compact office. I sat at the apex of the triangle, in an office visitor's chair—the chair was another cue that found its way home. Cues and omens.

There was a window that might have showed summer in San Francisco, from about six stories up, but the curtains were closed, and the room was gloomy, might've as well been a room in New York City. That was almost an omen, too.

Maceburger wore a three-piece suit, the jacket over the back of his chair so that in his vest and shirt sleeves he could affect his notion of an actual publisher. I suppose, as an exec for Ledbetter, Maceburger was a publisher in some sense. The slick, pernicious prick.

Me, I wore jeans and cowboy boots and one of my cowboy shirts that day—the rusty-red one with the black, furbellowed panel in it along the top—and I mention it because I ended up wearing that same shirt for a bunch of days. And I wore glasses—these same glasses. Wire rims.

Which have come through an amazing lot of shit intact, whereas if I'd been just hanging around the house, I probably would have sat on them and broke them.

Eickoff nervously patted his threadbare blond comb-over, and looked at me. Then looked back at the clipboard on his knee and waited. He wore a butter yellow shirt, a brown tie, brown slacks, loafers. Prominent wedding band. He had one leg tightly crossed, almost knotted over the other, and he seemed like he was breathing a little too fast; like if I stood up too quickly, he might scream.

I'd always pictured marketing guys and advertising execs as flippant, sleekly dressed young bachelor types, who skied on their vacations, all tans and smirky grins and a glibness that passed for confidence. And they mostly were like that. But Eickoff seemed more like a monochrome, witless accountant, wound just a little too tight.

He was wound way tighter than I realized. I mis-read the guy. Lots of people did.

Maceburger was polite but also unfailingly disdainful.... Do you sense my hostility to these two guys? You're not mistaken. It wasn't because they were the business guys and I was the editor with the glamorous Critical Faculties, the Understanding of the Artists.

No. It was because they sucked.

See, I was used to business guys. Mr. Ledbetter, my old boss—my boss for eleven underpaid but honorable years—was a business guy. He liked to make money, but he was not a slick, pernicious prick. In fact, he knew I'd done some time—less than two years, but real State Pen time—and he hired me anyway. He was consciously trying to give a guy a chance. He said it was because he'd read some reviews I'd written—I was the Dallas Morning Star's pet inmate book reviewer for awhile—and he liked them. That figured into it—but really he was just trying to give me a chance. Would this pernicious prick Maceburger have hired me eight months out of prison?

Fuck, no.

I thought about Meredith and Frankie and tried to get back on task. I dutifully chimed in, "Change can be good. Businesses need it."

"Ledbetter Books is still Ledbetter Books, though it has been purchased by Polymer International Industries," Maceburger went on.

I couldn't resist saying something to that. Which was maybe the first crack in my veneer. I should have maintained airtight integrity in my pressure suit. But I said, " It's still Ledbetter Books? Although...Mr. Ledbetter is no longer connected with Ledbetter Books, in any way. Except for his name."

I smiled to show it was a friendly observation. Though it wasn't.

"Right," Maceburger said, eyeing me speculatively. He looked at my cowboy boots. Every time I'd met him he always acted like he wanted to tell me not to wear the boots and then remembered the company had agreed to keep Mr Ledbetter's casual dress code. "...but uh—though we do want to maintain Mr. Ledbetter's, uh, deservedly respected standards, we have to face marketing realities."

I glanced at Eickoff. He was squirming a little, like he had to go to the bathroom. I felt like telling him, *Just get up and go, dammit.*

As I watched Eickoff, his eyes snapped to the window, and back to us. There was a distant sound of a siren, somewhere South of Market, and his hands tightened, knuckles white, on the arm rests. What was up with that?

"I...."Eickoff began. "There are, yes, in fact—certain realities...."

He seemed far away in that moment. As if trying to remember what those realities were.

I sensed some kind of hideous pressure in Eickoff, and took pity on him, turning my attention to Maceburger. "Who're we going to be realistic about first?" Thinking, even as I said it, that I really ought to gentle up my tone.

They could be thinking about getting "real" with *me,* after all. Ledbetter Books had been taken over. A take-over usually led to lay offs.

Maybe part of me was hoping they'd fire me. It might give me an excuse to go back to Austin. I'd been thinking about Texas a lot. The delicious contradictions of Texas.

In Austin, college town with college-rock scene, most people disdained cowboy boots and hats. So of course I'd had to be the guy that wore them. (I understood the cool of anti-cool way early). Lot of pride in barbecue in Austin, though. Secret "don't mess with Texas" feelings amongst those liberal-demo PhDs. Warm nights. Cicadas. Brash, noisy grackles like a gang of bratty winged children stealing your sandwich buns right off your plate at the picnic table behind the barbecue place where Janis Joplin used to wipe grease off that powerful whitetrash mouth and hoist her beer.

Bats at sunset, multitudes of them gushing, strobing up into the sky from under the bridge to the *oohs* of tourists, the *ee-ews* of kids holding their noses at the mustiness of a million guano sticky leather wings hitting the air at once.

Sudden changes of weather like a sultry woman showing her moods.

Undergrads laughing amiably at me in the college bars—where I was a half-assed grad student, already an older guy—because I talked earnestly about how westerns, in movies and books, were America's only true native artform except maybe for meatloaf: Perennial English major and binge crystal-sniffer Slim Purdoux sitting in the booth in his cowboy hat and boots holding forth about the honest romanticism of westerns; the "sacred austerity of instinct with a gun." Students in the early R.E.M. T-shirts laughing at me—and buying me drinks, and always glad to see me, though they insisted I was full of shit.

I wanted to go back.

But that was fantasy: I couldn't go back, because Meredith and Frankie were in San Francisco, in the little house she'd bought when she filed for divorce. She was invested in the foggy rolling hills of the Sunset District, she wasn't moving, and I wasn't going to move away from the boy, separation or no separation. I needed to see him safely to at least nineteen years old.

There had been no one to see me through, except Mom, the old man having vanished when I was nine. She was there as much as she had to be, and not a jot more.

Maceburger was nattering on about something. How the big book chains remaindered books in no time now, if they didn't sell fast enough. How we had to please the big book chains not the little stores which were dying out anyway. Darwinian publishing.

But I was still thinking about Texas—and Frankie. Wishing I could show Frankie all of Texas's rich embarrassments—like Crawford—and its embarrassment of riches, like Austin. But even if I could get Meredith to let me take him out of the state even for a visit—so far she'd refused, on the advice of her bitch of a Wiccan Lesbian therapist girlfriend—all my friends would've moved on by now. I was clean and sober hardworking Slim now, and I didn't take drugs anymore, and maybe the town wouldn't have that throb of intimate, laid back but relentlessly experimental energy now. And Austin was getting too big....

"The kind of books we need for the 21st century," Maceburger was saying, "are going to be...."

Books. I remembered reading to Frankie when he was little. He had an unquenchable thirst for stories, just good stories. Maybe he'd have become a storyteller, a writer, someday—something I'd wanted to do, and never seriously could...my standards being too high to tolerate my own writing.

I remembered going to father-son camp with him two years before. After the separation, I hadn't been able to afford it again. But that one summer we were happy. The two of us laughing at the chirpy drones of the summer camp staff; splashily paddling canoes, me and him, the two members of a two-member gang. I kept my authority, by a thread, but he was there with me; right there with me.... And then that winter his Mother decided I was a bad influence—on her and him both. And she kept me from seeing him much, after that, when she divorced me. And he never got over it.

Eickoff cleared his throat, glanced at Maceburger, who nodded almost imperceptibly.

A little red light went on inside me and I made myself listen.

"We're thinking," Eickoff said, looking hard at his clipboard, "that there isn't any room for Mark Dustin in the Ledbetter general fiction line, or Judith Mayfield."

"Say what?" Then I remembered: *Gently, gently.* I leaned back, and made a mild hand gesture that meant, *I understand, but after all...*and said: "We should remember that Mark Dustin *sells.* He has a following. *The New York Times* reviewers love him."

"He's been slipping," Maceburger said, shrugging. "Sales figures don't lie, Slim."

Eickoff wagged his head apologetically.

"It is a shame. I do read Dustin myself." He glanced apprehensively at Maceburger to see if this bit of self-revelation was approved. "But uh...."

I pointed out, "We don't give Dustin big advances. We actually make a profit on him!"

"I know." Eickoff stiffened, for no particular reason and seemed to concentrate hard on making himself relax, before finally going on. "But it's—a kind of a narrow profit. We have a mandate from Polymer— from the stockholders, really—to at least double the profit margin."

"To double.... At least?" I was genuinely amazed. I shouldn't have been.

Eickoff nodded stiffly. He squirmed in his seat, like he had to go to the bathroom. "Right, uh...now when I did the Goodslice Margarine account, I found that, uh, by tightening up the catalogue you—"

"Whoa, hold on now, you say you came here from doing marketing for Margarine?"

Eickoff blinked at me. "I still do it. I do general marketing for Polymer West Coast. I do some of the Goodslice, some of the Grecian Caress Soap line, some Dinkins Candy, and all the books from Ledbetter West Coast."

I took off my wire rim glasses to clean them on a tissue as I spoke, so I didn't have to look at him. "You market soap and margarine and candy...and books. All more or less at once?"

"It's all commodity," Maceburger put in. "There's no reason to get coy and precious about it, Slim."

"But at least bring in somebody with some experience in books...I'm sure he's an ass-bustin' margarine marketer but...no offense, Eickoff."

"No, no problem...." he said faintly.

He looked, though, as if he had a problem. Of some kind. It didn't seem to be me. Strange to think about it now, what with all that's happened.

Eickoff abruptly stood up—making Maceburger's head jerk back in reaction with the suddenness of it. "Just want to...."

"Go ahead, right down the hall to the right," I said, almost relieved myself.

"...the Men's room...."

Maceburger looked irritated but waved him on. Eickoff almost bolted through the door.

"Too much coffee or something," Maceburger muttered, looking after Eickoff. "He's been very tense lately. We had a bit of a...he walked off the job yesterday."

Now I was genuinely surprised. "That guy? He seems so milquetoasty."

"Seems to be having some kind of issues with his wife."

"It's going around," I said. "Look I don't want to talk about the guy behind his back but do you really think he—actually *any* marketing guy—should be making *editorial* decisions?"

Maceburger was exhaling windily through his nose, as if he'd tried to keep an irritated sigh down and only partly succeeded. "In fact, Peter Eickoff was chosen because he is a pretty darn literate guy...."

"Fuck, man, that doesn't mean he understands publishing...."

I was relieved when the phone on Maceburger's desk rang; I knew that Maceburger would answer it. He always took calls during meetings—during meetings with mere editors, anyway.

It was Polymer, for Eickoff. "He was just here—just ran off to the little boy's room for a moment. He should be on his way back by now. Hold on...." Maceburger pressed his intercom button. "Kenny? Is Eickoff coming back down the hall? He went to the men's—"

"Peter Eickoff?" came the tinny voice from the box. "He didn't go to the men's, he went out on the balcony. The other way. He's out there pacing and talking to someone..."

Maceburger frowned and stood, took a step to the window and

moved the curtain, tilted his head to look along the wall to the balcony. "He's out there all right...but there's no one out there with him so I don't know who he'd be...." Eickoff must've seen him looking, because Maceburger waved and made a 'there's a phone call for you' gesture holding his hand against his head. Then he sat back down at the desk, picked up the phone. "Yes uh—he'll be...okay, I'll tell him." He hung up, shaking his head. "Whatever."

"Anyway," I said, "about these *marketing realities*—did you say Judith Mayfield? You're eliminating Judith *Mayfield*? She just had a big write up on her in fucking *Vanity Fair,* man."

Maceburger elected to ignore the profanity creeping into my conversation. "It was a small 'write up'. It was just her commenting on the way women writers have dressed in the 20th century and now...."

"Sure—because people know she's sharp, she sees deep things in our cultural surfaces."

Eickoff came in, face mottled. He sat down, avoiding our eyes, looking just as squirmy as before. But then, he hadn't gone to the bathroom at all.

Maceburger glanced at him. After a moment he said, "You got a call—"

"From Alice?" Eickoff interrupted, rather shrilly.

"Alice? No. From Ferris at Polymer—but he said he couldn't hold, you can call him in about an hour."

Eickoff shuddered. Then he nodded way too briskly. "Oh, great, gee, thanks, I'll...good...."

"So we were talking about Judith Mayfield, um, Peter," I said. "Have you actually read her?"

"Sure, sure, I read *Garage Winds*. Great stuff. Great, great stuff. But uh, maybe she's not, you know, for Ledbetter, she's maybe more a Knopf writer...?" He sounded apologetic no matter what he said.

"What we're not seeing is a deep profit here, with Mayfield," Maceburger said dismissively. "Her last book—no one knew how to market it. Was it a novel? A *roman a clef*? A memoir? A 'Travels with Charlie' book about America? She won't be categorized...and that screws up our marketing, our distribution, the whole shebang."

I nodded patiently. "Which means she's an American original. Like Mailer...."

"Who doesn't sell very well now either. Look, those authors are going—they're outta here. And we've got a few more. I know you discovered both these writers, ten years or so ago, you were their editor, Slim, you nurtured their careers—I know it's hard to let go of that...."

"Which brings up another matter," said Eickoff almost sorrowfully. "This 'nurturing' thing. The new paradigm is about making that high score right away, or moving on to another possibility. We...just aren't going to be allowed, by Polymer, to 'nurture' people."

"You're saying...if the book is not a best seller *now*, the first book by the author right out of the box, we drop them?"

"That's about the size of it," Maceburger said. "That's the new publishing paradigm. You know, we have a corporate situation with stockholders to please—they have their own agenda, Slim."

"Speaking of 'the size of it'—not to make a bad pun here," Eickoff said, smiling like a stretched-out rubber band. "The books are going to have to be a certain length. Our research shows that a book that fits in the rack at supermarkets and airports just right, thick enough, with the right look, is going to move better. And the racks are built, anyway, for a certain number of a certain size...."

The phone rang, and Maceburger answered it.

Was Eickoff pinching his own thigh, outside of Maceburger's line of sight? It certainly looked like it. Like a man trying to control one pain by making a smaller, sharp one somewhere else.

But mostly I was dazedly taking in what he'd said. "The books will have to be a certain length...decided by the racks...?"

"Yeah? Billy boy!" Maceburger was saying, into the phone. "...how you doing? Sure. Sure. We're not sure yet who's going to New York and who's not...if he wants to—right. We want to keep our best selling writer happy. Yeah. I'll tell him."

I looked at Eickoff. Stage whispered: "Did he say 'Going to New York'?"

Eickoff seemed embarrassed at what he apparently perceived as eavesdropping, though Maceburger was right there, talking loudly in front of us. "They are going to reduce this office to the New Age Books line, probably, to compete with HarperSanFrancisco, and move the mainstream editors to New York. Midlist'll be laid off."

"No midlist..." I was a mainstream editor, but Hally Wenson was a friend of mine, and she was a midlist editor.

"Why no midlist? Wait, don't tell me...they're midlist. By definition, too narrow a profit margin. So no science fiction, no mysteries. No...westerns."

He shrugged in a 'that's right' kind of way. "Other people'll do them."

No westerns. Mr Ledbetter had liked the westerns, too. "So am I going to New York?"

"Uh...probably."

"Thanks Billy boy," Maceburger was saying. "I'll see we get somebody out there that Spaulding likes."

"Spaulding," I murmured. "Oh great."

Joel Spaulding. Best selling horror author. Pill-head. He had a way of fixing on things. And people.

Maceburger hung up. "So—Slim...."

I looked at him. "Now's the time when you ask me if I'm a team player, right?"

"That's the drill, yes," said Maceburger, flatly, not taking the bait. "Is this the time when you play Mr. Boho Individual and let us down? You going to start a gift shop in Sonoma, Slim?"

"I don't want to go to New York. I've got a kid here. His Mom has custody so I can't take him with me. I keep sane by convincing myself that my work is not without meaning. I don't want to stay here if it's going to be meaningless. It doesn't pay well enough to be meaningless."

"Spaulding wants you in New York," Maceburger said. "If we have to, we'll get Bunchly out there—he likes Bunchly too."

"Bunchly? My assistant? ...I guess that's a dumb question. How many Bunchlys could there be? So —Bunchly wants to go...."

"He doesn't want to stay an assistant. Who would?"

"Hell, Spaulding is welcome to Bunchly. But...I don't know...I do need the gig. Sure as shootin'."

"There isn't a lot of major publishing in San Francisco, Slim. It's mostly New York. The West Coast Ledbetter experiment hasn't worked that well."

Maybe I could get them to keep me in San Francisco and fly me out to New York to do meetings with Spaulding. I could call Spaulding and get him on that bandwagon. But I'd need time to pull that off. "Okay well look," I said. "Give me a day or two to digest all this...."

The phone rang again. Maceburger answered—and frowned when he learned it was for me. That was two not for him. "Yes he's here but he's in a meeting...what kind of emergency?"

I sat up straight. Who the fuck cared what kind of emergency it was. *Give me the fucking phone....*

But I simply sat there, quivering, waiting. I hadn't crossed over, yet. Finally Maceburger said, grudgingly. "Alright, hold on. Slim...it's for you. You can take it on that phone on the little table next to you there, just press...there ya go."

I knew the woman was a nurse, the moment I heard her voice. "Mr. Purdoux? We've admitted Frank Purdoux here—we're at San Francisco General...."

"Is it...what is it? What happened?"

"He seems to've toxified himself on something, we're not sure exactly, they're doing tests. He's not conscious so we can't ask him. Your wife would like you to come over...."

"Which...?"

"He's in the critical ward, third floor, B-wing."

"Critical. Is he...."

"That's all I can tell you on the phone, sir, you'll have to speak to the doctor."

"Frankie...."

"Will you be able to—"

"Yes! Yes I'm...coming over. Now."

I hung up and the other two had adopted the expected expressions. "Go ahead on over there," Maceburger began. "Don't give it a second—"

I was on my way out the door before he finished the first sentence.

2

The doctor was a small Asian man with a small mouth and a smaller smile. "Mr. Purd-owks?"

I wasn't going to correct his pronunciation right then. "Yeah, yes, where is my son?"

"I...."

"Jimmy?" It was my ex, Meredith, interrupting. Looking squinty-eyed and pale in the other doorway. Standing there hugging herself. Tall and wiry, like me, but with lank dark hair that stood sharply out against her white skin. It bristled right out at you when she didn't shave her legs. Except for both being sort of tall and skinny, and glasses, we didn't have much else in common. Except we both came from Austin.

She had been intensely progressive, politically— I was intensely cynical, politically; she took classical music appreciation classes and knew a scherzo from an adagio—I liked the Stooges and the Buzzcocks and Metallica and the Velvet Underground, used to play in punk bands, and I thought Frank Zappa was classical—and of course I could get into Johnny Cash and Hank Williams; she thought Andy Warhol was sexist—and me, I couldn't believe she thought that. Worse, she was a Wiccan, now. Basically a goddess-worshipping feminist witch. Which is just such unutterable horseshit. She was wearing a dark blue workshirt and jeans and sandals and an Isis moon goddess pendant around her neck.

I knew, when I saw her squinting that way. I knew he was dead and I knew that somehow she was going to blame me.

"It was polytoxia," the doctor said in a soft little voice. "He take a number of drugs...we think maybe all in these same pills...."

"How the fuck you graduate from medical school only speaking half-assed English?" I asked. I barked it, really.

He didn't even blink; he nodded to say he understood how angry I was and put a hand on my arm. "We think someone sold Ext-shaw-see, to him. They are many times now only little bit ex-shaw-see, lots of amphetamine, cough medicine too, mix in the pills. Maybe sometimes they take PMA too, another drug. So you see—Polytoxia."

"You're saying...you're saying he's dead."

"We try for half an hour to revive him...everything, everything. There was a blood clot in the lung from a breaking vessel there, and the blood clot goes into artery, stops heart, we try to break clot up, re-start heart but he came to us already gone...."

Frankie....

I turned to look at my ex. She was gazing mutely at the floor tiles. "Where did he take this shit, Meredith? Exactly where did it happen?"

My own voice sounded like a recording, to me. The room was a box with some white walls and white lights overhead. There were three people in the box. Me and this little Asian guy in the white suit, and my ex-wife. We were in this box and always had been; we'd always been here, talking about my dead son.

"He went off to...." Meredith was making long raspy asthmatic gasping sounds in between phrases. "A party without...." Pausing to breathe between what I now recognized as sobs, sobs of a depth that I'd never heard from her. "...without my permission."

A gasping sob. "He went from summer school...after class...to...some party of Victor's—Victor's Mom was working a night shift somewhere, nobody was home—I think Victor was the one who got them the...I don't know...I was frantic...didn't know...where he was...police...called.... He collapsed at the party, when he was dancing...four or five pills...."

"Maybe some more," the doctor put in, softly.

"Drugs. When did it go from pot to this ecstasy shit?"

I was in a state of raging detachment, though I stood statue-still, and now my voice was more than detached; it was flat as the surface of a subterranean lake. "I thought you had a counselor working with him...some flake from Marin, Meredith, right?"

She looked at me with a murderous emptiness. "I...you...you were his hero, the party animal...."

"I have been clean and fucking sober for eleven years—you're going to say he did this to be like me?"

"I will leave you to talk," the doctor says. "Remember grief makes people angry. I will be in—"

I grabbed the doctor's bony little shoulder. "I want to see him, doctor," I said. "Now."

The doctor looked at me. He looked like he wanted to refuse. Something to do with proper morgue procedures and authorized doctor's exams and death certificate signings or something. But he didn't say it.

He was wiser than that.

He nodded and gestured to a metal door; a door painted very, very white.

�֍ ✖ ✖

Meredith didn't come along. I figured she was calling her sister or her gestalt therapist. Or her fucking lesbian Wiccan priestess.

The hall contained little Filipino nurses and a black orderly and a middle aged white doctor who darted by as if he was afraid I was going to ask him for pain meds for my dying mother, and then there was a room, a cool room, with three gurneys in it, with sheets pulled up over three faces, making me think of three-card monte, pick the right shell and under it...is your dead son.

The doctor pulled back the sheet on the nearest body.

I was surprised by how much expression there was on Frankie's face. He looked puzzled, a little angry, betrayed. Cheated. There was a certain dulling, too, like a shape in wax when it's just a little warm; that was death, softening the edges of that final expression. Death undefines us.

Frankie was lying there...so very still. When he was feeling good, he'd been a dynamo of a kid. Skateboarding. Doing the tricks over and over till he splintered his skateboard into a ruin. Dancing. He danced to Everclear, to Moby. And softball. He'd been awkward at every other team sport, but something would snap into place when he played soft-ball, and he became Fred Astaire as a short stop. Then he dropped out of the team, last year, because Mr Glausinger was a judgmental, snarling old bastard and Frankie had a way of taking everything personally. He took my separation from his Mom personally.

I'm sorry about that, kid. Sorry about breaking up with your Mom. I didn't think it was like breaking up with you too. But I guess you thought it was.

Had I ever said I was sorry about it, to him? I couldn't remember.

I tried to make myself kiss him; touch him. I couldn't. My body wouldn't bend over. My hand wouldn't lift up.

I didn't need to confirm he was dead, anyway. He was long gone. There was no Frankie Wayne James Purdoux left in the world. There was just that tire-print of a parting expression.

I had just one other thought I remember now. That he was born in drugs, and died in drugs. Because I had gotten Meredith pregnant with him, in college, when we'd both been doing some hashish; when she'd seemed yielding and intellectually open and full of possibilities; while her bitterness slept. She'd gotten pregnant in a waking hashish dream; he'd died in a tortured mix of MDMA, amphetamine and cough medicine.

The doctor's almost tender touch on my arm steered me away from the body, and I went out the door, into the warmth of the hall. Away from the room where I'd seen Meredith.

I found an exit—emergency only—and its warning bell rang when I pushed through it, and I didn't care even slightly that it rang. I liked it ringing. It should ring. The hospital should be filled with that clangor, for all day and all night. It should be required.

I decided I needed to be moving. I had to keep a step, two steps ahead of the feeling that was coming. The thing trying to catch me....

So I decided to go back to Ledbetter, to quit the job, which I had only kept for my boy, all along; and while I was there I could just coincidentally get the Jack Daniels I had in my desk, a retirement gift all wrapped up to send to Mr Ledbetter. I wasn't going to send it to Mr Ledbetter anymore. Mr Ledbetter was on his own.

Yeah, the office. For starts. That was someplace to go.

I moved my body through the necessary places to get back to work. I walked a few blocks and waved down a taxi and took that. The driver was a late middle aged white guy who looked like he was having to work at not drinking on shift. He tried to talk to me and then he looked at my face in the rear view and shut up.

I arrived at the building, wordlessly paid the cabbie. I went upstairs, in the elevator, scribbled a note to Maceburger, handed it to Clueless Kenny, the vapid young gay guy who was Maceburger's assistant...

> *Maceburger:*
> *My son has died. I am done here. I stayed so I could be sure of a job, so I could provide child support. And maybe a role model: a working Dad.*
> *I'm not a Dad. That's all gone. Two things were meaningful to me, my son and my chance to cultivate good books. The world took my son from me, and you took the other. I might've gone on a sabbatical, and come back, except that you and Polymer have made my profession meaningless. Books are now bullshit. You and Polymer have turned Ledbetter Books into a steaming pile of shit. I can do better than shoveling fresh shit. Go back, in this note, to the word "meaningless." Re-read that word. Meaningless....*
> *Sincerely,*
> *Slim Purdoux*
> *dated: whatever the fuck this day is*
> *and who the fuck cares?*

...and Kenny read it, even though it was addressed to his boss and not to him, and blinked back at me in graceless confusion. "Uhhh...Are you, like, sure you don't want to—you know—talk to him?

He'll be back in a second—he just went down the hall real quick to—"

I turned my back, walked away from him. Went to my office, got the wrapped package from the desk drawer, tore it open, poured a coffee-cup full, and drank off about three shots worth, wham.

It was good timing, in a couple of different ways. I had just finished shuddering, was just lowering the cup from my lips, when the gunshots started.

It sounded to me at first like an irritated carpenter was really whacking something resistant with a hammer. Rap! Rap-*Rap!* Rap *RAP!*

"Huh," I said.

I poured some more Jack. When had I last talked to Frankie? The phone night before last.

What was the last thing I ever said to Frankie, I wondered. Was it something like, *"You gotta go to the damn summer classes if you want to graduate to the next grade, man. You screwed off most of the school year."* Something like that.

You screwed off most of the school year: Last thing his Dad said to him before he died.

I felt something catching up to me, and had to keep moving out ahead of it—and curiosity was a way to keep moving, a couple of steps in front. So I let curiosity pull me to the banging sounds, and saw Eickoff, with a big automatic pistol in his shaking hands, standing over the body of Clueless Kenny. Blood skirling around his loafers. Blood still pooling, flowing.

Eickoff was panting, staring down at Kenny's shot-up body.

"You going to shoot me too?" I asked, more interested than scared. I took another drink of the Jack D. "What the hell, it's your gun, I'm just asking. You want some of this here, Pete?"

Yew want some of this here, Pete? I was also interested to note that my accent returned a little when I got drunk. The first drinking I'd done for years.

"I believe...." Eickoff licked his lips. Staring at the bottle. "I would like a drink. Yes."

I handed him the cup. I was aware that he hadn't yet answered my other question. He seemed in no hurry to kill me but....

I could smell Kenny's blood.

I was a little afraid...of how little I was afraid.

And Eickoff was drinking, looking at me with wide eyes over the cup. His face was tear stained.

I felt I had to say something. Also it kept me busy, kept me moving, in some way, to talk. "My son's dead, y'know, Eickoff. He died today—from some shit he got into last night. He was, you know, all I stayed here for, all I fucking stayed *straight* for—that and the idea that I might be contributing a little something to art. That idea is gone...."

"I'm sorry about that," Eickoff said vaguely, kicking at the puddle of blood so that it spattered the side of Kenny's desk.

"...and my son is gone, Eickoff. He was pretty much all that I loved. See, the young jackass—I mean, goddamn him too, you know?—he got hold of some drugs and they were bad drugs and they killed him. So what do you think of them apples, Eickoff?" I swigged from the neck of the bottle. "My son's dead and he was all that was keeping me alive. He's gone, Eickoff. Wiped off the face of the Earth. Frankie."

He nodded sympathetically. "That sucks. That really sucks, Slim. It sure sucks."

"You just about nailed it there, Petey."

Eickoff cocked his head at the sounds of sirens. "I killed Mr. Maceburger too," he said conversationally.

"Yes," I said. "I can't say I'll miss him but I can't say I approve. There has to be a better way to cull publishers. But each to his own." I took a swig and grimaced. "Well hell, Pete—I take it something was bothering you."

He nodded gravely. "For a long time. I haven't slept...I mean, really, no sleep...in so long. You see, my Alice left me and wouldn't talk to me. I've had some problems, and they started to come back lately, but it's so hard to concentrate when I take the medication, I can't work, so I cut back on the meds, and then certain kinds of, you know, behavior started—and then she wouldn't see me...so I called her today, and she told me she had a restraining order...so I said that was the last straw, and it really was, and I told her I had this gun, and if she didn't come here to talk to me I was going to start killing hostages...and she didn't, so I did." He looked at the gun. "I did tell her, I warned her about that."

I thought about his behavior, earlier that day. Now I understood it. "So—did the good folks at Polymer know you were on medication?"

"No, no, I would never have gotten hired. I have a relative at Polymer, and I did some copy writing for an agency, those two things got me the job, but no one knew about the episodes...or the meds...no, no, no."

"You certainly seem more relaxed than in the meeting," I said. "Hold out your cup, you want another drink."

The blood continued to pool around his feet; as quickly as it pooled it was soaked into the carpet, but then some more kept coming, refreshing the red pool. Poor Clueless Kenny had a lot of blood in him.

Eickoff held out the cup and I poured. Some part of me was playing him a little. I had some instinct not to die just yet and some further instinct to keep him from shooting anyone else.

At the same time I felt I was in a kind of existential groove with

Eickoff. He and I were both stricken, and he and I knew a certain truth we probably couldn't have articulated for one another. And he and I both didn't give a fuck anymore.

I was carefully not looking at Kenny's body because I was afraid I'd see Frankie's face instead of Kenny's.

Eickoff took another drink.

"Whew...hard stuff...I've got a fresh clip in this gun," Eickoff said. "You want it?"

"Me?"

"See—I know now that Alice isn't going to come. She just isn't. She won't answer her cellphone or call back on her beeper and she isn't going to come."

"The police wouldn't let her anyway, man. I mean, they're on this by now...."

"That's right. So...." He held the gun out to me. I felt like a magic token was being passed over to me. A badge of office, a talisman of some kind.

I took the gun, thinking if I had it he couldn't shoot me or anybody else with it. I didn't think I wanted to live, but I didn't want to be sitting in an office building, gut shot and dying, either. (Or did I? Maybe there would be a certain satisfaction in it).

"It has a fresh clip in it," he said helpfully.

It was a blocky semi-automatic .44; heavy in my hand. But I was pretty comfortable with guns. Me and my westerns fetish, for one thing. I'd started as an editor for Ledbetter's line of westerns. Slave wages. But I loved westerns. I'd gotten some guns, back in Austin, soon as I was legal to have them, and spent a lot of time shooting at paper targets. Meredith had made me get rid of the guns, of course.

More sirens outside.

I squinted at the gun. It seemed to swell and shrink and swell in my hand. I was drunk. "Where's the safety?" I was drunk and not so drunk. But drunk enough I was having trouble seeing straight, and figuring the safety out.

"It's there—see it? But why would you want the safety? Can I have another drink?"

I gave him the bottle. It was starting to give me a headache anyway.

Then I heard the amplified police voices, from downstairs, and shouts, all with an official tenor.

Eickoff was swaying, beginning to shake. "Alice...."

I started to wonder how many other bodies there were. "Say uh, Peter—who else did you shoot? I have some friends in this building."

"Just that black Security Guard downstairs."

"I don't really...didn't really know that guy. Too bad, though."

"One favor...Mr...wait, I might have to throw up...no...no it's passed...Mr. Prodox—"

"It's pronounced Per-doo."

"Sorry."

"No big thang there, Petey. So uh...what favor?"

"Could you please shoot me?"

"Oh."

He looked pitiful, and like he needed putting out of his misery. How would a guy like him do prison? Hang himself first opportunity if the prison predators didn't get him.

I thought about Frankie. I raised the gun and pointed it at Eickoff. But it didn't feel like I had it in me to shoot him. To shoot somebody, it has to be in you; has to come out of you. It didn't seem to be in there for me to shoot Eickoff.

I thought I could shoot lots of *other* people though, if they fucked with me. I could shoot just about anybody who fucked with me.

People who had made a joke of my life; people who'd taken Frankie from me. Having Frankie meant I didn't have to live with a lot of regrets. I didn't have to regret marrying Meredith, because that would mean regretting having Frankie. And I didn't regret having him even now that he was dead. At least there'd been Frankie for a while.

It almost caught me then, the feeling, but it didn't because that's when the cops started shouting through bullhorns at the door.

"Stay out there or I'll shoot this hostage!" Eickoff shouted shrilly at them, though I was the one with the gun.

"Eickoff...." I began. But I wasn't sure how to advise him. "I can't do this for you." Then, in a boozy kind of way, I had an idea. "I know!—the cops'll do it for you! Here, take the gun back...."

He shook his head.

"No, you keep it. Kill me before they get here, please!" Eickoff said, licking his lips. "Please oh please...I'm scared of them. I might fall down and beg them not to kill me. I'm not scared of *you*. I could let you do it."

I didn't understand that logic at all. But Eickoff hadn't been taking his meds; he had his own logic.

The booze made me dizzy when I shook my head. "No, man—it ain't in me to kill you in, like, cold blood. If you had another gun and threatened me with it.... Then I could."

"This is the San Francisco Police Department! Come to the door and talk to us, in there! Do not hurt that hostage! If there are wounded people inside, let us help them! Don't make this any worse than it is!"

"How about...." Eickoff stumbled to the desk, stepping in the blood, and found a daggerlike letter opener. "I could stab at your eyes with this...."

Eickoff was just full of helpful suggestions.

The room spun a little when I shook my head. "No, man, look—we gotta surrender, here...."

But Eickoff came lurching toward me—stepping on Kenny's bloating stomach, his weight forcing air out of the corpse, so that the corpse said, faintly, *"Whoa-ohhhho...."* Something Kenny might've said in life, too.

"We're going to come in there—drop your—"

Then Eickoff slashed at me with the letter opener. I stumbled instinctively back and the gun went off in my hand and Eickoff shouted in triumph and fell on his face at my feet—

Shot down—I'd shot Eickoff down—

—and then there was a pale, very young cop-face at the door. The SWAT guys hadn't got here yet and this helmeted young guy was staring at me with his pretty blue eyes.

"Shit!" the cop swore. "Fucking hell!" Mad that he'd failed, so he thought, to save the hostage.

"No, I'm not the kil—" I began.

But a vase on the desk behind me burst apart: the young cop was already shooting at me. He'd seen me shoot Eickoff; he assumed I was the guy shooting people here. Figured I was the one who'd shot the guard downstairs.

Well shit. Wouldn't you fucking know it?

I felt a ripple of rage come up in me, almost an orgasmic feeling of relief, and I pointed the gun toward the cop, squeezed the trigger, making the gun kick in my hand, pieces of the door frame fly.

I missed the young cop, who ducked back around the doorframe, shouting to his friends.

"Fuck you fuck you fuck you and all your fucking dim bulb cop friends!" I shouted. "You guys become cops so you could find some fucking excuse to shoot people goddammit!"

As I shouted, I was moving through a side door into the long room along the hallway, with its strip of cubicles, backing down the aisle of cubies, gun in hand, and then I saw the door onto the balcony that we could take lunch on—one of those extraneous balconies put there by a show-off architect— and I was out the door and climbing over the rail of the balcony onto a motorized window-washing scaffold, where I found the switch and made the scaffold go down, way down to the alley....

...and I jumped down onto a closed dumpster from there, and—leaping almost joyously ahead of the black wave inside me—jumped on top of a cop car, denting its roof, and down from the car to run past the two gawping, startled cops sitting in the cruiser, hiding the gun in my pants under my untucked shirt—and around a corner to a crowd that was gathering—

And ran into the crowd, laughing, laughing uncontrollably, and grateful to Eickoff, knowing I was going to have plenty of people shooting at me, thanks to Eickoff, plenty of people to shoot back at, until somebody eventually put me out of my misery.

Frankie. Frankie.

Stay ahead of it. Run! Run and get some ammo and reload that gun....

"Thank you, Eickoff," I said aloud.

And I meant it.

And everyone in the crowd, not seeing the gun, just ignored me, thinking me some flaky street guy—and they just got out of my way, and I ran down into the BART station....

3

First time I saw Latesha and Wendell, they were standing at a sidewalk pizza by-the-slice window, and I knew something was up. They were drinking sodas, and Wendell was eating a slice. I didn't really care that much, when I worked out that something was up. I just said, "Huh," to myself.

I knew they weren't plainclothes cops or anything, this tall willowy African-black girl with the corn rows, her stocky high-yellow boyfriend with the blue plastic visor and the voluminous short-pants that went past his knees and that long shirt that, like mine, was untucked and, like mine, could be hiding a pistol. I figured he was maybe forty, a little too old for his clothes.

It was, anyway, just sort of interesting to notice their probable associate—the squinty red-faced white guy in a dingey red windbreaker that said Quebec Ice Hockey Finals on it—had followed me from the ATM machine down one of the filthier streets in San Francisco's Tenderloin, through the long shadows of the buildings...between which the setting sun blazed, from time to time...*And....*

...and that this asshole in the hockey windbreaker was now moving up onto my right, on the sidewalk, pacing me a few steps away, and he was making eye contact with these two finishing their sodas at the pizza place a few steps to my left....

Maybe my face was already on TV, a wanted guy with a reward. But I didn't think it could happen that quick. I'd only slipped the cops half an hour or so ago.

After that, I'd gone to a second-hand store, to change my appearance a little, and bought a used levi jacket to go over my cowboy shirt, and a used white Resistol cowboy hat—a little the worse for wear, somebody else's sweat marking the base of its crown—and some dark glasses: faux Oakleys. I had my own glasses in my shirt pocket and now I was thinking I was going to need them.

I was trying to avoid the cops for awhile, because while I was in the BART train, I realized I had a mission.

It involved a kid named Victor and some people he knew....

"Hey there Tex," said a voice behind me.

I turned to see the high-yellow guy in the visor, followed by the black girl, who was a head taller than him, and the blue visor guy was grinning at me.

"What's up, Tex?"

"People call me Slim," I said, aware that it sounded like dialogue from a Western. And liking it.

I could feel the white guy circling around on the other side of me....

I'm not sure how I felt the guy moving in on me back there. Nothing telepathic. It was just that my senses were so sharp now. I was so *there*. So present, so awake. The only thing blurring that *present* and that

40

rootedness in *being there* was a smoke that rose from inside me and sometimes fogged my head. It's funny how cold fury burns hot.

But right now everything seemed so crystal clear. The scraps of wax paper on the sidewalk, the gum pressed into blackened flat stamps, the posters for rapper MC-SWEE-TOOF on the wall of the alley: every wrinkle in the sloppily-glued paper etched in my mind; the rapper's carefully-selected angry grimace, his gold teeth.

Fuck it, I thought, let's not run from this thing, let's do it.

Maybe I could get a jump on my mission here—or go down with a gun in my hand. There could be some satisfaction in that. A little satisfaction is all I could hope for now.

"That alley looks like a good spot for you to jack me up," I said. "Let's do it there." And I stepped into the alley. I turned around so the back of the alley was behind me; the three jack-buddies were in front of me, in the mouth of the alley. It stunk so much of urine in there, I almost gagged—but that would've looked bad. So I didn't let myself gag.

I reached under the shirt and put my hand on the gun.

"He gotta piece," the dark-black girl said. Just an observation. She wasn't scared.

"This motherfucker's crazy too," the white guy observed. He had some kind of accent. French Canadian maybe. His upper lip was always squinched up like he was smelling something bad.

"Going in the alley, talking that shit," the black girl agreed. "What you think, Wendell?"

The blue visor guy, Wendell, shrugged and shook his head. Amused. He had a gun out already, a .38 revolver, just dangling in his hand by his side, pointing at the ground; he didn't even have his finger on the trigger.

"What you talking about, we jack you?" he said.

"Talking about find a stupider white boy," I said. "Canadian Red there was watching me at that ATM, saw me take out three hundred dollars."

"How he know I'm from Canada?" the French Canadian asked.

"How people know a Chinaman from China, you dumb motherfucker," the girl said.

Because I knew it would show my confidence to good effect, and because it would say I didn't have to wear shades to be bad, I reached slowly up with my free hand, took off the counterfeit Oakleys, replaced them with my prescription wire rims, put the Oakleys in the shirt pocket. And as I did that, I went on, real casually, "There isn't much more than three hundred in the account, this time of the month, so you can forget the part where you try to get my card and my PIN number. Just try for the three hundred. Go for it. Then the bullets'll fly from me to you and you to me." No quick movements. I looked at Wendell. "Because I sure as fuck do not care at all."

Wendell looked into my face. After a moment he nodded. "I expec' ya'll don't give a fuck. I'm wid dat. Whynch you just kick wid us then?"

"Because you think you'll wait for the right moment, and then...but I tell you what. Instead of jacking stupid white boys, why don't you go in with me, help me on my mission, and you can have pretty much all the money from it. I figure there's got to be some good cash there. Somewhere between 40 thousand and three hundred thousand."

"He onna mission," the black girl said.

I didn't know if I wanted anything to do with this street trash. Could be tiresome always having to watch my back. I was just fronting with them, right then, dangling a carrot so I could get them under control; get them in some place where I could decide if I was going to ditch them or not.

42

I only 49% wanted to die, right then. I still 51% wanted to go on my mission. Maybe they could be useful though. I probably needed some help, if only cannon fodder.

"How much money, 'baller?" Wendell asked.

"How much money does a drug dealer have in his house? It varies, what I remember. But always there's a pretty good pile. And then there's the dope. You can have all that if you want it. Sell that shit."

"You got somebody in mind?" the girl asked. Her face was expressionless. The whites of her eyes were ivory yellow.

"Yeah, I just got to confirm a few things," I said. Which was of course pure unmitigated bullshit.

"Latesha," Wendell said, "You let me ask the man the questions."

"I just askin—"

"I said shut up, bitch." He kept his eyes on me as he shut her up. "Tex...Slim, you want to get a drink?" As he asked it, he put his little revolver away under his shirt with one hand, made a kind of roller-coaster motion with the other hand, to show the row of thick gold rings on it; to bling-bling at me, maybe.

I kept my hand on Eickoff's .44.

"I got to put something in my stomach," I said. "Nothing but some whiskey a little while ago. I'm out of practice with that shit. Giving me a sour belly."

I saw an SFPD cruiser ease by, behind them. I took my hand from my gun, looked at the ground, like a tweaker looking at the white spots, so that my hat brim would hide my face.

The cops went on by. They looked bored. It's good when cops are bored.

Wendell, who wasn't stupid at all, glanced back at the cop car after it was almost passed, and then looked at me.

I put my hand back on my gun.

"Ah'ight," he said. Like: I get it.

"So I tell you what...." I smiled like a Bible salesman.

I was going to get over on the people who were set to rob me. I was going to pick them up in my slipstream and draw them along with me. That gave me a nasty kind of pleasure.

"I'm buyin' dinner, ya'll want some," I said. I decided I had to pretend I was equal to anything, so I dropped my hand from my gun and walked past Wendell, feeling him watch me, 49% of me wanting them to make a move on me, and started down the street to the little Chinese place on the corner. "Ya'll like that Chinese beer?"

※　※　※

I had managed to get down a bowl of Chinese chicken soup, the kind with the big gooey lumps floating in it, and half a pot-sticker. Behind the ORDER HERE counter, the chunky little Chinese lady who ran this Tenderloin greasy spoon had an expression on her face like she was enduring her third year in a re-education prison camp, instead of being a merchant in San Francisco.

"You ain much appetite," Latesha observed, looking at me. I could see a prison tattoo on her arm, a cross with a weeping Jesus over it, almost lost in her dark skintone.

She and Wendell and Canadian Red had eaten a buttload of food, greasy piles of sweet and sour pork and Mandarin beef and spicy shrimp—not like people who hadn't eaten in a while. It was just the way they always ate.

And they drank four or five Chinese beers each, none of them acting like it was strange at all that a guy they'd been planning to rob was buying them dinner, because in the Mix all kinds of things happened and you never knew who was your friend and who was your enemy for any too long. I hadn't been on the street like this for twelve or thirteen years, but except for some new slang, it was about the same old bullshit. You could have all kinds of fun with people, long as you didn't turn your back on them, or go to sleep with them in the same room.

I was wondering what would happen, late tonight or tomorrow, when I ran out of strength to keep going.

When I was asleep, I'd be vulnerable in other ways. I didn't know what'd happen if I fell asleep around Wendell and his friends. They might decide that the best, most logical, most prudent course of action was to disarm me as I slept, and beat me to death.

I was more nervous of drugs than of Wendell and his crew. It wasn't their drugs I was nervous of—it was mine. I might take drugs to keep going, and I was worried about how I'd feel then. Especially about how I'd feel after the drugs wore off. I remembered that vividly—the crash. From, anyway, my drugs of choice, speed and cocaine. When you've crashed from that shit you don't have it in you to hide from anything— it all catches up with you....

If you're wondering how I could even contemplate taking drugs after what happened to Frankie, all I can say is: *That's dope.* You can hate it—and still unquestioningly spend all your time and money trying to get it.

If I got into drugs, out here, chances were I'd lose sight of my mission, lose sight of anything but more drugs, more drugs, another hit, more drugs. Plus I was lame, highly unprofessional doper, when using; couldn't really take drugs and do anything else, the way some can, so I'd probably get way psychotic on them, and just fucking lose it, thereby attracting the attention of the police...who were looking for me anyway.

I'd just lucked past those cops at Ledbetter—just happened to hit on the wide-open moment. Another forty seconds and the cops would've had that place sewed up tight.

It was just possible, I thought—using my fork to idly squish the insides out of a half eaten potsticker—that SFPD hadn't identified me yet. The cops hadn't seen me clearly. I probably hadn't run past any security cameras. The other office hacks hadn't been around. But pretty soon they'd guess it was me, after they talked to some other Ledbetter employees.

"Skinny white guy in a cowboy shirt? That sounds like Slim Purdoux. I'm not too surprised. He was kind of a sour guy, kind of on a downer, and he was bitching about the Polymer takeover a lot, and I heard he used to take drugs, though I guess he was in recovery...and no one's heard from him either—oh wait, look at this weird note that he wrote Maceburger. Well there you go...and I heard his kid just OD'd or something. Wouldn't surprise me if he gave that kid the drugs that killed him...."

And I wondered...what was Frankie thinking about when he died?

When he collapsed on the rug at that party and heard people around him laughing as he puked and clawed at his chest, before they realized how serious it was.... Had he yelled out, in his mind, for his Daddy?

His Mom, who could be so brittle, so judgmental about me, about men, would soften around Frankie. We'd watched him try out for a skateboard competition together, both of us pretending we weren't afraid he was going to hurt himself veering and leaping in that hard pool of bone-busting concrete. And her eyes, when she turned to me, had some of the old, lost tenderness in them...Frankie must've thought of his Mom as a completely different person from the woman I knew....

Had he called out for her, when the blood clot bullied its way into his heart?

I was glad when Latesha broke into my thoughts. The thing had almost caught up with me....

"I'm fittin to go outside for a cigarette," Latesha said, taking a pack of Newports from her purse.

"You don' smoke cigarette in here!" the little Chinese woman barked—she was half Latesha's size but she wasn't going to take any shit off her.

"I jus' *said* I was goin' outside, woman, *damn!*"

Wendell and I both chuckled at that. "You watch out, she don't kick your ass," I said to Latesha.

Latesha took it good naturedly, and stood up. "I am watchin out too,"

Wendell said, "While you there, you get Dulcet from the Fat Pussy."

"That fuckin' place a mile from here."

"It's no fucking mile, girl, just get over there."

"Shit I'll go get her," Red said, licking his lips.

"No you won't," Wendell said. "You'd disappear into that place, start paying all your money for lap dances, grabbing titty, get into a fight with them bouncers, it go downhill from there."

"No I fucking won't—"

"That's what you'd do, so just drop it now, Red." He looked at Latesha like, *'You still here?'*

She shrugged. "Shit I'll go, but I don' know Dulcet want to leave, she makin good money this time of day."

"You bring her down here. I don't give fuck she don't want to leave. We not here, we'll be in the Boxcar."

Latesha fingered her unlit Newport. Her nails were long and curved and spangled. "Why don you call her, see if she...."

"Why don't you shut the fuck up, bitch?"

But even as he said it he reached into a big side pocket of his short pants, or long shorts, or whatever those things are, I never figured it out, and he brought out *three* small cellphones.

"That one ain like to be no good now," Latesha said, pointing.

He tossed the one she'd indicated onto his greasy plate, and tried one of the others.

They were all stolen, I supposed.

"This one inactive now too," he muttered. He tossed that one with the first and tried the third one. That one seemed to work. But whoever he was calling didn't pick up. "She not pickin up.... You get your ass over there now, girl."

"Ah-aight," Latesha said, and went outside, cigarette in her mouth; provoking the Chinese lady by firing the cigarette up with a Bic lighter before she'd gotten through the door.

"We'll wait over the Boxcar," Wendell said.

I'd seen the graffiti-splashed entrance of Boxcar Cocktails and Dancing on the way from the BART station, just off Market. From the outside it looked like a good place to go if you had an urge to get stabbed and lie bleeding awhile in beer-soaked sawdust.

Red looked mournfully through the window after Latesha as she walked down the street smoking. "Shit I wouldn'ta—"

"Red I'm tryin' to talk to the man, here," said Wendell, though he hadn't said much to me since we'd sat down. But now he turned to me and said, "You talk like a 'baller. You going to highball, then you deliver. You going to deliver what you promised there Tex?"

"I don't have to deliver anything to you, Wendell," I said. "I didn't promise you shit. But if you're there for me, you can rake in something good."

Red looked at Wendell. Apparently surprised that Wendell sat still

48

for someone talking to him like this. But again that look passed between me and Wendell. Two guys who really didn't give a fuck.

Wendell knew he could kill me—but he couldn't intimidate me.

I went on, my voice soft, "But you got to go with me somewhere first. I need to confirm one thing."

"Where's that 'we goin' at?"

"Over in the Sunset District. You got a car? We can take a cab we got to."

"Bensur, we gotta van," Red said.

Bensur? After a moment I realized it was his version of the French 'bien sur'.

What were the chances, really, somebody wouldn't spot me from some tv news shot, call the cops on me, running around town like this? Of course, I could turn myself in, and try to prove I was innocent and probably prevail in the end. The gun was likely registered to Eickoff. He'd have gunpowder-discharge on his hands from shooting. Shit like that. But how long would that take? It'd take too fucking long.

I was on a mission. I didn't have time to fuck around. And if I sat in jail waiting for something to get cleared up, that black wave would catch me.

"I got business to do," Wendell said. "I can't be running around the Sunset not knowing what I'm doing. The SFPD going to stop us, in that neighborhood. You never heard of some shit called 'racial profiling'?"

"So let Red drive."

"Ah sure," said Red. "But you know, there's some skip tracer motherfucker looking for us...."

Wendell turned him a look of disgust. "Shut your froggie Canuck mouth, motherfucker!"

A bounty hunter? That could make things interesting.

I pointed something out. "He going to look for you in the Sunset District? Probably not. He going to look for you around here? Probably is."

Wendell made a grimace that meant I just might have something there but he had to think about it.

"Les get outta here, get a real motherfucking drink," Wendell said. "The van's over by the Boxcar anyway."

※　※　※

Early evening. San Francisco summer. The unseasonable chill that had blown over the town the last couple of weeks was ended; it was a balmy night, everybody in shirt sleeves, lots of bare chests.

I walked along with Latesha, Wendell, and Red. I could smell Red: sweat that had decayed, and then covered over with a fresh layer. He didn't bathe much. Wendell smelled like a good-quality cologne.

We walked past the corner of Hyde toward Ellis. Bunch of Cambodian teenage boys—that was my guess, anyway, Cambodian—were sitting around a boombox on plastic milk crates, listening to hip-hop. Swee-Toof.

> *"I always hadda way*
> *I sho always know*
> *A motherfuckin chump*
> *fumma real high-roll...."*

The Cambodian kids might or might not've been a gang. They were wearing white or gold ribbed tank tops, nose rings, gold necklaces.

They looked at us with a loaded emptiness. I knew better than to make eye contact or even nod. Stay in neutral.

We kept on till we came to a concrete basketball lot, cracked and infiltrated by weeds. Red and Wendell paused to watch a pick-up game that was at some point of primal testosterone explosion, Asian kids and a few Chicanos whipping around each other, grunting and shouting, whipping in and out of the melee so fast I couldn't follow the moves.

"That boy with the dreadlock, he got some game ay?" Red said. He took a circular container of smokeless tobacco from a shirt pocket and thumbed some under his lower lip.

I was looking nervously down the street, checking the people out. I saw a black trannie, with afternoon stubble but eyebrows plucked pretty much to nothing, mincing along on big muscular legs, out of uniform in cut offs and a sweat shirt with the sleeves missing; prison tattoos on her biceps...when she—she, if you like—passed people she knew on the street, she said, "Hey Boo-boo! How you, Boo-boo!" in a sort of high pitched Yogi Bear voice. They all grinned back at her and waved.

I saw a couple of crack tweakers, a sagging white woman and a gaunt black man, fighting over bottles in a trash can. I didn't see any cops. But it wouldn't be long before they rolled on by again.

"How's about, let's get off the street," I said.

Wendell looked at me and shrugged and led the way again.

I was walking a tight rope. If I fell off, I'd be lost in Frankie dying, Frankie dead. If I kept moving, kept my mind focused on always the next thing and the next thing, I stayed on that tight rope. It was not good to stay in one place for long, and not only because of the police. I was afraid of five in the morning. I was going to have to go to ground somewhere....

Just keep moving. Eyes on that tight rope.

Then we went into the Boxcar. It was almost a shock how much better it was inside than it looked outside. I'd had the completely wrong impression from outside. It was a surprisingly comfortable place, with a fireplace—okay, the fire in it was fake, just rotating lights under red plastic logs, but it looked nice glowing at the far end of the long, dimly-lit boxcar-shaped bar room. There were only a few high windows, set with purple and green stained glass, giving the room a mellow Art Nouveau sort of glow. The bar was a nice one, of mahogany. There weren't a lot of beer signs. There was a mirror behind the bar, repeating some pretty expensive liquors. There were plush black leather booths at the back.

I was relieved to see no bar television; I didn't want to look up and see myself on a news flash.

Only a half dozen customers—the usual shaky old men, a bored middle aged black guy in a janitor's overalls, one bleary skeletal white woman in a skanky outfit who might've been a whore. She looked like she'd probably been up for a few days.

"Looks like they planned for a different clientele," I muttered.

Then I thought, maybe that isn't the smartest thing to say to Wendell. But he laughed. "You got that, woadie boy. New owner got it like this cheap. The people that put it here they thought the neighborhood was, you know uh—what you call that—"

I nodded. "They figured it was gentrifying before it was, huh? Shit look at that, over there, with its own little track-light spot on it, a print from...." I started to identify the industrial still-life as Ozment, from the Purist school, one of the post-Cubists—I had three years of Art History in Austin—but I decided that might make Wendell think I was showing off and putting him down, and I didn't want him primed to have to prove anything—anymore than he already was. "...some art-catalogue bullshit."

"They got that decorator shit going," he said, distantly, as we took bucket-seat leather barstools.

The bartender was a slender young black guy in a Hawaiian shirt, who kept chewing his lip; it was like he was waiting for someone in particular. Wendell, either having to front or having developed a taste, ordered the Remy's.

True to form, Red ordered Canadian Club. "That's real patriotic of you, Red," I said. "As for me, I don't drink Texas beer." I got an Irish coffee, which I had to explain to the bartender. The only coffee he had was the burnt-tasting stuff for drunks who wanted to try to sober up.

"Yeah this place," Wendell said, making a point of paying for the drinks, "it had a cigar room, where they had a deal was legal to smoke in there, and its still there but there's hardly no cigars left, they puttin a pool table in there."

"Whassup Wendell," the bartender said, "you goin get us that pool table?"

"I got a line on that pool table, I told you that, don't you get it nowhere else," Wendell said.

"Some bars, I heard, serve only oxygen," I said. "Flavored oxygen from a tank. You pay to suck air from oxygen masks."

"Now you fuckin wid me," Wendell said.,

"No, I heard that too," the bartender said. He glanced at me.

Had he spotted me when I was standing at the door looking around, remembered me from some TV news flash and called the cops? Is that who he was waiting for? But he hardly seemed to notice me, except to look at my cowboy hat. "I like your hat there, Tex," he said.

"Tex likes to be called Slim," said Wendell, who was genuinely fucking with me now.

"It's true," I said, "about the oxygen bars. They got tanks of scented oxygen, flavored air."

"It get you high?" Red asked.

"No," I said. "Might give you a headache."

"And people they pay for that shit, eh?"

"Believe it or not. It's over there in that *chi-chi* area they started up south of Market."

"I like to get into that business," Red said. "Selling air. Maybe they buy some farts from me eh."

Wendell laughed. Now he was looking at the door too, like the bartender.

I wondered about Wendell and Red. How'd those two improbable associates hook up? In prison? Not impossible—but I'd done a year and a half in the Central Texas State Pen, and though that was a long time ago I was sure it was the same scene anywhere, anytime: black guys stayed with black guys, for protection; white guys stayed with white guys for the same reason; Mexes with Mexes and so on. Most likely they'd hooked up in the Mix, on the street, probably around drugs, which bring all kind of people together. Which drugs, in this case? That was an issue. Some drugs were safer to be around than others. But then, did I care what was safe to be around?

Fuck no. I was a little worried about sleeping, about getting into drugs—but I didn't really give a fuck about anything in any serious way. What a great feeling that was, too. It was like I'd had some kind of abscess in me, some fluid build up, and it was being drained away, relieving the pressure: and that relief was about not caring what was safe.

But at the same time, I thought: I should've cared about *Frankie's* safety a fuck of a lot more.

Oh sure, I'd tried to protect him. But why hadn't I warned him, more, about dope? I *did* tell him—but I should've drilled it into his head till he was past sick of hearing it and then told him some more. He'd known dope was a roach motel—theoretically. But a kid sees his friends getting high and nothing *apparently* going wrong with them, so he figures maybe the adults were lying...or if he's mad at his folks, maybe he wants to do drugs just to fuck with his Mom and Dad.

I hadn't wanted to harangue him about it because I didn't want to lose him as my little gang-buddy, I didn't want to lose my son's friendship—so I lost my son.

"Well, fuck *me*," I said aloud, chuckling.

Wendell looked at me incuriously. I shook my head, and he looked back at the girl at the end of the bar, maybe wondering if she were worth the trouble to recruit into working for him.

He struck me as a kind of jack of all trades, who never hesitated to pimp his women but who didn't like to work at any one thing too long in any one place...always a step ahead of something, which was maybe something else we'd recognized in each other....

I drank some brackish Irish coffee—the bartender hadn't put any cream or sugar in it—and looked at the stained glass windows straining streetlight shine through in purple beams, and thought of a funeral chapel.

I was grateful to Eickoff again, because he saved me from having to go to Frankie's funeral. I would've had to force myself to go, and I don't think I could've gone without going postal on Meredith there. Or just imploding in some way.

And I didn't want to see Frankie Wayne James Purdoux in a coffin, I didn't want to talk about how he had loved life—which would only be about half true—and about how it was a loss to the world but he'd always be with us and....

I started getting seriously restless. Couldn't stay in here much longer.

I was sitting still too long in this funeral chapel of a bar. I was starting to *feel* too much. Relief at not caring—that was okay. But that feeling wasn't alone in there. There was a drunk-tank full of unwashed, retching feelings in me, fighting one another for the little window in the door, each one shouting idiotically for the guard in its turn.

"How long we got to wait in here?" I asked.

"She be along," Wendell said. "Whynt you tell me what you got going."

I shook my head. "I don't know...."

The bartender licked his lips, looked at his watch, and then asked Wendell, "You watch the bar, for a second, Wendell, I got to go to the bathroom, I don't trust that bitch-ho down at the end."

Wendell thumped fists softly with him. "I'm wid dat."

The bartender slid off to the bathroom. He looked, frowning, at Wendell, once, as if wondering, just before disappearing inside.

I reckoned bartender-boy was going to shoot up some dope, or maybe do a line of speed.

Wendell got up, stretched, went confidently behind the bar, tapped the cash register keys in some pattern that made the cash drawer open quietly, reached in the back of the drawer for the larger bills, shoved them in a pocket.

He looked at me. I shrugged.

He looked at the other people in the bar in a very flat kind of way, and they got the message and, like it was rehearsed, they all looked down at their drinks in unison.

Just to make sure, Wendell put a twenty and a ten on the bar. "Drinks for ya'll."

He closed the register and came around and I thought for sure we'd split then—but he just sat down.

"Now, how about if we go to a booth and you tell me what you got going, Tex?"

Something was close to catching up with me, inside, and I thought: anything, anything.

"Yeah sure."

We got up, went to an oversized black booth under a window; the booth had only a few knifemarks and cigarette burns in it.

I leaned back and said, "There's a drug dealer who takes his own shit. He's all fucked up. He's got no security anymore. He's got at least ten grand in cash around him, maybe as much as a hundred. He's got a lot of dope."

"What kinda dope?"

"All kind of shit. He's nobody you know, probably, and there's no way to connect us to him. He don't know me either." I was making most of this up as I went along except the parts about there being a dealer and this hypothetical dealer probably not knowing us. "I just don't want to go in alone. You never know for sure—he might after all have somebody to back him up. Might have an AK47, something like that."

Wendell looked at the table. He sipped a little Remy's. He looked at the door.

"You could be a cop."

"You know I'm not," I said.

He thought about it, and nodded. "But I don't think you any kind of pro in the life either."

"Not for a long time. I did less than two years in the joint."

"Texas?"

I nodded, making a stuck-out 'I'm impressed' shape with my mouth. "Good guess."

Wendell nodded. "And even before then maybe you weren't too..."

"You're right, I was no real pro. But things have changed with me. I'm a good pistol shot and I keep moving till I get what I'm going after, or I go down. I do what I say I'm going to do."

I considered telling him about what had happened with the cops and Eickoff. Might dazzle him a tad.

Or, might discourage him—he might figure I was too hot to chill with, so to speak.

At the moment I was inclined to keep him around. I wasn't sure why—sometimes you know you've hit the right combination, is all. It wasn't a question of liking him; it sure wasn't a question of trusting him. It was about chemistry, and a sense of experience. It was about confidence. His and mine.

"You don't fucking know me and I don't fucking know you," Wendell said—not saying it out of concern, but more just finding it remarkable. He drank some of his Remy's, and went on, "but I'm so fucking bored, and so close to the bottom of the pocket, I had told Red to watch the ATMs and find us one—and that going to be only three hundred dollar, at most. And we got to go, there's that bounty hunter, they ain't never alone. We cain't stay around here. So, Tex.... Where in Texas?"

I pushed my glasses back on my nose with one finger; something self deprecating in it. "Austin. I'm from Austin."

He snorted. "Bunch of college students and hippies. I was born in Dallas but I left there I was a kid. I been back to Texas a few times. Got a lot of relatives with something like your accent. Maybe thas why I'm thinking of going along with ya'll for awhile."

"So, we good to go? Then fuck it. Let's go."

"*Maybe* good to go. *Maybe* could be. Got to wait for my other girl. Think on it. I don't like to be fucking rushed—I like to do the rushing."

We didn't say anything for awhile. Then Latesha came in, blinking in the sudden dimness, with a bottle-blond white girl, black streak in her hair. Her name was Dulcet....

She was maybe thirty, had her hair rubber-banded up in those two little fanned-out tufts, on the top of her head, kind of a rave thing, that curious-puppy-ears look that was an ironic mock of innocence. Her expression was distantly annoyed and there was some kind of impudence in her eyes, that she used to keep the depression at bay. Her face was long, like a lamb's; her ears stuck out a little. But she was pretty. Her eyebrows were unplucked, and the same color as the streak in her hair. She had nice eyes if you didn't get lost in the expression. She was at least five foot nine inches, and her clothes were another burlesque: a little girl's blue and yellow frock, way too small for her, with the top unbuttoned to show her surgically enhanced cleavage; white tennysneakers with little white socks folded down at their lacey tops just above the shoe; stretching between the sneakers to the horizon of the billowy little skirt was a highway of long legs in blue stockings. Each long fingernail on her long slender fingers was painted a different color like The Little Girl had been playing with her Mama's manicure kit. She carried a small shiny plastic Barbie purse with a picture of Barbie and Skipper frolicking on the side of it, on a long yellow strap.

"She wear that outfit on the street?" I asked. "Around here?"

"She got a .25 AMC back-up pistol in that little toy purse," Wendell replied, in a soft aside to me. "Anyway, people know who she belong to."

I doubted if that would've stopped anyone. I doubted if Wendell ran the Tenderloin in any way. If anything the Cambodian gangs ran it now. But I nodded.

"Who's the four-eyed cowboy?" Dulcet asked, looking at me with no social shyness whatever.

I thought her accent was maybe Florida. She didn't wear much makeup; her lips were naturally dark pink. She had hazel eyes, and it looked to me like one of her cheekbones was slightly lower than the other. You had to look close to see it. That might be from an operation that went wrong. Or a beating.

I looked at her bare arms and didn't see any tracks. But if there'd been much of that she wouldn't have bare arms.

"Slim Purdoux," I said, and put out my hand.

She did a little girlish curtsey, ironic as her outfit, and briefly shook my hand. I could feel hand lotion still drying on her slender fingers.

"Pleased ta meet you Mr Cowboy." A mock of a little girl's voice. "I'm Dulcet Groans."

"She got an act, when she strip," Latesha said, seeming to feel an explanation was necessary. "Does that little girl thing."

"What?" I said. "No lollipop?"

"I'm her motherfuckin' lollipop and the only one, you keep that up there in yo cowboy hat, too," Wendell said. Not bothering to put threat in his voice. "Unless I say she give you some."

Dulcet said, "Tuck in your shirt, cowboy." Dropping the little girl tone.

"I can't," I said.

She looked right at the place where the gun was and nodded faintly and then opened up her purse—and got out some candy. "You like sour candy? This is super-sour, this stuff."

"No thanks."

I glanced at the bar. Red had that skinny whore on his lap, he was grinning at her with all his tobacco discolored teeth. She was chattering away and didn't seem to mind him. Her hand was on his back, not so far from his wallet. Red was kind of stupid in some ways, but my guess was she was going to be sorry if she tried to take his wallet.

The bartender hadn't come back from the bathroom yet. The few remaining patrons were looking at the bathroom—and at the cash register. Wendell had only taken the large bills.

"I'll bet they like that little girl thing, down at the club, there," I said vaguely, sensing the others were waiting for a comment from me.

"Sure they like it, they all perverts," Wendell said. "But fuck, I like it too."

Latesha laughed. "You so crazy."

An old black man got up from his stool and went to the restrooms, opened the men's room door— and there was the bartender on the floor, slumped against the wall, with a needle dangling in his arms, nodding. Not dead—just dreamland.

I looked away, so I wouldn't see Frankie, and watched as the people in the bar got up and, taking turns, looked at the bartender, then went around behind the bar....

Red dumped the whore off his lap; he'd pretty much forgotten she'd existed, you could tell, before she even hit the floor.

"You fuck!" she shouted, rubbing her fanny.

Red went behind the counter, grabbing bags of peanuts and a bottle of Irish whiskey.

"Get me that Remy's, Red, yo," Wendell called over to him.

The old black man had the Remy's bottle, and tried to hold it back. Red cold-cocked the old guy in the forehead with the bottle he already had, caught the other bottle falling in the hand that held the peanut bags without losing the peanuts; arms crowded with all this he came back around the other side of the bar, waited by the door.

"Let's go then, eh?"

Dulcet watched all this without reacting, except she clicked her front teeth together, click-click-click, sort of meditatively. She had a way of doing that.

"That jus' like the boy," Wendell said. "Getting peanuts. Without me that all he do, steal peanuts."

Latesha barked a laugh again.

"How come you made me leave work, Wendell?" Dulcet asked, chewing sour taffy like gum. "I was making some money for you."

"I s'pose we gonna go out to the Sunset district, see what we can see," Wendell went on. "Les get the van...."

He led the way to the door—I let him lead the way, right then.

I glanced behind the bar on the way out of the place, and saw the old man sprawled back there, his head bloody, stirring a little, cursing softly.

I looked into myself and saw no feeling for the old man, which was interesting. I was different today. I was, for sure.

Mostly all I felt, right then, was relief at moving, staying one step ahead of that certain something.

When we left, the whore was in the bathroom, with the door open, going through the bartender's pockets.

THE SECOND PART

Put On Your Glasses You Dumb Bastard

4

It wasn't just luck, finding Victor. I had dropped him and Frankie off at this little shopping center before and I knew Victor was here most nights till the cops ran them off around midnight.

"You can smell the ocean," Dulcet said, rolling down the van window. She was in the front of the old Ford van, beside Red, who was driving; me and Wendell and Latesha were in the back seat.

We were about twenty blocks from the ocean, in the parking lot of a shopping center dominated by a Safeway. The big red letters, lying about safety, shone morosely down at the parking lot. The supermarket was flanked by a dry cleaners, and a Taqueria; the shopping center had a shoe store, too, and a couple of shops that'd gone out of business, with For Lease signs in the windows. *Fogtown Comics 'n Cards* had not made the grade.

On the right side of the parking lot from us was a Shell station, and the teenagers congregated behind it, with skateboards and portable CD players. And there was Victor, as always, with half a dozen other guys and one defiantly-smoking pimply white girl with cerise hair. She was sitting on an overturned plastic bucket, flipping a light stick up over her head; catching it, flipping it up again.

There was an impromptu line of skateboarders doing grinds against one of those little cement bars they put at the end of parking spaces.

"Whoa Nigga! You can't do a 180 on that?" That was Victor, heckling some kid. "Nigger, you can do better than that!" Victor was a medium-sized kid with a slack mouth and spiked up hair, brown toward the roots, the tips bleached white. He wore a zip up windbreaker with the hood up over a D12 T-shirt, same kind of calf-length shorts as Wendell had, Airwalk skateboard shoes.

We pulled the van up near the boys, as if we were just watching the skateboarding.

"Mother*fucker!*" Victor was yelling, as he piled up trying to do a grind, scraping his palms. "Nigger—" This to a portly white kid. "—get out my way!"

"How come," Dulcet said, "all the shoes the kids wear now are, like, too big for their feet?"

"They shoes not too big on the inside," Latesha said. "Just the outside. Too fucking big for they little bodies."

"What I am wantin to know," Wendell murmured, lighting a joint, "is why the white boy say 'nigger' all the time, what up with that?"

"They ain even any of them black," Latesha said.

Wendell offered me the blunt. I shook my head. Still holding the smoke in, he passed it to Red.

Victor was looking toward us. "That's him there wearing the windbreaker," I said. "Go ahead, Dulcet."

She opened a window, lazily leaned her cleavage out the window. "Hey sugarbone! You Victor?"

He looked at her with a visible mingling of lust and naked suspicion. "Uh...yeah?"

The portly kid laughed. "He's not sure who he is."

Dulcet idly fluffed one of her puppydog hair tufts with her hand. "I'm from Bigass Skateboards. We're looking to sponsor you," Dulcet said. "We heard you were good. You want to come with us and try out?"

"I never heard of no Bigass Skateboards," the girl said, scowling at Dulcet. "They're, all, hoaxing you, Vic."

"I think I heard of it," Victor said. Though Dulcet had made the name up. He snapped the skateboard up with the tip of his foot, caught it in his hand, without looking at it, and walked over to us. "Ya'll get the ska'ers to try out this time of night?" He asked, seeing Wendell and Latesha through the window. Putting the black-talking act back on.

"That's Bigass Skaterboards for you!" Dulcet said. "That's our lifestyle! Come on—we're going over to the skate park."

"Which one?"

"Nearest one, fool," Latesha said. She opened the backdoor of the van.

I leaned back, keeping my face in the shadows, my hat brim tilted down.

Victor nodded, mouth open, eyes half glazed. His nostrils twitched at the smell of the pot. "Oh—that new park out at Sutro baths? Fuck it, les go. I'm your nigga."

Wendell laughed softly.

He climbed in the van, and squeezed in between me and Latesha. Wendell was in the seat behind us. Latesha closed the van door with a slam that made Victor jump, and we drove off, toward the beach.

Wendell leaned forward toward Victor. "So you my nigga huh?"

"If ya'll want to sponsor me for skateboard competitions and shit, yeah nigga. Shit yeah, dog. Can I have a hit off that blunt?"

Latesha laughed and passed it to him. "That a blunt huh?"

I said, "I thought a blunt was one of those little cigars, with some marijuana hid in it, and some other dope too."

"It used to be," Dulcet said, nodding, watching the boy smoke the dope. Pretty expert he was with it, too. "But now it just means reefer I guess."

Wendell was watching Victor with hooded eyes.

Victor looked at each of us, a little more nervous with each one. He finally noticed me. "Mr. Purdoux?"

"That's part of me," I said.

"Yo, you the one recommended me to be sponsored?"

I chuckled. "I recommended you, all right."

"Is Frankie going to chill widdus at the skatepark?"

I looked at him for a long moment. Finally I was able to answer him. "Frankie's dead, Victor. He died of polytoxic exposure to narcotics. Ecstasy and some other stuff all mixed together."

Victor coughed smoke. "What? He's dead? For serious? You're fucking with me!"

"You hadn't heard? Yes he is, Victor. He's dead. There's a lot about him and me you don't seem to've heard about...."

Victor gaped at me. Then something occurred him. He looked out the window. "This ain't the way to the skatepark."

"Hey bingo!" Red hooted.

"What's up with this shit, motherfucker?" Victor asked, with his best street bravado.

Wendell leaned closer to Victor. "What up with that gangbanger shit you talking you little cracker bitch boy?"

Victor blinked. The pot had slowed his reactions. "Uh...fuck. You dudes ain't sponsoring shit are you."

"That's right, Victor," I said. "That was an untruth."

"But I was good, wasn't I?" Dulcet said.

Latesha laughed. "Yeah! Damn! 'That's Bigass Skateboards! That's our *lifestyle*'!"

Wendell chuckled appreciatively. "You are good, Dulcet. That's my babygirl."

Dulcet stuck her hand out toward Victor. He recoiled. She said, "You want some sour candies?" She opened her hand, to show him a couple of wrapped up sour taffies.

He took them, automatically, "Uh, cool, thanks." He looked at me. "So—if you're not, you know...."

I nodded sagely. "We are on a whole different mission, Victor. I have some information in my head and I need you to confirm it. You can do that by telling me where Frankie got the drugs. From you, right?"

"What? Fuck no! We both got 'em at the same time. But he took more and he...I don't know...I threw mine up...."

Latesha laughed.

Victor scowled and added defensively. "Yo I was drinking hella Forties, man!"

"Oh shit, he drinkin 'Forties' too," Wendell said, shaking his head. "Boy, can't you find your own culture?"

"It's that Slim Shady motherfucker," Latesha said, pointing at Victor's T-shirt.

"Who'd you get the X from, Victor?" I persisted.

"...I...we...we got 'em from Abel at the Bike and Board. And I don't know where he got 'em."

I looked at him and I knew he was lying about not knowing where Abel got them. "Yeah you do, Victor. Where'd Abel get 'em?"

Victor looked at the door. I'm pretty sure he was imagining slamming that door open, jumping from the van. We were driving slowly down side streets, zig-zagging toward the beach road.

I shook my head. "Victor? Forget it. Don't think about going for that door. That's not going to work. Think about what I asked you."

He glanced at me—then away. When he looked back at me there were tears in his eyes. "Frankie's really dead?"

"I saw his body...." My voice caught, "in the...." I cleared my throat. "Yeah. He's dead."

Victor looked into the middle distance, likely thinking about Frankie being dead—and I could see him peering, for a moment, into eternity. He whispered, "Whoa. Fuck."

"Where'd he get 'em?"

Victor looked at the door again. "They're gonna kill me if I tell. I know because my cousin works for 'em too but they ain't gonna care they got my fuckin cousin there. Anybody talks about it...I mean, this guy's got connections with some people—those sick motherfuckers, they...." He shook his head convulsively. "No fucking way, Mr. Purdoux. Please."

I patted his shoulder. "That stuff about what they'd do to you's just bullshit to scare you, Victor."

Wendell looked out the window at a passing car. "That one not a cop, but who knows when one ride on by and get curious." He sighed and drew his pistol.

Victor was trying to seem unworried, unwrapping a sour candy.

Wendell smacked Victor on the side of the head with the gun to get his attention. Latesha barked her laugh.

The boy recoiled, shouting, at the impact. The blood stained his scalp almost immediately.

I looked inside myself again, to see if I cared. I saw nothing there. Felt nothing. I didn't care.

I leaned back in my seat to wait. We drove along the beachside highway....There were few lights here....

"What the matter, 'dog'," Wendell said. "I thought ya'll liked to get real with the niggas. I'm just keeping it real...nigga." He grabbed Victor by the throat with his left hand, with his right pressed the gun barrel to the side of Victor's head. Some blood ran down from the sobbing teenager's head wound, and parted around the muzzle of the gun. "You know what's real? My dick in you Mama's pussy. You know what else is real? I tell you what—I got some real for you. I'm gonna give you somethin' makes its own *real*. It's called *a bullet*, mother-fucker."

"Ricky Kwai!" Victor shouted. "They got a warehouse down by Richmond Point...Kwai and sons...."

"That 'confirm' what you wanted to 'confirm' there, Tex?" Wendell said, not taking the gun from Victor's head.

I didn't like the way Wendell said that. I looked at him and put my hand on my gun.

Victor's eyes were sliding to their corners to try to see Wendell's pistol.... His slack jaw was trembling, dropping a little spittle into his lap.

"That kid looks comical, doesn't he, Latesha?" Dulcet said, as if fondly amused with a toddler.

"He going to pee his pants."

"Hey now he don't fuckin pee in my van, ay!" Red called, sharply, over his shoulder. His voice was a little blurred by the smokeless tobacco he'd just thumbed under his lip.

We were just pulling into a strip parking lot at the beach. There was a faint scribble of silver on the waves from the young moon, and far down the beach a fire burned in an old steel oil barrel. I could just make out bottles glinting as they were lifted to firelit faces.

Red cut the van's engine and switched off its lights. We sat in a little glow from a streetlight about a hundred feet away

Latesha peered at the fire down the beach. "We way far off from those people," Latesha said. "They cain't see no license number from here."

Wendell was still watching me. "You don't know shit about this Kwai or the dealer, do you Tex."

Red turned to look at me. "I don't trust this cocksucker, Wendell. 'Tex'. 'Slim'. He don't' even know his own name. He's lying about shit, Wendell. He's making all this shit up eh? I don't want to be around him if we don't need to."

I ignored Red. "I know what I need to know, Wendell," I said. Figuring that was the right degree of ambiguity. I looked him in the eyes and waited.

Maybe Wendell had figured I had jerked him off about the money supposedly just sitting there for the taking. Maybe he'd resent that—and it would end here, in this van on this dark beach, with a scream from Victor and an exchange of gunshots.

So big deal. Let's do it then.

Wendell looked at me, his face hard to read in the dimness. "You know what you know, huh. You just a white guy lost his kid, looking for revenge. That's some fucked up shit for me to get into."

"I heard that," Latesha said.

I shrugged. "The money's there. I stand a better chance of coming out of it alive with the money, if I have some help. But you do what you want. Within reason."

But Wendell smiled. "Well shit. It's like I said, I got nothing else on. Let's see what we see."

"You guys, listen...." Victor began.

"Oh now it's 'you guys' and not 'what up my nigga'?" Wendell observed. "Fuck you, bitch boy."

Red turned in his seat and pointed his finger at Wendell. "You don't shoot his brains all over my van Wendell, eh? I said you the boss but this fucking van is all I got, ay?"

"Just shut the fuck up, Red, I'm gone take him over to that dumpster there. You get the motor runnin' but keep the lights off—"

"Hey, whoa!" Victor shrilled. "Don't!"

"Got to, 'brotha man'," Wendell said, grinning. "Because we going to have to kill some motherfuckers around all that dope money. If they is any. And with you knowing about us...uh uh. Noooooo...."

I looked into myself. Was I going to let them do this?

The side door made a rumble-rumble-*chunk* guillotine sound as Wendell slid it open and then he and Latesha were pushing Victor out. Victor yelled something I couldn't make out and tried to run but Wendell had him by the shirt tail.

"Look at that, Latesha!" Dulcet pointed at Victor's boxer shorts, exposed above the loose waistband, showing now under his shirt. "Isn't that cute, showing his undies like a homeboy? They all do that now— All the white teeny-peepees."

Latesha laughed. "'Teeny peepees'!" But the laugh seemed forced. She was looking after Wendell and Victor with a sort of blank sadness.

"Ooh," Dulcet said, pointing at the floor, "he dropped one of my candies still wrapped on the floor there, hand me that, I've only got a few more on me.... Thanks Lateshadoll...."

Wendell was dragging Victor over to a dumpster in the parking lot about fifty feet away. Cars passed but Wendell and Victor were in the darkness, on that side of the van; he was dragging Victor away from the streetlight into deeper and deeper shadow.

Victor yelled, *"Mr. Purdouuuuuuux!"*

I remembered Victor as a boy of 12 on a trip to the Marin County Fair with me and Frankie. Waving with Frankie from a whirligig as the garish ride-car whipped by. *"Yo, hi Mr. Purdoux!"*

I remembered him and Frankie showing me skateboard moves. Victor, who had no Dad, just as concerned as Frankie to have me watch him do a trick. *"Watch, Mr. Purdoux!"*

I sighed. And I drew my gun.

Latesha saw that, and reached for a gun somewhere low, stashed somewhere I couldn't see. She did it so I'd notice.

I said, "Just simmer. I want to shoot the little prick myself. He got my son killed."

Latesha relaxed and nodded sadly.

I got up and climbed out of the van and, hiding my gun in my left armpit, strode over to catch up with Wendell.

Victor was on the ground, Wendell standing over him. Victor trying to get onto his feet to run—in the position of a sprinter—and Wendell kicked him hard, knocking him over against the dumpster. "Ow shit please! Don't! I'm not going to tell anyone anything!"

"Wendell?"

He turned to look at me; I could just make out that he was frowning.

His gun hovered in some kind of midway space between Victor and me. It might turn to Victor or it might turn to me.

5

I made my voice apologetic. Man-to-man friendly. "I used to make sandwiches for this pitiful little fuck, here, Wendell. He's got a single Mom. She's...she was pretty nice to my kid. So I'm asking you not to kill her. Nobody's going to backtrack all the way to this dumb little asshole. And he'd never go to the PD on his own."

Wendell looked at me. Thinking. Victor was breathing hard. Listening hard.

Wendell looked past me at the van. "I...don't think I can do it, Tex...If I let him go after I walk him over here to do this...."

Victor wailed, hearing that, and tried to crawl away.

Distractedly, Wendell kicked Victor in the head so that he sagged, gasping, stunned.

"I understand," I said. "They're watching. I told 'em I was going to ask you if I could do it. Like a favor. Long as it's like under orders from you, right? I'll make it look good."

Wendell thought about that, frowning.

Finally he shook his head in quiet amazement. "Lookit that! I am just letting you fuck with me and fuck with me. I must really like you, Tex. But you second-guess me one more time? That's the end of your ass. You understand me?"

I played it like one businessman negotiating with another, all reasonableness. "Yeah of course. I hear you. I'm just asking a personal favor. This once."

He looked at me, then at the van. Then he nodded. He said, loudly, so the others would hear it. "You going to do it, Tex, then fucking get it done! I want that shit done, motherfucker!"

I nodded vigorously. He walked back toward the van.

Victor was blinking, coming back to himself. He turned to look up at me.

I hated the sight of him. Too simple to blame it all on him but—hadn't been for him, probably Frankie would still be alive. And it was easier than admitting who the real culprit was, right then. I said, slowly, thoughtfully: "Actually, thinking about it...I really *should* kill you, Victor. I know you're the little prick got Frankie started on drugs."

I raised the gun and pointed it—Victor screamed.

There was a ragged rust-hole in the dumpster, hand-width, right next to Victor's head. I shot into the rust-hole, twice, saying, between the shots, "Act dead, dumbshit."

Victor, whimpering, sagged as if dead. But you could still see him breathing.

"Hold your breath till we're gone, moron," I muttered.

Victor sucked it in and held it.

I strode with a grim, satisfied air back to the van.

It occurred to me I didn't have much ammunition left in that clip. I'd needed ammo but it might not be wise to tell Wendell that.

The people at the fire down the beach were shouting something I couldn't make out. They'd heard the gunfire, seen the flashes.

I half expected the van to drive off without me, but they waited, though the van was moving when I jumped into it.

Red backed up, turned, drove out onto the highway, then down a sidestreet, before switching on his headlights—and before I finally got the side door shut.

※　※　※

We were cruising slowly by Fort Mason, where yuppies and bohos went to see small, chic theatre productions, and gay guys went to orchid shows. We passed Fort Mason, turned, another block or two came to a strip mall.

"This the Sunset district?" Dulcet asked.

"Not exactly," I said. "This is the Marina."

Barry White was rumbling around a tune on KMEL. Wendell was singing softly along with it. "I admire that man," he said. "Barry's got style. He know how to talk to a woman."

I saw a smile ghost over Dulcet's lips when he said that.

"There's the *Bike 'n Board*, right there," I said, pointing at the strip mall.

I'd taken Frankie here for skateboard trucks and the hottest ballbearings and a T-shirt that said ARREST ME I'M A SKATE-BOARDER on it. And he'd reluctantly accepted an Element helmet and shin guards. Which he'd only worn occasionally. I'd been way more worried about him killing himself from cracking his head open skateboarding than getting into dope.

Red pulled up across the street from the shop. There was a light on

77

in the back room—I could see it over the unfinished wall behind the counter.

Frankie might've grown up to be a writer. He might've grown up to be a comic book publisher. He might've grown up to be a doctor who worked in Physicians Without Borders. Or he might've been a shop-owner, selling bicycles and skateboards in a little stripmall storefront like this—and loving it, and perfectly fine, perfectly happy, safe as anyone is...safe....

"I don't know what the point of this is, eh?" Red muttered, looking in the mirror at Wendell. "There's not going to be much cash in that place. It's just another place to get noticed by the cops, you know eh?"

He might've grown up....

"Red got a point," Wendell said. "We going to follow this up, let's go over to Richmond where the fucking money is."

"Red." I looked at Red. I thought it might be time to do the necessary, with respect to Red. I could feel he was the loose brick in my building. "What's the appeal, with Red, Wendell?"

I said it that way, talking about Red like he wasn't there, because I knew it would piss Red off.

And I needed to get started pissing Red off. Because Red didn't like me around. So I didn't like Red around. So I had to push him so he made his move when I was expecting it—not when I'd let my guard down. It's a pretty basic equation, really.

Red looked at me in some amazement. "Who the fuck you think you are, cocksucker?"

Wendell snorted. "Red's a good driver, and he's got nerve. He always been loyal."

"I ain't loyal to this Texas cocksucker," Red said.

"Red, find another epithet," I said, genuinely irritated. Cocksucker I could just barely tolerate, for a brief time. But Texas cocksucker?

"Whoa-ho, listen to that eh? Epithet! Suck my dick, Texas cocksucker!"

I decided this wasn't the time to let it escalate any further. "Wendell," I said, letting all feeling slide from my voice, "I need to find out from this guy Abel exactly *when* the money's going to be there. They'll have pick-up days."

"Now that's a point too," Latesha said.

"Shut up, Latesha," Wendell said absently. He considered, briefly, and then he nodded just once. "Okay, but I ain't here for any motherfuckin mission of vengeance for angry daddies," Wendell said. Meaning I was on my own in there with Abel. That suited me.

"I hear you, man," I said, getting out of the van.

"And don't fuck around," Wendell said. "We leave if we don't feel comfortable, you know?" He slammed the door behind me.

I nodded my head as I walked across the street. Looked up and down the avenue for cops.

No cops, no cars of any kind. I put my hand on my gun in my waistband.

The front of the shop was dark; just a small neon clock on over the back counter. Mountain bikes hung from racks; skateboards lined the wall over the counter; there were cases of skateboard-trucks, wheels, special ball bearings.

I walked around behind the shop. I saw Abel through the back window. He was using an electric screwdriver, tightening the truck screws on a skateboard vised to a workbench. There was a finished skateboard next to it. He was making house boards with his logo on them.

There was a bong on the bench, with smoke drifting from the top of it, like the last smoke from a chimney just after the factory's shut down.

I could hear music playing from a radio on a shelf over the bench. It was a local metal-rock station, which called itself "The Bone" for reasons no one but its marketing department understood. They were playing Slipknot, I thought. It was either Slipknot or Pantera.

The back door was open. "Hi Abel," I said, cheerfully, as I came in behind him, like I was an old pal coming for a visit.

He jumped, spinning around with the electric screwdriver poised out in front of him like a knife.

"Fuck! Who the fuck are you, sneaking up on me like that! I am fucking closed, dude! Back the fuck out that door!"

I laughed. He made a funny sight, all worked up like that with that little whirring tool in his hand, especially considering how I felt about him now.

Abel was an ex-surfer, now at forty-something a minor entrepreneur in the skateboard resurgence. He was chunky, darkly tanned, his head shaved on the sides, blond hair long on top and back. He wore surfer shorts and an open bowling shirt; under that a T-shirt for Dogbreath Skateboards with a picture of a cartoon dog riding a skateboard and flipping the world off.

Wendell had said don't fuck around so I pulled the gun and closed the door behind me.

"Alright that's it, asshole—" Abel blustered, setting himself for a fight—but looking more scared than angry. Especially after he noticed the gun. "What the fuck—you going to rob me you won't get much, man, it's not worth it."

"Abel," I said calmly, "You killed my son."

He took a step back and went pale. "Who the fuck...No, dude.... What?"

"Or—you and me killed him. You more proactively, selling him dope—me passively. Working together without knowing it, you and me, to kill my son. Eventually, the police are going to take care of my part of the justice, what with the shit I'm getting into. But I think, really, it's up to me to take care of your part. Don't you?"

He was stoned and it took a while for all this to sink in. "Man you ...got me totally mixed up with somebody."

"I know you, Abel. By sight. Victor says you're dealing the bad X."

"Victor! That little fuck! Victor is full of shit!" He looked at the gun in my hand. "He's full up to his little pin head with steamin' shit, dude! You think I'm dealing drugs, call the police on me."

"I don't have time for that."

"Goddammit what do you mean, killed your son?"

"You know my boy, Abel. Knew him. Frankie Purdoux? He's dead. He got the dope that killed him from you. Bad X. Not that you can't die from 'good' X. But this shit—doctor thinks it was particularly toxic."

"Look I smoke a little weed—I might even sell a little Thai stick now and then—" He was going onto the balls of his feet, probably thinking about jumping me, jabbing at me with that electric screwdriver. Maybe catch me by surprise before I shot him. "But I never...."

"We know about that warehouse in Richmond, Abel. Come on, man. I just want to know...when do the people who supply it pick up there money? I'll bet you know. You've got some connections out there...."

He was breathing hard. Almost hyperventilating. And he was thinking too hard: You could see the strain of it on his face. Trying to estimate...could he jump me?

"You can't, Abel," I said. "The safety's off, I can't miss at this range, and if you twitch, I'll shoot a hole in you. Now put that cute little Home Depot Sale Item down. Put it fucking down *now!*"

I extended the gun out in front of me, clasping it in both hands, and aimed at his head. If I had to shoot, I'd probably drop the muzzle to the center of his mass, to be sure of hitting him, but the psychological effect of a gun pointed between your eyes is profound.

I looked into myself, to see if I felt bad about any of this.

Nope. Not a damn thing.

"Okay—you're not going to drop the tool? Then I'll say goodbye right now, Abel—"

He dropped the electric screwdriver from slack fingers, his eyes now riveted on the muzzle of my gun. It was like he was trying to literally see down the dark barrel, see the tip of the bullet.

I thought about Frankie, and sorrow was utterly indistinguishable from rage—and I felt like pistol-whipping Abel to a pulp, instead of shooting him. And he kept looking down into the barrel of that gun.... There was no time to beat his head in.

I kept my voice carefully flat. "You ever think about what happens when a person gets shot, Abel? You better think about it if you plan to keep anything back, having to do with that certain little warehouse. A bullet, Abel, is like a battering ram. You know? Like for a castle?"

He nodded numbly, staring into the muzzle.

I went on, genuinely into my subject, "The bullet, like the battering ram, *smashes into* its target. It breaks through. I mean, in movies, they make it look like punching a neat little hole, almost surgical, but really it's a *smashing*. It *smashes* through the skin, it *smashes* through the soft tissue, it *smashes* through the organs, and it *smashes* through bone. Can you imagine how that'd feel? A flying battering ram smashing into *you*? And with a big ol' .44 calibre like this? It sets up shockwaves that explode through the body from that big hole. Sometimes it smashes right on out the other side...."

Abel made a squeaking sound in his throat. "I think...."

"Yes, Abel? Go on."

"I think they pick up the money Thursday night. Maybe four or five guys get together, count it and shit. They got a whole route they go on and that's the last...the last stop...to count it, turn it over to...."

A whole route? That would please Wendell. Lots of money. Me, I didn't give a fuck.

"And?"

"I swear that's all I know. But don't tell them, if you tell anybody that I told you this shit, they'll—"

"You are worrying for nothing, about that."

He relaxed a little, until I went on:

"...because I'm going to kill you right now, man, for what you did to my son."

"Hey—people buy shit off me they know it's not pharmaceutical!" He was waving his hands now, his voice getting loud and shrill; he was edging toward the door behind him that led into the front of the shop. "I don't make nobody take it! And he musta done that shit wrong!"

I nodded understandingly. "I would generally agree that an adult, they take their own chances with drugs. It's *their* lives, Abel, right? But a kid Frankie's age? He didn't know what he was doing. And you didn't really care to tell him. You don't really care about anything or anybody."

"There's money—right there. In that metal box there. See it there—on the work bench?" He wanted me to look away from him. "See it? I can get more tomorrow—a whole buttload more!"

I shook my head and my hand tightened on the gun—and he bolted for the door to the front room of the shop.

I have a thing about shooting people in the back. Not that I'd ever shot anybody dead before. But I'd known that I would someday. Some people just know it.

"Hey Abel—"

With my left hand I scooped the finished skateboard from the work-table, slapped it toward him down under his feet.

Abel tripped over it, fell down in the doorway, turned toward me. Scrambled up—

Squeaking: "Don't—it was your own—"

They say that it's hard to shoot someone the first time, and after that it gets easier. They're right, up to a point. Maybe it's especially harder for certain people, their first time. I did hesitate. I did.

He looked pathetic, scared. His face drawn into a white, involuntary grimace of fear.

But there was a big momentum in me; a momentum that was like a wall of black volcano glass, pressing down. And it didn't really matter, those feelings that made me hesitate. They were just some extra, peripheral feelings.

The main thing was to kill this motherfucker.

I shot him twice, carefully. First time he yelped, like a kicked puppy; before the second shot, he put his hands up instinctively to protect himself, palms outward—

I fired, and one of his fingers disappeared. The bullet that took off his finger finished its work: a battering ram smashing into his chest.

Abel fell back, and convulsed like a fish just yanked from the hook: I was surprised at how much he shook, there, on the floor. After a minute, he lay still. I could smell the shit as his bowels let go.

I looked at him. What had he started to say? *Don't! It was your own....*

My own fault? Was that what he was going to say? If so—he had a point. But it was something I already knew.

That's when I saw it—that finger I'd shot off had been carried along in some kind of slip-stream of velocity, and the bloody upper half of it, about from the middle knuckle up, was lodged in one of the holes in his chest, right over his heart, flipped around—

Abel's shot-off finger was pointing out of the wound on his chest, and right at me.

Life simply likes to *fuck with you,* sometimes.

I was distantly aware that Abel's radio was playing a Blue Oyster Cult song.

I muttered, "Some bands just refuse to die...." The chorus was saying, over and over,

> *One step*
> *ahead of the Devil*
> *one step*
> *ahead of The Man*
> *one step*
> *ahead of Evil*
> *You can only run as far as you can...*
> *you can only run as far as you can....*

I wanted to shoot the radio, then, but I just grabbed the metal box Abel had pointed to, put the safety on my gun, stuck the gun in my waistband under my shirt, and went out to the van. I had to keep moving.

You can only run as far as you can....

I'd just killed a man. Once before I'd shot a guy in the leg, years ago. I'd never killed one before.

I felt a little high, really.

※　　※　　※

"Four hundred and six dollars and change," Latesha said, as she finished counting the money from the little metal box.

"Ey, big fucking deal, okay?" Red snorted.

"You can have my share, Red," I said. "Buy yourself a personality."

It's not the line, it's the delivery. Dulcet laughed, anyway.

"Hey fuck you, cocksucker—I'll *take* your fucking share."

I smiled like Buddha and said softly and sweetly, "It was an offer made in all sincerity, Red."

Wendell chuckled at that, and shook his head. "Crazy editor boy."

I wished I hadn't told them, over dinner, that I'd been a book editor.

We were crossing the Richmond bridge from the Marin side, soaring over the blueblack San Francisco bay on an arc of steel.

"So that warehouse was in the phonebook, Dulcet?" I asked. It was time to ignore Red again.

"Sure, but it was an old phonebook. If they haven't moved...." She shrugged.

"That's where the serious money is."

Red snorted. "Yeah. Maybe."

Dulcet turned and lolled her head over the back of her seat and pouted at Wendell. "I want to get high, Wendell."

"You get high when I tell you, bitch."

"You get high sometime, editor boy?" Latesha asked me.

"Not really. Lost control of that shit a few times."

"Shit, I always lose control. Wasn't for Wendell I be shaking my heels at the ceiling for that glass pipe."

Dulcet laughed with a sisterly fondness.

"That skateboard shop guy going to talk to anyone, editor boy?" Wendell asked.

He gave me a particular look to mean, *You kill this one for real?*

"No, he isn't," I said. Seriously wishing they'd stop calling me editor boy. "He's not even going to ask what's for breakfast."

I gave him a little nod that meant, *For real this time. He's dead.*

I looked inside myself again. Still didn't find any regret about Abel.

What I did feel, though, was tired.

Maybe some drinks would help. I had to keep out ahead of that thing that was trying to catch up, inside me...and if I slept, it'd get me for sure...maybe a gallon or so of Irish coffee....

"How come they callin' you editor boy?" Dulcet asked.

I sighed. "Because when we ate dinner I was still a little drunk and I made the mistake of telling them I was a book editor till recently. After I got out of jail I got a break from—"

"Ooh! A book editor. You edit anybody famous?"

"Depends on what you mean by famous. Real famous—Spaulding. Joel Spaulding. I'm not his usual editor but for one book—"

"Joel Spaulding! I love his shit!"

"She always reading something," Latesha said affectionately.

Dulcet said, "Did you edit *Devil May Care*? I loved that one. When that guy turns into a tiny little bug-man and crawls into people's bodies and eats them up while he's in there and they can hear him saying 'how you like that, how you like that'? That's some funny shit."

"Damn girl, you makin' me sick wid that shit!" Wendell said.

"I didn't edit that one, no...."

Red was taking the first exit off the bridge, toward Point Richmond.

We circled around and down, followed the freeway for awhile, and then drove along the underpass beneath it. The towers and tanks of a refinery rose to one side; they always made me think of tubes in the back of an old-fashioned TV set, writ large.

If I'd been driving around with Meredith I could've remarked about how some artifacts, like industrial technology, only made you think of other kinds of technology; that was the referent that came first to mind, it was that far removed from human warmth. But though these people would've pretty much understood the remark, because they weren't stupid—with the possible exception of Red—they wouldn't have seen any point in saying it. Would've seen like jerking off to them. But Meredith liked to talk about ideas for their own sake.

Too bad I hated her fucking guts now.

Thinking about that, I hoped she hated me too. That'd be justice for Frankie: if his parents each hated the other.

"There's the cowboy's warehouse," Dulcet muttered. There was an almost sexual anticipation in her voice.

It was a squat, rectangular, tin-roofed wooden place. A rust pitted metal sign, from maybe thirty years ago, read KWAI & SONS over the loading dock at the parking strip. On one end wall was one of those old billboards they painted on the sides of buildings: the faded, peeling face of a cherubic boy; the boy was brandishing an orange soda bottle and under his grin was the slogan, "*FANTA, now* that's *refreshment!* " Complete with the quotation marks.

"Shouldn't be too hard," I said.

The warehouse looked pretty run-down, though not abandoned. Run down is good, because it means the place is porous. Lots of holes, ways to break in. Less chance of an effective alarm system.

Not that I wanted to get in and out without coming across anybody. There was no point in it, for me, if the dealers weren't around, even if there was a big pile of unguarded money sitting in the middle of the floor. I just wanted to get the drop on the sons of bitches.

We drove slowly around the place.

There was a big black SUV parked in its weedy strip of gravel parking, and one of those bull-like six-wheeled Ford pick-ups with the "extended cab". It was blue and its license plate read "BLUE OX". I could see a light in a painted-over corner window of the warehouse, where the office might be. No signs of new alarm systems. Nothing much else to see, except an outside door into the corner office—a last resort.

Across from the warehouse was a storage-rental business with a chain link fence around it. It was late, no one was around, though they might have a security guard.

Behind the warehouse was a vacant lot waist-high with weeds. On the other sides of the warehouse were cinder block buildings, one a modest plastic toy manufacturing plant; the other maybe another warehouse. Both looked deserted, closed down for now.

"Your skateboard man say when the cops patrol through here," Red asked, knowing I probably hadn't asked.

Latesha looked at me.

"You ax him that?"

"No," I admitted. "But he wouldn't have known. Cops aren't here now so maybe we should just go with the momentum. It's quiet now. We could just...go in. Right now."

"Now?" Dulcet asked, her eyes shining.

Wendell shook his head. "The money don't pile up till tomorrow night. So that when we going in."

Dulcet said, "Can we go over to Leon's? He's so close...."

"That what I fittin' to do," Wendell said, annoyed that she'd anticipated him. "We party a mite and rest up and we go in tomorrow night...."

But I didn't think I could make it that long. Not without blowing my brains out.

Or somebody else's brains. At least.

Still, we went to Leon's place, half a mile away, and thinking about it now I'm pretty sure that the bounty hunter was already watching the place when we got there.

6

I was having to keep a close eye on myself, because after years of sobriety I'd lost most of my ability to cope with whiskey—my old ability to keep my mouth and my impulses in check under the influence. I had drunk one glass and I was already on my way to drunk.

Red was indoors asleep on Leon's sofa, snoring softly. The rest of us were out back.

We sat under a naked yellow lightbulb on the big wooden back porch, talking and drinking; the others smoking pot. Wendell in a rocking chair, me in a woodframe canvas deck chair. Dulcet, wrapped in a long coat, lounging in a hammock. Latesha getting up from her deck chair, by Leon, to go into the kitchen.

Leon was a tall, very black guy, muscular but with a roll of beer fat; close cut nappy hair salted with gray. He was sagged in the overworked deck chair with a tumbler in one hand, a cigarette in the other, but he kept looking at me like he wanted to say something about what the fuck was I here for and did they know anything about me and was I maybe a cop—and then kept thinking better of it because of Wendell.

Leon's was up on the East side of the ridge that separated Richmond from the Bay. There weren't any houses real close by. It was an old two story wooden house, good-sized, with an up-sloping back yard, the front yard choked with flowering azalea bushes. The house was recently painted white and the picket fence was half-painted with the same color, as if they'd run out of the extra house paint partway.

Leon, who was even older than Wendell, had some Marvin Gaye softly playing on the living room stereo. Between songs there was the distant sound of cars; there were crickets, night birds in the ivy. I could smell the white flowers on creeper vines that had overgrown the rose bushes in the up-sloping back yard. They say that parasites dominate the biosphere.

The air smelled sweet up here. The night, though, was wearing thin. My head hurt from the liquor and I was getting hungry—and at the same time the thought of food made me sick.

Leon was Wendell's cousin, and he was part of the reason Wendell had picked the Bay Area after his crew's sudden exodus from Miami. From the general talk, I gathered Wendell had ranged across the south, Texas to Atlanta to Orlando to Miami. He'd had to go somewhere else, far and fast from Miami. I didn't know why the sudden exit from Miami, except that it had as much to do with avoiding Cuban gangsters as running from cops and bounty hunters.

"My man Leon here he put me up for six, seven weeks, when I first got here," Wendell said.

Leon took a drink, and grunted, then said, "More like four months but who counting?"

"You are, dog. You got some black tar?"

Leon hesitated. Frowned at me again....

Dulcet rolled her eyes. "He's all *right*, Leon, *fuck*."

He grunted. "And you know this how, girl?"

"She's not stupid, is how," I said.

Leon made a noise deep in his chest as he stood up. He had the look of a guy who was going to ask what I'd meant about *her* not being stupid.

"Just simmer, Leon, yo," Wendell said.

Leon glared at me; looked at Wendell. Then he pointed his finger mutely at me, and gave me a don't-fuck-with-me look—and went into the living room to turn the record over. It was an actual vinyl record on a turntable.

I wasn't popular with Red, and I wasn't popular with Cousin Leon. But the girls seemed to like me. And Wendell seemed amused by me.

Wendell needed me, too. He was no kid anymore. He needed a fat score.

Again I wondered about the television news. Had Leon seen me there? Was that what was behind the hostility? But he'd have said something about it. *Wendell you know this motherfucker went postal, shot a bunch of people at work? You can't turn your back on a wack motherfucker like that.*

But Leon's mistrust was probably more a matter of policy, made more pungent by the fact that I was a strange white guy who didn't act like the white guys he usually dealt with.

I was getting terminally antsy again. Maybe I should tell Leon *fuck you, I'm a cop. Here's some cop action if that's what you want.* And shoot him in the head. Because I gleaned that he sold black tar heroin.

He was a dope dealer. Part time.

It was just a sideline. His main job was AC Transit bus driver.

Leon came back and sat down with a double grunt.

I was about to just go for it—and get it all over and done with—and I even started moving my hand toward my gun—

—When Latesha came out with a joint for Wendell and a fresh tumbler of Johnny Walker Red for me, smiling, and I drank some of it and I felt like chilling a bit then. Wendell took his hit, handed her the pot, and she said squeakily, through the exhale: "You want a hit of this, editor boy?"

I shook my head. "And ya'll please stop calling me editor boy."

"What you going to do, if *I* want to call you editor boy?" Leon said. "Do tell."

He was checking me out by pushing me this way.

I waved my hand in a mild dismissal of Leon's crude little goad. "Call me Slim, or Jimmy."

"How about Slim Jim like those chewy things?" Dulcet said, winking. Taking up the little girl voice again: "You big bad stinky chewy stick, Slim Jim!"

Latesha laughed. "Slim Jim."

"If you must," I said, "Slim Jim. But not editor boy."

"I said what you going to do, make me call you different, editor boy? I call you what I want. Maybe four-eyes editor boy."

I glanced at Wendell. He looked up at the moon and studiously said nothing.

I shrugged. "You know, I don't think I'm going to get into a fist fight for anything, I'm not up for it. I'm fading too much. I'd lose, too. And I don't think I should *shoot* anyone just for calling me editor boy. Doesn't seem right. Especially as you're Wendell's cousin. So what does that leave me? I guess you call me editor boy."

"Oh, Leon, call him Slim. Or Tex," Dulcet said.

"Shut up, bitch," Leon said, just the way Wendell did. "Wendell your ho is backtalking me."

Wendell said, more dutifully than angrily, "Ho, shut the fuck up."

Dulcet seemed to get a certain satisfaction from hearing that, and shutting up when she heard it.

"'Kay," she said faintly.

"We going to have some harrow-ron—" That's the way Latesha said heroin. "—or not?"

"Editor boy going to have some?" Leon asked.

I had some rationale or other for saying yes. Social necessity of the moment or something. But I probably just wanted the dope. I told you, it makes no sense. It has its own logic. Like for example: *I'm going to get high on something different this time, and since it's not what I used to take, I won't get addicted to that.*

Or maybe:

Even though I'm doing the same thing I did before, getting flat-out fucked by this shit, this time it's going to end differently than all the other times.... Because this is a different time....

Or even:

I am on a mission to kill the dope dealers who killed my son. I hate dope. So now I'm going to take some dope. And that's why I hate it, and why I want to kill people who give it out, because it makes me want some now, even though dope killed my son...and that's why I must now...must now...must now have a hit...a big, strong hit....

Dope logic.

I leaned forward in my chair. "Yeah—I'll take one good hit, Leon."

He grunted. Then he pointed his finger at Wendell. "I bring out my dope, I get some pussy."

"You get some pussy anyway, these bitches do what I tell 'em to," Wendell said, starting his rocker going. It creaked on the wooden back porch, as if in reply to the crickets.

Latesha looked up at the moon. Said distantly, "Whatever my man say."
Dulcet shrugged.

"I don't want no motherfucking stripper pussy," Leon said. "Last time she said all that weird shit to me, I couldn't keep my motherfuckin wood. Made me feel like a motherfuckin child molester. So I want some cash too, Wendell. I'm almost outta shit, I can't afford to give shit away."
Wendell shrugged. "Latesha, give him all that cash Tex here got today."
"Okay baby." And Latesha got up immediately, went into the house, out front to the van. Less than two minutes later she came back and handed him most of the money I'd taken from Abel. She'd probably pocketed fifty or sixty dollars.

Leon folded the money without looking at it, and put it in a shirt pocket. He waited a while, so he could show he was in charge and hence would get the dope in his own sweet time.

Finally Leon grunted to himself, and got up, stretched, and lumbered into his bedroom. A few minutes later—Dulcet watching the doorway the whole time, waiting—he came back with a small metal tray. On the tray was a lump of black tar heroin, a small sheet of aluminum foil, and a torch-lighter.

"You going to shoot that gunk up?" I asked Wendell, conversationally. "Take a long time to cook it clean enough."

Leon shot me a glare, but got to work on the black tar, using a pocket knife to lay some of the lump out on a piece of foil....

Latesha said, "Wendell don't allow needles."

"That black tar'll give you abscesses, if you shoot it," Dulcet said, unconsciously rubbing an old scar on a bare thigh. She was watching Wendell's every move.

"We jes' chip on it, like ol' pros," Latesha said to me. She was watching Leon too.

Leon made the smoke rise, and Wendell inhaled it from the foil. He leaned back, his eyes immediately dimming.

Her voice husky now, Latesha added, "Wendell don't let us do the hard narcotics too often."

I nodded approvingly. Going to use dope, it's good to have a dope nurse.

We each chased the dragon rising from the burning black tar.... It tasted like opium to me but harsher, and it wasn't all that different.... I was already fucked up from the whiskey....

I sagged back in my chair, feeling like I'd crossed some kind of moral Rubicon....

That's right, it was doing dope that made me feel that way—not killing Abel.

Stoned, slumped in a deck chair, nose itching, slightly sick to my stomach, I told Wendell about the finger sticking out of Abel's wound. Abel's shot-off finger, pointing at me out of the bullet hole.

"You full of shit," he said, laughing.

"I swear it's true. You watch, it'll probably be in the papers." Then I thought: Dumbshit, don't mention the papers. Better they don't look in the papers....

"Because you *stuck* that finger in there, with your hand, motherfucker. That shit is ballistically impossible."

"Improbable, I grant you. But it *can* happen—because it did! It's like synchronicity. One of those weird coincidences that make you think life is playing games on you...."

Wendell nodded solemnly. "I do know that kind of shit for sure."

I almost told him about Eickoff then—that was life fucking with me, too. But I bit that one off.

I was getting sleepy from the dope and whiskey—but I was nowhere near actually sleeping. There were swastikas dancing around the edge of my vision. Scimitars flashed in the darkness. The moon breathed and exhaled, sucking in and out. I thought I saw Frankie slipping through the ivy...I thought I saw him riding that small luminous gray cloud across the sky...I thought I heard him crying....

Daddy....

It was the heroin. Just the breath of the dragon.

I took off my glasses, and rubbed my eyes. Looked up at that moon, not quite full. Without my glasses the moon was all distorted, doubled and tripled, so it looked like a fat yellow spider, the double exposure of its edges splitting to look like the spider's legs.

(About this time, I'm guessing, the bounty hunter was slipping up the side of the house...maybe he'd called the Bail Bondsman who'd hired him, a little earlier, and said, "I got 'em, and I'm going in...." Just to establish that this was all his. And he had that in his mind as he crept up the walk, with his shotgun in his hands.... *They're all mine and that's a big hunk of payday....*)

Stoned and drunk, I just started talking; it flowed out of me on the warm spring of dope and whiskey....

"When I was a kid—just, like, a teenager," I said, barely aware I was saying it aloud, "I wrote some poem about how when I took off my glasses, the blurriness, my nearsightedness, made things...sinister, weird. Like, when I looked at the moon without my glasses, the moon all double-imaged-up so it looked like a spider...just like now...just like now, too.... Glasses on or off, man, I always felt like the world was...alien, weird to me anyway...then. Even now a lot of times. But shit, back then I was 'specially...disassociative. I didn't feel a physical connection to things. I didn't identify with being a person in the world. Other people felt ordinary—and I envied feeling ordinary. I never felt ordinary—I mean, I

wasn't *special,* or wonderful, it was more like...out of it. Lost. Discon-
nected. Like some kind of bird blown from its migration path into a big
empty desert. The bird ended up in a desert when it was supposed to be
in some lush tropical place.... Things that were normal to other people,
like dances, school events, TV, shopping centers—they all seemed strange
to me. Cars seemed strange conveyances, weird shell-like accretions. I
couldn't understand why sports weren't important to me. I never felt
comfortable anywhere. I wanted the same things other people wanted—
love and admiration and acceptance—but always there was that feeling
of everything being out of focus, distorted a little, like I'd lost some
other pair of glasses...but when I got into literature, *then* I felt a connection, it was like I heard the music of life for the first time...but the fuckers
have taken that away too...they've ruined books.... It's that connected,
focused feeling I want. When I was younger, I found other things, things
that made me feel connected—drugs and rock 'n roll and guns...I used
to do some second-story work, when I was really young, mostly stealing
office machinery, petty cash from some lawyer's desk...and that's when I
felt awake and connected. But then I had this kid, I had a son, my boy
Frankie...and I felt connected to *him....* I loved him, see—so I did what
I had to for him. Went straight...but now he's gone.... They took him....
And when they told me he was dead it was like I was falling into this
hole in myself, like I had a black-hole with its super gravity in my gut
and my body, my mind, it was all sucking into it. Imploding. I was swal-
lowing myself. And I knew that to survive I could either go into...into
not feeling like I belonged on the planet again, or I could...I could go
on, ya'll know what I mean: a Mission—a memorial mission for
Frankie...and then the black sucking mouth was left behind and I...if I
pushed out the edges, if I looked for somebody to kill, something to go
after...for Some Weird Sin like Iggy said...if I was on the edge of com-

pletely going off—like today with that prick Abel—then, that's when, that's when...that's when I felt like I was in my own...my own...like I was real again, I was...like I had my glasses back on...I could see things right again, it wasn't all just a...just a nightmarish blur...."

Latesha was laughing silently. "He *so fucked up*! Cowboy all stoned up, yo. The 'bird is blown out of its migration'!"

I laughed too—we both laughed at it. It was ludicrous; it was funny. Then I stopped laughing, abruptly, feeling something crumbling inside me: I thought I heard Frankie's voice again, when a bird warbled, and the wind picked up and a fence post squeaked....

Dulcet turned her body completely around in the hammock stretching between the back porch posts, so her head was near me. Asked softly, "Cowboy...you feel bad huh."

It wasn't really sympathy. Dulcet just liked to know. Maybe she wanted to probe the wound.

"I...went on way enough already...."

"True dat," Leon muttered.

"...let's talk about something else, Dulcet," I said.

She moved her hand like a hula dancer, said lazily, "The boy's dead. I'm gonna be dead. Everybody going to be dead. Boogie man eat up everybody." Her eyelids sagged, her lower lip hung. She'd sucked three dragons down, to my one. I wanted to bite into that ripe lower lip. I wonder if I was capable of fucking anybody tonight. Maybe find out later.

(About that time, I think, the bounty hunter must've been setting himself in the darkness nearby, deciding how he was going to handle this...and hesitating, not wanting to bring the cops in but probably thinking maybe he should; wishing he'd called his partners to help him after all....)

"But maybe there's life after death," Dulcet said, not sounding as if she believed it.

Latesha said, "Why sure there is...." Said it so softly I could barely hear it. "Across the Jordan...."

"I don't know if I'd want there to be life after death," I said. "Life after death's just as likely to fuck with you...."

I was looking at Dulcet—because when I looked at her, I didn't see Frankie anywhere. She pretty much held my attention, her slim white legs, her lips, the teasing mystery in her eyes.

I managed not to think about Frankie most of the time, anyway, at least with the top part of my mind—it's a skill you get. Like, suppose you have a ripped-up, badly injured leg that hurts all the time, can't be fixed, pretty soon you get good at putting your weight entirely on the other leg—at balancing on one foot like a damn crane. You don't even know you're doing it after awhile. You lean away from the pain, and you do it expertly. That's something you can do inside yourself, too.

But still—in some part of yourself—you knew you were maimed.

I went on, "Personally...I think this life is all there is. I'm an Existentialist, I reckon, pretty devotedly...."

I noticed, distantly, that Wendell and Leon had gone inside, were talking softly near the record player in the living room. Maybe they were just discussing a choice of music, or maybe they were up to some shit. Hang with two guys like that, you should always know where they are and what they're talking about. But I didn't care, right then. I could feel the weight of my gun in the pocket of my jean jacket. There were, what, two bullets left. Just aim carefully, is all.

"What's that 'Existentialist'?" Latesha asked, taking over the rocking chair. "I heard the word a lot."

Dulcet said sleepily, "People use it all kind of ways. Doesn't seem to mean one thing."

I laughed and my laugh sounded crazy in my own ears. "You are so right! You got it nailed. It's come to mean whatever people want it to, like 'Zen' has. But what it's *supposed* to mean...something like...well, in modern times it's, uh, it's a philosophy of uh...." I couldn't seem to access that part of my brain just now.

Dulcet said, "Ohhhhh, it's about authenticity. Being real. Making decisions that make you more real. Seeing everything kind of absurd and making your own reality and shit. Recognizing that it's all up to us, in this life, 'cause death is certain and final and all that."

I looked at her.

She tinkled a laugh. "The stripper went to college and actually remembers some of that stuff! Yeah two years, almost three.... But I'm *tooooooo* happy being little Dulcet to do anything I don't wanta do...." She added, almost inaudibly, "...unless it's for Wendell...."

Latesha said, "What you said that Existentialism is, that's like Wendell is. He don't believe in anything but being Wendell as much as he can. Being real, that a big thing with him. Don't believe in nothing but this life. I try to save his soul one time, he said 'girl, you can't save my soul and if you keep trying I'm gonna save your motherfucking soul by sending your ass away from me.'" Latesha's voice was breaking. She was close to crying, as she rocked, the mournful creaking sound of the rocking chair making a torn paisley shape in my mind....

I thought I saw the moon climbing down the sky, on its eight white legs, but when I looked again, it was just squatting up there in its pale, dimly seen web of stars and stringy cloud.

"So you believe in Heaven?" I asked her.

The porch light seemed to hum a song I couldn't quite name. The light from the living room window rippled as a shadow crossed it; the shadow looked three dimensional, palpable. I drank a little more whiskey.

"I believe in Heaven and I know I ain goin', Slim Jim," Latesha said. "I ain' goin to Heaven. I chose the Life and I chose Wendell and this is my life and that's all they fucking is."

"If you believe in Heaven," I said, on an obscure impulse, "...you could go and...find your way to...I don't know—someplace where you could feel you were going to go to Heaven when you died. A church of some kind...."

"Oh I know where I'd go! The Easter Hill Church of Our Loving Savior, right down there in Oakland." She pointed over her left shoulder, toward Oakland. "I ran off from Wendell one time, a month after we get here, you widdat? I went to this gospel church down there and I could feel the Lord moving. But I called Wendell and he was just so sad. So I went back...I went back to him to let him beat me and put it right because he's my man, and I'll go to Hell for all eternity for him...."

She said it with complete conviction. *I'll go to Hell for all eternity for him.*

"So you think Wendell's an Existentialist, huh...." I said. "He's an interesting kind of player anyway. He dresses like a rap video but he seems to me like...old fashioned...."

"He's fifty-two, he oughta be old fashioned," Dulcet said.

Surprise almost penetrated my dreaminess. "Ya'll are yanking my chain. No way, girl. I thought maybe forty...forty-three or...."

"People always think that," Latesha said. "He going to live forever. He fifty-two."

I drank a little whiskey, to make the taunting song in the lightbulb go away. "What happened in Miami?"

Latesha shrugged.

"He was working a thing with us...me and Dulcet we pick up on tourist guys and then we slip 'em something make 'em sleep, take all their shit." Her voice as bland as if she was giving work experience in a job interview.

I think that's when the record ended. Not Marvin Gaye by now. Chaka Khan? It was, anyway, suddenly very quiet, except for the crickets, the birds. The rising and falling sound of a motorcycle passing somewhere way below us. A truck whining on the freeway.

Latesha went on, "The thing we had going, it worked damn good too. Dulcet got them in easy. But one of 'em woke up in the middle of the thing, in his hotel, an' he go a little crazy—that GHB shit, you know, it can make you crazy—and he grabbed open my purse and took my little piece, got a shot off at Wendell, so Wendell grab the gun away and beat his collegeboy ass dead with it...I don't think he plan to kill him but...well this was a Cuban kid visiting his auntie and his family they got their paid-for peeps in the local police to grip on that shit like a dog with a rat—and Wendell got arrested. We put up the bail and then we jump bail. And we come out here. He had put up all his money so he need a new start, something fat to start over, that why when you come around with—"

"You talk way too fucking much, you dumb little ho," Leon said, coming out on the porch. "Wendell you hear that shit what she say? She tell every motherfuckin secret you got."

Wendell muttered, "Shit!" as he came out, shaking his head in disgust. His eyes were lost in deep shadow as he lifted his arm to backhand Latesha for babbling his story out—

—And I was poised on the edge of turning my back...or doing something about it. I wasn't sure I could just stand there while he beat the woman up. Not that she would like it if I tried to do anything about it. But still—

"Look!" Dulcet said, pointing. "It's a little boy in the bushes! Looking at us!"

My heart stuttered, and I looked—we all looked, even Wendell, frozen with his arm still raised to strike—and I saw what did look, in the moonlight, sort of like a boy's face looking at us. But when the face shifted position a little we saw it was a gray fox, poking its head up above the ivy, checking us out. Its face was delicate. Its eyes gleaming gold. It opened its mouth as if to speak, but only panted.

"Look at that, it's a fox," Wendell said with a city dweller's awe.

I thought he seemed grateful for the interruption, as this way he didn't have to hit Latesha.

Leon grunted. "Sure, we got foxes and raccoons out here getting into our shit all the time. Motherfucking raccoons mess with the garbage can."

He picked up an empty flower pot to throw—but the fox was way ahead of him, and ducked into the bushes, vanished.

"Wow, a fox," Dulcet said, with something like authentic childlike wonder this time.

"Ya'll freeze right there, every last one of you!" quavered a voice from the darkness.

I was looking for the fox, still, and the voice from the night didn't register on me at first as quite real—it seemed like another heroin illusion. I was trying to ignore the hallucinations. "A gray fox, Dulcet... beautiful animals...I wish...Frankie could see...."

"Everybody stand up and put your hands on your heads!"

"Fuck!" Wendell muttered. "It's that motherfucking skip tracer."

Then it sank in. I stood up, and saw Wendell reach behind for his gun—and pat his bare waistband. He realized he didn't have it on him. The bounty hunter had stepped into the light now—

The first thing I noticed was he was a tall, refrigerator-sized white guy with a big belly. Fat, colorfully tattooed arms in a sleeveless shirt. A Safari hat. A short sharply trimmed black beard. Second thing I noticed was his shotgun. I looked down into its muzzle the way Abel had looked into my gun.

The bounty hunter had another gun on his hip, and what looked like a taser and pepper gas and a cellphone and a beeper all attached to his belt.

"This asshole has a fucking Batman utility belt on!" I said.

Dulcet laughed, her eyes bright. She got up from the hammock but she didn't put her hands on her head. She hadn't been carrying her Barbie purse, a few moments ago, but now she had it over her left shoulder, with her left hand on top of the purse. She had that little gun in there, I remembered.

Latesha was already standing up, open-mouthed, her eyes wide. "That same motherfucker!"

"Ya'll were dumb to come here, Wendell," Leon growled, shaking his head. "What you think, the motherfucker not going to find your cousin, come to your cousin's house?"

"We thought you were in Dallas, for a long time," the skip tracer said. His voice was kind of high-pitched. He seemed genuinely scared, his eyes darting around. "They're still...."

He broke off, realizing he'd given something away.

Wendell said, "I think this dumb ofay is the only one here."

I took just one side-step toward the door, and stopped. Waited.

"Nobody move," the skip tracer said. "No you're wrong, Wendell— I've got all kinds of backup here. And I can get the Richmond PD here in five minutes. Now we're gonna do this easy.... You folks going to get down on your knees, put your hands behind your backs...."

Nobody moved, though—except me. Wendell and Leon were now pretty much blocking the bounty hunter's view of me. So I took another sideways step to the back door. And stopped.

Moving made me realize how fucked up I was. Every step seemed to spin the world like a globe on a stand. My stomach seemed to revolve inside me too.

But on a certain level, I was feeling pretty good. Probably because I wasn't thinking about Frankie.

"Where's the other one?" the bounty hunter said. "The red-haired Frenchie Canuck."

"He went for beer," Wendell said. "What kind of deal we going to work out, homes?"

The "red haired Canuck" was actually snoring like a little lamb a few feet from me, just inside the door as I side-stepped through, squatted, put my hand over Red's mouth. He instantly came awake at the contact. Stared at me a moment in furious shock.

I put a finger on my lips. Then mouthed, "Bounty hunter." Tilted my head toward the back of the house.

He turned his head, under my hand, to look toward the back porch... I straightened, and went in a low, slow crouch, through the house....

It seemed to take a long time. The light was mostly in the back of the house, behind me; I was moving through a dark wooden corridor, past the shadowy shapes of unidentifiable furniture that seemed to change proportion as I passed. It felt like a long time getting to the front door, each step requiring some concentration. I was still stoned and the smell of Leon and dope smoke and dust on old wood seemed thick as wool in the air—feeling like something physical to push through.

But I got to the front door, and thought: Don't fumble with this. Stop and think, Slim.

I could just make out the door knob in the yellow-white of streetlight shine through an old glass transom. I found the knob with my fingers—the contact almost electric with sudden metallic chill—and turned it.

I heard a shout behind me, and an answering laugh of derision. "You all alone ain't you motherfucker!"

I got the door open, went out on the front porch, looked around. If the skip tracer had back-up, he had them well hidden.

I forced myself to move against the current of my altered state, and went into a primitive kind of stalking mode, a prickling energy rising up, a sense of the fullness of the present moment taking hold of me, filling me with the night's breath: life, given sharp definition by the imminence of death.

Still crouching, I went up the walkway along the side of the house toward the back, my gun in hand.

I saw the bulky shape of the bounty hunter, a silhouette from here, his left side to me. He was lifting the shotgun to his shoulder, forcing the issue.

He was trying to make his voice deep and scary as he barked, "Get down, *now*, or I swear I'm going to blow your fucking head off, Wendell!"

I was creeping up on him...and I felt good, now that the spinning had stopped. I was centered, awake, alive.

Thinking: *Made for this. I was made for this.*

Now he was looming over me like a building.

I put the muzzle of my gun against the back of his neck.

He shivered and I heard him hiss, "Shit!"

I said, in a reasonable, soothing tone, "That's right, big guy, you're in it deep. This gun is primed. Safety off. Toss the shotgun aside. Do what I say and you get out of this in one piece."

He was breathing hard, chest rising and falling, fast. "You give me your word on that? The part about me not getting hurt?"

"What's your name, man?"

"It's...Tuck. People call me Tuck."

"Like Friar Tuck? My word on it, Friar Tuck. If you cooperate, you're cool. We'll just leave you somewhere to chill for awhile, and you'll be fine."

I could see the outline of his Adam's apple go up and down, very distinctly. Then there was a rustling thump as he tossed the shotgun aside.

I stepped behind him, reached slowly across to pull his pistol from its holster with my left hand.

"Now drop your Batman utility belt. Slow."

Hands shaking, he dropped his belt—just as Red came out of the back door with a Mac 10 auto-pistol in his hand.

"I'm surprised you came here alone, Tuck, with all of us here," I said, genuinely curious. "Don't you guys usually come in packs?"

Tuck made a hissing sound through clamped teeth. "They wouldn't leave Dallas. I knew Wendell was here but they wouldn't listen." He added wistfully, to himself: "I almost had the collar...."

I heard Dulcet laugh from the porch. "He wants to be the hero and get 'em all by himself! What a cute little Safari-hat guy!"

Red was grinning—and he was cocking the Mac 10. The machine pistol was pointed at Tuck's gut. "I don't like fat guys following me around. The smell bothers me eh?"

Tuck must've seen something in Red's eyes.

"Don't!" Tuck said. "He gave me his word, man! Don't do that—I'll blow this case off—you can leave me tied up somewhere a long time...."

Tuck's trunk-like legs were shaking; I could hear the cloth rustling as his thighs rubbed together.

"Red," I said, "I don't believe in much, but I do believe in keeping my word. We'll truss him good and be long gone...."

Red shook his head. "It's not what you say." He kept the gun leveled and kept looking at me and Tuck, but tilted his head, spoke out of the side of his mouth to Wendell who stood behind him on the porch. "Wendell? What you want me to do?"

Leon said, "Just so ya'll do something quick as a motherfucker about this. And I mean fast."

"Look," Tuck said, "I'm fucking *outta here*! I've already forgotten you guys exist. I'm not really cut out for this job—I just, you know, I blew everything else I tried, I thought I'd try this but—"

"Shut the fuck up," Red said. "We don't want your whiny life story, eh? What I do with him, Wendell?"

I heard Wendell sigh.

I figure Wendell didn't particularly want to execute anybody but he couldn't seem weak. He'd already compromised too much.

"You know what to do, Red. Just do the stand-up thing— and don't ever put it on me."

Which meant: Kill him— but if it goes to court, don't say I gave the order.

7

Tuck was breathing hard....

I said, "Wait a minute, goddammit, Wendell—I gave my word—"

"But here's a thing," Red said, ignoring me, "maybe too much noise here, eh Wendell? Then there's this big fat slob's body. When you were eating all those cheeseburgers you didn't think about other people having to haul that fat ass around and dig a hole for it, bounty hunter, eh?"

The moon seemed to spotlight Red somehow: His grin was getting wider. His knuckles were getting whiter.

"I...look, you could ransom me," Tuck said. Tuck was breathing through his mouth, faster and faster.

"Ransom—that's always a sucker game, at least in this country," Wendell said.

"*What if*," Dulcet said gleefully, "you gave him his gun back and let him fight with you! I'd fight with him too! We could play army! With real guns!"

I'm pretty sure she wasn't kidding.

Leon snorted. "Motherfucker. You see what I mean about that woman, Wendell? She out of her mind. Ya'll get this motherfucking bounty hunter out of here. I don't want to *know* what you going to do with him."

Tuck was wheezing now...as I put my automatic in my waistband and shifted his pistol to my right hand.

Red meditatively thumbed some smokeless into his mouth, and said, "There's a cliff over the ocean, on the other side of that hill there, you know. We could take him there, tie something to his feet, and shoot him right off the edge—take care of his big cheeseburger-eating ass and get rid of him all at once...."

"That what you do—that what you do," Wendell said. "Whatever you gone do—get to it."

Tuck made a bleating sound, and tried to rush Red—

And the Mac 10 barked and rattled in Red's hands.

The skip tracer staggered back under the multiple impacts, scream-ing. His safari hat, cinched under his neck with a leather string, falling to hang awkwardly off the side of his neck—

I shouted, "Red you fucking *weasel!*"

And I leveled Tuck's gun at Red...only barely registering what kind of gun it was: a .45 revolver with a silver finish....

"Back away from him, Red!" I yelled.

"Goddamn this noisy shit!" Leon was hissing.

Tuck was on his knees now, clutching his gut, writhing. He was squealing, "Ee, ee, ee-ee...." over and over.

"Ooh, what a sound!" Dulcet exulted.

"Damn, girl!" Latesha said, clucking her tongue reproachfully.

You could tell that Latesha believed if you were going to murder someone there was a right way and a wrong way.

And me, I wasn't sure which way to jump. Tuck was on his side, was clawing up the ivy, thrashing.

It made me think of Abel. Only I felt kind of bad for Tuck—and I hadn't felt a thing for Abel.

"Goddamnit mother*fucker*," Leon said, growling it and stamping the porch so you could hear a board crack. "My neighbors going to be calling the motherfucking police, all that noise. Wendell, that's all now, I'm gone tell you straight up: get your shit-brains crew and this dumb bleeding motherfucker of a half-assed bounty hunter and get the *fuck* right on out of here!"

"Ah-*iiight*, Leon, shit, just fucking simmer, and let me think how we going to do this," Wendell said.

Tuck looked like a salted slug, on the ground, and Dulcet was tittering and I could almost read Tuck's mind: *I fucked up everything in my life and then it ends like this, people laughing at me while I bleed to death.* I was starting to laugh, in fact—but at myself, really.

Tuck was still squealing and didn't seem ready to die. Red was looking at me and at the gun in my hand—and I realized I had it aimed at Red and wasn't even conscious of it.

I mean, if you're going to point a gun at somebody's head, you should at least be mindful about it.

Red looked like he was gauging when to swing his Mac 10 toward me....

Tuck was doubled over, fetus-like around his wounds.

"Ya'll ever see that movie 'They Shoot Horses Don't They?'" Latesha asked. "I never saw it but I remember the title. I mean, the idea seems to come to mind."

And Red was poised to make his move—he was going to take me out.

And Tuck was squealing...bleeding, thrashing....

"Motherfuckers, do *something*," Leon hissed.

Wendell said, "Okay...what we gone do is...Slim? Yo...."

I nodded. I lowered the gun but kept it between me and Red. And I looked at Red and then jerked my head toward Tuck.

Latesha was right. Tuck wasn't going to live, even if he got to an emergency room.

Red stepped up to Tuck, put the gun against Tuck's head. Tuck looked up at him, and then squeezed his eyes shut and waited for it.

Red grinned and blew Tuck's head open, and after that Tuck was pretty quiet, except for two or three final spasms.

Red straightened up and squinted at me. "You were pointing a gun at my head, there, Tex," he said softly. Looking at me like a man looking at a dartboard in a bar, calculating the throw. Like it was no big thing, just a question of when and how.

I remember exactly what thought went through my head then.

I'm gonna have to kill Red. Because the second I turn my back on him....

There was a silence as everyone listened for sirens and tried to think about what to do next.

"Hey!" Dulcet said. "Look! Slim got a cowboy gun!"

I looked at Tuck's pistol more closely. It was a Colt .45 double action revolver—a reproduction of a gunfighter's Peacemaker. She was right. It was a damn cowboy gun.

※　※　※

Leon agreed to deal with the blood in the yard if we did the rest fast. There was an old scrap roll of linoleum in the crawlspace under the back porch.

A black widow spider walked daintily away from it as we rolled Tuck up.

"Roll him up just like a burrito," Red said. "Feels like he suck up lots of burritos the fat fuck."

"Red," I said. Just that: *Red.*

At the other end of the linoleum, he glared coldly at me, and then grinned. "Yeah you get your chance—Editor Boy...."

✳ ✳ ✳

Red's idea about the cliff still applied. He knew the way. He'd been here once before...on an errand.

Someone had started to build a house up here and run out of money. The access road was still there, overgrown at the edges, and the viney frame of the house, and nothing else. The site overlooked San Francisco Bay.

Wendell was at the wheel now. He backed the van up to the edge of the cliff; Red and I silently pulled the linoleum out of the rear of the van, letting it thump to the ground. Swearing softly, we dragged it onto the rocky outcropping over the bay.

Wendell drove the van back over to the road to wait. I could see Dulcet watching out the van's back-door window. I guess Latesha didn't want to watch.

Red looked at me, now and then, and looked away, but I knew what he was thinking. *Why do we need this asshole now that we know which warehouse it is?*

I shivered. My high was mostly gone. Sounds still had a certain re-verb quality and everything I saw—trees waving in breeze, house frame, curve of road, rocky cliff-edge, the setting moon, the Bay, Red, the roll of linoleum—it was all some kind of insignia in a code I couldn't understand.

The dawn was turning the sky to cobalt and aluminum above the East Bay hills. But the sun hadn't yet shown itself in person when the linoleum roll containing ol' Tuck and about two hundred pounds of new brick, intended for a chimney that would never happen, went bouncing end over end down the cliffside and into the bay.

I had given Latesha the automatic and I had Tuck's Peacemaker stuck in my waistband. I was looking down over the edge of the cliff, to see if the linoleum sank. It did, vanishing like the Cheshire cat's grin. And I realized Red was very quiet—and he was behind me....

I straightened up, not too fast, saying, "Tuck's gone, it's cool," as easygoing as I could. And I gently put my hand on the butt of the Peacemaker, stepped back from the cliff—

Then I spun, jerking the pistol—

You know, it happened to one of the great gunfighters too. I think it was John Wesley Hardin. Some Pinkertons were calling for John Wesley Hardin to surrender and he pulled a gun and its gunsight got stuck in his waistband. That's why they make holsters.

Red was grinning and leveling the Mac 10 at me, and I was trying to get the gun loose from where it was stuck on the inside of my pants.

Wendell, waiting at the van, shouted, "Red!"

Red half turned at that, giving me a moment to twist the gun free, cocking the hammer back as I drew.

Another gunfighter, Wyatt Earp, said that the man who took his time and aimed with sure deliberation was the man who won the gunfight.

Wyatt was right. Red fired a burst jerkily at me, but the bullets buzzed past me like confused wasps, into the sky over the bay.

I aimed at the center of his chest and squeezed the trigger.

At that range, the round hit him hard, and he was slapped right off his feet, backwards, dropping the Mac.

I went and picked the auto pistol up, and stood over him, watching to be sure.

"Don't," he said. "Don't. *Je suis rien*...Don't...."

But he was staring at the sky, and I had the weird feeling he wasn't talking to me. Maybe he was talking to a memory.

It took him about thirty seconds total to die, I think. "Don't," he said, one more time. And then he was done with his dying.

I grabbed him by the collar—felt the ebbing warmth of his body on my knuckles—and turned him sideways to the cliff edge. I used one cowboy-booted foot to roll him over a couple times, then right off the edge of the cliff. He splashed into the sea, bobbing up to float just above the spot where Tuck had sunk.

Then I looked at the van, maybe a hundred feet away. Were they going to take revenge for their old crew-buddy?

But Dulcet waved, "Come on!" from the back.

I waved, and walked back to the van.

I looked inside myself again to see if I was sorry I'd shot Red.

Nope. Not even a little.

I did notice one thing though. Some of my high had come back.

THE LAST PART

Bring It On Home

8

EDITOR SOUGHT IN MASS KILLING

The newspaper was on the counter, in the Travelodge office. I glanced at the headline, and then I looked hastily back at the registration form I was signing for the Sikh clerk. The turbaned clerk was a reticent man with pockmarked skin and a pointed beard.

Dulcet, who was wearing a coat and playing my wife, saw the newspaper too. She only smiled mysteriously.

I told the Sikh we'd been driving all night from Missouri so we were going to get some sleep, even though it was morning. I could smell the coffee from their continental breakfast nook. The clerk nodded, indifferent. He didn't care. He never glanced at the newspaper or looked closely at me.

I took a chance booking that motel room. Using my credit card with the Eickoff thing hovering in the background. But I didn't care anymore. I was terminally exhausted.

I was still scared of sleeping...but the exhaustion had come like a deep layer of volcanic ash, falling at first lightly, then more and more heavily; each black snowflake, weighing near nothing, conspiring to become the weight of the world—bearing me relentlessly down.

We got a room with two queensized beds. It was pretty much like all $59 a night hotel rooms. I got it for two nights so we wouldn't be disturbed.

We pulled the thick curtains really snugly so it was dark in there, except for a couple of milky shafts of light cutting down at the rug from the edge of the window and the light from the TV. Dulcet had switched it on the instant we'd come in.

Latesha showered. I sat on the edge of a bed, trying not to think about incompetent bounty hunters begging for their lives; trying not to see my son's waxen face in the hospital morgue. Sagging where I sat, barely able to keep from sliding to the floor. Wendell lay on his back on the other bed, remote in one hand, gun lightly under the other, flipping around on the TV. I thought he'd see me on the news but he started watching *Sesame Street*, laughing sleepily at the puppet vampire.

I could hear Dulcet pissing, as she talked to Latesha in the bathroom. I heard the toilet flush, then the squeak of her feet on the tub as she got in beside Latesha, and their tired voices as they washed each other.

Latesha came out first, with only a towel around her; she tossed it onto a chair, and lay naked on the bed near the bathroom, beside Wendell. Then Dulcet came out, barefoot in her panties, braless, went yawning hugely to the bed I was sitting on. Wendell turned the TV off, pulled off his shoes and lay beside Latesha, spooning, muttering to her; his gun under his pillow.

I made myself stand up; I tottered into the bathroom, undressed and showered, hand-washing my clothes in the shower at the same time; I wrung them out, and hung them up over towel racks.

When I came out, Wendell had turned off the TV and I went naked through the semidarkness to the other bed—naked, anyway, but for Tuck's gun in my hand, which made me feel dressed enough. I put the gun under my own pillow, and kept my hand on it, as I lay down next to Dulcet, spooning just like Wendell with Latesha. Dulcet had one hand under her own pillow.

"Maybe we should roll a joint, could we Daddy please?" Dulcet suggested. A little girl voice in the darkness.

"Girl, shut the fuck up and go to sleep," Wendell said muzzily.

"'kay Wendell Daddy...."

"'n if that white boy wants to fuck you, you just let him fuck you, I don't want no arguments waking me up...."

"'kay Wendell Daddy...."

He was already snoring even as she said it. Latesha was soon snoring in a kind of duet with him, her alto to his bass.

We all lay on top of the covers. If we had to jump out of bed, fast, covers would just get in the way, and it wasn't cold.

Dulcet reached back, found my left arm, and pulled it around her. It was not unpleasant.

"Tex...Slim Jim...." Dulcet said sleepily.

"Hmmm...." The ashen weight was mummifying me.

"Know what? I'm glad you got rid of that Red. I didn't like him. He was always asking Wendell to make me fuck him. I hate red pubic hair. And his mouth was all gross with that smokeless shit he chewed on."

I was almost asleep. "Glad to...be of service...."

"Know what else...?" Her whisper seemed to come from the blackness behind my closed eyelids. As if she were sharing my personal darkness.

"Whuh?"

"You know that Leon? You know what he said? When we were getting ready to leave and I was in the van and you were loading the back of it and he was talking to Wendell up front?"

"Don' even fuckin' care whuh he said...."

"He said, 'That Slim Jim boy is alright, after all. Ya'll better off with him than Red....'"

"Did he. I'm...all aglow from enhanced...self-esteem...."

She sniggered softly at that. I was almost asleep—the fear of sleep perched somewhere like a raven in the night: there, but hidden in the darkness by its color.

Then she said: "...how many them people you kill, in the city, at that publishing place? I saw it on TV in the dressing room at work...."

That brought me slightly more awake. I whispered, "Do...the others know?"

"I didn't tell anybody. I like secrets." Her voice was a play-whisper. "How many you kill? Tell me!"

"Not any. Well, one guy in self defense—the guy who did the real killing. The cops misunderstood the...the situation."

"That your story and you stickin' to it?"

"'s true...."

"Don't have to pretend with widdoo Dulcet...it's alright...they're all happier now...those people...they're happier dead...."

I wanted to change the subject. "Is 'Dulcet Groans', like, a stripper stage-name?" By the end of that question all my fatigue had rolled insistently back onto me.

"It used to be...not no more...." She yawned noisily, seeming to enjoy the sound. "You want to fuck me?"

"Honored...by the...offer...but.... I'm too...I'm too...."

"That's okay, we got time...tomorrow night or some other night...."

I went to sleep, thinking that we probably didn't have much time, at all.

I slept without dreaming for awhile. Then I came almost awake— just enough to surmise, a few hours later, that Wendell had awakened with a hard-on. He had anyway, shoved himself with no preliminaries into Latesha from behind. I heard her grunt with the entry—it must've hurt, some, there'd been no time for her to get wet—but she dutifully pumped her hips for him till he came in her, moaning, "Ooh, bitch...give it to Daddy...." as he came. And then he was asleep again, sawing logs almost instantly. He probably hadn't been fully awake for any of it. And Latesha too was back to snoring a minute or two later.

Dulcet too was aware of this small sexual ellipse, and she squirmed against me, in case I wanted anything, but I only hugged her a little, and she stroked my hand, and commenced snoring softly again.

I remember I heard kids laughing as they walked by outside our second floor room; heard their flip-flops slapping on the concrete.

They're coming back from the swimming pool, I thought. *Frankie loved to swim....*

Then I slipped back down into the pit of ashes again.

❋   ❋   ❋

"I've joined a special group of people who have a very very special relationship to God," Meredith told me matter of factly. "And just for the record, Slim, I don't like it when people call it a cult."

"You said special twice," I said. "That's so special."

We were in a sunny, wooded park, sitting at a picnic table. It was a hot summer day that buzzed to itself: bees, maybe. Cicadas. And the day groaned, too: an airplane passing overhead. I saw a water fountain in the background with flies thick around it but the flies weren't buzzing—they were whispering. I couldn't quite work out what they were saying.

Meredith glanced over her shoulder at the place in a thatch of ivy where two men knelt in a flowerbed, sawing at something. I didn't recognize the men. I could just make out the glint of tools in their hands.

I knew somehow they were sawing down deep into Frankie's body, though I couldn't see the body. I wondered distantly why I didn't feel much about it.

"You know," I said, "when my Mom died, I didn't feel anything. No grief. Or I didn't know I was feeling grief. But then I had trouble concentrating on anything for weeks, even watching a movie. I couldn't finish a book. I was weirdly clumsy, I kept dropping things...and then I realized, that was it...that's how it showed itself...."

"We can cleanse you of all that," Meredith said. "All that's necessary is a special operation. Do you see this little scar on my abdomen? Of course, sometimes—" She glanced toward the two men, the body.

One of the men was throwing red bits of body parts in the air, showering himself with them, and gibbering something that might've been some kind of prayer.

Meredith went on, "Sometimes the operation goes wrong. But if you'll just trust us, without thinking or feeling or caring, but leaving all that behind, we can promise you endless bliss...endless bliss...."

Then the two men stood up and now they were someone else—or had they been Red and Abel all along? The lumpen ex-surfer and the obtuse French Canadian gunsel...dragging soggy red bits of Frankie toward me....

"Daddy? Daddy?" said a bird on a bush. *"Daddy please, I can't breathe,*

help me, I'm so hot, I can't breathe, Daddy...I'm sorry—please just...help me...Daddy...."

"Don't," Red said. "Don't." Grinning as he said it. Coming closer with something in his hand—something—

"Tuck is one of us now," Meredith was saying.

"Daddy...."

※　　※　　※

It was one of those dreams you have to wriggle free of, like Houdini from a straight jacket. I twisted and turned and tore myself free....

And woke up with Dulcet straddling me.

"Hey Tex," she said, smiling down at me. "Poor ol Slim Jim! You having a bad dream?"

She was pinning my arms with her knees. Her hair was bed-frizzied; her breasts were pointing at me like they might go off.

She had my gun in her hand. She pointed it at me.

"Boomy!" she said.

She laughed and spun the silver revolver on her finger, like in the movies, but awkwardly.

"Don't do that," I said.

"You need to brush your teeth," she said. "I've got some toothpaste and a brush you can use, we brung it in from the van....Your clothes are not completely dry but I hung 'em over the heater...Wendell's in the bathroom. He always gets constipated after doing some of that kinda dope. Latesha's bringing us back some food and coffee...."

I pulled my arms out from under her, gently took the gun from her hand. "I hope it's a lot of coffee. A fuck of a lot...."

"Do you want to smoke some pot?"

"No...no thanks."

"Want a hair of the dog? Got half a bottle of really hairy hooch."

I shuddered, and shook my head. "*Fuck* no. For God's sake don't even talk about it."

"'Kay, Cowboy-ee!"

My stomach lurched. "What time is it?"

"About seven p.m...."

"You're kidding."

"No I'm not *even* kidding, Mr. Big Saddlehorn Cowboy. We got to get it together, Wendell says. They're going to be bringing all that ecstasy money to that place tonight. He says at least you better hope they do." She lowered her voice so she sounded like a child actress from a sitcom and said behind her hand: "He didn't wake up in a very good mood."

"Me either...." I wriggled out from under her, trying to think about the mission, so I could forget about the dream.

"Do you wanna fuck *now*?" she asked.

It was her way of being polite. Hospitable.

"Nah, I'm...hungover and...no thanks, hon, but I do thank you very kindly and I mean that."

"'Kay some more!" She reached out and tugged my forelock playfully. "Hangover owie! Come on, then, Mr. Little Bighorn Cowboy Guy. Wendell's finally getting out of there...I'll show you the toothpaste and where Wendell put the extra bullets."

9

We sat in the van for an hour, in a wedge of warehouse shadow cast by moonlight and streetlight, half a block from Kwai & Sons. Wendell at the wheel, me riding shotgun, the two girls in back. Latesha smoked Newports. I wanted to tell her not to, but decided it was probably better she had her nicotine fix. Her hand would be steadier.

We sat without radio or lights, just watching. We could see the little gravel-strip parking lot. The Blue Ox oversized pick-up truck was there alone. That one light in the warehouse office window....

I was feeling a little hung over, still. Spaced and sick to my stomach. The almond-paste croissant I'd eaten seemed to haunt me now. I was still just slightly stoned on the heroin. And all the coffee I'd drunk was churning in the there too.

But I sat there. We waited. It sucked. It was hard to stay out ahead of the black feeling when you're just sitting somewhere. An hour seemed like a year. It seemed like that fucking hour had seasons. I was only up to autumn when Wendell asked me the second time about the autopistol.

"You sure you don't want that Mac 10 of Red's," Wendell said, putting his plastic coffee cup down. "That fucking six-shooter only shoots...six."

Latesha laughed. "'Six shooter only shoots...six!'"

I shrugged. My clothes hadn't dried completely and the damp cloth was making me itch. I shifted around, scratching my back against the seat. And I said:

"Nope, I'm gonna use the Tuck the Bounty Hunter Memorial Pistol. I got a pocketfull of his shells."

"'Tuck memorial pistol!'"

I could hardly sit still. The razor-edged wave of volcano glass was looming up inside me again, and—

Daddy...?

—I needed to stay out ahead of it. I had to get moving.

Wendell glanced at me and muttered irritably, "You're squirming around, man, you making me nervous. You got to pee? Too much caffeine or what?"

"I'm just antsy to get going. It's got to be after ten...."

He looked at his watch and shook his head. "Fifteen to ten."

Still had the winter of that year-long hour to go through. Fifteen minutes that lasted three months.

"You want some chewy sour candy?" Dulcet asked. "I've got a few pieces left...."

"No thanks. I don't think you want me to be sick in the van."

"You nervous about this huh Slim Jim?" Latesha asked. "You don't need to be. I looked up in my astrology book—I use Wendell's birthday, my birthday, what day it is. We cool."

This annoyed me more than it should have. I almost snapped at her that astrology was bullshit and didn't she claim to believe in the Christian God and lots of Christians thought astrology was a tool of the Devil to get innocent people into the occult.... That kind of mean-spirited remark.

But Wendell saved me from myself. "What the Zodiac say?" Wendell asked, interested.

Latesha held a little pen light over an opened supermarket-register paperback. "It say 'A syz....' What this word, Dulcet?"

"Uh...Syzygy."

"What the fuck is that?" Wendell asked.

"I think it's about conjuctions of planets."

"Thas interesting," Latesha said. " I wasn't sure about that part. But it's good, it all good. It says, 'A syzygy of luscious convergences pours forth the fruit of the...the....'"

"The cornucopia."

"I can read it, shit! '...the cornucopia of good fortune on your enterprise. Wealth is a *possibility* if you play your cards right and do the footwork.'"

"That sounding right-on fine," Wendell commented, showing his age. "But ya'll better shut off that motherfucking light. You could see it from over there if they was looking."

She shut the little pen light off and lay back. Dulcet lay beside her, stroking her.

"That shit sounds *good* for us," Latesha said cheerfully. "What gun I got, Dulcet?"

"I guess you can have this Mac, the cowboy don't want it."

※　※　※

A cold, bleak handful of minutes before ten—and the black SUV pulled into the gravel strip at the warehouse. It parked beside the pick-up,

131

snug to the old loading dock. Its lights switched off.

A tall, crew-cut blond man in a tailored powderblue suit got out of the SUV from the driver's side; a short, chubby Oriental dressed in black jeans and a black button-up shirt got out from the passenger side. He was talking, the other nodding. And the blond guy was carrying a leather satchel.

Okay, Frankie, I thought. *A meaningless gesture is better than no gesture, sometimes. It's all I can do. Here goes....*

Wendell murmured, "You think they there to bring in some money—?"

"Yeah, and count it with what's already there," I said. "Let's go." I put my hand on the door handle.

He reached out and laid a hand on my arm, not too hard. There was respect in the touch. That was worth something.

"Hold your horses, cowboy...give 'em time to get theyselves comfortable. They talking to the people inside, distracted."

I felt like I was going to explode if I didn't get out of that van...I pictured it seen from outside, the windows splashed with blood from within...I chuckled.

Wendell glanced at me but didn't ask what was so funny.

To keep my mind busy, I tried to start a conversation about something, you know, meaningful. "Hey uh Wendell—did you ever notice that even if you *know* you have a self-destructive tendency, a character flaw, you usually can't do anything about it, and you keep doing it, keep acting out and like exhibiting that same fucking flaw even if your therapist has made you see it?"

Wendell looked at me. "You picking *this* moment to say some put-down shit about me?"

"You?" I was confused for a moment. "No, man. I was making conversation. About my favorite topic: Me. I just spoke, like, in the second person—I meant anybody, anyone."

"Anybody? I thought you said it was you."

"Hypothetically anyone but especially me, okay? I meant me. I just figure most people...are the same."

Latesha said, "I sure as a bitch know what he mean. I have a lot of behaviors I wanted to get rid of and never fucking could."

Wendell turned in his seat and scowled at her. "Something to do with me? About how you behave for me?"

"No...."

"Everything you *do* supposed to be for me, ho."

"I didn't...that's not what I meant baby...."

I felt sorry for Latesha. And I found myself wondering if I was hanging out with a pimp now, a misogynistic choice of companions, because I was so infinitely angry at Meredith.

I said, "I meant, Wendell—all my life I've had a tendency to get into modes of acting out where I just lurch into things. Haste and...and impulse. I had it in some kind of check for a long time. For my family. But now—now I lost them...it's like it was just waiting. I just want to plunge into the shit. I mean, there's running in bravely where you have to, and then there's dumbfuck *mindless* bravery—"

Wendell was laughing silently now. "Tex you are one weird white man. Shut the fuck up, get out the car, and let's go."

"I'm wid dat, dog," I said, doing my best Victor imitation.

I turned to see if Latesha thought that one was funny. She looked solemn. I'd had a feeling she'd regretted having to kill Victor. Maybe at some point I'd tell her I hadn't killed him after all.

But Wendell laughed aloud at my Victor imitation. As he laughed he checked to see if the .44 was fully re-loaded.

� ✗ ✗

Wendell had popped a window, sent Dulcet in. Enjoying herself silently but to some kind of ludicrous excess, she'd climbed in and opened a back door. No alarm had gone off.

The main room of the warehouse had a small fleet of vintage cars in it and nothing else. Classic cars, most of them in perfect shape. A Lincoln Continental, maybe from '71; an old, cherry condition '67 Thunderbird; a '57 Chevy; a really nice 60-something flat-black Ford Falcon; a Bentley touring car, maybe 1955, that looked like it was waiting to be restored. A vintage Rolls Royce Silver Shadow. There was even an old Packard.

Dulcet clapped her hands without making any noise, seeing the cars. Wendell made the fanning 'that's hot' hand-wave and grinned appreciatively. They assumed that they'd come out of this with a nice car, now, as well as cash.

Me, I assumed that some of us were going to die.

They followed me through the shadows along the closed corrugated metal gate that had once opened onto the loading dock. I wondered how they'd got the cars in here, then I remembered there was a ramp that went up onto one end of the loading dock, just wide enough to drive cars up.

We padded slowly toward the upright rectangle of light that was the open inner door to the office....

I glanced back at the others. Wendell had the .44 automatic in his hand; Dulcet had the AMC .25—probably kept the little gun because it looked like a toy, though in fact it'd kill you dead, properly used, as fast as any other gun. Latesha had the Mac 10.

Her expression was all business, focused. Dulcet, though, was big-eyed with delight, chewing her sour taffy, almost skipping. I was glad she didn't have the autopistol—not something to play with.

I had the Peacemaker in my hand; worn cowboy boots on my feet; my cowboy hat on my head. My wire rim glasses firmly on, too.

And all my dope spaciness, all my hangover, was gone now. Burned away in adrenaline.

We got close to the open door, out of the line of sight of whoever was in the office. I could hear voices.

"We got the CyberFlash to do," said a deep voice that sounded black to me. "Lot of people going to be there with money."

"I haven't decided on that one," said a smaller voice. There was something about the careful diction that made me picture the Asian guy, though his only accent was Northern California. But he would be at least third generation here, probably. He went on, "That's so high profile. There'll be celebs there...X at that event might get some attention we wouldn't want, specially if something goes wrong...."

"Oh, no, we *have* to service the Flash!" said a man with a fruity, self-congratulatory voice, sounding high himself. "The more celebs the better! Let them celebrate freedom!"

"You know, I'm starting to wish we didn't have to have this clown here," said a man I thought might've been the big blond guy, judging from the timbre and the probably-Dutch accent. "Here or, I tell you, anywhere. He gets high, he says stupid things, it is very risky. We count the money, Banyan—why don't you go to your rave, you're already high. You should be there."

"Word that," said the black voice.

"Oh my friends—open yourselves up to the moment!"

I knew they were glaring at him, then, whoever he was.

So I stepped into the doorway, the Peacemaker leveled. "Yeah, gents," I said with a soft voice, scaring myself with my own confidence, "'open yourselves up to the moment.'" I added in my thickest Texan accent: "And will yew all kindly put your hands up?"

Just as we'd rehearsed it, Wendell moved up close behind me, down on one knee with his pistol out at the end of his arms; Latesha stood behind him aiming the Mac over his head. She was rock solid. Dulcet knelt beside Wendell, between me and him but a little back, grinning over her little pistol.

Four men in the room stared at us. One of them was indeed a black guy, with the overstated bulkiness of a hardcore weightlifter; his close cut hair was dyed in stripes of white and blue. He wore jogging sweats, a muscle shirt under an open Oakland Raiders windbreaker that partly concealed a .357, probably a Smith and Wesson in a shoulder holster. I was peripherally aware that Latesha had her weapon aimed at the weightlifter. He had a calculator in his hand, though, instead of a gun.

Wendell was aiming at the big square-headed Dutch guy with the angry blue eyes and a bundle of cash in each of his hamsized fists.

I figured the Asian guy for the boss, the one ultimately responsible for what had happened to Frankie....

...besides me and Meredith, I mean....

...so I had my gun aimed at him.

And he knew it: The Asian guy was twitching visibly, his empty hands opening and closing.

Dulcet was aiming at the fourth guy, who stood on the far left, the one with the droopy, frozen smile: A tall—at least six foot five—middle aged, stooped, shaven-bald white guy in an *AREA: ONE* T-shirt and beltless tie-dyed pants. You know that kind of pants, with the really light fabric? I never *got* those kind of pants. And he had a fanny pack too. Kind of guy wears a fanny pack.

Not one of them had a gun in his hand.

They stood around a big oak desk, gaping at us, and the desk was cleared off to make room for all those stacks of money.

They had been counting the dope money, looked like at least a week's take. I could feel Wendell's happiness like a space heater in a cold room at the sight of the skyline stacks of money on the table.

He said, "Must be at least three hundred thousand dollar there. You see how a little planning, and waiting for the right time'll, how that pay a man, Tex?"

"When you're right, you're right, pard," I said.

I saw there was, after all, something else on the desk, behind the stacks of cash. I was pretty sure it was an Uzi; I could just make out the muzzle and breach.

Behind them, was another door, which I thought went out to a little wooden porch. I wasn't sure if it opened anymore. On the floor, near the door, was an open cardboard box, and in it were four big plastic jars, with something white in them. The dope or something to cut the dope with.

The muscular black guy was staring at me. "It's a motherfucking cowboy," the black guy muttered in wonder.

Dulcet tittered, behind us. "He is! He's a killer outlaw! He kills all kindsa people!"

"Shut up, ho," Wendell said. He cleared his throat, and went on, to the four guys in the office: "Ya'll lift your hands, like the cowboy says, move your asses back away from that desk, and anyone does anything not on that list is the first to get hisself cut down dead."

Then came the inevitable moment when they had to think about that. Which way to move? Raise your hands—or to go for your guns? They hesitated....

With easy deliberation, I cocked my gun. It made a loud noise in the waiting quiet.

The Asian guy heard that, and looked at my gun, which was pointed dead at him, and raised his hands. The others followed suit, though I saw the Dutch guy glance at that Uzi as if to memorize exactly how it lay.

We didn't want any shooting, during the robbery. One of us would probably go down, at least, if the shooting started. Then some neighborhood security guard would hear the shots. Call the Richmond police. Cue the car chase scene. No thank you. A non-violent robbery was less problematic.

Except, of course, that I planned to kill these strangers, all four of them, after the robbery, once Wendell and crew were safely on their way with the money.

Till then...if we could just ease quietly through the robbery part....

"We really should talk this over!" the tall bald middle aged pseudorave guy chimed in; his red mouth—one of those mouths that look like they have lipstick on them when they don't—barely moved when he talked. It was like he was talking out of his dilated eyes. He looked vaguely familiar to me. "Because what's up is, we all are working for the same thing, freedom and love and—"

"Banyan," the Asian guy said gently, licking his lips, "please be quiet now. Be very quiet and just do what we do...."

Banyan—was that some kind of exotic first name, or his family name? We blinked and seemed to consider the Asian guy's advice. "'Do what we do.' It's yes and no, with that, isn't it? There's a time for harmony and a time for individuality...." He cocked his head and his face got vacant as he spaced on that.

I let out a long slow breath. "Now ya'll step real slow and carefully back, like the Buffalo Soldier here toldya," I said.

Latesha giggled. "'Buffalo Soldier!'"

They glanced at each other—they were unnerved, I think, by what a good time we seemed to be having, which was the idea. We hadn't rehearsed that. It was just our style. Effective criminals should be natural psychologists. I thought I might write an essay on that from Death Row.

The Asian guy moved back. The others followed his lead again.

"Line up," I said.

"Why?" The Asian guy asked. Scared.

"Not so we can shoot you," I said. "So we can keep an eye on you." That was half true.

"Yo nigger," Wendell said, to the black weightlifter, "you reach you left hand, use two fingers, and I going to count they is just two, and you take that piece out by the tippy end of the butt, and you toss it on that desk there...."

The black guy's eyes clouded over. It was fury. He was getting pissed off.

Wendell shifted his gun muzzle from "Dutch" over to the black guy. "Girl, you help me kill that nigger there with that Mac? We get him first and then that Eurotrash motherfucker."

"Yes baby," Latesha said. "I fittin to shoot his crotch up first."

The black dude seemed to sag in his clothes; he eased his left hand to the shoulder holster, tossed the gun on the desk.

"Can I ask 'em one question?" Dulcet said, chewing her sour taffy.

"Go ahead," Wendell sighed. "Just git it out."

She beamed at the four men in the office. "How come you pissy puppies drive those dumb ugly trucks and those big ass jeepthings when you could be driving those pretty cars back there?"

"Those are *my* cars!" Banyan said. "Aren't they beautiful? They're a present from the Spirit of Ecstasy. I was planning to give one as a gift to each of these guys, but you know what, there are plenty of cars in the world…. Would you like one? All the keys are in that desk there. Let's talk it and walk it—individuality in harmony!"

"Banyan, shut up!" the Dutch guy said.

"Amen to that," I said.

Dulcet laughed snickeringly.

"I got a question or two myself, and then we can get to business," I said. I looked at the Asian guy. "You Ricky Kwai?"

He just looked at me, chewing the inside of his cheek.

I said, "I could always check the ID off your body."

He blinked. Then he nodded. "I'm Ricky Kwai."

"And that stuff in the jars, in the box there, that more of the pseudo-Ecstasy you sold my kid? The stuff that killed him?"

"Tex," Wendell said. Warningly.

I knew what he was thinking. If these guys thought I was on a vengeance mission, they'd figure they had nothing to lose by going for the guns.

And, as each second ticked by, we were perpetually half a second away from a bloodbath, while things stayed like this. The mutual exchange of death. I knew that too.

But I also had to know if this was Ricky Kwai. Right then I had to know.

"Ricky? Answer the question."

"What does he mean, pseudo?" Banyan said, genuinely puzzled. "It's the best pharm X friend."

"Oh fuck," the black guy muttered.

I nodded. "Oh I get it. They didn't tell you they were not only stepping on the shit, they were mixing it with poison?"

Banyan frowned. "Yes, I...." He looked at Ricky. "You poisoned someone?"

"If you guys want the fucking money, take it and get the fuck out," the Dutch guy snarled suddenly.

"I believe the man right, Tex," Wendell said. But he didn't move.

Banyan looked at me like he was a Baptist painting of Jesus, and said, "I thought it was good to make money on it because the X brings people together, it's a gift from the Spirits, to save us all, a communion wafer, a—"

"Even pure," I said, "it causes brain damage. And you're the proof." I stepped into the room. My arm was starting to get tired, holding the gun like that. "Buffalo Soldier, get your money."

Wendell nodded happily and stood, then stepped into the office, coming at the money, with me and Latesha covering him....

If there's a bunch of cold-sober guys in a hard situation, and one stoned guy, the stoned guy is always the one who fucks things up.

So the bald headed guy, with his droopy ear rings and his droopy smile and his nebbishy face, came half-stumbling toward us. "We're all going to glow as one, when the star in each of us becomes the galaxy of all of us—" he was saying. At least I think that's what he was saying.

I'm not sure, because my attention had riveted on the Dutch guy, who was using the blundering distraction of Banyan—

—Banyan lurching sparkle-eyed toward us with arms spreading for a group hug—

—to lunge for the Uzi, the Dutch guy scooping it up and in the same motion squeezing off a long burst at Wendell.

Most of the burst missed Wendell, sizzling the air around us, chewing up the frame of the door. I felt a hot poker in my right ear. I heard Latesha yell in surprise and pain.

141

Wendell caught three rounds, stitched across his left shoulder, his chest, his right side. He shouted, "Fuck, shit—!" and fired at the Dutch guy, catching him in the forehead near the right temple, the .44 round chiseling a corner of the Dutch guy's skull away, so that bits of yellow and bluewhite calcium and droplets of red sprayed back on Ricky who was covering his head with his arms, cringing.

Dutch staggered back, fired another burst at nothing in particular, making a stack of money burst into the air like a flock of startled butterflies. He didn't fall immediately, blinking as if simply surprised, his hands still swinging the Uzi around for another burst at us—

I shifted my aim to Dutch and squeezed the trigger, the six gun jumped in my hand, and the round punched right through his esophagus, and his head jerked back, and he spun and fell with a heavy thump—

As shot-torn bits of 100 dollar bills drifted down like parade confetti between us....

The black weightlifter had just closed his hand on the pistol he'd tossed on the table when a burst from Latesha's Mac made him do a sort of odd little dance, and he fell back against the wall, firing the pistol so that the window exploded outward....

Dulcet was half skipping into the room, her little gun making popping sounds, as she pumped rounds into Banyan, who was off in a corner, to my left, waving his hands at the gunshots as if to shoo flies away.

Ricky was crawling...crawling toward that back door...breathing hard. "Take the fucking money!" he rasped. "Just take it!"

I saw the black weightlifter was still alive, sitting on the floor with his legs splayed, shakily raising that gun again. I cocked my gun and aimed at his head—he moved, and I only hit his right eye.

The eyesocket instantly became a crater gushing blood, but the round

had gone downward, missing his brain—and he was firing the pistol—
sloppily, though—the rounds whistled close, smacked into my hat, made
pieces of ceiling rattle down—

I squeezed off another round into the black weightlifter, and he
bounced back against the wall, closing his remaining eye.

Gunsmoke snaked bluegray up into the air from the silver muzzle of
my Colt.... My eyes ached with it....

I heard Dulcet singing something and turned to tell her to get back
into the warehouse.... But I found I couldn't say anything to her, right
then....

"Ecstasy, happy trancedance ecstasy at the ravey dance!" Dulcet
chanted, kind of muffled because she was shoving some sour taffy candy
in her mouth with her free hand— the other hand firing her pistol. And
I saw that she had ripped off her blouse, she was topless, *she was stripping* during the gunfight and sort of dancing around to a music only she
could hear—and shooting, her bare breasts bobbing with each shot,
blood spattering the nipples—

"No that's...it's...." Banyan said, between each impact, sounding as
if he was trying to explain how sadly wrong she had gone.

A number of small holes on his torso spouted blood.

He was on his knees, his mouth open, looking so sad, so disappointed,
it seemed to affect her.

Dulcet took the half-chewed sour taffy from her mouth and put it in
his, as if to share.

"Want some candy now?" she asked. Sounding completely sincere.

He chewed once, twice, and he actually smiled up at her. "That's
so...it's sour but...you're so...sweet.... My Dad likes...."

Then he stopped talking, and just collapsed, like a remote control
toy with the batteries pulled.

I heard the black guy coughing wetly. The son of a bitch was game, pard: he wasn't dead yet. I turned to see his remaining eye burning up at me, as he tried to say something, not getting the words out. But I knew he was telling me he was going to kill me.

He raised his Uzi. The little submachinegun was wobbly—but it was pointed at me.

I aimed carefully, quickly but with deliberation, and, without time to cock the gun, I squeezed the trigger hard. It was harder to pull the trigger, without cocking the gun.

But the Peacemaker bucked in my hand and this time the round caught the weightlifter between the eyes: a nice round hole, only a couple of red oozing cracks zigging from it.

He quivered—and dropped his gun. Went still. His remaining eye staying open this time, rapt. As if he were attentive....

Maybe he was. Maybe he was attentive to something....

The room was choked with gunsmoke now; smelled of gunpowder and blood. I felt hot wetness running down from my ear.

Latesha was on her knees beside Wendell, who was trying to sit up. Latesha's face was wet with tears; it was screwed up like a weeping three year old's, and for a moment I saw the little girl she had been, once, in that face. A little black girl in Florida waiting for her parents to come home.

Ricky was pulling at the lock on the door to the outside. I walked toward him. "Ricky. Turn around...."

He got the lock open, now; was jerking at the handle. Fumbling. He was clumsy with fear. I almost wanted him to get away, he was so scared.

But I hadn't come this far to let him go.

"Ricky.... You killed my son. His name was Frankie. I hope he prays for both of us, Ricky...Ricky Kwai...."

"Shoot him, Tex!" Dulcet shouted gleefully.

That made me want to let him go, too. "Shut up, Dulcet," I said.

I walked over to Ricky, cocked the gun—

At the sound of the gun cocking, he tried to make himself small, cringing away from me.

I reached out, spun him around, shoved the gun into his open mouth, and pulled the trigger.

I admit it: I closed my eyes. As an Existentialist, I should've taken responsibility. And watched his brains explode out the back of his head to run stickily down the door.

I didn't watch it, though. But that's what happened to him.

I looked to make sure it was done, and then I let him drop and turned around to face, at least, the wreckage behind me.

10

Latesha was still weeping over Wendell. He was cursing her, telling her to get him up, get me up you stupid-ass ho.

And Dulcet was raking all that money—what wasn't shot up or blood-stained—into the three satchels it'd come in. The one they'd brought with them had held only part of the total. Then she turned to the dope....

"Dulcet!" I said sharply.

She pouted at me.

"Leave it for the police to confiscate," I said. "That's non-negotiable."

Dulcet hesitated. She hated to leave all that potential money....

Grimacing with pain, Wendell snarled, "Dulcet forget that shit dope and get your skinny little ass out to the motherfucking...." He broke off, gritting his teeth.

I knew we ought to be running and right now. Even in an area with few people around at this hour, that much gunfire was going to attract the cops.

But as I walked over to Banyan, every step was a struggle against a current that wanted to push me back, push me down on the floor...with the dead.

And I wasn't sure I wanted to leave here at all. I figured I really ought to stay and greet the cops.

My boots made sucking sounds in the blood on the floor as I walked unsteadily, slowly, over to Banyan.

Looking at all those little holes Dulcet had punched into him....

What had Banyan been saying at the end?

My Dad....

It seemed to prompt some fuzzy recollection—Oh no—

I recognized his face now, with the unnaturalness of his high gone from it.

Oh bullshit. That can't be right. No fucking way. Can't really be who I think it is....

I hunkered down and I unzipped his fanny pack. Found his velcro-closed bicyclist's wallet. Found his driver's license. Read the name on it.

Gary Ledbetter.

"Fuck," I said, out loud, standing to stare down at him.

Banyan. It was a nickname. I hadn't heard the nickname before tonight, but I put it all together now— because I had met this man once before. He was Mr. Ledbetter's second-youngest son. Ledbetter of Ledbetter Books. The son the old man had the trouble with.

Gary "Banyan" Ledbetter had persuaded his Dad to invest a lot of money—money blown, as it turned out—in trying to start a "Banyan fig" plantation over here with trees transplanted from Israel, because he was fixated on Banyans, he'd had some kind of stupid-ass hashish vision under a Banyan, and now, it seemed, people called him Banyan....

Mr. Ledbetter's son. I had persuaded some people to help me kill, among other people, Mr. Ledbetter's son.

His son who had drug problems—like Frankie had.

And it wasn't a coincidence—because Frankie sometimes came to work with me. Once, when I had to work through lunch, Frankie had gone to lunch with Mr. Ledbetter's son, who worked there, sometimes, on a kind of probational deal with his Dad.

And "Banyan" Ledbetter knew Abel—of course he did. He'd heard Frankie was into skateboards.

Really? You into skateboards? There's somebody you ought to meet, man. Friend of mine got his own shop.... Ocean surfer gone sidewalk surfer.... Got some interesting experience over there.... You like rave mixes?

So it was Frankie, probably, who'd introduced Victor to the drug, through Abel. Not the other way.

And I'd introduced Frankie to Gary "Banyan" Ledbetter.

Life likes to fuck with you....

Or maybe that thought was just a way to avoid blaming the real culprit.

"Come on, Tex...you crazy...motherfucker...." Wendell was whispering. "Let's go...."

A bag under each arm and another hanging from her right hand, Dulcet was looking down at Wendell, as if trying to comprehend: a single drop of blood trembling to fall from the tip of her nipple. Like if she had a baby, it'd breast-feed blood from her.

I thought I could just make out the sirens approaching. Still a ways off. But it wouldn't be long.

"I don't think I should go, Wendell," I said. "Ya'll go ahead. I think I should stay here and face all this. I never did want the money."

Latesha looked at me, her eyes red; there was blood dripping from her lips and she was newly missing a couple of teeth on the right side of her mouth. "Tex—Slim Jim—we gone need you now."

Her voice was bubbly. She spat out pieces of teeth.

"Jesus—you're hit, Latesha," Dulcet said, with real concern. "We gotta get you to a doctor...."

Wendell looked at Dulcet. "You...hear that...little white ho...she don't say take Wendell to a doctor...she already write me off." He said it almost fondly.

Dulcet said half-heartedly, "No way Daddy Wendell, I didn't write you off. No sir no sir—" She looked at the satchels of cash and couldn't resist adding, "—three bags full." Then she looked at me. "Tex, you got a hole shot in your hat—and your ear! Ooh, it's like they used one of those hole-punching tools...."

Wendell said, "I got another little hole punching tool right here for you, Tex...." Then he tilted his pistol up at me.

"What's up with pointing that gun at me, Wendell?" I asked.

"You got to go with us...can't...you talk to the police...they ID us...."

"You probably got prints all over here," I said, "and it's not as if your prints aren't in their computer. No time to get rid of them. I wouldn't tell the cops anything about you, anyway, man."

He lowered the gun, realizing I was right about the prints. He grimaced with pain. "Fuck you, then...Editor Boy."

Latesha said, blood foaming the corners of her mouth, "Tex? You got to help us with him."

The siren got louder....

I sighed, and decided I couldn't abandon Latesha, at least, and that meant going with them.

I remembered something Gary Ledbetter had said about the classic cars in the warehouse.

I went to the desk, opened the drawer, saw the brass ring of old fashioned car keys.

"Wendell," I said, "we're gonna travel in style, man. You want the Rolls or the Bentley. Your choice."

He smiled wanly at that. "I always wanted a Rolls...."

� ✕ ✕

Dulcet got the loading-dock gate open and the Rolls rolling while Latesha and I were carrying Wendell out. He groaned and ground his teeth with pain, as we loaded him in the luxurious backseat of the saloon car.

Dulcet had the Rolls moving down the street, *oohing* over driving the Brit car from the "wrong" side of its cab, before we got the car door closed.

We pulled around the corner maybe three seconds before the cops pulled up to the warehouse—that's what it looked like, anyhow, from the whirling lights I could see over the rooftop of the adjacent building.

Later I found out the cop had gone to the wrong building, at first. There'd only been a vague report of gunfire in the area. It took them awhile to spot the broken glass from that shot-out window. It's possible to underestimate police competency—but usually you can count on them to fuck something up.

In some ways, we were lucky.

✕ ✕ ✕

Wendell was propped up in the back seat, between Latesha and me. Latesha was leaning up against him, to help keep him upright. She had one hand on his leg, and the other on her swelling jaw.

"I wish I had a chauffeur's cap," Dulcet said, driving us onto the *80* toward Oakland.

151

There was a doctor in Oakland that Leon had told Latesha about, on the last working cellphone, before he'd summarily hung up with a "Just don't bring him here."

Dulcet went on, "A chauffeur's cap. That'd be cool. I could use it for part of a costume in my act too."

I glanced at her. She was still topless. "You're driving with your tits hanging out. Could be a smidge conspicuous. Pull over—put on my jacket here...."

"Oh, well, fuck, " she said, "okay, but it's not my look...." And right before the freeway ramp she pulled over long enough to put on my jean-jacket, buttoned most of the way up. She checked her hair in the rear-view mirror....

"Girl," Latesha said, "get this motherfucking car back on the road! Wendell's...he fittin to...he needs a doctor! Le's go!"

Dulcet put the car in gear, struggling with the clutch— it lurched a couple of times before she got it rumbling up the onramp. "I don't get to drive stick shifts much," she muttered.

I wondered how badly Latesha was hurt. But she was watching Wendell like a mother with a grievously sick child—and you could see the veins pulsing too hard at his forehead. He had lost a lot of blood. There was probably some pretty bad internal bleeding.

But he was still smiling. "Rolls Royce Silver Shadow...nobody going to call this bitch in stolen...not for a long time, if they ever do, right? This bitch here is mine. She mine...."

He ran his hand over the white leather seat. It was only slightly smeared with blood, here and there.

"How much...how much money we get?" he asked, his voice weaker. His eyes dimmer.

Latesha said, "Near half a million dollars...."

"Motherfucker...that a lot of money. You girls...you gone take your share, too. You put your money...in...you...invest it...Latesha...."

"We all gone invest our money together, baby," she said. Sort of mush-mouthed through her wrecked mouth, so it was harder to make out what she was saying now. But I thought, after that, I heard her praying for him.

Wendell noticed it too. "Don't you...save my soul...bitch, who you...." But Wendell put his hand over hers. "You sure stuck by me.... Look at this, a Rolls...we scored...like a motherfucker.... Those Cuban pencil dicks can kiss my black...Latesha? How much money we got? You count that money, Latesha?"

"I think it's near a million dollars, baby," she said, this time.

I saw Dulcet looking in the rearview mirror at us. Maybe those were tears in her eyes. Maybe they were gleaming at the talk of all the money they had in the trunk of the car. Closer to three hundred grand.

"Maybe...." Latesha was saying. "A million and a half...."

Wendell's voice was a croak now. "Tex...what you gone do with your share...."

"I thought we should stick together...all of us go to Las Vegas...start one of those Mustang Ranch places...Best Little Whorehouse in Nevada.... The girls can supervise...I can be head of personnel. In charge of hiring...."

Wendell made a raspy sound that might've been laughter. "Thas right...we gon to Vegas...Mustang Ranch...Wendell's...Love Ranch...."

"Barry White playing all day," I said. "It'll be great. We'll get you patched up and head out there tonight."

Latesha looked at me, and then looked away.

Wendell's voice was getting softer and softer. "My brother...wait'll he sees me drive up in this bitch...I'll toss him a roll...go out and have you'self a time motherfucker...damn he...look at this Raybobby, you rag-gedy ass motherfucker... look...this...." He closed his eyes. "Didn't get enough motherfucking... sleep...last night...fucking ho drain my...."

"You just rest now, baby," Latesha said.

Wendell didn't answer.

※　※　※

We carried Wendell between us, Latesha and I, his arms over our shoulders, his feet thumping, up a back staircase, into the office where the doctor was waiting—we'd arranged the whole thing through the doctor's beeper.

The doctor was a semi-retired elderly Chinese, in Oakland's scaled-down Chinatown, who didn't ask questions if you waved enough cash. And Latesha had brought in a paperbag full of 20s and 50s.

I'd started out on this Mission with a young Chinese doctor. Now the mission was old and so was the Chinese doctor.

Dr. Jiang said this was going to cost plenty, because we'd dragged him from his bed, but actually he was wearing a rumpled three-piece brown polyester suit, and smelled of cigarette smoke, and it seemed more likely he'd been playing Mah Jong with the boys in some basement casino. He scarcely glanced at the bullet holes in Wendell's clothes, the blood stains on all three of us. This was not his first post-shooting patch-up.

We stretched Wendell out on an antique white-painted metal examination table, a deeply worn leather pad under his head. On one wall there was a chart with the outline of a man on it, arrows from ideograms pointing to different blockage points for *chi* flows in the body; on the other was an old promotional poster for Ely Lilly showing various pills for various ailments.

Jiang had a neat little white mustache that made him look more like a Japanese World War Two General than a Chinese doctor. His office was over a Dim Sum restaurant, and it was so redolent of Chinese cuisine I felt both sick to my stomach and hungry at once.

The doctor pressed two fingers to Wendell's jugular, kept them there for ten seconds or so. Then he shook his head. But glancing at Latesha, he wisely put on a show of making sure, with his stethoscope. "He is dead, miss. Maybe fifteen, twenty minute," he said. "I cannot bring him back. If I could, his brain would be no more, you know?"

(..."You're saying...you're saying he's dead."

"We try for half an hour to revive him...everything, everything. There was a blood clot in the lung from a breaking vessel there, and the blood clot goes into artery, stops heart, we try to break clot up, re-star heart but he came to us already gone...."

Frankie....)

Latesha pressed another stack of bills on him.

"Try," she said.

Jiang shrugged and bustled around, opening drawers. He injected adrenaline into Wendell's limp arm. No response. Then he wheeled a tank over in its rack, put an oxygen mask over Wendell's slack face, and tried to force oxygen. No response.

Jiang looked at the money, deciding, probably, he needed to make sure it looked like he'd earned his pay, and climbed up on the table to straddle the body, pumping his clasped hands on Wendell's chest. Nothing. He shrugged sadly at Latesha. And shook his head again.

Latesha groaned, and took a step back. She stood there, swaying and I caught her when she fell, dragged her to a chair.

I said, "Hold still a minute, girl, lean back and open your mouth." And I looked in her mouth myself.

The bullet had shattered two upper right teeth, and it was lodged in the gold filling of a lower back tooth. I was a kind of blown away by that: There was the bullet, half crumpled, wedged like a dud rocket in an old wisdom-tooth filling. Ballistic oddities were dogging me.

"Not my specialty," Jiang said. "Tomorrow, a dentist—my brother-in-law, very good—"

I looked at him. I almost hit him. But instead I just looked at him. He got the message.

He muttered in Chinese and made her lean back in the chair while he probed in her mouth with a forceps, wrenching out the remains of the two smashed upper molars, then working on the wisdom tooth, prying at the crashed spaceship.

Latesha seemed to've mentally gone somewhere else; she twitched with the pain when he worked over her, but she never cried out, and her eyes never came into focus.

I wondered about Dulcet. She was supposed to be waiting outside in the Rolls. She had all the rest of that money with her. I hoped she'd still be out there when we got back to the alley.

The doctor finally dug the bullet out; looked at it in his forceps with arched eyebrows, then tossed it into a metal dish. He took out a big set of keys, said he was going next door to the office of a dentist—maybe the brother-in-law, since he had the key.

Then he stopped at the door, came back, took the money we'd brought for him, and took it out with him.

Maybe two, maybe five minutes passed. I was beginning to worry he'd gone for the police—when he came back with some temporary filling paste, and a little dental tool.

He worked on the tooth in an impromptu sort of way. He gave her some codeine pills. I made her swallow a couple.

She hadn't said a word the whole time.

Finally, the doctor put antiseptic on my ear. I looked at it in the reflection on a shiny chrome tissue dispenser. It was true: a neat round hole punched through the lobe. The little wound burned, but not much more than a new piercing would've.

The doctor had a couple of body bags—he made a point of claiming he'd never needed them before—and the two of us grunted through zipping Wendell in one. I carried Wendell's body down the back stairs, over my shoulder. I make it sound easy. It wasn't.

Showing unexpected tenderness, Dr. Jiang escorted Latesha, helping her down the stairs.

I realized then that the old Chinese pill pusher wasn't the venal, indifferent old prick I'd taken him to be—he simply assumed we were criminals, with whom he worked only for the sake of the inheritance of his children and grandchildren. And he didn't like or trust us.

But seeing Latesha's grief had moved him....

He helped her into the Rolls, in the alley, and patted her arm before closing the door.

Dulcet stared at the bodybag laid across the back seat, for one protracted moment, then turned firmly away.

❊   ❊   ❊

We drove Wendell's body around for awhile, more or less at random. We were quiet, even Dulcet. Watching for cops but not really caring where we went. The lower end of the body bag was on the floor; Wendell's head and shoulders, zipped away inside, leaned up against Latesha's legs. She had one hand on top of the vinyl bag, where his left shoulder would be. She just sat there, staring out the window, as we drove.

We only stopped once, on the old steel bridge over the estuary into Alameda. I got out, glanced around. It was late, dark. A Ford Bronco drove onto the bridge, passed us—then it was gone. I reached into the Rolls, got the guns out, and tossed them into the estuary. We didn't linger there.

Okay, to be perfectly honest, I tossed most of the guns in. I couldn't bear to toss Tuck's nice Colt .45 in. So I hid it under a girder, on a rusty ledge of the bridge, where no one would be likely to find it any time soon. I might want it sometime.

We finally fetched up at a "lookout point" turn-out, near the top of Grizzly Peak, overlooking Berkeley and Oakland and the Port. Berkeley was spread out below, mostly dark, glittering in clusters.

I could see the angular freight cranes jutting gigantically along the Bay, so tall they were crowned with bright lights to warn passing choppers. Beyond the long sweep of the Bay Bridge, the San Francisco skyline was sharply outlined in lights.

It almost broke Dulcet's heart, but Latesha, coming out of her fugue, insisted that we burn the Rolls—with Wendell's body in it. A Viking funeral kind of deal. *The Vikings,* with Ernest Borgnine, had been one of Wendell's favorite movies.

Dulcet liked the Viking funeral idea but she hated losing the Rolls. "Wendell was probably wrong that we got away clean with this car," I pointed out. "They probably have a list of the cars, by now, and chances are they're looking for this one...."

She pouted. "My beautiful Rolls...."

"It was Wendell's," Latesha said rather severely. Dulcet shrugged.

I didn't even consider saying, *Actually it was Banyan's Rolls.* In my mind, too, for no clear reason at all, it was Wendell's Silver Shadow.

Dulcet and Latesha almost fought over what to do with Wendell's cut. Dulcet naturally enough thought we ought to split it along with the rest of the money. I was pretty surprised myself when Latesha insisted on starting the fire with Wendell's share of the money.

She got her way. She took Wendell from the body bag, piled most of his share of the cash onto his chest. She lit it with his gold Zippo, and then lit a big handful of 100 dollar bills. Dulcet backed away from the Rolls, saying, "Whoa nelly, girlfriend," as Latesha stuffed the wad of burning 100s down into the gas tank—

I shouted, "Latesha, get the fuck away from that car...now!"

Murmuring a prayer to Jesus that would have pissed off the Vikings, Latesha was shoving the burning bills down into the tank with a stick.

I ran to her, grabbed her upper right arm in my two hands and yanked her back from the car, having to drag her, thrashing, to the cover of a couple of steel trash barrels.

One step, ahead of the Devil....

Dulcet was already crouching, calling a cab on the cellphone, telling them to send it to an address we'd picked out, up the hill. Still mad about burning the car and Wendell's share of the money, Dulcet snapped at the dispatcher when they didn't understand her the first time over the sound of the explosion—

As the Rolls gave out a deep throated whoosh and burst into flames.

But then she danced a little, in front of the pyre; wearing only my jacket and her short-shorts, a sylphic silhouette in front of a burning Rolls. Saying goodbye to Wendell her own way.

There was a dark, hard lump in the middle of me; it felt as if my stomach had petrified. It wasn't so much for Wendell—though I did feel something for him. It was just that, watching the car burning, maybe, after all, I felt some regret about not going to Frankie's funeral.

I shook my head, like I was trying to shake mosquitoes off. I forced the tears down. Thinking that I had to get moving again...keep moving out ahead of it....

We were only a half block up the hill when the police cars and fire trucks came....

One step, ahead of the Man...

...the cops and firemen staring, bemused, at the pyre of the burning Silver Shadow....

Where Wendell's body burned joyfully....

You can only run as far as you can....

※　※　※

The cab found us in front of a dark "mini mansion" in a stand of eucalyptus. The driver was an aging hippie, with braided white hair, the tips of his big white beard braided too.

"Look," Dulcet said, as we got in, "it's fucking Willie Nelson come to get us."

The cabbie chose not to take offense, and said, "Hey what's happenin'...late to go out on the town huh? But whatever's your... your...."

He broke off, looking us over—we were still blood spattered, shabby after the fight. We probably smelled of gunpowder and blood and gasoline. Dulcet clutching the remaining two satchels....

He stared for a moment, then he glanced in the direction of the burning Rolls, though from here it was just a flicker of flame down the hill, a tremble of red light through the dark tree trunks, below us; the counterpoint blue strobing of cop-car light-bars. He must've rubbernecked the pyre scene on the way here.

I gave him the same look I gave the doctor, and he said nothing and took us where we were going.

An address on the West Oakland flats.

✺　✺　✺

The Easter Hill Church of Our Loving Savior was a long narrow wooden building that looked like it had probably once been a middle-sized discount shoe store. At the bottom of the hand-painted sign nailed onto the false front, next to a Christian cross formed out of glued-on sparkly stuff, silver lettering read: THE REVEREND HUEY KEARNEY. Below that, there was a butcher-paper banner in the window: *Save Easter Hill Church! Come to the Bake Sale and Witness for the Lord! (Yes we will have Mrs. Hoaglin's Sweet Potato Pie!)*

We stood awkwardly in front of the makeshift church—a makeshift chapel for a makeshift denomination. Making the cab wait for us across the street.

There was one light on, in the back of the improvised church. But I couldn't see much in there.

"You sure they're in there, Latesha?" I asked.

She nodded. There was a certain peacefulness in her expression, now. "Reverend Kearney lives back there."

Dulcet shook her head in wonder. "You're not *really*, are you, Latesha?"

"I got no reason not to give myself up the Lord now," Latesha said. "Everything happen for a reason."

"No I mean—the money. You aren't going to give them your share of the money are you?"

"This place going to shut down, it don't get some money. The neighborhood 'round here can't afford to support it but they do some good here. Organize food drives for peeps got no food. They got a program to get the kids off the street."

"Whatever. I just don't like—"

"And she's getting my share too, Dulcet," I said. "I already put it in her bag."

Dulcet pouted. It was not a cute pout. "That going to get you off the hook somehow, Tex? Make you feel all right about what you've done— and what you didn't do?"

"Dulcet," I said tonelessly, "Shut the fuck up."

She looked at me—and her eyes softened. "'Kay!"

"Take your share, that *one* bag, and go sit in the cab. Maybe you can get Willie to sing for you."

"'Kay. Can we get something to eat later? I'm hungry as a wolfy."

"Sure. Go on now."

She looked at the satchels with a theatrical pout, then reluctantly gave one to Latesha. And started across to the cab. Turning around halfway across the street just long enough to say, "Bye Latesha!"

"Bye Baby." Latesha turned to me, kissed me on the cheek. "Thank you, Tex. I'm sorry about your little boy."

I swallowed. I wished she hadn't said that. I nodded stiffly and turned away. Looking at the waiting cab—but just standing there. Not wanting to get back in that cab, either.

Up the street, I saw a black teenager sitting on a small Y-handlebar bike, rolling it back and forth under him with little motions of his hips as he talked to his friends. His homies, I guess. They all had those black skullcap sort of things made out of stretch material on their heads, with the flaps that hang down in back. I never have figured out what the hell those things are. They didn't have those when I was in stir, back when.

Latesha patted me on the shoulder, then she went up to the door and knocked. I waited, to make sure she got in all right. After a few minutes I heard a gravelly voice, muffled through the door, "Who the hell that, this hour?"

"Reverend Kearney? It's Latesha? You remember me?"

I heard the door unlock, and open. "Girl what you doing here this time of night?"

"You said I could come day or night, if I wanted to pray."

"You want to pray with me, come on in. What you got there?"

The door closed behind them. I waited a moment. Then I heard him shout something I couldn't quite make out. It was a joyous sound unto the Lord, though. And I definitely heard the word 'miracle'.

I walked back to the cab, and got in. I leaned forward and tapped the cabdriver on the shoulder, reading his name off his identification card.

"Hey, Jason Winslow Becher," I said.

He looked at me. I noticed his bristly eyebrows; the marijuana stain on his mustache. "Yeah?"

"Did you call this stop in?"

"No—we aren't where we're going yet. But o' course, strictly speaking I'm supposed to tell them wherever I stop in case—" He broke off, and licked his lips.

I leaned toward him and fixed his eyes with mine. "In case? Not in this case. Jason Winslow Becher, you remember *no details* of this fare at all. You don't remember what the people looked like. And you didn't drop any of them here. You understand? You pretend I'm fucking Obie Wan Kenobie here and I'm erasing your mind. You don't fucking know. You got me?"

"Um…. Yeah."

"I mean this. Because if you do cross me on this—no matter what, or why—I'm going to find you and kill your ass dead. And that's a flat promise. Okay?"

"Right on," he said, though 'right on' made no real sense just then.

"Okay, let's go."

Dulcet had already given him an address, so the driver set off immediately. In a hurry to get this fare over with.

I looked wistfully through the cab's rear window, back at the storefront church.

I wished, then, that I could believe in the whole story about Christ. About repentance and forgiveness and Heaven. I wished I could believe in God. I still wish I could believe. But I can't.

I sure as Hell can't.

WHAT HAPPENS THEN

About an hour after dawn, we had breakfast, Dulcet and I. Coffee and a donut for me. Dulcet had a Denny's "grand-slam". Then we got another cab.

I dropped her off with a tall, skinny, nicely dressed black guy name of Jacques, with neatly jerry-curled hair. He didn't talk in Black English at all. Very community college business major, this guy. But he had the gold at his wrists, the gems on his rings. Apparently he'd once tried to buy Dulcet from Wendell. It seems he owned a small but thriving rap-music record company, with a sideline in girls. The girls did outcalls, also servicing the rap stars as required.

I was sorry to leave Dulcet with him—he had a kind of background hum of cruelty about him, despite his surface amiability, his limp handshake.

Dulcet planned to partner up with him, use the money to open her own strip joint. Help him run the girls. It was just as likely he'd simply take the money from her, but I didn't argue.

I just raised my shot-up cowboy hat to her, and said, "Ma'am," to make her laugh. And she did.

And then I left her there with her new pimp. Maybe I should've felt sorry for him, instead of her, come to think of it.

Very tired, but very awake, I walked through San Francisco, three and a half blocks, straight to a police station. I felt, somehow, as if Frankie was walking right beside me.

�֍ ✖ ✖

I simply strolled into the brand spanking new offices of the nearest SFPD precinct, and said I had some information on a homicide.

They said I'd start with a uniform, and directed me to an office down the hall. No one was taking particular note of me. They hadn't looked at any wanted posters lately, it seemed.

Down the hall I found the designated cop, a uniformed sarge just hanging up the phone. He was a plump, mustached, middle aged Latino name of Sergeant Garcia. I made no Zorro jokes.

He seemed like a bright, amiable guy. There were framed pictures standing on his desk and a couple of framed certificates on the wall.

I sat down across from him, said I had a story to tell him involving some nice fresh homicides. He nodded, smiling patiently, and said go ahead.

His face got hard, his eyes sort of flat, when I said, "I killed a number of people in the last couple days...."

He stopped me with a raised hand. "You'll have to repeat all this for a stenographer later...."

I said sure, fine. I didn't mind. But I wanted to get it all out now—

He seemed to hesitate. Then he got up and closed his office door. He went and sat back down and said, "Go on."

I talked for a long time. I told him about Frankie, then about Eickoff, and about shooting Eickoff and how that'd happened; and I told him about hooking up with a certain part-time pimp, and his two girls who happened to have some other skills too, and about my Mission for Frankie. I told him about killing Abel, because of Frankie, and about killing Ricky Kwai in cold blood.

I didn't tell him everything. I didn't give him Wendell's real name or the real names of his crew. I didn't tell him about the Bounty Hunter, because they might've connected that with Latesha.

I didn't tell him about Wendell's cousin, either. I just said we'd stayed with a friend of Morris's, somewhere in the northeast Bay—Wendell had become Morris, in my story.

The cop looked at me for a long moment, after I finished telling him the story.

Finally he said, "His name was Morris? That's who was burned up in that Rolls, up in the Berkeley hills?"

"Yeah. I never did know his last name."

He nodded, slowly, but he said, "You're not telling me everything, are you."

I shrugged. "What I can. All I ever will. Anyway, you guys are looking for me for those killings at Ledbetter Books, and here I am. We can start with that. I didn't kill those people there—except I shot Eickoff. Not really wanting to. I know it sounds improbable. But—that's what happened. Maybe they can prove it forensically or something. Just for the record—I didn't do those killings. I'll cop to killing Ricky Kwai, and those other guys. Some of 'em were basically self defense. But Ricky Kwai and Abel—that's basically some form of...well, I planned it."

"What became of the two girls?"

"One of them's gone straight, I think. She's...got religion. In another town. That's all I can tell you. The other...." I shrugged.

"Found herself another pimp?"

"Basically. Yeah."

"I figured." He picked up a pencil, tapped its eraser on the desk as he looked at me. He glanced at the door—then looked back at me. "You didn't actually watch the TV news, I take it? Read a newspaper?"

"No...I was—on a Mission."

"Then you don't know. Eickoff isn't dead. He survived. He's in pretty bad condition, but he's alive in a hospital under twenty-four hour police guard. He exonerated you completely. You're off the hook for that one. We're aware that some drug dealing scumbags were killed in Richmond—and one dealer in the Sunset we were about to bust ourselves. Richmond PD doesn't have any suspects. They're talking gangs. We were never looking to arrest you for the Ledbetter Books shooting spree. It was understandable, you shooting Eickoff under the circumstances. We just wanted your side of the story. Confirm things, close the case. Eickoff is pegged for those killings, not you. It never was you."

I stared at him. "Well shit."

He nodded. "That's right."

I thought about it, then I shrugged. "That's a good 'un on me. But—it doesn't matter. I am ready to make a statement to your stenographer, whoever else you want, about the killing in the Sunset, and the killings at Kwai and Sons warehouse. I murdered that prick Abel, and I murdered Ricky Kwai, Sergeant."

He leaned back in his chair. He looked at something on his desk. He sighed, long and loudly. He stood up. "I'm going to get the stenographer. You'll make a short statement and sign it. But you say nothing about our friend in the Sunset or Ricky Kwai or those assholes in Richmond. You just say what happened at Ledbetter's and you leave the precinct. We'll issue a statement about you. You will say you fled because you thought you were going to be shot down—but you are not a suspect in the Ledbetter killings. Technically the DA could probably *charge you with something for running off like that—but they won't. I was you, I'd leave town—the damn reporters will be all over you if you don't get clear."

"I...don't quite follow, Sergeant. I mean—why?"

He leaned toward me, tossed the pencil on the desk, and put his hands down flat on the desktop. "I'm a by-the-book cop. Always was, always will be. Except today, just for this. This's going to be the one exception I'm making. See, I helped Detective Carlson gather the facts on the Ledbetter books shootings, and I know about you and your son."

He reached over and turned a framed photo around on the desk, so it was facing me. It showed a good looking, slightly plump teenage boy, with an unconvincing mustache, wearing a lavender prom jacket and a ruffled prom shirt, the kind some Latinos liked to wear sometimes. He looked proud. He had a corsage in his hand. Photo taken, I guessed, right before leaving to pick up his prom date.

"Your boy?" I said. My voice breaking a little.

"That's right. He was. He's dead. Drugs. He didn't do them much, if ever before that night but—he got talked into it. Got blitzed, I guess, on beer, and his judgment was...you know...and then they gave him some...it doesn't matter what. But you know what? I'll never find the dealer behind it." He smiled, though he looked like he might cry. "But you...look what you did. Well sure: It's wrong. I'll confess to my priest. I'll ask for God's forgiveness. But I won't tell anyone else about it. Because it's my own little piece of getting even. Now I want you the hell out of my office, after we do the statement about Ledbetter books. And you don't say a word about the other thing. Never."

I looked at the picture of his boy. I nodded.

I'd do as he asked. But freedom was a terrible thing to me now. It meant I wouldn't be punished by the rest of the world for what happened to Frankie.

It meant justice would come to me when it was ready. And it would do with me as it pleased.

And now, finally, I was scared. I was so scared.

※　※　※

I rented a new TransAm with only a hundred miles on it. I drove northeast. On and on, toward the Nevada border.

I tried to drive faster than the thing that was pursuing me, inside, but it caught up and poised itself over me, now; caught up with me effortlessly, just because it was ready.

I drove deep into the desert. Out in the desert like that bird that got blown off course.

Finally, I parked the car in a big, empty, flat dry lake. There weren't even any rocks or bushes there. Just the smell of dust in the lowering sun.

I walked out into the desert, following my long, starved shadow. I fell to my knees.

It all poured out of me then, in dark waves, roaring through me. I started to sob.

Frankie...I'm sorry...Frankie...Frankie....

SAVING CHINA:
CANADIAN MISSIONARIES IN THE
MIDDLE KINGDOM

ALVYN J. AUSTIN

SAVING CHINA

CANADIAN MISSIONARIES IN THE MIDDLE KINGDOM 1888-1959

UNIVERSITY OF TORONTO PRESS

Toronto Buffalo London

ISBN 0-8020-5687-3

Canadian Cataloguing in Publication Data

Austin, Alvyn.
    Saving China : Canadian missionaries in the
    Middle Kingdom
    Includes bibliographical references and index.
    ISBN 0-8020-5687-3
    1. Missions, Canadian – China – History.
    2. Missionaries – China – History. 3. Missionaries
    – Canada – History. I. Title.
    BV3415.2.A87 1986   266'.023'71051   C86-093985-5

All photographs are from the archives of the United Church of Canada (UCA), except
for those on: pages 2, 8, 16, 109, and 324, from the China Inland Mission archives (at
the Overseas Missionary Fellowship); pages 124, 214, and 239, from the Anglican
Church of Canada archives; pages 143, 161, and 163 from the Scarboro Foreign Mission
Society archives. The photograph on page 22 is reproduced from G.L. Mackay, *From
Far Formosa: The Island, Its People and Missions*. Sam Tata took the photograph on page
323. The author acknowledges the assistance of the Donner Canadian Foundation and
the Joint Centre on Modern East Asia in the reproduction of these photographs.
    The Chinese papercuts from the 1930s used as chapter headings are from the
Anglican Church archives, except the Chefoo school insignia on page 325, which is
from the China Inland Mission.

This book has been published with the help of a grant from the Canadian Federation
for the Humanities, using funds provided by the Social Sciences and Humanities
Research Council of Canada, and block grants from the Canada Council and the
Ontario Arts Council.

For my parents, John, Lilian, and Emma Austin, and for my brother, Norman.

They told me the best stories they knew: their own.

Contents

Acknowledgments

'Without whom this book would not have been written' – the phrase rattles around in the brain of every writer. I would like to take this opportunity to thank those who gave me world enough and time to write. In a story of this diversity, that is a lot of people – former missionaries who told me their own stories, archivists who fetched material and pointed the way to further research, scholars of Chinese history and of Canadian church history who gave advice and read the manuscript in progress, editors who polished typewritten pages, and finally friends who offered encouragement when it was needed most.

All this would have come to naught if I had not had time. For that I would like to thank the Canada Council Explorations Program, the Ontario Arts Council, and the Donner Canadian Foundation for subsidizing the research and writing of this book. I would also like to acknowledge Margo Gewurtz and Peter Mitchell of the York University–University of Toronto Joint Centre on Modern East Asia, without whom there would be no Canadian Missionaries in East Asia study program.

For the world at an eastern Ontario crossroads, I would like to thank the trustees of Greenbush United Church – Eugene Horton, Lloyd Kerr, and Alan Hayes – who sold me their church building for my home. This edifice, I discovered, was the birthplace of one strand of the Canadian missionary movement back in the 1880s when the young Salem Bland preached his 'heretical' New Christianity to the younger Omar Kilborn. The late Clifford Hall remembered the departure of the first Methodist missionaries to China in 1891, because his brother William was supposed to be part of that group but decided instead to go to Korea. Dorothy Gordon, Ann Hay, Gordon Little, Mona Salmon, and their families made me feel part of the village, and helped me imagine what it was like when a young doctor set out to save the world. Here I could also imagine other villages, far away in time and space, where bandits camped down by the banks of Mud Creek. This a story of Greenbush.

Among members of the Overseas Missionary Fellowship, formerly the China Inland Mission, I would first like to thank my parents who searched their memories when I asked them to go a long way back to remember little things; David Michell and Isabel Taylor, who gave me access to the mission archives; the late Albert Grant, who gave me evangelistic posters, and Patricia Kennedy who read the manuscript and provided photographs taken by her grandfather; and for interviews, Dorothy and the late George Bell, William and Vera Tyler, Gordon Martin, Margaret Bunting, Cora Hanna, Karin McLean, Mona, Raymond, and Robert Joyce, Dr Edward Fish, and, of course, my brothers, Stephen, Norman, and Paul, who all my life have given me three separate pictures of life as a 'missionaries' kid.'

At the United Church archives, the staff was most helpful over a period of eight years, particularly Glenn Lucas, Mary Ann Tyler, and Neil Semple. Among former missionaries, I would like to thank: Barbara Jones Good, Katharine Hockin, Dr Helen Mitchell, Bea Mullett, Kathleen Spooner, Anne Davison Storey, Dr Stewart Allen, Bruce and Marnie Copland, Jim Endicott, Dr Robert McClure, Findlay Mackenzie, Lewis Walmsley, and Arthur Menzies (of the Department of External Affairs), and several members of the Jolliffe clan, Ted, Mary, Paul, Lee, and Jen.

Terry Thompson and Dorothy Kealey helped me through the MSCC papers in the Anglican church archives. Ruth Jenkins Watts allowed me to use her letters in Chapter 7. Dr Gordon White gave permission to publish extracts from Bishop W.C. White's correspondence in the Thomas Fisher Rare Book Library at the University of Toronto. Peter Brown's conversation about his father, Dr Richard Brown, was one inspiration behind this book.

Sister Fleurette Lagacé of the Missionary Sisters of the Immaculate Conception and Fathers Michel Marcil and the late Rosario Renaud of the Quebec Jesuits helped me understand two unknown cultures, Quebec and China. Sister Theresa Chu, of the Canada–China Program of the Canadian Council of Churches, shared her conversations with the church in New China, and helped me realize once again how the present is a continuation of the past.

Since a history is more than just a recitation of events, I am indebted to scholars who have posed the larger questions of the missionary movement: what is the nature of 'cultural imperialism,' of religious conversion, modernization, and, indeed, of Christianity itself? John Foster and Karen Minden wrote the two basic doctoral theses on Canadian missionaries to China, and both have contributed to this book. Others are: John Webster Grant, recently retired from the Toronto School of Theology, Ruth Brouwer, Stephen Endicott, Jerome Ch'en, and Donald Willmott, all of York University, Catherine Stevens of the University of Toronto, Thomas Quirk and Dorie Dohrenwend of the Royal Ontario Museum, Richard Ruggle of the Anglican church, and Bruce Lawrie and Cheung Yuet Wah who have both written on Canadian missions.

All my friends had to listen to my missionary stories, but some listened with interest to more than their share: Lois Cox and Keith Leigh, Gail Larrick, Hilary Russell, and William R. Young read preliminary versions of this book; Heather Chandler, Alyse Frampton, Carolyn Gibbs, Marcia Johnson, Margot Miller, Dora Nipp, Robert Bathgate, James Bracken, Doug MacDonald, Larry Ryan, Daniel Stainton, Brian Silversides, and Rod Stewart all contributed in other ways.

A special thank you to Maris Pavelson for his help with the French translations.

Finally, my editors at the University of Toronto Press have my admiration: Gerry Hallowell, who shaped my various drafts with his rare gift of insight and enthusiasm, and Margaret Woollard for her careful copy-editing of my syntax and typographical errors.

Another phrase haunts a writer: 'these people have helped, but the faults are all mine.'

ALVYN AUSTIN
Greenbush, Ontario
21 March 1986

A NOTE ON ROMANIZATION

Since this is a book of history, I have used the Romanization current during the period under discussion. Even this was not standard: with a relatively easy name like Chengtu, there were at least six different spellings; for more difficult names like Suchow (a French Romanization) there were eight or more spellings. Consequently, whenever a name is used for the first time I have included the *pinyin* Romanization currently used by the People's Republic of China in square brackets, thus: [CHENGDU]. Certain places that are too small to identify have been left in the original spelling.

Preface

'Bringing in Chinese,
Bringing in Chinese,
We shall come rejoicing,
Bringing in Chinese.'

(Sung to the tune of 'Bringing in the Sheaves')

When I began writing this book in 1978, nothing had been heard from the Christian church in China since 1966. As a result, I approached the subject as a piece of history. With the exception of a few individual pioneers, the Canadian missionary enterprise to China started on a specific day in 1888 as the first large party of missionaries was escorted in a torch-lit, hymn-singing parade down the main street of Toronto; it ended seventy years, seven months, and two days later, on 27 April 1959, when the last Canadian missionary slipped quietly across the border out of 'Red China.' One lifetime, the proverbial threescore years and ten, that was how long the missionary enterprise – which took as its prophetic slogan, 'The Evangelization of the World in This Generation' – had lasted.

In 1966, at the height of his personality cult, Mao Tse-tung [MAO ZEDONG] loosed his little-red-book-waving Red Guards to destroy the Christian church that had survived the communist 'liberation' of 1949. The government of the People's Republic of China abolished its own Bureau of Religious Affairs, outlawed public worship, confiscated the church buildings, and systematically crushed the Christian leaders. The Christian church in China had been, I felt, a victim of international politics.

In Canada, too, the missionary enterprise seemed a historical embarrassment. The Marxist interpretation of missionary activity as 'cultural imperialism' was widely accepted. The attitude of many Canadian churches was summed up in the history of the Salvation Army, *The Blood and Fire in Canada*, which admitted that 'some Salvation Army missionaries, Canadians among them, were terribly naive in their single-minded adherence to the notion that conversion alone would solve all the problems of the so-called "heathens" and their countries ... It was just such simplistic notions, in the face of obvious exploitation, enforced ignorance, uprooted cultures, tribal wars, extreme poverty and too sudden exposure to western values, which justifiably brought down upon them the wrath of their critics.'

One of these critics was Jerome Ch'en, educated by Canadian missionaries in West China and now professor of Chinese history at York University. In *China and the West*, he gave a thoughtful, devastating judgment:

Handicapped by their foreignness, their small numbers, the language barrrier, their intellectual mediocrity, their racial prejudice, their sectarianism and their growing bureaucratism, what little the missionaries had succeeded in achieving collapsed like a house of cards in 1949. Perhaps the worst obstacle they faced was the assumption that they must carry out their task of Christian conversion within the existing framework, which they could try to change only by changing the people living in it ... They were aware that all would be in vain unless China could be regenerated and a new China come forth, but in their occluded view they could only pray God to cleanse China by the blood of the blessed Saviour.

When the cleansing and regeneration did come, would the missionaries interpret it as being done by the blood of the Saviour? Why do the followers of the Saviour find no place in that regenerated country? The answer must be either that they were not truly the ambassadors of Christ or that the new China was not brought forth by the will of God.

We have learned since 1978 that followers of the Saviour do have a place in the regenerated China; indeed, in the reopening of China since the downfall of the Gang of Four, Chinese Christians are now regarded as patriotic enough to take prominent places in the 'friendship associations' with overseas countries. It was these same people who, forty years ago, were the friends of the foreigners.

Accompanying the reopening of contacts with the West has been a reinstatement of the Christian churches of China, both Catholic and Protestant, starting with the restoration of the Bureau of Religious Affairs. Individual congregations in many cities have been able to reclaim their churches, which had been confiscated twenty or thirty years before; they now hold Sunday worship services for up to two thousand people. According to Bishop K.H. Ting, head of the state-recognized Three Self (self-governing, self-propagating, self-supporting) Protestant church, there are now three million Protestants and up to nine million Catholics in China. Sixteen thousand churches have been opened between 1978 and 1984.

The Chinese government has appeared willing to re-evaluate the history of the missionary endeavour, not just its bad, imperialistic elements, but also its beneficial aspects. Of course, this is still tentative and in line with communist patriotism: 'There are many good people among missionaries, some of whom engaged in social welfare under-takings,' says Dwan Jin, first secretary of the embassy of the People's Republic of China in Ottawa, and thus an official spokesman for this new attitude. 'Some progressed from a sympathy for the sufferings of the Chinese people to sympathizing with and supporting the revolu-tionary struggles. Dr Jim Endicott is a distinguished representative of this group. Others were ... born in China, and their life in China helped them develop a deep affection for Chinese culture and the Chinese people. They have returned to their homeland as bridges between the people of China and the foreign countries. Mr Chester Ronning is a remarkable representative of this group. We welcome all those who are friendly to us. We especially respect those old friends who did good things for the Chinese people when they were in difficult times.'

The reopening of China has coincided with a willingness in the West to reconsider our own religious history. It is no longer enough to dismiss the missionary movement; we must seek to understand the nature of missionary paternalism – our paternalism – so that in our dealings with the underdeveloped nations we do not repeat the mistakes of the past. We must remember, too, that Third World Christians outnumber those in the West, and it is they who are beginning to guide the international church councils.

The eminent Harvard sinologist John King Fairbank described the foreign missionary as 'the invisible man in American history,' standing at the sidelines, the messenger, the bridge between East and West. The missionary enterprise was – and is – a complex organism, and its history can be approached in many ways. On the political level, it was a potent force for spreading Western ideas, not just of the faith but of science and medicine. Who can estimate the influence of the missionary woman who explained to an illiterate Chinese woman for the first time the concept of individuality and personality? Or the missionary doctor who started with a mud-floored dispensary and built it into a modern medical university?

Since the missionary enterprise was primarily a religious movement, one can discern in its history the conflicts inherent within Christianity between evangelical Protestants who sought to save the world by transforming individuals, and social-gospel liberals who believed that in order to 'regenerate' human society it was necessary to 'Christianize the social order.' When one includes Roman Catholic missions, the story becomes still more complicated. The danger with this approach, however, is that it tends to distort Chinese Christianity into an extension of European Christianity, with its historical national and denominational boundaries.

When the Woman's Missionary Society was absorbed into the general bureaucracy of the United Church of Canada in 1962, its functions had to be divided among six boards of the national church: finance, home missions, world missions, colleges, Christian education, and the new Board of Women. One could write a history of the missionary movement from any of those perspectives.

This book is not meant to be an academic treatise on how ideas crossed the ocean and converted the Chinese – seemingly without any human agents. Instead of exploring the big questions of imperialism and educational theory, I prefer to ask the little questions: how did the missionaries in the field feel about hitting a Chinese servant? What sort of schools did they set up for Chinese girls? This is a story of people. Some were so eccentric they seemed to have inhabited another world; others were 'solid' citizens who are almost recognizable as one's grandfather or maiden aunt. Some seem as current as the morning headlines, though they are talking of wars and dictatorships that happened fifty or sixty years ago. They are a fascinating group of people.

What some readers may see as a fault in this book, I have intended to make an advantage. This is not a history of Chinese Christianity, or even of Christianity within the Canadian missions; there are others far better qualified than I to write that story. If the Chinese people mentioned in this book seem like objects rather than subjects, that was deliberate. I have tried to present the Chinese not necessarily as they were but as the Canadian missionaries saw them and reported them in letters home. This perspective shows, I hope, the 'occluded' vision and narrow-mindedness of the missionaries in their reaction to the Chinese. One historian has called this a conversation between the deaf and dumb; we can see the Chinese frantically gesturing, trying to convince the Canadians of their perceptions but unable to find a common language.

This, then, is the story of 'us,' of Canadians in China. I believe it is important to understand who we were and what we did there in those threescore years and ten. It is an exciting story – of intrigue in high places and death in back alleys, of Christian charity and of modernization. It is, in short, the history in microcosm of one of the most cataclysmic events of twentieth-century history – the collision between China and the West. Christian missionaries, Canadians among them, tried to soften the blow, to save China by building a structure of modern education and modern medicine where none had existed before. The men and women they trained continued to be the educated elite even after the missionaries were forced to leave. Even today, in the 1980s, these people continue to exert their influence.

There are many areas of the missionary movement that need further research on both sides of the Pacific. Only then will we be able to listen to the Chinese voices. This book is a beginning.

'What a lot of Giant-souled fellows these [missionaries] were. No selfish motives coat-rolled their lives ... they realize they can invest their lives to the best advantage, for the uplift of a common humanity, and in the service of a common humanity's common Lord ... The business of these men is on earth, among men on Earth, but it is for eternity.'

D. Fuller McKinley, on attending the Mission Council of the West China mission, 1911

'We are flotsam in a whirlpool with which we have no connection.'

An American missionary whose husband had just been killed by Chinese soldiers, 1927

PART 1
The Saving Gospel
1888-1900

'Enlighten China and you have illuminated the eastern world. Move China and you move the world. Save China and the problem of the world's salvation is solved.'

Annual Report of the Canadian Methodist Church Missionary Society, 1896–7

1·Journeying Mercies: The China Inland Mission

'I suppose, of course, that you know, when I speak of foreigners I mean us and not the Chinese. It seems funny to think that we are *foreigners* now – and everything American, Canadian, English, or anything else is spoken of as foreign.'

Ruth Jenkins, writing home from Peking [BEIJING], 1921

On a cool, slightly rainy evening in late September in the year 1888, one thousand enthusiastic young people marched down the main street of Toronto in a torch-lit parade singing hymns to escort 'the first Canadian party' of missionaries bound for China to the train station. Though Canadians had been going to China in ones and twos for more than twenty years, this farewell ceremony marked the beginning of Canada's overseas missionary enterprise; never before, and not again for another fifteen years, would so large a party leave Canadian shores for the China mission field. Even now, almost a century later, the story of this departure is fresh in the minds of the children of the participants; they recount it as a not-quite-current event that might have happened yesterday. Onward Christian soldiers . . .

At the beginning of that summer, the Reverend James Hudson Taylor, the most famous missionary in the world since the death of Dr David Livingstone twelve years earlier in 'darkest Africa,' reluctantly agreed to make his journey from England to his home in China via the newly opened Canadian Pacific Railway – a saving of two weeks' travel time – and to speak at some meetings en route. Some had suggested that he use this opportunity to expand his English mission into North

Reverend and Mrs James Lawson, early 1900s

America, but Taylor dismissed this idea saying, 'The Lord has given me no light about it. I do not think it is His purpose thus to extend the work.' At age fifty-six, after thirty years 'in China's service,' Hudson Taylor was worn out.

Age, rather than diminishing him, had transformed him into the incarnation of an Old Testament prophet – if one can imagine the prophet Jeremiah in a frock coat and with a Yorkshire accent. (Actually, Dr Taylor often wore a Chinese scholar's silk gown; then, when he put on his button cap with a false queue hanging down his back, in the twinkling of an eye he turned into an oriental sage, all deferential politeness and strange idioms. Only his pale blue eyes shining with an unearthly fire gave him away.) He was a small man, only 1.57 metres tall, but he towered over his contemporaries by sheer force of personality and single-minded determination. Brusque, seemingly humourless, and always autocratic, he had one concern: the salvation of souls, specifically the numberless millions of inland China. Everything else was unimportant.

Twenty-three years before, having been invalided home from China, he had had a blinding vision on the beach at Brighton. That day, with ten pounds and a prayer, he had started the China Inland Mission (CIM). Since then it had grown to include three hundred missionaries located in fifteen of the eighteen provinces of China. Dr Taylor still ran it like a family business (the current director is Hudson Taylor, IV), carrying the accounts in his back pocket. Every morning and every evening he prayed for his missionaries individually, by name and by station; in the three months he was in America, he personally wrote eight hundred letters.

No, he shook his head sadly, he was too old to undertake such a new venture. Besides, six Canadians had already joined the CIM, travelling to London to do so, and others were welcome to do the same. As for Americans, even if they could accept his rigid regulations and conservative theology, they would do better to set up their own independent mission.

Taylor had planned to stay for a month in 'America,' but when he reached Canada in his second week, he found such 'deep well-springs' of missionary enthusiasm that he changed his plans and proceeded to establish a North American branch of the mission with headquarters in Toronto, under the direction of Henry Frost, a New Yorker. It was Frost who had first invited Taylor to America.

Seemingly by accident, Taylor arrived at a propitious time – one of those minor turning points in history when one generation gives way to the next. During the 1880s, 'the earnest eighties,' the complacent mid-Victorian church – what one might call 'the church sentimental' – was increasingly being taken over by the aggressive young people of 'the church militant.' It was the difference between saying, 'Oh, isn't it wonderful what those missionaries are doing to civilize the heathen?' and the young people's response: 'As a Christian, you are personally responsible for the salvation of the world. Think about it. Pray about it. Then, give or go.'

Throughout the decade, social reformers and evangelists had been challenging the churches of Canada to stop acting as comfortable way-stations for the faithful on the road to heaven. When the American evangelist Dwight L. Moody (of whom one recent historian has said, 'no American of his generation had a larger audience') came to Toronto in 1885, he preached his version of 'sanctified common sense' to 25 000 people, estimated at half the adult population of the city. There was a reason why the city was known as 'Toronto the good.' Out in the provinces, when Canada's own team of evangelists, Crossley and Hunter, took to the sawdust trail, businesses often closed early so employees could attend the meetings. The Salvation Army, with its street-corner tambourine preachers, had also, in the six years since it had been introduced in Canada, become a force in society.

The time had come, these preachers reiterated, finally to complete Christ's 'great commission,' the last command he had spoken after his resurrection: 'Go ye into all the world and preach the gospel to every creature.' The world was opening up at every hand; no part of the world was too remote or too intransigent to be penetrated by the gospel. This surely was the fulfilment of Isaiah 49:6 – 12 when the prophet wrote that in the last days 'the preserved of Israel' shall be a 'light to the Gentiles, that thou mayest be my salvation unto the ends of the earth.' In that day, when every highway would be exalted, the elect would 'come from afar: and, lo ... these from the land of Sinim.' (Though modern scholars tend to dispute this verse – or identify 'Sinim' not with China but a town named Syene in upper Egypt – *These From the Land of Sinim* was the title of three twentieth-century books on China.)

Taking salvation to the ends of the earth! What an awesome, God-given task for some young man or woman! The challenge had been eagerly taken up by the students in Canadian colleges, influenced by students in Great Britain and the United States. Taylor's first stop was Northfield, Massachusetts, where several years before D.L. Moody had opened a summer conference in the town of his birth. There, Taylor presided as an elder statesman over an 'inspiring assembly' of two hundred students, among them a few Canadians, as they founded the Student Volunteer Movement (SVM) for Foreign Missions. Over the next thirty years, the SVM became the primary recruiting agency for college students to the foreign field, sending out more than 8000 men and women missionaries under its motto: 'The Evangelization of the World in This Generation.' 'It seemed as if the only thing needed in a college,' one of the student leaders recalled of that momentous summer of 1888, 'was to strike a match and the whole college blazed up with enthusiasm for the evangelization of the world.'

Hudson Taylor himself had practically coined the phrase. *The Evangelization of the World* was the title of his story of the recruitment of the so-called Cambridge Seven in 1885. These young upper-class Englishmen were volunteering to give up stately homes and distinguished careers to live in poverty in a Chinese village. One had been captain of the Cambridge cricket team (and thus one of the most famous men in England); another had been stroke of the Oxford rowing team (and thus equally famous). 'Students ... are apt to regard professedly religious men of their own age as wanting in manliness,' an Edinburgh professor wrote, 'unfit for the river or cricketfield, and only good for psalm-singing and pulling a long face. But the big, muscular hands and long arms of the ex-captain of the Cambridge Eight, stretched out in entreaty, while he eloquently told the old story of Redeeming Love, capsized their theory.'

Taylor's pamphlet became an instant best seller on both sides of the Atlantic, distributed free to every YMCA. 'China was the goal, the lodestar, the great magnet that drew us all in those days,' recalled another student leader; as he and his friends would run around the track, they would encourage each other by saying, 'This will carry us another mile in China.'

Taylor found Northfield 'inspiring,' but he had no reason to change his plans until he reached his next stop, the Preachers' Conference at Niagara-on-the-Lake, Ontario. His message there, as always, was simple and graphic. The Chinese race had sunk into opium-induced, sin-besotted degradation. They lived without faith, without hope, without love. 'The gospel must be preached to these people in a very short time,' he pleaded, 'for they are passing away. Every day, every day, oh how they sweep over! ... There is a great Niagara of souls passing into the dark in China. Every day, every week, every month, they are passing away! A million a month in China are dying without God!'

Pointing to a large map beside his lectern, Taylor told the audience that the evangelization of China was not 'chimerical, and beyond the resources of the Christian Church.' This was his most famous piece of 'missionary arithmetic': the map was divided into 250 black squares, each representing one million Chinese; one tiny white star in the middle showed the 40 000 Protestant converts. If, he explained, 'one thousand whole-hearted evangelists, male and female, were set free ... for this special work ... and if fifty families were reached daily for 1000 days by each of the 1000 evangelists, every creature in China could be reached in three years.' If, as some estimated, the population of China was four hundred million, the task would take five years instead of three. It could be done!

The following day, a woman got up in the meeting to announce that she had discovered how to work for the Lord twenty-four hours a day: 'I work twelve hours here, and when I have to rest, my representative in India begins her day and works the other twelve.' The meeting broke into organized pandemonium as everyone became 'intoxicated with the joy of giving.' That day the audience contributed enough to support eight people in China for a year.

Instead of being pleased with this turn of events, Taylor seemed 'frightened.' After a night of prayer, he issued an appeal:

To have missionaries and no money would be no trouble to me, for the Lord is bound to take care of His own ... But to have money and no missionaries is very serious indeed. And I do not think it will be kind of you dear friends in America to put this burden upon us, and not to send some from among yourselves to use the money. We have the dollars, but where are the people?

At his third stop, in Hamilton, he found a Bible-study group at the Young Men's Christian Association 'united in earnest prayer that seven of their number might be privileged to go as missionaries to China.' Taylor took six, and came back for another half-dozen the following year. In Belleville, he visited the Marchmount Homes, one of the organizations that brought British orphans to Canada; out of this group, he 'called' the chaplain, the Reverend Robert Wallace, to sit on a temporary North American board, and took with him to China William Horne and Jeannie Munro, two of the orphans who had grown up and joined the staff of the institution.

Altogether Taylor received forty-two applications and selected fifteen of the applicants to accompany him. Thirteen were Canadians, two were

The first Canadian party of the CIM before leaving Toronto, 1888. *Back row: second from left* William Horne, *third* Hattie Turner, *fourth* Henry Frost, *fifth* Grace Irvin; *centre row: first* Jessie Gardiner, *fifth* Hudson Taylor, *sixth* Susie Parker; *front row: first* Cassie Fitzsimmons, *third* Jeannie Munro

from the United States. Believing that God had a place for enthusiasts in China, he gathered a group who could quote the Bible chapter and verse but had little formal education: the seven men included, for example, a grocer, a cabinet-maker, a mechanic, and a printer. The eight women (all unmarried, as were the men) had worked as teachers or stenographers, or had lived as 'spinster daughters' with their families.

Going out as members of a 'faith mission,' he warned them, they would have no guarantee of a regular salary. Since the mission refused to borrow money, even for daily expenses, it had no income except what was contributed by the faithful. Hudson Taylor went so far as to refuse to make a public appeal, preferring to let the Lord provide by stirring the hearts of the people. The Hamilton newspaper concluded that the members of the China Inland Mission depended upon 'chance providences for a scanty subsistence.'

Can you accept these regulations? Taylor asked each candidate. How is your health? How is your faith? Can you leave in a month?

The first of the farewell meetings was held on the evening of Sunday, 24 September, in the new Association Hall of the Toronto YMCA. The hall was only moderately filled until 8:00 P.M., when the churches of the city let out their congregations. Then the ushers were 'simply overwhelmed' by the two thousand people who crowded in. The meeting, a joyous affair, was presided over by the president of the University of Toronto, Daniel (later Sir Daniel) Wilson. 'It must be a source of happiness to those present,' Taylor said thrillingly, 'to know that God had honoured the city by choosing so many of its young people to go out to preach the gospel to the heathen. Within six months these young people would be able to put God's blessings before the heathen intelligibly, and shortly after would be numbering the souls they have saved. And who could estimate the value of a soul?'

The final communion service the following evening was more sombre, in keeping with its high purpose. The service in the old Knox Presbyterian Church, then located near the corner of Yonge and Queen streets, was attended by leading ministers of all denominations, unusual in a city often charged with denominational squabbles. The father of Susie Parker, the first candidate selected, moved the congregation to tears when he said, simply, 'I have nothing too precious for my Lord Jesus.'

After the parade down Yonge Street, the Union Station rotunda reverberated as the ministers spoke a 'panoply of prayer' over the heads of the little group. Grant journeying mercies, they intoned, to these Thy servants as they launch out into the unknown. Protect them from the perils of land and sea so that they may reach the heathen shores in safety. Then as a Salvation Army band struck up 'God Be With You Until We Meet Again,' the train pulled out of the station. The women on the platform waved their handkerchiefs, the men threw their hats in the air.

The little band was happy and congenial as the train crossed Canada. Hudson Taylor was impressed with the view of the Rocky Mountains from the train window. At Victoria, they had their first glimpse of 'the Orient.' As they were embarking on the ss *Batavia*, second class, hundreds of Chinese 'coolies' were being herded into the steerage for passage back to China. Iron grilles were locked over the entrances – to prevent a mutiny. 'Life is cheap in China,' the missionaries were told. 'You'll get used to it.' But throughout the trip, they found it disturbing to pass the vents where the stench of human sweat mingled with smoke from the subterranean cooking fires.

During the stormy, three-week voyage across the North Pacific, the young missionaries – those not confined to their beds, at least – would gather in the salon, sandwiched between the drinkers and the gamblers, for prayer and Bible study. Sometimes they beguiled Hudson Taylor into telling them stories of his experiences with bandits and mandarins, but he was preoccupied by a sterner message. 'Should not the little things of daily life be as relatively perfect in the case of the Christian,' he wrote on board ship, 'as the lesser creations of God are absolutely perfect? ... Is it not our privilege to take our rest and recreation for the purpose of pleasing Him, to lay aside our garments at night neatly (for He is in the room, and watches over us while we sleep), to wash, to dress, to smooth the hair, with His eye in view?'

At Yokohama, the first land they had seen since Victoria, Taylor received a telegram informing him that since their departure three CIM missionaries had died at their stations in China. News from cities all over the country told of menacing mobs appearing on the streets and threatening to destroy mission property. 'I never knew anything like it,' Taylor wrote to his wife in England. 'Satan is simply raging. He sees his kingdom attacked all over the land, and the conflict is awful.'

In the previous few years, as a result of the 'unequal treaties' between China and the Western powers, foreigners had been granted the right to live and own property in the interior, away from the designated treaty ports. Taking advantage of this God-given opportunity, Christian missions expanded rapidly in the 1880s. The CIM itself grew from ninety-six people in 1881 to 330 eight years later, by an appeal for seventy new workers in 1881 ('And the Lord appointed other seventy also ...'), and then for another hundred in 1885. It had expanded precipitately, and now, like a ship without ballast, the mission floundered when the storms of external persecution drove it onto the shoals of internal dissension. Another telegram announced that the London council was threatening to resign over Taylor's expansion into North America.

Steaming across Japan's placid Inland Sea, the group did not yet know, though they sensed it, that they were coming to China in what went down in mission histories as 'the tragic autumn of 1888.' They sang a new hymn, 'Jesus, Saviour, Pilot Me'.

Their first view of what was to be their adopted home was not favourable. Far out to sea, mud from the Yangtse [CHANG JIANG] River turned the ocean into a thick polluted soup; as the tug pulled them twenty miles upriver, land and sea merged, mud on mud. Just beyond a bend in the river, down the Woosung [WUSONG] Creek, lay Shanghai [SHANGHAI], gateway to China, fleshpot of the Orient, farthest outpost of European civilization. The flotilla of grey British gunboats looming above the junks and sampans in the harbour were a reminder that the phrase 'I am a British subject' was more potent, more universal, than 'Civis Romanus sum' had been in the days of St Paul. The buildings along the Bund, the boulevard that ran along the waterfront, seemed to have been plucked from the stately cities of Europe; indeed, some of the banks and hotels lining the avenue – what later came to be known as 'the million-dollar skyline' – had been transported in pieces from Paris and London and reassembled here. A few streets back from the water, Trinity Cathedral (Church of England) cast its benediction over the city.

Their first visit to Shanghai was a blur to the young missionaries and became overlaid with impressions of a dozen – or several dozen – later trips through the city. This time, they were not there to sightsee. Their first and most abiding impression was the overpowering crush of humanity. They had heard of 'China's millions' – that was the title of the CIM monthly magazine – but they must have found it inconceivable that within two hundred kilometres of Shanghai alone lived almost as many people as in the whole of Canada. Coolies swarmed everywhere like ants, human beasts of burden toting bales and carrying other men on their shoulders – literally. One worker was seen carrying a full-sized harmonium that weighed close to 136 kilograms. Grunting and sweating, nearly naked, the men accompanied themselves as they worked with a weird singsong chant that became part of the background to life in China. The chant was so common, even in the dead of night, that it terrified some missionaries; one called it 'the moan of China' – the horrifying sound of heathenism.

Carried rather squeamishly on their first sedan-chair ride, the Canadians were taken past the formal gardens along the Bund, where the signs read, in English only, 'No dogs or Chinamen allowed,' into a back street of the French Concession. There the mission had rented two Chinese courtyards until its new five-storey buildings were finished. Sleeping three and four to a room, the young people happily bedded down in what they described as 'a real Chinese house.'

Two days later they boarded British steamers to take them up the Yangtse to the mission's language schools. The women went to Yangchow [YANGZHOU], 80 kilometres inland, on the Grand Canal; the men went a further 240 kilometres, to Anking [ANQING], the capital of Anhwei [ANHUI] province.

'There was scarcely a grey head in the mission in those days,' wrote the mission historian, 'and everything seemed possible.' Nowhere was this more evident than in the language schools. The twenty-six young women at Yangchow were under the supervision of the Murray sisters from Glasgow, who themselves had been in the country for only four years; the seventeen men, ranging in age from eighteen to the mid-twenties, studied under the watchful eye of F.W. Baller, a crusty veteran. The residences, built in the hybrid style adopted from British India, with verandas on all four sides, were institutional-looking; but the Misses Murray and Mrs Baller added the homey touches, the pictures, table-cloths, and magazines that meant so much to the newcomers.

As soon as they were settled, each of the young people was fitted for a Chinese gown. Despite the derision of the rest of the foreign community, other missionaries included, the CIM made the wearing of Chinese clothes part of its policy. The women, pulling their hair into a bun, wore blue and white Chinese dresses. The men shaved the fronts of their heads and braided the rest of their hair into a queue; until their own hair grew in they wore caps with false pigtails pinned inside.

It is almost possible to identify an individual missionary's theology from his or her photograph: those wearing Chinese dress tended to be the most evangelical – people who could not compromise their theology; on the other hand, those who continued to wear Western clothing, and who could not compromise on cultural grounds as they saw it, were the liberals. Although he was accused of 'going native' – the worst insult in the colonial world – Hudson Taylor argued that 'the foreign dress and carriage of missionaries (to a certain extent affected by some of their pupils and converts), the foreign appearance of chapels, and indeed the foreign air imparted to everything connected with their work has seriously hindered the rapid dissemination of the Truth among the Chinese. And why should such a foreign aspect be given to Christianity?' Why indeed? In its broader sense, this was the essential question of Christian missions in China.

From the women's point of view, Mrs Hudson Taylor revealed, 'Things which are tolerated in us as foreigners, wearing foreign dress, could not be allowed for a moment in native ladies ... The nearer we come to the Chinese in outward appearance, the more severely will any breach of propriety according to their standards be criticised. Henceforth I must never be guilty, for example, of taking my husband's arm out of doors!' So, these prim Victorian women had to learn to curb whatever spark of spontaneity they had so they would not shock the (publicly) prudish Chinese.

Now, wearing their new Chinese clothes, just when they seemed to have attained their life's ambition, these new recruits found themselves immobilized. Since the sight of so many 'foreign devils' walking the streets might cause a riot, the students dared not venture beyond the compound gates. Consequently, they took their exercise in the yard, skipping, playing tag, or walking in circles. Tennis became known as 'the missionaries' game' because it was one of the few active, competitive games that could be played in a limited space.

Life in the languages schools was not slack, though. The students' day started with two hours of solitary prayer at 5:30 A.M. After breakfast, as one of their male recruits reported,

we all meet together, sing a hymn, read a chapter, expositions by Mr Baller – very good – exhortation, prayer and a hymn. After this, prayers in Chinese in the chapel, at which eight or more Chinamen and a few women are present; 9.0 – 10.30 private study of Chinese; 10.30 – 11.30, Chinese class with Mr Baller; 12.30 dinner. Time between class and dinner for study, and prayer. Prayer for the provinces immediately after dinner till about 1.50.

Then I may have a Chinese teacher from 2 till 3 or 3.30, and private study at Chinese till 5.0. The hour between this and tea is supposed to be for recreation, when we take a walk or run about in the small yard. Tea at 6.0 and study after as long as you like. So you see we are not idle . . .

The fare is good and sufficient. For *breakfast* we get good bread, a peculiar kind of bread, toast, porridge, or some meal, tea with condensed milk, meat or fish. *Dinner*: Meat or fowl, vegetables, potatoes, &c., and pudding; oranges, nuts and tea. *Tea*: Fish or meat, eggs sometimes, bread, butter and treacle. So we fare right royally; but we need it, when studying hard.

The devil invented the Chinese language, the common wisdom went, to keep the gospel out of China. As well as a prodigious memory, students of the language need to learn a new emotional behaviour. In Western languages tone indicates feeling: 'yes' in English, for example, can express different emotions depending on its inflection, but the meaning of the word remains constant. In Chinese, the sound 'i' has over seventy-five distinct meanings, from 'salt' to 'righteousness' to 'eye,' depending on which tone (four in Mandarin, up to eight in Cantonese) is used and how it is combined with other words to produce an intelligible, spoken meaning. In the written language, each of the words has a different character.

The language lessons with Mr Baller at least had grammar and syntax; those with the native tutors were incomprehensible. Traditional scholars down on their luck (else why would they teach barbarians?) would start the lesson by pointing to an object and say the word. The student would repeat it and repeat it, hour after hour, until the teacher was satisfied. Laboriously, the students began to translate the books they would need for their daily work: the New Testament, *Pilgrim's Progress*, the hymnary.

After months of study, when the students took their first Chinese prayers, they were likely to be taken aside and told that they had addressed the 'honourable' audience as 'devil people' or had preached an interesting sermon on the subject of Noah's dog. Slowly, they were learning the hardest lesson of their lives: 'Have patience. Remember you are in China.'

Since the language schools were nerve centres of the mission, filled with people in transit going hither and yon, the students gradually began to sort out the welter of names and places. The CIM formed one-quarter of the missionary force in China, and maintained seventy-seven stations in towns and villages across the country. Dedicated to pioneer evangelism where no white person had ventured, its people would make 'itinerations' into the countryside, often for months at a time, with no direction save accident and the hand of God. ('Consulting no one but his Maker,' was one description.) Every year or two, the perseverance of one missionary or the reluctant submission of a local magistrate would open up a new area, a new province, for foreign mission work. Then the cry would go up: 'Lo the fields are white unto harvest, but the labourers are few.'

The 'forward movement' of 1888 was in Kiangsi [JIANGXI] province, one of the southern provinces, located midway between Shanghai and Canton [GUANGZHOU], one province inland from the ocean. From the beautiful Poyang [POYANG] Lake in the north to the Kweilin [GUILIN] mountains in the south, Kiangsi was famed for its salubrious climate and lush hillside resorts: 'Where every prospect pleases,' the hymn states, 'and only man is vile.' Hudson Taylor's daughter-in-law sent up an impassioned plea for Kiangsi:

Fifteen millions of souls within its limits pass across the narrow stage of life ... *Fifteen millions!* It is with *them* my heart is tonight!

Twice the size of Portugal, this busy province has no less than *one hundred and three walled towns and cities*, besides almost countless large villages, hamlets and scattered homesteads.

One hundred and three walled cities. How many of them are occupied for

CHRIST? ... Alas, alas for the sad answer! In only *four!!* Thank God for the four! but are there still ninety and nine without a single light? left in these last days to utter heathen darkness? *Yes, still ninety and nine.*

Taylor considered designating Kiangsi as an 'American' area, just as he had granted the Church of England its own diocese in East Szechuan [SICHUAN] under the CIM. Manpower needs changed quickly, and North Americans were soon dispersed throughout China. Kiangsi, however, did retain strong ties to Canadian missionaries, a tie that has lasted down to the present day. All the 1888 group, most of the 1889 party, and fully three-quarters of those recruited prior to 1900 (some eighty Canadians, as well as Americans) were assigned to Kiangsi. Evidently Canadians made good pioneers; they also seem to have made good teachers and business managers, for large numbers were employed in the schools for missionaries' children in Chefoo [now called YANTAI] and in the business office in Shanghai.

True to his promise in Toronto that the young missionaries would be preaching to the heathen within six months, Taylor visited the Yangchow school in the spring of 1889 to assign the women to their first stations. Two years earlier, the mission had started a daring experiment of placing unmarried women in pairs at isolated stations along the Kwangsin [GUANGXIN] River, a tributary that flows into the south-east corner of the Poyang Lake. To many 'treaty-port missionaries' this seemed a deliberate courting of danger, but the mission designated Kwangsin 'the women's river' and prohibited its male staff from travelling up it. (James Lawson, for one, bent this rule in a moment of desperation when he went *downriver* to visit his fiancée.)

After a steamer ride from Yangchow to Kiukiang [JIUJIANG], where the Yangtse meets the lake, the women embarked on native 'slipper boats,' long, narrow, reed boats that were poled upriver. Travel in China was slowed to the pace of a walking man, so a day's journey would be thirty to fifty kilometres. Sometimes the Kwangsin River flowed past terraced hillsides aglow with spring rice; elsewhere it narrowed so that willows brushed the surface in scenes reminiscent of a Blue Willow plate. With its waterwheels, women at the well, and startled flocks of geese, the landscape was almost biblical. By that analogy at least it was comprehensible. Then, suddenly, it became inscrutably Chinese: when the boats moored in the shadow of a walled city, the foreign women would have to hide so they would not attract a crowd.

Three of the young women disembarked at a town called Kweiki [GUIXI],

Grace Irvin setting out on an itineration by wheelbarrow with her Bible woman, c. 1898

including Susie Parker. She contracted typhus shortly thereafter and died within a few weeks. When he heard the news, her father said simply, 'I have given my best to Jesus.'

Cassie Fitzsimmons and Hattie Turner, both of the Hamilton YMCA group, continued four days further to Yushan [YUSHAN], which had been 'occupied' two years earlier by a young Scotswoman, Katie Mackintosh, a remarkable woman in a mission filled with them. Small and wiry, even younger than the Canadians, she lived a completely Chinese life. Everything she did, her companion wrote, 'was planned with a view to the people round us, rather than our own convenience, hours of meals and meetings included. Katie was not impulsive, erratic, or unwise. She never allowed liberties. But while standing aloof in her gentle way she was thoroughly one with the Chinese, and full of fun, which they greatly appreciated.' The Chinese women would wander in and out of her room and exclaim, 'Truly, this is a little heaven.'

After the regimented life at the language schools, the young people were apt to feel at loose ends in their first station. To put it bluntly, there was little they could do. They were expected to help out with the regular meetings, the Wednesday sewing class, and the Saturday night evangelistic services, and thus find their own particular calling. They spent much of their time in the street chapel, encouraging the native preacher in three- and four-hour harangues or accompanying him on excursions to distribute tracts throughout the neighbourhood.

The street chapel, located in a shopfront in one of the suburbs outside the city wall, was furnished with rough benches and coloured lithographs on the walls. But, as one contemporary described it, this unpretentious building was

the missionary's fort, where he throws hot shot and shell into the enemy's camp; the citadel, where he defends the truth; the school, where he teaches the A.B.C. of heaven; the home, where he loves to dwell; the altar, upon which he is laid a living sacrifice; the church, in which he worships; the throne, on which he rules the minds and hearts of the heathen; the happy land, where he enjoys communion with his Maker; the hill of Zion, where he sings sweet songs; the gate of heaven, where the angels ascend and descend.

Inside their own courtyard, the missionary women would encourage the Chinese to come to them. And, surprisingly, they did come. The neighbourhood women came first, timidly peering around a corner to make sure they were not walking into a trap. Then, tottering on their tiny feet, chattering like a flock of magpies, they came inside for tea and 'polite words.' The missionaries would take them on a tour of their rooms, demonstrating the sewing machine, the baby harmonium, and the magic lantern. On subsequent visits, the women would stay all day, bringing their children and their sewing with them, gaily oblivious of the passing time.

The missionaries would constantly try to steer the conversation to 'the things of the Lord,' but the Chinese sisters would merely get a glazed look on their faces. 'I am only a woman,' they would say, 'a dumb mule of a beast. I cannot understand your ghostly talk. You should speak to my husband.' They would willingly fold their hands – though they would never close their eyes – and mutter a few prayers as part of the ritual of visiting the foreigners, but they were interested in more practical questions: Are you a ghost? Do you eat children? Do you pluck out their eyes? Can you see underground? Where is your husband? Are you a prostitute? Then after poking them in unexpected, private places, the boldest of the women would stroke the missionary's cheek and exclaim, 'Why, you are no different from us.'

One sudden move by the foreigners, however, like closing the door, and the whole group would silently take flight. The next day or the next week, they would return and the whole process would start over, with the same questions asked and answers given.

Each station had its regular visitors who came with eyes gazing out of downtrodden lives. Those who came for food or opium or whatever they could pilfer were sent away with a tract and a prayer. A few, a very few, came for spiritual food. One old woman at Yushan, a devout Buddhist who had given up meat when her husband died, came hobbling thirty kilometres every Sunday leaning on her cane and her grandson. Testifying that her Buddhist ceremonials had never given her peace, she gladly renounced her vegetarian vows and publicly ate meat in the mission courtyard to prove that she now believed in the Jesus religion.

Another 'enquirer,' a poor boy, lay on his filthy pallet in a corner of the Good News Hall, pale with dropsy. When he first heard of Jesus, he forgot his pain and began to speak of nothing but heaven. When he died, Miss Mackintosh said she was 'quite sure that there will be many children, blind men, and beggars around the throne of GOD whose names were never on a Church-book.'

The work was, to put it mildly, unrewarding. Those who had dreamed of two hundred converts a day had to be content with five or ten baptisms a year. And there were sometimes more severe disappointments: as when, after years of patience, the infant church was split by the defection of a trusted convert. At Kwangfeng [GUANGFENG], the Misses Turner and Fitzsimmons' first station alone, the women made the mistake of dismissing their colporteur – the book-pedlar they employed to distribute Bibles – while they attended a conference of North American workers in Shanghai. During their absence, the man spread wild rumours about them, 'revealing his true character,' and started a rival congregation. 'It is a sad case,' the district superintendent wrote, 'for he had formerly been so bright and earnest.' What was sadder was that this story could be repeated, with countless variations, in every station, every outstation, every church in China.

Before psychology came along, religious people ascribed a spiritual origin to their emotions; fear, despair, loneliness, anxiety, and doubt were sent by the devil to tempt the faithful. In their upside-down way, the missionaries described their suffering as 'blessed adversity' and grew strong resisting the devil. That Shanghai conference in 1891, which was attended by thirty Canadians and Americans, was the first time that some of these young people had seen their colleagues in two or three years, in fact the first time in Chinese dress. With their hair streaked with grey and their teeth unattended to, they were so changed they could hardly recognize each other.

If the women of the Canadian party lived with discomfort and discouragement, at least they had a roof over their heads and a daily routine. The men of the party had nothing. After a full year in the language school, they were assigned to 'open' the southern part of Kiangsi, 160 kilometres and five days' journey south of the women, where no Europeans had ever been before. For years, they wandered like religious pedlars; James Lawson, at nineteen the youngest and strongest of the party, was nicknamed 'Hudson Taylor's wandering boy' because he spent seven long years on the road. Perpetually homeless, he once fell sick with typhoid and was nursed back to health by his servant; in his delirium, he tried to walk to Shanghai until his sympathetic superintendent coaxed him back.

Lawson and the others would leave their worldly goods in an inn while they wandered far and wide. One particularly obnoxious inn in Kiangsi, known as the 'Queen's Hotel' after the high-class establishment in Toronto, became legendary. A real Chinese inn, if you know what I mean, old China hands would reminisce, is 'like our barnyard with all the stables and pens around the sides, and the carts, wheelbarrows, mules and donkeys filling up the empty space.' The main difference from a Canadian barnyard was the fact that the tumbledown shanties were not the barns but the hotel accommodation. Holes in the walls let in icy blasts in the winter and, seemingly, not a breeze in the summer. In the corner of the communal sleeping room, opium addicts would chatter nervously all night, occasionally prodding the missionary to make sure his soul had not fled his body. If the missionary managed to gain a private room, he might have to share it with a grunting sow and her litter. Still, he tried to find some humour in his situation: the fleas, lice, and assorted vermin casually picked off his body he called 'China's millions.'

The young Canadians were desperately lonely, but never alone. Besieged day and night by staring eyes and grabbing hands, their only private time was while walking before breakfast. Preaching to the crowds often became little better than a circus side-show. One missionary, red-haired and blue-eyed, would have to sit immobile while the Chinese preacher instructed the crowds. Sometimes the crush was so great they were forced to fling their tracts into the air, hoping that some printed words would fall on fruitful ground. From practical experience, the missionaries knew that as long as a Chinese crowd was kept amused it was easy to control. Consequently, they learned the tricks of an entertainer, performing little antics and playing instruments: one Englishman reputedly used to take out his false teeth and clatter them in his hand; another, a Frenchman, would remove his glass eye for public inspection.

The early 1890s were not the safest of times for a white vagabond to be wandering through Central China. In 1891, one of the regular rounds of anti-foreign, anti-Christian riots was sparked by a Roman Catholic agent's attempt to purchase a group of orphans for the orphanage at Hankow [HANKOU]. The excited mob fell on the first white people they saw; within days, mission stations for hundreds of kilometres had been pillaged and all missionaries forced to flee to the treaty ports. At the height of the turmoil, Hudson Taylor wrote to admonish his people to follow Christ's example. 'We are in our stations at God's command, and as His ambassadors, and therefore have both promise of, and claim to, His protection ... A holy joy in God is a far better protector than a revolver.' Once again, his pacific attitude put the CIM at the outer fringes of the foreign community, as businessmen and missionaries alike armed themselves with more than 'holy joy' as protection against the restless natives.

Not surprisingly, the South Kiangsi forward movement was not an overwhelming success. The seed fell onto stony ground, choked by weeds of xenophobia, parched by the drought of ancestral opposition. William Horne, the Scottish orphan, however, could still write of a 'grand time of rejoicing' when he held a prayer meeting with two servants and one 'interesting enquirer.' He concluded this letter by noting, wistfully, without a trace of irony, 'We have many indications that this world is not our home, and that we are not of the world, else it would love us.'

2 · The Old Homestead of China: The Presbyterians in North Honan

'Brother, if you would enter Honan, you must go forward on your knees.'

Hudson Taylor to Jonathan Goforth, 1888

When Hudson Taylor came to Toronto in 1888, he did not so much ignite 'fires of missionary enthusiasm' as simply fan the already glowing embers into flame. The welcome he received, the volunteers clamouring to join his mission, were proof that he was not alone in his world-saving vision. Yet if he had come even five years earlier, he would not have received the same welcome; the missionary ideal then had seemed little more than 'a waning relic of the enthusiasm and theology of past generations.' His presence at the Northfield conference and his recruitment for his own China Inland Mission were both symbol and catalyst of the resurgence of fervour. From that point onwards, the enthusiasm became a movement, and its growth was dramatic and inexorable.

Forty-four years earlier there had been a flurry of missionary interest in the Canadian churches when the Baptists of the Atlantic colonies sent Richard Burpee to join the American mission in Burma, under the famous Adoniram Judson; later that same year, 1844, the Presbyterians in Nova Scotia sent John Geddie to the New Hebrides in the South Pacific. (This latter mission had a particularly tragic history, and was widely mythologized for its 'Erromanga Martyrs.' Geddie had been sent to take the place of John Williams, who had been murdered and eaten by the native headhunters; and Geddie's own colleagues from Nova Scotia, George Gordon and his brother James and their wives, were similarly killed. The mission had a happy ending, however, when the

Reverend George Leslie Mackay, 'the black-bearded barbarian,' and A Hoa extracting teeth, Formosa, c. 1894 headhunters were converted not individually but in whole tribes. Geddie's tombstone read: 'When he came there were no Christians; when he died there were no pagans.')

The missionary interest, so marked in the 1840s, never really died out: perhaps because Canada itself had been recently carved from the wilderness, many church people appreciated edifying stories about civilization's triumph over savagery. When Alexander Duff, the great 'Apostle of India' came to Canada in 1855, his visit had a 'startling' effect, inspiring the formation of the first Canadian foreign mission society by the Presbyterians of the Atlantic colonies. It was not until eleven years later, however, that this society sent out its first permanent foreign missionaries, to Prince Albert, Saskatchewan. The following year, 1867, it inaugurated a mission to Trinidad.

Most people felt that, as one Scots elder remarked to a China pioneer, 'We have heathen enough of our own here, without going out of our way to send the Gospel to heathen Chinese.' At its worst, this betrayed an attitude of insularity, a concern only for the members of one's own parish; but on the other hand, it could be – and was – a call to reach 'the heathen' in one's own midst. In the excitement of the 1870s and 1880s that followed Confederation, especially with the annexation of the North-West Territories (the old Hudson's Bay Company lands, now the provinces of Manitoba, Saskatchewan, and Alberta) and the entry of British Columbia into Confederation, the Protestant churches of Canada laid important foundations for eventual national organizations.

In 1875, the Presbyterian Church in Canada was formed of a union of four strands of Presbyterianism, making it the largest denomination in the Dominion – at least until 1884, when the Methodists underwent a similar union. The Presbyterian form of government is a presbyterial or democratic one, in which each minister is free to speak in church councils, and decisions are made by majority vote. The new organization reflected this, with regional partition into Eastern and Western divisions, each with its own finances, responsibilities, and initiatives. This led to 'a rather unsystematic and illogical selection of far-flung mission fields': the Eastern Division, centred in Halifax, supported missions in the New Hebrides, Trinidad, and Korea (1893), while the Western Division, based in Toronto, was responsible for Formosa (1870), North Honan [HENAN] (1888), South China (1902), and India (1904).

By contrast, after its union, the Methodist Church of Canada became a highly centralized denomination, with a headquarters in Toronto and a mission society that was 'one piece of denominational machinery.'

Methodist church government, like that of the Anglican church from which it is descended, is hierarchical under bishops or superintendents. The Reverend Dr Alexander Sutherland, elected as General Secretary of the Board of Missions in 1883, was responsible for all the church's missions: these included domestic missions among the French Canadians in Montreal, the poor in Toronto, the Chinese in British Columbia, and some forty Indian stations throughout the North-West Territories, plus a mission in Japan, with, by the mid-1880s, an annual budget of $60 000. Until his death in 1910, Dr Sutherland ruled the board as a 'Missionary Statesman in an imperial, if at times imperious, manner.' 'Whatever the Missionary Society of the Methodist Church is today,' he proclaimed in 1906, 'by God's help I made it, and let no man rob me of my boasting.'

Of the major Protestant denominations only the Canadian Anglicans supported no missionaries. The English low-church Church Missionary Society (CMS) and the high-church Society for the Propagation of the Gospel maintained the missions in the North-West Territories, and the Canadian Domestic and Foreign Mission Society merely channelled funds to the mother church. Although the students at Toronto's Wycliffe College did establish missions in Mid-Japan in 1888 and in Fukien [FUJIAN], China, in 1896, the Anglican church itself did not take over responsibility for the western Canadian missions until after 1902 when it established the Missionary Society of the Canadian Church.

It is impossible to read through the church magazines of the 1880s without sensing the widening horizons that greeted the readers a century ago, not only as church people but as Canadians. The opening of the Canadian Pacific Railway in 1886 symbolized the expansion of Ontario Protestant ethics not just from sea to sea, but beyond, into the Pacific, Canada's other ocean. Here in the magazines' stories and pictures a new world unfolded, a world that could be redeemed. In 1882, when a 'daring proposal' that it was physically and financially possible to evangelize the world in twenty years was going the rounds of the religious press, the Methodist *Missionary Outlook* commented, 'We like daring things, and we like daring men. There is no danger that the Church will be too courageous ... It is the cowardice of the Church that we dread.'

Although the new missionary fervour of the 1880s found the Canadian churches in an expansive phase, it was not the denominations per se, or their mission societies, that spread the word. Rather the zeal came from outside the churches, from the young people, particularly the students in the colleges. It is fascinating to watch the new enthusiasm for foreign missions skipping across the Atlantic during the decade, gaining momentum with each crossing, passing from Hudson Taylor to D.L. Moody in America, then back to England and the Cambridge Seven, then to North America and the Meeting of Ten Nations, the North-field Conference in 1886 that is considered to be the birth of the SVM and thus the birth of the modern missionary movement. Always the missionary movement developed under the auspices of such international, interdenominational organizations as the China Inland Mission and the Young Men's Christian Association.

Naturally, Canadian students got the inspiration from both the British and the American examples. Four Canadians had attended the first Northfield Conference, called the Meeting of Ten Nations, because of the presence of children of missionaries from various lands, and they returned to their home colleges to found the Canadian Inter-Seminary Missionary Alliance. The movement spread from the theological colleges into the arts and medical faculties, leading to the formation of the Student Volunteer Movement. By 1888 the Presbyterian Knox College in Toronto had thirty-three students offering themselves as foreign missionaries. Queen's University in Kingston, the Methodist Victoria College in Cobourg, and McGill University in Montreal all had similar numbers of volunteers.

At first the churches did not welcome this new direction, or at least did not comprehend either its depth or its urgency. As late as 1896, Dr Sutherland 'cautioned' the Methodists against 'encouraging societies which are outside of the Church ... Such societies are almost sure to be disintegrating, and not connexional. He strongly advised all contributions to be made through the proper channels, otherwise irregularities and confusion were sure to ensue.' But the church leaders, and the churches themselves, were forced to respond when the students came to them with cash in hand, offering themselves to their own denominations.

Coincidental to the growth of the missionary movement, a style of architecture flourished for Canadian churches, a style that froze into stone the solid aspirations of 'this generation.' It is called 'Romanesque,' a heavy castellated style of arches and towers typified by Victoria College when it was moved to Toronto in 1891. No trace of spindly Victorian Gothic lingers about these hallowed walls. In John Wesley's day, plain seats had inspired plain preaching, and the idea of evangelism was redolent of brimstone and the gaping tomb. A century later, resonant Casavant organs drowned out a thousand voices raised in song, and the seats, like the people, were comfortably padded.

The revivals of the mid-nineteenth century had domesticated 'church-iness' and brought it into the family parlour in the form of Gothic crockets and Parian saints. By contrast, the revivals of the 1880s attempted to make people feel 'at home in the churches' by bringing the parlour into the church itself. Churches became social centres where one could spend every night of the week and where 'missions' was the topic of the day: missionary meetings, prayer meetings, committees, magic-lantern lectures, sewing circles, cradle rolls, magazines, books (*Missionary Heroes of the Cross*) were prominently featured.

It was in this atmosphere that the Canadian missionary movement was born. The institutions the churches built during this period, both the physical structures and the mind-set, continued to shape attitudes until the 1920s and beyond. The spokesmen – and it *was* primarily men who spoke in and for the churches – forged life-long friendships in the crucible of their youthful cause.

The Canadian Presbyterian missions to China were, in many ways, a bell-wether of Canadian China missions, and the group against which others could be compared. Interest had been first stirred up on behalf of China among the congregations of western Ontario as early as 1844, but nothing concrete came of this except a sentimental attachment. A generation later, in 1870, these same churches undertook a mission to the island of Formosa (Taiwan), at the time a province of China. But this effort had been too marginal, too indirect, both in China and among the home people, to be considered more than a pioneer beginning.

The real foundation of the China missions did not happen until early 1888, when Jonathan Goforth, influenced by Hudson Taylor, left Toronto eight months before the Taylor contingent's departure from the same Knox Church. Goforth, of the fortuitous name – he became known as 'Goforth of China' – was an unlikely leader; his friend C.W. Gordon described him as 'a queer chap – a good fellow – pious – an earnest Christian, but simple-minded and *quite peculiar*.' He had personal magnetism despite his shabby exterior, and relied not on staged oratory but on the power of his 'burning words' and 'right condemning forefinger.' He was, in the terminology of the day, 'a God-intoxicated man,' drunk with the spirit, who could be 'counted insane sometimes because of the tremendous earnestness of his fire and zeal.'

Although Goforth and his wife set out as pioneers, they, too, were not the first Canadian missionaries to China. That privilege seems to have belonged to nineteen-year-old Adelaide Galliland from Farmers-ville (now Athens) in eastern Ontario. Addie went out in 1865, one week after marrying the Reverend Virgil Hart of the American Methodist Episcopal church. Hart became a prominent 'missionary statesman,' opening a string of stations up the Yangtse River, but Addie disappears like a shadow into the pages of his biography. 'Their married life was a perpetual honeymoon ...' her son wrote. 'She was a helpmeet, indeed, and many of the institutions which he was instrumental in establishing, such as the famous hospital and college in Nankin [NANJING], owe their first inspiration to her.'

Twenty years before Mrs Hart, however, the Presbyterian churches of south-western Ontario had their own representative in China and he, the Reverend William Chalmers Burns, though only a visitor in Canada for two years, can be considered Goforth's spiritual grandfather. Like his uncle, the Reverend Robert Burns, long-term secretary of the Glasgow Colonial Society and later minister of Knox church in Toronto and founder and principal of Knox theological college, W.C. Burns was dispatched to Canada in 1844 in the wake of the 'Great Disruption' of the Scottish church to drum up support for the secessionist Free Church. From the beginning of his ministry, the twenty-nine-year-old Burns had emphasized 'the new birth' (a most un-Presbyterian doctrine), and his revivals among the Highland settlers of Upper Canada sound more like Methodist camp meetings, which, 'like the rushing mighty wind of Pentecost ... broke forth simultaneously in weeping and wailing, tears and groans, intermingled with shouts of joy and praise.' Welcomed like a member of the family into the communities of western Ontario – in Ingersoll, Stratford, and Owen Sound – Burns left them after two years because he felt called to 'a sterner and more self-denying service' in China.

Burns's arrival in Macao in 1847 coincided with a world-wide expansion of Protestant missionary activity. Exactly forty years before, Dr Robert Morrison had been the first – and for twenty-three years the only – Protestant representative in China. At that time, the British East India Company, which controlled all British trade 'east of Goa,' had publicly declared 'the sending of missionaries into our Eastern possessions to be the maddest, most extravagant, most costly, most indefensible project which has ever been suggested by a moon-struck fanatic. Such a scheme is pernicious, imprudent, useless, harmful, dangerous, profitless, fantastic. It strikes against all reason and sound policy.' A dour hermit of a man who was never known to smile, Dr Morrison tried to remain independent of 'John Company' for two years until he realized he could do nothing without its co-operation. Reluctantly, he joined its employ as its only British interpreter, hoping, he wrote home, 'to do away any adversion of the Directors of the East India Company to missionaries, when they found that they were ready to serve the interests of the Company.' Thus was forged the fatal link with the enterprise called imperialism.

Morrison's death in 1832 was followed by the demise of the British East India Company in China when the British government revoked the company's trade monopoly and began to consolidate its own commercial empire. During its tenure, the company had controlled the avarice of the dockside hagglers; now with the company's demise, the Orient filled with a new breed of freebooters, pirates, and opium smugglers. No longer content to abide by the stylized, intricate rituals of company trading, they invoked the full weight of the British empire to support them. They also brought cannons and 'international law' to batter down the gates of the Middle Kingdom.

A direct outcome was the First Opium War (1839–42). As a result of the British and French occupation of Canton, a new word entered the English language: 'loot,' of Anglo-Indian derivation. The China trade that had mesmerized the West for five hundred years, that had introduced silk and tea, gunpowder, moveable type, porcelain, and 'Chinoiserie' to the backward countries of Europe and America had come down to 'loot.' According to Hudson Taylor's estimate, opium brought from British India poured into China at the rate of one-half ton per hour every day for the next seventy years – until it was outlawed by the International Opium Agreement of 1907. Silver from the Chinese treasury poured out at a commensurate rate.

If Dr Morrison was the Adam of Protestant missions in China, W.C. Burns and the fifty or so other missionaries who arrived in the country immediately following the First Opium War were his fractious children. Morrison had been content to remain in one place; but this younger generation were restless wanderers. Burns himself opened a mission in Canton, spent a few years in Amoy [XIAMEN], travelled on to Swatow [SHANTOU], Shanghai, and Peking, and finally, when in his fifties, moved to Manchuria. 'I think I can say through grace,' he wrote, 'that God's presence or absence alone distinguishes places to me.' Burns introduced itineration, adapting to China the circuit-riding practice of Canadian Methodism.

Burns was remembered not so much for his effect in converting the heathen – it was seven years 'rewarded only by hopeful appearances and fair promise' before he made his first convert – as for his influence on Hudson Taylor, then a raw recruit. Floating along the rivers that fan out from Shanghai, Burns introduced Taylor to every village and told him 'of revival work and of persecution in Canada and Dublin, and in Southern China ... His views ... were seed-thoughts which were to prove fruitful in the subsequent organization of the China Inland Mission.'

Twenty years after Burns's death in 1869 and far from the scene of his labours, a pretty stone chapel was dedicated to his memory in a remote mountain village among head-hunting aboriginals of northern Taiwan. It was built by one of the strangest characters nineteenth-century Canada ever produced, 'the Black-Bearded Barbarian of Formosa,' the Reverend George Leslie Mackay. Just as Simeon had blessed the infant Jesus, so, too, Burns had christened baby Mackay many years before in the village church, in Embro, Ontario, of which this chapel was a copy.

Mackay was a 'Zorra boy,' and proud of it. Zorra Township, located east of London, Ontario, in the rich farmlands of Oxford County, had such a reputation for log-cabin success stories – Canadian versions of Horatio Alger – that at the beginning of this century they were published in a book called *Zorra Boys at Home and Abroad or, Success Illustrated by Example*. The entire township of fifteen hundred people had emigrated from Sutherland, the barren, northernmost tip of Scotland, when the notorious 'Highland clearances' displaced tenant farmers for flocks of sheep in the 1820s and 1830s. Within a generation, Zorra had produced thirty-three ministers (fifteen of the clan MacKay alone), twenty-four medical doctors, three millionaires, and two college presidents. *Zorra Boys* describes the secret of their success: 'Born in humble though Christian homes, reared amid hardships and sometimes want, they were unconsciously trained by a stern but kind Providence in those habits of temperance, economy and hard work which have brought them to the front in almost every department of life ... So far as known to the writer, no Zorra boy to-day is ashamed of either the porridge or the Catechism on which he was reared.' The greatest secret, deceptively simple, was not mentioned by the author: first they had to get out of Zorra.

Canada's missionary enterprise was dominated for fifty years by the stern but kind providence of Zorra, as exemplified by G.L. Mackay's kinsman, the Reverend Robert Peter MacKay, secretary of the Presbyterian Foreign Mission Committee from 1892 to 1926, and by the Reverend

Henry John Cody (a member of the only non-Sutherland family in Zorra), the foremost Anglican clergyman of his day and founder of his church's missionary society.

In 1870, when the twenty-six-year-old George Leslie Mackay applied as a foreign missionary to the Western Division of the Free Church, its Foreign Mission Committee had been in existence for sixteen years without a single missionary. After it had appointed Mackay to go to China, he took a farewell tour of the congregations to 'reprove, rebuke, exhort.' Instead of enthusiasm, he found indifference: the ministers called him 'an excited young man'; he in turn described them as 'the ice age' of the church.

From the moment of his arrival in Formosa, G.L. Mackay reported phenomenal success. Within a month he made his first convert, a Chinese of prepossessing appearance and 'more than ordinary intelligence' named A Hoa, who became his life-long disciple. A few months more and he had gathered a 'peripatetic school' of twenty or more students who followed him on his itinerations. 'Under a tree or by the sea-shore, or in the chapels, they received instruction in geography, astronomy, church history, anatomy, physiology, etc., but chiefly in Bible truth.' The procession of these men, headed by the black-bearded Mackay, wearing a pith helmet, 'would of itself excite interest in the numberless hamlets and towns through which they passed.'

'Our usual custom in touring through the country,' Mackay wrote, 'is to take our stand in an open space, often on the stone steps of a temple, and, after singing a hymn or two, proceed to extract teeth and then preach the message of the Gospel.' Having taken a little basic medical training, Mackay fancied himself a doctor, and when he was given an honorary doctorate in theology from Queen's University, he insisted that everyone refer to him by that title. In his lifetime, he claimed, he had extracted more than 40 000 teeth in twenty-five years; no wonder the committee at home concluded that in Formosa 'the forceps and the Bible went together.'

Five years after his arrival, Mackay took the unusual step of marrying a Chinese woman. 'Brother R. just sent me a note,' he wrote to the committee by way of explanation, 'saying there are "charming ladies in Canada, one of which would come out as my help-meet." I am not thinking about "charming ladies." I am thinking how I can do most for Jesus.' When he returned to Canada after eleven years in the field, Tui Chang Mia, now prosaically called Minnie Mackay, disarmed criticism by her earnest convictions and forceful nature.

Oxford County was especially receptive to Mackay's message, and on his return to Formosa presented him with $6000 for a school to be called Oxford College. One year later, with great fanfare, he opened a boys' school in Tamsui [DANSHUI], the capital city, that 'would do justice to any Ontario city.' The school, part of whose ethnographic contents are now in the Royal Ontario Museum, contained everything needed for the edification of the students, including 'globes, drawings, microscopes, telescope, kaleidoscope, stethoscope, camera, magnets, galvanic batteries ... There are idols enough to stock a temple, ancestral tablets and religious curios, musical instruments, priests' garments, and all the stock in trade of Chinese idolatry.'

Moving from success to success, Mackay was even able to take advantage of disasters. During the French invasion of Tamsui in 1885, the main city in his area, the local Chinese used this excuse to tear down his chapels. Mackay immediately presented a statement of losses to his friend the local magistrate, who 'without delay or argument paid as indemnity the sum of ten thousand Mexican dollars' ($5000 U.S.) With this sum, Mackay figured he could build 'two dozen fragile churches – one dozen ordinary ones or half a dozen *strong* and at the same time *artistic* churches.' The choice was obvious. Carving models out of turnips, Mackay designed, and then constructed, six stone chapels (of which the W.C. Burns memorial was one) with eighty-foot steeples 'of solid masonry' emblazoned with a Union Jack and the burning bush, the Presbyterian emblem. During the construction, the people 'would stand and gaze for hours in wonder and amazement ... "Look now," they said, "the chapel towers above our temple. It is larger than the one we destroyed ... We cannot stop the barbarian missionary."' Indeed they could not.

This is the official picture tailored by Mackay himself in his autobiography, *From Far Formosa*; however, a darker picture emerges, like a ghost in a photograph, in his correspondence with the Foreign Mission Committee in Toronto. The qualities that made him a 'missionary entrepreneur' also touched him with madness, a fact tacitly recognized at home. His egomania exploded whenever he was confronted with a Canadian colleague; as far as 'charming women' were concerned, he would not allow them on the field, except when they were a necessary part of their husbands' responsibilities. His first associate, an ordained minister and medical doctor, lasted two years before his wife died during the birth of their fourth child. The second was shipped home, delirious with 'brain fever,' after a running, two-year battle with the British consul and A Hoa. He spent his days 'buying snakes and feeding them; he spent much time over bugs, beetles, &c.' (He sounds like one contemporary in Shantung who endlessly counted the paving stones in his courtyard to make sure none had been stolen.)

The conflict with his third colleague, which came to be known in the church papers as 'the Jamieson Affair,' started innocently enough when Mrs Annie Jamieson wrote to the Woman's Missionary Society (WMS) saying that in four years in the field she had never been able to do any real missionary work. Unlike Mrs Mackay, she wailed, 'I did not grow up among the people. I have not been at their homes; I do not know their children and aunts and uncles and neighbours, and all about their family troubles. How could they be expected to come to me?' The secretary of the WMS sent back a soothing, carefully worded reply saying that if she were not 'so actively employed, as perhaps you yourself had anticipated, it is only because the methods of Dr Mackay differ from those of ordinary missionaries.' When the Reverend John Jamieson, feeling 'more and more the injustice done to Dr Mackay,' put this letter into his hands – after waiting for two years to do so – Mackay wrote a furious diatribe to the committee, concluding:

I have been *misrepresented, misunderstood* and *falsely accused* just long enough and in the interests of *Truth* I will remain silent no longer ...
    O base injustice!
    O base ingratitude!
And this church here in the midst of heathen pressing around made to feel and suffer on account of such statements from a Christian land.

Suddenly John Jamieson had his own startling announcement. Writing two and three anguished letters a week, he confessed that for six years he had been 'dreaming over the language' and had 'been the cause of injury to the church here, and been a stumbling block to others ... Such a disposition as this, along with my self-conceit and stubbornness have been very trying to all about me, especially to Dr Mackay.' When the committee's telegram recalling the Jamiesons reached Mackay he made another volte-face and telegraphed back: 'Jamieson working now; is a comfort and help; all anxious he should remain; hope you will allow him to stay.' He hastened to assure the committee that his relationship with the Jamiesons had been 'all along *neighbourly, friendly,* and *brotherly* fellowship between us – no clashing – no irritation, no "temper" during all these years ... It is one thing to be *grieved* and *burdened*. It is another thing to have a "missionary quarrel."'

The mystification of the committee turned to anger and bewilderment. Is Dr Mackay in his right mind? the minister from Owen Sound asked. 'Who counts the teeth he pulls, and what [do] those thousands of teeth carefully treasured have to do with counting up spiritual results?' The representative from Seaforth had the most logical answer: jealousy over the recent appointment of Goforth to Honan. 'Some people say Dr Mackay does not like so much attention being paid to Honan, and think he inspired these letters with a view of checking it and directing more to Formosa.'

In the end, the Jamiesons remained in Formosa – on half salary as they requested – until John Jamieson died three years later of tropical fever. Mackay lived ten years longer, until 1901, when he died of cancer of the throat. With him died an era. During his second furlough, in 1894, the Japanese had seized his tropical isle and moved the capital city from Tamsui to Taipei [TAIBEI]. The invasion, according to Mackay, led to greater success, 'broke through the wall of Chinese conservatism and made a *change of religion easier* ... Now hatred for the Japanese induced friendliness to the religion of the foreigner.' This hatred was one reason why Japan continued to regard Christianity as a subversive doctrine in Taiwan, and later in its colonies in Korea and Manchuria.

On Mackay's death the Presbyterian church began to regularize the Formosa mission, sending out batches of men and women to build it into an institutional organization. By 1912, there were fourteen missionaries on the field, five of them single women, and a middle school under the principalship of George William Mackay, the University of Toronto-educated, half-Chinese son of the black-bearded barbarian. The mission, now in Japanese territory, remained with the continuing Presbyterian church after church union in 1925 and was, until the Nationalist government moved to the island in 1949, the only Protestant mission in the northern half of Taiwan. The memory of the founder is perpetuated by the Mackay Memorial Hospital in Taipei, one of the largest in the Republic of China.

During his first furlough in 1881, Mackay had preached in a village church in Oxford County. 'It seems that no one has caught the vision,' he pleaded. 'I am therefore going back alone. It will not be long before my bones will be lying on some Formosan hillside.' Unknown to him, one person had caught the vision: Jonathan Goforth, then aged twenty-one, who was just about to leave Ingersoll for Knox College in Toronto.

Goforth was not a Zorra boy – he came from the next township – but he was raised on the same porridge-and-catechism Presbyterianism. The seventh child (of ten sons and one daughter) of a Yorkshire immigrant who had settled near the village of Thorndale, he had already acquired those peculiar mannerisms that would make him the butt of his fellow students' ragging. One night they dressed him in a sheet and forced him to run down the corridor; though this was only a student prank, Goforth took it more seriously; henceforth, he vowed, his role in life would be to plough 'a lone road ... an independent trail.' He threw himself into work at the City Mission, distributing tracts in brothels, disrupting gambling dens, and praying for the street urchins. When he started preaching to his fellow students, however, he was hailed before a 'judge' at midnight and warned 'against further breaches of good form.' However, he persisted with his lectures and gradually won the respect of his fellow students. He applied to the China Inland Mission as its first North American candidate in 1886, and his fellow students volunteered to raise his support themselves.

In the end, he decided he was too much a Presbyterian to join the CIM and started pressuring his own church to plant the banner of Presbyterianism in central China. That summer he met James Frazer Smith, a portly, straightforward medical student from Queen's University who was lodging in the Knox dorm. Placid and practical, Smith came from a similar Highland log-cabin background in 'Smith's Settlement' in Grey County north of Owen Sound. He too had a personal connection with W.C. Burns: his childhood meditation spot was a tree stump Burns once used as a pulpit. When Frazer Smith heard that the Knox students wanted to sponsor Goforth, he went to the Queen's University missionary association, of which he was president, and asked his own friends to support him. 'With subdued enthusiasm, and calm business-like manner,' the students considered Smith's request. 'We dare not go back,' they unanimously declared. 'There can be only one watchword for us now: FORWARD!'

That fall, representatives of the two student associations met with the Foreign Mission Committee, Western Division, of the Presbyterian Church in Canada. After a weighty discussion, the FMC still hesitated. It was all very well to have $2800 in pledges to support Goforth and Smith, but as Formosa showed, the salary of missionaries was only a small part of expenditures: of the $24 000 Formosa budget, only $2500 went to pay the foreigners, while more than $7500 went to pay the native helpers. With a total budget of $79 000, the FMC was chronically in debt, a situation that continued right up to the time of union with the Methodists in 1925.

In January 1888, after shelving the proposed mission for a year and a half, reports of a famine raging in 'our Honan' made Goforth approach the committee again. This time, it agreed he could sail immediately, taking the sum of money raised by the churches for famine relief. George Leslie Mackay had gone out under what was known in mission circles as the 'Old System,' which made 'free use ... of the more advanced and intelligent of the converts in the capacity of paid colporteurs, catechists, teachers, helpers, preachers and Bible women. All these agents were paid from Mission funds.' Determined not to fall into this trap again, the FMC warned Goforth to 'practise such care and prudence' as not to run into debt. He could hire no teacher except a language instructor; he himself was to be the agent of evangelization to the Chinese. All mission expenditures had to be approved in advance, even though it would take six months to receive a reply from Toronto.

Three months before he sailed, Goforth married a woman who seemed as unlikely a partner as Frazer Smith; she was Rosalind Bell-Smith, sister of prominent society artist Frederick Bell-Smith. Born in London, England, and raised in the cream of Toronto society, Rosalind had turned her back on a promising career as an artist at the age of twenty to dedicate herself to mission work. 'If the Lord wanted me to live the married life,' she wrote, 'He would lead to me one *wholly given up to Him and His service*. I wanted no other.' After only two meetings, she knew Goforth was the one. When he spent the money for her engagement ring on tracts, this was the first step, she stated in her biography of him, in 'his training of Rosalind.' At the time of their departure, she was two months pregnant; their journey was, she wrote, 'a terrible nightmare.'

In his naivety, Goforth had assumed he would be able to go directly to Honan where he could distribute the famine funds himself. When he and Rosalind arrived in Shanghai, Goforth was taken aback to learn that without the language he would be more of a hindrance than a help. So, he turned the money over to an inter-mission committee and took his wife north to Chefoo, where the American Presbyterians had a flourishing mission he could use as a jumping-off point for trips into the neighbouring province of Honan. Situated on the salubrious northern coast of Shantung [SHANDONG], the peninsula that points like an index finger to Korea, the foreign community in Chefoo had grown up around the China Inland Mission sanatorium and school for missionaries' children. This school, reputedly 'the best school East of Suez,' was located on one of the area's many white-sand beaches and attracted parents from all over North China, who built bungalows where they could 'escape from China' – from the heat, the flies, the cholera, and the crowds – during the summer.

The first Presbyterian reinforcements arrived in Chefoo in August: they were the Frazer Smiths and a nurse, Miss Harriet Sutherland. They had left Toronto on the very day that Hudson Taylor issued his appeal for CIM workers. In November, with the arrival of Dr William McClure, the respected superintendent of the Montreal General Hospital, and Donald MacGillivray, a gold-medal winner from Knox College and a 'brilliant' student of languages, they proudly dubbed themselves 'the Honan Seven.' Technically, however, they numbered eight, baby Gertrude Goforth being the uncounted member.

In theology and temperament, the Honan mission resembled the China Inland Mission, though there were important differences between them. The former was an autocracy with Taylor at its head, the latter organized into a presbytery – that is, a democratic council that voted on all aspects of the work. (For years, the single women were regarded as assistant missionaries and not allowed to attend presbytery, even though their work was being voted upon.) But the most telling difference was in education: all four Presbyterian men had university degrees; the doctors had double degrees – in theology and medicine. By contrast, out of a staff of 330, the CIM had four doctors and a handful of ordained ministers. Needless to say, no member of the 'first Canadian party' of the CIM rated a biography; the Honan Seven produced three full-scale works and hundreds of pages of memoirs.

It might seem strange that these two missions should come into conflict over one small part of the uncharted vastness of China. In 1889, Hudson Taylor wrote a stiff letter to the Foreign Mission Committee claiming North Honan as his mission's territory, citing the exploratory tours his people had been making for fifteen years. 'We, with the intimate knowledge of the province which many years' work has given, have not yet succeeded in occupying any *city*,' he wrote, and the 'unwise impetuosity' of the Canadians 'has alarmed the officials and greatly increased the difficulties.' After personally meeting with Goforth for

North Honan mission, c. 1892. *Back row: first from left* Harvey Grant, *third* Jonathan Goforth, *fourth* Rosalind Goforth; *centre row: first* Margaret McClure, *second* Dr William McClure; *front row: first* Dr Lucinda Graham

the first time, Taylor gave his blessing to the Canadians, adding the warning that if they hoped to gain a foothold in Honan, they would have to 'go forward on their knees.'

Where the experienced men of the CIM feared to tread, the hearty lads from Oxford and Grey counties marched with confidence. The two senior men, Smith and Goforth, were escorted on their first trip into Honan by the Reverend Arthur H. Smith, an American expert on things Chinese. He was in the middle of writing his classic, a book called *Chinese Characteristics*, which, right up to the 1930s, was considered essential reading for anyone concerned with understanding the East. Seen from a 1980s perspective, it is a nasty piece of racist business; to use one of its author's favourite words, it is 'craven.' 'Not consciously prejudiced,' Smith describes himself, and goes on to delineate the Chinese character in chapters entitled: Face, Disregard of Time, Absence of Nerves, Absence of Sincerity, Absence of Sympathy, Mutual Suspicion. The Chinese were filthy, cruel, lazy, callous, deceitful, stupid; their good works were a sham, a 'mixture of fear and self-love.' Such was the man who introduced the Canadians to their field.

By reputation, Honan was 'the most bitterly anti-foreign province' in China, comparable only with the 'warrior province' of Hunan [HUNAN]. The Canadians, expecting their trip to be 'rather thrilling, and probably far from pleasant,' found instead laughing, friendly crowds at every stop. This was mainly because Dr Frazer Smith had brought 'a good pocket-case of instruments, a small assortment of medicines, and three pairs of forceps for extracting teeth.'

What went on in the minds of the hundreds of people lined up in the courtyard of the inn, as they brought their boils and abcesses, their runny eyes and fevered limbs to the foreign doctor – what bargains they made with the devil – can only be imagined. But 'when people are suffering,' Smith wrote home, 'and probably have continued for a long time to suffer from some lingering disease, fear and prejudice are forgotten; and, although they will call the doctor "Foreign Devil," they will plead with him for help, and a goodly number will submit to an operation with the utmost confidence. Patients in China will, without an anaesthetic, bear unflinchingly a degree of pain that the bravest of westerners would collapse under.'

As Reverend Arthur Smith took the opportunity to point out to the waiting crowds: 'You see how many sick people the doctor has to turn away. Many of these cases he could help and cure, if he were living in your midst, and had a hospital where all who were sick and suffering could be treated.' At the suggestion that the 'foreign devils' might set up shop in their village, the onlookers reacted with horror. After a whispered conference, the headman 'kindly informed us that, as we had come from that splendid country so far away, we could not be familiar with this poor province, nor was it possible for us to understand ... that this particular locality would be very unhealthy for such honourable gentlemen to reside in.' When the missionaries refused to take the hint, he warned that 'some low-down characters' were already gathering to molest them. Choosing the better part of valour and chased by a brick-throwing crowd, they took a hasty departure out the city gate.

As a result of the glowing articles Smith wrote about this trip – 'It is a good land, let us go up and possess it' – the Foreign Mission Committee dispatched a party of eight the following spring, three married couples and two single women. (There were so many 'Macs' in the mission with the arrival of the MacKenzies, MacVicars, and MacDougalls that one wag suggested it should change its name to 'McAll Mission,' after a famous seaman's rescue in New York City. James Hattie, who went out in 1912, must have felt left out, for he legally changed his name to MacHattie while home on furlough.)

By the spring, the fifteen adults – Miss Sutherland, the nurse, had married out of the mission and was replaced by Mrs McClure, who had formerly served with the American Presbyterians in South China – were still lodged in two villages in Shantung. Not for another year were they able to take the first extended tour. Travelling in creaking, lurching wheelbarrows, the usual conveyance in North China, McClure and MacGillivray took the northern route, while Goforth and Frazer Smith went south, towards the Yellow River.

Donald MacGillivray described Honan as 'the old homestead of China,' the North China plain where Chinese civilization had begun three thousand years before Christ. Of the eighteen imperial capitals that China had had in its history, fifteen had been within the borders of the province. In fact, Anyang [ANYANG], the capital of the Shang dynasty (1766 – 1122 BC), was located just outside the city of Changte [ZHANG-DE], where the Canadian mission opened its main station in 1897.

Although Honan means 'south of the river,' one small triangle extended north of the Yellow River [HUANG HE]; this was the Canadians' destination. Bounded on the west by the Tai-hung [TAIHANG] mountains, the area was as flat as a prairie, with scarcely a tree or shrub. Everything, from the ground to the houses to the rivers, had assumed the dun yellow colour of the loess soil; the soil was so granular that in places the wheels of the carts had worn roadways twenty feet below the grade of the surrounding land. The soil was incredibly rich, producing two crops a year of millet, beans, wheat, and kao-liang; but because of its flatness, the area was also subject to the cyclical pattern of floods and drought. The Yellow River was aptly named 'China's sorrow.'

Everywhere, 'almost as numerous as farm-houses in some parts of Canada,' over 20 000 walled villages were home to seven million people. Throughout its early history, the North Honan mission emphasized rural work, not only because of the nature of the province, but also because of the background of the missionaries themselves. Of the thirty-seven who went out before 1900, twenty-one women and sixteen men, only eight came from cities – from Toronto, Montreal, and, if one could describe it as urban, Guelph. The rest, excepting six born in Scotland, hailed from small rural centres – from the Scottish enclave in the Eastern

Townships of Quebec, from as far west as Ormstown, and from such Ontario villages as Fergus, Elora, Listowel, and Ailsa Craig.

On this their first extended trip through the district, the missionaries made their first convert, a character who became known in the Canadian church as 'Old Blind Chou.' After examining his eyes, Dr Frazer Smith declared that his cataracts were ripe enough to be cut out with a simple operation. When Chou leaped back in terror, his grandson cajoled him, saying that his eyes were useless anyway, and if the doctor made medicine from them, he, Chou, would gain merit in heaven. So, in front of a crowd, Smith performed the first cataract operation in North Honan. Four days later when the bandages were removed, just as in biblical days, Chou leapt to his feet and shouted, 'I can see.' As payment, Smith told him, 'Believe in my Saviour, for if I did not love my Saviour I would not have come to China, and you would not have received your sight.' Three months later, on the missionaries' way back, Chou told them he was 'happy all the day,' and was now holding prayers with his family.

The other pair, McClure and MacGillivray, travelling south towards the river, encountered the rough winds blowing up from the Yangtse riots. In one city, Dr McClure tore down a placard 'of the familiar type,' which he described as 'a most violent and lying tirade ... accusing the doctor for using bloody methods in healing diseases (I had operated on several patients with inturning eyelashes), that I "dug out" people's eyes and *cut into* their *hearts*.' These troubles, McClure claimed, were stirred up by the local gentry, 'these learned ignoramuses'; 'the common people receive us gladly.'

After several more tours 'in Abrahamic ignorance of our destination, but with Abrahamic faith that God would bring us into a city of habitation,' Dr McClure was able to secure a derelict house in Chuwang [CHUWANG], a 'wretched' market town 'on the ragged edge of ruin' whose only distinction was that it lay thirty miles inside Honan. A few weeks after he had obtained the rental agreement – by subterfuge, through a middle man – a mob burst into the courtyard and destroyed every stick of furniture. The next day, MacGillivray, the gifted linguist, drew up a petition to the magistrate in his best literary Chinese:

We are not secret preachers of unlawful doctrine, but, as is well known, the Emperor himself in treaty has sanctioned the preaching of the Christian religion in the Empire, and whether you notice the matter or not, we are bound to carry it before a higher court.

Goforth and Smith happened to be passing the town in their houseboat and, in response to Dr McClure's laconic message, 'Please come,' burst into the candle-lit room where the magistrate was holding a knife to Dr McClure's throat unless he relinquished the lease. The credulous Chinese soldiers claimed these two foreign devils had been blown in along the telegraph wires from Tientsin [TIANJIN], and the magistrate himself, described as 'a piece of meat which could turn the edge of a knife,' was unnerved by the presence of such an august emissary as Dr Smith, whose large frame was enclosed in 'a fine maroon-coloured dressing gown.' (This costume, Smith remembered, 'did splendid service in many subsequent interviews with Chinese officials, and was a source of considerable amusement to our missionaries in those early years.')

For several days, the magistrate hemmed and hawed, offering to give the missionaries a feast and two hundred *taels*, but they dismissed this face-saving sum – they were demanding two thousand *taels* – and finally deputed Dr McClure to present a statement directly to the British consul in Tientsin. The consul immediately took their 'clear case' directly to Li Hung-chang [LI HONGZHANG], the Chinese foreign minister and the most important official in the empire. Li ordered them to be indemnified with 1800 *taels* of silver, and the local magistrate had to serve them a thirty-six-course 'peace and harmony' banquet – in their own court-yard.

The Canadians marvelled at the speed of the judgment, in 'two and a half months and three days,' according to the mission history, 'in a province inaccessible to gunboats and several hundred miles from the nearest foreign cannon.' Other missions waited seven or eight years with no resolution. McClure himself felt that being 'at the cannon's mouth' helped, but others suggested that Li had pushed because of the loss of medical instruments. In any case, the Canadians had a foothold in North Honan, and they were there to stay.

For someone raised in the fresh air of Ontario, the hot, pestilential climate of Honan could be debilitating; the early history of the mission is filled with stories of heroic deaths. The first to go was little Gertrude Goforth, 'that precious first-gift of God,' dying of dysentery before she was one year old. Scarcely a missionary family did not bury at least one infant: the Goforths buried five. (Descriptions of the death of these little angel children figure prominently in mission literature, sweetly counterpointing their folded hands against the darkness of heathenism.)

Even though the missionaries took summer holidays at Chefoo or in the mountains, practically deserting the mission for two months, they could not shake the effects of the climate. Two of the three couples who went out in 1889, for example, withdrew before their first term was finished. Of the next group, Dr Lucinda Graham, who went out to replace her invalided sister, was a merry individual who cut quite a figure in the mission by striding out for a walk around town (an action that caused the men consternation since, she confided to her brother, they 'very seldom go outside the compound themselves unless of course they have some special object.') Dr Graham was called to attend Mrs Malcolm, who was dying of cholera. Within a week, both women were dead. Their epitaph read: 'They went to China on the same vessel, were located in different centres in the same mission, and gave promise of marked helpfulness in mission work ... Lovely and pleasant in their lives here, in death they were not divided.'

The story of Donald MacGillivray shows how the climate, the overwork, and the primitive conditions could combine to affect a sensitive soul. Described as the best student of his class in Greek and Hebrew, he acquired Chinese with the same facility and, within one month of his first lesson, was reading the gospels in Chinese. He had originally volunteered to go to Honan on the same salary as the China Inland Mission people, $500 a year, or $300 less than the other single men in his own mission. Although he had done this voluntarily, at the end of five years he felt he could no longer live on this amount and asked the Toronto committee to increase his stipend. 'Our Church is too small to go off into departments,' he wrote to the secretary, 'some going to the *quarantined*, some to the *well-fed* ... If ministers and laymen at home begin casting off high salaries, etc. ... I should have the fullest sympathy and gladly live all my life as one of the many *brethren*.' After much wrangling, which left a bad taste all round in the mission, the committee did raise his salary, which he promptly donated to construct a hospital in memory of his mother.

The lone bachelor in the mission, MacGillivray took to itinerating to alleviate his loneliness: during one year, he spent 278 days travelling more than 10 000 kilometres. Utterly dejected, he wrote desperately to ask the committee to send him 'a true yoke-fellow to share my room and life,' offering to donate the salary himself. The committee sent the Reverend William Harvey Grant, who became the clerk of presbytery for most of his forty years in China. Obviously he was the right man for the mission, but the wrong companion for MacGillivray. '*There* he is ready to undertake all sorts of work ...' Grant wrote, 'and *here* am

I left at home in my loneliness, unprepared to do anything, left at home to keep house for myself ... Before this, he should have sent home for a companion of a different sort.'

MacGillivray's furlough was delayed for four years. Passing through Shanghai on his return, he was approached by Dr Timothy Richard, an English Baptist who was head of the Society for the Diffusion of Christian and General Knowledge. Richard asked MacGillivray to join his staff as a writer and editor of Christian and scientific material. In a culture in which the written word was sacred – even Christian tracts were not thrown out – 'one man may preach to a million' through literature, Richard argued, 'instead of to a few hundred in a street chapel, and at the same time keep an open door for the rest of his brethren working throughout the land.' MacGillivray, who had already compiled a Chinese–English dictionary, was the man Richard needed. 'Some have gifts of preaching pre-eminently; let them preach ...' he continued. 'Some have literary gifts; let these write books. Our friend Mr MacGillivray has these literary gifts. Are they not multiplied in their usefulness by being specially set aside for what he is best fitted for?' Reluctantly, presbytery agreed to release him, while keeping him on their roster: 'We consider Mr MacGillivray a host in himself,' Dr Percy Leslie wrote, 'and it will take quite a reinforcement to fill the gap.'

By 1900, the North Honan mission was a small but well-established group with twenty-three missionaries located at three stations: the district cities of Changte and Weihwei [WEIHUI, now called XIN XIANG], as well as Chuwang. Compared with the more energetic British and American denominational missions, it could already be considered a conservative backwater where the ideas of the founders became fossilized over the years. Partly because they were all of one theological mindset, partly because of the presbyterial form of government, policies changed slowly. Every male member of the mission felt it was his duty to speak on every matter that came up in presbytery, and agreed to abide by its majority decision. For one individual to approach the home committee directly, as MacGillivray had done in asking for a companion, was 'the unforgivable sin of a loyal Presbyterian.' These meetings must have been tumultuous affairs when Goforth got his dander up and pounded the table, for as Rosalind wrote, 'with his strong convictions concerning Divine guidance *of himself*, he naturally came often into conflict with other members of the Honan Presbytery, for what body of, say, twenty strong personalities could easily bend to one of their number, when some had perhaps equally strong convictions opposed to his?' Harvey Grant's written records, however, are reticent: the following resolutions were passed, he would write, and afterwards everybody stood up to sing the Doxology.

The deliberations of the Honan presbytery took up more time than those of the General Assembly of the whole Presbyterian Church in Canada.

3 · 'Our West China Mission': The Methodists in Szechuan

'Fire will spread, but *all must* take part in the work of spreading ... The world is open for the Gospel, all we need is Consecration, Missionaries and Money. Time is so short, the centuries are fast filling up; the dust of the *passed* away is all about us. O! if our ladies could but see how much more important it is to be up and doing at this work, than it is to be altering the style of a dress or remodelling a bonnet.'

Mrs J.L. Stoney, Dominion President of the Methodist Woman's Missionary Society

When the missionary fires blazed through the churches in the late 1880s, the Canadian Methodists blazed as hot as the rest. Missions had always been part of Methodist theology; John Wesley himself had said, 'The world is my parish.' But rather than establish poorly planned missions as the Presbyterians had done, the Methodists delayed a few years, building missionary support at home so that when the time came they could build an equally grandiose institution in the far corners of the earth. Whereas the Presbyterian Foreign Mission Committee looked with horror on its debt of $5000, the Methodist Foreign Mission Board regarded its debt of $20 000 as a challenge, 'a proof that God is opening for us ever wider doors of opportunity and is summoning us to ever larger responsibilities.' The secret was 'systematic giving.' As early as 1882, the motto of the church had been: 'A revival on every Circuit, and one cent a day for Missions from every member of the Church.' This seemingly insignificant sum would amount to $200 000 a year for the mission coffers.

Dr and Mrs Virgil Hart at Mount Omei, c. 1888

One of the innovations at this time to encourage regular contributions to missions was the church's introduction of 'duplex envelopes' – a Canadian invention widely copied in the United States – in which one pocket was for normal church work and the other pocket was for 'the other,' for missions.

When a group of people decides to establish a colony, how does it select a destination guided only by 'Abrahamic ignorance' and with the whole world to choose from? Did the Presbyterians sense beforehand that they would find the dusty, biblical plains of Honan to their liking? And the Methodists; did they know that hidden beyond the gorges of the Yangtse lay a Shangri-la where 'flowers forgot to bloom by the season?' The Chinese call Szechuan 'the ricebowl of China'; the Canadians nicknamed it 'China's Last Best West' because it was located on a longitude that when extended through the North Pole, passed through Maple Creek, Saskatchewan. Did the Canadians sense that their mission among the 'virile, enterprising, and hopeful' Szechuanese (not a bad description of the Methodists themselves) would provide work and prayer and success enough to become 'the largest, single mission field operated by a single church in the world,' and would endure to occupy the world-changing visions of their grandchildren?

By the 1880s, Methodists were 'the coming men.' Having shaken off their old 'Nonconformist' image along with their poorly educated circuit-riding preachers, in 1884 they followed the example of the Presbyterian brethren by uniting the divergent strands of British (Wesleyan), American (Methodist Episcopal), and Canadian Methodism into one Methodist Church of Canada. With 128 000 members and 800 000 adherents, it was the largest denomination in the country, outnumbering the Presbyterians by 100 000 and the Church of England by 200 000. As an illustration of the strength of the Methodists in Canada – or at least in Toronto – the *Canadian Methodist Magazine* claimed that:

Baltimore has 64 Methodists to 1000 of the population; Pittsburgh, 37; Detroit, 20; Buffalo, 18; Brooklyn, 18; Cincinnati, 22; Chicago, 14; Washington, 43; Philadelphia, 33; Rochester, 24; Cleveland, 22, and New York, 10. Toronto has about 300 to the 1000.

'The Genius of Methodism is her power to adapt herself,' stated Dr Morley Punchon, a leader of the Canadian Methodist church. Although governed by a centralized hierarchy, ever since Wesley's day the Methodists had stressed 'the priesthood of the people,' that is, the involvement of the laity as preachers, class leaders, and behind-the-scenes organizers. Now, declaring that 'Methodism is a social as well as a religious force,' the church organized the people into an army of foot-soldiers and social convenors, boards, committees, Sunday schools, Epworth leagues, and Chautauqua circles.

'We have heard a great deal about the Institutional Church,' editorialized the *Canadian Methodist*:

It has kindergartens, and working-girls' clubs, and young men's clubs, and boys' clubs, and parlours, and a gymnasium, and a reading-room, and perhaps a bowling-alley and a billiard-room, to say nothing of a kitchen and a monthly party called a 'sociable.' It has something on hand every night in the week. It educates, it entertains, it instructs. We believe in the Institutional Church.

But ... a Church is not an Academy, it is not a Club, and it certainly is not a Variety Show ... The more institutional it is, the more inspirational it needs to be ... The more of the so-called secular work the Church is doing, the greater the need for spiritual preaching in the pulpit.

By this time in history, many Methodists argued, an ecstatic conversion with weeping and confession of sin, such as characterized the early days of Methodism, was no longer an essential for the New Life. In primitive societies or among hardened sinners, it might still be encouraged, but surely their own children, raised in Christian families, could be 'educated into the faith' to become 'soldiers of a new holy war, of a new crusade, of a nobler chivalry than that of arms, the symbols of which shall be the white shield and the white cross – its great purpose to maintain purity of soul, and through that sign of grace to conquer.'

'When the citadel of our faith is attacked at home,' said Dr Punchon, 'let us go to our Missions to authenticate our theology; in these days of sad latitudinarianism, when spiritual religion is by many derided as a myth and a mockery, let us go to our Missions to authenticate our experience.'

The first of the connexional organizations to be turned towards foreign mission work was the Woman's Missionary Society (WMS); on its shoulders fell the responsibility for 'organizing the whole sisterhood of the church – the matrons, the young ladies, the girls at school, the little tots scarce out of their cradles.' Unlike its counterpart in the Presbyterian church, which was an auxiliary of the Foreign Mission Committee, the Methodists founded their WMS in 1880 as an independent body that was to work in harmony with the General Board while remaining responsible for its own fund raising, its own fund dispersal, and its own organization. This 'young shoot ... in the garden of the Church' was not universally welcomed by the men, many of whom thought it would steal light and air from other, more productive plants. Yet, within ten years of its inception, the Methodist WMS counted 16 500 members in 436 auxiliaries and 183 mission bands, and was raising $30 000 annually for missions, an astounding sum considering that the women were 'but gleaners in a well-reaped field.'

'The women's missionary societies,' according to John Foster, 'permeated their denominations with a missionary atmosphere. Every home was to be opened to the possibilities for the extension of the Kingdom abroad.' Even in isolated prairie hamlets, the WMS was likely to be the first connexional society to hold regular monthly meetings. 'Who can estimate the good done to a farmer's wife,' the president of the Dominion WMS wrote in 1892, 'as she ... hears of the loneliness of a missionary – loneliness and isolation so complete that she blushes to think that as she went to the meeting she was brooding over her own loneliness? ... If [our farmers' wives] were full of an intelligent knowledge of the world of missions, we should hear less of their falling into the opium habit, or of their losing their reason.' The antidote to loneliness, the next president wrote, is 'simply *work*. Give the Christian women in our Churches something to *do*; let them see and know about others; broaden the vision until it is wide enough, strong enough, to take in the whole world.'

By 1891, with a flourishing mission in Japan and extensive churches across the Canadian West, the Reverend Dr Alexander Sutherland, General Secretary of the Methodist General Board wondered whether the time had not come for the church 'to turn her eyes toward yet another part of the neglected field of foreign heathendom.'

There were already a handful of Canadian Methodists in China serving with the American Methodist Episcopal (North) mission. The most notable of these was Dr Leonora Howard, who went out in 1875 and who had the double distinction of being the second woman doctor sent to China by any denomination and one of the first two Canadian women to graduate in medicine. (She had to go to Michigan Medical College to do so.) She came to prominence a few years later when she was called to treat the wife of Li Hung-chang, the Chinese foreign minister; this providential request opened 'the homes of many of the best and most influential families' to the gospel. Similarly, when her story was widely publicized in church papers in the late 1800s, it also opened many influential homes in Canada.

Dr Howard came from the same church in Farmersville (Athens) in eastern Ontario that had sponsored Addie (Galliland) Hart, wife of the Reverend Virgil Hart and the first Canadian sent to China in 1865. It was Mrs Hart, the unsung pioneer, who was instrumental in founding the Canadian Methodist mission to West China. Dr and Mrs Hart were of the same generation as Hudson Taylor and George Leslie Mackay, and had displayed the same restlessness. They had started the Central China mission of the American church at Wuhu [WUHU], moving further inland every few years as new regions were penetrated, and finally reaching Szechuan in 1886. However, they had had to retire from the field in 1888 because of Dr Hart's ill health to a family farm near Burlington, Ontario. At that time, Mrs Hart was still in her mid-forties, seven years younger than her husband, so when the local minister, who was also a member of the General Board, asked for suggestions as to a choice of field, she helped persuade Dr Hart to come out of retirement to establish yet another China mission. 'And for Canada!' he enthused.

Dr Hart combined the expertise and vision that the Canadian church needed to establish its new mission. He knew the field 'intimately,' and could be considered a 'progressive' missionary. From the beginning, he had established schools and hospitals in every station he opened, and though he had the reputation for exceeding the annual budgets, that too showed the breadth of his vision. In 1891, when the Canadian Methodist church was building two colleges at home, Victoria in Toronto and Wesley in Winnipeg, it seemed logical to ask, Why not another in West China?

In the three years since the Honan Seven had gone out, the Christian map of China had filled in; gone were the days when a pioneer band could claim a province on the strength of prayer alone. In Chengtu [CHENGDU], which the Methodists selected as their destination, there was already a substantial missionary presence; in addition to the Roman Catholics, who had been there since the seventeenth century, there were four other missions: the China Inland Mission, the British Friends (Quakers), the London Missionary Society, and the American Methodist Episcopal. Division of the field was fairly common in China, and generally, despite occasional friction, worked out harmoniously. In West China, for example, missions were actually allotted specific city districts. Such 'comity' was often cited by the church councils at home, especially in this century, as an example of practical ecumenicism that could show the way to church union in Canada.

By the time Dr Hart volunteered to lead the mission, the General Board had four applicants, two of whom, Dr Omar Kilborn and the Reverend George Hartwell, were congregants of the same Farmersville church as Mrs Hart and Dr Howard. Just as the Presbyterians had Oxford County, the Methodists had Leeds, where Mother Barbara Heck had cradled the infant church after the American Revolution. It also had strong missionary-sending areas in south-western Ontario, adjacent to the Presbyterians, along the shore of Lake Ontario, around the Bay of Quinte, and later in the Canadian West. And, perhaps most important, it had Toronto: if the hinterland supplied the personnel, Toronto provided the organization. The thirty congregations of the city were regularly assessed for one-quarter of the annual mission budget of the church, 40 per cent of that one-quarter was donated by only three churches, Metropolitan, Sherbourne Street, and, later, Timothy Eaton Memorial.

The pioneer group of the West China mission that set out in September 1891 numbered nine: Dr and Mrs Hart and their grown daughter, Estelle, the Reverend and Mrs Hartwell, Dr and Mrs Kilborn, Dr David Stevenson, another medical man, and Miss Amelia Brown, a registered nurse sent by the WMS. After a series of 'never-to-be forgotten' meetings across Canada, the nine sailed from Vancouver on the luxurious *Empress of China*, the first ship of the Canadian Pacific 'Empress' line. In Shanghai, they found themselves in the midst of the evacuation caused by the Yangtse Valley riots and had to lodge in a crowded mission home where they were given a warm welcome 'such as Christians who meet once in a lifetime, amid the dense darkness of heathenism, know how to give.'

After three months, the British consul lifted his restriction against inland travel, and the Canadian party sailed up the Yangtse on the first leg of its 2900-kilometre journey inland. 'There was a sense of security,' wrote one missionary a few years later, 'which afterwards we sadly lacked, in the feeling that the great river was but an arm of the gentle Pacific which laved our native shores.'

The river steamers, captained by British officers resplendent in tropical whites and crewed by Chinese 'clad in rags and sunshine,' took a leisurely week to reach Hankow, eight hundred kilometres upriver. 'Here again we found a foreign concession,' a later missionary noted, 'with fine brick and stone buildings, wide, clean streets, sidewalks, and boulevardes carefully guarded by Sikhs.' At Ichang [YICHANG], a dirty provincial town located at the sixteen-hundred-kilometre mark, they had to unload all their baggage, some several hundred 'cases, trunks, grips, boxes, and parcels,' to pass through the third (but not final) set of customs, and then reload them onto river junks that would take them the next eight hundred kilometres to Chungking [CHONGQING].

The first sixteen hundred kilometres usually took two weeks; the last twelve hundred took at least two and sometimes three or more months. The top speed of the houseboats averaged five kilometres an hour. Some days, the crew counted themselves lucky if they gained seven or eight metres.

The Yangtse gorges became an important part of Canadian missionary mythology, for they emphasized how far away West China really was. 'Remoteness is to be judged by inaccessibility rather than distance,' wrote the Reverend Jesse Arnup, long-time secretary of the board. 'Measured by this standard the field chosen was certainly one of the uttermost parts of the earth.'

The awesome perpendicularities of the Yangtse gorges are one of the wonders of the world. Words are barely adequate to portray the effect of staring simultaneously up the three-hundred-metre cliff walls and downwards a hundred metres to where whirlpools exposed the rock of the river bed; or to describe the eerie effect as the shriek of the wind gave way to an abrupt and complete silence, broken only by the chant of the trackers. This whole stretch of the river was 'soaked in religion,' with makeshift shrines clinging to the steep banks. Despite its mystical presence, however, every square centimetre of soil was cultivated, often in terraces 'no bigger than a good-sized tablecloth' that were accessible only by rope ladders.

Few travellers passed through the gorges without a kind word for the lowly trackers. Beasts of burden paid in rice and opium, with huge welts across their backs, they were up and working from dawn till dark, pulling the boat step by excruciating step. Upwards of one hundred people, men, women, and children, each attached by a rope around his or her waist, strained at the traces while the boat bobbed at the end of the three-hundred-metre main cable. Scrambling over the rocks in their bare feet, through passages worn by thousands of years of use, they were 'under the guidance, command and whip of their foreman.'

Coming out of the Wind-Box Gorge, the wild turbulence subsided to a swift current as, around a bend in the river, the walls of Chungking towered above the golden sands. The setting of Chungking is majestic; the city stands on a peninsula formed by the junction of the Yangtse and the Kialing [JIALING] rivers, with mountains as the backdrop, the highest of which is surmounted by a slender white pagoda. The reality of the city was wretched. It was one of the four 'cauldrons' of China, 'a city of steps and swear-words,' unhealthy, unattractive, and dangerous. In this city of 700 000, through which was funnelled almost all the goods from West China including 90 per cent of the nation's salt and a good deal of the domestic opium, everything had to be carried up thousands of steps from the river to the city. A constant line of coolies carrying water buckets jostled sedan chairs of dignitaries and crates of food, and the millions of spilled drops turned the steps to slime.

Leaving Chungking, the travellers had the choice of going 640 kilometres overland by sedan chair, or continuing through the equally dangerous rapids of the Min [MIN] River, past the impassive 112-metre Buddha that guards the river at the base of the holy Mount Omei [EMEI]. Both routes took about two weeks, and both were uncomfortable.

The first reaction of most people on seeing Chengtu was surprise at such a metropolis so far inland. Capital of the largest and richest province of China, the city threw out 'pulsating arteries of commerce in every direction,' towards Tibet, towards the silk roads across Central Asia, and south to Yunnan [YUNNAN] and Vietnam. The Chengtu plain, 160 kilometres long by 95 wide, was a veritable 'farmer's paradise,' producing some fifty varieties of vegetables and forty fruits; 'something of the density of its population may be realized when we try to conceive of a province slightly smaller than Ontario supporting two-thirds of the people of the United States.'

The history of Szechuan stretched back to the beginnings of time, back to the period when the legendary Fu-hsi [FUXI] taught humans agriculture and Lao Tse [LAOZI] taught them the Way – the *Tao* [DAO]; but the ancient history of the province, the missionaries discovered, told little more about 'the development of the modern Szechwanese than the history of the Indians would throw on the life and character of Canadians.' According to an exaggerated account given in *Our West China Mission*, during the last years of the Ming dynasty, in the 1660s, the local bandit chief laid waste to the province, systematically butchering every Chinese inhabitant. 'The land became a wilderness ... In the more thickly populated districts of Eastern China, the people were simply taken from their homes, and with their hands tied behind their backs were driven to the vacant lands of Szechwan.' Thus, by a curious parallel of history, 'the people of this old land (as old as Canada) are really young (as young as Canadians).'

The comparative rootlessness of the Szechuanese made them friendlier and more mercantile than other Chinese, but as an old Chinese adage states – and as the missionaries soon found out – 'When there is trouble in the Empire, it is in Szechuan that order is first disturbed and last restored, where peaceful days are few and days of confusion many.'

Having already been in China for six months, the members of the Methodist party were eager to be up and doing as soon as they reached Chengtu. 'As a colt champs its bit with apparent relish,' Hartwell wrote, 'though untrained for active work, in like manner have we, in a limited degree, tasted the pleasures of preaching to the Chinese in their own tongue.' After only two weeks of hunting, Dr Hart rented a 'haunted' house that was large enough to accommodate three families, as well as 'a Sunday chapel, a street chapel, three schools, a dispensary, and a small hospital ward.' The name, translated as the Pearly Sands Mission, sounded auspicious, and after a good wash with carbolic soap, the old mansion was soon ready to receive its new tenants.

Even before they moved in, however, Dr Hart opened a bookstore where the curious public were free to browse among the books and periodicals. On the first day, 'at least a thousand persons dropped in ... and manifested considerable interest in the new book concern.'

On 3 November 1892, one year to the day after their arrival in Shanghai, the two doctors opened their first dispensary. 'The thought was,' Dr Kilborn wrote, 'that the direct teaching of the Word should always be accompanied, if possible, by the practical benevolence of the medical missionary.' Even before they had left Toronto, Dr Hart had written enthusiastically of medical work as 'one of the best chisels ever devised to cleave the flinty mountain of heathenism.' And, preparing the church for budgets that would later soar astronomically, he continued, 'Wherever we open chapels they will need funds to fit up dispensaries ... Five hundred dollars will fit up one ... Have we not twenty devoted Christians who would like to put as many dispensaries into that richest valley of the world? We shall need a plain but well-equipped hospital at Chenten [sic], able to accommodate one hundred patients. Such a building can be put up for $6000.' After describing a 500-seat chapel at $3000 and a school at $4000, he closed with the plea, 'If it will pay to send the men, surely it will pay to give them a modest start.'

The first dispensary proved premature, because the work became so absorbing it interfered with the men's language lessons, forcing them to 'worry along with a sort of pidgin Chinese, chiefly a collection of

WMS home in Chengtu, the first house built after the 1895 riots, c. 1897

phrases used in the hospital; utterly unable to preach a sermon or ...
carry on a conversation with a Chinese on any subject other than medical.'
The next venture, into education, was more successful. When the
Presbyterians opened Honan, the FMC specifically forbade them to open
a school, but the Methodists considered educational work 'a very
essential part of the propaganda.' Accordingly, in early 1893, they hired
three traditional Confucian scholars on condition that each one bring
twenty pupils to start a school. In the mornings, the boys – and two
girls! – recited the Confucian classics, including the emperor Yung-
cheng's [YONGZHENG] classic *Sacred Edict* condemning Christianity, at the
top of their voices; in the afternoons, the missionary men would, in
quite a different fashion, try to inculcate 'the fundamental truths of
Christianity' and a smattering of arithmetic and geography. By the end
of the year, the school had one hundred students, including a class
of thirty girls under the instruction of an educated woman teacher,
a great rarity in China. 'We trust this is the nucleus of our coming
university,' Hartwell dreamed enthusiastically.

The first reinforcements, who arrived in Chengtu in February 1894 after an exasperating six-month delay in Shanghai and shipwreck in the gorges, contained at least two people who were instrumental in founding that coming university. Undoubtedly the most prickly of the individualists who went out in the first decade was the Reverend James Endicott, a Devonshire man who had emigrated to Lucan, Ontario, at the age of seventeen. 'In a rare moment of self-revelation,' he once told a friend that he had left the Old Country because 'he did not like to have to touch his cap or take it off to the "Gentry."' At twenty-two he had been accepted for the ministry and attended Wesley College in Winnipeg, where he helped found the college YMCA and the Student Volunteer Movement. Two weeks before his departure for China, Endicott had married Sarah Diamond of Lucan. On the field, Endicott founded the Canadian Mission Press, which, as the largest foreign press west of Hankow, eventually turned out millions of pages a year in Chinese, English, and such diverse languages as Tibetan and Miao.

The other important member of this second party was Dr Alfretta Gifford, described as the best doctor in the mission, male or female, who became engaged on the upriver trip to the recently widowed Dr Omar Kilborn. After a wedding on the lawn of the British consulate, on 24 May, the Queen's birthday, they left the next day to open the mission's second station at Kiating [JIADING, now called LESHAN], where Dr Alfretta Kilborn established the first hospital for women in the province.

Kiating, where the colossal Buddha guards the river, was an important commercial centre for the manufacture of white wax. More importantly, it was a Chinese holy city – 'a haughty religious centre,' the missionaries described it – the pilgrimage site and gateway to Mount Omei, one of the four sacred mountains of China. Dr Hart was entranced by Mount Omei and became friends with the Buddhist priest in the temple at the two-kilometre-high summit. (Although there was some question as to how he acquired it, Dr Hart brought this priest's cane back to Toronto for the burgeoning collection in the mission rooms.) This friendship eventually led to the establishment of a Canadian mission summer resort on the mountain, including rental of some of the temple buildings, for the next fifty years. To listen to the people who spent their summers there, especially those who did so as children, it sounds as though Mount Omei must have been near to heaven; if you stand on the peak, the sunlight casts your shadow, circled by a perfect rainbow, onto the swirling mists below.

By 1895, the mission was strong enough to issue an appeal for twenty-five missionaries in the next five years. By the time the appeal was published, however, the mission had been forced to flee downriver to Shanghai. Mistaking the Canadians for Japanese (!), the ignorant Szechuanese started a riot outside the mission compound to protest the Sino-Japanese war. When a mob burst through the mission gate, Dr Kilborn fired his rifle over its head and ran for help. That night, the entire foreign population of the city, twenty adults and eleven children, huddled on the city wall listening to 'the inhuman din of human voices' wreaking havoc below. Seeking refuge in the magistrate's official residence, or *yamen* [YAMEN], they were incarcerated in three tiny rooms for ten days until he could arrange an auspicious day for their departure from the city.

On their arrival in Shanghai, Dr Hart remarked that 'God moves in a mysterious way.' He himself took the mission's grievance to Peking, where his old friend, Charles Denby, was the American Minister Plenipotentiary. 'It is not in a vindictive spirit that we are acting,' he explained to the mission board, 'but to rescue China from the greater perils in store for her if such proceedings are not stopped. Mob violence has been chronic with her for forty years; it is growing and becoming one of the chief features of her action towards all foreigners ... A money settlement only will not help us for future work. We must be respected and be treated as men if we are to be successful.' In the usual dichotomy, the women clothed their determination in softer words: 'We will return,' Sara Brackbill, the WMS educational worker wrote; 'no sacrifice is too great to be made that these dear people may be won to Christ.'

As a result of the Chengtu riots, the Protestants received an indemnity of 40 000 *taels* ($36 000) and the Roman Catholics, using the pretext of converts' houses destroyed, received 800 000 *taels*. Thirteen men were beheaded in the city square and forty more were beaten with the big bamboo stick. The governor was degraded and removed from office. In its annual report, the mission board called this settlement the 'greatest victory' of 'missionary diplomacy.' Even twenty years later, at a time when many missionaries were beginning to question the use of 'the gunpowder gospel,' Dr Kilborn looked back with satisfaction. 'And so we were driven out,' he wrote in *Our West China Mission*,

taking with us the clothes in which we stood – nothing else. But, to the chagrin of the officials, and the amazement of the common people, the former were obliged to pay in good money for our lost property, and the latter saw us return in less than a year, to replace and rebuild on a larger and better scale

Dr Virgil Hart and staff of the Canadian Mission Press in Kiating, c. 1895

than before ... Foreigners were no longer despised; on the contrary we were respected and even feared.

The Canadians began rebuilding with a vengeance. Within a year of their return, they had under construction, in Chengtu alone: a church (called First Methodist) and a chapel; two boys' schools, one with a dormitory for ten boarders; a twelve-room hospital with waiting rooms, chapel, and in-patient wards; a girls' school and orphanage; a women's hospital; and missionary residences in three centres in the city.

With such expenditures, the church at home was becoming alarmed that the bills were some $30 000 in excess of the indemnity. In addition, a Miss Crossthwaite of the China Inland Mission was touring the Methodist churches of Ontario stating that the CIM could support two missionaries on the salary the Methodists paid for one. 'Our brethren in China are excellent men,' wrote Dr Sutherland to Dr Hart, 'and we have the utmost confidence in them, but in their eagerness to have what our friend Dr. [C.S.] Eby [head of the Japan mission] calls sufficient "plant" they may incur expenditure beyond what the indemnity fund, with other claims upon it, can bear.' In particular, medical supplies 'savoured of *downright extravagance,*' he concluded in a later letter: 'medicines must be used far more freely among the Chinese than among people in this city.'

The twenty-five recruits the mission asked for did not come before 1900; ten years after its founding the mission numbered (according to *Our West China Mission*) 'only twelve, or nineteen, including the Woman's Missionary Service.'

The period from 1895 to 1900 was one of constant upheaval in Szechuan. The missionaries learned to live through these 'days of confusion' as though they were normalcy itself. The doctors made their rounds in the hospital wards and tried to ignore the stage-whispered gossip. The WMS women continued to fuss over the children in the Jennie Ford Orphanage, and the neighbourhood women still came for demonstrations of the sewing machine. But in 1900, they stopped coming altogether.

4 · Foreign Devils

'At present the field is clear for Anglo-Saxon suprem-
acy ... But there are perils in the way, the chief of
which spring from its own nature. Its methods of
aggrandizement rest upon the deification of force.
Fighting blood is in its veins ... In our language today
may be found more than half a hundred Anglo-Saxon
words which mean to give a flogging; such as beat,
baste, box, bruise, bleed, cuff, cut, cane, cudgel, clip,
carve, kill, rap, maul, hide, whip, strike, smite, switch,
smash, knock, thrash, and drub; they show what a
wealth of thought and feeling the Anglo-Saxon race
has lavished upon aggressive modes of life.'

Canadian Methodist Magazine, July 1896

To the older generation of 'old China hands,' one mission history stated,
'the year 1900 holds the same significance as does the flood in Old
Testament chronology ... All China missionary history dates before or
after 1900.' In that hot, horrifying summer, the Society of Harmonious
Fists, known as the Boxers, came screaming out of the villages of the
North China plain, twirling their broadswords and chanting, 'Burn, burn,
burn. Kill, kill, kill.' All over China the structures of Christendom came
tumbling down: chapels, cathedrals, orphanages, hospitals, schools,
residences, and summer resorts. Two hundred and forty missionaries
and fifty of their children perished in the conflagration. Some thirty
thousand 'secondary devils' – Chinese converts – were martyred.

By 1900 the foreign community in China had grown rich and arrogant.

Staff of the Chungking hospital, c. 1909

From the first five treaty ports of the 1840s, it had grown to encompass the whole country. It owned property in almost every major city, sometimes even whole cities, like the French and International concessions of Shanghai, Hankow, and Canton. Foreign nationals – English and American, French, Dutch, Spanish, German, and, the largest group, Japanese – swaggered through the treaty ports secure in the knowledge that they could commit no crime under Chinese law. If a drunken sailor killed a prostitute or his captain set fire to a trading junk, he was protected by extraterritoriality, 'extrality' for short. It was, in the words of one historian, 'a glittering life, all things considered.'

In this class-ridden, closed colonial society, the lives of the foreign residents took on the texture of a Kipling novel. J.O.P. Bland, a British journalist living in Peking, described in his diary an incident, when out duck hunting, in which his companion 'blazed away at a bird with a Chinaman for background. Chinaman badly pickled ... I had a dollar which I at once gave him and quieted the crowd.' He was lucky; few people did carry cash; they had no need for it, since they paid for everything from a rickshaw ride to the servants' wages, with an omnipresent 'chit.' They spoke to 'the natives' in the brutish 'pidgin' (a corruption of the word 'business') Chinese of the 'missee go fetchee down topside' variety.

The Christian churches maintained an ambivalent attitude towards 'the vices of the scoundrel whites in the sea-ports of the Orient.' These people were, after all, their parishioners. In the larger centres, many missionaries were bound up with the 'Shanghai mentality' that regarded the world beyond their own enclave as a 'heathen colossus'; books like *Chinese Characteristics* only confirmed their suspicion. In the smaller centres, such as Chengtu, the missionaries had a more intimate relationship with the British authorities, playing soccer at the consulate with the sailor boys on leave, but though they tried, consciously, to bridge the gap between Chinese and foreigners, they, too, were often bewildered. 'We are placed in a country,' one woman missionary wrote, 'among a people, where the very atmosphere is vile, and the more we go among them the more we are forced to breathe corruption. It takes some time to realize ... we are losing moral tone. The daily sights and sounds to which we are exposed become familiar, and after a time we cease to be so shocked at what formerly would have made us blush for shame. Can you imagine it?'

This 'loss of moral tone' manifested itself in various ways. One 'gentle-spirited Norwegian' told a Canadian in Szechuan 'that after being out here for a few years he got into such a dulled spiritual condition that he would, on occasions, knock down or beat a Chinese.' Physical violence, mentioned often enough in mission literature to indicate it was not uncommon, was not the besetting sin of the missionaries. Rather their sin was pride, engendered from having too many people imploring them on bended knee, too many magistrates offering them 'peace and harmony banquets.'

The missionaries' pride was bolstered in 1899 when the Chinese government conferred official status on them, making a bishop or superintendent the equal of a provincial governor and ordinary men and women equivalent to a district magistrate. The Roman Catholics eagerly adopted the yellow hat button and closed sedan chair for the glory of Holy Mother Church. The Protestants, caught unawares, cast envious glances on these symbols – Dr Hart of West China wrote approvingly, 'What other government has bestowed such privileges upon ministers of the Gospel?' – but eventually turned them down for fear of confusing their message behind dragon robes and silken palanquins.

As it was, their message was already confused by their identification with the Western powers, an alliance one missionary called 'The Society for the Diffusion of Cannon Balls.' That man, Dr S. Wells Williams, dean of the American community, had been the translator for the American treaty that ended the Second Opium War in 1860, in which he had included specific clauses, called 'toleration articles,' legalizing Christianity and granting missions the right to own property inland. At the time he had strenuously defended the need to humble China; violence, he wrote, was 'almost necessary, for we shall get nothing important out of the Chinese unless we stand in a menacing attitude before them. They would grant nothing unless fear stimulated their sense of justice, for they are among the most craven of people, cruel and selfish as heathenism can make men, so we must be backed by force if we wish them to listen to reason.'

By 1900, there were about two thousand Protestant missionaries in China, as well as one thousand Roman Catholic priests and nuns. Canada was a junior member of the missionary force, numbering about 120 people. Sixty were in the China Inland Mission alone, scattered from Chefoo to the mountains of Kweichow and Yunnan. Twenty-three were in the North Honan mission, and nineteen in West China. In addition, six or eight were working under the (Anglican) Church Missionary Society in the southern coastal province of Fukien.

Lottie Brooks and the Reverend Howard J. Veals preaching in Chengtu, 1910s

In Nanking, the proud 'Southern Capital' 240 kilometres up the Yangtse from Shanghai, a small but influential group of Canadians had gathered in missions belonging to the Methodist Episcopal church, the Disciples of Christ and the Christian and Missionary Alliance (CMA). These three churches, all American, had attracted Canadians as the founders of their China missions. Nanking, once ranked with Honan and Hunan as bitterly anti-foreign – one Roman Catholic missionary noted that it was as if, 'loitering on the sombre and gigantic walls of the city was a host of bad angels ... crying lugubriously, "in vain, in vain!"' – was pioneered for the Protestants by Dr and Mrs Hart in 1886. By 1900, their boys' school had grown into the nucleus of the University of Nanking, under Dr Hart's successor, a scholarly twenty-two-year-old from Napanee, Ontario, named John Calvin Ferguson (a relative of an Ontario premier, G. Howard Ferguson), who was then at the beginning of a brilliant career; he became president of Nanking University, and an advisor to the Manchu government and, later, to Chiang Kai-shek. In addition, he became one of the western experts on Chinese art, acting as agent for such institutions as the Metropolitan Museum of Art in New York.

Dr Ferguson's counterpart in the Nanking Medical College was Dr

William Macklin, of London, Ontario, who was the first representative of the Disciples of Christ missions in 1886. He came to some prominence among the reformers at the Manchu court (along with Timothy Richard of the Christian Literature Society, the renamed Society for the Diffusion of Christian Knowledge) for his translation of Henry George's single-minded apologia for 'the single tax,' *Progress and Poverty*. (This 'hundred days of reform' was suppressed by the empress dowager, and the young emperor was imprisoned until his death ten years later, in 1908.) The Christian and Missionary Alliance was itself founded by a Canadian, Dr Albert Benjamin Simpson, who was born in Prince Edward Island and raised near Chatham, Ontario. The CMA mission was founded in 1888. Its first representative, Dr William Cassidy, a Toronto school superintendent, died en route to China, from smallpox contracted because he had insisted on travelling steerage; but his widow continued on with her two small daughters. She later married a well-known minister from Nova Scotia, Z. Charles Beals, author of *China and the Boxers*, and together they founded a missionary dynasty.

Many missionaries were not content to remain in the big cities, feeling themselves instead 'called to be pioneers.' To use one of their own metaphors, they could not reap in joy where they had not sown in tears. Some were angry, God-driven men, but others, mainly women, pushed beyond the pale with gentleness. The story of one of these, Dr Susie Carson Rijnhart, founder of the Disciples of Christ mission to Tibet, is representative of the nineteenth-century missionary enterprise: so much love, so much sacrifice, so few results.

Born in 1865 in Strathroy, Ontario, a small town near Chatham, Susie Carson never wavered from her childhood decision to become a medical missionary, and in 1893 she married Petrus Rijnhart, a headstrong Dutchman who had been 'summarily dismissed' from the China Inland Mission and was now working in a Toronto factory. One week after their marriage they sailed for Tibet, the 'last stronghold of the wicked one.' After a six-month journey across China by river steamer and overland cart, they reached the far north-western city of Lanchow [LANZHOU], the jumping-off point for central Asia and the silk routes across the Gobi desert. Pausing briefly, they moved to Lusar, the first mud-brick town in Outer Tibet, where they became friends with Mina Fuyeh, a Living Buddha, whose residence, the golden-roofed Kumbum monastery, dominated the town. Although he told the Rijnharts he was 'charmed' by the gospel story, he found no need to convert; in fact, Dr Susie does not mention one convert made in four years in Tibet.

In the spring of 1898, the Rijnharts set out with their one-year-old son on the trip that had been their objective since the beginning, across 'the wilds which no man knows,' over the mountains to Lhasa. Taking enough supplies for two years, six hundred *catties* of barley (360 kilograms) and three hundred *catties* of rice, they set out with sixteen pack ponies, five horses, and three guides, followed by their dog, Topsy. Leaving the cultivated fields behind, they soon came to the 'uninhabited districts' where for days at a time they would climb through mountain passes with names like Buddha's Cauldron, perpetually shrouded with fog and littered with bodies of yaks that had fallen to their deaths.

Their guides deserted them, taking the horses and supplies, and their son died during a nocturnal snowstorm. They buried him in a drug box lined with towels and covered his grave with boulders to protect it from the wolves. Miraculously they managed to reach the southern caravan route from Chengtu to Lhasa, where the local nomad chief implored them not to journey any further or he himself would be killed. So, turning away from Lhasa, without tents and with few supplies, the Rijnharts once more entered uninhabited territory on their way to Chengtu, Szechuan.

Sighting a nomad encampment across the river, Petrus told Susie to wait while he went to get help. For three days she waited where she was, her revolver in her lap, 'alone with God.' Although the nomads denied seeing her husband, they helped her push on to the next town, where she was put in the custody of new guides, 'truly wicked men' who tried to rob her of her last possessions, her revolver and telescope. Finally she reached the CIM station at Tachienlu [DAJIANLU] two months after Petrus had disappeared; she was so covered with mud that the English could not tell whether she was Tibetan or European.

In May 1900, in broken health and with no news of her husband after a year, Dr Rijnhart left China. In Toronto, where she became a minor celebrity, she said in her quiet, earnest way, 'It was my husband's burning ambition to be of service to Tibet, whether by his life or his death he said it did not matter.' As a memorial she wrote *With the Tibetans in Tent and Temple*, one of the more interesting Canadian travel books. She herself returned to Tibet escorting two new Disciples, where she married James Moyes, the CIM man who had greeted her at Tachienlu. Her health was precarious, and in 1908 they returned home to Chatham, where she died two months later at the age of forty-three, possibly in childbirth. (Moyes's application to join the West China mission mentions a three-month-old son: the mission turned him down because of his lack of formal education.)

In 1899 when the news of Petrus's disappearance had first reached Toronto, the *Canadian Methodist Magazine* echoed the thought of many in the denominational missions: 'It would, in our judgement, have been much wiser to have gone out under some Missionary Society, which can exercise direction, oversight, and some degree of protection, than in this free-lance style ... Our own missionaries in the disturbed Province of Sz-chuen [sic] are not without serious peril, but they are also laying the foundations of a great and successful mission by which the highlands of Tibet may be successfully entered.'

Within two months of Susie Rijnhart's departure from Chengtu in May 1900, the West China mission itself was being evacuated downriver, for the second time in five years. The Methodists, however, were travelling under the escort of British gunboats.

Attempting to understand the history of Christianity in China without considering the Chinese reaction is, as Professor Margo Gewurtz of York University has pointed out, like listening to a conversation of the deaf and dumb. A dialogue with heathenism would, of course, have been impossible to these early missionaries. Locked inside their compounds, terrified by mobs and firecrackers, affronted by idols and 'heathen ceremonials,' most missionaries had little inkling of how their word spread beyond their walls. Thus, when the Chinese people rose up against the foreigners, the missionaries saw no pattern behind seemingly unrelated incidents.

In his study of American perceptions of Asia, *Scratches on Our Minds*, Harold Isaacs called the period between the opium wars and the Boxer revolt the 'Age of Contempt.' The missionaries had no background either in Chinese studies or comparative religions. In fact, all they knew before they arrived could be gleaned from Sunday School lithographs and performances of *The Mikado*. Now, to say that the Holy Land at the time of Christ barely resembled Honan or Kiangsi in 1888 is to state a truism; but when the missionaries' sense of history was shaped by the Bible, naturally their perceptions of present day China became blurred. In their cosmology, they could only compare 'the heathen colossus' to Babylon and Gomorrah; they accepted implicitly St Paul's dictum that God gave the ungodly

over to a reprobate mind, to do those things which are not convenient; being filled with all unrighteousness, fornication, wickedness, covetousness, malicious-ness; full of envy, murder, debate, deceit, malignity; whispers, backbiters, haters of God, despiteful, proud, boasters, inventors of evil things, disobedient to parents, without understanding, covenant breakers, without natural affection, implacable, unmerciful.

'By grace are ye saved through faith,' St Paul wrote later in his Epistle to the Romans, and again, 'faith cometh by hearing, and hearing by the word of God.' What did it matter to the missionaries what an individual had done before his or her conversion? All alike were sinners, and in faith alone was the power to transform lives. Thus, once they had passed a probationary period of one or two years to show their 'newness of life,' ex-opium sellers, ex-opium addicts, ex-criminals of all sorts – even murderers – were allowed to become church members. The most contentious and painful church policy was one refusing admission to men who had more than one wife – although their wives could be accepted. By sending one of his wives back to her family, the husband was condemning her to a life of shame.

The conversion of these 'brands from the burning' was often sudden and dramatic, like St Paul's subjection to a blinding light on the road to Damascus. Jonathan Goforth recorded the 'humbling' conversion of one man, a 'proud' Confucian scholar, in his *Miracle Lives of China*. Mr Shen, the head of the county information bureau, had been invited for dinner and discussion. 'When dinner was ended I opened my Bible and commenced to talk with them,' Goforth wrote. Mr Shen challenged him, 'saying that he had read John Stuart Mill, Darwin, and others, and that he did not believe there was any God, nor heaven nor hell, but that this life ended all.' With constant reference to the printed word, Goforth explained how the solar system was no more governed by chance than the railway from Peking. Then, moving on to *The Wonders of Prophecy*, he showed how Ezekiel had prophesied the destruction of Tyre hundreds of years before it happened. Looking up with tears in his eyes, Mr Shen said, 'I believe there is a God.' Banging his hand down on the table, he said, 'No other book in the world is going to save China but this book.' Within a year, Mr Shen was responsible for the conversion of twenty other scholars in his district.

Conversion of a scholar or other member of the gentry was rare in this early period, but the churches were strangely democratic institutions, attracting people from all classes, from rich peasants down to rural poor and, in the cities, from merchants to such outcasts as barbers, butchers, and actors. Even women were encouraged to join: many men were persuaded to postpone their baptism until they could join the church with their family group. (Missionary work was strictly segregated and continued to be until well into the twentieth century. The women missionaries worked exclusively with the Chinese women and children. This was symbolized by the partition – sometimes a curtain – down the aisle of the church sanctuary that separated the women and children from the men.)

It would be a mistake to characterize all converts as 'rice Christians.' Mission literature is filled with stories of individual heroism, of one convert standing up to his or her mother, wife, husband, family, and, in certain extraordinary cases, whole village. Not surprisingly, many of these people seem to have been on a spiritual quest long before their conversion – going against the general apathy of the Chinese towards religious questions – and to have embraced such divergent paths as Buddhist vegetarianism, Taoist pilgrimages, and Confucian secret societies. Some had been employed as idol makers or story tellers – which necessitated a change of vocation – and all had images, ancestral tablets, and household shrines in their homes. Many had been anti-foreign, and were thus reversing their attitude by following the foreigners' way. There was considerable movement between the Roman Catholic church, known as the Lord of Heaven Religion, and the various Protestant denominations, known collectively as the Glad Tidings Religion, especially in the outlying areas where missionary visits were infrequent.

Having convinced themselves that they were living in an apostolic era, the missionaries passed on to their converts the conviction that they too were part of this divine drama. This was not as difficult as one might think and accounts, in large measure, for an apocalyptic strain in Chinese Christianity, a concern for the ecstatic and the miraculous. Even a humble convert could claim that Jesus appeared to her in a dream, clothed in white raiment, saying, 'Why do you not go to worship?' Local preachers would stage contests with the Taoist priests to call down rain on the parched soil.

When Hung Siu-ch'uan [HONG XIUQUAN] first appeared in the late 1840s as leader of a Christian rebellion, called the Taipings, the Kingdom of Heavenly Peace, many missionaries (including W.C. Burns) welcomed him. Later, when he went too far, calling himself the messiah, the brother of Jesus Christ, they turned against him, joining the Chinese government and the British Victorious Army under General Gordon to exterminate every trace of his heresy.

Hung was outstanding for his extremism and his rebelliousness, but his character traits and methods were shared in a muted form by many other preachers. Outstanding among them, for example, was Pastor Hsi, the China Inland Mission's earliest convert in Shansi [SHANXI]. Like Hung and Mr Shen, Pastor Hsi Shengmo was a Confucian scholar. Before his conversion in 1879 he had been an opium seller and was known for his hatred of foreigners. Afterwards, he retained this suspicion of missionaries, not only refusing to co-operate with them, but actually banning them from his area. He learned everything about their religion from books. Calling himself 'overcomer of demons,' he became particularly adept at casting out devils in true biblical fashion and at faith healing. Using this power and a supply of 'anti-opium pills' from the foreigners, and financing his endeavours by the sale of his wife's jewels, he opened an opium refuge in his home town. Opium was so prevalent in that area that, 'according to common report, eleven out of every ten smoked opium!' Within ten years, once he had obtained the recipe for the anti-opium pills, Hsi had a lucrative business going, running forty-five opium refuges in four provinces, including North Honan. He operated them like utopian communities, called them Middle (i.e., Chinese) Eden, and laid down stringent schedules for the inmates (women and children included), consisting of hymn singing, agricultural labour in his fields, and domestic cleanliness. Hsi became so revered that his followers started to call him Living Jesus, a practice he discouraged, at least publicly.

The missionaries could keep a rein on their army of colporteurs and Bible women and preachers; they could supervise the education of these associates and correct them when they mixed up the Bible stories. They could even control people like Pastor Hsi, at a distance. But they had no control over their message once it went beyond their street-corner preaching into the minds of the Chinese people. 'I heard only yesterday of two men who had taken in $1000 by selling tickets of membership to the Methodist Church at $1 each,' wrote Gertrude Howe from West China in 1899. 'No doubt one of these tickets is relied upon to secure its possessor against unnumbered ills, and neither the buyer nor seller knows or cares to know anything about the doctrines of the church to which admittance presumably has been purchased.' Nevertheless, she concluded, 'in secret places, the leaven is yet working ... until the whole be leavened.'

There was a deep anti-Christian folk tradition among the Chinese that can be traced back three hundred years to the seventeenth century and the days of the early Jesuits. The missionaries experienced only the tip of the iceberg when a cry of 'Kill the foreign devil' would whip a peaceful crowd into 'a wild, shrieking, gesticulating mob.' 'We got so used to being pelted with mud and gravel and bits of broken pottery that things seemed strange if we escaped the regular dose,' wrote one pioneer. 'We went out from our homes bedewed with the tears and benedictions of dear ones, and we came back plastered over, metaphorically speaking, with curses and objurgations from top to bottom.' It would be an exaggeration to say that missionaries were spat upon every time they went outside their courtyards, but they *were* always under suspicion, and one spark could set off a conflagration.

Peering through the compound gates, catching a piece of printed scripture, the Chinese people engaged in their own one-sided conversation with Christianity. The Chinese traditionally have neither a concept of sin nor a word for it, equating it instead with crime. Thus, they stumbled over the basic concept of Christianity, since they had committed no crime, felt no guilt, and had no need to be saved. More confusing still were the multiplicity of Christian sects, which could not even agree on the same name for their god, and the complexity of doctrines and dogmas that were cloaked in such language as:

the body of Christ, the bride of Christ, the bride of the Lamb's wife, the general assembly and Church of the first born, the city of the living God, the family in heaven and earth, the golden candlestick, the habitation of God, the temple of God, the heavenly Jerusalem, the pillar and ground of truth, and many others.

As early as 1724, as a result of the so-called Chinese Rites controversy within the Catholic church and the pope's proscription of ancestor worship, the Yung-Cheng emperor had issued his *Sacred Edict* condemning Christianity as 'heterodox' and contrary to the Way of the Sages. (This edict became part of the compulsory canon for anyone writing the Confucian examination system and was taught in many Protestant mission schools until the system itself was abolished in 1905.) By the late nineteenth century, anti-Christian antipathy permeated all levels of society. The highest officials hated the missionaries because they were always bringing court cases, backed by the foreign consuls, demanding restitution when a convert was 'persecuted' by his neighbours. The local gentry and wealthy people hated them because they saw Christianity as a new and seditious secret society.

The common people, engaged in their own 'deaf and dumb conversation,' had a simple view: in the world of real people, humanity assumed one form, dark haired and dark eyed. These pale creatures with their red hair and foetid breath could be nothing less than ghosts, demons, hobgoblins – in short, 'foreign devils.' If the magistrate or trader knew that the foreigners were indeed corporeal beings, his superstitious wife and servants were not so certain.

The most persistent rumour about the missionaries, one that can be traced back to 1660, was that they plucked out the eyes of Chinese for use in alchemy and medicine. This strange tale had a logical if twisted origin from the Roman Catholic ritual of baptism *in articulo mortis* – at the point of death. From the Chinese point of view, the priest would perform magical incantations over a dying person, sprinkle him or her with holy water, and cover the face with a cloth. Then, while pretending to pray, he would secretly extract the eyes and replace them with a coin. Inevitably, during a riot, the grounds of the mission compound would be dug up to uncover the cemetery of the victims, and jars of preserved cherries would be paraded through the streets as evidence of stolen eyes.

Prior to one of these riots, the missionaries would notice that the local gentry would post placards on the city's walls in order to stir up the people. The most common of these placards, which the foreigners called 'Death Blow to Corrupt Doctrines,' appeared regularly all over China between 1860 and 1900. It was such a vile document, 'a farrago of obscene calumnies,' that the missionaries could never bring themselves to translate it in its entirety.

By a pun in Chinese, the Catholic name for God, *T'ien-chu* [TIAN-ZHU], 'Lord of Heaven,' became transformed into 'Pig of Heaven,' and 'God's religion' became 'the Pig's grunt.' In the first panel of the placard, beneath a picture of a crucified pig stuck with arrows, worshipped by piglet followers, 'Death Blow' tells the story of Jesus:

The heir apparent Jesus was the incarnation of the pig in heaven. He was very licentious by nature. Of all the wives and daughters of the high officials of the country of Judea there was not one who did not fall prey to his lust. Subsequently his licentiousness extended to the king's concubines and he schemed to usurp the throne. Therefore a high official memorialized, making known his crimes. He was bound upon a cross and fastened to it with red-hot nails. He emitted several loud cries, assumed the form of a pig, and died. Frequently, he entered people's homes, where he did unnatural things and engaged in illicit relations. As soon as a woman heard his pig's grunt her clothes would unfasten of themselves and she would let him satisfy his lust before coming to her senses. The followers of the pig therefore exhort people to worship him, making use of this as a pretext for satisfaction of their greed and lust.

But if crosses are chiselled into your doorsills and steps, the pig incarnate and his followers will be seized with fear and will not approach ...

Their dog-fart [i.e., nonsense] magical books stink like dung. They slander the sages and worthy ones and revile the Taoist immortals and Buddhas. All within the four seas and nine provinces hate them intensely.

No wonder women and children screamed when missionaries appeared in the village marketplace. No wonder the people flocked to the Boxer cause.

In the drought year of 1899 gangs of teenaged boys had first appeared in the dusty villages of Shantung, proclaiming themselves invincible against foreign bullets. Gesturing wildly, scarlet sashes trailing in the air, they put on an effective show, even according to British observers. Their message was summed up by the four golden characters inscribed on their turbans: Protect the pure, exterminate the foreign. If China could regain the mandate of heaven, then the parched fields would bloom, and the children would have food.

At first, the Boxers had been a rebellion directed against the 'foreign,' i.e., Manchu, dynasty. But the crafty empress dowager wooed them to her side and hitched her dynastic star to their cause. In the name of the imprisoned boy emperor, she declared war on Great Britain, the United States, France, Germany, Italy, Austria, Belgium, Holland, and Japan. 'For forty years,' she said, 'I have lain on brushwood and eaten bitterness because of them.' Now, in an edict issued to the governors of every province, she stated: 'The foreigners must be killed.'

The most spectacular episode of the Boxer year was the siege of the foreign legations in Peking, an episode that entered the annals of colonial heroism alongside the Indian Mutiny and the Siege of Khartoum. Inside the legations and in the Northern Cathedral where the French bishop sheltered four thousand people, life was grim for two months of unremitting warfare. The women (including, it seems, two from Toronto, Miss Hattie Rutherford and a Miss Gowans) scurried about the rubble as angels of mercy, carrying sandbags and tending the wounded. The male missionaries, the backbone of the committees, manned the barricades, shooting at anything that moved.

The Peking siege thrilled the world's imagination; the slaughter in the provinces of China horrified and sickened it. Fortunately only two governors obeyed the Empress's edict before one courageous man changed it to read, 'The foreigners must not be killed' – but in Shansi and Hopeh [HEBEI], the two provinces closest to Peking, the death toll rose with each passing day. Of the 300 foreigners killed, 243 were missionaries – 136 Protestant adults, 53 children, and 54 Catholic priests and nuns. They were hunted down like wild animals, burnt alive, shot, disembowelled, and beheaded. Their heads were hung in triumph from the city walls.

The China Inland Mission, which had boasted that in thirty-three years not one of its people had died by violence, had eighty-nine adults in Shansi. Forty-six died. One group of twenty was brought into the governor's *yamen* and ritualistically beheaded in his presence. 'I was very restless and excited while there seemed a chance of life,' wrote one American woman in a letter found after her death, 'but God has taken away that feeling, and now I just pray for grace to meet the terrible end bravely.' A young Englishman wrote, 'I am like the ox, ready for either – the plough or the altar.' 'The less of time, the more of heaven,' they encouraged each other. 'The briefer life, earlier immortality.' Even little children rose to their preordained role in the great drama. Five-year-old Kennie McConnell was heard to rebuke his killers, '*Papa puh chuen siao Kennie*. Papa does not allow you to kill little Kennie.'

It was through providence that only three Canadians were in Shansi. CIM missionary Alec Saunders, an old friend of Jonathan Goforth, suffered forty-nine days of 'wandering in deserts and mountains and caves and holes of the earth' in what he described as 'a thousand miles of miracles.' The other two, William Peat of the Hamilton YMCA and Margaret Smith of New Hamburg, both died violently.

The venom spread beyond Shansi to engulf the Presbyterian mission in neighbouring North Honan, and the story of the Presbyterians' escape is typical of what many people in North China had to go through during those terrible months. At the beginning of the year, the people had dismissed the Boxer uprising as a cloud no bigger than a man's hand, even though the province had been 'in a state of great unrest' for several years. When a telegram came from the British consul in Tientsin in July warning them to flee for their lives, they hesitated for another two weeks, 'with little sleep and much prayer,' until events turned so nasty that the largest party handed over the mission keys to the magistrate and took flight. A second party, numbering thirty-seven people, included a group of British engineers from the nearby coal mines and their armed guard of four horsemen and eight soldiers. This procession of thirty carts trying to pass inconspicuously through 320 kilometres of hostile territory 'greatly increased our danger,' the missionaries charged later.

One baking hot morning, as Jonathan Goforth led his group from the inn, the streets of the village were a solid mass of people, 'ominously quiet.' As soon as the foreigners' carts entered the crowd, Goforth became the target for the onslaught; his pith helmet was slashed to ribbons and 'it was a miracle that the skull was not cleft in two.' Dr Percy Leslie, the youngest and strongest man in the mission, received 'fifteen wounds, great and small,' one of which practically severed his right hand. Mrs Cheng, Goforth's nurse, showed great heroism by throwing herself over the baby and taking the blows on her own back.

Goforth managed to crawl to the next village, where all day he lay deathlike in an airless mud hut. Dr Leslie, lying on a plank door, spent 'a day of great suffering by the roadside.' The next day they were taken into an inn so crowded that 'falling rain could not reach the ground'; all except Dr Leslie, but including the children, were lined up 'shoulder to shoulder on the narrow veranda. Till darkness dispersed them, we remained facing that great seething mob.' Leaving that city in 'the dead of a very dark night,' they managed to avoid the men lying in ambush and reached the main party who had gone on ahead. Once they crossed the Yellow River into South Honan, where the officials were less bloodthirsty, the trip became safer, though still excruciatingly painful. One month after they left their stations they arrived in Hankow.

By August every mission station in China had been evacuated, even those in the south and the west that were never in any danger. Three thousand foreigners huddled in the ports of Shanghai and Hankow. 'There is no use talking settlement,' one woman missionary wrote, 'until we have the heads of Prince Tuan and the Empress Dowager.' If regicide was too strong, then China should be forced to move its capital to a more accessible centre so that Peking, the symbol of infamy, could be levelled like ancient Carthage and the ground strewed with salt.

In retaliation for the 'unprovoked' declaration of war, the Western powers sent their armies to hack their way to Peking, where they indulged in a fury that made the 'looting' of Canton sixty years before seem like child's play. A boy from Brantford who had joined the American marines described the scene at Tientsin for his parents: 'You can't imagine what this city looks like ... Dead Chinamen are lying around the streets, and every day the river receives a consignment of their bodies ... Pigtails are scattered all around in the streets like pieces of rope ... I would send a silk robe if I could put it in a letter, but as I can't you can keep this bit of ribbon as a souvenir of the fall of Tien Tsin.'

Once the armies reached Peking, all the imperial palaces, which had been deserted by the court, were looted. The empress dowager's bedroom became a urinal, and the Temple of Heaven, the holiest spot in the empire, an American horse stable. The British looting of the city was 'the most scientific': the ancestral tablets of the dynasty were taken to the British Museum, 'an act of more than justifiable reprisal,' A.H. Smith stated, 'for Chinese treatment of the foreign cemetery, and also perhaps the most stunning blow which the system of ancestor worship ever received.'

Outside the city, 'casual exploitation by arrogant detachments of foreign soldiers moving about a prostrate countryside' led, according to a captain in the British army, to 'robbery, assassinations, and nameless outrages ... numbers of innocent and peaceful non-combatants were slaughtered ... whole districts were ruthlessly and needlessly laid waste.'

The Western press could excuse these exploits, drape them with patriotic bunting, on the grounds that the soldiers were only doing what comes naturally. But when missionaries led looting expeditions, scepticism turned to cynicism at this 'gunpowder gospel.' Mark Twain, a well-known agnostic, caricatured the 'Blessings-of-Civilization Trust' run by muddle-headed romantics and money-grubbing opportunists. In particular he excoriated W.S. Ament of the American Board, who used his knowledge of Peking to loot the wealthiest mansions. Sir Robert Hart, Inspector-General of the Maritime Customs (and thus an employee of the Chinese government) defended Ament by saying that he had been 'set apart by the Legation authorities to take charge of whatever looted property was brought in for the use of the Legations – a tribute to his honesty and capacity.' Another missionary wrote an article entitled 'The Ethics of Looting.' (All in all, this weak defence sounds like what the historian Pat Barr described as 'the inattentive right hand.')

This criticism stung the churches. Indeed, many of the statements coming from China were embarrassing in their vindictiveness. In order to stem the criticism, the churches launched a campaign to publicize the uplifting side of China missions: the sacrifices of the missionaries, the trials of the converts, the beneficial effects of Western medicine. 'The Church has been stirred as never before in modern times,' wrote Luella Miner, a prominent American missionary, summing up the general attitude, 'and has heard in this record the call of God to more strenuous and devoted effort to redeem the lands thus purchased by blood and suffering.'

In his first public statement on landing in America, Dr Hart of West China cautioned that 'those who say the least now will be in a better position to talk later on.' The Methodist West China mission, which had been evacuated at great expense and little danger, discouraged its people in Canada from speaking out, at least until the beginning of 1901 when it became apparent that the Boxers were no longer a threat. Then, it published in great detail the death of 'our first martyr,' an itinerant Bible seller. When, on the return trip back to Szechuan, a daughter of Dr W.E. Smith was drowned, news of her death, too, was given wide circulation.

The Presbyterian Church in Canada, whose members had walked through the fiery furnace, was especially reluctant to let its missionaries speak, pleading that they needed rest after their ordeal. No doubt, after its experience with George Leslie Mackay, the Foreign Mission Committee was wary of letting people like Goforth loose. So, with a dozen eyewitnesses in Canada, the committee 'could think of nothing better,' according to the Reverend George Macdougall, a former Honan missionary, 'than to send them at once to isolated places [in British Columbia as substitute ministers] to keep the Church at large from seeing or hearing them.' But the congregations were pressuring the committee to send out deputations on speaking tours of the country. Macdougall implored the committee to let the missionaries tell their story. 'There need not be anything sensational but the simple story of events and of what had been achieved, and of how the Chinese Christians had stood up to the test of tribulation would be enough.' The committee relented.

In a meeting in Toronto, Jonathan Goforth thrilled the audience, according to the *Toronto Daily Star* reporter who covered it, taking 'the ground that the terrible occurrences in China were in themselves an evidence of the deep impression that Western teaching had made upon the Chinese Empire.' But even so the reporter pointed out the discrepancy:

He made one statement that had an odd sound: 'All we require is that the powers shall give the governors and mandarins to understand that our work is sacred, and our persons sacred, and we ask no special favours whatsoever.' If missions are to be established by gun-boats and field-guns and the sacredness of the missionaries' person and work forced upon the recognition of rulers who are adverse to them, the heathen mind might regard these things as 'special favours,' and might be further confirmed in their erroneous belief that the missionaries are the political agents of the foreign powers that plant them by force in the Chinese provinces.

However, Mr. Goforth told a story of surpassing interest and made plain to his hearers the great charm the work has for all who are engaged in it.

A comment like that, with its sarcastic undercurrent, would not likely have appeared five years later when missions rose to become the foremost 'mission' of the churches.

PART 2
The Social Gospel
1901-1927

'Yes, China is awake! The great stream of reform is rapidly gaining force; it will soon be at the flood. No doubt there will be many wrecks, even some good boats will overturn in the eddies and rapids but the cesspools will be cleaned, the worthless, rotten crafts will be strewn as driftwood along the shore, soon to feed some industrious man's worthy fire, and in good time, the stream with its course cleared, will be able to continue in its strong, deep, useful way in peaceful plenty to the sea.'

Mrs Grace Smith of the West China mission on the occasion of the first football game in Chengtu, 1906

5·Loved Ones in the Homeland

'Little Builders all, are we, –
Building for eternity!
Children of the "Mission Bands,"
Working with our hearts and hands ...
Building in the Hindu land,
Where the idols are as sand;
And mid China's millions, too,
Living temples rise to view;
Building in Japan as well, –
Ah! What stories we could tell! ...
And, one day, our eyes shall see,
In glad eternity, –
"Living Stones" we helped to bring
For the palace of our King!'

M.A. West, 'The Little Builders,' 1882

Few people in the West are interested in China for its own sake, for the wisdom of its philosophy, the beauty of its art. It is too ineffably, incomprehensibly, 'Not Like Us.' By the same token, many *are* interested in China's relations with us, and in how deeply the sleeping dragon is roused by Western influences, be they opium or medical science. The missionary enterprise at once capitalized on this nascent interest and shaped it in its own image. The enterprise itself and the images it propounded were not static, but changed as China moved towards revolution and beyond. The underlying message was unchanging, however: the Chinese *were* like us; they, too, were hungering after

Meeting of the West Toronto Epworth League, 1906

righteousness, and when they became Christianized, even superficially, they would save China. The strange truth is that they did.

When the traditional Confucian educational system was abolished by the Imperial Chinese government in 1905, this created an overnight need for Western learning among the 'better classes.' Accordingly, mission work shifted its emphasis from merely 'preaching the word' to education. Christian missions could be all things to all people: they could educate China's children, heal its sick, care for its orphans, strengthen its leaders, reform its family life, clean out its cesspools, revitalize its economy, and introduce the latest agricultural methods. 'Yes, China is moving,' George Bond told his Canadian Methodist readers in his 1909 study book, *Our Share in China*. 'And it is for the Christian Churches of the West to direct the movement. Christian schools and universities in China itself, to Christianize this movement for western education and to train the eager minds of China's young people under Christian auspices and Christian influence, are of immeasurable strategic importance ... We may have young China under our influence in young China's most plastic and impressionable years, if we will not grudge the men or the money.'

By the beginning of the First World War, the international missionary enterprise was a proud ship sailing the oceans of the world, a well-oiled piece of machinery with many 'willing workers' fuelling the engines. Comparing this enterprise to modern multinational corporations, the American historian Valentin Rabe commented: 'The multimillion-dollar budgets and complex inter-relationships of this world-wide conglomerate were the characteristics less of a spontaneous movement than of a giant service industry.' But it was a corporation with a heart and a moral purpose that, though narrow and self-serving at times, could also be mobilized to alleviate a good deal of human suffering.

Perhaps as many as one-third of the older generation of missionaries who had fled the Boxers in 1900 never returned to China: Dr Hart retired from West China along with his wife and daughter, as did two of the four male doctors. Even those who did return to their stations soon started to pass away: George Leslie Mackay, for example, died in 1901, and Hudson Taylor in 1905. (Dr Hart died at the family farm near Burlington in 1904; Adelaide died ten years later.)

Despite this attrition, Protestant mission ranks grew steadily, from 2000 in 1900 to 3300 five years later; by the mid-1920s they had swelled to 8300. Up to the beginning of the First World War, most of these new missionaries continued to be British: in 1905, for example, 1800 missionaries or 55 per cent of the total force were British; there were 1300 Americans, and only 200 Continental Europeans, the majority of the latter Germans and Scandinavians. By 1919, the proportions of British and Americans were reversed, with 3300 Americans, (50 per cent) and 2200 British (33 per cent); 750 Europeans (17 per cent) made up the total. From that point onwards, Americans formed the majority of the mission force.

Within this phalanx, Canadians occupied a special place. The growth of (North) American missions in China is more astonishing when one realizes that almost one-quarter of British missionaries in 1919 (almost five hundred people) were in fact Canadians. Canada's contribution to the world missionary enterprise, like its contribution to the First World War, was larger than its share: it has been said that in proportion to their size and resources, the churches of Canada sponsored more missionaries than any other nation in Christendom.

During the nationalist fervour of the late 1890s, epitomized in the political realm by Prime Minister Sir Wilfrid Laurier and stirred up in part by Canadian participation in Queen Victoria's Diamond Jubilee, the idea was circulated in mission circles that Canada could be the 'linch-pin' of a new Anglo-American alliance whose 'high mission' was 'to give light and liberty, peace and good government, civilization and Christianity to all races of men.' One American missionary bishop wrote to his Canadian colleagues that, 'looking at you out of straight, honest American eyes, and talking out of a loyal American heart,' he looked 'for the time when the Stars and Stripes and the Union Jack, side by side, shall make every yard of water and every acre of land safe for prayer or for trade.'

As Canadian nationalism itself developed in the first years of this century, the churches refined their role, not just as a linch-pin but as independent fellow workers. At a conference of laymen billed as 'Canada's own missionary convention' and held in Toronto in 1909, the churches formulated a 'national missionary policy' that gave equal emphasis to home missions within Canada (a situation that other nations did not have to consider) and foreign work. Newton W. Rowell, the leading Methodist layman and future leader of the Ontario Liberal Party, warned the assembled delegates that God had blessed Canada with 'a large share of the world's wealth, all the material resources necessary to accomplish the task of world evangelism, and their own salvation depends on its right use.' He concluded that, in the same manner 'as the Roman was called to teach the world law, the Greek to teach the world art, the Hebrew to teach the world religion, so we in Canada, if true to our opportunities, may be called to lead the world in the work of world-wide evangelization.'

The task the laymen took upon themselves was truly awesome: they assumed on behalf of the Canadian Protestant churches the responsibility for the evangelization of forty million people throughout the world – five times the population of Canada. 'The attractiveness of mission work,' explained James Shenstone, treasurer of the Massey-Harris Company, 'to world-conquering businessmen should be its far-reaching, its courageous, its gigantic plans ... The world needs winning, and we men need a world to win ... We are big enough for the biggest thing that God intends us to do.'

By 1919, according to *Canada's Share in World Tasks*, an interdenominational mission study book, the five main denominations of Canada – Methodist, Presbyterian, Anglican, Baptist, and Congregationalist – supported directly in their own connexional missions overseas 768 missionaries in ten countries and each year raised a combined $2 million for their support. China was by far the largest field, outstripping even the Canadian North and West. Since the Baptists and Congregationalists had no missions in China, the 321 Methodist, Presbyterian, and Anglican missionaries represented one-half of the missionaries of their respective denominations. The West China mission alone had more than 200 members. These three denominations co-operated in two universities in China, and operated on their own 270 schools and thirty hospitals; they owned property at twenty stations and hundreds of outstations.

In a sense, Canadian missions did become a link between British and American interests, at least to the extent of explaining each group to the other. There were some 175 mission organizations in China at the time, 82 of them American and 32 British, with overlapping denominational and national groupings. The 18 Lutheran missions, for example, represented seven countries, the 12 Presbyterian missions, six. (England, Scotland, Ireland, New Zealand, the United States, and Canada). Canadian missions not only co-operated along these denominational lines, but also through a wide variety of international and interdenominational channels, including the YMCA, the Student Volunteer Movement, the Christian Literature Society, the Canadian School of Missions, and the Associated Boards of Foreign Missions of the United States and Canada.

A majority of the Canadian missionaries who went out under these denominational missions were truly 'this generation,' born at the same time as the missionary movement. They brought a deeper meaning to the slogan 'The evangelization of the world.' No longer did it merely mean that every person would hear the Gospel. It meant, stated the *Missionary Outlook* in 1907, that 'the Church of Christ will have super-seded old forms, the passing away of "old things" and the making of all things new. Idolatry, superstition and all forms of heathenism will have become matters of history alone.' Rejecting the 'grim doctrine of an endless hell for the unreclaimed heathen,' this new theology – which its proponents called 'the social gospel' and its opponents called 'modernism' – sought a Christianizing of society through its institutions and government structures. The social gospel 'rested on the premise that Christianity was a social religion, concerned, when the misunder-standing of the ages was stripped away, with the quality of human relations on this earth. Put in more dramatic terms, it was a call for men to find the meaning of their lives in seeking to realize the Kingdom of God in the very fabric of society.'

Richard Allen, a Canadian historian who has written extensively on the social gospel, pointed out in *The Social Passion* how

the earthbound movements of the disinherited and those who rose to champion them might, in their rough struggle for justice, express some of the profoundest religious yearnings of man, while the hallowed institutions of religion might behave in ways that were not simply unbecoming but worldly and damning. The sacred might be very secular, and the secular sacred. All alike shared in the social guilt of an imperfect world, and the way from death to life, from the present social order to the Kingdom of God, lay through awakening the 'social consciousness' and harnessing oneself to the social problem with the yoke of social self-concern.

The Reverend Samuel D. Chown, General Superintendent of the Meth-odist church, called the social gospel 'the voice of prophecy in our time.' The Reverend Charles J.P. Jolliffe echoed this when he closed his autobiographical notes with the exhortation 'Long Live the Social Gospel.'

Not all of these recruits were social gospellers, but even those who were not tended to be team workers chosen by the home boards on the criteria of likeability. 'Can you cheerfully acquiesce in the decision of the majority?' asked the Methodist application forms. Karen Minden, in her doctoral thesis on medical workers in West China, concluded from the letters of reference attached to their applications that they were 'solid' people – a resonant term – amiable and adaptable in personality, 'calm, cheerful, kind, devoted, genial, co-operative, popular, "all-round," well-liked and respected.'

These liberal denominational missions were only part of the story, however. Debate within the churches at home and in the missions overseas was often acrimonious between the social gospellers and the evangelicals who felt that the original purpose of missions, the salvation of individuals, was being discarded in favour of the larger vision of Christianizing society. The churches themselves, as well as the missions, usually went towards the social gospel, but many people within them co-operated in an alternate structure of evangelical ventures. These ventures attracted a diverse range of evangelical Anglicans, Methodists, and Presbyterians, as well as traditionally conservative groups like the Baptists, Brethren, and Free Church adherents. Even the Pentecostal movement in its beginnings was interdenominational. Support for these evangelical organizations did not preclude support for one's own denomination: David Yuile, a wealthy Montreal businessman, endowed one whole station of the Presbyterian mission as well as sponsoring his niece, Margaret King, in the China Inland Mission because she found her own Presbyterian mission too liberal. Similarly, S.H. Blake, the leading Anglican layman, and T.R. O'Meara, principal of Wycliffe College, as well as the Presbyterian R.P. Mackay, sat on the boards of the CIM and of the Toronto Bible College.

Because these evangelical efforts were often small and fragmented, like the independent People's Church in Toronto, they formed a complex network. The Christian and Missionary Alliance typified this complexity. Founded in 1887 by Dr Albert Benjamin Simpson, a Canadian Presbyterian minister who had been consecrated to God by John Geddie (the pioneer missionary to the New Hebrides), the CMA was an interdenominational alliance based in the United States. From the beginning it attracted a significant Canadian following and sent out Canadians as pioneers of its China missions in 1888. The CMA never became a denomination, even though it built churches and congregations from Ontario to British Columbia. Much later, in the 1940s, its most famous evangelist was Charles Templeton, Canada's answer to Billy Graham.

In the China field, the China Inland Mission focused much of this evangelical interest (as did the Sudan Interior Mission for Africa and the Evangelical Union of South America for South America). Until the mid-1910s, when the West China mission experienced an extraordinary growth, the CIM remained the largest Canadian mission. It was the great colossus to which other missions had to react, either positively or negatively: the controversy in the 1890s in both the Presbyterian and Methodist churches over the rate of mission salaries was but one example. This sort of criticism continued in the form of questions about the wisdom of the denominational missions' expansion into institutional work after 1905.

It is difficult to estimate exactly the Canadian presence within the CIM because, once in the field, the Canadians melded into what was basically a British colonial mission. As part of his expansion into North America in 1888, Hudson Taylor also expanded into Australia, New Zealand, and Continental Europe, where he accepted as associate missions eleven Lutheran and Free Church groups from Sweden, Norway, Finland, and Germany. Its associate missions made the CIM consistently the largest mission in China; it grew, slowly, from 800 missionaries in 1900 to 1200 in 1927. Canadians predominated in the North American groups in the early years, but this changed after 1904, when the mission's headquarters moved from Toronto to Philadelphia. On average, Canadians made up about 10 per cent of the CIM proper, somewhat less if the associates were included: 60 Canadians out of 672 CIM and 153 associates in 1905; 103 Canadians out of 765 CIM and 368 associates in 1925. Americans varied from 10 per cent at the beginning of the century to 20 by the 1930s. These figures do not include spouses of Canadians, British citizens who had taken on Canadian citizenship during their careers, or the considerable number who retired to Canada because their China-born children emigrated to Toronto rather than to England. Because they were not stationed together as an identifiable group, a considerable number of Canadians married their station mates from Australia (one Australian man in Kweichow had three Canadian wives), Great Britain, South Africa, the United States, Poland, and Holland.

The story of Canadian missions to China becomes even more complex with the establishment of Canadian Roman Catholic missions, although by 1919 these represented but a handful of pioneers. The Canadian Roman Catholic missionary enterprise started later, in the 1920s and 1930s, but the two strands of Canadian Catholicism were evident in China from early in the century. The first North American Catholic missionaries to China were two French-Canadian Franciscan Sisters of Mary who went out in 1902, followed a few months later by Father John Mary Fraser, the first priest. (The first American missionaries, from the Maryknoll Missionary Society, did not go out until 1911.) By 1919, Father Fraser had returned to Canada to found the Almonte Foreign

Mission Society, which shortly after moved to a suburb of Toronto and was renamed the Scarboro Foreign Mission Society, the only English-Canadian mission board.

Canadian Protestant missionaries in China represented all regions of the country, from British Columbia to Nova Scotia – and extended their influence beyond these borders to Newfoundland. Each of these areas contributed a different aspect of the national character. The Presbyterians had a rich recruiting ground in the old Scottish areas of Nova Scotia, around Halifax and in Pictou County, on the south shore of the Northumberland Strait; the seafaring expertise of the east coast missionaries was put to good use in the seaports of Canton and Hamheung, North Korea. The North Honan mission was staffed mostly by people from the Eastern Townships of Quebec – from Montreal south-east to Coaticook near the Vermont border, and westward to Valleyfield and Ormstown – and from the younger (post-1840) settlements around the Huron tract of south-western Ontario – from Guelph to the Bruce Peninsula, and down to London and Zorra Township. The mission attracted several prominent missionaries from Montreal, among them Mrs Percy Leslie, daughter of the Ogilvy department-store family, and Dr Ferguson Fitten Carr-Harris. The only major Scottish area not represented was the conservative (and mainly non-Free Church) Glengarry settlement of eastern Ontario; even so, it did provide several missionaries to the China Inland Mission.

The Methodist church, too, recruited widely both in the Maritimes and, especially, in southern Ontario. Ontario-born Methodist missionaries in China came from several broad areas: the triangle of eastern Ontario extending from Cornwall to Ottawa to around the Belleville – Bay of Quinte area up to Peterborough; and the whole area west of Toronto. (Considering the preponderance of Ontario people in the West China mission, it is hardly surprising that the given names of Wesley and Egerton Ryerson were quite common.) Right up to the 1920s, south-western Ontario continued to be by far the most fruitful recruiting area for foreign missionaries; recruiting groups included the Anglican Diocese of Huron, the Disciples of Christ, the Christian and Missionary Alliance, and the CIM. Many of the increasingly numerous (after 1900) contingent from western Canada were often transplanted Ontarians who had served their probationary ministry in Saskatchewan or Alberta; among these were James Endicott and the Jolliffe brothers. Others like Mrs Edith Sibley, daughter of prominent Winnipeg pioneer missionary,

J.M. Harrison, or Harriet Woodsworth, granddaughter of James Woodsworth ('The Apostle of Systematic Giving') and niece of James S. Woodsworth (the leader of the CCF), were only one generation removed from 'the old Ontario strand.'

Despite their geographic diversity, most of these missionaries shared a remarkably similar background. Most came from middle- and upper-middle-class rural or small-town families, 'farm homes of the best type' (like Dr Jeannie Dow) with libraries and magazine subscriptions to open up the minds of the children to the wider world. Although many did go on to college or university, further education was not automatic, and most worked their way through school. Most of the missionaries, too – it almost goes without saying – were of British stock; the celebration of the Queen's (Victoria's) Birthday was a patriotic event among Canadians overseas. There were, however, a few exceptions to this general pattern, among them, for example, Petrus Rijnhart (who was born in Holland) and a few Swedish Lutherans (or Norwegians like Chester Ronning) who were products of the Fransen revival in the United States. The most remarkable exception to the pattern was Dr Victoria Cheung, a Victoria-born Chinese woman who had been a ward of the Oriental Rescue Home and had gone on to graduate from University of Toronto Medical School. The churches tried to recruit Chinese Canadians for their China missions, and for a while there was a regular exchange of pastors, especially with South China, but Dr Cheung and the China-born Reverend Paul Kam of the Scarboro Fathers were the only Chinese employed as fully accredited missionaries by Canadian boards.

If the hinterland provided the personnel of the foreign missionary movement, much of its ambition, propaganda, and finances were supplied by Toronto. In the area one could describe as 'uptown Toronto' (bounded on the east by Sherbourne Street, on the north by Bloor and Dupont streets, on the west by Bathurst Street, and on the south by College and Carlton streets), there were, by the 1930s, some twenty-five missionary-sending institutions, organizations, societies, and training centres, as well as thirty churches, some of them the most missionary-minded of their respective denominations. The institutions clustered around the University of Toronto included the theological and deaconesss training colleges of the Methodists, Presbyterians, Anglicans, and Baptists, the interdenominational YMCA and YWCA, the Canadian School of Missions, the China Inland Mission on St George Street, and the Toronto Bible College up Spadina Road. The missionary churches included: Knox and Bloor Street Presbyterian; Trinity, Sherbourne Street, Central, Broadway Tabernacle, and Bathurst Street Methodist; St Paul's and the Church of the Messiah Anglican; Walmer Road Baptist, and Cecil Street Disciples of Christ.

Because of the physical proximity and the interdenominational co-operation of these Toronto missionary societies, the Protestant churches of Canada encouraged involvement in the missions program literally from the cradle to the grave – beginning with 'cradle roll' and ending with bequests in one's will. Missionary propaganda played on every emotional string, from the lofty and the practical to the maudlin. Long before they reached the age of reason, little children were told heart-rending tales of heathen children; even Canadian orphans in the Marchmount and Barnardo's homes were encouraged to save their pennies for China. Church women were given a somewhat more sophisticated version of the same stories, with emphasis on the horror of women forced into the seclusion of purdah. Church men were kept apprised of the missions' world-changing, business-like practicality; one oft-quoted statistic was that the cost of Christianizing the Sandwich Islands (Hawaii) would be more than repaid from the profits of one year's trade a generation later. For the young people, and indeed for the whole church, missionaries were a shining example of people 'living for God and doing something.'

Yet, despite the young people's movement and the laymen's movement, the notion persists that missions were 'women's work,' supported by 'the widow's mite' and staffed by lonely spinsters. Indeed, from the 1880s on – right up to the present – roughly two-thirds of missionaries in the field were women, half of them unmarried. R. Pierce Beaver, professor of missions in Chicago, postulates that the foreign missionary movement 'was the great cause to which American churchwomen were devoted for a century and a half ... It began as the first feminist movement in North America and stimulated the rise of various other streams in the nineteenth-century struggle for women's rights and freedom.' The avowed intention of the Woman's Missionary Society – the nomenclature is significant, for the wms movement waged a strong battle to keep the singular, and political, 'woman' – was nothing less than 'the elevation of the status of Woman in heathen lands.' Although the women's societies could not be called feminist in the modern, narrow sense, they can be understood as a broad movement for the education, emancipation, and enfranchisement of women throughout the world. As such they had a profound impact.

The wms local branches (which the Anglican Women's Auxiliary 'likened in its own way to that of the Empire, with its self-governing units') gave their members 'ordered freedom' to manage their own business affairs, often for the first time, 'teaching people to bear responsibility, and laying it upon them as they are able to bear it.' These little groups brought their members out of the kitchens and taught them how to raise money and how to speak in public (who can estimate the effect of praying aloud for the first time?), and in general encouraged them to think about the world that lay beyond the next village. In 1914, the Toronto *Globe* praised the Protestant WM societies for raising half a million dollars in 'a most business-like manner and with a freedom from hair-splitting over non-essentials that so frequently come up in men's societies ... Think of this band of women all over the Dominion working quietly, steadily, and prayerfully through the years, and no doubt some of the male portion of the church will say that they know of them, but only that they are organized.'

The WMS movement can be traced back to the Boston Female Society for Missionary Purposes, which was founded in 1800 (one year after the Church Missionary Society), and the Halifax Wesleyan Female Benevolent Society, founded in 1816, which was the first Canadian organization. These 'Extra-Cent-a-Day' and benevolent societies were consolidated into the formal Women's Boards (of which, by 1900, there were thirty-five, co-operating in the Conference of Woman's Missionary Societies of North America) during the American Civil War, when American women in both the North and the South 'received a baptism of power. They were driven to organize, forced to co-operate by their passion of pity and patriotism ... in ... distributing aid to the soldiers.'

The first Canadian WM societies were the Baptist Missionary Aid Society of the Maritimes and the Woman's Missionary Society of Montreal, both founded in 1871. Five years later the newly united Presbyterian Church in Canada organized the first denomination-wide WMS, followed by the Methodists in 1880 and in 1886 by the Anglican and Congregationalist Women's Auxiliary.

Just as women were beginning to organize and to enter the institutes of higher learning, holy scripture itself was changed to condone the expansion of woman's sphere in the churches. The old King James Bible had translated Psalms 68:11 as 'The Lord gave the word; great was the company of those that publish it'; the Revised Version of the Old Testament of 1885 interpreted it as, 'The Lord gave the word; the women that publish the tidings are a great host.'

The women were indeed a great host, but the early WMS organizers often found they were like grown-up children who could prattle away during the meeting – 'get right down to visiting' – and when asked to pray could not utter a syllable. As late as 1908, Miss Janie Thomas, head of the Anglican deaconesses' residence, wrote to Principal T.R. O'Meara of Wycliffe College that 'in England women never (that is, *most* women) become *adults* ... In this country ... it is usually seen to be a weakness, and I am sure we all feel our own deaconesses must have developed in them this sense of responsibility. Of course, it opens up a possibility of failure. All freedom does that.' O'Meara gave her a paternalistic pat on the head and suggested that serving afternoon tea might be a significant step in the women's development: 'We are anxious that these young girls who come to us should learn the emenities [sic] of the orderly drawing room and perhaps from the fact of having a simple cup of tea and learning how to pour it out and hand it about will help in developing these softer and gentler charities so essential if they are to be more acceptable as refined people.'

Because of their frugality, it was reported that the women's fund-raising apparatus spent only two cents out of every dollar for administration. As the men's mission boards filled office buildings, 'once a month a band of ladies would meet at someone's home to mail out 20 000 leaflets ... Even when the organization assumed national proportions, its executive still travelled cheaply, stayed in members' homes rather than hotels, and had no broadloom in their offices.'

The story was told of one children's mission band whose leader gave each child one cent

as their talent with which to work for Jesus. At the end of six months they brought back their earnings ... One little girl bought a sheet of tissue paper with her cent. She twisted this into lamp-lighters, which she sold for ten cents. With the ten cents she bought some wool, and crocheted a pair of bootees, which she sold for twenty-five cents. With the twenty-five cents she bought some cretonne, which made a laundry bag, which she sold for fifty cents. She invested this in more cretonne, and made ten more laundry bags, which she sold for $1, and she gave the treasurer $1.01 as the receipts from her cent ... The boys planted seeds, and sold flowers, and made tops out of old spools; [made] kites, whittled out sail-boats, ran messages, made dish-mops.

From such droplets, mighty oceans grew. 'The figures in the WMS President's report,' crowed the Toronto *Globe*, 'sounded as if it must be the statement of, say, the Provincial Treasurer or some other big concern, so large were the figures. Think of $148 480.23 of a balance.'

In order to keep the attention of the members, WMS meetings tended towards theatricality. One typical program presented by the Little Light Bearers of Canning, Nova Scotia, consisted of 'singing, readings, recitations, and two dialogues ...

A very pleasing feature of the entertainment was the rendering of a piece of music called 'The Light Bearers.' The children entered the main audience-room from the class-rooms, each bearing a lighted taper, and singing, while others, out of sight, responded, in plaintive tones, to imitate the cry of the heathen ... 'The Heathen's Box,' as the children call it, into which each had contributed from their own means, was opened, and found to contain $5.60.

A more sophisticated program was 'an imaginary missionary trip around the world' taken by the Methodist women and children of Canada in 1907. In February they crossed the prairies, visiting the Winnipeg All People's Mission and the Brandon Industrial Institute and ending with a tour of Victoria's Chinatown. In March they crossed the Pacific to picturesque Japan and travelled up the Yangtse gorges to West China. ('Chentu [sic] is the capital of Sz-chuan [sic] – this name we committed to memory ...') The next month was devoted to India, and after the summer they progressed to the islands of the Pacific and Africa, and then back across the Atlantic. A side trip in November introduced the Grenfell missions in Labrador, and then it was on to Montreal for a peek at work among the French Canadians, Chinese, and others. At Christmas they returned home for a 'Missionary Thanksgiving.' This trip was intended to give the participants 'information about the conditions of child life in the several countries visited, to tell them what is being done by missionaries.' Boys and girls acted as conductors and news agents, by reading a short story or gave a few facts about each country; large CPR maps showing the route could be obtained from Dr Stephenson's office.

Who can calculate the effect of such a trip on a youngster in Ingersoll or Moose Jaw, especially if it was reinforced by the presence of some missionary dressed in 'native costume'? In a sad, strange way, it would be like reading a guidebook to Canada that listed only the churches.

One way of measuring the effect of missionary propaganda would be to consider the many missionary leaders who had grown up with this world view and had gone on to join the Student Volunteer Movement in college. According to its leader, John R. Mott, 'Next to the Christian home the Movement has been the principal factor in influencing life decisions for missions.' By 1919, more than eight thousand college-educated men and women had sailed from the United States and Canada under the SVM banner, some '75 per cent of the men missionaries of North America and 70 per cent of the unmarried women missionaries.'

Rather than sending people on its own resources, the SVM attracted college students who would in turn offer themselves to their own boards for service. Every four years – the life span of one college 'generation' – the Student Volunteer Movement held a mammoth rally, which became the focal point of religious life in campuses across the continent. These conventions grew in strength from the 691 delegates to Cleveland in 1894, to 2957 in Toronto in 1902 (with the Boxer uprising just two years in the past), and reached 9000 in the last of the old-time rallies in Des Moines in 1920.

The Toronto convention was typical of the early ones. The stage was draped with flags and bunting, representing the hoped-for alliance of British and American churches. The 494 Canadian delegates, one-sixth of the total (the usual percentage of Canadians at conventions in the United States was one in twenty), represented fifty-four institutes of higher learning in six of the seven provinces of the Dominion. (Alberta, Saskatchewan, and Newfoundland were not yet provinces; British Columbia sent no delegates.) The 50 people from Quebec and 14 from the other provinces were vastly outnumbered by the 431 delegates from Ontario, 261 of them from seven colleges in Toronto, the denominational and medical faculties of the University of Toronto and the Toronto Bible College among them.

Declaring that 'enthusiasm is not noise,' John Mott, a burly man with the instincts of a general – meeting him was like being let 'in to see God' – emphasized the quiet moment of decision. One young speaker summed up the students' mood: 'We are young, active, and vigorous; we are educated and disciplined. We possess an *esprit de corps*, caused by our contact with our confreres abroad.' Even the *Toronto Daily Star* reporter put aside his objectivity to rhapsodize:

The platform in Massey Hall these days commands a farther skyline of life and service than any meeting in legislature or parliament. The real statesmen are here. It is they who deal with big affairs, and put their hands on vast enterprises. What are our poor parish politics compared with this world-wide sweep? What is our trade policy compared to the evangelization of the world in this generation? Is it any wonder that such a movement has drawn to it the best and the brightest?

At the close of the meeting, $60 000 was raised in pledges in ten minutes while a telegram was read from the Christian students of Shanghai: 'One million students, the leaders of 400 million people, suddenly awakened. Pray.'

Back in the 1880s, when the SVM had first started, the denominational leaders had been wary of the movement; but by 1902 those days were long past. The Methodist church, for example, that year created its own Young People's Forward Movement for Missions (YPFMM). This Canadian innovation was widely copied in the United States and Britain and led to the foundation of the Young People's Missionary Movement of the United States and Canada, which by 1908 had enrolled 100 000 in mission study courses. By that time, the Methodist YPFMM had raised more than $3 million for missions and supported 107 missionaries in West China, Japan, and the Canadian West.

The YPFMM was the inspiration and life's work of Dr Frederick Clarke Stephenson, of whom an American mission leader had said, 'the foreign missionary enterprise owes more to your Dr Stephenson than to any other living man.' While still a medical student, Stephenson was turned down by his board because it lacked the money to send him to China; so he turned his entrepreneurial skills to raising money for missions. Unlike the SVM, which emphasized the silent moment, the YPFMM societies were often criticized for their 'minstrel shows and entertainments.' Their offices became a storehouse of missionary 'stuff': books, pamphlets, magic-lantern slides (in boxed sets of up to six dozen), postcards, stereopticon views, photographs ('of picturesque Szechuan ..., many are gems for framing'), posters, and maps, as well as an extensive collection of costumes that could be rented for a nominal fee. (The American Baptists had a similar collection of four hundred 'specialized types of costumes for artisans, beggars, brides, children, coolies, laborers, merchants, monks, officials, priests, school-teachers, village people, and the rich as well as the poor.')

The YPFMM organizations were great believers in the value of 'visual education': in this category were gigantic missionary expositions, like the one that filled the Sunday-school auditorium of Broadway Methodist Tabernacle in Toronto in 1912:

Exact counterparts of the native huts of Japan, China, India, and Africa were erected, and are on exhibition with their accompanying furniture, and occupied by members of the church in native costume. Many interesting curios are also on exhibition, among the most interesting of which is a model of the method of bandaging the feet of Chinese women to keep them from growing ... A chop suey restaurant, with the regulation chopsticks, is included in the China exhibit. Moving pictures of the missionaries at work were shown, including films of the Chinese Revolution.

(It is hard to realize that chopsticks were as exotic as moving pictures of the Chinese revolution.)

The motto of the Young People's Forward Movement for Missions – 'Pray. Study. Give.' – was expressed as the three legs of a tripod: prayer and giving had to be informed by study. Starting with the mimeographed, four-page *The Missionary Leaguer*, Stephenson launched an ambitious publishing program to provide study material. Expanding from one page in the General Board's *Missionary Outlook*, by 1903 the YPFMM had its own *Missionary Bulletin*, a 200 to 300-page quarterly of letters and pictures from its representatives in the fields. The year 1903 also saw publication of E.W. Wallace's *The Heart of Szechwan*, first in a series of paperbound books published by Stephenson. They were intended, one of his authors said, 'for busy people, anxious for facts in small compass and short order.' By 1911, the movement had sold more than 20 000 copies, at thirty-five cents each, of its textbooks; by 1924 it had passed the one hundred thousand mark. The most famous of these books, and one of the few that can be read as more than a curiosity today, is J.S. Woodsworth's *Strangers Within Our Gates*, the seminal study of Asian and East European immigration into the Canadian West.

The young people's movement and the women's movement were the backbone of missionary enthusiasm, so much so that many church leaders felt that religion was being 'left too much to women, children, and young people.' The time had come to galvanize the men of the church. At an international call to prayer in 1906, the Laymen's Missionary Movement of the United States and Canada was founded. As it spread through the churches over the next fifteen years, the LMM made foreign missions 'a matter of respectability, civic and Christian duty, and even patriotism ... The impression was left that the only serious obstacle to the evangelization of the world was the lack of necessary funds.'

The slogan of the LMM was, 'Enlisting the whole Church in the supreme work of saving the world.' During the first campaign, which culminated in Canada's National Missionary Congress in 1909, every congregation of the participating churches – involving up to seven denominations and including the Salvation Army in some parts of the country – was canvassed, and more than $3 million was raised for missions. The Methodist churches of Toronto doubled their missionary offerings, though nationally the increase was less dramatic: from $469 000 to $682 000 annually. The Anglican Missionary Society of the Canadian Church garnered five times more in 1912 than it had ten years earlier. The Presbyterians, hopeful that the campaign would replenish their depleted coffers, felt disappointed that it did not 'put us on Easy Street.' The additional revenue did lead to a spurt of building activity in Formosa and Honan and in the new Canton mission (opened in 1902), and in turn increased the mission debt from $12 000 in 1907 to $53 000 six years later.

With its emphasis on 'practicability and business-like administration,' the laymen's movement had a profound effect not only on mission givings, but on the structure of the boards. In the Presbyterian Church, the 'saintly' Dr R.P. MacKay had long been an advocate of interdenominational co-operation through such organizations as the Student Volunteer Movement and the Associated Boards of Foreign Missions of the United States and Canada, of which he was a charter member. An assistant was brought in at this time, a young minister named Allan Egbert ('Bert') Armstrong, who was serving concurrently as the first secretary of the LMM. He remained secretary of the Presbyterian, and later United Church, board until his retirement in 1947.

In the Methodist church, the laymen's influence was more dramatic. For twenty-five years, the Missionary Society had been concentrated in the hands of Dr Alexander Sutherland, under the slogan 'One Society, One Fund, One Policy.' At the 1906 General Conference, the two leading laymen, N.W. Rowell and Joseph Flavelle, bitterly attacked the seventy-three-year-old Sutherland's administration as inefficient. 'The progress which is being made is due to the weight, mass and innate zeal of Methodism rather than to the laying of far-seeing plans, the quick adjustment of means to ends, the clear thinking which make zeal irresistible and multiply the effects of energy.' They proposed that the society be divided into home and foreign missions, with Sutherland as secretary only for the latter. 'Anything with two heads is a monstrosity,' declared Sutherland in his own defence. Nevertheless, he was shouted down, and a young minister, T.E. Egerton Shore, was brought in as his assistant.

After Sutherland's death in 1910 and Shore's early retirement three years later, the mission society was brought under the control of two men who between them continued to run it until 1952, just days after the last United Church missionaries left China. The senior was the Reverend James Endicott, formerly of the Canadian Mission Press in Chengtu, who had been recruited by the LMM during his furlough as speaker and fundraiser. Dr Endicott served as secretary of the board from 1913 until his retirement in 1937. Known as one of the best orators of his time, he represented 'the voice of the Church' to many of the older generation. He was also elected chairman of the Associated Boards and, in the troubled period after Church union, second Moderator of the United Church of Canada. His assistant and successor was Dr Jesse Arnup, a 'brilliant student' from Victoria College, 'a strong speaker and bubbling over with well-regulated enthusiasm.' Arnup had never taken up a pastoral charge, but had been involved in the laymen's movement since its inception. Arnup, too, became a powerful voice in international affairs, and was elected Moderator of the United Church in 1946.

Reading through the lists of the committees of the LMM, one is struck by the recurrence of the same names. John Foster's landmark thesis on the marriage of men, money, and missions – 'the consecration of wealth' was their term, 'the imperialism of righteousness' is Foster's – lists these men and the companies they controlled through a network of interlocking directorships. The Methodist church especially was able to attract prominent 'names' to its committees, including at least three millionaires who were 'at the basis of Canadian finance': Senator George A. Cox, board member of forty-six companies; Chester Massey, scion of the prominent farm-implement manufacturing family; and Sir Joseph Flavelle, who made his millions through pork processing. These men, and others who followed them, adopted foreign missions as their personal charity, anonymously slipping a thousand dollars into a building fund or to cover a debt in the same way that other families adopted the Barnardo's homes or, later, Rotary clubs, art galleries, and symphony orchestras.

The list of 'names' who chose missions as their charity is long and impressive, and includes founders of the three major Canadian-based multinational companies: Massey-Harris (now Massey-Ferguson), Brazilian Traction (now Brascan), and Moore Business Forms (now Moore

Corporation). Foster seems to impute a sinister motive to their interest in foreign missions; they were working, he wrote,

in a close alliance with their contemporaries in the British Empire and in American commercial and capital markets, and in the context of British and American political and military power. They lent money, sold insurance, borrowed capital, marketed pork, purchased hardware and invested in utilities in Britain and the United States and expanded into the Caribbean, Latin American and Asian markets in which British and American capitalists were also expanding. China was simply another part of this unfolding world of opportunities ...

While enjoying the privileges for Christianity, cotton textiles and life insurance which had been gained in China by British, French or American negotiators or guns, the Canadians in China believed that, unlike other Western powers, theirs was a nation without a bad history in the 'heathen world.' Canadians were particularly susceptible to the belief that their hands were clean, that they were neutral and beyond the compromises of collaboration with imperial expansion. Canada's unique and short history made it 'superior' to the other powers. Canadians were, therefore, uniquely suited to the imperialism of righteousness.

Public charity cloaking private greed is an old story; but did these rich mission supporters have no more in their Methodism than money, no social idealism in their social gospel? Though it is hardly credible now, in those distant days before the First World War, they credited their own peculiar Anglo-Saxon variety of Christianity with the kindness life had shown them. So, along with their ploughs and insurance policies, they offered the world the love of Christ, the greatest gift of Western civilization.

These Christian laymen *were* different from their non-religious colleagues. 'Holy Joe' Flavelle, for example, ran Canada Packers like a Methodist class meeting, 'holding earnest discussions with his officers about the state of their business souls.' He once told a group of young businessmen: 'You are a trustee holding time, talents, and equipment for the good of others. The only real apology for your existence is the service you will render.' As a group, mission advocates felt that passing on their wealth to their own children would rob them of initiative, so they often dispersed their fortunes to charity.

Like the British aristocracy who trained their younger sons for the Indian Civil Service, the mission lay people also gave freely of their children to the foreign fields. Muriel Wood, daughter of E.R. Wood, president of Dominion Securities, served in West China, as did Vida

Coatsworth, the second Mrs Sibley, daughter of Emerson Coatsworth, a former mayor of Toronto. Another Toronto mayor, R.J. Fleming, sponsored his daughter in Honan, where she worked with the Reverend R.P. MacKay's daughter, Mrs Andrew Thomson. Margaret Wrong, 'the saint of Uganda,' was a sister of Hume Wrong, Under-Secretary of State for External Affairs, a granddaughter of Edward Blake, premier of Ontario in the 1870s, and a grandniece of S.H. Blake, leading Anglican layman.

The cause of foreign missions first began to falter on the battlefields of the First World War. As Fred Deacon, a prominent stockbroker, complained to Joseph Flavelle, there just didn't seem to be any families 'trained to give' any more. Flavelle, chairman of the board of West China Union University, explained to Joseph Beech, the president, that the war had pressed people

to such an extent, that it has been difficult for many to continue support of church and philanthropic enterprises as before the war, while many who came into new wealth are without special sympathy with church efforts, and therefore without the disposition from within to assist materially the work which the Church undertakes. There is, I think, as you may know, the additional spirit of unrest which the war produced, that has caused a highly critical feeling to be developed towards Church enterprises, and to question, both from within and without the Church, its capacity to discharge the high duty which it undertakes to perform.

'All these conditions,' he concluded, 'call for patience.'

The Protestant churches entered the post-war period with 'The United National Campaign: An Inter-Church Forward Movement' in 1920. The campaign slogan was 'An active Christianity will mend the world.' This was to be the last of the great fund-raising campaigns. By the end of the decade, with the coming of the Depression, foreign missions were in disarray, beleaguered from within and without, understaffed and underpaid, their buildings overseas falling into disrepair or irretrievably secularized.

In China, as in Canada, the international Christian student movement trained a new generation of radicalized leaders who equated true Christianity with the destruction of imperialism. When the World Student Christian Federation met in Peking in 1922, the Chinese formed their own Anti-Christian Student Federation to express their own sense of nationalism. It is us, they said, who will save China.

6 · Revival in North Honan, Mass Movement in West China

'China, as she is now, is in a most pitiable condition. In every department she is unsound and unclean. Her public and private life are both corrupt. Outwardly she has an appearance of virtue, but it is not even skin deep. As long as the present conditions continue there can be very little advance in Christian work. The twentieth century could not permit a nation so corrupt to exist. China is too near civilized nations to remain as she is. A change must come.'

Rev. George Hartwell of West China, fleeing the Boxers, 1900

The new century that dawned with enthusiasm in the West slunk into China a camp-follower of the conquering army. The Boxer Protocol signed by the defeated emperor forced China to pay an indemnity of $67 million over the next forty years – until the year of Pearl Harbor – for the destruction of foreign life and property, and to compensate the Western allies for the cost of raising the invading army. To ensure payment, the powers took over the Imperial Maritime Customs and the salt gabelle, basically making them into debt-collecting agencies for the West. In addition, China agreed to change those aspects of its society that restricted Western access; henceforth, foreigners could go anywhere, do anything, and would be given armed escorts to do so. Silver coinage that varied from one city to the next was replaced by a standard national currency, a post office was set up, and railway construction became a priority. Before 1900 China had one short, unfinished railway from Peking to Tientsin; in 1902 more than fourteen hundred kilometres were

William H. Leonard with 'my gang,' the workers building Hart Memorial College in West China Union University, c. 1914 constructed by British, French, American, and Japanese consortia, and sixteen hundred kilometres the following year.

Within a few years drastic changes began to be seen even in village stores, where Pear's soap and tinned milk, printed cotton and rubber goods jostled dragon bones off the shelves. By the end of the decade, almost every home in the empire had at least three foreign products: opium from India, British-American cigarettes, and, thanks to Standard Oil's campaign, 'oil for the lamps of China.' By the second decade another product had become ubiquitous: Pink Pills for Pale People, the dyspepsia pills that made Brockville, Ontario, famous throughout the world. For many reasons, not all of them ethical – since they relied on hard-sell techniques and the natives' credulity – the Fulford Company that made the pills found the Far East its most lucrative market and claims that to this day pills in China are pink. (Needless to say, the names of the Pink Pills' people do not appear on the lists of laymen mission crusaders; in the field, little love was lost between missionary doctors and company 'drug reps,' who tried to recruit the doctors with promises of salary increases.)

Foreign fashions, as interpreted by the models of the treaty ports, also caught on. Chinese men, wearing pigtails and silk robes, could be seen dressed 'head-and-foot' in bowler hat and leather shoes. Sometimes, to their great amusement, foreign dignitaries would be invited to a feast 'in the foreign style,' only to be presented with platters of strawberry jam and tinned milk!

Once the fever of 1900 passed, a few voices began to repeat the ancient formula: 'The blood of the martyrs is the seed of the church.' By the time the missionaries were allowed to return to their stations, the phrase was on every tongue: the time for vengeance is over, they said, now we must rebuild.

First the troubling matter of indemnity had to be resolved. The China Inland Mission, hardest-hit of the missions, announced it would seek no reparations whatsoever. Other missions, following the advice of the Associated Boards of Foreign Missions of the United States and Canada, decided to put in claims for property but not for the loss of life. Though this policy was widely defended at the time, Arnold Bryson of the London Missionary Society felt that 'in retrospect the indemnity demanded from, and paid by, the Chinese authorities ... is undoubtedly regarded by many as a serious mistake, for which we have paid heavily in its effect upon the spiritual life of Church members ... The payment of these sums throughout the district sowed the seeds of a mercenary spirit in the churches, which has seriously retarded the anticipated harvest from the blood of the martyrs.' (Missionary claims were generally less extravagant than those of commercial people, Paul Varg notes, citing as an example a young mining engineeer named Herbert Hoover who demanded $52 000 for lost wages; he settled for $10 750.)

Nevertheless, despite considerable reservations, the Presbyterians in North Honan did submit their claim for $74 486. When the British Claims Commissioner disallowed $11 000 for travel expenses, the Toronto committee suggested making up the amount by pressing for compensation for Dr Percy Leslie's injured hand. The mission was incensed. 'Are we now going to use the outbreak in China as a means of paying the furlough expenses of our missionaries?' wrote Dr Leslie in return. In the end the mission settled for $50 000.

The five men who returned to North Honan in September 1901 were escorted by a 'triumphal procession' of fourteen Chinese gunboats; they received an official welcome from the governor himself. A few months later, they joined the throngs to watch the imperial court returning to Peking in a 'river of silk' from its exilic 'tour of inspection' beyond the Great Wall. When the missionaries refused to bow for the imperial procession, the empress dowager, the old harridan herself, caught them with her gimlet eye. The Reverend James Slimmon bowed, 'giving her something of a military salute, to which she promptly responded by giving a sweet little bow, and favouring us with a bright friendly smile ... my companions ... had gone one better than my salute. They had returned her smile, actually smiled on the Empress Dowager of China!'

Despite the imperial smile, the missionaries found a dispirited church, some of whose members had recanted in their absence and signed 'declarations meant to convey the impression that they had consented to forsake the error of the Christian religion.' These backsliding members were 'kindly but firmly' suspended from the church. Nevertheless, Slimmon described the first communion service in apotheistic terms: 'Amongst the Christians present,' he wrote to the Foreign Mission Committee

were men who had been hunted in the fields like wild beasts, haled before magistrates, fined, robbed, beaten, tortured and persecuted in every possible way ... I seemed to catch a glimpse of that great multitude, which no man can number, of all nations and tribes, and peoples, and tongues standing before the Throne ... And these Honan Christians were among their number ... Has our work been in vain? ... Does anyone grudge the money that has been spent on this field, the suffering endured, the lives laid down? ... If so, let us look on these two hundred Christians gathered in the church that Dr Menzies has built and remember that God who has given us these first fruits never grows weary, never gives up.

By early 1903, with the missionaries back in the field, the work in North Honan could resume in earnest. In addition, two new missionaries had arrived from Canada as a partial replacement for the six who had left the field permanently.

The next few years, rewarding ones for the mission, saw the building of a Chinese church under its own synod that became independent of the missionary church in 1907. This 'Three-Self Church' – self-governing, self-propagating, and self-supporting – was mainly a rural phenomenon, as, out in the countryside, the initial one or two converts had grown into congregations supporting their own pastor. The missionaries themselves concentrated on the cities; four new stations were opened before 1914, for a full complement of six.

When the imperial Manchu government abolished its old examination system in 1905, it consigned its old learning, the application of Confucius to modern life, to the dustbin of history. The United States generously offered to help by turning back its Boxer Indemnity Funds to educate Chinese students in American universities. This open-handed gesture was shortly matched by France and Britain. (At this time, because of the notorious head tax and exclusion laws, there was no more than a handful of Chinese, most of them church-sponsored, in Canadian universities.) But these overseas students were only a drop in the bucket. Where could China turn when it needed Western learning? To the mission schools.

Mission schools had always been a contentious issue in North Honan – the 'Cinderella of mission work.' And when the Christian-run China Educational Association called for the mission boards to send out 'trained educationalists' to start professional schools, the Presbyterian FMC replied tartly, 'Our Board sends out a grade of missionaries that are supposed to be competent educationalists.' From the beginning, the committee in Toronto had warned its missionaries not to start schools that would become 'a charge upon the finances of the mission.' The missionaries themselves, moreover, were not inclined to open schools whose main purpose was to teach English to rich young men. Their motto was: 'First the church, then the school.' But schools restricted to the children of converts were in an untenable position, because the converts were

Great Grace writing the names of the Apostles for his junior Bible class, early 1900s

mostly the poorest of the poor, barely able to give up their children's earning power, let alone pay tuition in the mission school.

Only the schools started by the women missionaries for Chinese girls managed to escape this dilemma. The mission boys' schools were replicas of the traditional Chinese schools and employed Confucian scholars to instruct the boys in the classics, while the missionary came in to teach English and Scripture. But since China had had no girls' schools, there were no such restricting models for mission schools to copy. In addition, at least in the North Honan mission, the male missionaries regarded 'women's work' as a subsidiary part of 'the work,' and allowed the women more latitude than they allowed each other.

At first the WMS workers started kindergartens and women's classes more as day-care centres than as formal schools. What the women learned about world history or the germ theory was incidental, the missionaries reasoned – that would come later. First they needed to learn they had a soul. As a corollary to this, they needed to learn that men and women were equal in the eyes of God. 'God loves you as much as He loves your husband,' the missionaries would say; 'Christian husbands don't beat their wives, they hold family worship together with them.' Then, since both the missionaries and the Chinese women would be busy with sewing, the missionaries would teach them handicrafts with the materials at hand. Mrs Joseph Mowatt started an industrial school in Hwaiking [HUAIJING, now called JIAOZUO] for the wives of opium addicts, to provide these poor women with food and shelter; the school was supported by Hwaiking shops – in Vancouver, Toronto, and Montreal – which sold their needlework. This school lasted for nearly fifteen years, until the Depression, despite the opposition of many male missionaries who could not see any direct benefit in terms of increased numbers of converts.

The West China mission, the Presbyterian women countered, did not restrict its schools to Christians. In fact, its schools were of the highest standards in order to attract non-Christian children who could, by precept and example, be educated into the faith.

When the first Methodist men arrived back in Szechuan in early 1901, at a time when the Presbyterians were scattered from India to Canada, they found themselves besieged by thousands of 'so-called enquirers' begging to join the church. 'We did not hear one unkind word,' one wrote home, 'and the people seemed glad to welcome the foreigners.' Not all the inquirers were sincere in their attraction to Christianity, wrote James Endicott (who was still on the field), for 'many a rascal under cover of his connection with the Church has bullied the ignorant and timid, and even brow-beaten the Magistrate. In some cases, even, men who had never been near a church or missionary, got possession of a Bible or hymn-book, and armed with this made the magistrate understand that he was a man not to be trifled with.'

Nevertheless, the missionaries did welcome these inquirers into their chapels and into their homes. Within a few months, Dr Omar Kilborn gave up his medical practice to teach eighty young men. One day, 'a man of rank, and also of wealth' approached him for use of the mission press to publish a newspaper whose 'avowed object is nothing more nor less than the education of the people – the masses! And, therefore, he said, the paper should be put into the simplest every-day language ... Here is our great opportunity,' Dr Kilborn concluded, 'if only we had the men and the women to meet the demand. The people come to us freely in every department of our work, they crowd to the hospital, they flock to the church, eager applicants for instruction in English and mathematics are turned away with their fees in their hands.'

So eager for Western learning were these young men that they would come at six in the morning, and 'Not a few attended our Sunday services, and acquaintances and friendships formed among some of these have contributed not a little to the opening up of the way for the Gospel in a large circle.' (In another letter Kilborn mentioned almost off-handedly that 'as a result of necessary pruning, suspending and expelling,' the Chengtu church had a total of thirteen members.)

Kilborn believed that the greatest tool for reaching the Chinese was education, spreading the word in its physical as well as its spoken form. '"Books of the Times" are very greatly in demand,' he wrote of the Chengtu bookstore. 'I am now circulating more than four hundred copies monthly of good Christian magazines. These all pay for themselves, and now that the business has increased so, there is a margin of profit. On Scriptures and tracts there is no profit, but even a little loss. On scientific books, histories, geographies, books on philosophy and literature, there is a decided profit.' At Kiating, Dr W.E. Smith, more evangelical than Kilborn, refused to carry scientific literature in the bookstore; it gives 'the missionary more trouble looking after than the Christian literature, as it is dearer, and a temptation for men to steal it. The Christian literature is so cheap it would require a very mean man to steal it, and if he did it might do him some good morally and would not be much of a loss to the mission.'

By this time, through their various connections, the Canadian missionaries had become acquainted with a number of upper-class people; even the governor of the province, known as 'the loves-to-kill-men Viceroy,' came to visit. Despite his reputation, the missionaries were impressed by his zeal in modernizing the city, installing gas-lamps 'at more or less regular intervals along the streets,' and stationing uniformed police at every corner. (The foreigners described them as 'splendid' and 'very efficient,' but unfortunately Dr W.F. Adams could not take them seriously because their 'little straw hats' reminded him of 'schoolboys at home.') By an accident of geography, the Canadian mission was more aware of these changes than other foreigners: they were awakened every morning by the Chinese soldiers in the parade ground next door playing German brass-band tunes.

This 'mass movement' in Szechuan brought forth an exuberance of plans for the future. 'Perhaps I cannot do better than enumerate some of our wants,' wrote Dr Kilborn in a letter accompanying an architect's rendering of the proposed Chengtu hospital. It must be a modern institution, he wrote, with a 'waiting-room, guest-room, consulting-room,

Official opening of the WMS hospital in Chengtu, 1914, with the Szechuan governor and members of the foreign diplomatic corps. *Fifth and sixth from left*: Drs Alfretta and Omar L. Kilborn

operating-room, minor operating-room, dark-room, and drug store-room ... As to ward accommodation we ought to have as the minimum sixty beds in large wards, say four wards of fifteen beds each; ten roomy, airy private wards for men or women of official class; further accommodation, which need not be nearly so elaborate or expensive, for thirty patients who come in to break off the opium habit.' The building would cost, he estimated, $15 000, 'a considerable financial outlay'; by the time it was finished six years later expenditures had exceeded $25 000.

In 1906, the Canadian Methodists despatched, in one joyous 'gang,' nineteen new missionaries who set the Yangtse gorges ringing with the Victoria College cheer and 'The Maple Leaf Forever'; 'living in a foreign country amidst a heathen people, ' one explained, 'teaches one patriotism like nothing else can.' This group was the first of many batches; some larger, some smaller, that sailed each September; the 1908 party, the largest ever to sail from Canada, consisted of twenty-seven people

– eight married couples, five bachelors, and six single women. So, at a time when the North Honan mission was still under the influence of the original Honan Seven, the West China mission expanded from nineteen people in 1900 to two hundred twenty years later.

The 1906 party contained a number of remarkable people, including Hattie Woodsworth, niece of J.S. Woodsworth, and Charles J.P. Jolliffe who, with his elder brother, Richard Orlando, founded a missionary dynasty in West China that eventually counted more than one hundred members. Rupert Carscallen became one of the founders of West China Union University in Chengtu and, on his retirement from the field, principal of Ontario Ladies' College. Dr Ashley Lindsay, going out as the first dentist in all China, was to establish a dental course at that same university.

None were as promising as the shy, bespectacled leader, Edward Wilson Wallace, son of the dean of theology at Victoria College in Toronto. Wallace was going out to set up 'a complete system of grading and curricula for Primary and Secondary Schools' for the western provinces of Szechuan, Yunnan, and Kweichow [GUIZHOU] – no mean feat for a twenty-six-year-old! Wallace had already demonstrated his skill by writing the young people's study book, *The Heart of Szechwan*, three years previously, before he had even seen the field.

Where the Chinese government attempted to reform the educational system 'from the top down' – as was graphically shown in Chengtu, where the provincial Szechuan University was built on the ruins of the old examination halls where the candidates had been locked for three days while they wrote their exams – the mission schools reversed this process. They started training children in kindergartens and building primary schools as the students moved up the educational ladder. The two processes were complementary, with the result that by the 1920s they met in the middle.

E.W. Wallace, after an apprenticeship in one of the old-fashioned mission schools, was named secretary of the West China Christian Educational Union, an interdenominational body that was responsible for the curricula in all mission schools. The course of five years of primary school, four of higher primary, and five of middle school, leading to four years at university (seven for medical doctors), was based on the American model. Each of these schools offered instruction in Christianity and the Chinese classics, world history, science, geography, physical 'drill,' and 'Chinese etiquette,' as well as English in the upper grades.

The kindergartens in West China, which were 'efficient and up-to-date,' used the Montessori method. The children were taught 'elementary drawing with crayons, hymns, songs, games, and stories drawn from the New and the Old Testaments ... We teach cleanliness, ... each child having its own face-cloth and tooth-brush, and little white apron ... Thus we strive to bring these children into a cheery, beautiful atmosphere of love and interest, where we may train their muscles along with various senses and faculties.'

Besides imparting knowledge, the mission schools tried to inculcate such virtues as devotion to service and discipline. 'The only idea of discipline that the average Chinese father has,' wrote E.W. Wallace of his first little school, 'is to warn and threaten and do nothing for nine days, and on the tenth to fly into a terrible passion and almost murder the offending child ... So, when the foreign teacher mildly remarks that lying will be punished, it seems not to dawn on the boys' minds that he means what he says, and it is a very surprised boy who discovers that our "yea" means "yea" and our "nay" means "nay."' This sense of discipline was emphasized, perhaps unconsciously, by the military-looking school uniforms.

The West China mission expanded rapidly, as the laymen's movement at home kept pace with the expenditures, opening four stations in 1905, two the next year, one in 1908, and one in 1910. It added its last three stations in 1913 by acquiring the London Missionary Society property in Chungking. In 1905, the mission had two schools with a registration of 60; by 1916, it had one hundred primary schools with 3500 pupils, exclusive of the WMS schools. The mission wrote expectantly of having 200 000 students by 1928, one child in ten 'securing an education under Christian auspices.'

'I dislike building!' wrote Dr Will Adams, who had been forced to give up his medical practice to become superintendent of building construction. He found 'something very "crawly" about building out here.' He had to count every nail twice – the second time as nailheads in the boards – and every plank, while also trying to teach the workmen Western construction methods (concrete foundations, tin roofs – imported into China by the Pedlar Company of Oshawa, Ontario – bricks, wood, lath-and-plaster, glass windows, etc.). When he surveyed the pile of half a million bricks brought for the construction of the Chengtu hospital, he had a nervous collapse and had to be sent home. His place was taken by Walter Small, 'Mission Builder' (as he signed his letters), who had apprenticed as a builder in England before emigrating to

Saskatchewan. Finally in 1909, the Canadian church sent out Frank Abrey, one of the first full-time mission architects in China.

Before the Boxers, mission buildings had been in modified Chinese style, with each room opening onto a central courtyard; but within a few years the West China buildings looked like fourquare Ontario farmhouses, with Chinese embellishments. Though modest by Canadian standards, 'to the eyes of Chinese countryfolk, the stations appeared as strongholds of capitalism.' The property at Penghsien, for example, which measured ninety metres by thirty-five, had formerly housed sixty families (!), each living in one room two and a half metres square; when the mission moved in, it had to demolish yards of mud-brick walls and remove six cemeteries to open the place up 'for light and air and tennis.'

The mass movement was not confined to West China, but affected every mission to a greater or lesser degree. Even the China Inland Mission opened schools for converts' children; and North Honan moved cautiously into educational and medical work. But institutionalization brought forth bureaucracy, which many of the older missionaries felt undermined their very purpose. 'Has the heroic in Missions passed away forever?' asked Harvey Grant. 'I can see a distinct loss of the power and presence of God,' wrote James Slimmon, 'since we began to give up evangelism as the main work of the Mission and went in for institutional work and forming organized churches. Perhaps 90 [per cent] of our energies are given to this, and the remaining 10 [per cent] given to direct evangelistic work.'

Jonathan Goforth, still the dominant force in the mission, became an increasingly stormy presence when, at the age of forty-five, a 'strange restlessness seemed to take possession of him.' Reading of a 'great awakening' in Wales, he discovered through prayer and fasting that 'the spiritual laws governing a spiritual harvest are as real and tangible as the laws governing the natural harvest.' He proposed that he and his family take up residence in each of the villages in turn, holding revival campaigns for a month or two, and then move on. When Rosalind his wife heard the plan, she wrote many years later, 'my heart went like lead.' When one child died and a second became deathly ill, Jonathan thundered at her, 'The safest place for you and the children is the path of duty. You think you can keep your children safe in your comfortable home at Changte, but God may have to show you you cannot.' She meekly took her place at his side.

In 1907, Goforth was asked to escort Reverend R.P. MacKay of the Foreign Mission Committee on his first tour of the East Asian missions, starting with Manchuria and Korea. 'Jonathan Goforth went up to Manchuria an unknown missionary, except to his own narrow circle,' Rosalind wrote. 'He returned a few weeks later with the limelight of the Christian world upon him.' This is no exaggeration.

Goforth's Manchurian revival was one of the first outpourings of the movement that came to be called Pentecostalism, and as such ignited further sparks around the world, in Africa, among Black Americans, and in India. It can be argued that this revival owed more to the apocalyptic nature of Chinese Christianity (as exemplifed by Pastor Hsi performing miracles) than it did to the Christianity of the Western churches, with its search for scientific explanations. One can argue further that Pentecostalism would not have arisen without the missionary movement, since it gave 'proof' of biblical literalness, unchanging 'yesterday, today and tomorrow.' In this respect, it is significant that the first revivals were in mission countries, particularly in Manchuria and Korea, that had long been considered the success story of foreign missions. (South Korea, with the flight of Christian refugees from the North, in particular from the Canadian Presbyterian mission in Hamheung, has become the first 'Christian' nation in Asia to have a majority of its population adherents of the Protestant churches.)

Jonathan Goforth brought his revival campaign back to North Honan, with startling results. Murdoch Mackenzie, 'a level-headed Scot who held tenaciously to strict Presbyterian ways,' compared these meetings to 'the suddenness and violence of a thunder-storm ... It started with the one or two. Then came the burst from many hearts – all the pent-up emotions held so long in check. There was no restraining it, and no attempt to do so.' Dr Leslie agreed that the Chinese church needed revival, 'But how explain the missionaries praying; some in Chinese, some in English, men and women, strictly Presbyterian, ordinarily restrained, with Scotch reserve sticking out at all points, raising their voices with the multitude.'

The churches in Canada greeted news of this revival with mixed emotions. One missionary in West China characterized it as 'preaching fever,' though that mission, too, had its own charismatic revival. It was a different story, however, when Goforth returned to Toronto two years later and tried to revive the church at home using the same methods. One need not wonder at the 'marked stillness' that reigned when he addressed the General Assembly; the leaders of the church, with their clerical collars acting like tiny neck braces, must have been in shock when Goforth urged them to confess their sins publicly. 'I do not remember another man who came home with such an asset, and who made so little of it,' Dr R.P. MacKay concluded in a letter to Donald MacGillivray in Shanghai.

In Honan, a year after the revival, as Dr Menzies sadly noted, the Chinese 'continued to confess but it was the other man's sins they confessed.' Murdoch Mackenzie felt that 'spiritual apathy took the place of zeal for Christ and love for his people.'

While on furlough, Jonathan Goforth had accused several of the professors at Knox College of teaching the heretical doctrines of the 'higher criticism,' and, on his return to Honan, he seemed 'to consider it his duty to hunt for heresy' among the members of his own mission. Three missionaries were eventually brought before presbytery to account for their beliefs; one resigned, but two remained on the field, to the continuing suspicion of the older missionaries. In the most serious case, in 1915, John Bompas, the 'kindly, intellectual' principal of the Changte Middle School, was heard preaching 'the idea that Christ was sacrificed for men's sins is immoral.' But Bompas replied that Goforth was telling outsiders that 'none of the young men the Board was now sending out are sound in the faith.' In the inquiry meeting of presbytery, Murdoch Mackenzie, a master of conciliation, reported that Mr Bompas had not 'departed in any signal way from the teaching ordinarily attributed to the Presbyterian Church; but his way of stating it is not in accordance with what was once the way of stating it.' Since Goforth and Slimmon were both absent, the motion carried – with the only negative votes by two of the single women – on condition that Bompas never speak of his contentious ideas; this proscription was not lifted until ten years later.

Things were changing fast as China moved towards revolution. The students who had been studying abroad – 18 000 in Tokyo alone in 1907 – were returning home with 'half-digested ideas, and much swagger, cigarettes and cocksureness regarding things foreign.' These young people, Goforth decided, would be his new constituents. He told presbytery that he wanted to be released from its control 'for several years and probably for life to carry on special evangelistic work ... in a much wider, it may be, a world-wide field.' The mission, he felt, was trying 'to compel me to take up a field in the ordinary way and henceforth spend my time in Honan else cut me off from membership.' Sadly, realizing that their control over Goforth 'can only be nominal and never real,' presbytery voted to 'release him ... and would wish him a hearty God-speed.'

And so Jonathan Goforth left North Honan to traipse through China with his wife and five children like 'gospel nomads.' In 1918 he severed his formal relations with the mission because, at the age of sixty, he could no longer delay his task of 'sharpening the tools for others.'

The predicted revolution came in 1911, led by a South Chinese Christian named Sun Yat-sen, who had learned revolution while printing Bibles at a mission press in Canton. For years, decades even, Christian missions had allied themselves with the progressive forces of Chinese society: the reformers at court, the iconoclasts, the disturbers of the peace. Yet, when the revolution did come, they were caught between their desire for a democratic, Christian government – as the Republic promised to be – and their fear of a revolution against established authority. Although they could accept, as Dr Charles Service reported, that 'One thing is certain, *viz*, that almost ten Chinese out of ten are against the Government; and they say so openly,' they could not go that extra step to welcome the revolution. In fact they did not know what to call it: 'Some newspapers use the term *Constitutionalists* rather than *Revolutionists*. Which do you think best?' queried Dr Richard Wolfendale, head of the Chungking hospital. Whatever the term, most missionaries agreed they could not trust Sun Yat-sen and his Revolutionary Kuomintang [GUO-MINDANG] Party. 'I do not belong to the Christianity of the churches,' the 'Father of his country' stated on many occasions, 'but to the Christianity of Jesus, who was a revolutionary.'

Such talk terrified those for whom the Boxers were still a recent memory. 'Masses of undisciplined men to whom murder and pillage are normal occupations will then sweep across the province,' predicted the British consul in Chungking at the beginning of the revolution, 'and an outbreak of anti-foreign feelings can only be a matter of time.'

Only a matter of time! Predictably, the first shots of the revolution were fired in the bell-wether region of Szechuan, in Chengtu, in a pitched battle between the short-lived Railway League and Manchu soldiers. Within a week, the western half of the province, the Canadian mission territory, was in open revolt. On 7 October, the commander of the Manchu forces, a cruel general known as 'the butcher,' defected and declared the secession of Szechuan from the Chinese Empire. Three days later, on the mystical Double Ten Day, the tenth day of the tenth month – according to the newly adopted western calendar – the Republic of China was formed in Hankow with Sun Yat-sen as president.

Since it was summer when the Railway League revolted, the Canadians in Szechuan had been vacationing at the resorts on Mount Omei, but when they returned to the cities in September, they found the situation so explosive that they asked protection from 'the butcher.' He, under the pretext of protecting them from danger, kept all the foreigners in Chengtu 'bottled up' in their own compounds for three full months before allowing them to get out on the third downriver evacuation in the mission's history. This time, the missionaries recognized that they had to leave not because of the 'recrudescence of Boxerism' that the consuls had feared, but because of the local situation. The new Kuomintang governor issued them with a passport urging the authorities along the route 'with insistence' not to impede them and to be 'sedulous in protection, so as to avoid giving rise to foreign complications, and all will be well.'

This evacuation was more dangerous than that of 1900, if only because the refugees, travelling in a flotilla of forty ships flying Union Jacks and containing 149 foreigners, their baggage, and servants, were more visible. (The refugee group, somewhat smaller than the normal foreign population of Chengtu, included 56 Britishers, of which 25 adults and 8 children were Canadians, 35 Americans, 12 French, 3 Germans, 1 Russian, and 42 Japanese.) The group was several times fired upon by unknown factions from the shore, and five-year-old John Jolliffe was killed. Rather than blaming the Chinese, as they would have done ten years earlier, the missionaries blamed the British captain of their escort, the ss *Widgeon* a notoriously trigger-happy gunboat along the upper Yangtse; the escort boat had deserted them, sailing on by without even dipping its flags to warn them they were in 'a district infested with marauders.'

'You certainly have had your share of river travel in the last few years,' the secretary of the board wrote to Dr Charles Winfield Service, 'but this last experience will probably be remembered throughout your life as the most exciting of them all.'

In the Canadian Presbyterian mission in Honan, the situation was quite different. Though the mission was only 640 kilometres from Peking, it was shielded from events there as though by an ocean. In Honan, the revolution came like a thief in the night. Cities changed hands with a stroke of a vermilion pencil; regiments defected without a shot. The missionaries were in no danger, except in the outlying districts, and made no plans to flee.

But even in old Honan, the changes brought by the revolution soon became evident. Robert McClure, son of Dr William McClure, has a wonderful child's-eye view of those changes. Coming back into Honan in 1912 at the age of twelve after a two-year furlough, he was struck by the 'craziest' impact of western fashion. On the train, young men would rush off at each station grab the nearest men by their pigtails and hack off this symbol of Manchu servility. Once the queue was gone, Dr McClure remembers, 'you had a variety of hair styles that has never been equalled ... The other mark of being an absolutely modern Chinese was to wear long underwear during the winter. But how would people know you had the underwear if you wore it inside? So they wore it outside. It was the craziest thing to see literally dozens of men – and these were the snobs of the city – who wore their long johns outside, with perhaps an umbrella in their hands – that was also a mark of status – and a felt fedora.' This was the day of 'the dollar watch,' he recalls; the flashlight, the bicycle, everything that was new and Western.

The mission boards in Canada were in favour of the new regime at first. Don't panic, T. Egerton Shore, secretary of the Methodist board, told Dr W.J. Sheridan:

No one in this country and I presume the same is true of the Missionaries in China questions for one moment that the Revolution will bring the Chinese people a long step in advance towards civilization. Neither do we question that this Revolution is partly the result of Christian missions, for they have been the pioneers of civilization in China and have introduced the ideas and institutions from the West, which have given the keener minds of China a desire for a new order of things. How then can we question that the Providence of God is working in and through this Revolution to a greater blessing for the people?

For the first year or so, the Republic seemed to be working. The slates of the old government were wiped clean, and then wiped again as bureaucrats and militarists jockeyed for position. When Sun Yat-sen, a southerner, realized that he could not gain military ascendance over the northern generals, the Peiyang [BEIYANG] clique, he magnanimously relinquished the presidency in favour of Yuan Shih-k'ai [YUAN SHIKAI], a former Manchu general. Now, once again, Yuan betrayed the trust placed in him and named himself emperor of a new imperial dynasty. He might have succeeded had his ambitions not been greeted with derision by the other generals. Whatever kind of government China was to have, it would not have Yuan as emperor.

Despite Yuan's orthodox Confucianism – he instituted 'worship' of Confucius in government schools, making it impossible for a Christian child to attend them – and his questionable character, the North Honan mission regarded him almost as a favourite son, because his ancestral residence was only a few kilometres from the main mission station at Changte. His call for a world day of prayer (27 April 1913) for 'the election of strong and virtuous men to office' was given wide prominence in the Canadian church; and *The Story of Our Missions,* a Presbyterian WMS study book for 1915, praised him because China needed his sort of 'supervised democracy' to give 'tutelage' and 'wise guidance to the people.'

Yuan died in 1916, reportedly of 'chagrin,' and on his death the country disintegrated. The Republic of China remained a government in name only, controlling little beyond the city of Peking. Sun Yat-sen waited in exile in Canton. The hundreds of warlords who had been building their armies seized whatever territory they could. The warlords were often depicted in the West as comic-opera buffoons, as in a way some of them were; one swaggering general in Chengtu, for example, launched his own 'hundred sons movement' so that his wives could staff his army in perpetuity. Yet, somehow out of this chaos, one of these warlords would have to become the leader of a reunited China. Anxiously, the missionaries scanned the horizon. Would it be Wu Pei-fu [WU BEIFU], the strongman of the north-east? He had the army; but could he beat Chang Tso-lin [ZHANG ZOULIN]? Would they join forces against the southern revolutionary party under Sun Yat-sen? Would China become Armageddon?

For a while the brightest hope lay with Feng Yu-hsiang [FENG YUXIANG], a giant over two metres tall, who was at different times the warlord of both Szechuan and Honan. Feng, the so-called Christian General, was one of Jonathan Goforth's 'miracle lives of China.' Hearing of Goforth's revivals among the students, Feng had asked Goforth to speak to his soldiers. The power fell upon Goforth that night, and soon he was baptising Feng's soldiers by the battalion, five hundred at a time, with firehoses. Feng's Christianity did not appear to be a political ruse; he seemed a genuinely humble man who, according to Sherwood Eddy of the Student Volunteer Movement, 'seems to unite the stern discipline of Oliver Cromwell with the mystical devotion of Chinese Gordon and the Christian character and quiet dignity of Stonewall Jackson.' His soldiers were not like other soldiers, they would march into the city in ranks, singing gospel hymns. They were polite, never stole anything, and wove cloth in their spare time. 'If we would impress our Christianity upon the armies of China, we must come behind in no military detail,' Goforth advised him, 'even to our shoelaces.'

Meanwhile, China plunged into darknesss. 'The Republic has come decades too soon,' wrote Dr Kilborn in 1919. 'The people were not prepared, and are not yet prepared, for a democratic form of government.' The optimistic spirit of Christianity marching hand in hand with reform gave way to 'disillusionment and timidity.' The students in the mission schools had no sooner given up their parents' superstitions than they learned that such Western intellectuals as John Dewey and Bertrand Russell, both of whom had visited China, felt that Christianity itself was a superstitious relic. Missionaries began to realize, perhaps for the first time, that the opportunity for the evangelization of the world by 'this generation' might already have passed.

This very lack of success became a clarion call for a new generation. In *Canada's Share in World Tasks*, the interdenominational mission study book for 1920, Harry Priest warned the churches to keep their faith in missions. 'Old orders are changing, giving place to new,' he wrote. Recent events 'have placed new emphasis upon the necessity of Christianizing not only the social life, but the corporate life of nations and their international relationships ... the teachings of Jesus alone contain the principles on which true democracy can be built, and in Him alone is the power "to make democracy safe for the world."'

7· New Labourers for the Vineyard

'Then over the sea to far China we go,
And we help Bishop White all the good seed to sow.
Honan is the name of his Diocese new,
And "he's-got-so-many-people-he-doesn't-know-
    what-to-do."
He's Canada's Bishop, the first one we've sent,
So, of course, we must help him, I'm sure you'll con-
    sent,
For the children of China must hear of God's love,
And the bright home prepared in the blue sky
    above.'

Letter Leaflet (Canadian Anglican Women's Auxiliary),
1914

The first overseas missions were usually started in response to one firebrand stirring up the churches in the homelands. A powerful speaker like Jonathan Goforth or Omar Kilborn might be able to rouse a whole denomination and set forth with cash in hand; lesser lights who inspired only one or two people set forth with the expectation of hand-to-mouth living in a Chinese village while they waited for the mail.

That was the way Sister Aimee went out. Raised near Ingersoll, Ontario, 'with one foot in the Methodist Church and one foot in the Salvation Army,' fifteen-year-old Aimee Kennedy became attracted by the preaching of Robert Semple, a store-front evangelist some twenty years her senior. In 1907, two years after their marriage, they went to Hong Kong with the backing of a few Pentecostal congregations. Before he had a

Pastor Y.P. Wang and his son, Stephen (son-in-law of Bishop Lindel Tsen),
Anglican Diocese of Honan

chance to learn the language, Semple died, leaving a destitute and pregnant widow. Aided by the kindness of strangers, she made her way home. She never forgot her stay in China, and twenty years later she returned, this time as the famous 'Hollywood evangelist,' Aimee Semple McPherson, to lay the cornerstone for a Shanghai branch of her own Church of the Foursquare Gospel.

By the twentieth century, with missions becoming increasingly professional organizations – the Semple attempt could barely be described as a 'mission' – most new missions were created in response to a request from the field. This was the case with both the Canadian Presbyterian mission in South China, and the Anglican one in Honan.

The South China mission – or the Macao mission, as it was first called – was inspired by a retired American missionary, Dr Joseph Thompson, who ran the mission to the Chinese in Montreal. His converts there asked him to send people to work among their relatives in the villages of the Canton area. (Similarly, the Chinese in Montreal who were Roman Catholics inspired the Sisters of the Immaculate Conception to establish a mission to the same Canton area, thirty miles from the Presbyterians.) When the first missionary, the Reverend William McKay and his wife, both from Pictou, Nova Scotia, arrived in Macao in 1902, they found their original destination, the village of Sunning [XINNING], already staffed by the American Presbyterians, so they set up base in the nearby city of Kongmoon [JIANGMEN], an island that was then being opened up as a British trading depot between Canton and Hong Kong.

Though the South China mission remained small, seldom exceeding a staff of twenty, it illustrated how one mission could multiply its usefulness in various ways. On its own, it operated two stations, each with one boarding school for boys and one for girls, and a hospital; in co-operation with other missions, it supplied personnel to the Canton Union Theological College and the general hospital in the same city, where at one point all three male doctors were Canadians.

The South China mission also demonstrated how a second mission could provide an alternate perspective on events in the field. Situated on one of the major channels through the river delta, right next to the British consulate, more than any other Canadian mission in China it was bound up with the visible presence of Western imperialism. Consequently, it often showed the typical treaty-port mentality, since the missionaries knew that in times of danger they could easily flee to Hong Kong or Macao. But Canton was also the home of Sun Yat-sen and his revolutionary Kuomintang; so, when the Honan people were worried about the rise of a militant nationalism in China, the Toronto committee could write explaining the events in Canton. This cross-conversation became more conspicuous after the formation of the United Church of Canada in 1925, when the two Presbyterian missions and the Methodist West China mission joined forces.

Women missionaries were always the strength of the South China mission, a fact pointed out to the North Honan men. 'We shall have to change the name of our Mission to the "United Sisters,"' wrote Ethel Reid in 1913. 'They tell me, a few years ago, the "United *Brethren* Mission" in Canton were left without a man on the field so that the brethren were all sisters.' Things never reached this point in Kongmoon, but for a while the Reverend William McKay was the only man on the staff of six. Women were also the strongest supporters of the mission in Canada, in particular the Woman's Missionary Society of Montreal. Sometimes Dr R.P. MacKay of the Foreign Mission Committee must have felt they took too keen an interest, when the formidable secretary, Mrs Elliott Busteed, contradicted his public statements with what she called 'the actual facts which I have from authentic sources.'

Matters came to a head when the FMC announced in 1910 that as part of its fund-raising campaign, it would give to whoever donated the cost of either of two hospitals in Kongmoon the privilege of naming the hospital. Mrs Busteed 'immediately ... set on foot a scheme to raise $2000 among the members of St Paul's ... to build the hospital as a memorial to Mrs [Marion] Barclay, our esteemed pastor's wife.' Although the FMC could find no guarantor for the second, a men's hospital, it authorized the beginning of construction, presumably on the women's hospital. The Montreal women were willing to put up with delays and spiralling costs in the field – this was on the eve of the 1911 revolution – but when Dr Jessie McBean sent a personal letter to Mrs Busteed informing her that only one hospital, a general one, was being built, the latter sent a sternly worded communication to Dr MacKay, announcing that she 'would not care to inscribe [this hospital] as the Marion Barclay Hospital.' In the end, the general hospital was never built, and the men's wing had to wait another twenty-five years. The Marion Barclay Hospital for Women opened with great fanfare in 1912, with thirty-three ward beds and twelve in emergency; it had its own electrical generating plant, one of the first in the city, and a modern operating room, and it was run for many years by the diminutive Dr McBean.

When the fires of missionary fervour blazed through the Canadian churches in the 1880s, the Anglican church never seemed to catch fire. As late as 1911, S.H. Blake, the denomination's leading layman, felt that his church as a whole seemed 'dead and cold in regard to that matter which bulked so largely in the mind of our blessed Saviour – the witness of his death and resurrection in all parts of the world.' Until the Missionary Society of the Canadian Church was formed in 1901, the Canadian Anglican church was 'the English Church,' the missionary-receiving daughter of the Church of England; most of the voices coming from the pulpits and church councils were British. In 1881, when the Canadian Domestic and Foreign Missionary Society was asked to assume responsibility for some of the missions, it felt that the new diocese of Algoma was already enough of a burden.

One flame did burn brightly, however; that was Wycliffe College, the low-church seminary in the University of Toronto. Founded in 1884 by S.H. Blake, it built its own buildings in 1888. That same year the Wycliffe College Missionary Association sponsored two of the graduates to open a mission in Japan; six years later it sent its first representative to China. By 1900, John R. Mott of the Student Volunteer Movement 'was able to say in a public meeting that no college in proportion to its size had sent more men to the foreign mission field than had Wycliffe College, Toronto.' By its fiftieth anniversary, the roster read like an honour roll of the Canadian church and included seven overseas bishops, three in China (one of whom was Chinese), three in Japan (one Japanese), and a native bishop of the Church of South India.

In 1895, Wycliffe students were shocked by news that the Reverend Robert Stewart of the Church Missionary Society, along with eight other adults and two children, had been brutally massacred in the southern coastal province of Fukien by a secret society calling itself 'The Vegetarians.' The year previously Stewart had passed through Toronto trying to raise interest in the mission. A member of the Anglo-Irish aristocracy – his brother-in-law was surgeon to Queen Victoria – Stewart had epitomized muscular Christianity in its Anglican form; to replace him, the Wycliffe students sent one of their own, the Reverend John Richard Shields Boyd, son of a prominent Toronto judge and son-in-law of the Bishop of Huron. J.R.S. Boyd was stationed with his family – including his wife's cousin – at Stewart's old station of Kucheng [GUTIAN], 160 kilometres inland from Foochow [FUZHOU]. The following year the Wycliffe students sent a second man to Fukien, the Reverend William Charles White.

The Canadians in China worked under the Church of England in a colonial outpost that included British, Irish, Australian, South African, and Indian co-workers. The low-church Church Missionary Society, one of the largest internationally, operated several missions in China, notably that in Fukien; the high-church Society for the Propagation of the Gospel had one in Shantung, and the American Episcopal church operated three in central China.

These missions, hiding behind their granitic facade of God, Queen, and Empire, often seemed more concerned with their own membership, than with ecumenical ventures. Only with the China Inland Mission did the Church of England enter into formal co-operation, when its diocese in East Szechuan, headed by a CMS bishop, fell within CIM territory. Even this modest co-operation had strict limits: for example, the Reverend Dr T.R. O'Meara, the 'broad-church' principal of Wycliffe, who was also a member of the Toronto CIM council, wrote regretfully in 1915 that he could not attend the annual meeting if it included an interdenominational communion since such action would launch the college into 'public controversy.'

The second Wycliffe missionary, W.C. White, was one of the most remarkable, most complex men in Canada's China missions. The son of a carpenter, he was born in England, in Ivy Bridge, Devonshire, in 1873 and raised in Norwood, Ontario, a small town near Peterborough, where he was remembered as an ambitious young man with a winning smile. His parents seem to have been 'Christmas-and-Easter' church members, but Will made up for their indifference with his own extroverted evangelism. After a stint as YMCA secretary, he entered Wycliffe at the age of twenty, where his 'good square talks' did not sit well with his fellow students, who took to calling him a 'Methodist.' White's diaries of the period are filled with agonized self-examination. White wrote on one occasion, 'Oh! Lord Jesus! Keep me from thinking I am anything. I am nothing but a miserable sinner. Keep me low at Thy feet.' His greatest sin, even at that age, was pride.

When White arrived in Fukien in 1897, he was stationed 160 kilometres, or eight days' travel, inland from J.R.S. Boyd, in the Kienning [JIANNING, now JIAN'OU] mountains, where the fragrant Oolong tea grows. Suddenly his diaries open up, and we see the world through the eyes of an intelligent, inquisitive young man who began to feel as at home in Buddhist temples as in proper CMS sitting rooms, and who preferred the company of Chinese to that of his English colleagues. At his second station, Longuong [LUOYUAN] on the sea coast near Foochow, White started a leper school, surely the most self-abnegating mission work ever devised, to give inmates of the camp, which was located 1.6 kilometres out of town, some way of supporting themselves (since, on account of 'their deformed limbs,' they could not walk out to beg). 'Their condition is most pitiable,' he wrote.

In 1907, the British and American bishops of the Chung Hua Sheng Kung Hwei [ZHONGHWA SHENGGONGHUI], the Anglican Church of China, called on the Canadian Church 'to join in the extension of Christ's kingdom in this land, by sending a Bishop and Clergy to undertake work in one of the Provinces in which there is at present no missionary work of this communion.' But the MSCC felt it could not 'see its way under present circumstances to binding the Church in Canada to the large, unknown, and growing responsibility which would be involved in undertaking the missionary work of an assigned district in China.' The laymen, led by the indefatigable S.H. Blake, persuaded the society to defer its decision at least until it had a report from the field detailing costs and location.

At the invitation of the Canadian Presbyterians in North Honan, W.C. White went to consider the provincial capital of Kaifeng [KAIFENG], located a few miles south of the Yellow River, which was the Presbyterian boundary. Kaifeng had the distinction of being the last provincial capital to be opened to missionaries; as late as 1902, a sign on the city walls declared, 'No scripture sellers allowed in here.' Since then it had been 'occupied' by the China Inland Mission, the American Lutherans, and the Southern Baptists.

With its yellow walls rising from the yellow plain, Kaifeng seemed like many other dusty North China cities. But behind its walls lay one of the great treasure houses of Chinese culture, a centre of art and learning that had once been capital of China, and had been cosmopolitan at the time when Christ was born. Within the missionary community, Kaifeng had an added significance as the home of the last surviving colony of Chinese Jews, which, after maintaining its separate identity for a thousand years, had begun to diminish after the death of the last rabbi in the 1850s.

White was excited by the prospects of Kaifeng. With the opening of the Lunghai [LONGHAI] railway, which ran west from Shanghai to Sian [XIAN], he pointed out, Kaifeng was an accessible city that was welcoming to foreigners. Chengchow [ZHENGZHOU], eighty kilometres west of Kaifeng and at the junction with the north-south railway from Peking to Hankow, would make an ideal second centre. (Chengchow is now the capital of Honan, a major industrial centre; Kaifeng, while still an important educational city, has fallen to the position of district capital.) The Canadian church, White stated, could open a modest mission with three missionaries for $12 000 annually, and could expand through co-operation with the other missions. Eventually, he felt, the church could establish a union university in Kaifeng. It was an ambitious yet sensible plan, and the bishops, who came to the MSCC meeting prepared to oppose it, 'afterwards confessed to their inability to rise up and do so ... because the very Spirit of Pentecost pervaded the assembly ... Thus did meet Honan the old and Canada the young, together to build on Honan's plains a Church, young in life and experience, but as old as "The faith once delivered unto the saints."'

A year later, when the mission was almost a reality, Archbishop S.P. Matheson, Primate of the church, still hesitated when White's original $12 000 estimate had soared to $45 000 for eight missionaries and a plant in three cities. 'Thereupon, the Hon. S.H. Blake, with chivalrous devotion, undertook to make himself responsible for any deficiency that might exist in the income of the Society at the end of the year; [and] ... Rev. Canon Scott, of St. Matthew's Church, Quebec, sent a thrill through the whole Church by proposing that his congregation should dispense with a new organ which they were about to procure and devote the money, $6000, towards the buildings of the new Mission in China.' The proposal carried unanimously. A few days later in St James' Cathedral, William Charles White was consecrated the first Canadian bishop to be assigned to an overseas diocese. (Within a year, Heber Hamilton of the Wycliffe Japan mission became the second.) White was named Bishop *in* (not *of*) Honan.

Bishop White and his wife arrived in Kaifeng, somewhat inauspiciously, in the middle of the night in a blinding sandstorm. Dr Whitfield Guiness, superintendent of the China Inland Mission hospital in the city and son-in-law of Hudson Taylor, offered to put them up until they were able to lease the property next door. 'The landlord would not rent the house to us,' White wrote to the MSCC, 'without having a clause inserted in the rental agreement that it was not to be a place for the preaching of the Gospel.' Two weeks after moving in, accompanied by four Chinese priests he had brought with him from Fukien and his four household servants, Bishop White held his first preaching service.

Significantly, White did not bring a single foreign colleague with him from Fukien. The world-wide policy of the Church Missionary Society, under which he had served, was to utilize 'native helpers under European supervision.' Though this system could lead to paternalism, its intent, as White showed in Honan, was to build a Chinese church that would be self-governing, self-supporting, and self-propagating. Rather than 'complacent and inefficient foreign personnel,' White explained to the MSCC, his real colleagues would be the pastors he brought from Fukien: 'The day for direct evangelistic work by the foreigner in China has gone.' As John Foster has commented, White's aim was to build an institutional church; 'but a Chinese Church armed with the Gospel, rather than a battalion of Canadian missionaries, was to be the means.'

The first Canadian party who came after Bishop White's arrival in Kaifeng had a rather shaky start: two unmarried sisters, Maude and Annie Sedgewick, both contracted typhus and had to withdraw within the year; and a third single woman, Mrs Beatrice Jones, a widow who (as she wrote in her application) had been 'married just seven weeks and then once more became free to offer my services for work abroad,' came down with smallpox and tuberculosis and died at a Swiss spa where she went to recuperate. The others, however, all gave twenty years of service each, the Reverend George Simmons as canon of the cathedral, and Miss Katherine Robbins as principal of the girls' school.

Bishop White, wrote Lewis Walmsley in the official biography, *Bishop in Honan*, 'approached the building of a mission with his usual careful planning, inexhaustible energy and dynamic enthusiasm.' Charles Taylor, who wrote about Bishop White in *Six Journeys: A Canadian Pattern*, echoes this. White was 'no desk-bound administrator ... For years he bounced along the rough country roads on a motorcycle, much to the amazement of the peasants and (one suspects) to the gratification of his own sense of showmanship.'

By 1913, when the mission was three years old, Bishop White could write confidently that despite initial prejudice 'the Mission plant has developed considerably' since the revolution, 'and the Mission is in favour with all people from the Governor of the Province down.' He himself had been decorated by President Yuan Shih-k'ai for his chairmanship of the famine relief committee during the famine of 1911. The mission had stations in three cities, Kaifeng, Chengchow, and Kweiteh [GUIDE, now called SHANGQIU], which was also on the Lunghai railway line 145 kilometres east of Kaifeng. In the capital itself, the mission owned three properties, including the ruins of the Jewish synagogue. In 1913 alone, White started construction on four buildings: an orphanage, a women's hospital, a boys' boarding school, and the nave of the future Trinity Cathedral. In addition to Bishop and Mrs White, there were thirteen missionaries on the field, Canon Simmons and his wife, five single men, and six single women.

Ironically, Bishop White's very success almost precipitated his downfall. Having the title attached to his name changed him; he was no longer the earnest, evangelical soul but a prince of the church, one of the youngest men to hold the office. 'Like many men who have felt called of God to a special destiny,' writes Lewis Walmsley, 'and been promoted rapidly to positions of prominence, Bishop White guarded jealously the authority his church had bestowed upon him. He assigned duties and delegated responsibility, but shared none of the prerogatives of his office. This made him appear a dictator to some on the Honan mission.'

In the correspondence of the MSCC in the Anglican church archives, there is a slim file in Canon Gould's papers, marked 'Important – Keep in Current Files – Private – Constitutions and Canons, Diocese of Honan.' The file also contains a letter from Primate Matheson dated 7 May 1915, asking each missionary in Honan for 'a candid and strictly confidential expression of your views concerning the causes of, and remedy for, the conditions' in the mission.

Of the nine replies, few have anything good to say about Bishop White; every one suggests he be recalled and be replaced with 'a strong man "full of faith and of the Holy Ghost" to take charge during his absence.'

Those are strong words. By that time, emotions were running so high in the mission, according to an American Lutheran who was helping out in the boys' school, that 'some of the missionaries do not exchange greetings or pass the time of day when their duties bring them into contact.' According to the other letters, Bishop White treated his Canadian workers as 'Juniors,' gossiped behind their backs that they were 'dreadful,' and 'tried to keep their work under the closest supervision.' He was 'instable,' vacillating, 'a man who changed with every changing wind.' Though too Anglican to question the fact that a bishop had supreme authority, the missionaries did allow themselves to object to the way this particular one chose to wield it. In particular, White had to learn how to 'rule his own house,' as St Paul said, and curtail his wife's 'neurotic' and 'willful' behaviour.

'Bishop White went to China very young,' wrote the 'spiritual' Canon Simmons, one of White's strongest supporters, 'since when he has spent very little time comparatively among his own people ... Irrespective of either feelings or rights of those working with or under him,' he continued, '(at least it has seemed so), he carries out his plans varying as they may from time to time, without consultation, although the consummation of such new plans may be construed by the interested parties as the breaking of pledges given.'

One might be tempted to dismiss this file as another outbreak of 'missionary quarrels,' except for this underlying theme of broken faith. 'Our mission in Kaifeng opened with a lie,' wrote Bessie Benow, a deaconess in the girls' school, referring to the original rental agreement. 'This has been the policy followed by the Bishop throughout. He has considered no promise binding but has broken faith with the CIM in Kaifeng, the [American] Baptists in Chengcheo [sic], the Presbyterian Mission north of the river, and with his own workers. We are known among the Missions as a mission which does not keep faith.'

To their credit, the missionaries did not blame White for trusting his Chinese pastors over themselves; that was one area where White never broke faith. But in his dealings with other missions, he refused to accept any co-operative venture that would limit his authority as bishop of the whole province of Honan. To the Baptists in Chengchow, he wrote, 'Either I did not make myself clear, or else there is a misunderstanding as to our footing in Honan. I did not ask *permission* from your Mission to start a preaching hall ... What I did was practically to notify you of the step I was taking, and did so hoping that it might meet with the approval of your Mission.'

The story of the Kaifeng hospital was more complicated, and illustrates how instructions from Canada could be misinterpreted once they got to the field. White's heart was never in medical work; it was too expensive for one thing, and, he felt, better left to the Chinese themselves. His accounts of the 1911 famine, however, so moved the church at home that St Paul's Church, Toronto, raised $6000 for the establishment of 'the Honan Medical Mission.' White settled on a hospital site in Kaifeng, in the South Gate suburb, first renting the property and then purchasing it; it was the only one 'with electric light plant and other conveniences.' However, White had originally acquired the site with the help of the CIM on the understanding that he would undertake no medical work. 'My only objection to this,' White wrote to Canon Sydney Gould, secretary of the MSCC, 'and it is only a sentimental one, at its best, is that it will bring our large hospital close to the CIM small one and in a sense overwhelm it.' What he did not explain for another two years was that his proposed hospital lay between the CIM facility and the road. Overwhelm it indeed!

When the CIM objected to this breach of comity, White attacked his erstwhile friends on theological grounds: 'Day by day I am more and more astonished at what I would consider the unScriptural and unspiritual methods of the CIM'; and, in a later letter, 'Now the CIM here, though they have missionaries who call themselves Anglicans, are supposed to work along Baptist lines, though really they are Plymouth Brethren in practice ... Consequently I feel it better for us and our work to have nothing whatever to do with them on any lines of outward agreement or federation.'

Once the foundations of the hospital were dug, Bishop White engaged an English doctor, Margaret Phillips, to supervise construction. Dr Phillips is an interesting figure, if only because she was one of the few missionaries described as a 'feminist.' She came highly recommended from the Society for the Propagation of the Gospel mission in Shantung, with a reference from the famous Dr William Osler in London, and had already built two hospitals in China. However, she could be abrasive and, according to her housemate, Miss Benbow, was subject to 'frequent, uncontrolled, violent outbursts of temper.' The Bishop in turn belittled her work and disputed her diagnoses (having taken some homeopathic instruction in Toronto, he felt himself qualified as a medical practitioner). Relations between them deteriorated to the point that Canon Gould had to go to China to mediate a conciliation that placed the doctor and the bishop on equal footing in the hospital board. As soon as he left, White resigned from the board saying, according to Dr Phillips, that he could take no 'responsibility for the hospital and that it must be run as a separate institution from the rest of the Mission.'

When the hospital did open in November 1914, it attracted few of the hordes who came to the CIM hospital (which White had disparaged as 'hardly more than a *Dispensary*'). If things had been better planned, wrote Dr Paul V. Helliwell from the small hospital at Kweiteh, there would not be 'two large women's hospitals *side by side* at Kaifeng, and no other such for hundreds of miles in all directions.'

By this time, the MSCC had been hearing rumours from various mission and non-mission sources in the field, and on the same day that the Primate sent his letter to the missionaries, he sadly sent one recalling Bishop White to face a special meeting of the society. When White met the committee in September, he was exonerated for the most part, except for tactlessness. The troublesome Dr Phillips, along with a priest described as 'as unfit for the missionary calling as the armless man is for a boxer,' were both fired from the mission. The Kaifeng hospital was closed, its name and function moved to Kweiteh, and the building converted into a boys' school.

White returned to Kaifeng a chastened man. By the same token, he had learned his lesson; there is no indication that anything approaching 'the conditions in Honan' in 1915 ever occurred again. The Anglican mission became widely respected, not only within the province and the Anglican community, but also throughout China, as a forward-looking operation. Even so, I suspect that this packet of letters – 'Important – Keep in Current Files' – was saved for future reference, for at odd moments an incongruous remark slips out. Twenty years later, when White was about to retire from Honan, he suggested he should be named 'bishop emeritus.' Canon Gould noted sharply that the mission 'must be kept clear of any possible activities, welcome or unwelcome, of a bishop emeritus and his "wife."'

By the time Ruth Jenkins arrived in Kaifeng in 1921, the 1915 incident had long since been forgotten.

Miss Jenkins was not an important missionary, even within the Anglican mission; she served one five-year term, three years of it in language study, had a one-year furlough, and then returned for the first year of her second term before the great evacuation of 1927. She is, though, respresentative of the most significant group of new mission workers of the 1910s and 1920s: the single women. You could see 'gangs' of them everywhere foreigners gathered in China – at the summer resorts, in the language schools, in the mission councils. 'An awfully nice bunch of girls,' Ruth Jenkins called them: laughing, talkative, interesting women.

Every week Miss Jenkins would sit down and write a long chatty letter to her mother detailing the doings of 'dear, dusty old Kaifeng'; and these letters illustrate the daily life of an ordinary single woman missionary better than a hundred pages of formal reports to the mission boards. Such letters they are! – a compendium of gossip and exclamation marks. Miss Jenkins came from the cream of Ottawa society. Her mother was Annie Lampman Jenkins, doyenne of the city's opera society; and her uncle was the poet Archibald Lampman. From them she had inherited a flair for language, and she enlivened many parties in Kaifeng with her 'yards of screamingly funny doggerel.'

Her letters capture Bishop White – 'Bip,' she called him – in his lighter moments. On first meeting, she announced that he was 'a darling ... and is full of energy, really "up and doing."' She quickly became 'the pet of the See House' – there is a hint that Bishop White favoured her at least in part because of her upper-class background – and was always being asked to play the piano for visiting dignitaries. She and her housemates, 'the Lao Fu Men maids,' threw one memorable Christmas dinner at which they had not only Bishop White but the 'austere' Canon Gould romping on the floor playing silly parlour games. Christmas was an important part of missionary life – descriptions of foreign and Chinese Christmas observances abound in mission literature – and Ruth outlined how she would carefully fold the wrapping paper each year and store the decorations, the red candles and the party favours. On this particular occasion, after a traditional Canadian Christmas dinner, with chicken instead of turkey, the hosts passed out toy instruments to the guests, who promptly dubbed themselves 'The Squealy Shriekwell Society of Musical Highbrows.' 'The Bishop, being the oldest member of the mission and the head of it, was presented with a beard, he being the revered and respected patriarch of the Squealy Shriekwell Society. The Canon, being the official scribe, ... received a tiny notebook, on the outside was written *Speeches, Reports and Other Tales* ... We had loads of fun over this and nearly laughed our heads off.'

Though White had a reputation for misusing the talents of his workers (putting 'nurses to work as matrons of girls' schools and teachers in hospital administration,' as one missionary told the author), Ruth never criticizes the fact that she spent her first years in comparative idleness because White required his workers to have 'a clear three years for the language,' one year longer than other missions. All the while, he kept shunting aside questions as to her final duties, giving her such part-time tasks as teaching singing and doing book-keeping. 'Imagine me keeping accounts!' she wrote. 'We do many things out here that we would never dream of doing at home, simply because there is no one else to do them.' Finally, after she scored perfect in her third and final exam, she announced that 'I am to commence work amongst the students in the government and other schools in ... a sort of YWCA, a club embracing many different kinds of activities and appealing to the educated classes.'

Having given her her assignment, the bishop thereafter seems to have taken little further interest, and it is sad to read of her efforts to gather a group of women by putting up, in the government schools, notices offering English and music lessons. She enlisted a friend, a Miss Sia, daughter of the Kuomintang foreign commissioner of the province, as her entrée to 'the higher class people … the good families.' The YWCA never got off the ground, and the following year Ruth Jenkins became principal of St Mary's Girls' School when another missionary went on furlough.

If spent in usefulness and good works, spinsterhood was regarded as an honourable estate. Yet a young woman could go to China and become a doctor or a school principal – prove herself in a hundred ways – and still be bound to her parents. Many was the missionary called home to give up her career for family duties. 'Darling, darling Mother,' Ruth wrote at the age of thirty, 'I do appreciate and will always appreciate the sacrifice that you are making in letting me come to China, and be away from you for so many years.'

The position of a missionary with one of the Woman's Missionary societies was, the common saying went, like being in a convent without walls. A recent feminist caucus has claimed their lives were more astringent than that: a single woman 'made no vow of celibacy, yet faced virtual charges of betrayal if she married. She had not joined an order and therefore did not have the explicit and intentional support of her sisters.'

That is not quite true. Women missionaries did form a sisterhood, a network of friends and acquaintances that stretched twenty thousand kilometres and cut across denominational lines perhaps more effectively than the men's friendships. From isolated inland stations, they kept in touch across the vast distances by letter (many of these were mimeographed for further distribution by the WMS at home) and by regular visits. The highlight of the year was summer vacation at one of the resorts, where there was (as at Kuling [GULING]) a designated 'spinsters' row' of bungalows.

Immediately after Christmas, according to Ruth Jenkins' letters, the single women would start making plans for the summer; money had to be saved, outfits tailored or revamped (the Peter Pan collar enlivened an otherwise drab Chinese cotton dress), and housemates arranged. About the middle of June, the whole mission would decamp, except for a skeleton staff who stayed behind; this was true not only for the Anglican missions, but for virtually every station in China. The Presbyterians in North Honan favoured Chikungshan [JIGONGSHAN], in the mountains of southern Honan, where the Goforths held regular revivals. The West China mission, isolated beyond the gorges, had several resorts in Szechuan, including Mount Omei and, closer to Chengtu, Douglas Heights.

Each resort had its own personality and, in her four summers in China, Ruth visited the best in North and Central China: Peitaiho [BEIDAIHE], with its emerald mountains enshrouded with fog; and Chikungshan, on the northern coast of Shantung, with its sparkling beaches; Kuling, with its emerald mountains enshrouded with fog; and Chikungshan, Kuling's poor country relative.

'The costume for the afternoon,' wrote Ruth Jenkins from Peitaiho in her first summer, 'was middies and bloomers.' These resorts offered missionaries (and other foreign residents) an 'escape from China in China,' a chance to get away from the servants and let down their hair. (Or, more to the point, a chance to wear dresses with short sleeves and higher skirts.) In Kuling, for example, where she spent one summer with five 'girls' in a rented house, one had brought a Victrola 'and we set it going whenever we feel gay and giddy, and dance around, either together or alone, doing fancy dancing.' A few weeks earlier she had asked her mother for a book on palmistry: 'We get crazy streaks out here,' she explained, 'and just now we have the craze for reading hands.'

Reading between the lines one can sense how compound-centric were the lives of the single women. 'Our life here,' she wrote after two years in Kaifeng, 'must be much like village life, I think. We feel as if we owned the place and resent anyone coming here we don't know. Occasionally on the street we meet a strange man, a foreigner, probably a businessman passing through Kaifeng, and we stare at him with questioning glances, as much as to say, Who are you and what are you doing here? and we are not content until we know who the stranger is!'

'My bedroom walls are done now,' she reported in her first spring. 'My room looks a perfect picture, with its fresh pink walls, the pink cretonne curtains and cushions and the white furniture. My beautiful pictures look so well on the pink walls and are a constant joy to look at. At night time, the light shining out of my pink shade sheds a pretty rosy glow over the whole room.'

Ruth was an athletic woman but, like the CIM pioneers of the 1880s, had to take her exercise in the compound courtyard. Tennis was her passion. During the 'constant terror' of 1924, when the city was right in the middle of a civil war, her only activity, she recorded, was 'Monday, school and tennis. Tuesday, school and tennis. Wednesday, school, prayer-meeting and tennis. Thursday, school and tennis. Friday, school and tennis. Saturday, did odd jobs, tea and tennis.'

The political scene is also revealed in Ruth Jenkins' letters – she is constantly presenting her mother with large chunks of Chinese politics, as well as clippings from Chinese newspapers – yet the troubles of 'poor China' seem to be distant, perhaps reflecting the modulated tone of the bishop. She did have a few rough weeks in 1922 during the First An–Chih civil war, when Kaifeng was besieged; on one occasion, the Anglican compound became a refugee camp to fifteen hundred women and children. 'The gorgeous moon seemed to shed its glory in mockery over the terrified city all night ... There was not a stir from those hundreds of women and the occasional cry of a child was quickly stifled. There was no panic, only patience.'

She took her furlough in 1925 and thus missed 'the year of looting,' but returned in the middle of the civil war between the North and the South. Politics recedes from her letters at this point because she falls in love with the Reverend Horace Watts, a recent arrival. 'This has been a very happy week,' she wrote, 'in spite of fightings and rumours of fightings. I have seen a good deal of Horace and somehow or other we have been drawn very close.' Two weeks later, Bishop White ordered the evacuation of the mission and, after a short delay in Tientsin, Horace Watts and Ruth Jenkins returned to Ottawa where they were married on the lawns of the family estate in Kingsmere. (The Reverend and Mrs Watts were sent to Japan in 1928 and served there until 1940, when he was made secretary of the MSCC; later he became Bishop of Caledonia. Dr Ronald Watts, formerly principal of Queen's University, is their son.)

Marriage was not the life goal of most single women missionaries – they did not go to China to 'get a man.' But a significant proportion of them did marry, usually within their own missions. The China Inland Mission, which still clung to the regulation that all missionaries, male and female, should go out unmarried, encouraged marriage once the two-year probation was passed. In addition, many women did marry outside their mission, which led to a complicated policy to determine which society would pay the woman's travel and language-school expenses. But the decision to marry had to be weighed by the single woman; with marriage she automatically gave up her special privileges as a missionary in her own right to take up the duties of wife, mother, and help-meet to the male missionary.

8 · The Apostolic Vocation: Roman Catholic Missions

'Let us remember that our Church was born like the Church on Calvary, in tears and in blood ... For a flourishing and healthy Church to grow in the soil of China with the fabric of French Canada etched into its fabric, we here must also repeat the deeds of old and take on the hearts of martyrs. We must put aside our selfish reckoning, we must forget what we did yesterday and think only of giving generously today, giving without limit ... a heart burning with the desire to see our race plant the Church of God in China just as our glorious ancestors planted it here.'

Joseph-Louis Lavoie, SJ, in *Le Brigand*, 1937

Roman Catholic missionaries had been in China for six hundred years before the arrival of the first Canadian representatives of Roman Catholicism in the aftermath of the Boxer rebellion. The Catholic presence had not been continuous, however, for the church had been banished from the empire for longer periods than it had been allowed in. The Franciscan friars who followed the path of Marco Polo enjoyed a certain popularity at the imperial court of the 'foreign' (i.e., non-Chinese, like the later Manchus) Mongols. When the Mongols were conquered by the Ming [MING] in 1368, the seventy-year-old Franciscan mission vanished with barely a ripple, and it was not until the Jesuit Matteo Ricci reached the court of the Ming emperor nearly two and a half centuries later that foreign missionaries were allowed to preach Christianity in China.

Fathers of the Scarboro Foreign Mission Society and Grey Sisters, Chekiang

To put this second wave into perspective, Ricci arrived in Peking in 1610, and in the same year the first missionary landed on the shores of New France. The two events were not unrelated. Both missions were manifestations of the global commercial, military, and religious expansion of Renaissance Europe in the late sixteenth and early seventeenth centuries and both were dominated by members of the Jesuit order. The Jesuit *Relations* (or letters home) from America, New France, and Paraguay virtually created the myth of the 'noble savage' in European intellectual circles; the *Relations* from China created the other, opposite Enlightenment myth of the 'civilized pagan.' In imitation of Chinese mandarins, gentlemen of Europe began to braid their hair into a queue, a fashion that became a hallmark of eighteenth-century Europe and America.

The Society of Jesus was founded in 1534 – the year Jacques Cartier planted his cross on the shores of Gaspé – and given papal sanction six years later by Ignatius of Loyola as 'an essentially missionary order' to convert the infidels. Francis Xavier, the order's first missionary and one of its co-founders (later named as one of the patron saints of New France), was despatched by the pope to the Portuguese colonies in the East. Often described as 'the first modern missionary,' Xavier established a string of stations from Goa, in India, to Japan, but he died in 1552 on a rocky island named Sancian [SANSHAN], ninety-five kilometres south of Macao, without ever entering China, his life's goal.

The fast-barred gates of China opened a crack when the Portuguese were granted residency at Macao, an equally desolate island that was separated from the mainland by a wall. After forty years of clandestine explorations and small foundations by various Jesuits, Ricci was given an official escort to take him to the Ming Great Within, the emperor's forbidden city. Although he got no further than kowtowing to the empty throne chair (the Wanli [WANLI] emperor no longer received delegations from outside the court), he did manage to have several gifts – of ostrich feathers, holy pictures, clocks, and even a harpsichord – taken into the emperor's presence. As a result, he was granted an imperial stipend to maintain a mission in Peking where he could teach Chinese scholars the secrets of Western learning.

In order to convert China from the top down, the Jesuits developed a policy of cultural accommodation. They became the epitome of Chinese scholars, dressing in the silk gowns of the literati rather than their order's traditional black robes. 'What could be more absurd than to transport France, Spain, Italy, or some other European country to China?' the

Propagation of the Faith instructed its missionaries. 'Do not introduce all that to them, but only the Faith, which does not despise or destroy the manners and customs of any people, always supposing that they are not evil ... Do your utmost to adapt yourselves to them.'

As other religious orders entered China, the 'Chinese Rites controversy' arose, focused on charges by the Dominicans and Franciscans that the Jesuits had adapted themselves so closely to Chinese ways as to enter into heresy. In particular, by condoning ancestor worship they had in effect allowed pagan Chinese into the Christian heaven. The other orders, confined to working in the rural areas, saw how superstitious ancestor worship really was. After nine successive popes had wrestled with the question whether it was a religious ('worship') ceremony or one of filial respect, Benedict xiv ruled in 1742 that the Jesuits were wrong; this ruling, along with other factors, led to the abolition of the Jesuit order seventeen years later. Meanwhile, the Yung-cheng emperor, incensed that his personal judgment had been countermanded by a foreign prelate, issued his *Sacred Edict* proscribing Christianity.

Almost a century passed between Yung-cheng's edict and the reintroduction of Roman Catholic missions on the coat-tails of renewed western expansion after the First Opium War. This new generation of priests, and an increasing number of religious women, were a different breed from their predecessors. They were bound by the rites settlement of no compromise: in fact, until 1939 when, as one of his first pontifical acts, Pius xii resolved the controversy once and for all by rescinding Benedict's decree, each missionary at the beginning of his career had to preach a sermon affirming his opposition to ancestor worship and to all aspects of Chinese paganism.

This intransigence towards Chinese ways reflected the spirit of ultramontanism that had enveloped the Vatican in the mid-nineteenth century. All over Europe, the Catholic church was under attack by the anti-clerical states, the *Kulturkampf* in Germany, the Laic Laws in France, and Garibaldi's armies, which were gobbling up the Papal States in the name of a free and united Italy. The response of Pope Pius ix was to withdraw from the political realm into the spiritual and, as a self-imposed prisoner of the Vatican, to hurl anathemas against all who dared suggest he 'reconcile himself to, and agree with, progress, liberalism and civilization as lately introduced.' It was not possible, he stated, *Non Possumus*, for the church to compromise with a secular state.

This led to an anomalous situation in the foreign missions area. Ever since Pius vi had signed the Concordat with Napoleon in 1814, the Vatican had recognized France as the protector of its missions 'east of the Levant.' Over the century, the great mission centres were established in France, especially La Sainte-Enfance (translated into English as Holy Childhood), which made Lyons the financial headquarters of the Far Eastern missions; and older orders – the Missions-Etrangères, the Foreign Missions Society that supplied much of the manpower, for example – were strengthened. France clung to this religious connection overseas even as its own society was becoming secularized through the Laic Laws, which dismembered the vast holdings of the religious orders, first by stripping them of their role in education and then by confiscating their properties.

Nevertheless, France regarded Catholic missionaries – the majority of whom were French – as its emissaries, and was always willing to use their troubles to extend the might of Imperial France. Indeed, the 'toleration clauses' that S. Wells Williams talked about in 1860, which guaranteed protection to Christian missionaries and their converts in China, were actually inserted into the Chinese version of the French treaty ending the Second Opium War – even though the French version was the legal one – by a priest acting as the delegation translator. After that, in the 1880s, France used missionary troubles as an excuse for its seizure of Indo-China.

The Chinese government agreed to French diplomatic protection of Catholic missions, going so far as to allow Spaniards and Italians to travel on French diplomatic passports. (As late as the 1930s, certain Canadian missionaries were still registered with the French rather than the British consulate.) China continued to make concessions to the Catholic church until, in 1899, it gave official status to Catholic missionaries, making a bishop equivalent to a provincial governor and granting a local parish priest the same rank as a district magistrate. The Protestants, as we have seen, reluctantly declined this honour, but the French priests seized upon it for the glory of Holy Mother Church. Using his new legal status, the foreign priest would often 'intrude himself into the Chinese court and sit beside the magistrate to hear the case' brought against a non-Christian who was 'persecuting' one of his converts. The convert usually won.

The growth of Catholic missions in China roughly paralleled that of the Protestant missions: consolidation in the treaty ports in the period between the opium wars followed by a penetration into the outlying areas that was greatly accelerated in the 1880s. During the suppression of Christianity, small scattered communities of Catholics, visited perhaps once in a lifetime by a smuggled priest, had survived under councils of elders and virgins. These congregations (*chrétientés* in French, or 'Christendoms') numbering as many as 200 000 individuals in 1840, became the foundation of the renewed Catholic missionary effort. In addition, after considerable diplomatic pressure, the old religious orders were given back properties that had been confiscated since the 1740s; in Shanghai, for example, the reconstituted Jesuits regained the ancestral estate of the Zi [XIU] family (converts since the early seventeenth century) and there built their 'fortress' of Zikawei [XIUJIAHUI].

But such foundations were the exception rather than the rule in areas remote from the treaty ports. Suchow [XUZHOU], the French-Canadian Jesuit mission five hundred kilometres north-west of Shanghai, showed the typical progress of Catholic missions: when the French missionaries arrived after 1882, they found no trace of the Christian community that had been founded as early as 1598 by Matteo Ricci and had had two separate churches, one for men and one for women. 'Not one descendant of the 1000 Catholics of 1703 kept the faith or one relic of the past: crucifix, chaplet, prayer book. They couldn't even identity the location of the former buildings.' The officials in Suchow city were unremittingly hostile towards Christianity during the 1880s and 1890s, and the French priests were almost forced to build up Christian communities in the countryside.

Because of its early inception and the aggressive tactics of the French priests, the Catholic church grew rapidly in China, always counting ten times the number of Protestant converts and reaching one million during the 'mass movement' of 1907. The Boxer rebellion had been especially virulent in Catholic areas, leading to wholesale massacres of certain communities. Forty-seven foreign priests and nuns were martyred (four of them, along with fifty-two converts, were canonized in 1955), and as many as twenty thousand Chinese converts. The Catholic missions demanded, and received, an enormous indemnity for these deaths and the destruction of property; the money was turned towards the building of new church complexes incorporating schools, churches, orphanages, and catechumenates.

The First World War marked the end of France's century of missions. The Separation Act of 1905, which severed the links between church and state, had resulted in the breaking of diplomatic relations between France and the Vatican. Over the next twenty years, the church systematically removed the missionary organizations from France, bringing Sainte-Enfance directly under the control of the Propaganda in Rome and building up the foreign mission seminary in Milan. In 1914–15, most of the younger, healthy French missionary priests were conscripted back to France, which decimated the China missions. When the call came from Rome for other nationalities to step into the breach, the church in Canada was ready.

By the end of the 1920s, after a decade of internationalization, more than a dozen countries were represented in the China missions, among them Hungary and Mexico. Other countries, notably Germany and the United States, sent out Catholic missionaries as well as Protestant ones, but only Canada sent out representatives of each group who differed both in religion and in race and culture. Fully seven-eighths of the Canadian Catholic missionaries to China, 389 out of 446 in 1941, were members of French-Canadian orders. In China as in Canada, the famous 'two solitudes' were still in effect: when English Canadians encountered French Canadians in the interior of China, sixteen thousand kilometres from 'home,' the only language they could communicate in was Chinese.

The existence of this *petit coin de l'atmosphère du Canada* in *la brousse*, the 'bush,' – or as another noted, in English, 'Canadian soil in the midst of China' – resulted from a unique set of circumstances in French Canada, not the least of which was French-Canadian wanderlust. The exploration of the interior of North America was but an early expression of the trait that led some 600 000 Québécois (one-third of the population) to emigrate to the United States. Like island dwellers, French Canadians have always been fascinated with tales from far away, whether from the *pays en haut*, the Canadian North West, or a Massachusetts mill town like Lowell, or China. 'We are nomads, we have the desire to leave, to travel, to move,' commented Father Benoît Lacroix, professor of history at the Université de Montréal.

By the same token, French-Canadian society – a society whose motto *'Je me souviens'*, 'I remember,' looks to the past – was closed in on itself, afraid of the outside world. After the British conquest of Quebec in 1763, the British had tried to force the French to assimilate, going so far as to nominate bishops and clergy who supported this policy. Comparing the position of the Catholic church in French Canada in the late nineteenth century to a century earlier, the historian Marcel Trudel noted, 'it is hard to imagine that from the conquest until 1840 it had been deprived of everything, condemned to stagnation, ceaselessly humiliated by the government, and it may be forgotten that at times its very existence was threatened.'

But it had survived, and under the saintly, autocratic Bishop Ignace Bourget of Montreal it gave the people a vision of themselves as God's chosen people, poor, simple, uncontaminated, bound by the holy trinity of Faith, Language, and Family. Theirs was a practical faith – 'in France, they wrote, here they acted' – passed down from generation to generation through the rituals of the family, the signs of the cross, novenas, and crucifixes, not only in the houses but in public places (schools, hospitals, courtrooms) as well. 'There were not so many foundations of contemplative religious orders,' continued Father Lacroix. 'The tendency in French Canada in this period was to go out among the people, to be of service. They were drawn more toward the active Martha than towards Mary, seated and contemplative. It was the Gospel of the glass of water, the Gospel of service.'

The consolidation of the Catholic church in Quebec continued after Bishop Bourget's death in 1870, strengthened by the abolition of the short-lived provincial Ministry of Education five years later, which put education under the religious orders. This in turn led to 'a religious awakening among the people: the creation of new dioceses [fifteen in this period], the advent of new religious communities, the multiplication of retreats and parish visits, and above all of the missionary impulse towards the Canadian North-West. All this was very important in the collective imagination.'

American Catholicism always had the reputation within the Catholic church of a certain liberalism, but the Quebec Church was reputed to be one of the most monolithic, untainted by contact with the modern world. Father Philippe Côté, superior and eventually bishop of the Jesuit mission to Suchow, hastened to reassure his readers that though he was born in Massachusetts he was American in name only. 'Américain, moi?' he wrote in the order's mission magazine, Le Brigand:

Never in my life! I must confess that one fine day my grandfather went for a walk to Lawrence, and stayed there. My father, too. Is that my fault? As soon as I was old enough to walk, I found myself living in Victoriaville where I took my first classes, before going on to finish them in Levis ... American? When I am just as much a Côté as all the Côtés on both côtés, both sides, of the St Lawrence?

By temperament and training, French-Canadian missionaries shared a common culture whether they came from New England or Cap-au-Diable where the loup-garou howled in the night. It was a pre-modern culture, with a rural mythology symbolized by the village church. In this society, where the priest was the intercessor between mankind and God, the religious vocation brought the highest honour to an individual, a family, or a whole community. By 1900, there were two thousand priests in Quebec, and 6500 nuns, an average of two priests and seven nuns to every one thousand people. Half the teachers in the primary schools and 90 per cent of college professors belonged to a religious order. The missionary vocation, with its possibility of sacrifice and martyrdom, was seen as the epitome of Catholic devotion.

French Canada had been born as a missionary venture and, as in the beginning, missions remained in its life-blood. Down through the centuries, from Marie de l'Incarnation's missions to the Indians in the early seventeenth century onwards, French Canada had sponsored 'foreign' missions. 'The inspiration came from Rome, but the reality was Québécois. The proof was the missions to the North-West. Nothing could be more Québécois, more French Canadian.' As members of French orders, the first overseas missionaries were two Sisters of Providence who went to Chile in 1853; they were followed by members of various orders en route for other Latin American countries, French colonies in Africa, and Japan in 1897. The first overseas priests, two Jesuits, who went to the Zambezi in 1883, were followed by Holy Cross Fathers destined for the Holy Land and White Fathers assigned to Equatorial Africa. By 1960, on the eve of the secularizing 'Quiet Revolution,' there were 5000 French-Canadian missionaries in sixty-eight countries, with an annual departure of 250; thirty orders had more than 50 members each overseas.

Although the orders were all based in the province of Quebec, or were Quebec branches of international orders, not all their personnel came from within the province. With few exceptions, however, they were francophone. Of the ninety-three priests and brothers who served in the Jesuit mission in China, for example, seventy-five were born in Quebec, five in Ontario, two in Manitoba, and one each in Alberta and Prince Edward Island. Five came from Franco-American communities in Massachusetts and Vermont, and five were from Europe (Belgium, France, and Germany).

Within the province, some of these orders were relatively parochial, attracting most of their personnel from one specific area. What is surprising, however, is how deeply this missionary spirit permeated the consciousness of Quebec. As the administrative centre of Quebec missions, Montreal held a position roughly analogous to that of Toronto in Protestant missions; but Quebec City was the old heartland of Catholicism. There the Franciscan Sisters of Mary had a large convent on the Grande Allée, the main boulevard of the upper town, and the Jesuits opened a Musée des Arts Chinois in their suburban St-Foy headquarters. Of the 876 sisters who joined the Missionary Sisters of the Immaculate Conception between 1902 and 1984, almost one-quarter (209) came from Quebec City; other dioceses represented were, in order, Montreal (146), St-Hyacinthe in the industrialized area east of Montreal (87), Rimouski (71), Joliette (50), Nicolet (45), and Chicoutimi in the remote Lac-St-Jean region (39). Fifty-three sisters came from other provinces of Canada, 34 from Ontario and 12 from New Brunswick; none came from the United States.

Going from rural Quebec to rural China was for many, as Jesuit missionary Father Michel Marcil commented, 'like going from St-Pierre-les-Becquets to Arthabaska.' It was a foreign country, to be sure, but it had much that was recognizable: illiterate peasants, agricultural festivals and markets, the seasonal work of seed-time and harvest. Although the missionaries used the word *païen*, pagan, almost as a technical description of any non-Christian, they reacted to the unfolding world with curiosity, friendliness, and a genuine concern for the downtrodden. Although this was a confined world seen from inside the convent or cathedral compound, nevertheless, Catholic missions in China had a reputation for knowing the secrets of their individual locality, the military manoeuvres, opium smuggling, and clan rivalries.

French-Canadian missionaries took with them to China a view of mission work that was, unlike that of either English-Canadian Protestants or French Catholics, tempered by their own history as a subject people. 'All the foreigners come here to exploit us, to make themselves wealthy, and they treat us like inferiors,' commented one non-Christian Chinese. 'Only the Belgians and the Canadians don't seem to come to exploit us or enrich themselves.'

French Canadians could salute the Union Jack in Hong Kong – 'majestic as Albion,' wrote Father Emile Gervais of his trip to the China missions, 'we reached, not without a feeling of security, a British land' – or could melt into the French presence in Shanghai; but when they crossed the borders out of Quebec they became aware of the fragility of 'the spiritual French islet' of North America. Once they reached their stations in *la brousse*, they were apt to dissociate themselves from imperial power, keeping communications with the British or Canadian consuls to a minimum. In 1939, for example, during the Japanese occupation of North

China, one anonymous Quebec Jesuit came across an anti-British demonstration with signs that read, 'Down with England, Enemy of Peace' and 'Drive Out the English'; turning to his companion, he said with 'bitter-sweet pleasure,' 'You know, you'd think we were in Quebec.'

'When I am an American missionary from California, I have the United States behind me, you see,' explained Father Marcil in a recent radio interview; 'but if I am a missionary from Marieville, will I have Quebec behind me?'

Having preserved the simple faith for so many centuries, French Canada by the beginning of the twentieth century had inherited the mantle of 'teacher of the nations.' Quebec foreign missions were, as Canon Lionel Groulx asserted as the subtitle to his history *Le Canada Français Missionnaire*, '*une autre grande aventure*.' 'The Canadian miracle of the spiritual and national survival of the French-Canadian people, isolated in the great American mass,' wrote Father Emile Gervais, 'is made manifest, is revealed, and above all is affirmed in the expansion of its apostolic and religious vitality to the ends of the earth.'

The first French-Canadian missionaries to China were two Franciscan Sisters of Mary who were sent out in 1902 to replace French sisters martyred by the Boxers in Shantung; they were joined a few years later by two Franciscan priests. By 1950, there were some four hundred French-Canadian missionaries in China working under twelve different orders. There were three French-Canadian ecclesiastical districts, each with its own bishop: the small Franciscan mission in Shantung, which never exceeded eight men; the important Jesuit mission in Suchow; and the Missions-Etrangères mission in central Manchuria. These orders of men were granted specific fields by their French confrères; the women, on the other hand, were invited by a bishop to undertake work in his diocese and thus tended to have small convents in many centres. The Missionary Sisters of the Immaculate Conception, the largest Canadian order (of either men or women), helped the Jesuits in Suchow and the Missions-Etrangères in Manchuria, and had houses in Canton, Hong Kong, Macao, Shanghai, Japan, and the Philippines. The Missionary Sisters of Notre-Dame-des-Anges worked under French bishops in Kweichow province in the south west, and in Kwangsi [GUANGXI] province, between Kweichow and Kwangtung [GUANGDONG], as well as in Hong Kong, Canton, and Macao. The Franciscan Sisters of Mary had fifty Canadian sisters in twenty-three centres, from Harbin and Chefoo in the north east to Chengtu and Kunming [KUNMING] in the south west. In addition to these large missions, there were four other international orders that had at least one or two Canadian sisters: the Soeurs Antoniennes de Marie in Manchuria, the Sisters Adorers of the Precious Blood in Hopei, North China; and the Carmelite and Sacred Heart Sisters in Shanghai.

Just as Canadian Protestant missions started with the zeal of one or two, so too French-Canadian foreign missions were inspired by one woman, Délia Tétreault, a shy unassuming nun whose religious name was Marie-du-Saint-Esprit. She must have been one of the more remarkable women ever to hide behind a wimple, for she was responsible, directly or indirectly, for founding all four of the Quebec-based orders that were 'specifically devoted to the missionary apostolate.' Her influence was officially recognized when, on 19 May 1985, the first steps were taken towards her beatification and possible canonization.

Born in 1865 in the village of Marieville in the diocese of St-Hyacinthe, eighty kilometres east of Montreal, Miss Tétreault, whose mother died when she was two and whose father emigrated to the United States, was raised by her godparents. In the convent school she was, according to a classmate, already 'a model of religious fervor, of faithfulness to duty, and of heart-sprung charity ... Already, one could sense that this young girl was marked with the sign of God. Her habitually downcast eyes easily gave the impression that her gaze was turned inward to that secret sanctuary where she kept tryst with her invisible Guest.'

Remarkably for one who founded her own religious order, she herself did not take her final vows until she was thirty-seven and at last free from family responsibilities. Prior to that had been sacristan at Béthanie, a Montreal charity. This, she felt, was preparation for 'the work' she had dreamed of since she was fifteen, the establishment of two societies, one for men and one for women, 'to serve the missionary interests of Holy Mother Church.'

Her struggles to realize her dream are an object lesson in the role of women in religious life. Archbishop Paul Bruchési of Montreal was lukewarm to the idea of a Quebec-based missionary order, because he was afraid it would become 'an added financial burden for the Archdiocese,' but he did permit her to gather a group of companions to work for the eventual foundation. Two years later, in 1904, the newly elected Pope Pius x intervened personally and ordered Bruchési to found the order. Normally, founding a new religious organization is a complicated and time-consuming business – as Father John Fraser discovered when he tried to obtain authorization for the Scarboro Foreign Mission

Society – but as soon as Bruchési presented the documents, Pius x responded, 'Let the work be founded and all celestial blessings will descend upon the new Institute which you will call, Society of the Missionary Sisters of the Immaculate Conception.' Thus was born the first North American Catholic foreign mission society.

Pius x was using the foundation of the MIC Sisters, as they are usually abbreviated, as a signal that he was trying 'to open the windows of the Church' (fifty years before John XXIII coined the phrase) to its wider universal responsibilities. Shortly thereafter, he elevated certain countries, including Canada and the United States, to their own hierarchy, that is, raised them from the status of missionary-receiving countries to that of missionary-sending ones.

There was an indirect if sometimes complicated relationship between Roman Catholic foreign missions and Protestant ones. Mother Marie recorded a conversation she had shortly after sending out her first sisters to Canton. A visiting priest had reported that the Canadian Presbyterians had just raised $15 000 for their foreign missions. This money, he continued, 'donated by their adepts to the Propagation of the Faith Association far from impoverishing their local churches had on the contrary invited unheard-of prosperity ... And what are we, Catholics, doing? ... How insignificant are our own receipts for the Propagation of the Faith! A large college sent in a paltry $2.00; a prosperous establishment forwarded $5.00; a well-to-do parish presented a derisory offering ... While we ignore our obligations towards the mission field afar the Protestants display restless activity, gathering funds, making important foundations, sending their emissaries to the Far East in notable numbers.'

The real growth of Catholic missions began in the mid-1930s; until that time, as the provincial of one seminary wrote, the mission effort remained fragmented, 'supported by a relatively small number of the faithful (usually the relatives and friends of missionaries) who give often and a great deal ... The apostolic spirit doesn't yet inspire the mass of our people. They need missionary education.' By the time the support apparatus was in place, the Missionary League of Students counted 160 000 members in the province of Quebec.

As part of the internationalization of the missions in the 1920s, Benedict xiv and his successor, Pius xi (who was described as 'the pope of missions'), stressed the indigenization or 'deoccidentalization' of foreign missions. In 1926, as one of the first acts of his reign, Pius consecrated six Chinese bishops and started the first steps towards canonization of the Boxer martyrs; he also beatified the Jesuit martyrs among the

Hurons of New France. 'It would be truly wrong to judge indigenous people as beings of an inferior race and limited intelligence,' he instructed in his important encyclical, *Rerum Ecclesiae*. 'The native priests one day must become the heads of the Churches which your sweat and sorrow have founded, the heads of the Christian communities of the future.'

One indication of this new movement towards indigenization was the founding of the second Quebec missionary order, the Missionary Sisters of Notre-Dame-des-Anges (MNDA). Florina Gervais, born in Césaire, ten kilometres from Marieville, had been one of the first MIC Sisters in Canton, where she had been assigned to teach novices. She had formed a friendship with one of these, a young Chinese woman named Tsan Tsi Kwan, a third-generation Christian; when Miss Tsan was refused admittance into the order as a regular postulant, both women quit the order and returned to Sherbrooke, where together they founded the new order with the authorization of the bishop. Shortly afterwards, the MIC Sisters also started admitting Chinese women as regular members, so that by 1950 one-third were local recruits.

So far, Mother Marie-du-Saint-Esprit had been responsible for the foundation of two orders; in 1928, a second of her sisters left the order to found the Missionary Sisters of Christ the King in Gaspé, which did not have missionaries in the China fields. But the reverend mother continued praying for what she called 'the other work,' a seminary for training secular priests, that is those attached to a parish rather than to a religious order, a congregation of men to complement her own women.

Several attempts had been made over the years to establish a branch of the Missions-Etrangères of Paris, the pre-eminent Foreign Missions Society, in Canada; but in 1919 Mother Marie convinced the bishop of Mont-Laurier (a region north of the island of Montreal) that the hour was now opportune 'for the Canadian Church to begin cancelling its debt for the priceless gift of Faith received of yore from the courageous missionaries of the Old World ... God did not want the Canadian seminary to be grafted on an old tree, but desired something new.' '*Québec ça fait,*' she stated; 'Quebec could do it.'

Independent congregations like the MIC Sisters, supported by contributions from the faithful, were one thing; but a seminary would have to be paid for by the whole church. 'Since you want a Canadian Seminary,' Monsignor Bruchési said to Mother Marie, 'find me the priests needed to establish it.' Providentially, a few days later, a young parish priest stopped at the mother house for a cup of coffee. This charming, deferential man, she decided, would found the seminary. Aldemar Lapierre was obviously the correct choice: he was the first entrant into the Missions-Etrangères in 1921, the founder of its mission to Manchuria four years later, and in 1936 the first Bishop of Szepingkai [SIPINGKAI].

The year 1924 was significant for Canadian Catholic foreign missions. On 7 September, in an impressive ceremony attended by three cardinals, twenty bishops, and numerous clergy, the seminary of the Missions-Etrangères was consecrated. It was, and is, an imposing stone structure situated on a strategic site overlooking the Rivière-des-Prairies in Pont-Viau on Laval Island north of Montreal; within a few years the building was flanked by impressive novitiates belonging to the Clerics of St Viator and the MIC Sisters. Two weeks after the consecration, many of the same bishops assembled in suburban Toronto to dedicate the equally impressive seminary of the Scarboro Foreign Mission Society. Other events of 1924 included the opening of the Notre-Dame-des-Anges convent in Lennoxville (an event that caused considerable stir in the predominantly *anglais* Eastern Townships) and the beginning of the Jesuit mission in Suchow.

When the French Jesuits had returned to China in the 1840s, they had been granted the huge area of Kiangnan [JIANGNAN], which consisted of the provinces of Anhwei and Kiangsu [JIANGSU]. After the First World War, they started to dismember it, 'carved rich populous slices out of its bulging flanks,' and handed them over to their confrères from Italy, Spain, Hungary, California, and Quebec. The Canadians were granted a rural area around the city of Suchow in the northern corner of Kiangsu, 480 kilometres north west of Shanghai. It was a strategic but isolated location, at the junction of the Peking-Hankow railway and the Lunghai railway from Shanghai, whose next stop west was Kweiteh in Honan. The area allocated to the Canadians had already been highly organized by the French fathers and, with its 14 000 converts, was the eighth largest of the 120 ecclesiastical divisions of China.

Between 1918 and 1920, the Canadians had sent six fathers to scout out the territory, but in 1924 only two remained in the field. The others had returned to Quebec to set up the support structure for the new mission. For the Jesuits to turn towards foreign missions required no change in purpose: in 1940, for example, their exhibit in the Montreal Mission Week exhibition showed a monolithic figure of Atlas holding up the world; according to the legend, one-seventh of all Catholic missionaries world-wide were Jesuits. As early as 1926, seven months after the ground-breaking *Rerum Ecclesiae*, the order had issued its own internal ordinatio, *On the Training of Missionaries in Chinese Studies*, which was 'essentially a directive for more systematic field adaptation.' This directive was of more than passing interest because it was written by the pioneer of the Canadian China mission, Father Edouard Goulet.

Father Goulet was thirty-seven when he arrived in Shanghai in 1918, accompanied by a young scholastic. After a year's language study, he was sent to Suchow to work with the French priests. In 1923, he was called to Rome as secretary-general of Jesuit missions. A capable administrator, he supervised the far-flung missions even during the dark days of the Second World War; more important, he was a progressive force, actively promoting the ordination of indigenous priests, so that by the time of his death in 1957 they made up one-third of the entire Jesuit order.

Another pioneer of the Canadian mission was to play an important role within the order. Father Georges Marin, born in 1895 in Lowell, Massachusetts, was sent to China as a young man of twenty-five before he had finished his final theology training. He spent three years at Zikawei outside Shanghai and returned to Montreal for final formation. He was sent back to China in 1926 as the Visitor, the superior of all Jesuit missions within the country. He, too, was an innovator and consolidator, who founded the Chabanel language school in Peking, the first Catholic school for the systematic study of Chinese. He remained in China until the communist revolution and gained a reputation as a theologian; the paleontologist Teilhard de Chardin called him the 'Navigator' of the Jesuit missions.

From 1924 to 1931, when the French Canadians took over full control of the Suchow mission, they sent two or three men a year, enough to replace retiring French priests; from 1932 up to the Second World War, they sent up to fifteen men annually. Some, like Father Goulet, went out in middle age, having completed the full fourteen years of Jesuit formation before leaving Canada; others, like Father Marin, went as unordained scholastics to finish their theology training in China.

Before the Chabanel language school, the Suchow mission fathers took their training at Zikawei, which has been described as 'one of the largest agglomerations of Christian works in the world.' Built on the ancestral property of Paul Zi, a Ming scholar convert of Matteo Ricci in 1600, Zikawei contained within its ten-kilometre-long walls fourteen churches, numerous chapels and schools, seminaries, orphanages, and the Aurora University, with its 80 000-volume library and meteorological observatory, the largest private one in the world. Many American priests hated Zikawei and nicknamed it 'The House of Ten Thousand Customs.' It was a 'fortress,' they felt, 'a monument to ... the futility of seeking past grandeur in minute observance of fossilized customs.' The French-Canadian Jesuits, however, were more in tune with the French spirituality of the place; when they were interned there during the Second World War, they treated it as a second home, rejoicing that at least the war had brought them back into one community.

The story of foreign missions in Quebec is a story of teamwork, of orders and seminaries; the China missions of the English-Canadian Catholic church are much more the story of one individual, Father John Mary Fraser, who, almost single-handedly 'awakened [English] Catholic Canada to its wonderful missionary destiny.'

Born in 1877 in a working-class area of Toronto, Father Fraser, son of a Scottish builder, was the ninth of eleven children, five of whom entered the religious life. At that time, anglophone Canadians had to study for the priesthood either in Montreal or in Genoa, at the Brignole Sale Collegio. Fraser chose Genoa and sailed there shortly after his twentieth birthday. Five years later, he returned to Toronto designated as a 'missionary at large' by the Propagation of the Faith and assigned to Ningpo, China.

Father Fraser spent his first terms working under the Lazarists as curate of the baroque French cathedral in Ningpo [NINGBO], a busy treaty port in Chekiang [ZHEJIANG] province 150 kilometres south of Shanghai. He was a charismatic man, and shared much of the same Scots temperament as a Goforth or a Mackay. Like them, he combined a single-minded zeal for souls with a personal brusqueness that made him difficult to work with. He wanted, he said, to come 'straight on like St Paul.' (He was almost Protestant in another respect; he was a teetotaller – most unusual for a Catholic – 'like a dyed-in-the-wool Presbyterian.')

By 1910, Father Fraser became fired up with the idea of establishing missionary seminaries and made a 'flying but very fruitful visit to Europe and America,' where he was partially responsible for founding the Maryknoll Missionary Society and the Irish Foreign Mission Society at Maynooth. However, he made no attempt to canvass English Canada until seven years later, when he returned with a message that was more urgent and more specific. The time had come, he said, for Canadian Catholics, who had been 'spared by God's mercy from the horrors and devastation which the war has carried to other Catholic lands ... to do their bit to save from destruction the work of generations of apostolic zeal in the lands still subject to heathen superstition.' Everywhere he went, from Prince Edward Island to southern Ontario, the response was enthusiastic. His tour culminated in the offer by the Archbishop of Ottawa of an unused twenty-four-room convent in Almonte, which he named the Almonte China Mission College.

By contrast with the foundation of the MIC Sisters, Father Fraser personally spent a year in Rome trying to steer the foundation of his society (based on the Milan Foreign Mission Society) through the Vatican bureaucracy. Finally, he was granted the small field of Chuchow [CHUZHOU, now called LISHUI], a mountainous region in the diocese of Ningpo, part of his old field. He returned to Canada ready to open a seminary with one student, a young Chinese named Paul Kam, and one professor, a Spanish Lazarist he had met in Hong Kong. Within a year, the Almonte building was too small, and by a fortuitous set of circumstances Fraser was enabled to purchase a dramatic piece of property overlooking the Scarborough Bluffs, east of Toronto, where he built the Scarboro Foreign Mission Society.

Father Fraser, then nearing fifty, took the first party of priests to China, a Spaniard and a Newfoundlander, in 1925. 'Unknown to the Society's many supporters,' states the history of the SFM, *Assignment in Chekiang*, 'the mission in Chekiang soon became and was to remain a recurring headache.' Relations between Fraser and the younger men were 'often strained and sometimes stormy,' a situation that led to a visit of inquiry by the society's 'foster founder,' Father J.E. McRae, rector of the seminary. Reluctantly, the society recalled Father Fraser, citing in the letter to him, 'the discord and lack of Christian harmony' that were 'rife' in the field. 'So persistent were the complaints,' the board concluded, 'that we could remain silent no longer.'

Father Fraser remained controversial and a loner throughout the rest of his life. He returned to Canada in 1930 and toured the country for two years, raising money for the society, until he received an invitation to work in the neighbouring diocese of Hangchow [HANGZHOU] in China. Except for a four-year internment by the Japanese in Manila during the Second World War, he remained in this field until 1949 'pursuing what he did best – individual evangelizing, unencumbered by any regional superior named by the controllers in Canada.' After the communist takeover, he went to the ravaged city of Nagasaki, and died in Japan twelve years later at the age of eighty-five. 'I'm always building churches,' he said of himself.

The daily routines of a Catholic missionary were quite different from those of a Protestant. Except for a few evangelists like Father Fraser, they did not go out on the streets to preach the gospel; instead they taught the catechism. Protestants, according to the mission historian, K.S. Latourette, tried 'to reach every Chinese with the Christian message,' either through literature or the spoken word; but Catholics 'placed their chief emphasis upon winning converts and nourishing a Church.'

There were voices within the church calling for accommodation with indigenous ways – such as the arrangement of candles on the altar and the style of church architecture – while maintaining the Latin Mass and the ecclesiastical hierarchy. Father Goulet, the Jesuit superior in Rome, was one who hoped the church would become 'Chinese in China as it is French in France, German in Germany, as it has in our own day become American in the United States.' But most missionaries, at least until 1946, when the Chinese hierarchy was instituted, felt 'more or less imprisoned in a system' established by the earlier French missionaries. 'We had to operate according to the rules of this system, like it or not,' one Scarboro father recalled. 'Like most systems, it had its good and bad points.'

Going from the confines of some 'Rome-in-China' like Zikawei into 'the bush' of China was at least as traumatic for Catholic missionaries as for their Protestant counterparts – perhaps more so, since their spiritual life was guided by the community. Once at their stations, they saw paganism at every turn: in the marketplace theatricals, in the familial ancestral tablets, in seasonal ceremonies. Father Fraser described in a letter home the first time 'I saw a person committing the sin of idolatry. It was an old woman prostrating herself before an idol. I'll never forget the feeling that came over me – I felt like vomiting.'

Although conditions varied from one area to another, since each mission reported to its own superiors, Catholic missionaries basically followed the catechumenate system. The keystone of this was the catechist, a local man or woman, usually married, who gave up his or her usual occupation to work for the church. The catechist was the missionary's language teacher and interpreter, companion, go-between, and guide, at least in his early years. 'The catechist knew the people and their problems,' wrote a Scarboro father, 'and he also knew our problems.' He had learned his religion well and was able to put it across well. We would have been pretty helpless without the catechists.'

This system meant that the foreign priest was often removed from the daily life of his converts. He might supervise the final stages of their catechumenate, when they came to live within the mission compound for a month or two, but he remained an aloof and distant

A Scarboro father with his catechism class

figure. Catholic missions, like Protestant ones, had a central station like Suchow city or Chuchow, and a number of outstations, each of which had dependencies of fifty to one hundred Christian communities, with anywhere from eighty to several hundred families. One priest might be responsible for ten to twenty thousand converts.

In time-honoured tradition, the church tried first to convert families rather than individuals, and then to gather them for mutual support into villages with a significant Catholic constituency. As the church grew, it would purchase land, often in North China with funds from the Boxer indemnity fund, and move Catholic tenants onto it, thus both strengthening the church and providing it with a continuing source of revenue. The church was not interested, necessarily, in converting pagans overnight with a blinding flash of conviction; rather it nurtured them slowly, transforming their children and grandchildren through education.

Whenever the priest made a visit to one of these stations – having often walked for two or three days to do so – there would be a great clamour to greet him. The children would rush out and grab his hand, the old women and the young men would hurry him to the house of the prominent Christians. 'The routine at each of the stations is the same,' wrote Joseph Venini of the Scarboro Foreign Mission Society.

'Confessions and Communions, perhaps a soul to prepare for its last journey, or it may be a marriage to regulate. There is usually a baby or two, born during the absence of the priest and baptized privately by the catechist or one of the Christians. They are brought to the chapel ... to be "supplied," that is, having the ceremonies of the Sacrament supplied.'

The China missionaries placed great emphasis on the sacraments. But in trying to combat pagan superstition, Catholic missionaries sometimes unwittingly substituted another, Christian superstition. One Quebec Jesuit noted that the Chinese, Catholic and non-Catholic alike, regarded 'medals of the Father as the most efficacious amulets against the present evils. "Very well," I tell them, "first get down on your knees and confess, get married, baptize your children, and then afterwards the medals."' A Scarboro father depicted the attitude of many converts: 'Has baby a tummy ache? A gulp of holy water will soon quiet him.'

The first and foremost sacrament was baptism. The object of Catholic missions was 'to send the most possible of these souls to paradise'; baptism even at the moment of death guaranteed that the soul would go winging straight to heaven. In one description out of thousands, Father John Fraser wrote early in his career of stopping in a peasant's house where he saw a haggard old man 'near the end.' Father Fraser asked if he wanted to become a Catholic. 'To my great joy he replied, "Yes." I then sent the catechist to instruct him in the necessary doctrine, and in half an hour he returned saying that the man wanted to be baptized ... I found upon inquiries that he had been a good man, never injuring anyone. After saying a few words of consolation, I poured the saving water over his head.' Thirty years later, he described journeying forty kilometres by bus, at a prohibitive cost of $10, to administer the sacrament. 'It was well worth the expense,' he wrote.

Only a priest could perform certain sacraments, such as Mass and marriage, but religious women, catechists, and even lay Christians could perform baptisms. Appalled by the common practice of female infanticide, the first European sisters in China would go out into the streets and baptize any baby they found abandoned. Once it became known in the neighbourhood that they were interested in unwanted infants, pathetic bundles would be left at their gates. On their excursions outside, the sisters would carry straw baskets to bring back more packages found under bridges or in garbage dumps.

By the twentieth century, orphanages and leprosaria had become important parts of Catholic missions. They were significant even in the

Unidentified sister with Chinese orphans, Chekiang

Chinese milieu. Most of the babies received by the foundling homes had been so maltreated before their arrival that they died within a few hours. Those who survived were farmed out to foster parents or wet-nurses until they were old enough to bring into the orphanage proper, where they were trained in the catechism and in needlecraft. These orphanages often supported themselves with the proceeds from selling the children's work. Once they reached a marriageable age, usually in their early teens, the girls were betrothed to local Christians, especially those who could not afford the high bride prices demanded by marriage brokers; the bride price, generally about one-third the going rate in the locale, went back into the orphanage funds. In some places, the local Catholic orphanage was the main source of unmarried girls, and many a pagan became baptized in order to marry.

One would like to know more about these orphanages. Were they the same as those in Quebec? Did they produce the same sort of institutionalized children, so transfixed by the good sisters' rule books they could barely survive life on the outside? It would be easy to accuse the sisters, living in pre-Freudian ignorance, of perpetrating heartless atrocities, snatching children from their mothers. But that is far from the truth.

The MIC Sisters ran three Holy Childhood homes in Canton, as well as others in Manchuria and Suchow. The society's magazine, *The Precursor,* is filled with heart-rending stories of these homes, which in Canton alone received forty and fifty children a day for a total of seven thousand in the year 1923. 'Our crib is rich in human miseries,' starts one typical account. The first child was horribly burned by his parents trying to drive out his demons; he 'is going to die, the poor little unfortunate; but his soul, worthy of angels' gaze, will leave his languid body without regret. Lightly will it soar to join the heavenly phalanx.'

Sometimes money changed hands in these transactions, often through a middle man or agent; the sisters defended this by saying they were paying expenses of food and travel for the orphan to be brought to the orphanage. In Chinese eyes, however, the fear arose that they were buying children; and some of their own accounts would support this. One woman, for example, brought her daughter, hoping to sell her for sixty dollars. A deal was made in the end to pay her 'forty dollars and seventy-six cents, a pair of shoes, five dresses (already much mended) and two cotton aprons.' The little child cried for a week.

Probably only a small percentage of the babies were actually purchased in this manner, yet mission propaganda at home emphasized this aspect of the work. School children in Quebec and, to a lesser extent, in English Canada were encouraged to 'buy' a Chinese orphan for a one-dollar contribution; in turn, they received a photograph of 'their' orphan and had the privilege of naming him or her. (The last of these campaigns, supported by Sainte-Enfance, was conducted in the late 1950s, almost a decade after Catholic orphanages were closed by the People's Republic of China.)

The sisters called their orphanages 'the vestibule of paradise,' 'the Kingdom of the Little Ones.' In times of danger and social upheaval, the numbers of the 'little moribunds' doubled and trebled, until there were sixty or seventy in one room, two and three to a crib. Yet the sisters could not turn away others; still, they would scour the streets looking for the dying. The accounts emphasize the positive, however:

How happy they are here, these poor little ones! We call them our 'little birds! – they neither sow nor reap; they see, as yet, only the silver lining of life; from morning to night their slender fingers trace characters or glide over bobbins that weave fine laces for the churches of Canada. But it has not always been thus for them. How many of these children before coming to us have known scarcely anything else but a miserable slavery! Several, only ten or twelve years old, have already been sold three or four times to very cruel masters! It is easy to understand their happiness in finding themselves now in the house of Him whom they call 'Tin Tu' – the Master of Heaven.

Even allowing for the exaggeration implicit in the sisters' accounts, one must accept that the children *were* better off under their care than they had been before. Who else would care for these unwanted, brutalized babies? Who else would take them into their homes and hearts? And if they did die, at least they were assured of a place in heaven according to Catholic sensibilities, and their place in the orphanage would soon be filled. In their self-denying way, the sisters did the best they could under horrifying circumstances.

9 · Clinical Christianity: Medical Missions

'If the ancestral faith in magic is destroyed by conversion to Christianity, it must be replaced by scientific medicine.'

Report on Medical Policy in West China, 1936

Charity, the concern for human well-being in this world as well as the next, has been part of the Christian message since Christ himself went about healing the sick and feeding the poor. Traditional Christian charity, like the Good Samaritan, does not question the causes of human misery: Why are there bandits on the road? Why did the Pharisee cross to the other side and avert his eyes? What would happen if all bandits were put into prison? Rather it tries to help in the most obvious way: there is a man lying bleeding beside the road; what can I do?

In the mission fields, this sort of charity, well-intentioned but with limited resources, expressed itself in foundling homes and dispensaries. With the expansion of Protestant missions in the twentieth century and the coming of the social gospel, which does question causes, these small works were no longer good enough. The construction of hospitals as modern as those in the home countries, noted Margaret Brown, the historian of the North Honan Presbyterian mission, 'symbolized the new place of Medical work in Mission policy. The change in purpose came so gradually as to be almost imperceptible. Medical work was no longer to be a mere means to an evangelistic end. It was in itself to be a living expression of the Christian Gospel and must, therefore, maintain the highest standards.'

Dr Frank F. Allan with patients, Chengtu

Dr Robert McClure of the same mission described this change in more scientific terms:

The big problem in the early days of medicine in China really was how scientific you would be. This was an ethical problem with the individual doctor and it was always a struggle. For instance, every time you raised your standards, you raised the cost and therefore the price to the patient. As medicine came into China, you first of all had antiseptic medicine, because that was what was being practised in Canada at the time. The sterilized sheet, the drapes, and that had not yet come into Canada. Then as antiseptic medicine was accepted in Canada and rapidly followed by aseptic, with sterile techniques and scrubbed hands and sterilized drapes, you had this tremendous struggle. Should the mission hospital adapt and enter the new field that it made available? The new field of abdominal surgery and that sort of thing. At each of these stages of progress, some doctors opted out. They said, 'We came here to preach the gospel and use medicine as a vehicle: it's not necessary for us to use a scientific medicine.' Very few did opt out, some merely dragged their feet.

It is a question Canadian hospitals still ask: when is the cost of health-care facilities too high?

Roman Catholic missions answered the question simply. They never went into modern medicine. The Grey Sisters, a small nursing and teaching order from Pembroke, Ontario, working under the Scarboro Fathers in Chekiang, operated a small dispensary where they handed out quinine tablets and worm pills, and the MIC Sisters ran leprosaria in Canton and Manchuria, but that was about the extent of Catholic medical missions.

The Protestants, on the other hand, went in for medicine in a big way, building hospitals at many of their stations and taking clinics into the remote villages. Mission policy repeatedly stated that these facilities should meet the highest standards. A Canadian Methodist pamphlet published in 1919 called "Spend Ten Minutes in China," put the point succinctly: 'Unsanitary hospitals are a reproach to Western medical science and to Christianity.' But, as Dr McClure said, many Western doctors, especially those who went out before the beginning of the twentieth century, had a great moral dilemma in incorporating these modern hospitals into the scheme of Christian missions.

Missionary doctors and nurses were generally a breed apart from the run-of-the-mill evangelists. They expressed their faith through their fingertips, rather than in street-corner preaching. They measured their success not so much in souls saved as in bodies healed, diseases conquered, and hospitals built. A few, particularly those recruited to fill a specific need, were not particularly religious, and did no proselytizing beyond handing out tracts with their prescriptions. Better educated than other missionaries, they often rose to prominence in foreign and Chinese social life; but, because they were accustomed to giving orders, they also often ran afoul of their Chinese staff – as happened with one normally reserved doctor, who hit a nurse in the heat of an operation and thus precipitated the evacuation of all missionaries from Szechuan in 1927.

Although medical missions did not conquer China at the point of a scalpel, as the doctors hoped, they did open up the country to Western medicine and built an 'infrastructure of health-care facilities' where none had existed before, a system of hospitals and clinics that survived through the communist revolution. Truly, the missionaries did fulfil their stated ambition, 'the multiplication of ourselves.'

Between 1875 and 1951, 120 Canadian medical doctors served in China. Sixty were in the West China Methodist mission, and 35 in the two Presbyterian missions in North Honan and Canton. The Anglicans in Honan and the China Inland Mission each counted 9, and 7 individuals were in various other missions, including the American Methodists, the American Presbyterians, the Disciples of Christ, and the Church Missionary Society. An astounding 100 of these doctors were recruited prior to 1927; after that year the Canadian churches all but stopped actively recruiting medical personnel.

Almost 60 per cent of these doctors, thirty-four in West China and thirty-six in the other missions, graduated from the University of Toronto and its affiliated medical colleges, Trinity Medical College and the Ontario Women's Medical School. McGill University in Montreal, the second ranking medical college in Canada, had seventeen alumni in China, most of them male and serving in North Honan. (These men, among them Dr Carr-Harris and Dr Percy Leslie, also seem to have come from wealthier families.) Of other medical schools, Manitoba supplied four male and four female graduates; Dalhousie in Halifax, two and five; Queen's, six men; and the University of Western Ontario, two men and one woman.

Probably no graduates were such active boosters of their old alma maters as doctors serving overseas. Harvard, Yale, and Oberlin universities all established medical colleges in China – Harvard-in-China,

Yale-in-China, and Oberlin-in-China. Although they never formally named it Toronto-in-China, Varsity grads did build and staff the medical college of the West China Union University. The Toronto men and women formed an elite, 'an inbred group,' one of their non-Toronto colleagues recalled, and were constantly admonishing their co-workers, 'In Toronto, we did this ... ' The roster of wcuu, reported a Rockefeller commission studying medical facilities in China, read 'like a roll-call of a University of Toronto alumni association.' When one thinks of those college cheers resounding through the Yangtse gorges, it scarcely comes as a surprise that the Toronto graduates suggested reproducing 'all the leading features' of University College, 'including the door and the architectural variety,' in the wcuu medical building. (Calculating that this would cost half a million dollars, the Reverend Alexander Sutherland wrote that 'the suggestion ... rather takes away my breath, and you know I am not easily alarmed.')

Despite this homogeneity of background, missionary doctors were anything but similar in character. Some seemed the epitome of the typical country doctor, with well-trimmed moustache and black bag always at the ready. Others gained a reputation as garrulous glad-handers, 'hustlers' in the parlance of the day, who thoroughly enjoyed their foreign stint and kept regular office hours with Wednesday afternoons off for tennis. Most were serious, somewhat bookish, 'reasonable' people who dedicated themselves to living by the Hippocratic oath.

A number of these missionary doctors, fewer than mission apologists would imply but many more than one might expect, were people who could (and sometimes later did) reach the top of their profession at home. Dr Ashley Lindsay, the first Western dentist in China, for example, was founder of the wcuu dental college and, after his retirement, editor of the *Journal of the Ontario Dental Association*. Edison and Gladys Cunningham, perhaps the wisest and best loved of the 1930s generation of West China doctors, both taught at wcuu, he in physiology, she in gynaecology. Dr Irwin Hilliard, of the prominent social-gospel family, was proof that Canadians were indeed creating the same structures overseas as their brethren at home: at the same time as he was building up the Fowchow [FUZHOU] general hospital, his sister, Dr Marion Hilliard, was transforming Women's College Hospital in Toronto into a world-recognized institution.

Sometimes brilliant parents begat a missionary dynasty. William McClure, gold medallist from McGill, discoverer of the cure for kala-azar, a dust-borne degenerative disease of the spleen, was the father of 'Dr Bob' McClure, who strode through China like a native, and of Dr Janet Kilborn, who married Dr Leslie Kilborn, son of the renowned doctors, Omar and Retta Kilborn. Dr Charles Winfield Service, who died at his post after thirty years of service, fathered Dr Charles William Service, known as Bill; both were remembered as gentle souls who made the world a better place for having passed through it.

One other prominent Canadian doctor in China should be mentioned, though strictly speaking he was not a missionary. This was Davidson Black, another Toronto graduate, whose palaeontological studies at Peking Union Medical College led to the identification of Peking Man. By giving these random bones an evolutionary pedigree, Dr Black left his own mark on history.

Some missionary doctors were extraordinary in another sense. They were the eccentrics, the misfits, the complainers, the other-worldly introverts, the glory hounds who worked with one eye set on getting an honorary degree from home: Dr Ferguson Fitten Carr-Harris, the best-trained doctor in North Honan (and twice decorated for valour in the First World War), was so eccentric that the mission could find 'no place where he could fit in.'

The most prominent of these eccentrics was undoubtedly William Edward Smith of West China. The sixth of nine children raised by a jolly but barely literate Irish widow on a dirt-poor farm near Peterborough, he had the Zorra boy's hunger for knowledge and, once that was satisifed, the same zeal for spreading the word. He went to China in 1896 and for forty years was one of the mission's most prolific correspondents. Among his writings was his autobiography, *A Canadian Doctor in West China*.

'W.E.' was a complicated man, outgoing and forward-thinking in many ways, but intensely evangelical in others. 'My mother used to tell me not to turn the hands of the clock backwards,' he wrote, 'as it injures the works; be that correct or not, I can assure you it was hard on me to be turned back four or five centuries.' From his hundreds of references to time – passing, flying, slipping away, never enough – he seems to have been obsessed by it: he put two clocks up on his compound gate, one that showed the correct hour and another face showing the time of the next meeting. He presented clocks as prizes to deserving Chinese.

Dr Smith had no time, he wrote on many occasions, for any work that interfered with his preaching. This included medical work. In 1927, five years after the death of his first wife, he married one of the women doctors, Ada Belle Speers, and handed over the operation of the hundred-bed Tzeliutsing [ZILIUJING] hospital to her: this seems to be the only case on record of a male doctor giving up his practice when he married.

Thirty-two of the Canadian doctors in China, one-quarter of the total, as well as all of the nurses, were women. Of the fifteen physicians who served in the two Presbyterian missions, twelve remained unmarried and the other three gave up their practices on marriage. Of the thirteen in West China, five married women continued as full-time doctors and five retired; two of the three unmarried ones served for only one term, leaving Dr Anna Henry as the only long-term unmarried woman doctor.

Charles Mills, an American Presbyterian in Shantung, summed up the general male missionary attitude towards women doctors in the field. 'If I were at home,' he wrote, 'I would never employ a lady physician. And the very designation is repulsive to me. But giving the ladies medical training for work on mission grounds strikes me as different.' Another American idealized these Florence Nightingales of the Orient, as 'not mere pretentious adventurers, but regular, well-educated physicians, actuated by the purest motive, immolating themselves upon the altar of humanity in order to lay the foundations for bestowing the blessings of a western medical knowledge upon the millions of their ignorant, down-trodden sisters in heathen lands.'

This vision of medical missions was inculcated into all women doctors along with their medical training. In *The Indomitable Lady Doctors*, Carlotta Hacker calculated that of the two hundred women graduates of Canadian medical colleges before 1912, one-quarter studied medicine 'explicitly so that they could serve usefully in the mission fields.' Idealistic though they may have been, the women doctors abroad were stubborn individualists: anyone who braved the college dissection-room jeers and the cold silence of the medical fraternity earned the right to be an individual. One need only think of Susie Rijnhart in the wilds of Tibet, or Margaret Phillips, who tried to wrest control of the Kaifeng hospital from Bishop White. Or Retta Kilborn, matriarch of the Kilborn clan, a doctor herself, the wife of a doctor, the mother of a doctor, and mother-in-law to two more (Dr Leslie Kilborn married twice). After her husband's death, she remained at her post for fifteen years until she had trained her successor, her daughter-in-law.

Long before the missionaries came, China had a system of medicine that, especially in internal medicine, was better than Western treatment. The early missionary doctors, peering into the 'native drug stores,' holding their deaf and dumb conversation with Chinese culture, could only see 'herbal remedies' and pagan superstition. Chinese medication, according to Omar Kilborn, consisted of such things as 'cast-off snake skins, turtle shells, monkey and tiger bones, and deer horns.' The most powerful poultice was 'thousand-feet earth,' that is 'earth trampled by (presumably) a thousand human feet. This precious medicine is found immediately outside or inside a doorway.'

Since the foreign doctors were allowed to treat only those patients not cured by traditional means or those who had been brought to the point of death by mistreatment, they saw only 'an unending procession, a boundless sea of ... diseases and putrid sores.' With rudimentary tools, the early doctors often resorted to remedies that came out of their own European pre-scientific tradition of 'heroic medicine.' As an emergency treatment for cholera, for example, W.E. Smith would open up the patient's gut and pour in saline solution, restoring the bodily fluids in the same way intravenous feeding does now.

The Chinese had no tradition of surgery, however, and surgery was the greatest miracle of the foreign doctor's stock-in-trade. The Chinese were terrified of the knife and would suffer the most bitter pills to avoid it; but with one deft stroke, the foreign doctor could dispel pain and centuries of ignorance – and in the process create a whole new mystique.

The most common – and most dramatic – of the operations was the removal of cataracts, making the blind to see. Dr Robert B. McClure recalls that in his father's day, the usual Chinese treatment for cataracts had been to dislocate them, 'really just giving the fellow a poke in the eye ... The cataract that had been neglected for years was a very ripe cataract and very easy to do. As the living standards rose and people became more sophisticated, they would never tolerate a blind eye. Therefore they would want their cataract done earlier.' By the time he himself arrived as a doctor in the 1920s, this 'cataract backlog was cleaned up ... In our hospital, for instance, we did about one or two cataracts a week ... perhaps eighty a year.' His father might have done that many in a month.

The most common of the medical stories from China, as popular in 1950 as in 1890, was the rescue of the opium suicide: A midnight call at the doctor's house rouses the dogs. The doctor follows a man with a lantern through the deserted streets and is ushered into the private apartments of a mansion. The patient, the young daughter-in-law, has swallowed a ball of opium to avenge her shame. She is as pale as death. The tiny room is crowded with Taoist priests and mourners shrieking to bring back her soul. The air is heavy with incense. The doctor orders the room cleared and gives the patient an anti-opium pill – the drug is unspecified, but it seems to have been a form of morphine because morphine was known in North China as 'Jesus opium' – and then pumps out her stomach. By the cool light of dawn, the doctor returns home. The variations were endless: the patient might be dead, or the sunlit afternoon would contrast with the human drama, or the male doctor would not be allowed to actually touch the patient but would have to treat her through a curtain. There were as many morals to be drawn from this tale: China's besotted degradation, the West's complicity in the nefarious opium traffic, the saving light of Christian medicine.

The young missionaries who came out after 1900 brought a new medical professionalism. In the few years since the first missionaries had gone out, Canadian medicine had itself changed from antiseptic to aseptic, from germ killing to germ free. No, the young people argued, a little dirt is not all right in a medical clinic. Dr Charles Winfield Service, University of Toronto class of '02, for example, took cleanliness to the point of 'fussiness'; 'Every time you look out of the window,' one hostess complained to him, 'you wash your hands.'

The younger doctors were 'shocked' by what passed for hospitals in China: ramshackle mat sheds with the patients' relatives camped in a corner of the courtyard. In 1908, when Ashley Lindsay arrived in Chengtu, his dental laboratory, he wrote, 'could hardly have had the status of a third-rate woodshed in Canada. The floor was of mud, literally so when it rained, and the rafters (for there was no ceiling) were as black as the soot and creosote of many years of open fires could make them.' Though these facilities may have done yeoman service in the past, they were no longer good enough.

'The aim of the medical missionary,' the Methodist *Missionary Outlook* stated in 1903, 'is to work out the Gospel of God's love through caring for and healing the body, and to lead those he helps to the Great Physician of their souls. His medical knowledge is the weapon he uses to break down superstition and prejudice, and prepare a way for the truth which shall make free. We cannot over-estimate the value of medical missions; they are the key to the homes and hearts of thousands.' The preacher was apt to lose his audience, Omar Kilborn noticed in his apology for medical missions, *Heal the Sick*, 'but just across the street, or perhaps in the same compound as the church, is the mission hospital, where every week a practical illustration of the same message is being given on the bodies of scores and hundreds of Chinese. The hospital is complementary to the church.'

What Omar Kilborn sensed, though he was a member of the older generation of doctors, was that the hospital was equal to the church in the scheme of missions. In the old-style dispensaries, the foreign doctor was still perceived in the familiar, paternalistic pattern of Confucian 'benevolence.' The implementation of user fees – twenty cash, for instance (about one cent Canadian), would allow the patient unlimited clinic visits – meant that 'the patient who pays even 100 cash a month is much more grateful for what is done for him than is the man who gets everything free ... And, moreover, he is not tempted to fawn upon us, or to be hypocritical in his gratitude. He can look us fairly in the face and thank us.' This professional relationship meant that just as the mission hospitals did not discriminate Christian from non-Christian in their treatments, so the people were no longer under any obligation to believe in the doctor's religion.

Running a hospital was an expensive proposition, and part of the growing independence of the mission hospitals came from the need to run them as self-supporting institutions, with the mission providing only the plant and the salaries of the missionaries. 'I was told I could do anything with my hospital,' Dr Stewart Allen recalled of the 1930s, 'as long as I kept it in the black.' To the foreign doctor it made eminent sense that, as Dr W.E. Smith said, the fees of 'the rich young men being treated for venereal disease' should help defray the cost of treating 'the deserving poor' at no charge. This led to intense efforts in the 1920s, once the construction phase was over, to enlist prominent members of the gentry to sit on the hospital boards, hoping thus to get them and their friends to contribute to the hospital upkeep.

The ideal for institutional medical work in China was to have one or more large hospitals at the central stations, preferably in conjunction with a teaching facility, and smaller 'station hospitals,' equally modern but on a smaller scale, similar to one that might serve a medium-sized city in Canada.

As usual, the West China mission led the way in establishing a professional class of institutions. By 1916, it had opened its full complement of ten stations, each of which had (or expected soon to have) its own hospital. The Chengtu hospitals were the showpiece not only of the mission, but of the entire province of Szechuan. The general men's hospital, located in the campus of the West China Union University, was a magnificent, multi-pavilioned, two-storeyed edifice built to the plans of the Toronto architects Helliwell and Gordon. It was reputed to be the best hospital west of Hankow, eight hundred kilometres distant. About fifteen minutes' walk away from the men's hospital, the women's hospital had opened the previous year 'with great éclat, the Governor and leading officials showing by their presence and speeches, their appreciation of the work done for their women and children.' Within a year, its sixty-bed public wards were already overcrowded, and a further expansion had to be planned.

The mission had two other large hospitals, the antiquated Chinese-style one built by the London Missionary Society in Chungking, and a modern 150-bed combined hospital in Tzeliutsing, in the rich salt-mining district. Despite initial opposition, the Tzeliutsing hospital was well patronized by the local gentry and officials of the salt gabelle, who on their own had raised $10 000 silver for the construction of the women's wing. This, R.O. Jolliffe wrote, was 'so far, the crowning manifestation of the good feeling of the people of this place toward the missionaries and their message.'

At the other stations, the mission maintained medical work that ranged from dispensaries in adapted Chinese buildings to modern sixty-bed hospitals like the one in Yuinhsien [RONGXIAN]. The quality of the medical plant depended on many factors, including the goodwill of the people and the 'hustler' qualities of the resident doctor. In all stations, whenever the doctor left, the hospital closed. The 'chequered career' of the medical work at Kiating, the conservative religious centre at the foot of Mount Omei, was typical of the progress of these station hospitals. Medical work was started there by Dr Omar Kilborn in 1895 and carried on until, a few months later, the riots drove out the foreigners and destroyed their buildings. Work commenced again in 1897, under three successive doctors, only to be interrupted again by the Boxers in 1900. The work of the first year or so under Dr W.E. Smith consisted mostly of 'repairing and altering the Mission buildings ... Here once again we see,' *Our West China Mission* noted, 'the lamentable fact of a doctor ready for full work set at the task of securing property, re-modelling buildings, and erecting a plant in order that he may begin his real work of ministering to the sick.' There was another two-year break in 1903–5 when Dr Smith went on furlough, a one-year break when his successor, Dr Charles Winfield Service, took his furlough, and another two-year interruption during the 1911 revolution.

This pattern of sporadic interruptions seems to have been common among many mission hospitals in China. In North Honan, during its first few years, the ratio of doctors to preachers had been about equal, but by the early 1900s, the mission was often hard-pressed to maintain the hospitals in the three main stations. For twenty years, Dr Jeannie Dow was the only practising woman physician in the mission – though there were two other woman doctors who had retired from active service after marriage – and during the First World War Dr James R. Menzies, one of the older men, was the only male doctor in the field. Wuan [WUAN], an out-of-the-way, unpleasant centre, the only small hospital in the mission, shut down every summer when the doctor went on vacation.

This regular closing down of operations, Omar Kilborn wrote, 'strongly emphasizes one of the greatest needs of our West China medical work, viz., ample facilities for missionary doctors to multiply themselves by training young Chinese doctors. Our evangelistic and our educational fellow workers have splendid facilities for preparing Chinese associates and workers in their departments, but the medical department has not been permitted to do this until very recently, and even now the attempt made is very inadequate.' This sense of the inadequacy of medical training seems to have been fairly widespread, for in North Honan one Chinese doctor complained that the evangelists had lectures every year, but the medical assistants 'had no prospects before them but forever to be washing patients' sores.'

The normal way for a doctor to train his or her own assistants was to pick a few boys, and maybe the occasional girl, from the mission schools and train them by imparting what he or she had learned in medical school. Dr Kilborn knew well the predicament of a lone doctor, 'not only physician and surgeon to his own institution, but also evangelist, steward, head-nurse, and superintendent and supervisor of floor-washing, laundry, kitchen and food supplies, chief pharmacist and dispenser, etc.' He himself had done 'just enough to realize the hopelessness of "the one-man medical school" as an adjunct to a large, busy hospital.'

Canadian missions participated fully in two medical universities in China, the Methodists in West China Union University and the North Honan Presbyterians in Cheeloo [QILU] University (which held its degree-granting charter from the University of Toronto) in Tsinan [JINAN], Shantung province, and part time in Canton University. In addition, Canadian individuals were involved in virtually every missionary medical college; Dr William Macklin, for example, participated in Nanking and Dr Davidson Black at the Peking Union Medical College. In the hierarchy of teaching and scientific standards, the PUMC, which graduated only 315 doctors in twenty-five years, was in the first rank, in a class by itself; Cheeloo was in the second rank; and WCUU, because it was in the far reaches of West China, tended to be ranked somewhat lower.

The Canadian Methodists, in addition to supplying the main building of the WCUU medical school, provided its professors of anatomy, physiology, biochemistry, obstetrics, surgery, and bacteriology. When the first college building opened in 1914, the medical school started with nine students housed in 'two miserable little rooms.' Three years later it had grown sufficiently for Dr Lindsay to open the first school of dentistry, and E.N. Meuser, formerly with the American Methodists, to start the faculty of pharmacy.

In the park-like campus of West China Union University, as at Cheeloo, the students studied the prescribed medical course – using English textbooks (a cogent reason for teaching English in the lower grades) – set out by the University of Toronto, with the same emphasis on anatomy and laboratory work; acquiring a cadaver for the students, which had to be used for several successive classes, was a recurring headache for the university administration. The earliest students were often the sons of Christians who had come up through the mission school system and, in return for subsidies, agreed to work so many years at one of the station hospitals. The dormitories were modest, so as not to give these students 'the habit of living beyond what they could command after leaving college.' Within a few years, the college started attracting 'the sons and daughters of the best families,' necessitating a separate women's medical school and more generous accommodation for the men.

This first generation of Chinese doctors, those who graduated before the 1920s, were, like their brethren in the ministry, a transitional group, caught between two worlds. Some followed Western ways, reading American novels and dancing to jazz. Others became caught up in bolshevism. But all were cut off from the world of their ancestors, even of their living parents. After all, how can one explain the theory of molecules to one's grandmother who still prays to a mud idol?

Many of the graduate doctors went to work for the mission hospitals, but this was not always a satisfactory arrangement either. Whatever their personal and professional qualifications, Chinese doctors were often condescended to by the white doctor in charge and by the Chinese patients as well. 'My Chinese colleagues might be smarter,' wrote Irwin Hilliard of the 1940s, but 'the Westerner was top dog.' This led to

Dr W.R. Morse giving a lecture in anatomy at West China Union University

personality conflicts and petty jealousies. It could also lead to more serious misunderstandings, as, for example, when the Chinese doctor accepted gratuities, 'tea money,' from the patients, only to be reprimanded by the missionary and told to return it. 'Our Chinese doctors and nurses love to be very generous with the medicines to the patients and give it free in order to do good deeds,' wrote Dr W.E. Smith. 'It helps their popularity but you can see how difficult it is for the Canadians to be always asking for money and the Chinese giving everything free.'

The story of the Yuinhsien hospital, one of the best small medical facilities in West China, was an extreme example of what could go wrong with Chinese doctors under foreign management. By 1915, the plant at Yuinhsien consisted of a dispensary and a fifty-bed hospital. When the foreigners evacuated the station in 1927 – this was the hospital where Dr P.S. Tennant's untoward shoving of a Chinese nurse led to massive demonstrations against 'foreign brutality' – they left it in the charge of Dr Liu Yue-ting, one of the first medical graduates of West China Union University. During their year and a half of absence, Dr Liu managed to keep it open, the only hospital in that part of Szechuan to remain so, and, moreover, to enhance its reputation among 'people of all classes.' As a reward, the mission granted him a year's postgraduate study, but Dr Liu felt slighted and shortly thereafter resigned on the grounds of ill health. A few months later, however, he was well enough to open his own rival clinic across the street from the mission hospital.

By the 1930s, the mission had withdrawn foreign missionaries from the Yuinhsien hospital as part of its retrenchment policy, leaving it in charge of Dr Chang Kwang-lin, a Christian and a graduate of WCUU. A secret opium addict, he 'allowed the institution to reach the last stage of dirt and neglect.' He died of an opium overdose, leaving behind 'two families [he was also a polygamist], a mountain of debts ... and a state of affairs that was not good for the name of the Christian church.' Dr Lo, his successor, embezzled funds from the endowment to build his own clinic. The next doctor, angered at having to share the former missionary residence with another doctor and his family, 'sued his wife for divorce, carried on an affair with the pastor's daughter, and was subsequently beaten and imprisoned by the townspeople of his native place. There he committed suicide.' By 1949, the mission had withdrawn all foreigners, including the evangelistic staff, from Yuinhsien, and the communists opened a 'people's hospital,' 'borrowing' the supplies they needed from the defunct mission hospital.

Despite the hard work, many doctors found something satisfying about the old-style hospitals-cum-dispensaries. Patients were not dislocated from their daily lives, not put to bed in sterile white sheets; their relatives were with them, sharing their room or camped in the compound. In addition, the doctor was freer than in a large hospital, where he became a desk-bound administrator supervising a staff that, with nursing students, could be as large as a hundred or more.

Mission medical colleges were dedicated to turning out highly qualified practitioners who could extend medical science in China, but many people felt that the system was too elitist and too impractical. 'While millions of people died of preventable disease and millions more went blind from trachoma,' Pearl Buck wrote, 'the doctors went on with their high professional standards. That is, anyone who practised medicine must be a graduate physician.' Every mission had critics of 'the big-plant mentality.' In West China, when Dr W.E. Smith argued for small dispensaries, his colleagues accused him of advocating 'mud-floored, store-front clinics,' as though these had no value. Dr Smith responded that when the Chinese came to take over the foreign institutions, as assuredly they must, the facilities would have to be simple and inexpensive enough for the Chinese to operate.

Pressure to modernize mission hospitals came from many directions,

Caroline Wellwood and nurses of the wms hospital, Chengtu, 1917

from medical literature, from graduates of the medical colleges, from the Rockefeller commission. More pressure perhaps than was wise was applied by the boards at home, a practice that could be disastrous when their directives overruled the opinions of those who had to implement the policies. In Kongmoon, the South China Mission bowed to the Montreal Woman's Missionary Society and erected a women's hospital rather than the general one it had intended. In the Anglican diocese of Honan, Bishop White had not originally planned for medical work, but under pressure from the missionary society he chose the most convenient site for a large institution in Kaifeng.

The China Inland Mission sidestepped the whole issue of hospitals. It was an evangelistic mission and had no desire to create an autonomous medical adjunct. The cim operated three large institutions: a sanatorium in Chefoo mainly for foreign residents, the hospital in Kaifeng, and the Borden hospital and leprosarium in Lanchow, in the far north west.

The mission also operated several smaller hospitals that were closer to the dispensary model, in such provinces as Yunnan and Kweichow, where it was the only mission. Both these latter were constructed and operated for many years by Canadian graduates of the University of Toronto – Dr Walter Clark in Tali [DALI], Yunnan, and Dr Edward Fish in Anshun [ANSHUN].

Why one Toronto graduate would choose to work at the West China Union University and another to go to the nether reaches of China depended on many factors, not the least of which was the evangelical zeal of the doctor. Yet, sooner or later, both had to face the same pressures to modernize and adapt medical technology to primitive conditions. The career of Dr Edward Fish encapsulated the history of missionary medicine in one lifetime. He went to Kweichow province in 1911 as part of the CIM forward movement among the non-Han tribespeople. At that time, there wasn't a single wheeled vehicle in the whole province, not even a wheelbarrow; the next doctor was three weeks distant. For twenty-four years, Dr Fish worked in his walled hospital serving a constituency of ten million people. Suddenly, with the fall of eastern China to the Japanese in the late 1930s, the isolation of Kweichow was shattered by Japanese bombers. With the influx of millions of refugees from 'occupied China,' Dr Fish's hospital was inundated by three nursing schools evacuated from Nanking and Shanghai. As head of the province's medical war effort, he was given one of the three automobiles in the area. Consequently, propelled by forces beyond his or the mission's control, Dr Fish built his erstwhile clinic into a complex of hospitals and teaching institutions.

To most observers, it was obvious that medical work in China needed to combine the two approaches. What is surprising in retrospect is that Christian missions did not develop a two-tier system of medical education. After the revolution of 1949, the communists touted the introduction of 'barefoot doctors,' local paramedics who worked in 'the spirit of Dr Norman Bethune' to bring medicine to the hinterlands.

Dr Robert McClure of the North Honan mission claims that he 'sort of patented the idea' of barefoot doctors a few years before Dr Bethune arrived, which he called the Hwaiking Rural Medical System. Bethune, working in the neighbouring province, could conceivably have heard of this innovation and adapted it to his part of war-torn China. The success of a mission hospital was measured, Dr McClure discovered, at least in Chinese eyes, by the number of Chinese doctors and druggists who set up shop across the street from it. Some, like Dr Liu in Yuinhsien, were 'real' doctors – that is, graduates of a medical college – but most had gleaned a little knowledge of Western medicine from a year or two of apprenticeship in a mission hospital. They proudly advertised their expertise in the way way Indian civil servants added 'BA Oxon., failed' to their titles. Rather than opposing these 'quacks' as most mission doctors did, Dr McClure found a way to co-opt them quite productively. Recognizing that most of the men he was training would be going into private practice, he said, 'we encouraged them ... I then came to this group and said, "I don't care what you say, but statistics show your actual ambition is to go out into private practice and make money hand over fist. I think you can do it. I think you can be of service to your community while you do it."'

Dr Bethune tried to turn out doctors in one year, nurses in six months, but that was teaching on the run, guerrilla-style. Dr McClure, in peacetime, took considerably longer:

five years of training, with a basis of one year lab training and one year lab experience, and then he went through as a junior in the operating room. Finally he finished up doing the simple operations. We had a repertoire of about twenty-five operations. We said, 'These you will learn, anything beyond that you will never touch. ... It means death for your patient and only trouble for you. Anything beyond that you send into the hospital.' ... Remember this man was a little lighthouse of not only Western medicine but of hygiene. What they did in hygiene was something terrific. They did typhoid vaccinations. They set up decent latrine pits in places. They went all out to get a decent water supply, usually beginning with their own little homestead. From there evolved electric lights and pumps because these people all wanted electric lights ... It also meant that for the hospital for its part 80 per cent of the work coming in was referred. The man had taken the patient's history and knew what our charges were. The patient came prepared and there was no surprise.

Unfortunately Dr McClure's training system was not copied by other missions. It may be said that most missionary doctors could never bring themselves to trust their Chinese 'assistants' to go out with mission encouragement but without mission control. Not until the 1930s, when the missions moved into 'rural reconstruction,' did many doctors consider public health and preventive medicine as an important component of missionary medicine. Yet that would have been exactly the area where they might best have achieved their goal of 'the multiplication of ourselves.'

10 · Marching as to War

'I want you to sit down with me for a few minutes to try to realize what it feels like to live in a country whose internal peace is uncertain, where law and order are apt to be interrupted several times during an ordinary life-time. If you have lived in Canada all your life, this will be no easy task. For war, rebellion, or brigandage in Canada is almost unthinkable. But in China it is not so. The Chinese are accustomed to the idea of war – not with a foreign nation – but civil war, war between the North and South, war between provinces, war with the aborigines.'

Dr Omar Kilborn, letter from Chengtu, 25 August 1914

'After 1911, after the first revolution had taken place and the Republic was formed, then we saw the execution squads and armed soldiers. From then on, I've always associated China with armed men, armed men, armed men.'

Dr Robert McClure, *Reminiscences*, 1970

Once Sun Yat-sen handed over the presidency of the Republic of China to Yuan Shih-k'ai in 1913, the nation started to disintegrate. The South seceded from the republic, the North was plagued with famine, the whole country was overrun with greater or lesser warlords. Not until 1927, when Chiang Kai-shek led his Northern Expedition against the

General Yang Sen, warlord of Szechuan, early 1920s

warlord armies, did China regain a semblance of centralized government.

Yet in 1914, insulated behind their high walls and protected by foreign gunboats, the missionaries were in some respects less affected by these events on their doorsteps than by those happening on the battlefields of Europe. China by this time had newspapers, fourteen in Chengtu alone, carrying news from British and German sources and enabling any literate Chinese to get 'a fair idea' of the causes of the war. This was shown by an essay written in English in October 1914 by a mission schoolboy in Chuchow, a small city in West China, a 'verbatim copy' of which Dr Wallace Crawford forwarded to Toronto. This, he concluded had 'enough truth in it to make us all overlook any errors, grammatical or otherwise':

Now, there is a great battle in Europe. This began because the Prince of Austria went to Servia with his wife. One man of Servia killed them. Austria was angry and so fight Servia. Germany write a letter to Austria, I will help you. Russia write a letter to Servia, I will help you. France did not want to fight but they got ready their soldiers. Germany write a letter to France, You don't get ready or I will fight you in nine hours. Germany to fight them, pass Belgium. Belgium say, I am not a road, I am a country and Belgium write a letter to England about Germany to them. So England help Belgium.

To many Chinese, the sight of these 'Christian' nations battling each other seemed to confirm that white men used religion to cloak their native belligerence. In 1915, for example, when Donald MacGillivray of the Christian Literature Society gave a series of lectures in North Honan on 'the fruits of Christianity, viz., a regard for human life,' he had to delete all references to the war because he was besieged by 'Christians and non-Christians alike' asking 'how one or two nations could hold several others at bay, and why no way of talking peace had been discovered.'

At the beginning of the war, most missionaries in China tried to ignore the supercharged emotionalism of war fever. For the China Inland Mission, which had more than one hundred German nationals in its associate missions, glossing over racial and denominational differences was crucial: it published an open letter reminding its supporters of the many 'godly German saints to whom the world owes an unpayable debt ... In the present day, some twenty-six missionary societies, having a total membership of some 2115 foreign and 8766 native workers, and having 246 000 communicants carry on active service in the regions beyond. These are facts which are not to be forgotten.'

The Rev. R.P. MacKay, secretary of the Canadian Presbyterian Foreign Mission Board, wrote an equally conciliatory letter to the 'brethren' in the field, telling them, 'We are not at war with the Germans, much less the German missions ... You will no doubt have many occasions to explain to the Native Christians the nature and origin of this war, and it will be well to make occasions in order that misapprehensions may be removed.' In addition, he suggested, Canadian missionaries might join their British and American counterparts in 'raising a fund to aid German missionaries in their distress.'

Because of their proximity to Hong Kong, as Agnes Dickson wrote from Kongmoon, the Presbyterian missionaries in South China were aware of the war more immediately than 'the people in many parts of Canada. In the first place, there was the panic over the possible dearth of food supplies, and the rush to lay in a stock against the evil day ... Then we had the excitement, and interest, of watching the movements of all the different vessels which passed Long Island. The torpedoes went out each night at sunset, to guard the different passes; and the searchlights played unceasingly from sunset to sunrise, at the harbour entrances ... All our foreign gunboats are off the rivers, but the situation is much as it was. Robberies and kidnapping continue in the outlying districts, but all is quiet about here.'

Not only in British Hong Kong but in the German colony of Tsingtao [QINGDAO], the war reached its fingers quickly into East Asia. Two weeks before the beginning of the European war, Japan seized the German 'China Station,' in the name of peace in Asia, promising to return it to China 'eventually.' Japan's intentions became clear the following year, when it presented its notorious Twenty-One Demands, which, by demanding that China 'employ Japanese advisors in political, financial, and military affairs,' would have made China a virtual dependency of Japan. Yuan Shih-k'ai agreed to a watered-down version of the Twenty-One Demands, an action that contributed to the further decline of China's internal politics.

The reformist, republican forces symbolized by Sun Yat-sen feared that Yuan and the reactionary warlords were joining Japan and the Allies against Germany in order to consolidate their own power and crush the reformist camp. In any event, China remained out of the war until August 1917, when Germany declared unrestricted submarine warfare against commercial shipping in the Pacific. Prior to its declaration of war, however, China did make a significant contribution to the Allied war effort, a contribution that is barely mentioned in histories of the First World War because it consisted not of heroic fighting men but of lowly labourers, in the so-called 'coolie corps.' By the end of the war, there were more than 100 000 Chinese in France in battalions of five hundred to two thousand men. Almost every Allied camp had its 'Chinese Johnnies' cleaning the latrines, laying railroad tracks, and mopping up the battlefields. Their arrival was shrouded in wartime secrecy; they just appeared one day, and their departure after the war was equally silent. Transporting them from China across the Pacific, through Canada by train, and then across the Atlantic in convoys was a massive operation, yet hardly a word reached the newspapers. It was as if these men did not exist.

As the carnage in Europe dragged on, the shortage of able-bodied men grew critical and Britain and France started searching for new sources of manpower in Africa and Asia. In early 1917, the British army opened a recruiting office in Weihaiwei [now WEIHAI]. Since China was still neutral, the British signed each volunteer to a private contract, at a wage of ten cents a day plus twenty dollars cash on embarkation from China. In the first few months of the war, many French and German missionaries had been recalled by their respective governments to act as army chaplains, and a few British and Canadians had signed up, like Dr Ferguson Carr-Harris of North Honan. Now the British government called on its nationals in China to join the Chinese Labour Corps (CLC), because Chinese-speaking missionaries were considered to be 'the critical element in a scheme the British considered of great importance to their war effort.'

The China Inland Mission tried to dissuade its men from 'leaving their posts on the field for service in armies at the front ... The issues abroad, in China and elsewhere, are as great and critical as any in the allied and central powers, and indeed are more important, being in the spiritual realm and having eternal issues at stake.' Only a handful of the five hundred male missionaries of the CIM signed up for the British army, and those who did, like James Goby and H.G. McMaking, the only CIM Canadians to join, had to resign from the mission to do so. The mission did not lack patriotism, however, as the number of missionaries' sons who did join the British army shows; eight Canadian lads, including the son of William Horne, one of the members of the 1888 party, joined the CLC as the trains passed through Ontario.

Each man, and each mission, had to decide for himself what response to make to this appeal for King and country. Those in South China, who spoke the dialect of that region, were pretty well useless as translators. The West China mission was so far away that only seven men joined the CLC. One was John Parker, a fifty-seven-year-old Englishman who had come out under the London Missionary Society in 1890; another was Harold Deeks Robertson, later secretary to the Hon. Newton W. Rowell at the founding conference of the League of Nations.

The staff of the North Honan mission, which was situated near the recruitment territory, felt strongly that they should 'do their bit.' Of the thirty-two male missionaries, sixteen joined the CLC. 'Years ago,' wrote mission secretary Murdoch Mackenzie, one of the pioneers of the mission, these men

had listened to the voice of the highest King, and in obedience to His command had come to China. They studied Chinese for the express purpose of making Christ and His great salvation known to the Chinese people in North Honan ... An opportunity, such as does not come often in an ordinary lifetime, has now led them to ask whether their lives, and all the knowledge they have gained of Chinese, may not be turned to account in the struggle now being waged. Britain is about to put forth its maximum effort. The weightiest issues for our Empire and the World depend on the result. No one worthy of the British name would shrink from considering the question of duty at such a time. It has been taken up seriously by all our brethren, and their response is only that which was to be expected of them.

The response may have been expected, but no other mission, not even the staunchest British ones, responded as vigorously.

The departure of so many of the youngest men was a 'tragedy' for the mission, cancelling a planned forward movement and all medical work except among the women. Evangelistic work was 'practically suspended.'

Altogether more than one hundred British and American missionaries joined the CLC, and among them Canadians occupied a significant place. Gillies Eadie, formerly principal of the Changte boys' school, was director of the recruiting office (euphemistically named the British War Emigration Agency) in Tsingtao until mid-1920, when the last Chinese were repatriated. 'He handled all the paperwork, kept all the accounts and oversaw the distribution of some twenty million dollars a year. He was responsible for seeing that the Chinese in France and their families in Chihli, Honan, and Shantung received the money due them ... Thus, in large measure was entrusted to two Canadian missionaries, Eadie, and at war's end, [J.A.] Mowatt [who was seconded to run the Tsinan office], "the good name of the Empire in Shantung."'

Amid a fusillade of firecrackers, the labourers left Tsingtao and Weihaiwei on Canadian Pacific Empress steamships, painted battleship grey, in contingents of from 300 to 3200; they were shipped out, according to an eyewitness, 'practically as freight.' After being assembled at Ivan Head military camp on Vancouver Island, they were taken to Halifax in sealed trains that took precedence over all other traffic. The journey across Canada, reported the *Halifax Herald*, was 'absolutely cheerless ... The Chinese are herded like so many cattle in cars, forbidden to leave the train and guarded like criminals ... Throughout the whole period it is safe to say that not one kindly smile or word of cheer is cast in their direction.'

Only on rare occasions did news of the 'ghost trains' hit the Canadian papers, such as the (erroneous) report that twenty-five 'Chinamen' had frozen to death when their unheated train had been shunted into the Maine woods. This news, like all other accounts of the passing trains, was 'assiduously' suppressed by the Canadian press censor because, he claimed, he already had 'ample proof that enemy sympathizers (Chinamen resident in Canada and the United States) have endeavoured to get in touch with the parties of Coolies passing through Canada with a view to inducing these men to mutiny.'

In the beginning, the British army brass were afraid that missionaries would be too soft to control the barracks life of the Chinese, especially 'a Company which has a sprinkling of Tientsin stiffs [professional gamblers] who think nothing of taking the whole of a coolie's savings off him in one night's play.' The brass quickly discovered that, with a few weeks' training, missionaries could 'deliver the goods'; missionaries, in fact, according to Dr Ernest Struthers, were credited with being 'the backbone of the enterprise.'

The missionaries had justified to the home churches that their going to France would enable them to work with a class of people they would not have been able to reach in normal times. In addition, they could act as chaplains to the Christians, who averaged about 10 per cent of the recruits. 'These are testing days for some of our Christian Chinese here in France,' Captain Herbert Boyd wrote to the Presbyterian Foreign Mission Board in Toronto. 'If there were before the war many things they did not know of Christian nations, they are rapidly enlightened these days. It is not a Sunday School, or Mission School or missionary compound they have now in which to learn Christianity or Christian nations, but war and increasing war.' In addition, the missionaries also conducted YMCA work in the larger camps. 'Lectures were delivered on such subjects as "Why We Are at War," "The Laborers' Part in the War," on western customs and ideals, the importance of observing rules of sanitation, etc. Every evening had its lecture, concert, motion picture show or social gathering ... Strikes, riots, fights, and much grumbling were not only eliminated, but the general morale of the Chinese greatly improved.'

All in all, most people connected with the Chinese Labour Corps agreed it was a success, even if it was not as crucial to the British war effort as had been touted in the beginning. The Chinese had worked under adverse conditions, 'winning golden opinions for themselves here for their capacity to do work and for their unfailing cheerfulness under all circumstances.' One cannot measure the lasting impact on the average Chinese labourer, but for at least one interpreter, a young Chinese named Chou En-lai [ZHOU ENLAI] who was recruited by the YMCA while studying at a French university, the experience led to his association with the Chinese communist party. Another YMCA worker, Dr Jimmy Yen, used the experience to follow a different course: working through the missionary educational system he developed a simplified literacy course based on 1000 of the most common characters.

For the missionaries, too, the experience was formative. The Reverend T.A. Arthurs felt that in six months in France he had learned more about 'the Chinaman ... than in the previous four years in China ... What could not I do now had my life been more fully consecrated to God.' Unfortunately, Arthurs was unable to take his new-found resolve back to North Honan, for he died of pneumonia at Le Havre one month after the armistice, the only Canadian missionary to die in France. Right up to his last letters, though, he repeated, 'I am more glad than I can say that I am in France today.'

By the middle of 1919, after supervising the cleaning up of the French battlefields – including the planting of rows of white crosses – by the Chinese workers and then escorting them back across Canada to China, the North Honan missionaries returned to the work they had abandoned two years before. The Reverend Arthur Lochead spoke for all of them when he wrote that he had come back 'in the firm resolve and fervent hope that this next period of service shall be the best I can render. The years are passing swiftly, and the next few years shall be our best.'

During their absence, the women of the mission, the single women and the wives of the men on active service, as well as the older male missionaries like Dr J.R. Menzies, had worked to maintain skeleton operations. During the same period, however, Honan, strategically placed straddling the Yellow River and caught between the contending parties, was a plum to be plucked by anyone with the might to do so. Two events in the mission in the year 1920 dramatized to the returning men, as well as to the Canadian church, the sorry condition into which China had sunk. The first was the murder of Dr Menzies; the second, more global tragedy was the worst famine in North China in forty years.

On the evening of 17 March 1920, just as the missionaries at the Hwaiking station were preparing to retire, the women were startled by burglars breaking the windows of the WMS house. Dr Menzies, hearing their screams, came running across the narrow divide and was shot by the lookout. If these had been ordinary bandits like those who swarmed in the mountains around Hwaiking – 'like maggots in the garbage,' Robert McClure commented – the mission would have accepted the tragedy as unavoidable. But they had been wearing grey soldiers' uniforms, which indicated at least some connection with the Chinese army. The British minister in Peking blamed the provincial warlords and their 'over-numerous and under-disciplined soldiery now over-running the interior of China, who merely act as a recruiting ground for brigands whom they do nothing to suppress.'

At the memorial service in Bloor Street Presbyterian church, attended by Mrs Menzies and her daughters, the Reverend George C. Pidgeon, one of the leading churchmen of his generation, called on the Young People's Society to raise $30 000 to build a hospital in Dr Menzies' memory. The Presbyterian Foreign Mission Board, taking its cue from the British consul's statement, demanded restitution from the government to help defray the cost of erecting this hospital. The murder, Dr R.P. MacKay wrote, 'was the result, was it not, of the government having allowed a band of marauders to kill and plunder?' Just as they had done in 1901, the missionaries in the field opposed the board's demand, by a vote of forty to two. They recognized that in the grim reality of the new China, the government could not assure protection for foreigners, even from its own renegade soldiers. This obstinacy from the field so angered the home church that the chairman of the mission committee in the congregation angrily threatened to withdraw the funds it had already collected for the hospital: 'I know if the people in Bloor Street Church knew the attitude they [the Honan presbytery] took, there would not be any Mission in Honan so far as Bloor Street goes, or any hospital either.'

The following year, Bishop White, in his station south of the river, mentioned the tragedy to the provincial officials; by this time he was practically the advisor to the Christian General, Feng Yu-hsiang, who personally donated $20 000 to the Presbyterian mission, half for Mrs Menzies and half for the hospital. Dr Menzies' death prompted the provision of North Honan's first modern hospital, complete with X-ray equipment and electric lights, and was followed by the appointment, as Menzies' replacement, of the energetic young Dr McClure. (Mrs Menzies, too, stayed on in the mission for fifteen years and was one of its best nurses.)

The second of the post-war calamities to befall the mission was the great North China famine. Honan had been in the grip of the drought-flood-drought cycle since 1916, but the drought of 1920–1 was the most severe since 1877, affecting some twenty million people. The spring wheat 'simply dried up and disappeared'; the autumn millet withered in the ground. Then, in the midst of nature's ravages, the hand of man added to the people's miseries when Honan became the battlefield for the first major civil war of the warlord era. The inability of the warlords to move food and their diversion of relief supplies to their own armies caused more suffering than the drought itself.

When faced with famine in their districts, the early missionaries had distributed food and money personally to the starving people, a procedure that, as Bishop White had found in 1911, was 'good advertising for the church' whether the people were 'interested in your religion or not.' (The green beans he distributed became known thereafter as 'Anglican beans.') The Presbyterian mission had always mistrusted such direct distribution of foreign money; as early as 1895, it had stated during another famine that 'all emotional charity on our part has been steadily repressed and none of the sufferers from privation has been taken into mission employ.'

In 1919, the incumbent at the small station of Tao-kuo [DAOGOU, now HUAXIAN], the Reverend Andrew Thomson, had tried an alternative approach of employing people in such make-work projects as building roads and spinning cloth: with $10 000 he had fed and housed some nine thousand men, women, and children. To the returning men, this work scheme seemed a perfect way of implementing the social lessons they had learned in YMCA work in France. The mission made a house-to-house survey of its part of the province, counting chickens, evaluating furniture, and recording the physical condition of the people. By this

Grace Sykes vaccinating refugees during the famine of 1921, Wuan, North Honan

time, the peasants were subsisting on a gruel made of bean pods, millet husks, thistle roots, and persimmon rinds. There was not one animal in fifteen villages.

The people of Canada responded to the China Famine Relief Fund, which was set up by the churches and run by the banks, more generously than could have been expected. The fund collected $666 923, all of which went to the missions in North and South Honan; an additional $300 000 was collected from Christians in China. Altogether in the six counties of North Honan, the missionaries and the native Christians distributed 11 000 tons of grain and $800 000 in cash to 1 212 316 people.

Distribution of food – public charity – fitted in with the old Buddhist concept of good works, but the people were amazed that the missionaries would go to all the trouble of building roads and bridges at the same time. The thirty-two kilometre road from the mission station at Wuan to the railway at Hantan [HANDAN], the largest project paid for by the mission and suitable even for motorcars, became not only 'a walking advertisement for Christianity, but a riding, driving, pushing one as well.' The mission employed one thousand men, women, and children to break stones for the roadbed, and another seven or eight thousand to build the earthworks and level the ground.

At Changte, in the heart of the famine district, Dr Leslie closed down the hospital because, he said, he had 'neither the time nor the energy to save men individually when they needed to be saved in the mass.' He organized a food kitchen in the city where, as one of his colleagues wrote,

People from a particular village came on a particular day, under the direction of their own village headman, [and] would stand patiently and quietly for hours, waiting their turn with no anxiety, knowing that in due time their opportunity would come and they would get full measure ... [This was] in marked contrast to the confusion worse confounded that prevailed amongst the rabble allowed to run riot whenever grain was given out by non-Christians. Sometimes in the crush lives were lost.

Four American Lutheran missionaries south of the river died of typhus, but because of the public-health campaign in the north, only one case was found in the entire territory. The missionaries paid a bounty for dead lice, and more than one million were brought to the mission stations in a ten-day period. At the food-distribution centres, the people were each given five coppers to get deloused.

By June 1921, the famine was officially declared over, and the missionary men and women could rest from their labours. The Christian church had been weighed in the balance of human misery and not been found wanting; the Chinese Christians, as distinct from the foreign missionaries, had proved themselves and earned the gratitude of the officials and people alike. The church was recognized as an institution of benefit to the people of North Honan.

Bandits, famine, personal danger, masses of humanity, these were the ordinary perils of life in China. They were not unexpected. To them were added in the 1910s and 1920s the armed men that Dr McClure talks of at the beginning of this chapter. For longer or shorter periods, every part of China, every province, and every mission station were devastated by warfare.

Honan was a battleground of four large-scale civil wars – in 1920, 1922, 1924, and 1927. Nominally, Honan remained in the northern camp; its warlords were appointed by the shadowy government in Peking and in theory owed fealty to that government – when they were not conspiring to take it over themselves. During the 1920s, Honan was under the control of all the major warlords, among them Wu Pei-fu, Feng Yu-hsiang, and Chang Tso-lin.

In Honan, though civil warfare was catastrophic, it was at least only sporadic. Szechuan, on the other hand, was divided among seven major and several minor warlords, and the fighting was localized and almost continuous: between 1911 and 1937, the province sustained more than four hundred civil wars. Though Szechuan was technically in the northern camp, for several years the warlords had to bolster their strength with troops from Yunnan and Kweichow.

The history of Luchow [LUZHOU] is representative of the fate of many centres. A small commercial city strategically located two hundred kilometres upriver from Chungking, Luchow changed hands five or six times in the early 1920s. Edward B. ('Ted') Jolliffe, son of mission superintendent the Reverend Charles Jolliffe, remembers how as a boy he made a collection of bullets that landed in the mission compound. 'It was commonplace to hear bullets or shells going overhead,' he recalls. On one occasion, he watched out of his bedroom window as a warlord army that had erected a pontoon bridge to cross the little river was slaughtered. 'There was a great roll of rifle fire and I could see what looked like white flags above the pontoon bridge. That was water ... being raised up by the bullets that missed, but many of the bullets found their mark. I could see men tumbling into the boats, into the river, falling on the bridge. There was no doubt about the result because the local Red Cross Society, of which my father was a vice-president, buried over one thousand men the next day.'

How the foreign missionary reacted to events around him depended on a number of factors, not least of which was his or her native courage. Bishop W.C. White in Kaifeng, and Dr William Macklin in Nanking energetically conducted negotiations between contending generals, ferrying white flags of surrender from one side to the other, reassuring the residents that their city would not be pillaged. Dr Robert McClure, by now chief surgeon at the Menzies Memorial Hospital in Hwaiking, made a deal with one local warlord that he, the doctor, would join the general's army as *Honorary* Chief Medical Officer in return for regular cash payments for the hospital's treatment of the wounded. (This arrangement, according to McClure's biographer, 'did not receive undue emphasis in reports from the Mission Council Secretary to the Secretary of the Foreign Mission Board in Toronto.')

Although C.J.P. Jolliffe was regularly warned by the British consul not to meddle in Chinese politics, he was 'a bit of a natural-born diplomat' who made friends with bandits and warlords and thus was drawn into events in which he had no wish to be involved. 'I remember more than one warlord walking up our front walk accompanied by his heavily armed bodyguard,' Jolliffe's son continued, 'to interview my father, or sometimes to tell him what he was willing to do, and this message would be discreetly conveyed by one of my father's friends to the other side.'

Similar arrangements were not uncommon, but such action could also have untoward repercussions. 'Mediation between Contesting Parties,' wrote the British Consul-General at Chungking in 1921, 'is a deadly practice which has an irresistible attraction for certain missionaries.' He then described several incidents concerning unnamed missionaries in Szechuan, one of whom could have been Jolliffe:

During the Szechuanese occupation, a large portion of a city was flooded by a sudden rise in the river and the defending troops were compelled to withdraw to higher ground, temporarily evacuating the city. A missionary went out to the Yunnanese who were attacking, informed them that the city was empty and asked them not to shell it. He then marched into the city at the head of the Yunnan troops. He next instituted a Red Cross Society, enrolled members at 25 dollars a head, and issued Red Cross flags to each member. In return the different members housed a wounded man. Next day the Szechuanese returned, drove out the Yunnanese, tore down the Red Cross flags and murdered every wounded man they could lay their hands on.

Consul-General Hewlett also condemned the universal practice of sheltering refugees in the mission compounds in times of danger. To allow refuge only to Christians would have given rise to further complications, so the missionaries opened their doors to anyone who came. Thus, on occasion, rich merchants and defeated generals with their retinues and carts full of goods would encamp in the missions for several months. 'The pride of the Szechuanese has been deeply wounded,' the consul warned, 'and though they are making full use of the missions and are flocking to their compounds and churches, they are only indulging a form of contempt, rendered all the more bitter because the superficial sincerity of this hypocritical friendship is proportional to the depth of their supercilious scorn.' He concluded, bluntly,

'None of these incidents serve [sic] to enhance the reputation of missions in Szechuan.'

Although most missionaries characterized Consul-General Hewlett and others as alarmists, they nevertheless followed his instructions and accepted, at least tacitly, his assumption that lying below the surface of the Chinese friendliness was a latent anti-foreign feeling. According to Consul-General Hewlett, 'First oust the extraprovincial [i.e., the Yunnanese], then oust the foreigners,' was a common slogan in Szechuan.

Ever since China's humiliating treatment at the 1919 Paris Peace Conference – which, among other things, handed the former German colonies of Weihaiwei and Tsingtao to Japan – a sense of nationhood had been growing among Chinese students and intellectuals. This nationalism, which was quite different from the old Chinese ethnocentrism, started with the May Fourth Movement commemorating the date of the Treaty of Versailles. That movement not only stimulated a renaissance of Chinese education and literature, but also articulated for the first time a 'public opinion' in the country. Unfortunately, this opinion expressed itself as a campaign to expel the imperialists (meaning the British).

One wing of this anti-imperialism was specifically directed against Christian institutions. 'Gold and iron make our bodies slaves of the foreigners,' stated the manifesto of the Anti-Christian Student Federation; 'the Gospel enslaves our souls.' The federation was founded in 1922 in reaction to two events that year that seemed to emphasize the imperialist nature of Christianity. The first was the convening of the World Student Christian Federation in Peking, the other the publication of a massive tome entitled *The Christian Occupation of China*, in which maps and demographic charts detailed every aspect of mission work and showed what still was left to be 'occupied.'

For the rest of the decade, anti-Christian demonstrations were the order of the day at mission stations throughout China. These could take the form of a 'student storm,' a boycott of classes – which could be begun on almost any pretext, from the undue emphasis given to studying the Babylonian Wars in the compulsory Christian history course, to the quality of food in the boarding school. A servants' strike was another common type of protest. The West China mission sustained one particularly severe strike in 1924 when the entire servant population of all foreign institutions in Szechuan walked off their jobs in protest against the actions of the Canadian mission's builder, W.H. Leonard. (The other missionaries sided with the Chinese against Mr Leonard,

WMS boarding school in Tzeliutsing, Szechuan

voting that he be recalled immediately. Citing his 'unfortunate disposition,' Dr Kyle Simpson, the doctor at the Fowchow station, wrote that
he himself had heard Leonard 'call the workmen Water Buffalo, and
fools. I have also heard him ask a man if he wanted him to hire a
wet nurse for him ... I think you will agree with me that is not the
kind of thing which is likely to inspire Mr. McAmmond to invite a
man to preach occasionally!')

Such demonstrations occurred at every station throughout China,
especially at times like Christmas and Easter and during annual conferences. (Many missionaries noted cynically how often student strikes
seemed to coincide with examination time.) Usually these were non-
violent, little more than heckling at the mission gates, but they could
easily turn into shoving matches between mission personnel and the
'crowds of coolies, soldiers, farmers and students marching about the
streets with their fife and drum bands, carrying flags and banners on
which were written such slogans as "Down with Imperialism," "Down
with militarism," "Down with the YMCA," "Down with Christianity,"
"Down with the running dogs of the imperialists."'

After the Russian Revolution, about which atrocity stories were spread
widely in China by the thousands of White Russian refugees, most
foreigners were only too willing to ascribe any anti-imperialist movement

to 'bolshevik agitators' stirring up the 'dumb, industrious peaceful millions of China,' even though they might also recognize, as one missionary in Canton noted, that 'the Christians, including many of the prominent leaders, all over China are behind this anti-foreign movement, in this respect differing from the Boxer Movement.'

Although the rest of China was subject to civil warfare, it was in the treaty-port cities that the foreigners faced the anti-imperialist struggle in its most violent form. It was there, in Tientsin, Shanghai, Hankow, and Canton, that western penetration produced a festering sore. One woman recalled these cities in the 1920s with images of 'Harbours full of warships and gunboats, grey and threatening. A half-baked pink-faced youth kicking a rickshaw coolie. A foreign woman in a street car saying to a decent Chinese woman who pressed against her, "Don't touch me, dog." ... A stout and comfortable gentleman in snug dress-clothes saying, "the only thing the East understands is force" – the East, the home of hospitality and religion.'

After Sun Yat-sen retired from the presidency of the Republic of China in 1913, he withdrew to his home base in Canton with little more support than his faithful Canadian bodyguard, the belligerent Morris 'Two-Gun' Cohen. Using an alliance with the 'progressive' local warlord, Sun set up his own rival republic in which he kept alive his dream of reuniting China under the Kuomintang party, whose platform was based on his Three Principles of the People: Nationalism, Democracy, and 'the People's Livelihood.' But without an army, Sun's power remained illusory and extended little further than the Canton city walls.

Sun appealed to the western democracies for help, but they could not see beyond his anti-imperialist rhetoric. Typically, the Canadian reaction followed the British example. Dr F.C. Stephenson of the Young People's Forward Movement for Missions characterized Sun's followers as 'dreamers,' and applauded the non-Christian Wu Pei-fu because his attitude 'towards the Anglo-Saxon race and the missionaries is distinctly friendly, while that of Sun Yat-sen is uncertain. When dreamers run amuck, they become destroyers.' (The Canadian government, too, was concerned about Chinese nationalism, especially when it began to surface among the Chinese in Canada, virtually all of whom came from the Canton area. In 1918, when white Canadians from Victoria to Lethbridge were reporting that large numbers of young Chinese men were taking flying lessons and applying for passports, the Canadian government outlawed the Kuomintang as a subversive organization.)

In desperation, Sun turned to the help profferred by Soviet Russia, his last chance and, possibly, his last choice. Stalin sent his emissary Mikhail Borodin with orders to bring the fledgling Chinese Communist Party (founded in 1921) into a 'common front' with the Kuomintang. In an agreement hammered out in 1923, the CCP would control the party propaganda, and the Soviets would supply money and armaments to build up an army – Russia was excluded from the Versailles embargo on shipping arms to China – starting with the Whampoa Military Academy, the first modern military school in China. This agreement was an alliance, not a merger, between the two parties, and the Kuomintang continued to have a dominant right wing of compradors, merchants, and bankers who had grown up 'under the wing' of foreign investments in China.

The spark that ignited what Woodrow Wilson called 'the combustible material in China' occurred on 30 May 1925, another in the growing list of 'national humiliation days,' when British police in the International Concession of Shanghai opened fire on a demonstration of five thousand people. 'Give them a bit of lead,' the chief of police is said to have ordered, laconically, between golf games. 'That's what they understand.' Twelve people were killed.

The effect of this relatively minor incident was immediate and electric. It started an 'unquenchable fire' that threatened once again to engulf Christian missions in the blood of the martyrs. For the two years from 1925 to 1927 China was ravaged by civil war; missionaries got caught in the cross-fire. Eventually, all seven thousand had to evacuate their stations, and it was two or three years before some semblance of normalcy returned. When it did, it was according to new rules.

Within days of 30 May 1925, spontaneous anti-British demonstrations broke out in every part of China. As far inland as Szechuan, Dr Kyle Simpson reported, 'the effect is seen and felt on all sides.'

Our Evangelists and preachers are having a tough time of it, Christianity and Christians are being reviled and vituperation is being heaped on them on every side. Our schools have been broken up, some of the teachers and scholars becoming the worst enemies of Christianity, publishing and preaching all manner of lies ... I had no idea so much patriotism could be worked up in this country in so short a time. The oppression of the soldiers has been severe, lawlessness and robbery are rife on every hand, but a few students run amuck in Shanghai and a few other places and civil wars cease and all the present troubles are forgotten in every city all over the land, and the merchants and coolies everywhere take up the cry of the students, 'Kill the foreigner.'

The vice-president of West China Union University, the Reverend James Livingstone Stewart, wrote, 'Even those students who have been educated by the mission and supported in part by the missionaries have been influenced by this trend of thought and now the red influence from Russia has inflamed this feeling. Even the servants and workmen know that the foreigner in their land is not all-powerful and not beyond the processes of law. To hit one of these employees to-day means vastly more than it did ten or more years ago. Indeed, one's influence is gone once one uses force on one of them.'

Despite the boycotts and the general air of unrest, West China was far from the main events of the year 1925; its turn came the following year. The two Canadian missions in the eye of the storm at the outset were the Presbyterian and MIC Sisters missions in Canton. The 1925 demonstrations erupted with dizzying suddenness in Canton. After Sun Yat-sen's death in March, a struggle for his mantle ensued; in June, the Kuomintang army took control of the provincial government of Kwangtung and marched into Canton – 'led by three hundred bolshevist officers,' the MIC magazine *The Precursor* stated as a fact. Ten days later, on 23 June, British police once again opened fire on a Chinese demonstration. The foreign consulates in Canton, which were located on the small island of Shameen [SHAMEN], separated from the mainland by a canal, were protected by twenty foreign gunboats; the British police fired from this island, killing fifty-two and wounding more than one hundred on the mainland.

'The Chinese newspapers are filled with the wildest reports,' the Reverend William McKay, founder of the Presbyterian mission, wrote from Kongmoon, 'and the whole population from officials to coolies seem to believe them implicitly. For example the version of the Canton affair which is circulated and which even all the Christians believe is that when a peaceful procession of unarmed students was passing along the street across the canal from Shameen the British guards on Shameen without the slightest provocation opened a murderous fire on them.' When McKay tried to explain that the British consul, an eyewitness, swore that the demonstrators had opened fire first, the Chinese pastors would smile 'incredulously' and say, 'Of course they would say that.'

The official foreign version, copied in *The Precursor* from the Hong

Kong newspapers, featured a screaming mob of fifty to sixty thousand men, led by three thousand uniformed students of the Whampoa Military Academy under their Russian officers – '*masked* and on horseback.' When they came opposite the legations, the cadets turned to face Shameen and, at a signal shot, 'took their rifles from their shoulders and opened fire ... The battle, a real battle between Chinese marine officers and soldiers, and sailors and volunteers from England, France, Portugal, etc., lasted three-quarters of an hour.' Three foreigners were killed.

All foreign commercial and industrial activity in Canton ceased. Hong Kong, forty miles away, the 'fortress of Britain in China, was totally immobilized. Not a wheel turned. Not a bale of cargo moved. Not a ship left anchorage. More than 100 000 Hong Kong workers took the unprecedented action of evacuating the city. They moved en masse to Canton.'

The Shameen incident polarized the Christian community, dividing missionaries from Chinese, even separating nationalities among the missionaries themselves. The Canton Christian College, partially supported by the Presbyterian mission, had a student delegation among the marchers, two of whom were killed; the following day, seventeen American professors at the college issued a statement condeming the British. 'If the whole incident was, as the British claimed, a Bolshevik plot,' the president remarked, then 'in the indiscriminate use of machine guns, the British played right into it.' This statement, it was widely felt, showed the effectiveness of the strategy of divide and conquer; when the professors were evacuated to Hong Kong, 'they took quite a beating' from the rest of the foreign community, and the police gave them twenty-four hours to leave the colony.

The Canadians in Canton and Kongmoon, being British, accepted 'implicitly' the British version of events. 'All true friends of China welcome the appearance and development of a spirit of true nationalism in China,' wrote the Reverend Thomas Broadfoot, principal of the Kongmoon boys' school, in *Forward with China: The Story of the Missions of the United Church of Canada in China*; what was happening in Canton, however, was in his view not true nationalism but 'insidious and virulent propaganda' originating in Moscow. The Kuomintang, as the Reverend Duncan McRae wrote in June, was 'so wrapped up with the Soviet movement that it is considered by many to be a turn to communionism [sic].'

Similarly, the Roman Catholic sisters used the terms bolshevik and Kuomintang interchangeably. 'The Cantonese-Russians have been victorious,' wrote Sister Marie-du-Rosaire, superior of the convent. 'The

Cantonese are aided by the Russians, who are terrible, and although we love the Cantonese, we pray to God to exterminate the Russian bolshevists. Right now, everything is controlled by the gold of Russia.'

Within a week of Shameen, almost all missionaries had left Canton. Dr Oscar Thompson tried to keep the hospital open, but without water, food, electricity, or servants, he could do no medical work. Even Dr Victoria Cheung, senior female physician in the mission, could not maintain the Marion Barclay Hospital in Kongmoon and moved to Hong Kong with the rest of the foreigners.

The only foreigners still at their posts were the French priests and six French-Canadian sisters living inside the cathedral compound, and two more sisters at the Shek-lung [SHILONG] leprosarium. For six months, those in the cathedral barricaded themselves inside the compound, where fifteen hundred people, including two defeated generals, also took refuge. 'We are afraid of a bombardment by the powers, as they were forced to do in 1900 when the Boxers spread terror everywhere,' wrote the sister superior.

While the storm raged outside, the sister in charge wrote, 'it was a real rest for me to be among my dear orphans, busy with their work, which they do while praying and singing holy canticles.' In the end, they remained, even managing to feed the children with rice smuggled in by local Christians.

By the beginning of 1926, 'the better thinking Chinese themselves' had regained control over 'the low elements' (as the missionaries characterized them) and the missionaries were allowed to return to their missions. The boycott against British goods continued for another year, during which time the mission folk had to live under constant surveillance. 'The relations between the Canadian missionaries in Kwangtung and the mass movements,' John Foster wrote in his history, 'were as distant, as free of confrontation and of direct contact as the missionaries could manage.' Medical work was suspended, but educational work started anew in the spring, with a fraction of the student body.

After Sun Yat-sen's death the see-saw struggle between the left wing and the right wing for control of the Kuomintang party continued throughout 1925, but the following spring, in a well-timed coup, an unknown general named Chiang Kai-shek dramatically seized power. Chiang Kai-shek was not yet the omnipotent generalissimo, nor even yet a Christian. In contrast to Feng Yu-hsiang, he was known in missionary circles as 'the Red general.' His past history was a blank, except that he had recently returned from Moscow where he had gone to study the workings of the secret police, and that on his return he had been the founder of the Whampoa Military Academy. It was not forgotten that these students – led by Chiang himself – had instigated the Shameen incident.

Once he consolidated his power base in Canton, with Russian help, Chiang launched the 'Northern Expedition,' long dreamed of by Sun Yat-sen, to conquer the northern warlords and unite China under the five-striped Kuomintang flag. The main branch of his army, under the tactical direction of the Russian Galen, fought its way due north from Canton, aiming for the industrial cities of the middle Yangtse valley. This was a truly revolutionary army, the forerunner of the communist armies that swept across China over the next quarter century. As Mao Tse-Tung wrote at the time, 'a revolution is not a dinner party, or writing an essay, or painting a picture, or doing embroidery; it cannot be so refined, so leisurely and gentle, so temperate, kind, courteous, restrained and magnanimous. A revolution is an insurrection, an act of violence by which one class overthrows another.'

The progress of this army northwards confirmed the worst suspicions of the foreigners in China. When it reached Hankow in January 1927, it took over the foreign concession by force; shortly afterwards at Nanking, the troops loosed a bloodbath, a 'rape' of the city in which a number of missionaries were killed. Among them was John E. Williams, the American vice-president of the Nanking university who refused to hand over his gold watch to the looters. 'We are flotsam in a whirlpool with which we have no connection,' wrote his widow.

By that time, the eye of the whirlwind had shifted from Canton to the Yangtse, and the unrest was felt as far inland as Szechuan. 'Conditions in this part of China have changed very considerably within the past few months,' wrote Dr William Birks from Fowchow in the summer of 1926, 'and would be quite a surprise even to our missionaries who went home only a little over a year ago ... The result is that some of the time as one walks along there is that nice little prickly feeling that goes up and down one's spine.' In Chengtu, 480 kilometres further upriver, the students at the university, under 'pressure from the Red influences,' organized an anti-imperialist association that called a strike of the entire student body. Their manifesto 'vilifying' the missionaries called the British nation 'always fierce and unnaturally cruel.'

In June of 1926, Mrs Edith Sibley, a well-known member of the mission, was shopping on the main street of Chengtu, barely ninety metres from the mission compound, when a man 'dressed in the garb of a coolie' came up behind her, and with one stroke of his broadsword cut off her head, which he then threw into an open latrine. He was shot by Chinese soldiers before he had gone a block, but before he died he revealed that he was a member of the secret Red Lantern Society and that he was a 'runner from hell' who had come into the city specifically to 'take life.' The mission reacted calmly to this most gruesome event in its history. Though some saw this as a 'recrudescence of Boxerism,' the majority of the missionaries accepted the fact that he was a madman – he had once been treated in the mission hospital – acting alone. Nevertheless, citing 'the growing frequency of these attacks on foreigners,' the British Consul-General demanded the imposition of martial law in the city; though he withdrew his demand when he realized there was no one able to enforce it. Weakly, he advised the British to withdraw downriver and, when no one took his advice, added that he would help any who wanted to leave.

Later that same summer, the British themselves committed another blunder as serious as the Shameen incident. The warlord of Chungking, Yang Sen [YANG SEN], who was known as a friend of foreigners, captured two gunboats belonging to the Butterfield and Swire Company near the city of Wanhsien [WANXIAN], the first city on the Szechuan side of the Yangtse gorges. In order to release the hostages, the British navy engaged Yang's ships in a battle in which several of the hostages were killed. Then, in retaliation for the original 'barbarous attack,' the British proceeded to shell Wanhsien, killing three thousand people, most of them civilians.

Many missionaries, of whatever stripe, began to alter their opinions of gunboat diplomacy as the 1920s unfolded. Richard Orlando Jolliffe, older brother of Charles, for example, who in 1919 had described the local cruiser as 'the neighbourly policeman, calling round to see,' commented after Wanhsien, 'this gunboat business seems to take all the moral and spiritual stamina out of one. How can we preach the Gospel of "Love" to people who have been made to suffer by our own countrymen?' (Jolliffe recorded a telling comment early in his career made by an unnamed Chinese: 'Oh, yes, we believe in your teaching; we believe in policemen.') As evidence that it wished to be less associated with British imperialism, the West China mission changed its name from *Ing-kuo* [YINGGUO] (British) to *Chia-na-ta* [JIANADA] (Canadian). Similarly, Canadian and American missionaries issued separate statements calling on their respective governments to repeal the extraterritorial privileges.

(The United Church of Canada passed this resolution on to the Canadian government, which had no influence as a British colony to repeal these treaties.)

Other missionaries, more timorous by nature perhaps, felt that their safety and their neutrality – their very presence as 'guests' – depended on the gunboats. This issue came to a head in the 1926 annual council meeting of the West China mission, a few months before Mrs Sibley's murder. The Reverend James Gareth Endicott, son of James Endicott, was a first-year language student at the time, and would not normally have been given a chance to speak. Always the most headstrong member of the mission, Endicott was unable to contain himself, his biography states, and asked permission to speak. 'I never read anything in the Bible which says, "Go ye unto the world and shoot the Gospel into every creature," ' he ended provocatively.

In the stunned silence that followed, Dr C.B. Kelly, one of the respected older men, rose and slowly said, 'I'm prepared to leave it to the idealists like young Endicott to try to work with the Chinese on a new basis. I'll be interested to see what happens. But for myself, I'm not prepared to work here without some protection for my wife and children. When the gunboats go, I go.' Dr Kelly spoke for the majority.

Therein lay the tragedy of the 1920s: no gunboats, no new basis. In the aftermath of the 'rape of Nanking' early in 1927, the progressive missionary community in that city rescinded its demand to end gunboat protection, and meekly embarked on those hated gunboats for Shanghai. By that time, the West China mission was also on its way downriver for the fourth time in its history.

Though the situation had remained tense throughout 1926, the West China mission had made no evacuation plans beyond sending some of the wives and children back to Canada for an early furlough. By this point, the mission had more than two hundred adults and almost as many children, so the cost of travel would exceed $50 000 Canadian, none of which was recoverable from indemnities. Besides, as university vice-president the Reverend George Sparling noted, the university had managed to remain open through the various storms, and, 'Every such crisis passed makes our position more secure and we may have more of them.'

In addition, the missionaries felt they could trust the goodwill of the people and, above all, of the local authorities. The new Kuomintang general, a representative of Chiang Kai-shek's government, though not noted for his friendliness to foreigners, had invited them to stay in his own compound if worse came to worst. 'It is my personal duty to render assistance and give all possible protection to all foreigners no matter what circumstances may arise,' he had stated.

In February 1927, however, in reaction to the inflamed conditions downriver, the missionaries were forced to leave, which they did in thirty-eight boats. By the time they reached Shanghai, the city sheltered several thousand foreign refugees, and was an armed camp, with 'barb wire and sand bags' blocking every street leading into the International Concession. The hysteria emanating from the city was as vengeful and bloodthirsty as anything twenty-seven years earlier when the Boxers had rampaged through the country. 'Across the barbed-wire barricades,' observed the American journalist Harold Isaacs, 'the foreigners were generally convinced, as one of them put it, that they were going to be murdered in their own beds by their own servants ... and were quite certain that their fair little islet of foreign justice and rectitude was about to be overrun with insane mobs thirsting for the white man's blood.'

Yet five Canadian missionaries, thirteen Americans, and three British Quakers did remain behind in Chengtu, defying consular orders even when a telegram came saying, 'Whatinhell isdelaying youfivemen?' (They were later honoured within the mission as 'gold star missionaries.') They had decided to take the general at his word, the Reverend W.J. Mortimore wrote, obviously in high glee. 'So here we are to see things through. Our reliance must be on the good-will of the officials and all classes of people. It will be worth while to see how much this counts for in case of war, which seems to me not unlikely.' Frank Dickinson, professor of agriculture, reported that he had dined with 'the Great Man' (the local warlord) and had 'thawed him out' with a conversation about cross-breeding apples.

Like their colleagues in Szechuan, the missionaries in Honan had lived for two years in the knowledge that any day serious trouble would erupt. They had remained relatively isolated from the events of 1925 and 1926, except for the occasional wave that swept up from the Yangtse, and had relied for their information on papers like the *North China Daily News*. Consequently, in many ways they remained as 'insensitive' to Chinese nationalism as any treaty-port missionary: they felt Sun Yat-sen was nothing but 'that misguided agitator.' Southern bolshevism might be different from Northern Boxerism, but the end result would be the same: the extinction of Christian missions.

The North Honan mission especially was prone to equate the Kuomintang with secret societies and mass movements. It was still dominated by those who had personally suffered through the Boxer escape: Harvey Grant, Murdoch Mackenzie, and James Slimmon were all nearing seventy. 'We, of course, wish to see the North win,' wrote Harvey Grant at Christmas 1926, 'for Feng and the Cantonese we believe to be Bolshevists out and out. And if they win we will receive Bolshevist treatment and life in China will not be pleasant if even bearable.'

In 1926 and again in 1927, Honan was occupied by the army of Feng Yu-hsiang. Feng had changed considerably from the touted Christian general who had left the province in 1922. He too, after a visit to Moscow, had seemingly gone over to the communists. He had reorganized his army on the Russian model and renamed it the Kuominchun [GUOMINJUN], the People's Army. His final defection, in missionary eyes, came in 1927 when, sitting astride the path from Hankow to Peking, he joined Chiang Kai-shek's Kuomintang.

The North Honan missionaries tried to warn the church at home about Feng's change of allegiance, but ten years of pro-Feng propaganda, mostly from Jonathan Goforth, had left too deep an impression. 'The first thought at home was to keep the knowledge from the Church and general public, lest it affect the budget,' wrote Margaret Brown, the mission historian. 'Those in the field were distressed by this news.' In one unpublished letter, Harvey Grant wrote, 'My eyes once turned very much toward Feng to save China, but they do not turn to him now. On the other hand I regard him rather as a source of great danger both to the peace and to the integrity of this unhappy land.'

The missionaries became more distressed after their evacuation in April 1927, when they learned that Feng had allowed his troops to loot the mission stations. Prior to this, 'soldiers of various armies had visited the mission stations out of curiosity or for medical treatment ... but for more than twenty years none, no matter what faction, had never [sic] harmed anything. It remained for the Nationalist Army to set a precedent.' When the soldiers did occupy the stations, they took pot-shots at windows, burned everything – doors, floors, furniture, books – and even tore down walls. 'It seems incomprehensible that Feng's army would be guilty of such conduct,' wrote the board secretary, A.E. Armstrong. 'Surely he can give instructions with reference to property that he knows so well has been used for the good of China.'

The mission's anxiety about Feng was not its only worry. Judging from its correspondence at this time of revolution, the missionaries tried to stop other movements within the church itself. The first blow to their status quo came from Canada, where the two Presbyterian missions in China had been joined with the Methodist West China mission under the aegis of the new (1925) United Church of Canada. The ultimate decisions in the mission – about work allotment, finances, institutional framework, etc. – had always been made by the all-male presbytery, which reported directly to the General Assembly in Canada without going through the Foreign Mission Board. The United Church ruled, however, that the mission must disband presbytery and be governed by a council that included all active members of the mission (in other words, excluding the wives). The male missionaries and a surprising number of the older women workers dug in their heels, 'once more using the delaying tactic with difficult decisions,' for two years until they met with the new Moderator of the United Church, James Endicott. (Instead of being angered or bored by their endless discussions, Dr Endicott was amused, and said that he could always be certain that every detail had been thoroughly thrashed over.)

A much more serious threat came from the Chinese church. By this time, the synod, the Chinese-run and -supported side of the work, had evolved 'a highly organized church system' with 123 self-sustaining congregations. But since the Canadians made the ultimate decisions, many Chinese leaders felt, as a historian commented, 'like serfs in the community of saints.' This led to the establishment of a breakaway independent church that, in Weihwei at least, attracted the majority of Christians. This church had four expressed goals: to destroy Church imperialism, to recover religious autonomy, to love God, and to love China. Harvey Grant, citing the immoral conduct of its leaders – one had three wives, another had pilfered famine funds – called them 'church-wreckers.' Finally, this independent group broke off all contact with the mission, refusing even to accept the financial grants in aid because they had strings attached.

'We are proud to be British citizens these days,' wrote Dr Grant as he left for evacuation in April 1927, almost relieved to be leaving the conflicts behind; 'we can thoroughly approve British policy in China now ... it may be necessary for G.B. and other countries who are following her lead to speak loudly with guns before the desired end is reached. And it is essential that we should all be out of interior China while this proceeds.'

How different from the attitude of Bishop W.C. White in the Anglican diocese south of the river. Living in a cosmopolitan centre like Kaifeng,

White was known as an arbitrator; though not exactly a friend of Feng's, he kept in touch with him even during his communist phase. Consequently, although Kweiteh changed hands six times in as many months in 1927, the station remained relatively unscathed.

White was also more sympathetic to the independent Chinese church, which had actually started in the Kaifeng YMCA, though it was connected to a much larger movement throughout China. Rather than rail against the movement, White recognized that 'the more *intelligent* Chinese Christians are now very outspoken in their desire to be free from foreign control.' The domination of the church by the missionaries, he had said the year before, 'is the greatest obstacle to Christianity in the minds of the thinking classes, for the strong nationalistic spirit of present China is violently anti-foreign and therefore anti-Christian. Until this stigma, as they view it, can be removed, the Church in China cannot be the Church of the Chinese nation. One feels that dark days are ahead for the Church in China.'

Then, just when things seemed blackest, Bishop White made unprecedented concilations to the Chinese synod: as early as 1925, he was making preparations for a future Chinese bishop and actively 'devolving' responsibility onto the synod. Early in 1926, he gave the Chinese 'a voice in the appointment of foreign missionaries, men or women, to the work in the diocese.' The Canadian mission, he said, would thus become 'purely an auxiliary of the local Chinese Church.' By the time the consular order came to evacuate the mission, White had much of this church structure in place, including an obvious successor, the Reverend Philip Lindel Tsen. White's faith was confirmed when he ratified the election of Tsen as assistant bishop of the diocese, the first true Bishop *of* – not just in – Honan, and the first non-European elected bishop in the pan-Anglican communion. (By the time the formalities of consecration had taken place, two other Chinese had been named assistant bishops of American and British dioceses in China, but Tsen was 'the first and only one to be supported from a fund under the control of the Church in China, and not from funds that come from the home Missionary Societies.')

Rather than waiting in exile in Tsingtao with the rest of his missionaries, Bishop White returned to Toronto, where he continued to pressure the church to accept the idea of a Chinese bishop.

Among those remaining in China, George Simmons, canon of the Kaifeng cathedral, wrote, 'There seem to be about three cliques of mission workers, ... optimists, moderates and pessimists. The first group say they will be back at work in two years, the second say six years, and the latter say "never."' But factions aside, the same question lurked in everyone's mind: 'You can imagine how hard it will be to work with those people in any degree of harmony in the near future,' summed up the Reverend William McKay.

PART 3
The Political Gospel
1927-1959

'It is regrettable that ugly politics has to come into our lives.'

Dr Jean Millar Kilborn to Drs Ed and Gladys Cunningham, 1 April 1952

11 · New Life: The Nanking Decade

'The Moderator of the [United] Church, the Rev. Dr [James] Endicott told us with tremendous emphasis that a new day was coming in China ... The new day will not be turned aside by talking about the turmoil and bloodshed, or by shouting bolsheviki either ... The New China will be such as the Chinese people will have it, and not as the Western nations want it. And no Christian missionary in the China of the future can justify himself save as he has fundamental within himself an intense sympathy with China in her aspirations for freedom and the better day.'

The New Outlook, 3 August 1927

'Now that civil war is raging in the southern part of Honan, China is once more in its normal condition, and affairs are as usual here – irregular trains, spasmodic mails, military officers, units and supplies being hurried forward, wild rumours circulating, authentic news scarce, and a general air of expectancy everywhere.'

Harvey Grant, clerk of North Honan mission to Board of Foreign Missions, United Church of Canada, 1929

As the foreign refugees huddled behind the barbed wire of Shanghai in that fateful spring of 1927, calling for international war, the strangest thing happened. Nothing happened. The war went away.

Teaching in the Anglican Diocese of Honan

When Chiang Kai-shek entered the city on 26 March, the streets were ominously silent. A week earlier a strike of 800 000 Chinese workers had paralysed the city. Kuomintang flags flew from every flagpole. The provisional government under the communist leader Chou En-lai held an uneasy peace over the 'native' suburbs of Chapei [ZHABEI] and Woosung. In the concessions, the foreign authorities had made a pact with the notorious Green Gang, 'the Chinese Mafia,' to police them and prevent a leftist uprising.

Unknown to the foreigners, however, Chiang Kai-shek had made his own arrangements with the Green Gang. For two weeks after his arrival in Shanghai, Chiang issued a flurry of self-serving statements of unity with both the right and left wings of the party; but then, in a night of 'White Terror,' he turned his back on his Soviet supporters. At 4:00 A.M. on the night of 12 April, a siren pierced the air; it was the signal for a well-orchestrated attack by the Green Gang goons against the leftists. The political underground did not stand a chance against the criminal underworld. The gutters ran with blood and few escaped. (One who did was Chou En-lai.) Within a few weeks Chiang had similarly purged the party structures in Canton, Hankow, and Nanking. He was now the supreme commander of the army and chairman of the party.

Six months later, Chiang Kai-shek made the most brilliant move of his career: he married May-ling Soong. She had all the right connections: family, wealth, and power; as well she was a stunningly beautiful woman. Her father, the late Charlie Soong, was an American-educated minister – the first Chinese pastor of the Southern Methodist denomination – whose Bible-printing Commercial Press had netted him a personal fortune that enabled him to give major financial support to Sun Yat-sen's revolution in 1911. May-ling's oldest sister, Ching-ling, had added to the family lustre by marrying Dr Sun; that she had been disowned by the family – and in fact became a vehement critic of Chiang – was ignored by the Kuomintang political press. May-ling's other sister, Ai-ling, the family manipulator, was married to H.H. Kung, one of China's richest bankers; her brothers, T.V. and T.A. Soong, were also gaining a reputation as financial wizards. For better or worse, and for richer rather than poorer, Chiang had decided to marry into the Soong family.

There was one impediment, however: May-ling's mother, known as 'Mammy,' who was described as 'a grand, puritan Christian of the highest principles,' refused to sanction the marriage because Chiang was still legally married to two previous wives (making May-ling into a lowly third wife in Chinese eyes) and was also living openly with a concubine.

Mammy was persuaded, none the less, to put aside her principles when she asked Chiang whether he would become a Christian. Without a trace of hypocrisy, which she would have seen through, he made no promises except to study the Bible and, if persuaded of its truth, become a Christian. He did so two years later.

The glittering wedding of Chiang Kai-shek and May-ling Soong was well attended by the foreign members of Shanghai society, among whom were at least two Canadians, Dr and Mrs Harrison Mullett, who were in exile from West China. In recognition of Chiang's newly professed anti-communism, the foreign powers gradually relaxed their gunboat grip on the port cities. They had misjudged him, of course. He was not and never had been the 'Red general'; he had merely used the communists for his own ends. Once he had supreme power, he 'hijacked the revolution' (from the leftist point of view) and set up a dictatorship of the right, not the left. He was the strongman the missionaries had for years been calling for.

Once the smoke had cleared, many within the missionary community began to question why they had been brought out of the interior, at great expense to themselves, as 'hostages to the necessities of British diplomacy ... so that the Great Powers might threaten armed intervention in the carrot-and-stick diplomacy which was undermining Nationalist unity and moving Chiang Kai-shek toward compromise with foreign interests.' The missionaries had always known, they professed, that the moderates in China – 'our merchants,' the South China people particularized – would triumph over the turbulent 'lower elements.' One month after the purge of the communists, William McKay wrote from Canton, 'It looks almost as if the better-thinking Chinese have awakened at last to the real danger to their country from Bolshevism rather than from the foreign powers or even the so-called unequal treaties.' As a further concession, Chiang tacitly agreed not to press for repeal of these treaties if the powers curbed their most flagrant abuses (such as missionary mediation in civil wars), and if foreign institutions in China, mission schools and hospitals in particular, became Chinese institutions in policy and personnel.

One of the voices of reason that summer was that of Dr James Endicott, former head of the Canadian Mission Press in Chengtu, long-term secretary of the Methodist Foreign Mission Board, and now the second Moderator of the United Church of Canada. He spoke with the authority of the church and his tone was distinctly accommodationist. 'I believe in God. I believe in China,' he told a gathering of West China people in Shanghai. 'Nobody will make me believe that China has rejected Jesus or rejected you because you are too much like Jesus. If it is difficult it is not because you are too much like Jesus, but too much like John Bull ... The word British must mean less, and the word American must mean less, but the cross of Christ must mean more and more.'

One of Dr Endicott's purposes in coming to China at this time was to meld the three disparate China missions, the Presbyterians in North Honan and Canton and the Methodists in West China, into one United Church organization. (This melding had already started, at least symbolically, with the union of the two founding families of the West China and North Honan missions through the marriage of Dr Leslie Kilborn and Dr Janet McClure.) Consequently, when Dr Endicott spoke to the North Honan people – who were proud to be British – he brought a sterner message: 'If you leave the impression your Christians cannot be trusted,' he warned them, 'and that these people when they become strong nationalists that they [sic] also become bolshevists ... then it is the strongest condemnation of what we have been doing among them for the last ten years. If I were a Chinaman and had to make my choice, I would be a nationalist right from my heart out.'

Right now, Endicott reminded the missionaries, while they were away from their posts, the Chinese church was still carrying on, still paying its pastors, even running mission hospitals. And furthermore, the Chinese themselves were taking the initiative for the creation of the two large church unions, the National Christian Council (NCC) and the Church of Christ in China (CCC), the one that the United Church missions had joined. (The CCC was a union of Presbyterians, Baptists, Congregationalists, and the Canadian Methodists.) Distanced now from the day-to-day conflicts, the North Honan mission passed a resolution 'expressing their faith in the Chinese Synod and requesting them to assume full responsibility for carrying on the work at the Stations in their absence.'

The North Honan people were not the only ones who did some soul-searching during their exile at the coast. Devolution occurred more slowly in some missions than others – grudgingly in South China, stubbornly resisted in North Honan, constitutionally in the Anglican diocese, bureaucratically in West China – but between 1926 and 1929, every church made important concessions to Chinese nationalism. Even the Roman Catholic church under Pius XI in 1926 consecrated the first six Chinese bishops and issued the encyclical *Rerum Ecclesiae*, which called for the deoccidentalization of foreign missions.

'We reëxamined ourselves and our methods,' a CIM missionary said at the time. 'Realizing that we had had a mistaken attitude in this matter of missionary control, we tried faithfully to make needed adjustments. The advance of the Chinese Church, since then, has been phenomenal.'

This meant, in practical terms, that by the time the missionaries arrived back at their stations, the Chinese church (excepting the Catholic) was *the* church. It made the decisions, allocated the money, assigned the people; the missionaries were there by permission. Although still influential – they sat on the councils and worked directly as evangelists – as a group they were now adjuncts, employees of the Chinese church. While 'devolution' was happening within the church, the same thing was happening in mission schools and hospitals, this time by government decree; in order to conform to the state system of education and medicine, the principals of the schools and the heads of hospitals must all be Chinese.

Some of these Chinese, recalls Dr Robert McClure, 'appeared to us to be flatly anti-foreign. And they were. Some of them were pretty belligerent ... And to hear this from your dear colleague whom you had known as a boy, whom you had helped support through mission primary school ... and then he said we must get rid of the foreign missionaries, ship them back to Canada. This sounded like pretty drastic stuff.'

Many missionaries could not adjust to this new reality; Dr Kelly who had challenged Jim Endicott at the 1926 West China council was one. Of the 8300 missionaries who were evacuated to the coast in 1927, fully three thousand never went back. The West China mission alone lost forty people, one-quarter of its work force. (The breakdown is interesting: 47 per cent of men and families retired, but only 23 per cent of the single women did so.) Some left for what one might call ideological reasons – they were pointedly 'not invited' to return by the Chinese church – others for more personal reasons. They could no longer take the daily tensions of life in China, they had the responsibility of a growing family at home, they had already put in twenty or thirty years in the field. The reasons why people left cut across the divisions of the workers and included not only the hard liners, but also outspoken accommodationists like Dr Kyle Simpson and Edward Wilson Wallace. Even three of the five 'gold star' missionaries who had remained in Chengtu retired at their next furlough. Eight of the twenty-four doctors followed suit, as did three of the founders of West China Union University.

There were similar departures from the renamed North China mission; twenty out of ninety-six missionaries left the field permanently, including at least two irreplaceable men. One was the Reverend Donald Mac-Gillivray, 'the best-known Canadian in Shanghai,' who retired full of years (to Tunbridge Wells, England) after forty years in China, the last ten spent as general secretary of the Christian Literature Society. Perhaps the most tragic loss was the Reverend John D. MacRae, president of Cheeloo University. Described by his fellow missionaries as a 'brilliant' scholar and 'the strongest all-round man in the mission,' he had managed to keep the university open throughout the troubles of 1925-7, going so far as to apply for government recognition to do so. By this time, he himself was beginning to experience 'paranoic fixations,' and was sent back to Canada. He died nine years later, aged fifty-eight, in the Ontario psychiatric hospital in Whitby.

Nevertheless, five thousand missionaries did return to their stations. Once again, neither age nor politics seemed to determine who stayed. At least three of the original CIM 'first Canadian party' of 1888 went 'home' to Kiangsi, as did four of the Honan Seven. Dr William McClure went back to teaching medicine at Cheeloo University, and even Jonathan Goforth came tottering back – literally: he was almost blind, and crippled with arthritis.

In 1925, when the North Honan mission had joined the United Church, only the Goforths had opposed union. Jonathan returned to Canada to speak on behalf of the continuing Presbyterian Church in Canada. Early in 1926, as Chiang was launching his Northern Expedition, Goforth received a telegram in Canada from Feng Yu-hsiang asking him to return to China to work among Feng's soldiers. Rosalind was in a typical position, lying on the sofa waiting for an ambulance to take her to the hospital, when the telegram arrived. 'What shall I do?' asked Jonathan. Poor long-suffering Rosalind, 'after covering her face for a moment, as if in prayer, looked up and said with decision, "I'm going with you."' One week later they sailed for China.

Evidently, Goforth had not heard of General Feng's defection; in any case, he could not accept that his old friend, one of the 'miracle lives of China,' had lost 'his first love.' But, according to Harvey Grant, when Goforth arrived in Feng's camp, he 'realized almost at once that the former cordial relations between himself and General Feng no longer existed. The General no longer desired to hear the Gospel from Dr Goforth but desired to convert Dr Goforth to an appreciation of Russian

Sovietism. Finding however, no common ground … he treated Dr Goforth with scant respect.'

Was there, Rosalind asked, 'no place left to us in this great needy land?' After a year of searching, Goforth was invited to occupy one station of the Irish mission in Manchuria, where, twenty years before, he had started his famous revival. 'What a weak band we were!' wrote Rosalind. 'The leader, an old man nearing seventy, with a semi-invalid wife [she was carried in on a stretcher]; a "Salvation Army lassie" – Miss Graham from New Zealand; a Dutch lady – Miss Annie Kok; and one young recruit – Rev. Allan Reoch, as yet struggling with the language.' This was the beginning of the continuing Presbyterian Church in Canada mission to Manchuria, located in Szepingkai (which happened also to be the centre of the Quebec Missions-Etrangères operation). It was a small, 'spirit-led' mission closer to the China Inland Mission model than to the United Church pattern (and supported in Canada mainly by Knox Church, Toronto, which was also the strongest Presbyterian supporter of the CIM). After six years there Dr Goforth was so blind he had to be led around by a boy, and his wife was confined to her bed. Only then did they retire to Toronto. Two years later, still dreaming of another call from the field, Dr Goforth passed away in his sleep. For fifty years he had been the most transfixing Canadian missionary of his day, and at his funeral his old friend Dr A.E. Armstrong epiphanized: 'I think of today as being Jonathan Goforth's *Coronation!'* Memorial services were held around the world, from Canada to China via England and Australia. Rosalind rallied – once more – long enough to write her husband's biography, before she, too, slipped away.

After taking control of Peking in April 1928, Chiang Kai-shek controlled the first real government of China since 1911. To emphasize that the Kuomintang was southern-based, he moved the capital city to Nanking, the old Southern Capital; in the process he downgraded Peking from Northern Capital to Peiping [BEIPING], 'Northern Peace'. The capital remained at Nanking for ten years, until the Japanese invasion of North China forced Chiang to flee with his government to the safety of Chungking. One recent historian has characterized this Nanking decade as a period of 'transitional semi-stability.' This stability was not always discernible to those on the ground; 'So much for the four-hundred-and-seventy-eighth civil war which this Province has experienced since the Manchu Government was overthrown in 1911,' commented Dr I.E.

Revelle from Szechuan in 1932. In China, as in Europe and America, the 1930s were a time of social upheaval and financial depression.

As the Canadian missionaries began to straggle back to their stations in 1928, a year or more after their departure, they found their first view of the new China anything but cheering. As the five men who came back to Changte, North Honan, found, 'All houses had been looted, from cellar to attic, of clothing, beds, bedding, sewing machines, dishes, cutlery, bicycles, in fact of everything the soldiers fancied ... Pianos and organs had been maliciously smashed to fragments with hammers. Books had been destroyed though all valuable dictionaries were missing from the waste heap, thus confirming the testimony of the local people that there were students in the army ... The foreign cemetery had been desecrated and basements of hospitals and houses used for latrines.' The mission estimated the damage at $150 000 gold.

The independent Chinese church, which had grown in their absence, remained hostile to the returning missionaries. The moderator of the Chinese synod refused to meet with them and ordered them not to 'engage in any active work.' Until the mission turned over complete financial control to the Chinese church, the latter would live without funding from Canada. When synod requested permission to communicate directly with the Board of Foreign Missions in Toronto, the board replied that 'the missionaries on the field are the representatives of the Canadian Church and bear the Gospel tidings. The BFM will be glad to receive communications directly from the Chinese church, but it will naturally look to its representatives for opinion and advice.' As to turning over finances to the Chinese, the board stated that 'it lays down certain rules and safeguards which the Mission is not at liberty to abrogate at will.' The dispute became so severe that the head of the Church of Christ in China was asked to negotiate a compromise. Eventually the Canadians did agree to turn over operational funds to the Chinese church according to its own budget.

In the Anglican diocese, the 1927 destruction had not been as severe as in the north, but just as work was starting again in 1929, Feng Yu-hsiang revolted against Chiang and occupied the Anglican compound in Kaifeng. 'After blowing up railway bridges, and destroying and removing other property,' Bishop White wrote, Feng's troops 'proceeded to the West of the Province, thereby allowing us to take possession of our schools again. Since then, armies have been moving to and fro, and it has been a constant task to keep our buildings from being occupied by these different military units.' All over the country, he wrote a few weeks later, 'official China seems to look on Mission property as public property.'

'The outstanding event of the year for this Diocese,' according to Bishop White's 1929 annual report, was the consecration of Reverend Lindel Tsen as Assistant Bishop of Honan. Ever since Tsen had come to Honan from the American mission in Hankow, wrote White, 'he has proved to be a tower of strength to the Church in Honan, and a great comfort to me personally. He is a learned and wise leader, a splendid executive, and a deeply spiritual chief pastor.' In 1930, Bishop Tsen was the only non-white bishop to attend the Lambeth Conference in London, England.

White's argument was not with the Chinese church, but with the Chinese government, over the regulation of mission schools. Ever since 1924, the Kuomintang had been issuing regulations trying to control mission schools. Many denominational missions agreed to go along with the instructions, appointed Chinese principals, and secularized their institutional structures. The Anglicans and evangelical groups like the China Inland Mission felt the time had come for the missions to divest themselves of the non-religious works. 'Our Educational Work of the past,' wrote White, 'has been an important factor in building up the Church in Honan,' but now 'radical readjustments should be effected to meet this new situation ... This will mean the "scrapping" of some of our educational plant. We should remove everything that may be in the nature of a liability on the Mission or the Chinese Church, and salvage everything possible.' In Kweiteh, he said, the damaged school should be razed and the material used to construct a new church building. 'This action,' he concluded, 'will insure an equipment of property the whole of which will be fully used, and which, if such an emergency should arise, could be handed over to the Chinese Church.'

Three years after Tsen was consecrated bishop, White announced his own retirement, saying that the past few years had been 'almost continuous physical and mental strain, and the time has come when ... I should retire to more peaceful service in the homeland.' He stipulated that the Canadian church should not name a Canadian as his successor – there was no likely candidate – as this would be 'unnecessary and ill-advised, as well as a retrograde step ... A missionary bishop is no longer necessary in this Diocese, ... a Chinese bishop can do the work.'

After much debate, the Canadian house of bishops concurred with White's recommendation, but turned down White's further suggestion that he be named 'bishop emeritus,' since, he claimed, he would 'be making journeys to China for the purchase of further supplies for the

Ontario Museum and could at the same time visit the Diocese in Honan.' White's retirement was anything but tranquil. Judging from his correspondence, he continued to act as advisor, if not exactly bishop emeritus, keeping in touch with daily events in Honan, issuing instructions to the MSCC and to individual missionaries in the field, and writing long avuncular letters to Bishop Tsen.

In addition, White undertook in his retirement a second career that would have daunted a much younger person, as director of the first department of Chinese studies in Canada at the University of Toronto and, allied with this, as curator of Chinese art at the Royal Ontario Museum. White had become a collector of Chinese art and artifacts, at least on the amateur level, shortly after his arrival in Kaifeng, when he purchased the synagogue site and liturgical articles belonging to the last remnant of the Chinese Jewish community. Arguing that Christianity was the historical successor of Judaism, he installed the two large memorial stele (one of which could be dated back to 1487 and recounted the, at the time, one-thousand-year-old history of the Jews of Kaifeng) in special porticos on either side of the entrance to Trinity cathedral. During his 1924 furlough, Bishop White was approached by Dr Charles Trick Currelly, curator of archaeology at the new museum in Toronto. Currelly's own ambition was to build the ROM into a world-recognized institution, and he asked the bishop to act as his agent in China. White accepted this new assignment with his usual forcefulness and enthusiasm and, over the next ten years, sent back thousands of objects that he hoped would give the average Canadian 'an intimate glimpse of the common life of China over a period of 4000 years.' This collection included some breathtaking objects, unknown in any museum outside China and illustrated in every standard (Western) history of Chinese art: robust Shang bronzes, Han tomb tiles, processions of Tang figures, fragile polychromed bodhisattvas from the Sung dynasty, and, most astounding of all, three huge fresco wall paintings that are among the greatest treasures of Chinese art.

Bishop White's collection, supplemented by other missionary collections – George Leslie Mackay's Formosan artifacts and the James Mellon Menzies collection of oracle bones – have given the Royal Ontario Museum one of the largest collections of Chinese art outside China. Yet, even putting aside the troubling question of whether the Anglo-Saxon race has the right to be the custodian of the Chinese past (China was in such turmoil, the argument runs, that these objects would have disappeared) the ethics of this collection are still controversial. Bishop

White has often been accused of being a grave robber, which technically he was not. He happened to be in the right place at the right time: two years after his retirement, in 1936, the Kuomintang government brought in its first laws controlling the export of cultural treasures. Until that time, anyone was free to purchase anything that was for sale and ship it anywhere in the world; this was but another expression of the 'open door' policy.

The path of an object from a Chinese peasant to a museum collection was murky and complicated, and at this late date it may be impossible to unravel; 'Secrecy played an important role in collecting, and valuable information was often obtained through hired spies and informants,' states Bishop White's biography. We do know that many unscrupulous Chinese did pose as 'curio dealers,' among them the sinister crippled millionaire Chang Ching-chang [ZHANG JINGZHANG] also known as Curio Chang, who used his position as curator of the Imperial Palace Museum in Peking to stock antiquities shops in Paris and New York. And there were the underlings: corrupt officials who would forge a document; soldiers who sold their loot on the black market. Art collecting, like interference in local politics, could have serious consequences: in 1923, General Feng Yu-hsiang accused Bishop White of possessing ' "treasure," the same being government property.' When the bishop denied holding the 'treasure' and Feng's troops seized it while in transit, the general 'issued a proclamation stating that, if such an offence as that committed by Bishop White should be repeated, in the event of future troubles protection would be withdrawn from the Christian Missions.'

Nevertheless, the other side must also be stated: in the rush to modernize China, the old *was* despised. North China in particular was littered with the detritus of 4000 years or more of human habitation, and every time a die-straight railway was built, hundreds of tomb mounds would be levelled, exposing their contents to the elements. Motor roads swept away city walls, memorial arches, and wayside shrines; temples were desecrated and idols smashed, all in the name of 'progress.' Bishop White did not instigate this tomb-robbing – as archaeologists in, say, Egypt did – although he was its beneficiary. More than that, White and others like him were the first to apply scientific methods to Chinese archaeology at a time when native scholars numbered only a handful of poorly trained 'experts.'

The change in emphasis from active collecting in the 1920s to academic research in the 1930s exemplified in Bishop White's career occurred in China as well as in Canada. With the skyrocketing prices of Chinese antiquities, and the cultural-properties laws, western-style museums were established in China in the 1930s both by the government and by the Christian universities. The museum of the West China Union University, for example, included such diverse artifacts as a dinosaur skeleton from Alberta, souvenirs of the First World War, and rare Tibetan scroll paintings gathered by expeditions into the Western mountains.

White's career was mirrored by other Canadian missionaries, Dr John Calvin Ferguson in Nanking, Dr Davidson Black in Peking, and, especially, by the Reverend James Mellon Menzies of the North Honan mission. Menzies (no relation of Dr James R. Menzies of the same mission who was killed by burglars) arrived in the Presbyterian mission in 1910 and was allocated to the main station at Changte. Under its ancient name of Anyang (by which it has been known since 1949), Changte was the capital of the Shang dynasty (1766–1122 BC), which is regarded as the 'semi-legendary' beginning of Chinese history. As he was walking in the fields near the so-called Waste of Yin, Menzies would find small dessicated shards of bone, as numerous as the Iroquoian arrowheads on a southern Ontario farm. For centuries the peasants had been selling these 'dragon bones' to herbalists who ground them into a fine powder and used them as an aphrodisiac. But J.M. Menzies was struck by the runic scratches on the bones and, after many years' study and consultation with Chinese literary scholars, he discovered that these were the so-called 'oracle bones,' the incised sheep scapulae and tortoise shells used in divination, and that the scratches were in fact the earliest form of Chinese writing. Dr Menzies was seconded from the Presbyterian mission to Cheeloo University, where he helped train the first generation of Chinese professional archaeologists. After his retirement from the field, he joined Bishop White at the ROM.

The contribution of these two men to a scholarly understanding of ancient China was enormous, a fact that the People's Republic of China tacitly recognized in 1974 when it allowed the travelling exhibition of archaeological artifacts unearthed since 1949 to be shown in the Royal Ontario Museum; it did make the stipulation, however, that the two collections were to be kept entirely separate. In return, China would not demand the return of its 'plundered cultural heritage.'

The United Church of Canada came into being on 1 June 1925 as a progressive institution whose official organ was entitled *The New Outlook*. It was a mission-minded church, as symbolized by the head of the

Moderator's gavel, which was composed of ten kinds of wood, each from a different overseas field, and had a handle of hard Canadian maple. The Methodists, being hierarchical, came into the union as a corporate body; the Presbyterians and Congregationalists, however, allowed each congregation to decide independently whether it would join. The wrangling was particularly severe in the Presbyterian church and lasted for several years. At first, all overseas missions were given to the United Church, but according to the final decision, the continuing Presbyterian Church retained those in Formosa, the British Guiana sector of the Trinidad mission and part of Central India. The United Church was given the former Methodist missions in Japan and West China, the Presbyterian fields of North Honan, South China, Korea, Trinidad, and Central India; and the Congregationalist mission in Angola.

Throughout the 1920s and 1930s, the United Church of Canada became one of the strongest supporters of the modernist wing of foreign missions, as exemplified by the Student Christian Movement. The SCM of Canada was founded in 1920 out of the ashes of the old Student Volunteer Movement for Foreign Missions, by, among others, Davidson Ketchum and S.H. Hooke, both of whom helped found the influential leftist *Canadian Forum* in the same year.

From its inception, the Canadian SCM was committed to world brotherhood and world peace: one of its first acts was to raise money to help German students after the end of the First World War. The SCM, 'a movement not an institution,' sought to reconstruct society according to a 'theology of radical reform, a modernist compound of Christianity, Bergson's creative evolution, and a touch of prometheanism which seemed to derive from Nietzsche. It was a theology which obviously contributed much to the birth of the new secularism which attended the decline of social service.' 'SCMers' were characterized as 'brainy idealists' who, according to an early 'manifesto,' had embarked 'on a world-wide quest for the ultimate values of life, based on the conviction that in the life and teachings of Jesus are to be found the means to a full realization of life.'

The greatest contribution of the early SCM was undoubtedly the Bible-study methods organized by a reserved disciplinarian named Henry Burton Sharman. Up to this time, Bible studies had tended towards the inspirational, but Sharman forced his students to put aside their preconceptions, two thousand years of dogma, to approach the life of 'Jesus in the records,' the synoptic gospels, as though they were reading them for the first time. Who is this man? What is He saying? he would ask at every juncture. Some people complained that Sharman's methods were apolitical, but the approach itself, with its emphasis on looking at Jesus as a man rather than as a divinity, also forced many people to reach their own conclusions about such political issues as war and peace, exploitation, and imperialism.

In the mission fields, in West China in particular, the Sharman study had a strong appeal; in fact, the use of the name Jesus, rather than Christ or one of His other names, appears in mission writings (such as the Shanghai speech of Dr Endicott, Sr) almost as a code word for Sharman's *Jesus in the Records*. 'We got that method into our bones,' wrote Earl Willmott, 'and it goes on into our daily jobs now, as we seek to help it permeate the structure of society through the groups we work with "in the world."' Willmott, along with Jim Endicott, Jr, and Dr Leslie Kilborn, was the leading proponent of the method in China, translating each volume of Sharman's works as it appeared and organizing study groups at the summer resorts. Like young Endicott, who had trouble even getting ordained because of his undogmatic views, Willmott often ran into difficulties with theological conservatives; in 1925, only four years after his arrival in West China, he published an unsigned article in *West China Missionary News*, a monthly digest of news by and for all missions in the area, claiming that belief in the miracles of Jesus was a stumbling-block to the Chinese. In 'A Conversation' with a middle-school student, he reported, the boy had said that most of the members of the Christian Endeavour society 'are fed up with religious meetings. Every morning, twice on Sunday, and Wednesday evening. When they hear the bell they all say, "Oh shoot, another 'worship!'" An awful lot of them hate the name "Jesus."' In addition, the boy claimed that Chinese preachers talked 'continually' about the supernatural stories in the Bible only to please the foreign missionaries and, besides, 'a lot of the country teachers and preachers have had *very* little education, they don't know what else to talk about.'

Such an article was not calculated to endear the Jesus-study movement to the evangelicals – indeed, on several occasions Earl Willmott was asked not to return to the field by the mission secretary, only to be overruled by the council. But such criticisms of the missionary endeavour, fuelled by the anthropological and sociological critique of missions as culture destroyers, were increasingly common in the mainstream churches. Between 1927 and 1935, articles in *The Christian Century*, the leading progressive religious monthly in the United States, testify to this: 'Can a Missionary Be a Christian?' it asked in 1930. 'End Mission Imperialism Now!' it demanded four years later. In the next issue, it announced, 'I Don't Want to Christianize the World!'

In addition, in the public mind, a new view of China and the Chinese people was emerging as exemplified in the stories of Pearl Buck, daughter and wife of missionaries. Divorcing herself both from her girlhood roots and from her husband, John Lossing Buck, a prominent professor of agriculture at Nanking University, she described from personal knowledge the eccentricities and rigidity of many missionaries. The Chinese she presented as humble, good-natured, persevering peasants. Her stories like *The Good Earth* were not written to 'convert any readers to the missionary cause.'

Responding to the mounting criticisms of foreign missions, seven leading denominations in the United States and the Associated Boards of Foreign Missions of the United States and Canada set up a joint fact-finding inquiry, the Laymen's Commission. Its two-volume report, *Re-Thinking Missions*, published in 1932, was 'the high watermark of Protestant liberalism,' It is a curiously balanced report, each criticism tempered with praise, every commendation countered with damnation. Of the thousands of missionaries the lay investigators spoke to in China, Burma, Japan, and India, the report said:

there were many of conspicuous power, true saintliness and a sublime spirit of devotion, men and women in whose presence one feels himself at once exalted and unworthy. It is easier to say this, than to say the rest of the truth; the greater number seem to us of limited outlook and capacity; and there are not a few whose vision of the inner meaning of the mission has become obscured by the intricacies, divisions, frictions and details of a task too great for their powers and their hearts.

Asking the rhetorical question whether missions should continue, the inquiry stated, 'is somewhat like asking whether good-will should continue or cease to express itself ... there is an always valid impulse of love to men: one offers one's own faith simply because that is the best one has to offer.' Thus when the inquiry finally did decide that missions should continue, even to their having 'permanent function and methods,' the good outweighed the bad only by the weight of a human soul.

As the commission issued its report in monthly instalments, a storm of criticism broke, even in liberal circles, directed not against missions but against the methods of the inquiry. Dr Wallace Crawford spoke for the West China mission when he stated:

It is true that one member of the 'advance guard' did visit this part of the country, and had a very good 'general' insight into the general work of the missions in West China. He visited the usual 'show places' of West China but did not get off the beaten path to see real missionary work. His visit to the Women's hospital consisted of having afternoon tea at the home of the medical ladies, and then in the semi-darkness of the afternoon, made a cursory investigation of the hospital. He was a layman and knew no more than the average layman would know about the work of a hospital. And not one of the fact-finding commission came within a thousand miles of the work of the United Church in West China ... The Medical workers of the United Church of Canada, West China Mission, would welcome an appraisal commission who would come from Canada and make thorough, and minute investigation of our work. We have no fear of any exposure of the work, either in quantity or quality, which we are doing.

The United Church Board of Overseas Missions (the disuse of the word 'foreign' was another sign of the changing times) was equally appalled by the inquiry, coming at this time of financial depression. The board had already reduced the salaries of its overseas workers by 10 per cent, then by a further 15 per cent; then, in a final ignominy, it had asked them to contribute to a relief fund for underpaid ministers in Saskatchewan. (The West China missionaries contributed $1700, and the Chinese churches also made a substantial contribution.) The secretary, James Endicott, wrote a strong reply to *The Christian Century* – which it never published – condemning the inquiry's 'unpardonable strategy' in publishing the report in instalments, and adding that Pearl Buck's 'unqualified endorsement' did little to give it credibility.

Fortunately, just at that moment, the University of Toronto chose to grant an honorary doctorate to Dr Robert Gordon Agnew, a West China dentist, for his statistical analysis of tooth decay among Chinese and tribespeople in Szechuan. 'Not only has honor come to them [the Agnews] because of this,' wrote Endicott to the mission, 'but also to the whole mission and to the West China Union University.' This, he felt, had given the whole missionary enterprise 'quite a boost in very influential quarters.'

The United Church never did send a fact-finding commission to tour the foreign fields, unless one considers the flying, wartime visit of Dr Wilder Penfield, the Montreal neurosurgeon, on an 'errand' for the National Research Council in 1943. But then, Penfield was hardly unbiased: Canadian missionaries, he wrote, 'have given the Chinese people the best example our civilization could produce – considerably better than we deserve!'

As the liberal denominational missions were beginning to retrench in the 1930s, the evangelical ones continued to surge ahead. The 1920s had been a time of change and experimentation, of church unions and church divisions; the 1930s, a decade of financial and spiritual depression, was one of conservatism and back-to-basics evangelism. As Paul Varg wrote of the American missions, the 'humanism and relativism, so fashionable in the 1920s, were now in full retreat.' This shift towards conservatism affected even the United Church, which symbolically changed the name of its official organ from *The New Outlook* to the passive *The Observer*.

Ironically in the same 1932 letter to the West China mission in which he voiced his opposition to the Laymen's Commission report and announced the doctorate awarded to Dr Agnew, Dr Endicott noted the growth of a new religious movement in Toronto, the 'Oxford Group Movement.' Founded by the British evangelist Frank Buchman, the Oxford Group (later called Moral Re-Armament) would barely rate a footnote in the history of Canadian religion, but its phosphorescence in the mission fields added another, continuing strand to East Asian messianism. Under the slogan 'Life-changing on a colossal scale as an answer to world problems,' Buchman aimed his message at the 'up-and-outs,' wealthy socialites who, once converted, were expected to hold weekend 'house parties' for fifty to two hundred friends who would, in 'absolute honesty,' work themselves into a fever pitch, singing hymns and confessing sins. The Oxford Movement whirled through the churches of Toronto for a couple of seasons in the early 1930s on a cloud of 'hectic heartiness and mass gaiety,' infiltrating 'society' churches like Timothy Eaton Memorial and Sherbourne Street United, and St Paul's Anglican.

Many missionaries welcomed this new movement, with its promises of 'life-changing' anti-communism. Dr A.E. Armstrong, secretary of the United Church Board of Overseas Missions, reported on 'The World-Spanning Christian Revolution' and 'the new cells of vital Christian life springing into being through the Oxford Group all across the Far

East . . . Kaifeng, Peiping, Nanking, and Shanghai were some of the twenty cities in China where there are Oxford Groups . . . Chiang Kai-shek and his wife have a Quiet Time together every morning and have four copies of "For Sinners Only" in circulation among their friends.'

The Reverend Gerald Bell, secretary of the mission council, wrote from Chengtu that many West China missionaries, 'both those who have been on the field, as well as those returning from furlough recently, have been greatly influenced by the Oxford Group and give evidence of greater consecration to the task in hand.' Bell reported that he himself was 'considerably disappointed' with the movement: 'Its refusal to recognize any corporate responsibility for social and economic conditions in our complex modern life is a great weakness.'

The Oxford Group was symptomatic of the contending revivalist sects that were attracting large attendances among Chinese during the 1930s. John Sung, a brilliant, manic preacher in the mould of Billy Sunday, who had been briefly hospitalized in the United States for 'religious mania,' carried his emotional revivals to Manchuria and as far south as Indonesia. Andrew Gih, one of Goforth's protégés, captivated the China Inland Mission people in Central China with his Bethel World-wide Evangelistic Bands. Probably the most revered of the Chinese preachers was Watchman Nee, a simple expositor of the scriptures who founded the Little Flock, a utopian community that combined Sharman-style Bible-study courses and first-century-Christianity communal living. (Perhaps because the Little Flock was too similar to its own utopia, the communist government made a special point of eliminating the group after 1949.)

The liberal paper *Chinese Recorder*, like many liberal missionaries, was highly critical of the 'emotionalized individualistic religion' of these various sects: 'In numerous places, we learn, "emotionalism has run riot, sexual excesses have been confessed as having been practised under the guidance of the Holy Spirit," hymn singing has taken the place of study and those Christian leaders lacking the gift of tongues, ecstasies and visions have been repudiated . . . Occasionally women serve as leaders.' China in the 1930s was not the only mission field to be swept by messianic, pentecostal cults; in West Africa, for example, in Nigeria and the Gold Coast, 'voodoo' cults based on bizarre combinations of Methodism and native beliefs enjoyed a vogue.

(There was also a curious parallel between the Chinese revivals of the 1930s with those of a century earlier in America. In China as in America, the first churches had been built with a central partition separating the sexes. When these were taken down in the United States and Canada in the 1830s and 1840s, there was a mighty revival among the people; the same thing happened in China. In both cases, taking down the barriers in the churches represented societal barriers that were collapsing, a collapse expressed on the individual level by the confessing of sin.)

The revivals in China were encouraged by the multiplicity of pentecostal sects in the homelands, many of which sponsored one or two missionaries in China and elsewhere: the Pacific Coast Mission Society of British Columbia, also known as the Pentecostal Holiness Mission, had four people in Hangchow, and the Pentecostal Assemblies of Canada had two. Canadians were also found in the American Assemblies of God and in Aimee Semple McPherson's Church of the Foursquare Gospel.

Just as the old Student Volunteer Movement had been formed among the universities, the evangelical wing of missions tended to coalesce around the Bible colleges that were springing up throughout the 1930s in Canada and the United States. The Bible-college movement had begun at the same time as the missionary movement, in the 1880s, inspired by the same fervour and often initiated by the same people. The Toronto Bible College (TBC) was founded in 1893 by the same people who started the Canadian branch of the China Inland Mission in order to train what D.L. Moody called '"gap men," people who are trained to fill the gap between the laity and the ministers.' Its board and teachers, which were broadly interdenominational, included Presbyterians like its principal, John McNichol, and R.P. MacKay of the FMB, Anglicans like T.R. O'Meara and S.H. Blake of Wycliffe, as well as Henry Frost of the CIM and Roland V. Bingham, the founder and director of the Toronto-based Sudan Interior Mission. TBC had always been mission-oriented, and by the 1930s 90 per cent of its graduates had served overseas: more than one hundred of its graduates were in China with the CIM; and many others (particularly missionary wives) were working in Canadian missions of every denomination, even in West China.

Nothing showed the growth of evangelical missions more than the call by the China Inland Mission for 200 new missionaries in 1929–31 to replace people who had retired during the 1927 evacuation. It was the first such call in twenty years. The first year only 35 recruits sailed, mostly from Britain; 47 went the following year. In 1931, an astounding 117 sailed, mainly from the United States and Canada, to make exactly one short of the projected total. This was at a time when mission offerings had plummeted because of the Depression; when one of these new people wrote home complaining of the conditions in China, his brother told him to stay in China because things were much worse in Canada.

The coming of 'the Two Hundred' meant a proportional increase of the CIM from 14 per cent of the total missionary population in 1922 (960 out of 6636), to almost one-quarter in 1935 (1359 out of 5816); if one includes Pentecostal and other associated groups, the percentage is closer to one-third. Their arrival also shifted the balance within the mission, making it more American in personnel and outlook. It had always had a strong following in Toronto and southern Ontario, but this new recruitment showed a marked movement westward, especially from Alberta and British Columbia.

Nevertheless, the CIM missionaries of the 1930s had more in common with the pioneers of the 1880s than with their contemporaries in other missions. If Hudson Taylor had thought of himself as Jeremiah decrying the wickedness of the world, the second Director General, Dixon E. Hoste, who took over the mission in 1900, was like Moses leading the chosen people into the promised land. When D.E. Hoste prayed he would adopt the posture of Moses at the battle against Amalek (Exodus 17: 8–16), with arms outstretched and, like Moses, would ask other men to hold up his arms, for when they grew heavy the battle faltered. The mission had made a few attempts to reform itself – it had joined the National Christian Council (one of the two church unions in China) during the self-examination period of the 1920s, but left shortly thereafter because the NCC had no credal statement for membership. On the personal level, the missionaries were still bound by the regulations set up by Hudson Taylor: no marriage until the two years' probation was completed, no bobbed hair for the women, Chinese dress while at the stations, and personal poverty. Hoste also made a point of telling new missionaries that if he had a pretty 'home thing,' like a table cloth, he would rather throw it into the muddy Yangtse than be tied through it to worldly possessions.

In the 1930s, the China Inland Mission was still a pioneer agency. Many of the two hundred were assigned to a new forward movement among the non-Han people of China: the Miao, Lisu, and Lolo tribes-people in the mountains of Yunnan and Kweichow, the Moslems in Honan, and the Tibetans in Kansu and Central Asia. Some (like the later Wycliffe Bible translators) learned to speak seven or more of these tribal languages, and were the first to 'reduce' them to writing. (The Miao claimed that they had once had a written language, but that it fell into a stream and a fish ate it.)

Christian missions had remarkable successes among these tribes-people – described as 'God's prairie-fire' – probably because they were already outside the Chinese social structure and thus were willing to learn at the missionary's behest. 'No one unfamiliar with such regions,' commented a mission history, 'can ever know what those devoted pioneers had to face of loneliness, suffering, and danger, as they travelled on foot, for weeks and months together, over mighty mountain ranges and through deep ravines and fever-stricken valleys ... But the joy of finding precious jewels for the Lord Jesus, in many a busy market and village clinging to the mountainside, richly rewarded all the toil and sacrifice.'

Living on the outer edges of civilization, the CIM missionaries were buffeted by whatever winds of nationalism and violence swept through their tiny corner. Morris Slichter, a former Toronto florist, was killed by bandits in Kweichow during the evacuation of 1927, and his wounded wife and children were held prisoners for three weeks. A few years later, in a sad tale that received wide publicity, John and Betty Stam, who had been married for only fifteen months after a five-year courtship, were brutally murdered by communists who had infiltrated their village in Anhwei, in central China; their infant daughter, dubbed 'the miracle baby,' was rescued three days later, having had neither food nor water in the meantime.

Discussion persists as to whether Chiang Kai-shek was a 'true' Christian or merely a 'rice Christian' supreme, cynically embracing Christianity to curry favour with the West. Or were his motivations too tangled to be clearly identified? Too many people wrote too many accounts of the private life of the Generalissimo and Madam, at prayer and Bible study, to doubt the sincerity of his beliefs. From the beginning he surrounded himself with Christians, Catholic and Protestant, Chinese and foreign. In his cabinet, he had his Methodist kin, T.V. Soong and H.H. Kung, as well as people like Hollington Tong. Antonio Riberi, the papal nuncio, and Bishop Paul Yu-pin of Nanking, head of Chinese Catholic Action, were 'close friends' of the Chiangs.

What is remarkable about the missionary descriptions of Chiang is their familiarity: 'Our Chiang Kai-shek.' Over the years, the Chiangs appeared at hundreds of missionary functions, from kindergarten graduations to prayer conferences and concerts; in the process an astounding number of Canadians seem to have shaken their hands.

Under the benign and increasingly pro-Christian eye of the Nanking government, Christian missions did some of their best work. The watchword of the decade was 'rural reconstruction,' rebuilding the

Generalissimo and Madam Chiang Kai-shek at home in Chungking

countryside after twenty years of wars and famines. Many missions, North Honan, had started as rural missions concentrating on building up churches in the villages, but over the years, with the increasing institutionalization exemplified in a plant of church-school-hospital and ancillary buildings, they had moved into the cities, where they concentrated on building up an elite of Christians. Fully two-thirds of all missionaries lived in cities in China, which housed only 10 per cent of the Chinese population.

This new call to redeem the rural churches came at a time when most missions, the Canadian United and Anglican denominations included, were working with half the staff they had had before 1925. This meant, as Bruce Collier, one of the bright young missionaries recruited in the 1930s for West China put it, that many missionaries were merely holding the fort: 'Picture the scene: the enemy attacking and the defenders cut off from supplies and reduced in numbers. Heroism demands the holding of the fort to the last man. Thus we see a pastor in a large, brick, foreign-style church, preaching to a congregation of twenty. We see a mission with its staff reduced by half occupying the same number of stations and carrying on the same quantity of work as formerly ... These sacrifices are very noble. But let us pause to ask just what it is that we are sacrificing; what is our standard of values?' *The New Outlook* refused to publish this article, claiming that it distorted the picture.

But Collier's opinion was shared by others, among them Frank Dickinson, professor of agriculture at WCUU. Dickinson recognized that many of the missionaries then on the field were 'almost on the last lap of service,' and that the Chinese pastors, 'these Ancients in Israel,' had 'gone into a state of "dry rot." Or it may be that they have gotten into a "rut," which has been described by someone "as a grave with the ends out."' The crying need, he felt, was for younger men who could '"sell" the preaching game to our best students ... Do not send "weak sisters" but choice preachers who can "put it across."' They never came.

'Dick' Dickinson was a good example of the creative initiatives of the 1930s, of how missionaries extended their influence – 'like leaven,' was one of their favourite metaphors – far beyond their own personal sphere. Starting in the 1920s, Dickinson had been engaged in experiments in grafting fruit trees, apples, oranges, plums, and the 'native "pomelo"' onto hardy Canadian root stocks. He moved in the 1930s into cross-breeding cows ('cowology'), chickens ('the Chinese chicken is what I used to call the dung-hill type'), and pigs. Much of this work was accomplished with little or no cost to the mission, since he managed to cadge 'a modern Noah's ark' of animals, two by two, from various Canadian breeders.' 'Like the Gospel,' he wrote to the board, 'we offer help wherever we can – "without money and without price."' He offered trees from his experimental farm at the West China university to anyone willing to learn how to manage a scientific 'orchard scheme.'

Dickinson, in a smaller way than Bishop White or Dr J.M. Menzies, also proved of value to the Royal Ontario Museum when White sent him a request for a panda skin for the museum. For one exhilarating summer, Dickinson's compound at the university was home to six pandas, brought from the foothills west of Chengtu.

While Professor Dickinson was training assistants to improve the livestock of China, medical work was also devolving to the Chinese doctors and nurses, freeing the Canadians for public health work. Dr Gladys Cunningham, for example, would escape the ivory tower of West China Union University to organize 'well-baby clinics' in the villages where she would set up a booth, with posters and such equipment as a weigh scale, formula bottles, and diapers. 'The clinic is not for

sick babies, but for well babies and its object is to keep babies well,'
Dr Cunningham wrote. The babies

... are undressed and weighed and some history taken of them the first time
they come. Then each day they are weighed, examined by a doctor and the
mothers are advised as to food, clothing, bathing, sleep, and just the ordinary
things of baby hygiene. You see, the matter of baby hygiene, as we know it
in Canada, is just a new world here ... In this well-baby clinic, we are trying
to teach the mothers ... how to keep the baby clean and well and so make
stronger happier people. It is very delightful to see the way many of them
respond to teaching and really keep their babies as well as any Canadian baby
you ever saw.

Perhaps the most remarkable achievement of the Nanking period was
the appearance of what can be described as 'the new woman' of China,
as exemplified by Madam Chiang herself. After their girl students had
graduated from the mission schools, the missionary women started
college-level courses for them, both in nursing and infant care and in
more academic studies. These classes grew into the beginnings of
women's colleges by the 1910s. During the educational upheavals of
the mid-1920s, the missions made their colleges co-educational, with
women the equals of the male students. The mission councils hesitated
over co-education, mainly because of their own fears of the sexual nature
of Chinese men. However, these fears proved groundless, and by the
1930s the women students, cool and self-possessed, hair bouncing as
they walked, were as common on the Christian campuses of China as
they were in Canada.

Nowhere was the equality of women stressed more than in the medical
faculties, in large part because of the women medical missionaries seeking
to multiply themselves. Margaret Brown of the North Honan mission
commented that the whole nursing profession was the result of the
missionaries' influence. This was 'an even greater achievement than the
introduction of modern medicine; medical schools would have come
sooner or later. But young women would not have taken up nursing
without the example set them by Christian women from the West.' The
philosophy of these medical schools was typified by the stated objectives
of the North Honan School of Nursing:

To give a training which would, *first*, open the eyes of the nurses to the physical
and spiritual ignorance and misery around them; *second*, make them feel their

Miss Ding and her sisters, Anglican Diocese of Honan, 1930s

responsibility towards these conditions; and *third*, teach them how most effectively to relieve and banish them.

One of the first graduates of the school was the granddaughter of 'Old Blind Chou,' the mission's first convert. 'It was thrilling to see the girl of seventeen,' Miss Brown remembered, 'who, when first corrected, threw herself on the floor in tears, develop into the quiet self-controlled supervisor of women's wards.'

In March 1935, Chiang Kai-shek announced to a gathering of Catholic and Protestant missionaries the formation of a new organization – the New Life Movement – that would combine his initiatives with their own. Hailed by the Christian community in China as a 'large-scale program to modernise China and attain equality in the family of nations, through *making* China progressive,' the New Life Movement promulgated a list of regulations, ninety-six in number, governing every aspect of the people's lives. The people were to refrain from smoking opium and tobacco, and from spitting and urinating in public; they were encouraged to brush their teeth, to wash their bodies, and to take daily exercise.

The first director of the New Life Movement was the Reverend George Shepherd, 'the one trusted American' in Chiang's 'innermost circle,' who retired when the government moved to Chungking in 1938. He was replaced as personal advisor to Madam Chiang by Jim Endicott. As the movement grew less spontaneous – or as its veneer of spontaneity wore thin – Chiang made it into a formal agency of the Kuomintang to promote 'Military Discipline, Increased Production, and Cultural Training.' Endicott felt that this military shift made the New Life Movement into the equivalent of the Brownshirts of Italy, and after a particularly stormy confrontation with Madam Chiang – 'This was something worth eavesdropping on,' wrote the American journalist Emily Hahn, 'a man, a European ... disagreeing with her!' – in which he told her to follow her Christian conscience and keep the organization away from the fascist mentality, Endicott resigned in 1940. 'His impression of the Kuomintang party by now,' states his biography, 'was that it had little more social conscience than a cholera germ; if the New Life Movement under Madam Chiang ceased to lead in service and with goodwill that cut across party lines, then his usefulness as an advisor was finished.' That may have been his private opinion, but publicly at this point Endicott kept these views to himself.

Most missionaries did. Chiang Kai-shek was too valuable an ally against communism for the missionaries to carp about his strong-arm tactics. He had recently rescinded the regulations forbidding mission schools to teach religious subjects and had promoted religious ceremonies within the government. As Jim Endicott had been warned by a senior United Church administrator, 'We must be loyal to our own, you know.'

12·The Days That Are Evil

'War, with all its terrors, is not a subject that we care to discuss with our readers, but if we are to be true friends and comrades of the boys and girls in China, we must try to understand a little of what they are called to pass through at this time ... At first perhaps it was interesting to see great airplaines flying over their town or village, and to run down into the little dug-outs in the backyards of their homes, but when the airplanes came over three, four, or five times a day dropping those awful death-carrying bombs, and nights had to be spent in dark, cold dug-outs, it ceased to be fun ... Little ones had also to flee with their parents and many a night was spent in the cold, with insufficient clothing ... disease is rampant, and in that large camp [in Shanghai] there are as many as thirty deaths a day.

Some of our missionaries have been going around seeking to brighten up the place, putting attractive Gospel posters in every room. The boys and girls are fascinated with these pictures – they stand gazing, wondering what they mean, while missionaries explain the way of life through Jesus Christ.'

R.E. Thompson, 'What War Means to Boys and Girls in China,' *Young China* (CIM), 1938

The Nanking decade ended as it had started, in war. This time, war was three-sided, with battlefronts that shifted among the Japanese, the communists, and Chiang Kai-shek's Kuomintang. For eight long years,

Mission compound and hospital at Luchow, Szechuan, after bombing, 1939 from 1937 to 1945, the guns were not silent. They rumbled in the night, shaking the hills with power; they came cracking down the back alleys, whining in the jet stream, exploding with kaleidoscopic destruction. It was an all-compassing war. Little ones did perish, and older ones and women in their prime, combatants and civilians alike, millions of them. The dogs grew 'unnaturally fattened by feasting on human corpses.' There was no refuge.

By this time the Christian churches had become, if not bastions of Chinese society, at least part of its national fabric. The large Protestant unions, the Church of Christ in China, the National Christian Council, and the Anglican Chung Hwa Sheng Kung Hwei, were led at the highest levels by Chinese personnel, and Chinese ran such former missionary institutions as the YMCA, the Christian universities, and the hospitals, schools, and publishing houses. During the 1930s foreign missionaries had retreated into the background of their own volition. The Catholic church, although still dominated by the foreign hierarchy, had 28 out of 138 ecclesiastical divisions under Chinese bishops; 2000 of the 5000 priests and 4700 of 6700 nuns were Chinese.

Missionaries now identified themselves with Chiang Kai-shek's form of Chinese nationalism, so that when the Japanese invasion came each had to decide whether to stand with the Chinese church and the Chinese nation amid the ruins, or flee with the refugees to Free China, that part of the country not occupied by the Japanese. Most stayed, and thereby proved themselves 'true friends' of China in its hour of need. They were among the first and most vocal opponents of Japanese expansionism, bringing the invasion of China forcibly before the conscience of the West.

We have become sated with war, bloated with body counts, but in 1931 – before Abyssinia, before Guernica, before Hiroshima – the invasion of Manchuria was without precedent. It so shook the unity of the League of Nations that the great powers refused to take any action beyond a resolution condemning Japan's action. When that resolution came before the league, Canada – which a year before had issued its most stringent Oriental Exclusion Act prohibiting all immigration from Asia into Canada – refused to support it. According to Dr James Endicott in Toronto, 'Quite a lot of our newspapers are on the whole pro-Japanese. They lay stress upon the fact that but for Japan, China would have lost Manchuria to Russia in any event, and then the argument from the large financial investments made weighs heavily with them.' He continued that Newton Rowell, the Canadian delegate at the founding of the League of Nations, had gone as far as he could in a speech to the Canadian Club in which, 'while he did not go out of his way to condemn Japan he made it clear that no satisfactory justification could be found for the belligerent and drastic program which the military party was following.' Two years later, when the matter came before the league again, the new Canadian prime minister, R.B. Bennett, did support the resolution but refused to impose sanctions. Japan, for its part, quit the league.

The effect of the Manchurian events was immediately apparent as far inland as Chengtu, with student strikes and military drills occurring with increasing frequency. 'From the beginning there has been no disposition to put any hope in the efforts of the League of Nations,' reported H.D. Robertson, who had been Rowell's Chinese translator at the league. This led to feelings of 'despair and helplessness.' Dr Gladys Cunningham noted that the parades were anti-Japanese, 'but you know how the Chinese are. Any anti-foreignism tends to embrace us all and we have been rather more observed on the streets these last few days than for some time. More "dog," and "prostitute" and "foreign baby" and "devil" and such like has followed us than is customary.'

There were two Canadian missions in Manchuria, in the eye of the storm, but their personnel were as bewildered by the takeover as anyone else. Prior to its downfall in 1911, the Manchu dynasty had kept Manchuria – with its unpopulated grasslands, where Manchu boys could be taught the arts of war – as its tribal homeland. It was opened for settlement under duress, and by the late 1920s the number of Chinese, Koreans, Japanese, and Russians flooding in reached a million annually. Szepingkai was a new city of a hundred thousand people on the South Manchurian railway between Mukden [now called SHENYANG] and Harbin [HAERBIN].

The Japanese invasion happened so swiftly that its effect on the missionary population was almost negligible. Rosalind Goforth deliberately did not mention it in her biography of her husband, trying, she said, to 'avoid touching on things political.' Mrs Goforth seemed less concerned about the international ramifications of the invasion than the 'perils and disturbed conditions' that followed in its wake, the barbed wire and searchlights 'against attacks by the threatening hordes of bandits.'

The Missions-Etrangères and their helpers the MIC Sisters had a much more distinctive Canadian presence in Manchuria, with some fifty missionaries at ten stations up and down the railway line from Szepingkai. But they too seemed to have been more concerned about the lawlessness than with the war. Writing from Mukden, one of four cities where the MIC had convents, the sister superior wrote (in no doubt heavily self-censored letters) of their initial fears during the invasion, of hiding the holy vessels, and of the solemn procession of the Rosary around the compound with bullets whizzing overhead. But once the Japanese had taken control, the sisters – who, taking no chances, had flown British, French, and Vatican flags – praised the politeness and respectfulness of the invaders. 'If personally we have nothing to fear from the Japanese,' wrote the superior, 'we do, however, have much to dread from the brigands who do not fail to take advantage of the abnormal situation.' Another sister questioned, without irony and without understanding, why the 'perfect discipline' of the Japanese troops in restoring order was not 'reason enough for the Chinese to pardon the invasion of their country.'

Over the next ten years, the mission prospered under the Japanese government, 'as long as we didn't act like enemies,' one sister wrote many years later. Three more Canadian orders came to join them, the Brothers of the Christian Schools, the Clerics of St Viator, and the Soeurs Antoniennes de Marie, and they opened five new stations, especially in 'the bush' north-west of Szepingkai; the Canadian population of these missions more than doubled, reaching 124 by 1941.

Since the Sino-Japanese war of 1894, Japan had been using 'provocations' against Japanese citizens in China – the largest group of foreigners in the country – as an excuse for military retaliation. After the invasion of Manchuria, these military actions multiplied rapidly, so that within in a year Japanese bombers were attacking Shanghai and Canton. This led to a new wave of 'Anti-Japan, Save-China' boycotts throughout China, resulting in more 'provocations' against Japanese citizens. By the mid-1930s, Japan controlled extensive areas of North China, by dint of political influence if not by overt annexation.

Chiang Kai-shek had told his generals in Manchuria not to resist the Japanese, and this continued to be his policy throughout the early 1930s. He concentrated his energies, rather, on exterminating the communists. The Japanese invasion, he said, was a wound on the body of China, but the communists were a cancer of its soul. After the 1927 white terror, Chiang had cordoned the communists off in the remote mountains of Kiangsi and Anhwei, but in 1934 they broke out of the noose and embarked on their historic Long March, ten thousand soldiers and their families walking thirteen thousand tortuous kilometres through twelve provinces, from Kiangsi, down through the south-west and then back north and east to Yenan [YANAN], a city of caves in the loess-soil cliffs. Throughout the route of the Long March, the armies scattered hundreds of missionaries from their path, including two hundred China Inland Mission people in Kweichow and Yunnan. Some who did not get out of the way in time were taken along as unwilling participants; Grace Emblem, a Canadian nurse, was released after a few weeks, but a Swiss minister, R.A. Bosshardt, remained with the soldiers for almost two years, walking six and a half thousand kilometres through five provinces.

In order personally to inspect the campaign against the communists in Yenan, in December 1936 Chiang Kai-shek went to Sian, the capital of Shensi [SHAANXI] province. His own generals, led by Chang Hsueh-liang [ZHANG XIUELIANG], the 'young marshal' whom Chiang had ordered not to resist the Japanese in Manchuria, kidnapped him and held him incommunicado until he agreed to form a common front with the communists against Japan. When he was released on Christmas Day 1936, Chiang testified that his Christian faith had sustained him during 'the deep waters' of his confinement. He compared his kidnapping to Christ's temptation and resolved to continue his 'struggle against evil, to overcome temptation, and to uphold righteousness.'

Chiang's release was the dramatic incident he needed to galvanize his popularity. Spontaneous celebrations broke out throughout China. 'There was tremendous excitement in the city last evening when the news ... came through,' wrote the Reverend Gerald Bell, mission secretary in Chengtu. 'I do not remember having seen anything quite so spontaneous or whole-hearted as this celebration.' The China Inland Mission agreed that these celebrations were a sign of 'a patriotism new and altogether unique in China ... nor should the fact be overlooked that this new patriotism reached its highest expression in Christian circles.' Roman Catholics, too, included themselves as celebrants. The Jesuit fathers in Suchow, for example, organized a prayer vigil for Chiang's release, and were thanked afterwards by a large-character proclamation on their gate: 'If our leader Chiang Kai-shek is delivered, it is due to the prayers of the Catholics who prayed all through the night for his deliverance.'

Chiang's release was in fact brought about by the intervention of the Chinese communists acting on direct orders from Moscow. After a face-saving delay, Chiang formed the Second Common Front with the Chinese Communist Party, which lasted officially until 1945.

Japan saw this new alliance as yet another provocation, and it invaded in order to 'save' China from communism. During the night of 7 July 1937, while on midnight 'manoeuvres' near Shanhaikuan, where the Great Wall meets the sea, Japanese troops were supposedly fired upon by Chinese border guards; by morning tens of thousands of crack Japanese soldiers were pouring over the wall. Contemptuously announcing it would 'beat China to her knees in three months,' Japan moved swiftly and mercilessly into North China. By the middle of August, it had established a naval blockade of the China coast from Tientsin to Canton, paralysing China's foreign trade. Ten thousand troops, bolstered tenfold within a month, advanced step by step through Shanghai. Japanese planes bombed Canton and flew ominously low over Hong Kong's Victoria Peak.

The bombing raids were catastrophic in their intensity. One attack on the New World Amusement Centre in Shanghai, in the middle of a Saturday afternoon, left three thousand dead. At a conservative estimate the city sheltered one hundred thousand refugees in Salvation Army camps, each housing ten to twenty thousand people. The 240-kilometre advance from Shanghai to Nanking, 'once the most populated area on earth, was the graveyard of almost a million Chinese.'

Once again, as they had done six years previously, the foreign powers enunciated the self-righteous doctrine of Non-Recognition: war had not been declared by either China or Japan – not even when Japan occupied half of China – and until a state of war existed, they would remain neutral and continue shipping war materiel to both sides.

In January 1938, Nanking fell to the Japanese in a particularly gruesome attack, and Chiang moved the government first to Hankow, eight hundred kilometres up the Yangtse, and then in August safely beyond the gorges to Chungking.

By the summer of 1938, in addition to those in Manchuria, several Canadian missions had fallen behind Japanese lines, including the North Honan mission, the Jesuit mission in Suchow, and the Presbyterian and Sisters of the Immaculate Conception missions in Canton. Later that year, when Chiang Kai-shek ordered the dikes holding back the Yellow River, the barrier that blocked the Japanese advance, to be dynamited, the river changed its course, putting the eastern half of the Anglican diocese, including the cities of Kweiteh and Kaifeng, north of the river

Ruins of the Chungking church, with Reverends D.L. Dsen, Gerald S. Bell, and S.Y. Din

and thus in Japanese hands. Further south in the Scarboro mission in Lishui, the bombers were coming over in regular convoys. 'If there should be another world war we know where we'll go,' the superior of the mission, Monsignor William C. McGrath, had written in his 1935 book *The Dragon at Close Range.* 'To Yanchinuen [one of the remote stations]. Neither death rays nor Lewisite nor the deadliest of those poison gases will ever disturb the serenity of this recess among the impossible mountains.' In the revised edition two years later, he corrected himself: 'Even remote places in China are no longer safe from roving bombing planes.'

The Japanese advanced according to a predictable pattern along the transportation corridors. They came down the railway line from Peking into North Honan, and from Tientsin into Suchow; once they had taken Shanghai, they advanced up the Yangtse and along the east-west railway line that ran through both missions. Before the Japanese troops arrived, each area was heavily bombed. At first the planes came at exactly the same time each day – say, at three o'clock; then without warning, they came at dawn, in the middle of the night, and five or six times a day.

This provided a tactical advantage, terrifying the civilian population so that they offered little resistance when the ground troops eventually entered an area.

The Chinese fled before the invasion in one of the largest human migrations in history, estimated at twenty-five to forty million refugees. In her grimly titled book *Harvest at the Front*, Margaret Crossett, an American member of the China Inland Mission, described the stream of refugees passing her station in Anhwei:

Day after day the refugees came, some with limbs missing where they had been struck by fragments of bombs; some the sole survivors of large families ... Men, women, and children tramped by with bundles of bedding and clothing on their backs, or loads of things in baskets hung from poles across their shoulders ... By evening the city was as the city of the dead ... Carpenters could not make coffins fast enough to bury the dead, and many bodies were thrown outside the city for the pigs, dogs, and vultures to dispose of. My husband would not let me leave our compound those days. He said the sights were too terrible.

Still Mrs Crossett stayed at her station, trying to preach to the passers-by. 'There is a greater enemy than the Japanese who is trying to harm you ... Attempts to preach to these people were almost useless,' she concluded, 'as they were too upset to pay attention to what we were saying.' Instead, she allowed the people to use the mission wall as a notice-board: 'Li family going to Hankow; Ho going to Hwang-chwan.'

By the summer of 1938, the North Honan mission had evacuated its territory, and its personnel remained at the resort of Chikungshan throughout the fall and winter. With the closing of mission hospitals, there remained few medical facilities within the occupied areas – Dr Robert McClure described them as 'a den of horrors' – and the wounded soldiers and as many civilians as could cling to the roof of the train were brought behind Chinese lines for treatment at the mission hospitals in Free China. May Watts, secretary of the Anglican diocese, would go down to the station in Kaifeng late at night, to meet the trains of

the wounded soldiers in transit ... They were pitiful in the extreme. There were one thousand men on the [one] train and the worst cases were just lying on straw in freight cars, some cars with tops on them and some open box cars, while others were in ordinary passenger cars. The Government service corps had provided bread for them and our Church Service Group prepared hot water for them ... The train was not remaining at Kaifeng so we immediately telegraphed to Chengchow to the International Red Cross and the Baptist Mission Hospital to meet the train and help do the dressings for these poor men who still had several days' train journey before them before reaching military hospitals in Hankow.

At Chengchow, Dr Robert McClure was Field Director of the International Red Cross. 'Dr Bob' was already a legend in the China field – bolstered, no doubt, by the 'breathless' fourteen-page account given of him by Christopher Isherwood and W.H. Auden – with his flaming red hair and knee-high leather boots. He was – and remains, though now in his eighties – an amazing man with more energy than two people half his age. Born after his parents, Dr William McClure of the original 'Honan Seven' and the former Margaret Baird, had fled from the Boxers, young Bob was raised in Weihwei and learned to speak the language like a native. This ability stood him in good stead when he brought the Buddhist Red Swastika society together with the other religious groups in the American Southern Baptist hospital in Chengchow to organize Red Cross relief; it was hard to say which group the 'sticky' Baptists mistrusted more, the Roman Catholics, the Seventh Day Adventists, or the Buddhists. Speaking the dialect was also useful whenever he crossed enemy lines to inspect the hospitals in the so-called 'red triangle' north of the Yellow River.

The Japanese were content to hold the cities and the railway lines; but the countryside beyond became the domain of the anti-Japanese guerrillas. Technically part of the common-front alliance, these guerrillas were part of Chiang Kai-shek's Nationalist army; but in reality he seemed to spend as much effort fighting them as he did the Japanese. Consequently these troops, the only resistance behind Japanese lines, owed their loyalty to the Eighth Route Army, the communist forces based in Yenan, and to its general, Chu Teh [ZHU DE].

On one trip into the communist area, Dr McClure recruited Dr Richard Brown of the Anglican hospital in Kweiteh for a flying trip to Yenan to tally medical supplies and devise a plan for getting Red Cross donations to the Eighth Route Army. By this time a few missionaries in China were willing to change their opinons about the communists as a result of the common front. Dr Wallace Crawford, for example, one of the older missionaries in West China, wrote that there was now 'no more compulsion' about the communist party 'than there is in a church school.' Only one missionary, however, saw the alliance as a call for work among the communist armies. Dr Brown returned to Kweiteh, now in Japanese control, where he became increasingly restless. 'Medical work under the J[apanese] is finished,' he wrote to Bishop White in Toronto. At the suggestion of Logan Roots, the American Episcopal bishop of Hankow, and with the majority approval of his own missionaries and the blessing of Bishop Lindel Tsen, Dr Brown was granted a three-month leave-of-absence to work among the communist troops.

A hearty, portly surgeon, Dick Brown had made his furlough trip in 1935 via the Trans-Siberian railway specifically to see the 'anti-God museums' of the Soviet Union, and on his arrival in Toronto had rather shocked the religious community when he made the pronouncement that there were no communists in China, at least none in the Russian mould, only 'discontented farmers and ex-soldiers. They are much the same as communists here in Canada. They know nothing of what Communism really is.'

On his second trip into Shensi, Dr Brown caught up with Dr Norman Bethune, who had already been sent, without an interpreter, towards Yenan. Just as McClure had done a few days before, Brown found Bethune in the middle of a 'pub-crawl.' His first impression was not favourable – twenty-five years later, Dr Brown remembered Dr Bethune as rude, arrogant, and 'psychopathic' – but he agreed to accompany Bethune to Yenan and stay with him as his translator. On the night they arrived there, in their candle-lit interview with Mao Tse-tung in his cave, Dr Brown assured Mao that he had not come as a communist: 'to the contrary, very anti Communist, but definitely as a Christian Doctor armed with the Christian doctrine.' He was excused from attendance at political meetings, and even given permission to hold an Easter service for the two thousand Christians among the troops, one of them a pastor of the Anglican mission.

Except for one short trip to Hong Kong to purchase drugs, Dr Brown stayed in the red triangle for almost a year. He worked with Bethune for three months building a base hospital – the first Bethune Peace Hospital – and thereafter went his own way, treating the wounded in the mountain villages that had been commandeered as open-air hospital wards.

Back in Toronto, Bishop White wrote to the missionary society that he had 'serious misgivings' about Dr Brown's venture, and stated that 'the duty of all agents of the MSCC [was] to devote all their energies to the relief of suffering in places or posts to which they are appointed.'

Expressing 'great relief' to hear that Dr Brown had no official connection to the Eighth Route Army, the MSCC delineated 'the principle that the mission and the missionaries must be kept absolutely clear and independent of military action of any kind whatsoever.'

When Brown received the resolution of the Toronto committee six months later – he was so remote the mission had had no contact with him during that time – he wrote back a scathing, eloquent letter of resignation.

I am firmly of the opinion that this work is of a very definite Christian character and is infinitely more preferable to acting as caretaker to a group of buildings which so many missionaries are doing at present ... May I remind the subcommittee that China is at war, her very entrails ripped and gushing blood, and that this is the time for professing Christians to show a little love to her ... Christmas is coming ... I think of the warmth and beauty of St James and then the smiles and the hurry and scurry of cars and people to gourmandize on the flesh of cows and fowl. Yes and to drink deeply of each other's wealth in rich blood-red wine. God save and protect me from further visions of Christians at a Christmas binge ... As for me, I do not know where I shall be celebrating the blessed birth or what I shall have to eat if anything but I do know that ... whatever the fare I shall thank God he did not leave me entirely hungry as so many are today in China.

The MSCC accepted Dr Brown's resignation with considerably more thoughtfulness than it would have before the spate of letters it had received endorsing Dr Brown's work. 'Full marks for Dick!' wrote Bob McClure. The Reverend George Andrew, canon of the Kaifeng cathedral, who had found the committee's resolution 'reasonable' while in Toronto, now felt Brown was performing 'a most needed and helpful act of mercy to a people in the most abject distress.' The English bishop Ronald Hall of Victoria was so moved by Dr Brown's sermon in the Hong Kong cathedral during Brown's trip there to purchase drugs that he personally wrote to the MSCC: 'I myself longed to be a doctor so that I could offer to join him and so preach to the Eighth Route Army the Christian message in the only language their ears are open to receive, viz., Christian charity in love and healing ... God himself, I believe, has opened this door into a new Mission field, i.e., into the pagan land of the soviets ... if Dr Brown had been able to speak in Toronto as he spoke here, the whole Canadian Church would have been behind him in love and encouragement and prayer.'

The most telling praise came from General Chu Teh, leader of the communist forces, in a speech to a missionary conference in Sian: 'The Eighth Route Army has no prejudice against missionaries. On the contrary, we welcome them and wish to co-operate with them. For our war of resistance not only fights for the independence and freedom of the Chinese nation, but also for the maintenance of world peace. In this respect our goal is just the same.'

Dr Richard Brown resigned from the mission as he indicated he would. Since he had no further income, he made one more trip into the war zone, and then retired to private practice in Tsingtao, behind Japanese lines, to support his wife and three children, 'merely waiting until after the war,' he told the MSCC.

One year almost to the day after Dr Brown resigned, Norman Bethune died in a mountain hut in the far reaches of Shansi. His death passed unnoticed: even Dr Brown heard no word of it for ten years. It was one of the minor tragedies of history that these three University of Toronto doctors, who met in a common cause in war-torn China, should be blinded to co-operation by their personality differences. They were, for example, the only three men for hundreds of kilometres who could have built a hospital system. It is tragic, too, that the missionary doctors could never see that Bethune's character became purified by the fires of China – just as their own had been – so that on his death he was spontaneously elevated to the rank of saint and martyr. His example, his laughter, his dedication – and even perhaps his flamboyance – inspired countless millions of Chinese to acts of selfless devotion. If for no other reason that that, Dr Bethune was Canada's greatest missionary.

When the Japanese first moved into North Honan, they were overtly friendly to the missionaries, if they co-operated in filling out voluminous forms and stayed inside the city. Within a short time, however, the central authorities in Peking began to organize anti-British uprisings in the occupied areas and these finally drove out the Canadian missionaries.

The reaction of the Japanese to foreign missionaries varied from place to place, depending on the location, the personality of the district commandant – and whether he was a Christian – and the nationality of the missionaries themselves. German, Italian, and French missions were unhampered, whereas British, Canadian, and American stations were subject to servants' strikes, rowdy demonstrations, and red tape.

In the United Church South China mission, the main station at Kong-moon was allowed to keep its hospital open, even adding a new children's ward; but at Pak-kai [BAQI], ten miles away, the missionaries were confined to their compound for six months and allowed out only to purchase supplies.

The position of the Jesuits in Suchow was complicated by the fact that as Roman Catholics they were representatives of a 'supra-national' religion recognized by the Japanese government, and also, at least in the initial invasion period, were protected by the French flag.

Canadian Catholic missions in China continued to grow throughout the 1930s: in 1933, when Quebec was suffering deeply from the effects of the Depression, it sent forty-seven priests and nuns, the largest party of Canadian missionaries ever, to East Asia. As late as 1940, the Scarboro Foreign Mission Society sent eleven men to Lishui, the last party it would ever send.

The Jesuit mission in Suchow had matured during this time and was now a respectable size, with thirty-one Canadian priests in Suchow itself and another twenty-two in Peking and Shanghai. Two years before the Japanese bombardment, the superior of the mission, Father Philippe Côté, had been consecrated Bishop of Suchow and the brick church elevated to the status of cathedral. 'The faith was solidly established,' wrote Father Rosario Renaud, the mission historian: '54 000 Christians gathered around eighteen centres, each with a church, residence, catechumenate and central school, and from ten to twelve schools in the *chrétientés*.' There were 550 schools run under Catholic auspices in the diocese.

The coming of the Japanese altered mission work, wrote Father Edouard Côté; prior to that time 'we went to them'; afterwards 'they came to us.' This statement is given mute credence by the statistics for Suchow: baptisms *in articulo mortis*, which had been averaging 1500 during the early 1930s, rose sharply to 4500 in 1938 and 5700 in 1939, the largest number ever in mission history. (During the early 1940s, the numbers dwindled to 300.) 'During these troubled years,' stated a mission retrospective, 'the people sought protection, and the Catholic Church indeed gave them one. For a whole year, the bishop's compound and the college of Suchow served as a refuge during the aerial bombardments and the first months of occupation. The number of refugees would be about a thousand, reaching two thousand after the capture of Suchow.'

At first the Catholic missions won praise from the Japanese. 'I subject a city or village to a bombardment of artillery and planes,' said the incoming Japanese general; 'fires are burning everywhere: so when we enter, I'm sure to find the Catholic missioner in his church, and protecting his Christians. I congratulate you and we respect such people.'

When the authorities found out that the missionaries were not French, they subjected them to 'aggressive' harassment – anti-British harassment, the chief of the demonstrators specified, not anti-religious – which included a servants' walkout that forced the Canadians to do all their own work. The Japanese posted a placard on the gate stating that all refugees had to be out of the compound within a month. 'It is probable we would have had to leave the place ourselves,' wrote one of the fathers, 'if it had not been for the unexpected intervention of some soldiers who thus found themselves at odds with the higher authority who directed this movement.'

Over the next year and a half, relations between the Japanese and the Canadians see-sawed; when Suchow city was quiet, the smaller stations were in turmoil. 'Providence was taking care of things,' wrote Father Edouard LaFlèche, 'to bring our enemies around, but at a great sacrifice.' One evening in October 1939, as two Jesuit fathers and one brother were returning home by bicycle, they were suddenly hit by a hail of bullets. Brother Edgar Gauvin fell mortally wounded. The assailants, a group of Japanese soldiers who had been taking pot-shots at passers-by, 'ran up and saw with amazement that they were dealing with three Canadian missionaries. They knew that it was an accident without evil intent on either part.'

Thereafter, 'though there were still difficulties, the influence of the Church grew and the apostolic work was filled with promise,' and the improved relations culminated in the construction of a new coeducational school in the cathedral compound. 'All the same, it was quite obvious that there was only a question of opportunism' in the Japanese friendliness, said a report on the anti-foreign tendencies in Suchow. The Japanese 'realize that the Church in China is a force; that the Church is an element of order, organization and stability. They want to take advantage of that ... It must also be said that in general the name of the Church, and the papal flag on our houses and cars ... helped facilitate travel and the transport of goods essential to the work of the mission. Most of the time, identification certificates given to our Christians are as valuable as official certificates. Medals and crucifixes have saved many lives and many houses.'

A number of Canadians learned to speak Japanese, including Léo-

Paul Bourassa, who had been wounded with Brother Gauvin, and who wrote a book called *The Japanese Soul* (*L'Ame Japonnaise*), which he dedicated to the local commandant, General Hirabayashu. After the war many Catholic clergy, both Chinese and foreign, were accused of collaboration with the Japanese. Though there is little in the Jesuit mission archives in Montreal – at least in those sections open to researchers – to indicate that the Canadians were collaborators, there is a pamphlet, called simply *The Sino-Japanese Conflict*, written by a Canadian Franciscan, Father Urbain M. Clouthier, that offers a glimpse of the pro-Japanese mind of at least a few Québécois missionaries. It is a strange, astounding piece of writing.

Calling the Kuomintang party a 'battery of Free-Masonry,' the author gives a rambling, simplistic history of relations between China and Japan since the 1890s. The Manchurian incident was occasioned, he wrote, by the boycott of Japanese products and 'many criminal assaults ... against Japanese officers ... Victorious after six months of warfare, Japanese troops freed Manchuria from Chang's [sic] grip ... The League of Nations, that Super-Masonic Government, wanted to intervene with the idea of favouring China ... However, its attempt was lamentably unsuccessful against the firm attitude of Japan, who very courteously indeed abandoned Geneva.' Between that time and the 1937 war, Japan had tried 'many times to settle the affair by a friendly arrangement; but alas! she always found in her path an irreducible diplomacy of indecision.'

Finally, the good father concluded in ringing tones:

Of all the countries, Japan is actually the only one who is fighting hard and with unity outside her own country against Communism. Although it is a pagan country, while the other so-called Christian nations are either neutral or accomplices, alone Japan stands couragaeously on the side of common sense which condemns Communism, alone Japan stands with the Pope, who has condemned Communism, alone Japan is taking the side of Christ himself whose teachings are the direct condemnation of Communism ... Yes, gentlemen, let us give our undivided sympathy to such a generous and brave nation whose only aim is to crush communism so that China and Japan may live!

One of the most enduring images of war-torn China – enduring because it was made into a splashy Hollywood movie called *Inn of the Sixth Happiness* starring Ingrid Bergman as a semi-literate English missionary named Gladys Aylward – was of a heroic missionary woman leading her band of orphans through the mountains, bombers flying overhead, cheerfully whistling 'This Old Man.' This scene was no mere Hollywood fiction. Orphans, nicknamed by Madam Chiang 'warphans,' were the greatest tragedies of the war; there were thousands of them in every bombed city, moribund infants born on the road, girls who had to turn to prostitution, the crippled, the blind, and the insane.

Hundreds of single missionary women felt their duty was to stay with the refugees and share their troubles. One of these was Greta Clark, a bustling, heavy-set deaconess who had run the Anglican Door of Hope orphanage in Kaifeng for many years. 'From experience,' she wrote in 1939 as the city filled with refugees, 'I knew that the best way to help women was to gather them into a school.' When the city fell to the Japanese a few months later and the authorities threatened to close the orphanage, she took her charges, one hundred of them, to Chengchow, eighty kilometres west. Throughout the war, she remained as close to the shifting battle lines as she dared, always within the sound of the big guns, working with the women and children. At one point, she started her own refugee camp, serving five hundred meals a day; 'To do this,' she wrote, 'I sold almost everything of value I possessed.' Miss Clark was the most evangelical member of the Anglican diocese, and she named her nameless orphans with the surname Su, as in Ye-su, Jesus. She taught Bible lessons to the refugees, as well as the Thousand-Character simplified text for illiterates. Impromptu, peripatetic schools like hers seem to have been unexpectedly successful, for after the war the Kuomintang government announced that, partly because of them, some forty-five million people had learned to read since 1937.

Travel in all its ramifications became a preoccupation of missionaries during the war years. 'The Church Goes Travelling,' was the title of one Anglican slide show. Correspondents wrote of hair-raising experiences taking devious routes from occupied China to Free China. After the fall of Shanghai and Canton, for example, the Reverend Gerald Bell described his one-month trip from Shanghai to Chengtu escorting sixteen adults and nine children and two hundred crates of luggage ('everyone in our Mission sent orders for goods of all kinds, but especially groceries'). The party included two new missionary couples, the Irwin Hilliards and the Ralph Outerbridges, and Mrs Lorena Edmonds, a widow with three children whose husband had died while crossing the Pacific. By this time, the Yangtse River route to Szechuan had been closed, and the party had to travel via Hong Kong to Haiphong, in northern Indo-China, up the Mekong river to Hanoi, across the continental divide by truck to Kunming, and then by flat-bed train and aeroplane to Chung-king. It was a trip filled with long waits and uncertainties because of the size of the party, but once it was over, Bell wrote of his gratefulness for 'travelling mercies that were ours. There were many anxious moments, but all worked out well, and we have all arrived safely.' The day after he arrived in Chengtu, the Japanese bombed the city.

A few years later, Margaret Brown, the United Church representative to the Christian Literature Society, was prevented from returning to Shanghai after her furlough – this was just after Pearl Harbor – and had to transfer the CLS to Chengtu. 'The only way to get to Free China,' she wrote, referring to herself throughout in the third person,

was by air 'over the Hump' from Calcutta. Boats at this time did not want civilians, especially women. Finally she went [from Toronto] to New York, New Orleans, then on a Chilean boat through Panama and disembarked at Val Paraiso [sic]. Then over the Andes to Buenos Aires, and from here to Capetown and Durban on a small Argentine freighter. At Durban she got passage on a British troup [sic] ship and arrived safely in Bombay. She went from here to Calcutta by train, stopping over three days at our Central India Mission. Five terrible weeks were spent in Calcutta which was then the centre of the great Bengal famine. Finally, one night she flew over the Hump to Chungking, and later to Chengtu. She arrived six months and five days after leaving Toronto.

Canadian missionaries were part of the migration to Chiang Kai-shek's Free China. Those who fled to the western provinces of Yunnan, Kweichow, Szechuan, and Kansu included not only millions of Chinese but factories and universities, government offices and consulates. Theodore H. White, then a young journalist for *Time* magazine, described the moving of the largest textile mill in Shanghai to Chungking. After being dismantled in February 1938, 'it packed its 8000 tons of machinery and bundled them off down the railway to Hankow. In May it kissed the railhead good-bye and set off by steamer upriver to the gorge mouth. In August it was repackaged again to fit some 380 native junks, which took it up the tumbling gorges to Szechuan; 120 of the boats sank in the gorges, but the junkmen raised all but 21 and carried on. The convoy arrived in Chungking in April, 1939 ... The new industries, resettled in Szechuan, were a Rube Goldberg paradise. Steel factories were built with bamboo beams; blast furnaces were supplied with coal carried in hand baskets.'

Heady though the sweet air of freedom might be, for the big-city sophisticates from downriver – the slit-skirted jazz girls and the high-rolling bankers – the move was like stepping back centuries. Even many treaty-port missionaries found the 'backwoods' of Szechuan quaint and somewhat shocking.

The settling-in process was not accomplished without some difficulty; in particular there were problems in finding accommodation for the universities that had evacuated. West China Union University became home to five downriver universities, including Nanking and Cheeloo. The Nanking students were housed 'in a building that will ultimately become the laundry of the proposed University hospital, and the staff ... in a building that is ultimately to be used as the residence and teaching building of a new school of Agriculture.' Within a few years, despite red crosses painted on the roofs of the buildings, the once park-like university campus became bedraggled from the bombing; eventually a large wall was erected around the perimeter to keep people from using it as a public park.

All the missions in West China benefited from the influx of coastal refugees and money; the United Church mission, which was the largest in Szechuan, expanded correspondingly. At one point in 1938, two of its missionaries were personal advisors to Madam Chiang Kai-shek: Jim Endicott as head of the New Life Movement, and Bob McClure in charge of the 30 000 warphans in the northern area around Honan. The Chungking hospital, the largest in the city that was now capital of Free China, had outgrown its dank premises within the city during the 1930s, and moved to a new building across the river, using the old hospital as a 'feeder' clinic. With the coming of the refugees, the hospital acquired two eastern nursing schools and opened a new, fifty-bed tuberculosis wing and an institute of hospital technology. Yet Dr A. Stewart Allen, the only foreign doctor on the staff – and for a while in 1938 the only foreign doctor in all of Chungking – managed to operate the hospital throughout the war despite 'hand-to-mouth' funding from home and an uncooperative staff.

The war changed the face of West China, not just of the United Church mission. The tiny stations of the China Inland Mission, the only mission in Yunnan and Kweichow, were also dragged into the twentieth century. Dr Edward Fish's station at Anshun, for example, became a strategic point on the Indo-China and Burma roads into Free China. An airport was built on the site of the old city wall, and Dr Fish's clinic-type hospital became the home of several downriver nursing schools.

Although few Canadian missionaries in Japan supported Japanese aspirations in China, most preferred discreetly to keep silence about Japanese militarism; it was better, they felt, for the Christian church in Japan to survive muted than to invite persecution. As it was, the Japanese government ordered the Protestant churches to organize into a single body and to break off ties with the missionaries, 'to escape the stigma of foreign connections.' When it tried to do the same with the Catholic church, there was a swift, Vatican-ordered indigenization of the clergy, so that when the Allies withdrew from Japan the church would not be left without a hierarchy. With native clergy, 'then, war or no war, the work of the Church could go on.'

Because there were few pro-Japanese voices among the missionary community in East Asia, most of the propaganda coming from the Canadian churches, Catholic and Protestant, became vociferously pro-Chinese. Feeling that their cause was the only just one, the China missionaries took to the pulpits to denounce Japan in the strongest possible terms. Margaret Brown, for example, who had already written several popular novels about how a Chinese wife named Mrs Wang resolves the problems of daily life in the light of Christian teaching, turned her hand to another about the siege of Shanghai, 'Heaven Knows,' which takes its title from the Chinese shrug in the face of incomprehensible tragedy. It tells the story of an illiterate peasant woman, caught in the bombing of the New World Amusement Centre, who is taken to a Christian refugee camp by white-clothed nurses.

Jim Endicott, too, although he had had differences with Chiang Kai-shek and felt he had no more integrity than a cholera germ, was willing to defend him on national radio. 'I have recently returned from the most bombed and blasted city in the world, Chungking,' he said on the CBC radio program 'We Have Been There.' 'You can count on Chiang Kai-shek to lay an enduring foundation for democracy in China. He will bind up the wounds of the Far East with malice towards none and with charity for all. To me, he stands there in the midst of his bombed and blasted capital a great and heroic figure, clothed in the qualities of a Lincoln.'

As early as 1932, missionaries in Szechuan had been writing to their home missions in Canada and the United States stating that they had found 'Made in u.s.a.' on many unexploded Japanese bombs. 'We believe it is a moral duty to distinguish between the aggressor and his victim, and to take appropriate measures regardless of consequences,' stated the Fellowship of Reconciliation at the West China Union University. According to many American missionaries the question was asked continually in China: 'When will America stop assisting Japan by sending them equipment, and thus bring this terrible slaughter and destruction to an end?'

Canada, too, was selling war materiel to Japan, including oil, scrap metal, and good Canadian nickel. As late as 1940, Dr Bob McClure stated, 'I have been digging Canadian scrap out of Chinese bodies and I expect soon will be digging it out of British bodies.' This statement contradicted the Canadian government's declaration that it had not shipped one ton of nickel for months and further that it had taken 'far-reaching precautions' against shipments elsewhere being transshipped to Japan. Dr McClure was summoned to Ottawa to explain himself. This encounter with Under-Secretary of State O.D. Skelton and his assistant, Norman Robertson, as recounted in the biographies of McClure and Robertson, is still a cause célèbre forty years later.

During its formative years after 1931, the Canadian Department of External Affairs had been consistently staffed with men who shared the same social-gospel background as Canadian missionaries, had sat on the same scm executive with them, and had worshipped in the same churches. Vincent Massey, Hugh Keenleyside, and Hume Wrong all came from families in which the missionary spirit was active, as did O.D. Skelton himself. Skelton's daughter later married the officer specializing in Far Eastern affairs, Arthur Menzies, son of the archaeologist James Mellon Menzies (whose appointment in 1973 as Canada's ambassador to the People's Republic of China was the culmination of his career at External Affairs). Mackenzie King had his own China connections; but, typically, they were more secular: his sister, Jennie, had married George Tradescant Lay, son of Horatio Nelson Lay, one of the legendary nineteenth-century traders. This may explain, in part, why King seemed to have more of a 'treaty-port attitude' towards Asians than did the DEA.

Admitting that McClure was in a truculent, 'intemperate' mood, Munroe Scott states that the North China Director of the International Red Cross – for such was the position from which he spoke – had a polite meeting with Skelton and Robertson and then was ushered into Mackenzie King's office. King did not deny the doctor's claim, but

Drs C.M. Hoffman and A.E. Best greeting members of the Friends' Ambulance Unit, Burma Road, 1943

stated that ten times the amount of nickel had been shipped. Looking at McClure, King – 'this roly-poly, oily politician,' McClure described him – warned him that his information was true but a state secret under the War Measures Act and that Dr McClure would have to recant his statement or go to jail for treason. McClure felt 'he had never seen anything so spineless in his life and compared him to "the dignified Chiang Kai-shek" whom no one could claim lacked backbone.'

With a 'less than candid effort,' Dr McClure signed a less-than-complete retraction: 'I am now satisfied that the Canadian government is taking every possible precaution to prevent Canadian nickel reaching Japan . . . I am, therefore, desirous of expressing my apology to the Prime Minister and his Government.'

Here J.L. Granatstein, the biographer of Norman Robertson, takes up the battle. McClure's account, he writes, 'is not only insulting and defamatory to both Robertson and Mackenzie King, but it also seems to be untrue.' For one thing, no Canadian nickel *had* been shipped for months; further, a memo from O.D. Skelton to King suggests that McClure probably never met King at all. Moreover, McClure's account begs the question why King – a politician's politician – would 'put a loaded gun into the hand of a man who could do irreparable damage.'

Not knowing Norman Robertson's character as does Professor Granatstein, I am tempted to believe his account may be literally closer to the truth: why would Mackenzie King put a 'loaded gun' into McClure's hand? In addition, the doctor was drawing his information from the time when he *was* extracting Canadian nickel from Chinese soldiers a year earlier in Honan. Yet Dr McClure claimed at the time – and still claims today – that he met with King; he may have forgotten details, but it is unlikely that he would forget meeting King under such circumstances. There is, too, a ring of truth to the peppery doctor's moral denunciation of the Canadian government's concern for trade rather than peace and justice.

Perhaps the best judgment was rendered by the Reverend Jesse Arnup, who had taken over as foreign-mission secretary on the retirement of James Endicott in 1937. Dr McClure, he wrote to West China, 'is one of those impetuous fellows who blurts a thing out without thinking it through ... On that incident itself, I would have been prepared to have defended him before the PM, or anyone else, but for the embarrassment it might have caused our Japan and Korea people if a missionary secretary should be quoted in the press on the subject of Canada's aiding China's enemy when China is fighting for democracy and has all along merited our backing instead of our opposition via Japan. That is to say, Bob was right in the general with reference to our shipping nickel and copper and a lot of other things to Japan throughout 1940, but wrong in the specific instance.'

One year to the day after McClure's meeting in Ottawa, the Japanese obliterated Pearl Harbor.

13·Redeeming the Time

'By military necessity, and for your own safety and comfort, you and your family as enemy nationals are hereby ordered to live in the Civil Assembly Centre. There every comfort of Western culture will be yours ... The Civil Assembly Centre, being the best home for those who live in it, must be loved and cherished by all of them. Each person shall take care of his health and live in harmony with each other. There shall be no disputing, quarrelling, disturbing or any other improper demeanours.'

Instructions given to British and American nationals by the Japanese authorities, 1942

As the news crackled over the BBC shortwave that the Japanese had bombed Pearl Harbor on the morning of 8 December 1941 – on the other side of the international dateline – an impenetrable barrier fell between Free China, the territory controlled by Chiang Kai-shek, and Japanese-occupied China. 'So life changed again,' wrote Mrs Dorothy Bell, a China Inland missionary in the far northwest. 'We were learning that nothing is normal but the abnormal.'

One of the frequently quoted verses during the war years, chosen as its annual text by the China Inland Mission, was from Ephesians: 'Redeeming the time because the days are evil.' For eight years, this was the preoccupation of the missions: to bide time, to hold the fort, and to wait, watch, and pray.

For those just ahead of the Japanese lines – from Honan westward

'Warphans' in Tientsin refugee camp

into Shensi and Kansu, and in South-Central China from Kiangsi to Kweichow – it meant an intensification of the war, continual bombing raids, and abject poverty. 'We were always prepared to go out in the fields when the air raid came, and we kept a tin of biscuits, our passports and a blanket ready,' remembers John Austin of Kweichow. 'We simply went out in the fields and sat on the gravesides while the planes passed overhead.'

Like many others, the well-known Bell family of the China Inland Mission, brothers John and George and their families, living way out in the panhandle of Kansu, had to take in boarders, three young men who had been forced to flee from their own stations. As rations dwindled, Mrs George Bell recalls, 'when bread was no good, we dried it in the oven, rolled it into crumbs and mixed malt syrup with it, then ... made a sort of "grape-nuts" ... We made cakes with a little honey and saccharine, but I left those to the men.' Mrs Bell also remembers that she was never without her knitting, unravelling sweaters to make anew. Again like many others, the war brought the special privation of split families; as the war dragged on, the Bells were separated into three groups, the father in China, the mother and the three younger children in Toronto, and the four older children interned at their school behind Japanese lines. 'I do not like to think of those days,' says Mrs Bell simply.

'"Busy" might describe our doings these days ...' the Reverend William Simpson of the Anglican mission wrote from Chengchow in Honan, still in Free China, in October 1942. 'We thought we came to preach the gospel, but in these times of famine conditions it seems to have but little place in all the round of business and banking and book-keeping and planning and committees ... Famine is the big word in Honan today, Famine is the word on our lips most often, Famine is what we're trying to fight, what we're scheming and planning and by no means least praying about each hour of our working day ... I don't want to paint a gloomy picture but it is pretty bad. The ravages of war were not enough (we still get alarms and planes, and can nightly hear the fighting) but we are now facing an unthinkable winter ... It is not at all uncommon to start out now and to be stopped on the road by people who in their desperation just won't let you pass ... Naturally it is hard to have people beseeching that you help to keep them from starving and to have absolutely no hope of helping them.'

The Anglicans and United Church people tried to keep a token representation in western Honan, in Chengchow, and Loyang, but by the end of 1943, their position in these cities became precarious and the missionaries made their way further west to Kansu or Szechuan.

The Scarboro mission in Chekiang also tried to maintain a token representation when thirty of the fathers and Grey Sisters departed for West China in May 1943. At least three fathers managed to stay at their stations throughout the bombing raids. 'For years and years on end Dolu village has enjoyed its placid existence, barely touched by the changes that have affected the outside world,' wrote the Reverend Kenneth Turner, later the first Bishop of Lishui. 'When a [Japanese] foraging party entered the valley attempting to take grain and cattle, there were some who resisted ... In retaliation every house in Dolu and in six neighboring villages were one by one set ablaze ... There was no evidence of any attempt to set the church on fire ... Half a year has gone by and Dolu is emerging from its ashes. Around the church, emblematic of what gives meaning to life and suffering, the villagers have begun to raise their little cottages.'

For the Scarboro missionaries the flight to Free China was a perilous 2400-kilometre trek through three provinces that took six months. Their destination unknown, they travelled 'on foot, by bicycle, and river boat, by bus, truck and train, until they reached Yuanling in the west central province of Hunan.' There they were welcomed by Bishop Cuthbert O'Gara, the Canadian-born head of the American Passionist mission. The priests remained in Hunan until 1944, when once again the tides of war shifted and they were enabled to return to Lishui.

The war brought a new group of Canadians to China who might be considered to be missionaries in the broad sense, since they were impelled by a religious calling: the friends of the Friends' Ambulance Unit. A number of Student Christian Movement of Canada leaders had signed a pacifism manifesto in 1935, and when war came four years later they continued to resist military service. The Canadian government interned these conscientious objectors in lumber camps in British Columbia and northern Ontario, then offered them the alternative of service in the FAU, which had recently been brought to China by the British Quakers. The FAU men, and a few women, earned a remarkable reputation for having the death-defying ability to drive a cranky charcoal-powered truck through the gorges of the Burma Road without a breakdown – of either the personnel or the truck.

Reading through the letters and articles written by missionaries during the war years, one is struck by the sense of adventure and terror. One is also struck by the sense that something is missing: not just the words physically snipped out by the censors – though it does come as a shock to pick up a letter that hangs in shreds – the lacunae are larger than that. Up to this time, missionary correspondents gave a running account of the political scene – who's a communist, who's not, who's a big shot, who we like. Now, like the Chinese people, the missionaries lined up patriotically behind Chiang Kai-shek, the shaper of 'China's Destiny' (the name of his curiously anti-foreign wartime testament).

For those living in Szechuan, the war entered a new phase after Pearl Harbor: the bombing stopped, the war became something distant, something far away. Szechuan had always been cut off from the rest of China, locked in its mountain fastness, but now that Szechuan *was* China as far as its government was concerned, this isolation intensified into 'a feeling of remoteness ... a certain unreality.' Contact with the outside world was reduced to two slender lifelines – along the Burma Road with its treacherous hairpin turns, and by plane 'over the Hump,' over the roof of the world and Mount Everest to India. Every letter, every item of war materiel, every individual, had to be brought into Szechuan by one of these two routes.

In this hot-house atmosphere, the Canadian missionaries constituted the most distinctive national presence as late as 1940, but as the other Allies joined the war, bringing in American and British men and money – especially money – theirs was a presence without real power. Shunted off to the sidelines, they continued 'the Work' as quietly and unobtrusively as possible. When the Kuomintang instituted compulsory military training in the mission schools, the missionaries acquiesced, and turned it into another exercise in character building; only the British Quakers were exempted, when they threatened to pull their college out of West China Union University if such training was imposed.

For Chiang Kai-shek to impose censorship of the press was one thing; to gain missionaries as his propagandists was brilliant. He and the Madam assiduously cultivated the missionary population of Szechuan, flattered their sense of self-sacrifice, and praised their relief efforts. He asked the National Christian Council to enlist one thousand Christians 'as morale officers in the Chinese army ... to supervise the spiritual needs of Chinese soldiers.' In turn, the missionaries praised Chiang and his wife as the only hope for China's salvation. 'China will win this war,' Dr Gordon Agnew had declared in 1943. 'Unlike the leaders of the Japanese, her generals are Christian and are striving to hold fast their national life and culture.' Chiang had the qualities of a Lincoln, Jim Endicott had affirmed in 1941 – and he, if anyone, would know.

Thereafter, as things got worse and Chiang became reactionary, the missionaries refrained from speaking or writing of politics. Instead of

Staff of West China Union University and other downriver universities, Chengtu, 1943. Dr Robert McClure is holding the lower left-hand corner of the flag of the Republic of China

discussing the political situation, the Chungking business manager, Gordon Jones, tabulated the comings and goings of the staff. Instead of political action, Earl Willmott organized Sharman Bible-study classes, and Dick Dickinson rambled on about the New Life Dairy Goat Association and his efforts to turn 'the Yellow Chinese Cow into Black and White.' Instead of writing partisan books like 'Heaven Knows,' Margaret Brown went back to editing *Happy Childhood* and *The Christian Farmer* magazines. Lewis Walmsley, principal of the Canadian School for missionaries' children, translated the poems of Wang Wei.

Only on the subject of money – 'the worthless coin of this realm' – did anyone venture near political judgment. 's.o.s.!!' wrote Mrs Katherine Willmott, 'we can't live on our salaries'; this was at a time when even a broken bicycle brought $1500 u.s. in the black market. In one year – 1942 – the mission increased its salaries from $1425 per family to $2800, an increase of $70 000. Even this was not enough, and some young couples (so a distraught father informed the board) were selling off their wedding presents to make ends meet.

'It is hard to write of this whole situation,' wrote Gerald Bell,

without getting 'het up' about it. There are some things one might say but which are better left unwritten. Suffice to say, the ballyhoo from London and

Washington that comes over the air leaves most people quite cold out here. The head of this Government still holds the responsibility and administration of all, but one cannot go far down from him. Apart from the salaried people, the people in West China were never so well off in terms of such money as is in circulation is concerned. Laborers, rickshaw pullers, merchants – all are enjoying a perfectly lovely time throwing money around like water.

As for the black market, 'Not much use in calling it "dark" here, because the biggest ones in the business are connected with the government banks.'

Even such veiled criticism is rare. 'Were I to go into details,' wrote Dr A.E. Best, 'I feel sure our friend the censor would just cut it out, so why waste time and paper?'

Canadian missionaries were encouraged in their inclination to praise Chiang by a subtle pressure from the boards at home. 'I have been to London to see the Queen,' wrote the United Church's Dr Jesse Arnup of his trip to Ottawa to meet Madam Chiang on her tour of the United States and Canada in June 1943. May-ling had made a big splash south of the border, staying at the White House, speaking before the assembled House and Senate, her passage covered in full colour and intimate detail by *Time* and *Life* magazines. Henry Luce of *Time* had always been one of her greatest admirers and, just as he did for many others, he 'puffed' her inordinately. Jesse Arnup was only able to meet her in the crush of a formal reception – 'let me tell you it was much easier to get in touch with her in Chungking than in Ottawa' – but declared that she 'of course, captured all hearts with her winsome manner' in her speech to the Houses of Parliament.

Later, the following year, A.E. Armstrong warned the West China mission against spreading rumours about the Chiang's 'marital relations and also political corruption and graft in China.' Five months before, Madam Chiang had left the Generalissimo, staying first in Brazil, then at the Kung family mansion in New York; during this year-long exile, however, ten months of it spent in the United States, not one word appeared in *Time* or *Life*. Chiang Kai-shek had taken up with his second wife – the one he had not divorced to marry May-ling Soong – and was living with her and their newborn son. All this was secret, however, and Armstrong was pleased that Dr H.H. Kung, May-ling's brother-in-law, had branded the rumours 'an unmitigated falsehood ... I hope Albright for the IMC and Mickle for the FMC [Foreign Mission Committee] will lose no time in countering this because of the very serious effect it will have on the public generally and its unfavourable reaction on Christian missions. Perhaps they have been too much idealized but notwithstanding that it was natural for a people, especially Christians, to hold them up as ideal Christian leaders.'

A second pressure coming from Canada was exerted by the Department of External Affairs in the form of the new Canadian Ambassador to China, Victor Wentworth Odlum. Prime Minister Mackenzie King had toyed with the idea of appointing a missionary as ambassador – Dr Leslie Kilborn and Dr E.C. Wilford were the most frequently mentioned names – but instead appointed the sixty-three-year-old Odlum, a military man who had fought in the Boer War and had risen to the rank of Brigadier-General in 1916. After that Odlum had become an insurance executive, editor of the *Vancouver Daily World*, member of the B.C. Legislature, and, in 1941, High Commissioner to Australia. By his own admission, he never had any China connections – the Prime Minister had originally planned to send him to Tokyo because his mother had died there 'and Mr King felt I would have a point of contact with the Japanese' – and had a temperament unsuited to life in wartime China. 'I am very direct and matter of fact, and these are two things I am told the Chinese do not like,' he wrote in one of his first letters back to the department in Ottawa.

The Canadian missionaries took General Odlum under their wing as one of their own even before he left for China: he had attended Victoria College with some of the older missionaries in 1900–3. Odlum arrived in Chungking early in 1943 and for the next year, until he had an embassy built in an area called Fairy Grotto and could raise 'the Canadian flag for the first time in history over a diplomatic establishment in China,' he lived and worked in a small unfinished house in the United Church hospital compound. In fact, General Odlum was surrounded by missionaries: his embassy interpreter was Dr Kilborn, his third secretary was Ralph Collins, a YMCA missionary's son born in China, and his counsellor was Dr George S. Patterson, who had served as a Methodist missionary to Japan and later as general secretary of the Canadian YMCA.

Ambassador Odlum's major goal in China, as far as the Canadian government was concerned, was to foster goodwill for Canada that would lead, it was hoped, to increased trade after the war. Odlum himself sanguinely wrote that 'China can do for the Canada of the future what Europe has done for the Canada of the present.' The best way to do this was to provide aid to China through the wartime Mutual Aid Board. Odlum found that the main opposition to this came not from the Chinese government – Chiang Kai-shek was so ready to receive foreign aid that President Truman nicknamed him General Cash-My-Cheque – but from the three major foreign powers in Chungking – the Americans, the British, and the Soviets. 'The Americans now look upon this field as their own, both for the war and the post-war period,' Odlum wrote in his first despatch. 'While the three groups jockey for position, Canada is simply not in the picture. She is looked upon as being "in the belly" of the u.s. (as an eminent Indian journalist expressed it to me) or as a very minor tone in the British chorus.' In order to raise Canada's profile, he negotiated, with Ottawa's approval, two $50-million shipments of artillery and other aid to China. But neither Odlum nor Ottawa had expected the American veto against what it considered interference in its monopoly to ship munitions to China, or the American refusal to fly Canadian munitions 'over the Hump.' Consequently, the thousand trucks and artillery sat in warehouses in India until after the war, and a sea route was once again opened to China.

General Odlum never did understand China. He was not an analytical type but a man of action, and from the beginning of his tenure he emphasized that 'analysis presupposes the possession of facts, and facts are about the last thing one can get in China. Even the fact seen with one's own eyes one day is belied by the contrary fact seen by the same eyes the next day. The wide grey "margin of doubt" dominates the whole picture.'

So, like another man who never understood China, his friend the American Ambassador, Major-General Patrick J. Hurley, with whom he would swap military stories, General Odlum opted for the only white figure in a grey landscape: Chiang Kai-shek. On one memorable occasion after the war, Odlum and his first secretary, Chester Ronning, were invited for a private picnic with the Generalissimo and Madam Chiang at the mountain resort of Kuling. Odlum was 'charmed' by the setting, by the lawns (sod was brought up the mountain at great expense to clothe the barren hillside): 'With a light breeze in the trees, the sound of running water, touches of light appearing through dark clouds and giving a mysterious atmosphere to the fresh green of the lawns ... There was nothing peculiarly Chinese about it, but it was very attractive.' Odlum was particularly impressed by Madam Chiang, 'by her fiery words, by her flashing eyes,' as she countered one by one 'the attacks that had been made on her herself [sic],' and her 'almost pathetic' sadness when she talked of 'the failure of the Communists to keep their word ... and of the hardships which the people of China were suffering because of the turmoil they created.' The Generalissimo was more taciturn; but Odlum told him to buck up, to make 'the necessary show of strength,' and to 'hold the Communists in their recognized part of North China with one arm and devote all the rest of his powers and resources to building up his own China ... He could make his China so happy, so well governed and so comfortable that his Chinese of the Northern China would want to join his China of the South. After all, I suggested, the people of the Northern China were still his Chinese.' General Odlum even had a good word for Dr Ch'en Li-fu [CHEN LIFU], the dreaded head of the secret police, 'the Bad Man of China': 'I have been telling you for a long time now that Ch'en Li-fu is no true reactionary,' Odlum wrote to External Affairs in Ottawa. 'This afternoon he was not only not reactionary in argument, but he swung over to my side of the case and commenced to prove that he was anything but a reactionary in outlook – that he was, in fact, a liberal.'

While the Canadians in Chiang Kai-shek's Free China were negotiating their way through the landmines of Chinese domestic policies, those in Japanese-controlled East Asia were enmeshed in a different sort of international politics: they were enemy aliens. As the Japanese swooped down upon Hong Kong, Indonesia, and the Philippines in the months after Pearl Harbor, their numbers grew to an astounding 140 000: British (estimated at 100 000 at war's end), Americans (33 000), Dutch, French, and, after their surrender to the Allies in 1943, Italians. The Sikh police in Shanghai, although British, were not considered enemies; instead the Japanese made them guards of the internment camps.

As many as one thousand Canadians were caught behind enemy lines, not including military prisoners of war like the two thousand Winnipeg Grenadiers in Hong Kong. Three-quarters of them were missionaries; the rest were employed by a variety of companies – Canadian Pacific Steamship Lines and insurance companies, British shipping concerns, Dutch rubber plantations, and the Chinese customs service.

Every Canadian mission in East Asia, with the exception of the tiny continuing Presbyterian, had representatives among the more than 750 missionaries and their children in the Japanese Empire. The statistics as found in the Canadian government records in Ottawa provide a fascinating look at Canadian missions at one crucial moment in time. The Protestant churches had made a point of withdrawing their people from Japan in the months leading up to the war. Consequently there were only twelve Canadian Protestant missionaries in Japan itself, all of them (according to Dr Arnup) single women 'exercising their female prerogative to upset the apple cart. It looks as if a group of them will stay no matter what happens.' Fifty-two missionaries were in Korea and South-East Asia, and 115 in China itself. Of those in China, 28 belonged to the United Church of Canada and 2 to the Anglican church; 68 individuals, 40 adults and 28 children, were members of the China Inland Mission.

Because of the Roman Catholic policy of remaining at the missions whatever government came into power, fully three-quarters of the Canadian missionaries were Catholics, 572 priests and nuns representing thirty-one different orders. Almost 200 were in China and Hong Kong; the rest were divided among Manchuria (129), Japan (136), French Indo-China (71), and the Philippines (49). By contrast with the Protestants, there were only 90 Canadian Catholic missionaries in Free China, members of the Scarboro mission, the Missionary Sisters of Notre-Dame-des-Anges in Kweichow, and a few Franciscan sisters in Chengtu.

People who had remained steadfastly at their posts could expect to be detained when war came, but the saddest stories were of those caught accidentally. Dr Harrison Mullett, on his way from Chengtu to Toronto, exchanged his ticket for a plane later the next day; that night, Hong Kong fell. Dr Richard Brown, setting out alone from Tsingtao a few days before Pearl Harbor, managed to cross the Japanese lines; his wife (a German-born nurse named Elsa), and their three children zigzagged across the China Sea and caught the last passenger ship out of Hong Kong. In Manila, in the least-familiar setting possible, Mrs Brown was captured in the Japanese blockade. Ten Holy Cross priests and nuns en route to India were caught in the same city. (One of the priests, in a gruesome and uncharacteristic civilian cruelty, was tortured to death in early 1945 in the euphemistically named National Psychopathic Hospital.)

At first the Japanese did not know what to do with these civilian aliens. The morning after Pearl Harbor, the Jesuits in Suchow were visited by three officers of the Japanese Military Service who assured them that nothing had changed, but warned them not to leave their compound. At the Anglican hospital in Kweiteh the same morning, a nurse in charge of the hospital, Susie Kelsey, the only Canadian in the city, was 'carried away in a Japanese truck as a prisoner of war.' Bishop Lindel Tsen, who had already been 'dehabilitated' from the cathedral compound in Kaifeng in an earlier Japanese attempt 'to extirpate what they considered extraneous elements,' now found himself 'prevented from entering the hospital compound by a contingent of Japanese guards armed with machine guns.' Miss Kelsey was released after two months and, by the summer of 1942, was allowed to go for walks outside the mission compound. 'I still have a policeman to look after me but he considers his duty done if he greets me affably when I pass him,' she wrote in a letter she managed to smuggle out. Since this was the only hospital still operating in eastern Honan, 'the hospital is carrying on as usual, even busier than it usually is in the summer. We are nominally under a Japanese organization who keep a staff of five or six in the w.a. house, but they have little to do with the hospital work beyond keeping an eye on our finances, making out reams of statistics and occasionally treating a J. or Korean patient. It is an expensive household for the hospital to maintain but worth while as it enables us to carry on as usual. They have forbidden preaching in the clinic but otherwise do not interfere with the hospital evangelism.'

The Japanese rounded up the usual suspects first, the muckamucks of the Hong Kong and Shanghai Bank, 'educators, ex-marines, missionaries, ne'er-do-wells, newspapermen,' as well as those bombed out of their homes, and brought them to commandeered buildings at such places as the Columbia Country Club in Shanghai, where they slept in the 'bowling alleys, locker and billiards rooms.' As for the rest, it took until mid-1942 just to locate and register them and issue them with blue arm bands, marked with 'a' for American, 'b' for British, and so on. Then they were gathered together into Civil Assembly Camps, starting with the people in the remote areas, especially any place controlled by communist guerrillas.

These camps, eventually numbering thirty throughout the Japanese empire, contained as heterogeneous a collection of western exotics as the East could command: British diplomats, bank presidents, and university professors; Eurasian good-time girls; Jews fleeing Nazi Germany; bishops and missionary doctors rubbing shoulders with lounge lizards and remittance men; fastidious spinsters sharing quarters with White Russian prostitutes and Chinese wives of British sailors. The camp at Weihsien, an American Presbyterian compound in Shantung that gathered people from all over North China, had two complete bands, a Salvation Army outfit and a black jazz band that had happened to be playing in a Tientsin nightclub. (Canadian and American-born Chinese, like Dr Victoria Cheung in Kongmoon, had a difficult time.

Generally, they were not interned, but were also not granted residency certificates; without a certificate they could neither travel nor find employment.)

Each of these camps had its own personality, depending on its location, its inhabitants, its commandant, and, not least, on the quality of its buildings, some of which were already in ruins, 'filthy, verminous and rat infested.' The Pootung [PUTONG] camp in Shanghai was in a tobacco factory that had been abandoned for a decade; by the time the inmates arrived, one-third of the ceilings had collapsed. Stanley Camp, located on a rocky outcropping that once had been the Hong Kong jail, was crowded with four thousand inmates, but was favoured with a warm climate and its own private beach. Most of the camps were located in foreign mission compounds, among them the Canadian Academy in Kobe, Japan, which housed only sixty people and was considered the most humane.

The Weihsien [WEIXIAN] Civil Assembly Centre in Shantung – 'The Courtyard of the Happy Way' was the ironic text over the entrance – was of more than passing interest to Canada, for it was home to about two hundred Canadians: Jesuits and Scarboro Fathers from the Chabanel language school in Peking; Dr E.B. Struthers and the Reverend George King, professors at Cheeloo University; Susie Kelsey of the Anglican mission, Dr Margaret Phillips, who had set up private practice in Tientsin; and some thirty adults and children of the China Inland Mission. One of the oldest residents was the eighty-year-old Mrs William Taylor, who, as Jessie Gardiner, had gone out in the first CIM party in 1888; she was one of the lucky ones, for she was interned along with five members of her family, including two granddaughters. Weihsien camp also had several prominent inmates, among them Eric Liddell, the Olympic runner (a protagonist in the movie *Chariots of Fire*), who had sent his Canadian wife, Florence, back home before the war, and Arthur and Mary Wright, the Harvard sinologists. Dr Leighton Stuart, president of Yenching [YANJING] University, and Dr H.S. Houghton, director of the Peking Union Medical College, were kept in a special confined area of the camp and were not allowed to communicate with the other internees.

The largest single group of Weihsien residents were the boys and girls of the Chefoo schools, the CIM school for missionaries' children, twenty of whom were Canadians. Since their foundation in the 1880s by Hudson Taylor, the Chefoo schools – one for boys, one for girls, and one preparatory school – had earned an enviable reputation as the only place 'east of Suez' to be granted the privilege of administering the Oxford examinations for entry into that university. Although a few parents happened to be visiting Chefoo in December 1941, and thus were interned along with their children, most of the school students had no contact with their families from 1940 to 1945.

A few days after Pearl Harbor, the headmaster of the school, P.A. ('Pa') Bruce, was taken away and held for six weeks. By the time he returned, the Japanese army had confiscated the cricket field for a Shinto shrine. Not until November 1942 did it expropriate the entire fifteen-acre site and send the staff and students, numbering some 150, to the resort community of Temple Hill across the bay, where 70 children lived in one single-family dwelling. Finally in August 1943, the inmates were transferred to Weihsien, a two-day steamer trip around the Shantung peninsula to Tsingtao and then by train 210 kilometres inland.

Before the war, the schools had been cut off from contact with other foreigners. 'It was easy to stew in our own juices,' recalled Gordon Martin, the Oxford-educated Latin teacher and later headmaster (now retired and living in a converted caboose on his daughter's farm in Bruce County, Ontario). 'We lived in our own compound. We couldn't afford to join the businessmen's club – actually we regarded the club as a wicked place where people went and drank.' Coming into Weihsien Civil Assembly Centre, he continued, 'was good for us, I think, because we were cheek by jowl with the world, the flesh and the devil.' David Michell, now Canadian Director of the Overseas Missionary Fellowship, vividly remembers the shock of walking into the camp at the age of nine and seeing women in high heels and lipstick: 'We had never seen people who dressed differently – or [encountered] their language. We didn't know what was swearing and what wasn't swearing. We had never heard swearing. So we had some very interesting adjustments to the outside world.'

The school tried to keep itself intact and separate from 'the outside world,' but the confines of the camp made that difficult. Once the smaller children reached a certain age they were moved, according to camp policy, into the adult wards, where they might share a 2.4-metre-square room with three other single men or women. The teachers, aided by the university professors, kept the school going throughout the life of the camp, even to the extent of obtaining special permission from Oxford University (through the Swiss consul) to hold matriculation exams, with the marks to be reported after the war. The school flourished during these years (partly because there were no distractions) and graduated three classes.

For everyone in the camps, ordinary life stopped. Forbidden to communicate even with the coolies who came to carry out the night-soil, the Westerners had only each other – and they soon fell to bickering. But they survived by organizing their lives with committees and entertainments and a thriving under-the-barbed-wire black market, clothing themselves in ragged immodesty and eating 's.o.s., the Same Old Slop.' Because they were used to organizing, missionaries immediately came to the fore as directors of the camp committees, of which the Discipline Committee was the chief, followed by Sanitation, Food, Education, and Recreation. The discipline committee, mediator between the Japanese commandants and the inmates, conducted roll-call and looked after camp security.

Some missionaries chose a self-abnegating service, latrine or kitchen duty. Eric Liddell was one who would do more than his share, offering to make coal balls of coal dust and clay for the older people. In the same Weihsien camp, an Australian Trappist monk, released from his vows of silence while in the camp, ran an egg-smuggling operation under the fence. Once, when he was caught red-handed, his vow of silence was restored and he said not a word until thrown into solitary confinement. There he sang all night in a voice loud enough to be heard throughout the camp. Within a few hours of his release the next morning, he was back at his job.

After the initial jostling for position, the camp inmates found that missionaries were, as the Chefoo teacher Gordon Martin recalled many years later, 'no more Christian than a haughty mule when selfish interests were threatened.' They would push into the queue like anyone else if it meant an extra ration for the little ones. And they could act like this and still maintain a judgmental attitude toward others, holding Bible-study groups, the only gatherings permitted by the Japanese after the minstrel shows and ballet concerts were found to be subversive.

On entering the camps in 1942–3, each person was allowed to bring only what he or she could carry. Women with babes in arms, the old, and the sick were correspondingly reduced in their possessions. Most brought only the clothes they would need for a few months (by which time they hoped the war would be over) – a few tins of milk and butter, a summer outfit for the children, a couple of pairs of shoes. Some gold, a diamond ring, or a bundle of pounds sterling might be smuggled in, sewn into the lining of a coat or a doll's outfit. Other families showed more foresight: one group of teenage brothers brought a gramophone dangling from a bamboo pole; 'Stardust' became the theme music for every camp gathering, until the grooves were worn out.

As their clothing became frayed and the mosquito netting ripped, as the tin cups lost their enamel and the shoes their soles, the people had nothing with which to replace them. In such poverty, where a used sardine can was worth its weight in gold – as a cup, a shovel, a toy for the children, or a safety-deposit container – food became the main preoccupation. At the beginning of the war, the authorities provided two meals a day of bread, rice gruel flavoured with pork, and tea; one pig fed the whole camp for a week. Eventually, even fish bones were fried for food. Queueing up for six or seven hours at a time, for food, for water, or for roll-call, became a daily routine. At least it passed the time.

During the first year of internment, as William Sewell, an English Quaker professor at West China Union University, wrote of Stanley Camp in Hong Kong, 'the resilient young men and women had a power of recovery which few of the older people possessed. They played softball nearly every day ... and they took part in concerts and ballets. They were like gods and goddesses those days. The unhealthy fat and sloth of our pre-war living had gone and there was a physical perfection which was shown to advantage by the scanty clothes which were all we had to wear. Bare legs and usually bare feet, brief shorts, and for the women, a gay sun-top, made us feel that we were not in Stanley but in Arcadia.'

In 1942 and again in 1943, the American government arranged through Argentina a repatriation of its nationals from Japan and China (but not from Indo-China or the Philippines), in return for Japanese civilians in the United States. As a courtesy, it allocated two hundred places, out of the two thousand per trip, to Canadians. Those to be repatriated were selected by the Japanese according to 'broad humanitarian directives ... those under close arrest; interned women and children; the seriously ill; and interned men ... long separated from their families.' The repatriates were taken on a Japanese ship, the *Awa Maru*, to Goa where they transferred to a Swedish mercy ship, the *Gripsholm*, which took them via Rio de Janeiro to New York City. The first trip, which gathered most of its people from Stanley Camp, was shrouded in such secrecy that Dr Mullett walked into the Toronto United Church House before the committee knew he had been released.

The second voyage received much more attention, and the *Gripsholm* was the only ship allowed to sail the oceans with all its lights blazing. Ottawa sent Herbert Norman down to Rio to escort the Canadians to New York. The Japanese authorities used this repatriation to clear the Americans out of Stanley Camp, and the final sixty Canadians (including the late Sun Yat-sen's bodyguard, 'Two-Gun' Cohen, who now described himself as a Yiddish-speaking 'banker'). But they also chose individuals, seemingly at random, to relieve the overcrowding in all the camps of China, Manchuria, Korea, and Japan. There was considerable jostling among internees for consideration, but in the end it made little difference. Two children of the CIM Bell families were returned to Canada, leaving seven behind in Weihsien. Some people refused repatriation, but Susie Kelsey was taken against her will because, she wrote, 'these petitions are seldom granted.'

By mid-1943, despite the less-crowded conditions in the camps, according to Professor Sewell's account, 'the days of Arcadia were passing. The young gods and goddesses were becoming too gaunt to be lovely, though there was still a valiant attempt to keep the place gay like a fancy-dress ball with clothes made from bath towels and curtains, and from some Red Cross clothing which had come.' Two years later, when the war was turning against Japan, the care of the internees diminished in importance. Few people ate in groups any more, Sewell continued, 'for co-operation is not easy when there is insufficient to eat ... At the beginning we had thought that internment was going to be good for us all. We should learn through suffering and living together a better way of life. Now we saw that while some of the best among us had been made better, many were not refined but degraded, the thin covering of culture having fallen away. Internment had gone on too long.'

Two weeks after the war had officially ended, the inmates of the camps began to hear rumours through the grapevine that the war might soon end. Outwardly, life went on as normal. The guards still patrolled and made roll-call. Then a few days later when the American planes came dipping their wings and dropping forty-five-gallon drums of food – which exploded on impact – into the camps, the aviators who parachuted in were greeted with exuberance. The leader of the rescue team at Weihsien, an old Chefoo school boy, was welcomed by the brass band playing the national anthems of every nation. At Yangchow, the church bell, which had tolled only once in three years – mysteriously, on V-E Day – rang forth, as the Japanese commandant ceremoniously handed over his samurai sword.

At liberation, Sewell wrote, 'smart suits, ties and leather shoes came out of hiding-places and some of Hong Kong's élite once more took on old airs with their new clothes as though their lessons had not been really learned.' It must have been eerie for the rescuers to be greeted by these cadaverous men and women in their Sunday best, and to be given a special meat concoction of 'Same Old Slop,' only to become violently ill with dysentery; it must have been equally strange when these same people, having regained their health, later donned their camp costumes to preach to fashionable congregations.

For most of the inmates, the adjustment to freedom was a difficult process. One small boy, terrified of the noisy celebrations in the camp, asked, 'Mummy, when will peace be over? Can't we have war again?' The worst problem was caused by the rich food – especially when children tried to eat the chewing gum and ketchup included in the drums dropped from the planes. For many, the physical and emotional scars of internment lasted for years; they would be sitting in class or a church service and their minds would wander back to the searchlights, the sirens, the barbed wire.

The wartime experience of Canadian Catholic missionaries in occupied China was complicated by the fact that four months after Pearl Harbor the Vatican signed a concordat with Japan, the end result of the 'indigenization' of the clergy the Japanese had demanded two years previously. To the Vatican, a concordat is a humiliating treaty signed under duress with a hostile power to regulate spheres of interest 'in fields where conflicts tend to arise.' *Historia concordatorium historia dolorum*, notes Anthony Rhodes in *The Vatican in the Age of the Dictators*: 'Concordats generally result in a surrender of Church privileges in return for permission to carry out its evangelical mission and educate the young in Christian principles. For this no sacrifice is too great, and Pius XI said he would negotiate with the Devil if the good of souls required it.' Less than ten years after he made this statement, Pius signed his infamous concordat with Hitler.

Generally, Vatican diplomatic channels were able to arrange a somewhat more lenient treatment for Catholic missionaries than could their Protestant counterparts during the early part of the war; but after the fall of Italy, this power lessened. In fact, arranging for its priests and nuns to be cloistered in their own compounds meant 'a greater degree of confinement than was the case' in the camps. The MIC Sisters in Hong Kong, where they were seen to be British, spent the war in Stanley, yet their sisters in Canton, where they were under French protection, were more or less 'free' and continued to run their leprosarium, orphanage, and six-hundred-pupil girls' school.

'You are probably asking yourselves how we were able to feed our large family of 220 orphans and twenty sisters during four years,' wrote the sister superior in her first letter after the war. 'Every method imaginable was used to procure the resources necessary to buy our daily rice. The school only closed its doors for holidays, and the classes were filled and well distributed. The orphans, each of whom got a ration of ten ounces of rice a day, were admirable in their courage and their resignation. They worked hard: needle-work, sweaters for sale outside, quilting for half a day for the little ones, all the industries were put to use. In spite of this, we would not have been able to supply our needs without the help of generous benefactors and continual collections ... After the fall of Hong Kong ... our Sisters went down the roads, under the bridges, in the hidden corners and the ruins of burned Canton where the poor hid themselves to die; and how many baptisms they made!'

Up in Manchukuo, held by the Japanese for ten years before Pearl Harbor, where the Christian churches had a reputation of being 'unpatriotic' in not supporting state Shintoism, the reaction was immediate and severe, starting with the imprisonment of Bishop Aldemar Lapierre on 10 December. However, the authorities seemed to have differentiated between religious fathers, brothers, and sisters, for each group received quite distinct treatment. Three days after the bishop's arrest, all the Canadian priests in Manchuria, about sixty in number, as well as the Belgians, were brought to the seminary compound in Szepingkai. Bishop Lapierre, who had suffered a heart attack in prison, was released, but had to stay in his room and was forbidden to communicate with his priests; this interdict was lifted on Christmas Eve. In June 1942, the Japanese evacuated the seminary because it was too close to the South Manchurian Railway, and the Canadian priests spent the duration of the war in the bishop's compound in Szepingkai, which, being inside the city, was more protected. (The Belgians went to Mukden.)

Having said this, it is hard to account for the Japanese treatment of the teaching Brothers of the Christian Schools; perhaps they just fell through the gaps of the Japanese bureaucracy. At least two of the brothers were interned in seven different camps, in Mukden, in Szepingkai, and in Japan, where they had gone in expectation of repatriation. One of the saddest documents is the deposition made after the war by Brother Marie-Médéric (Emilien Douville):

When captured (Dec. 11th 1941) I was suffering of rheumatism (very badly). They promised to send me to an hospital ... They didn't cure ... I was interned like others and had to sleep on the floor ... Badly healed ... lack of food ... underfed ... no medical attention ... refused help of a dentist ... Graft on the part of the authorities (from officials down to the last guard). All complaints useless – even worse afterwards ... Sergeant Watanabe (WATANABE) of YAMAKITA CAMP must be tried as war criminal ... [Ellipses are in the original.]

The Japanese authorities do not seem to have regarded the humble sisters as being much of a threat, for some of them, especially in the outlying areas, were allowed freedom to continue their work throughout the war. The Soeurs Antoniennes de Marie were allowed to live in their own convent and to walk to the bishopric to cook for the priests. The MIC Sisters were allowed to continue their dispensary and catechumenate until late 1943; but after that, as guerrilla activity increased, the remote sisters were gradually moved into the Szepingkai bishopric. As late as 1945, however, some twenty sisters were still free at four different stations. But Sister Bertha Crévier balances their freedom with the fact that the four sisters at Paichengtse [PAICHENGZI], the farthest from Szepingkai, were so isolated that they had no letters from Canada for nine years, four of the Japanese War and five of the Chinese civil war. 'Nothing, absolutely nothing came to us,' she wrote in a recent article, 'not even a letter nor the least help.'

Suchow, like Shensi and Honan, was a communist guerrilla zone. For most of 1942, the Canadian priests were allowed to remain at their larger stations 'except those too distant from Japanese posts who were assembled together in cities occupied by the army.' Just as in Manchuria, the Jesuits confided their churches to the indigenous clergy and to the German priests of the Society of the Divine Word; the MIC Sisters handed over their work to the Chinese Présentandines and the Polish Sisters of Notre-Dame of Kolocsa.

Throughout 1942 and the first part of 1943, relations with the Japanese authorities were 'encouraging enough,' and the priests were allowed to go out of their stations to visit the villages, provided they came home by nightfall. Later, when they were confined to their compounds because of recurrent bandit scares, they still could communicate with the Apostolic Delegate in Peking, and they received some money from the Swiss consul in Peking. But this was far from sufficient to support the thirty priests sequestered within the cathedral compound in Suchow city, and the local Christians were encouraged to remit part of their wheat harvest to help support them.

In March 1943, the 'most painful trial' of the mission's history occurred when three Canadian priests were executed by a local military man at the 'bush station' of Fenghsien [FENGXIAN]. At first both the Jesuits and the Japanese refused to give the Swiss consul any information, even the names of the priests, 'fearing the consequences.' The annual report attributes their death to vague 'reasons not yet well known.' What had happened was that the priests had accepted the offer of some Chinese gentry to finance their school and had invited them and the Chinese 'puppet officials' to dinner. But no Japanese had been invited, an oversight that angered the district governor. That night he had them arrested for 'scattering of anti-Japanese propaganda and connivance with Chinese guerrillas,' and shortly thereafter had them killed and their bodies taken to the mission with the notice that the communists had done it.

In any event, relations quickly deteriorated and, two months later, all the Canadians in Suchow, thirty-seven priests and seven sisters, were transported to Shanghai. 'They will be escorted, but with an escort so benevolent and so trustful they will hardly notice,' the Japanese general of Suchow promised. He himself remained friendly and 'went so far as to call on His Excellency the Bishop before his departure ... On the train, [the missionaries showed] neither elation nor lamentation; there was singing, holy chants intoned by Father Hauser, to the amazement of our "sympathetic" military guards.'

The Jesuits from Suchow were joined by the younger scholastics from Shanghai, and all were interned at Zikawei. For those who had spent their first formative years in China within its walls, it was like coming home. 'Twenty months of rest, if not for the body, at least for the soul,' wrote Father Rosario Renaud, the mission historian. 'Even in internment, we enjoyed relative freedom. We had our books and our leisure, the joys and comforts of the communal life in a religious setting.' Nothing, he wrote in his annual letter, 'will give, it seems to me, a better idea of this simple, tranquil, regular, studious, somewhat monotonous life, than to outline, so to speak, the "diarum" that we usually have in our ordinary houses of formation and study.'

Brother Léo Fontaine cultivated his vegetable garden as he had done in Suchow, while the fathers disappeared into the voluminous library and compiled an index of Chinese literature since 1919. Others studied mission history and Chinese customs. Bishop Philippe Côté was allowed out of the complex occasionally to celebrate mass at the Tousewei orphanage or at the convent where the Canadian sisters were interned, in another part of the city.

The Weihsien camp had been liberated by a graduate of the Chefoo school; equally appropriately, at the war's end the Zikawei compound was visited first by a priest of the Suchow mission, Father Armand Proulx, an American citizen who had left Suchow just before Pearl Harbor and made his way to Szechuan, where he became a chaplain in the American army. When he was parachuted into Shanghai on 15 August 1945, the Feast of the Assumption, he found his fellow priests completely cut off from the rumour mill that was seething in the Chinese city. 'The end of the war came as a surprise to everyone,' wrote Father Renaud in his annual report.

Within two weeks, the bishop and three priests had started on their way back to Suchow, followed by the other priests and nuns in parties of ten or twelve, bringing with them 'all the commodities much sought after or appreciated in ordinary times, whether they travelled by covered or open truck, standing or seated, by reserved coach or mail train, always in the middle of a pile of bags.' By 22 September, all the missionaries were back in the mission ready to take up active work again.

14·The Last Days: Silence

'It surely should not be odd to Canadians that there is a diversity of opinion on matters political in this province, among Canadians ... it has been taken for granted that the civil war in China is a clear-cut struggle between right on the 'Left' and wrong on the 'Right' ... I would like to make a plea for clearer thinking on the part of the church people ... do not consider us a group of unthinking, selfish and hypocritical folk, who take the name of Jesus on our lips and act in utter disregard of His principles as they affect this country.'

Dr Gladys Cunningham, 'A Missionary Looks at China,' *The Observer*, 15 February 1949

During the 'haywire' conditions of the Sino-Japanese war, many mission groups had been planning for post-war reconstruction, planning that was often, according to Margaret Brown of North Honan, 'too little and too late.' For instance, in one conference of Anglican missionaries on furlough and a few Chinese pastors that was held in Toronto at the beginning of 1945, there is not one mention in the recorded minutes of communism, even though large portions of the diocese were already under communist control.

Often the reconstruction plans were pipe-dreams of devolution. Setting the tone for many, the Reverend Gerald Bell, secretary of the West China mission, recommended privately that the church divest itself of its overgrown plant. The first to go would be the smaller station

Missionary family leaving Szechuan

hospitals. 'So long as we had the field of Western medicine to ourselves, it was our duty to continue this form of social service to society wherever we could, either with Chinese or foreign personnel. Now that the Government, both National and Provincial, is moving actively into this field, it is likewise our duty to reconsider the whole question of medical work. Just where we fit into the picture is not yet determined.'

If Christian missions had not yet figured out their role after 140 years, post-war China was no place to learn.

By the time the Jesuits arrived back in Suchow, less than a month after the Japanese surrender, half of their territory was in communist hands; three of the six North Honan stations were occupied by the Eighth Route Army. Through the last half of 1945, the Kuomintang, backed by massive injections of American aid (and some Canadian in the form of 170 Mosquito planes and Mutual Aid foodstuffs), pushed the communists back into the mountains of Honan and Shensi as the Japanese had done, and confined the actual fighting to Manchuria. There was talk, talk, and more talk; sometimes it seemed like a war of verbal attrition. Talk at least delayed the fighting, although fighting inevitably started again and, by 1947, it was only a matter of time. The hand-to-hand fighting of North China, the brutal consolidation of communist power, gave way in 1948–9 to the more or less peaceful annexation, piece by piece, of China south of the Yangtse. The communists were poised to capture Nanking, Chiang's capital, but still he demanded more talk, more negotiations, more time. Then when his time had run out, he asked the foreign embassies to accompany him to Canton and to Taiwan – then still legally belonging to Japan, since no peace treaty had been signed – pleading with them to roll back the communist scourge.

On 1 October 1949, the communists proclaimed the People's Republic of China in Peking. In November, they took over Chiang's last stronghold of Chungking. On Christmas Day, they marched into Chengtu.

Though much church property had been destroyed by the war the Christian church in North China had continued to grow, slowly, even without the presence of foreign missionaries. The Japanese consolidation of the Protestant denominations had brought such diverse groups as Pentecostals, Methodists, and Seventh Day Adventists into the same organization. In Free China, too, ecumenical co-operation had been hastened by the churches' joint efforts to distribute relief through the United Nations Relief and Rehabilitation Agency (UNRRA) and the United

China Relief organization. Even the Roman Catholics began to shed their isolation and sit on the boards of these agencies.

UNRRA had 'for a long time refused the assistance of all private relief agencies in their attempt to meet the needs of post-war misery, but eventually there was formed a National Clearing Committee of Private Agencies,' that included the Canadian Aid to China Committee. Canadians were represented on many of these committees and boards. The United Church of Canada supplied Anne Davison, the first accredited social worker sent overseas by any Canadian church, to the American Advisory Committee, and Dr Robert McClure to the Friends' Ambulance Unit. Fathers John H. McGoey and Gerard McKernan of the Scarboro Foreign Mission Society were both active in the Catholic Welfare Committee; the latter, in particular, 'flew thousands of miles in a matter of three months [in 1947] and carried out successfully his most difficult task of arranging equitable distribution of residual UNRRA–CNRRA supplies.'

When the United Church missionaries returned to North Honan, they found 'scattered congregations, ruined buildings and impoverished masses.' During the early years of the war, the church had grown, even establishing refugee camps and literacy classes. As the war dragged on, the congregations were divided by a charismatic sect whose members 'spent hours in prayer and were intolerant of those who did not.' Frictions between the Chinese Christians and the returning missionaries were minimal, but inevitable: 'For fourteen years "Resist, Resist" had been the slogan,' stated one leader. 'Now there was no further need for resistance. The war had ended too soon. We're not ready for it.'

The missionaries were not returning as they had in 1929 trying to hang onto outworn privileges; they were invited back as old friends. Dr Isabelle MacTavish, Miss Grace Sykes, and Dr Robert McClure were all veterans of twenty years, and of the younger men, the Reverend Norman Mackenzie had been born in the mission.

Dr McClure preceded the others back into the province as director of the Friends' Ambulance Unit hospital in Chengchow, with a budget of $8 million for the rehabilitation of mission hospitals in Honan. By the spring of 1946, his team, which included Canadian doctor Walter Alexander as superintendent and his wife, a registered nurse, as well as one English doctor and eight Chinese nurses, had done 'an excellent job' of restoring the Changte hospital and turned towards Weihwei, the only one that had continued throughout the war, with 'some semblance of idealism ... Apparently, years of trying to deceive the Japanese [had] left some room for misunderstanding and mutual suspicion,' however, and Dr McClure had to fire the Chinese doctor who had 'at times risked his life to prevent the Japanese from gaining control.'

'With trained mechanics and trucks,' wrote Margaret Brown in the mission history, 'the FAU were able to forge ahead. The Evangelistic Missionaries had to walk or cycle or use wheelbarrows.' 'Was the Canadian Church only interested in Medical work?' asked the Chinese leaders. Why had so much been spent on the hospital when the church had neither doors, roof or windows? Why, echoed the missionaries, when they had asked for $40 000 and fifteen missionaries had the Canadian board sent only $5000 and five missionaries, some of whom were 'too old to have been sent in the first place?'

This disparity between the medical and evangelistic work was increased by the flying visit of Dr Stewart Allen, superintendent of the United Church hospital in Chungking. The Canadian Red Cross had sent Dr Allen to tour 'the hospitals in China ordinarily supported by Canadian funds and to report on their present conditions, needs and prospects, with a view to assist with equipment and funds.' In addition to North Honan, Dr Allen also visited the Peace Hospitals in the communist areas that had been founded by Norman Bethune in 1938–9. The communists, he reported enthusiastically were 'eager to welcome doctors, nurses and rural workers and they wanted them quickly.' Dr Allen's picture of life in 'the red triangle' contrasted so sharply with the North Honan people's own encounters with the communist forces that they were flabbergasted; eight years under the Japanese, the Chinese stated, was easier than twenty months under the communists. The guerrillas were evil 'beyond all words to express,' wrote Grace Sykes.

In that fateful summer of 1947, the communists moved south along the railway line. The North Honan missionaries had long since declared their opposition to populist movements – from the Boxers onward – and when the collision came, they were obviously on the wrong side. At Weihwei the mission 'acquiesced under severe pressure' to let the Kuomintang army install a big-gun emplacement in the compound because of its strategic position. Consequently, when the communists attacked the city, the battle swirled around the mission compound and the two Canadian nurses evacuated the hospital patients in a pitiful procession out of the north gate. Though the Kuomintang pushed back the communists, and the missionaries returned to their homes for two weeks, they were eventually forced to abandon the city.

At Changte, the fighting came a week or two later, and the Canadians vacillated about whether they should move out. One group caught a passage on a U.S. military plane, while four more flew out on the last American plane on 6 May. The last two Canadians, Dr Isabelle MacTavish and the Reverend Norman Mackenzie, remained until 15 June, when they hitched a ride in a truck with the departing Chinese staff of the hospital.

The following day, the North Honan missionaries gathered in Kaifeng and held an emotional council meeting to disband the North China Mission of the United Church of Canada forever. The first Canadian mission had fallen.

The attitude of the Chinese communists towards religion went through several stages between 1945 and 1951, always guided by the principle that religion, like everything else, must 'serve the people.' At first, since the guerrillas had been in hiding for the eight years of the Japanese war, their initial contacts with the missionaries tended to be positive; this was shown by Dr Allen's trip through the Peace hospitals. As a result of this friendliness, Mao Tse-tung promised that the followers of the five religions of China – Buddhism, Taoism, Islam, Protestantism, and Roman Catholicism – would 'enjoy the protection of the people's government as long as they are abiding by its laws.' Thereafter, in every constitution the freedom to practise religion was guaranteed, along with the equal, contrary freedom to propagate atheism.

As the war intensified in 1946-7 – and as missionary attitudes hardened – the communists started what seemed like a systematic persecution of the churches in their 'liberated' areas. They would seldom use the pretext of religion but, in the brutality of a military occupation, anyone suspected of collaboration with the Japanese, Kuomintang, or western imperialists, or who was opposed to 'the will of the people' – as landlord or money-lender, hospital director or intellectual – was imprisoned and sometimes executed: in North Honan, for example, two Chinese doctors who had criticized the communists to Dr Allen were executed as soon as he left the province.

Even today, Dr McClure mourns the destruction of the church in North Honan. The purge carried out prior to the communist accession to power, he says, 'was a real revolution in which everyone who opposed them, practically, was eliminated, liquidated, sometimes by torture, sometimes by straight execution. The estimates go as high as forty million [for all China]. The Chinese explain it by saying that there were people who could not adjust to the new conditions, and those who could not adjust had to be eliminated. It was a very small number, because it was only five or ten per cent. Five or ten per cent of four hundred million ... is an awful lot of people. It included most of my friends, my doctors. Many of my country doctors had survived the war but were liquidated during that period. Our Christian Church was liquidated during that period.'

'Communism as carried out in these parts,' fulminated the Reverend George King, head of the Cheeloo divinity school, 'is for the people an enforced slavery, regimented and controlled by cruel torture, torture unto death. There is no freedom of religion, thought, speech or action. The destruction of the church organization or any agency under its control is one of their avowed purposes. The implementation of these policies comes not all at once, but in successive stages culminating in a show trial of those whom they choose to name as offenders in their policies, a public trial which is in fact judicial murder.'

This overt hostility towards the Christian churches softened gradually, as the communists came to power and began to act like a legitimate government. To this end, at the request of the Chinese Protestant leaders themselves, the communists opened a dialogue with the churches after 1949. 'There's nothing wrong with you, except your friends,' Chou En-lai told a gathering of these leaders, referring, of course, to the foreign missionaries. Using the term that dated back a century, he told them they would have to form a truly 'Three-Self Church.' Stripped of its imperialist connections, its foreign finances, and its foreign influence, the Christian church must become a 'patriotic' institution, self-governing, self-supporting, and self-propagating.

Since there was only one Protestant denomination, this movement spread rapidly, not only among left-leaning theologians like Y.T. Wu and T.C. Chao, but among evangelicals like Marcus Ch'eng of the China Inland Mission. Anti-imperialist rhetoric had been part of Protestant propaganda since the 1920s, so the government's demand was nothing new: 'We expect Chinese Christians to march under the flag of opposition to imperialism and love of the fatherland, and ... to join up with the People's Government to work together to build the new China.'

The Three-Self movement culminated in the declaration known as the Christian Manifesto, drawn up in May 1950 by five Christian leaders under Y.T. Wu, head of the Christian Literature Society of Shanghai. Not exactly a conciliatory document, it is a reasonable one for its time and place. It was 'unfortunate,' it stated, that 'Christianity consciously or unconsciously, directly or indirectly, became related with imperialism in China ... From now onwards, as regards their religious work, Christian churches and organizations should lay emphasis upon a deeper understanding of the nature of Christianity itself ... and ... should emphasize anti-imperialistic, anti-feudalistic and anti-bureaucratic-capitalistic education, together with such forms of service to the people as productive labour, teaching them to understand the New Era, cultural and recreational activities, literacy education, medical and public health work, and the care of children.' By the next year, a supplementary covenant signed by 400 000 Protestants, half the membership, pledged each member to 'help the People's Government to get rid of spies and special agents, and be on the alert to prevent reactionary elements from using the church in their destructive activities. We will clear the church of all renegades, so as to preserve the purity of religion.'

The reaction of foreign missionaries to the movement was almost uniformly negative. It was a continuation of the deaf and dumb conversation they had been having with Chinese Christianity since the beginning. Many missionaries could never recognize that the Three-Self movement was Christian, not just a communist plot to control religion. They could never believe it was meant to 'save' Christianity, make it viable in a revolutionary society, rather than deny and destroy it.

And so this barrier came down. The Chinese Christians were going one way – unless they were willing to suffer martyrdom, they had to live in and with their culture – and the missionaries became an 'embarrassment.' This word was used so frequently at the time that it almost lost its meaning, but it is important to understand that the continuing Chinese church was 'ashamed' of the churches in the West. In order to 'save face,' it had to denounce them. To this end, nothing was too trivial – many a missionary was accused of wearing fine underwear while giving castoffs to the Chinese – or too remote to be dredged up. The church had always had malcontents and leftist sympathizers, and some were only too ready to denounce a missionary to his or her face; but most Christians, if pressured by their communities, would weakly denounce some missionary long-since dead or retired from the field. They preferred to break off contact with individual missionaries, even friends of twenty or thirty years, not to recognize them when they passed on the street, not to call or attend worship with them. 'And so, you just lost your friends,' one missionary recalled.

Nowhere was this deaf and dumb conversation more apparent – or sadder – than in the Anglican diocese of Honan, the one Canadian mission that had always prided itself on maintaining good relations between the Chinese and the home church. To put this into perspective, we must go back to 1945, the end of the Japanese war.

'Now we can join the angels again,' wrote Bishop Lindel Tsen from the Kaifeng cathedral in his first letter after the war. 'Thank God who has guided us through the perilous years of war as He did for the Israelites in the wilderness.' Now and for the future, he continued, the diocese would need 'the actual presence of foreign missionaries who are more effective in dealing with intruders. Here in Kaifeng ... all the other buildings ... are still in the hands of those who should not be there. But those occupants are not Japanese. It would not be difficult to get them all back if we could have Bishop White with us here, even for a few weeks.' Like an old warhorse hearing the bugle, Bishop White was ready. Within a month, he had arranged a leave of absence for himself from the University of Toronto and a furlough for Bishop Tsen in Canada. 'I am not in any way seriously sick,' Tsen wrote to thank him, 'but just fatigued and exhausted.'

From the beginning everything seemed to go wrong with White's new mission. The large party was held up by red tape, and only two colleagues from the old days, Archdeacon George Andrew and Miss Greta Clark, joined him. In Shanghai, he learned – apparently for the first time – that the communists were threatening Honan. 'There was no inkling of a clash imminent in Honan between the National Government and the Communists,' he wrote from Kaifeng. 'This meant that the disruption of communications and the active conflict ... upset all our plans.' The bishop's entry into the city, which had been planned by the Kuomintang general, had to be cancelled; the next day the guerrillas cut the railway line.

White had been a progressive twenty years before, but now, with two distinguished careers behind him, with his three-and-seventy years weighing on his shoulders, and with his second wife left behind in Toronto, he was certainly not the man to deal with soldiers standing at the mission doors with bayonets. Bishop White remained in Kaifeng for thirteen months, from June 1946 to July 1947; 'we were fighting against time,' he said. To his wife, he wrote more bluntly: 'I don't like this China a little bit, and my desire to live here has evaporated! for I don't think it will be much better in my lifetime, and I want a few years, *D.V.*, of quiet restfulness.'

The last six Canadians remained in the city until the beginning of

1948, when they too were forced to leave. The story of the church in Honan in those last days belonged not to the foreigners but to the Chinese who inherited it. Bishop Tsen was still in Toronto when Bishop White returned, and shortly thereafter made his way back to Kaifeng. The following year, just after the final evacuation of the Canadians, he attended the Lambeth Bishops' Conference in London. While crossing through the United States, however, he suffered a heart attack, and was brought to Toronto to live with his son Chien-yeh Cheng, known as C.Y. Cheng, who had recently arrived on a two-year scholarship at Trinity College 'to investigate the social and religious work' of the Anglican Church in Canada.

One would like to imagine the meeting of these three bishops of Honan – for C.Y. Cheng was consecrated assistant bishop of Honan in 1951. He left Toronto after only six months, which he spent mostly 'making a study on his own of all the Communist literature he could find.' He had been receiving so many letters from friends in China, he wrote to Bishop White, asking 'Is it not true that communism is something more wonderful than Christianity?' 'We can easily see the confidence of the writers in the new People's regime,' he continued. 'We must recognize now that something great is now happening in China, something entirely new to our past experiences and we can no more deal with it only according to the "common sense" ... Imagine how much we can learn at this critical time which we can learn nowhere else and no time else.'

It is easy to sense C.Y. Cheng's optimism as he packed his bags and set forth to join the New China. It is less easy to understand the pain of his father in February 1951, two years later, when he returned to Shanghai in a wheelchair. How did he resolve his divergent heritages? With his Anglicized name and English ways, he looks from his photographs to have been the model of episcopal rectitude, standing in a pose characteristic of Chinese pastors, holding his Bible to his chest. The last he was heard of, he was living with his daughter in Shanghai, in the same tiny compound as two other Chinese Anglican bishops and the head of Chinese Freemasonry.

On his death in 1954, aged sixty-eight, the paper *T'ien Feng* [TIANFENG], *Heavenly Wind*, published a glowing obituary. 'Long before the liberation, and right in the time when savage imperialists were robbing many of our good fellow-workers and fellow-believers of their patriotic spirit,' it said, Bishop Tsen 'was already much concerned with our people's liberation ... We have to be even more thankful for the bountiful mercy which granted him the light of the Holy Spirit, lighting his heart so that at a very early time he already received the revelation of truth and saw the resplendent future of the Fatherland and the new heaven and earth of socialism.'

C.Y. Cheng was ordained assistant bishop of Honan in the Kaifeng cathedral by his father's successor, Bishop Francis Tseng (no relation), a graduate of Wycliffe College in Toronto and formerly pastor of a wealthy Leaside congregation. Together, the two of them launched a vitriolic denunciation of Bishop White. Forgotten was his famine work, forgotten the building of a self-sustaining church; they had seen the collection of the Royal Ontario Museum and 'realized,' now, that White had only used the cloak of religion to plunder. He had been a robber of graves and a robber of souls.

Bishop White commented when C.Y. Cheng was consecrated that 'no doubt there is some connection between his rosy colouring and his new appointment.' Later, reeling from the news that Kaifeng was leading the country in instituting Sino-Soviet Friendship Month in the churches ('We who are Christians, in our prayers ought to thank God for Sino-Soviet Friendship ... '), he wrote sadly that the news was 'so ominous we shrink from reading anything new, lest something more dreadful should come to light.'

An old man nearing eighty, Bishop White would sit for hours at a time in the gallery named in his honour in the museum he did so much to enrich, staring at the thirty-foot high mural of the serene Buddha of the Future.

The Christian church in China was trying to talk, but Bishop White, like many church people in Canada, had already stopped listening.

The communists appear to have harboured a special hatred for the Catholic church; it must have seemed to them a monolithic structure designed to usurp a control of the people that rightly belonged to the state. Whatever the reason, any atrocities they had committed against Protestants paled beside the vengence they wreaked on Catholics.

At first things did not seem too bad. In Suchow, for example, when the Jesuits returned in September 1945, they established a wary peace with the guerrilla soldiers. Only at Howchiachuang [HEJIAZHUANG], known as Le Roc, were the resident priests imprisoned by a people's court for 'troubling the hearts of the people, and many other crimes.' These two were released and returned to Canada, to be replaced by Father Aurélien Demers, one of the older men, who 'sought to re-establish good relations with the communists.' In spite of minor difficulties, they allowed him to continue visiting his *chrétientés*, the Christian villages.

One can sense the symbiotic relationship, and the respect, between the communist guerrillas and the Chinese Catholics in a letter written in 1948 by the mission superior, the Reverend Father Edouard Côté, to T.C. Davis, the new Canadian ambassador. Referring to the 555 schools the mission had run before the war, he said, 'Those schools were fundamental to the welfare of the youth, and, very often, of the grown-ups too, who would after a day's work in the fields, gather at the school-house, and there would get the elementary principles of sound social doctrines. The Reds had no chance to spread their subversive doctrines where there was a school. To get a hearing from the peasants, they had to declare that they were friends of the missionaries ... All our missionaries are convinced that if we gave the youth a serious education, it would go a long way in checking the progress of communism, and that it is one of the best ways to save China.'

Since Suchow city was located at a strategic junction of two railway lines and was largely destroyed by Japanese bombardment, the Japanese had transformed the city during their eight-year occupation, widening the streets and constructing eight- and ten-storey red-brick and cement-block public buildings. Consequently it was relatively easy for the Kuomintang to hold the city, which they did until the final, bloody battle of Suchow in November 1948.

Up in Manchuria, it was a much different story, as the Missions-Etrangères mission lived under five governments in as many years: Japanese, Russian, Chinese communist, Kuomintang, and communist again. When the Chinese communists had first appeared at the convent of the Immaculate Conception in Szepingkai, they had politely said, 'Don't be afraid, you are from the Catholic mission, and are therefore part of our family ... Don't worry, it's not you that we are looking for.' ('They call us their friends,' the sister whispered parenthetically, 'a title which is scarcely flattering to us in normal times, but which, none the less, was very useful to us that night.')

As in Honan, however, the attitude of the communists stiffened in 1947, a year that went down in Catholic history as 'the year of the martyrs – a time of terror and torture that tested the Chinese Catholics and removed from them, forever, the slurring stigma of the name "rice Christians."'

In one minor incident, Father Antonio Bonin, the resident priest at Changchun [CHANGCHUN], 160 kilometres north along the railway from

Szepingkai, was imprisoned on the evidence of his radio transmitter. He described his year-long ordeal as a classic case of 'brainwashing': chained hand and foot with other 'hardened' political criminals, he would have to attend 'courses in Marxist indoctrination, long interrogations and written confessions,' interspersed with hysterical accusation meetings when he would have to sit immobile 'as a pillar of salt.' By the beginning of 1948, the Canadian sisters had been evacuated from the outlying stations, and the missionaries' numbers had dropped from forty-seven Canadian sisters to eleven, and from forty-two priests to seven. 'The fuse is still burning,' wrote Bishop Aldemar Lapierre of the Missions-Etrangères.

The 'explosion' proper began with the casual destruction of the Trappist monastery of Notre-Dame-de-la-Consolation in the desolate mountains north of Peking. Brother Alphonse, born Albert L'Heureux, was among the five foreign and twenty-eight Chinese priests who died during the month-long 'death march.'

Born in 1894 in Coaticook, Quebec, the youngest of four children of a poor widow, Brother Alphonse had announced at age eighteen: 'I am going to join the Jesuits and, I hope, die in China.' After fifteen years' study in Montreal, he was sent to Suchow in 1933, at the age of thirty-nine, where he spent six years in the 'bush' stations. The only way to leave the Jesuits in those days was to join a strict order like the Trappists and, he wrote to his sister from the monastery, 'in this immense silence how easy it is to take care of one's soul, to think of heaven, to live for eternity.'

From the beginning of their occupation, the communists cast covetous eyes on the well-tilled fields of the monastery. After the 'usual farcical mass trial,' the French abbot was condemned as a Japanese collaborator – though like the rest of the community he had been interned during the war in Weihsien camp – and was chained to the frozen ground for two months as punishment. A second mass trial condemned all seventy-seven priests to death. Eight were executed immediately, and the rest were forced to evacuate 160 kilometres with their hands bound behind their backs with fine wire, though some were upwards of eighty years old. 'We know that you are not afraid to die,' the guards taunted, 'but we can beat you and torture you until you have nothing but a spark of life and would be happy to die.' Brother Alphonse was one of the first, signalling his comrades that his end was near. He died peacefully, 'just like that other man in your chapel on the figure-ten [cross],' the guard admitted.

The Catholic church in China prepared for martyrdom. Just as he had done for Japan in 1940, Pius XII elevated the Chinese church to its own hierarchy in 1946, under the papal internuncio, Cardinal Antonio Riberi. In an equally profound move, he resolved, after two centuries, the Chinese Rites question: ancestor worship as practised in China was not a religious ceremony; now the clergy were encouraged to use 'pagan rituals and correct them by Christianization. It is better ... to amend what is in many parts good and can always be an element of strength and social equilibrium.' These edicts had a double-headed message to the faithful. On one hand, the church was recognized as strong enough to withstand persecution, even if cut off from contact with Rome. On the other, by making peace with their own ancestors, with the Chinese past, they were tacitly warned to make no compromises with the present. The Catholic church had survived the Japanese war by the concordat, but by Catholic practice, a concordat could never be signed with a communist regime.

Catholic literature of this period seems motivated by hysteria, incomprehension, and fear of the corporeal devil himself. 'The persecution of the Church in China is an example of pure disinterested hate,' wrote Gretta Palmer, a prominent member of the American 'Catholic Revival,' in her book God's Underground in Asia. 'Catholics number less than one per cent of the population. They are not rich or powerful people. They are not armed. They are not organized into guerrilla bands, and have no wish to be. The only threat they pose to Communism is a spiritual one.'

The church took on a messianic aura. The Legion of Mary, a militant form of Catholic Action for young people, was introduced in 1948 so the lay people could become 'shock troops' of a new holy war. It gained strength from the 'apparitions, revelations, and miraculous manifestations' of the Virgin throughout China. Miracles happened spontaneously. Mrs Palmer compared the Church in China to 'Rome of the first 300 years. The people are living in an age of faith. They don't want to escape martyrdom. Grace is in the air. There are other Agneses and Cecilias, ... people I believe I'll be praying to someday.' One church in Shanghai erected a life-sized reproduction of the catacombs, to remind the faithful 'that they were not alone.'

In 1949 just before the communist victory, Pius XII excommunicated all Catholics who joined the communist party or signed any of its documents. 'Offer unto God as a sweet-smelling burnt offering [suave holocaust] your difficulties, your suffering, your pain,' he consoled the people, 'so that He in His mercy will grant the Church of China peace, tranquility and freedom, and that He may open the eyes of the world to the fact – which is as clear as sunshine – that the Church does not seek the things of this world, but those of Heaven and that, according to her mission, it is towards her heavenly home that she prays and directs her children by the acquisition of virtue and the practice of good works.'

'Week by week the list of Chinese martyrs grew, no book, no magazine could keep up with it.'

By the time they came to power, rather than trying to destroy institutions opposed to them, the communists set up a Bureau of Religious Affairs to 're-educate' the people and, in the eyes of the missionaries, to subvert them. By mid-1950, with most of the Protestant leaders signing the Christian Manifesto, the People's Republic tried to institute a similar Catholic Patriotic Church. Looking back with hindsight, many Catholic historians blame the 'intransigence' of Cardinal Riberi for the plight of the Catholic church, saying that, 'a simple talk between him and Chou En-lai, over a cup of tea, would have solved everything.' In fact, there was a rumour a few days after the founding of the PRC, seemingly started by the American Bishop James E. Walsh of the Catholic Central Bureau, that Cardinal Riberi had 'recommended early recognition of the new Chinese Government to the Vatican'; Cardinal Riberi denied the rumour at once, and nothing further was said about recognition.

Instead, Riberi enunciated the Catholic 'line: hold on, hold on as long as you can, in spite of danger and suffering, do not abandon the flock.' 'Three Times No,' thundered the bishop of Shanghai. 'Do not listen! Do not speak! Do not sign!' When the government ordered the Legion of Mary to register as a 'secret and wickedly counter-revolutionary organization,' the school children lined up with their satchels and blankets at the prisons. In the first six months of 1951, 160 foreign priests and 12 bishops were imprisoned, as well as 30 foreign sisters.

The communists moved swiftly against the institutions of the church – the schools, the retreats, the catechumenates, and, especially, the orphanages. In March of that year, five MIC Sisters who worked at the Holy Ghost orphanage in Canton were arrested and paraded through the streets like Joan of Arc, deprived of their veils to cover their shorn heads. Three were released, but two were brought before a mass show trial in front of four thousand 'frenzied' people. This trial, which marked a new phase of Catholic 'persecution,' was the first one broadcast into

Hong Kong. The sisters' servant screamed his macabre story that he had taken eight sacks every day to the graveyard, each containing four to six corpses of dead babies. Chinese children were toured through the 'slaughter-house' and shown 'the death pit.' In the end the two sisters were given the 'lenient' sentence of five years for the murder of 2116 babies under their care in the year 1950 alone.

Their imprisonment became an international incident when Canadian Ambassador to the United Nations Lester Pearson brought it before the Security Council. Curiously, no one ever disputed the fact that 2116 babies *had* died in the convent, by the sisters' own count; what they did debate was the circumstances. Only a few months before the Chinese authorities had inspected the orphanage and had reportedly 'praised' the 'sanitary conditions.' In fact, the orphanage had such prestige that the Canadian ambassador to China had suggested taking over its operation as an official Canadian aid project. On Christmas Day 1952, almost two years after their arrest, the two sisters were escorted to the border of Hong Kong, still dressed in their prison garb, and were deported from China 'forever.'

The Canadian Franciscan mission in Shantung likewise ended in a fiery reckoning. Father Didace Arcand, one of the pioneers who had arrived in China the very day in 1911 that the Manchu emperor had been deposed, had during his forty-one year apostolate 'constantly nourished the desire for martyrdom; there were times when his some-times foolhardly recklessness almost got him his wish ... he ran, he flew towards the tortures which earned him the crown of martyrdom.' After six months in prison, he was 'taken from his cell to be dragged through the streets, hounded by crowds and subjected to other tortures. As a result of the blows received, he fell unconscious in the street and died without regaining consciousness.'

In Manchuria, the fuse that Bishop Lapierre had seen burning back in 1947 exploded when he himself, founder of the Missions-Etrangères mission and bishop for eleven years, died of malaria while incarcerated in a 'miserable hovel, the last vestige of his bishopric.' The remaining four priests, three Clerics of St Viator, and four MIC Sisters were 'chased' out of Szepingkai as soon as their passports could be arranged.

'The ruins continued to accumulate,' Canon Lionel Groulx intoned. 'The end of everything was approaching.'

In December 1951, in the Jesuit mission in Suchow, still surprisingly intact, Bishop Philippe Côté was arrested on the steps of the cathedral by two hundred soldiers, charged with refusing the sacraments to three 'progressive' priests who had joined the Three-Self movement. The remaining twenty-four priests (among them one Chinese Jesuit) and six sisters were brought in from the smaller stations and placed under house arrest in the cathedral compound. In ones and twos over the next year and a half, they were deported. Bishop Côté himself was imprisoned for twenty months, but was spared a trial by signing a carefully worded document confessing the crimes of Father Oscar Doyen, who had left China five years before: 'According to Communist law, a chaplain in the American Air Force is an agent of a foreign power, therefore a criminal. As Father Doyen was a chaplain of the American Air Force, therefore according to Communist law Father Doyen is an agent of a foreign power.' The ascetic fifty-eight-year-old bishop was taken directly from his prison cell to the train, 'and that was how the grand criminal, who they wanted first to humiliate in a great show trial slipped unnoticed and quietly into the wings,' commented the mission historian.

Perhaps because it was close to the Shanghai orbit, the Scarboro mission in Lishui, Chekiang, also sustained a relatively easy time, although two priests were imprisoned for 'Instituting the Legion of Mary, being an agent of President Truman, of Chiang Kai-shek and of the bandits; anti-revolutionary activities.' Even under house arrest, Bishop Kenneth Turner was able to keep in touch with the Chinese Christians: 'sitting by the window that overlooked the lane past the cathedral, Bishop Turner said he could exchange meaningful signs with Chinese Christians who were passing by. A hand on the breast was the agreed sign of sorrow for sins. Seeing this, the Bishop would silently repeat the sacramental words used to absolve the penitent. Local Christians could do no more than exchange such furtive signs without risking arrest, he said.'

The Catholic church in China had become, in the words of a Vatican honour roll, 'the Church of Silence.'

'You shall not go out in haste,' said the prophet Isaiah, 'and you shall not go out in flight.' The final evacuation of foreign missionaries lasted from 1949 to 1955, and was such a mammoth operation that the Chinese government set up the China Travel Service to oversee the evacuation.

The event that precipitated the departure of three thousand Protestant and two thousand Catholic missionaries (including some six hundred Canadians) was not the proclamation of the People's Government in October 1949, but the beginning of the Korean War eight months later.

Up until that time, the government permitted at least some mission activities – those pertaining to medical and charity work – to continue under surveillance. It even asked certain individuals it considered friendly to stay in China; five in West China, for example, were asked to remain, including dental professor Dr Harrison Mullett, Dr Leslie Kilborn, and Earl Willmott, professor of English at the university.

China's entry into the Korean War was – and is – considered by the Chinese to have been prompted by American interference in what had been a civil war between North and South Korea, and by General MacArthur's incautious advance towards the Yalu River, the border between Korea and Manchuria. China was under attack and retaliated in self-defence. This event, and its conflicting interpretations, ricocheted against the foreign missionaries. They were enemy aliens once more, and the communists worked to neutralize them, prohibiting them from all contact with Chinese Christians. By Christmas 1950, 'the reluctant exodus' had begun.

Before the Chinese allowed anyone to leave the country, he or she first had to obtain an exit permit, a procedure that could take months or even years. 'They did not want us to leave, yet they did not want us to stay, either,' recalled the Reverend John Austin of the CIM. Each man, woman, and child had to submit his or her life to an official scrutiny that involved lengthy interrogations and lists of all addresses since the age of eight. The attitude of the interrogators seemed calculated to humiliate the missionaries. Each person had to post an advertisement in the newspaper announcing his or her departure, and face any accusers who came forward. Then, and only then, could the missionary leave.

The trickle of evacuees became a torrent in March and April 1951. They came by the tens and twenties, busloads and trainloads of them streaming across the little iron bridge over the ditch that passed for a creek, with barbed wire on either side, that separated the Hong Kong New Territories from 'Red China.' Some came running across, laughing and weeping and kissing the flag. Others were carried on litters, or hobbled on swollen limbs. Still others came handcuffed, prisoners to the end. On two days in March, one hundred children and teachers from the China Inland Mission Chefoo school came in double lines, each carrying their three most important possessions: Bible, passport, and toothbrush. By the end of the year, the torrent had slowed once again to a trickle, and at the end of 1952 there were only a handful of missionaries left in China, almost all in jail.

With seven hundred missionaries and three hundred children in the field in 1949, the China Inland Mission approached this final evacuation as yet another venture in faith. The money for the passage of all its people – as well as for the purchase of new buildings in Singapore – came from the most unlikely source: the communist government itself offered to rent the spacious six-storey mission headquarters in Shanghai as a hospital for six years, two years' cash in advance. To the mission's surprise, the communists continued to remit the full amount every year.

The mission had many stories of personal heroism in those days. 'You cannot tabulate loneliness,' the mission magazine said epigrammatically. Mrs Irene Cunningham was allowed outside her room once a day to carry food through the streets to her husband in prison, her three small children at her side. The last two missionaries of the CIM to leave, in July 1952, Dr Rupert Clarke and the Reverend Arthur Matthews, out in the Central Asian province of Tsinghai [QINGHAI], spent two years incarcerated in their emptied rooms, sixty-five kilometres apart from each other. To both it seemed as though the authorities had locked them up and forgotten them; they were forbidden to cash bank notes or to purchase food. Yet, despite the terror, the starvation, and the loneliness, not one missionary fell sick and died in China. As one saying in the mission goes, 'neither a hoof nor a husband was left behind.'

As soon as the mission announced the 'withdrawal,' it also announced its intention to expand activities to the Chinese diaspora in East Asia, to Malaysia, Thailand, Japan, and Formosa. It is eerie reading through *China's Millions*, the CIM magazine, for this period. There are many articles about the 'new outreach,' and reprints from years before (including one meditation by Hudson Taylor written in 1888). There is no mention of what was happening in China; only a few cryptic comments disclose the clenched teeth:

At the end of April [1951] approximately three hundred of our missionaries and a little over one hundred children were still on the mainland of China. Prolonged delays and 'hope deferred' are not easy to bear. Some are in particularly trying circumstances ... May we be very faithful in this, bearing up before the throne of grace these missionaries and children as well as the sorely tried church in China.

There was a feeling in the organization, widespread but seldom mentioned in public accounts, that the mission – which now changed its name to the Overseas Missionary Fellowship – was emphasizing these new fields to the detriment of those missionaries who decided not to go to a new country or learn a new language. There was often ill will on both sides when a pastor came home and was reduced to selling Fuller brushes door-to-door, or when a forty-year-old nurse, after twenty years spent running a hospital in China, could barely get work as an assistant nurse in British Columbia.

The sad fact of the matter was that few people in Canada wanted to hear the missionaries' 'truth about China' any more. The post-war period was one of 'new beginnings,' new outreaches, and it was better to put aside the past and get on with the present than to dwell on the supposed 'lessons to be learned from China.' 'I don't hear anything,' wrote the English Bishop Ronald Hall of Hong Kong to the Canadian MSCC, 'and I refuse to be a listening post. Remember Lot's wife who looked back.' Lot's wife was a common metaphor in those days.

These were dangerous times to speak out on behalf of 'Red China.' Debate in the United States was stifled by the powerful China lobby with its Committee of One Million, who signed a petition against allowing the People's Republic into the United Nations. In the United States, the missionary voices tended to be extreme; they included people like Walter Judd, a retired missionary surgeon turned senator who passed on information to McCarthy; Henry Luce of *Time–Life* who looked back nostalgically to his old Chinese amah; Pearl Buck and, posthumously, John Birch, a missionary whose death at the hands of the Chinese communists was taken up as the first American martyrdom of 'a war that is still being waged.' Moderate spokespeople like K.S. Latourette, the mission historian, or the sinologist Owen Lattimore were denounced by the McCarthy witch-hunts as part of the 'left-wing conspiracy' that had 'lost China.'

As one American newspaper noted in 1951: 'On medieval maps the parts of the world that were still unknown or unexplored were marked with an inscription: *Hic sunt leones*, Here are the lions. Now we can write: Here are the Reds. And that's all.' This continued to be the U.S. policy towards China for the next twenty years. As late as 1966, one respondent to a Gallup poll summed up the general attitude: 'Here is a big, hostile country, going ahead, developing, without our knowing very much about what is going on. It is frightening to think about.'

The fury of the cold war did not occur in Canada as severely as in the United States, at least as far as China was concerned (the Soviet Union was another matter, especially after the Gouzenko case), and this moderation can be attributed in major part to two institutions that permitted (if they did not exactly encourage) debate: the Canadian government in the form of the Department of External Affairs, and the United Church of Canada. These two were not unrelated: Dr Jesse Arnup of the Board of Overseas Missions wrote early in 1950 to West China, 'Did I tell you about my trip to Ottawa to urge upon the government the question of recognition of the new regime in China? I found a curious situation. The Minister, Lester Pearson, is the son of a well known Methodist minister; his deputy [Escott Reid] is the son of an Anglican minister; his Secretary is Jerry Riddell, whose father was Principal of Wesley College, Winnipeg; the specialist on the Far East is Arthur Menzies, son of Jimmy [J.M.] Menzies of Honan; his Number One man in Japan is Herbert Norman, Dan Norman's son; and his leading representative in China is Ronning, who is the son of a missionary. I felt quite at home among them all.'

This situation in Ottawa was in distinct contrast to the United States, where the missionaries' sons in the State Department, like John Service and John Davies who had established the 'Dixie Mission' to open discussions with the communists, were considered part of the enemy; the messengers were denounced as 'soft on communism.' Ottawa was a disinterested observer of the civil war in China, and therefore had much less to lose. But, if the men in External Affairs were willing to listen, it was even more important that their informants in China had the courage to speak.

They had their man in Chester Alvin Ronning, son of Norwegian-American Lutheran missionaries in Central China. After his mother's death and his father's retirement, Ronning's family had moved to Valhalla, in the Peace River country of Alberta. Young Chester graduated from the Camrose Normal School and went to China under the YMCA in 1922, where he was stationed at his birthplace of Fancheng [now XIANGFAN], Hupei [HUBEI] province. Although he had retired after the Northern Expedition in 1927, he had sympathized with the reformists, and afterwards, as Principal of Camrose Lutheran College, he was elected as a CCF MPP in Alberta. When General Victor Odlum asked for a Chinese-speaking first secretary for the embassy in China, almost by accident Chester Ronning went to China.

As a prairie populist, Ronning found himself with sympathy for the revolution and, almost as soon as he arrived in Chungking in November 1945, he started discussions with the communist leaders, especially with Chou En-lai, who was stationed there as Mao's negotiator. Ronning's views clashed with Odlum's, but Odlum was replaced in 1947 by a much more congenial ambassador, the Honourable Thomas C. Davis, who had been an appeals court judge in Saskatchewan and Odlum's successor as high commissioner to Australia.

As he wrote to Ottawa in one of his first despatches, Ambassador Davis was confronted with trying to make sense of what was happening in China. It was T.C. Davis's personal feeling that 'Chinese Communism is an evil thing; also that the Nationalist Government is evil, but that I have to decide whether the two are equally evil ... I am of the opinion that the Nationalist Government is the lesser of two evils, and that if I were called upon to advise the Government of Canada which of the two to aid and support, I would without hesitation urge the support of the Nationalist cause.' When he discussed this with Chester Ronning and G.S. Patterson, they asked, 'On what basis do you make this decision? If on the basis of cruelty and brutal practices, they state that in their opinion there is nothing to choose between the two ... if a decision must be made between the two, it must be made on the basis of Communism on the one side and the system of a degree of free enterprise within an authoritarian state, as prevails in China.' In the end, 'with hesitation,' Davis wrote, he would still support the government, in the increasingly vain hope that Chiang Kai-shek would reform it and oust the reactionaries (many of them members of his wife's family). His despatches, and those of Ronning, also reported the other side, the communist position.

Davis's policy shocked many people, including General Odlum, now Ambassador to Turkey; six months after this letter, Odlum started a barrage of letters to Ottawa and to Davis himself, complaining that Davis's views were 'almost a direct contradiction to the one I submitted to you when I was in China ... *Mr. Davis is now reporting the very stories which were told me nearly four years ago,* and which, I then discovered, emanated from ... the dissident, or left wing, element in the American Embassy – the element which General Hurley denounced when he returned to Washington ... The propaganda of the Communists caught on ... And it received a final coating of respectability from a small group of very fine, able, devoted but leftist members of the Canadian Missionaries in China.' General Odlum felt so strongly that, at the end of 1948 when the Kuomintang regime was collapsing like a house of cards, he wrote an unauthorized personal letter to Madam Chiang Kai-shek urging her to return to China from her American exile to stand beside the Generalissimo. 'It must be the two of you, acting as one – you inspiring, and he carrying the flag and doing the hard administrative work ... I want to see the Generalissimo win – to be the historic figure who will successfuly introduce Western democracy to the Chinese people.'

In place of such sentimental claptrap, Ambassador Davis was writing 'bleak' despatches from Nanking, trying to report the 'disjointed mass of inconsistencies and double talk' that passed for 'peace negotiations' and 'cleverly devised political manoeuvre[s].' In particular, he excoriated Chiang's attempt to characterize the situation in China not as a civil war but as a world war between Soviet communism and Free World capitalism. He sympathized with the disenchantment of American Ambassador Leighton Stuart, former president of Yenching University, 'who has had more faith in the Generalissimo than any other man I know,' and like him recommended that his government face the inevitable and recognize the new government as soon as it was established. This recognition, he urged, must be not only *de facto* but also *de jure*, differentiating between the communist 'regime' and the communist 'government' of China: 'I am afraid that Uncle Sam is going to smell to high heaven before this show is over,' he wrote at Christmas 1948; his prescience was noted by an External Affairs official in a pencilled marginal comment that said simply, eloquently, '1955.'

If there ever was a 'lost opportunity' in China, it happened in the first months of 1949, before and after the fall of Nanking. In a concerted gesture of solidarity, all the foreign embassies remained in Nanking – except, significantly, the Soviet embassy – despite intense pressure to follow the Kuomintang, thus continuing their *de jure* recognition of the KMT. Britain, with its worries about Hong Kong, and India, with its concern about Tibet, were the leaders in the move to recognize the new government.

The United States, consumed by fear of communism, took the opposite position of delaying recognition. In the end, it refused to heed the advice of its own ambassador, the gentle, indecisive Dr Stuart, and listened instead to career diplomats who had 'such a hatred for Communism and Russia that they cannot conceive of the United States being forced to recognize a straight or camouflaged Communist Government.'

Canada's policy, like that of other Commonwealth members, was aligned with that of Britain, and in one final attempt to mediate an Anglo-American policy, Ambassador Davis sought to soften the American position. As Ronning was the foreign diplomat best able to speak Chinese, he became the liaison officer between the Western diplomats and the incoming communists, who refused to speak English; 'You speak Chinese or you don't talk now,' Davis reported to Ottawa. And how

Ronning could talk! Through contacts built up over years, he talked with the Americans, with the British, and with the Indians. He talked to the Foreign Nationals Bureau, he talked to Chou En-lai in the middle of the night, he talked to Mao himself. Then, after Davis was recalled to Ottawa for 'consultations' – since according to protocol he was accredited to the Kuomintang government – and Ronning was named chargé d'affaires, he poured out his talk in reports to External Affairs. He almost became a 'one-trick pony' in his single-minded pursuit of Canadian recognition of the People's Republic. 'When you stand for months at receiving end of bombs falling from planes sent by corrupt and discredited regime and see wanton destruction of life and property long after civil war has ended,' he wrote in one spirited telegram, 'you pray daily that all support which recognition may give will be withdrawn, remnants of [the Kuomintang] Government thrown out of China and recognition granted to the real Government.'

As the precious months slipped away, Ronning's pleas fell on ears that were not deaf, merely preoccupied. In Ottawa the isolationism of Mackenzie King's government was shifting to the internationalism of Louis St Laurent, which shaped a broad, continental North American foreign policy. Canada could entertain private doubts about American policy, but in public forums like the U.N., it would have to toe the line as a 'junior member' of the alliance, hoping to act as a 'counterweight' in private. Escott Reid, playing the devil's advocate in Ottawa, even queried the basic assumptions for recognition of China: 'It is hard to see that there is any Western national interest served by assisting the Communist regime in China to become stable or get anywhere.'

Then, having driven China into the reluctant arms of Russia, American policy opted for silence, enunciated in Truman's 'hands off' doctrine. Stalin saw Mao as a rival for the leadership of international communism, and in early 1950, he forced Mao to trek to Moscow for a niggardly, cash-basis Sino-Soviet treaty. Ronning contended that Mao would take an independent line, like a 'Tito-in-Asia,' and advised he remain in Nanking to negotiate Sino-Canadian recognition with the Chinese based on 'equality, mutual benefit and utter respect for territorial sovereignty.' Chester Ronning was still talking, desperately; he had rented a house in Peking and was ready to move there when the clock struck midnight and moved on.

On 2 January 1951, Ottawa cabled Ronning to return to Canada 'in view of your long period of service abroad and continued separation from your family.' On 26 February, he lowered the Canadian flag for the last time from the Nanking embassy, hoping that a new embassy 'will soon be re-established in the new capital of China.' He did not mean Taipei. Since Ronning by this time was considered the agent of a hostile power, despite the personal regard felt for him by the Chinese, he was subjected to an intensive nine-hour search at Canton. On arrival in Hong Kong, he was greeted with a telegram from Ottawa:

I am sure you appreciate need to be circumspect in dealing with press. You will be subject of great interest and probably closely questioned. Please confine your statements to press to platitudes until you have seen us.

Another voice fell to mouthing circumspect platitudes.

The 'indefinite' postponement of Canadian recognition of the People's Republic of China did not end debate, which came up regularly in parliament and in the United Nations, especially after the cessation of the Korean War. But each time the debate became more tenuous, more abstract, based on third- and fourth-hand reports.

Although one can state with some assurance that the vast majority of Canadian missionaries supported Chiang Kai-shek personally, and in varying degrees still supported his regime, there were few missionary demagogues of the right in Canada. One was the Australian-born Reverend Leslie Millin, the best orator of the China Inland Mission, who spoke of the communist concentration camps and brainwashing sessions as though he had actually experienced them. (He was convicted in the late 1950s, in British Columbia, of fraud in a pyramid-sales scam for a product called Nutri-Bio, a vitamin supplement whose profits were to be used to beam gospel radio into China.)

Canadian Catholics, too, were uniformly against communist China; but again, unlike such American Catholics as Bishop Fulton Sheen and Francis Cardinal Spellman, who became outspoken cold warriors, their voices tended to be restricted to the classrooms and pulpits of their own church. Monsignor William C. McGrath, former superior of the Scarboro mission, took a statue of the Pilgrim Virgin of Fatima on extensive tours of Canada and the United States, preaching 'Fatima or World Suicide': 'Ten years more, that's about all!' he predicted in 1955; 'Fifteen, maybe, at the outside! By then the Reds will have taken over America. No war. No hydrogen bombs. No mass slaughter – till after the victory has been won ... The men who sold five hundred million Chinese into Communist slavery will finally betray America ...

in China a Red officer recently told a departing missionary ... "We will be one hundred times as cruel when we take over America."'

In 1957–9, in face of renewed debate in Ottawa, the Catholic missionary orders, in company with La Sainte-Enfance launched an extensive Canada-wide crusade that encouraged elementary school children to 'buy' Chinese orphans, and parishioners to send identically worded statements to their MPs: 'As a Catholic and as a Canadian, I protest most vehemently against Canadian government's decision to recognize the godless Red China Government. Think of the future!" This was also the time of renewed military activity over the shelling of Quemoy and Matsu, and in one of his few public statements, Bishop Philippe Côté of Suchow reportedly suggested that 'an atomic bomb or two dropped on China would do nothing but good for humanity and that the Chinese themselves wanted it' to free them from their communist oppressors.

Most Canadian missionaries, however, eschewed demagoguery, preferring to keep their own counsel, and to wait and pray. Like Bishop White, they drifted off into the past: as one Honan missionary wrote to External Affairs in 1950, 'The greatest mistake we [Canada] could ever make is to disregard the *real* China, by the *real*, I mean, the *old* China, which in a small nucleus *STILL* exists in the old Nationalist party.' The School of Chinese Studies (later the Department of East Asian Studies) at the University of Toronto, the only school in Canada to teach Chinese, followed the same policy. From its founding in 1934 to the mid-1960s, it was under three successive missionaries: Bishop White, Lewis Walmsley of West China, and William A.C.H. Dobson, who had gone to China under the CIM in 1936. With its close connection to the Royal Ontario Museum, the school became world-renowned for its studies of ancient China: White on Shang culture, J.M. Menzies on the oracle bones, Walmsley on T'ang poetry, Dobson on Mencius. Chinese history seemingly ended in 1949; beyond that was spoken of as 'the current regime.'

(Notwithstanding this trend, Dr Walmsely gave an eloquent plea in 1958, after a trip to the People's Republic of China: 'We can inform ourselves,' he said on the CBC-radio 'University of the Air' series, 'by every possible means of what is actually going on there, keeping our vision clear of preconceived prejudices, rather than isolate ourselves from them with non-recognition of their peasant government ... I believe the time has come when it is an essential to survival to understand communism and cease to shun it as if we were uncertain of the ground whereon we stand.')

A number of Canadian 'sympathetic observers' did come out of the Chinese revolution. Not surprisingly, most were United Church of Canada members who chose to question the church's 'establishment' line in what came to be known as 'the Endicott controversy.'

Chiang Kai-shek's wartime capital in Chungking had scored deep divisions in the West China mission. On one hand the missionaries had the thrill of being at the heart of the action, able to influence the events of history over tea with Madam Chiang. On the other hand, they could see firsthand the corruption of the Kuomintang regime: the graft, the bully-boy tactics, the mysterious disappearances, and the inflation that spiralled beyond human comprehension – from $4 Chinese National Currency to one U.S. dollar during the war to $3 000 000 CNC to the U.S. dollar by 1948. But Szechuan was riddled with underground groups; and by listening to these cells, some Canadian missionaries allowed themselves to be re-educated.

The leader of this group of 'very fine, able, devoted but leftist' missionaries (as General Odlum called them) was the Reverend James Gareth Endicott, always the most outspoken member of the mission. It was a small group, numbering perhaps eight or ten out of the fifty United Church missionaries in the late 1940s, and included Earl Willmott and Katharine Hockin of West China and two North Honan people, William Mitchell and Donald Faris. These people had certain things in common; they were all teachers, for example. Half were second-generation missionaries, but all were deeply influenced by the SCM Sharman method of Bible study. Once one learns to question the ground of one's faith – 'Who is this man Jesus?' – then it is easier to question accepted political dogma: What is the Christian mission to 'the people' when the government is corrupt (or, alternately, when it is a 'people's government' that is good but godless)?

Most missionaries, when forced to choose sides, stuck at the 'godless-ness' of communism. Others, especially medical people like Dr Leslie Kilborn, stuck at what they perceived as the anti-scientific basis of the new regime. Dr Kilborn, too, was a second-generation missionary; he had come out to China in the same ship as Earl Willmott in 1921 and had remained equally conscientious in Sharman studies. But, as a medical doctor, Kilborn's questioning was directed towards scientific examination. Like his father before him, Dr Leslie had no dialogue with Chinese medicine; he considered acupuncture and herbal medicine bunk and superstition. And what he saw under communism was a lowering of standards, a return to the days of folk medicine and 'barefoot doctors,' a situation he could neither understand nor condone. He would be willing to work under a communist government as long as his Christian, scientific message was permitted.

Dr Kilborn's approach, like that of most missionaries, was to face the end of his life's work by working feverishly to build an institution that would survive, a memorial to Christianity in China. The small political group was more vocal, and their questioning led them, like Jim Endicott, to 'active participation in political controversy.' After his stint with the New Life Movement at the beginning of the Japanese war, Endicott became such a vitriolic critic both of the Kuomintang and of Chiang Kai-shek personally that he was marked by the secret police and, on one occasion, threatened with an unexploded grenade on his speaker's podium.

But Endicott had resigned from the mission and from the ministry in 1946, to publish *The Far Eastern Newsletter* in Shanghai. It is still a matter of debate whether the mission or the board suggested he resign; in effect it was both, in the person of the Reverend Gerald S. Bell, long-term secretary of the mission and by then acting secretary of the Board of Overseas Missions in Toronto (replacing Dr Jesse Arnup, who was the moderator that year). Bell warned Endicott unofficially that his actions were 'jeopardizing the influence of the whole Christian movement.' When pressed, the mission executive expressed their support for Endicott, resolving that members of the Christian 'fellowship should be willing to lead in all movements for the uplift of the people ... In the pursuit of those ends we realize that members ... may often find themselves in opposition to entrenched selfish interests.' But such assurances were not enough, and Endicott resigned because, as he said, he felt 'called to take an active part in the struggle for human betterment in the field of social and political movements, areas of life that are considered unsuitable for ministers to be active in unless possibly they happen to be on the "right" side.'

All this was kept secret; but two years later, when Endicott made a cross-Canada tour 'boasting' that within a year the 'monster' Chiang Kai-shek would be dead, or in jail, or in exile, the board in Toronto chose to silence him. Reluctantly, thoughtfully, patiently, as one would do to a member of the family – yet none the less firmly – Dr Arnup took up his pen to write a letter to the United Church, 'a statement with reference to the campaign being conducted across Canada by the Reverend J.G. Endicott, formerly a missionary of the church.' This statement in *The Observer* reminded its readers that Endicott had made exaggerated statements before and that Dr Arnup could not agree with his characterization of Chiang Kai-shek as a 'Lincoln' in 1941 and a 'monster' in 1948. In addition, Arnup published the correspondence between Endicott and the board to show positively that he had not been 'kicked out of the United Church and its missionary work,' as he had alleged.

On the face of it, Arnup's statement was a matter-of-fact document, couched in formal language; in reality, however, it was harsh and uncompromising. It was printed baldly with no explanation, no previous mention of Endicott or his campaign, and no discussion of what he was saying or why. One can understand the reason for the silence of the CIM *China's Millions* or the MIC *Le Précurseur* – terror; but the reticence of *The Observer* signalled more than just an argument between Jim Endicott and Dr Arnup; it highlighted the collision of the United Church's traditional Christian socialism with dialectical Marxism. Endicott was tainted – 'pinkist,' Arnup called him privately – and by his resignation put himself outside the church. But the contagion spread among United Church ministers and lay people and coalesced to become one strand of the Peace Movement of the 1950s, the first 'Ban-the-Bomb' movement.

Dr Arnup sought to silence Endicott, to catch him in his own contradictions. 'He is suing the Toronto *Telegram* for calling him a Communist and he is technically,' Arnup wrote to Dr Kilborn. 'I believe he is not a member of the Board but he is what we would commonly call a fellow traveller.' (Endicott was not a communist, as he stated many times. 'I am a Christian. It is not possible to be both.') To H.J. Veals, acting secretary of the mission, he wrote: 'On Monday last his father [Dr James Endicott] spoke to the Ministerial meeting in Toronto and took Jim's side 100 [per cent]. I felt rather badly in view of the fact that we have tried for about ten years to draw him out of retirement to make an occasional missionary address but without success. Then when Jim got involved in controversy he took the platform and made it a little more difficult for us.'

The Observer, the most influential religious magazine in Canada, tried to steer a middle ground between Endicott and Arnup, publishing letters and articles for and against both positions. In fact, some of the letters to the editor are quite vituperative, like one that claimed that 'a large part of the Church is identified with reaction and the old order, which order will pull the house down with it in its inevitable and final collapse.' (A curious point arises here: Dr Arnup always claimed that most of the correspondence he received was 'wide and sympathetic ... Only two men thought it was hard on Jim and they are of a decided pinkish hue. Most writers commended it for its gentle treatment of one who has gone out from us.' Most of the letters to *The Observer*, however, are decidedly hostile. All this was very hard on Dr Arnup personally, as he wrote to Earl Willmott: 'I am not a reactionary. During recent years I have usually voted socialist in this country; not so much because I was a convinced follower of the socialist party, but in order that I might say to the older parties, "A plague on both your houses."') In addition, *The Observer* did publish warnings to the church to face the inevitable. In July 1948, while denying Endicott's campaign, it published an editorial, 'In China Now,' which said, 'The crucial need for our Church literature about China seems to me to be the preparation of the minds of our people for the collapse of the Government in China, and the possibility of the wiping out of our organized work there.'

In all this debate in *The Observer*, however, missionary voices were almost entirely absent; the debate had been taken out of their hands. There is no mention, for example, of the fall of the North Honan mission, except one terse sentence about the deputation visiting East Asia in 1947: 'if possible they will visit Honan missionaries who are at present evacuated from that area.' Even Jim Endicott was conspicuous by his absence, except for an occasional attempt to refute slanderous charges; rather he is a nameless shadow behind such subversive groups as the 'peace congress' and the Stockholm appeal to ban nuclear weapons, or a sort of shorthand symbol for a particular faction, as in 'Endicott and the others.'

Missionaries only appear out of a vacuum to prove a point: the Reverend A.C. Hoffman, a twenty-five-year veteran, asked: 'Why cannot J.G. Endicott in his attitude claim a single member of our South China missionary group? ... frankly, I would respect him much more so, if he would somehow make it quite clear that he is a devoted Communist, *but for certain reasons*, had not actually entered into Communist membership.' (One might ask the same question in expectation of a different answer: why did the South China mission, alone of the three United Church groups, reject the communist liberation?) Dr E.C. Wilford, dean of medicine at WCUU, agreed that, 'About 90 per cent of our missionaries *on the field* are pro-Chiang Kai-shek and were very annoyed at some of the "stuff" appearing in your valuable periodical.'

These letters were published at a time when others in Chengtu were writing, as Dr Gladys Cunningham did: 'I believe there is a very small proportion of the missionaries of the United Church of Canada, who are in Szechuan now, who approve of the Kuomintang or its policies. Few of them but believe that Chiang has long ago served his days of usefulness.'

Over the next year, both Dr Arnup and *The Observer* perceptibly softened their stance against the communist regime. In November 1949, Arnup wrote an 'optimistic' letter to the field after an interview with Ambassador T.C. Davis, who had recently returned from Nanking. 'When the Communists see that great institution you have there [the West China Union University] they are not going to do anything to disturb it,' Davis had told him. Further, he had said, 'He hopes the time will soon come when we can resume our work in areas now evacuated and urges that we hold our men in readiness.' At the beginning of the New Year, Dr Arnup wrote the first of his many letters to Ottawa strongly urging the Canadian government to recognize the communists as the government of China.

But the United Church was not alone in West China, and in the last days the missionaries found themselves fighting on two fronts, against the communists and against 'a hoard of refugees' from North China 'who represent a "type of Christianity" new to most of the people around here,' Dr Kilborn wrote. 'They are extreme fundamentalists and the burden of their message seems to be that the world is ending tomorrow or the day after and that the most of us including all missionaries not of their denomination are going to be swept up in the holocaust and will suffer eternal damnation. Not long ago I heard one senior missionary in Chengtu say that the two greatest problems facing the youth of Szechuan were Communism and Fundamentalism.' (The same apocalyptic urgency was evident in the fundamentalist churches in Canada; one sign in Toronto's People's Church read: 'Ministers – Leave your pulpits! Doctors – Leave your patients! Teachers – Leave your pupils! Craftsmen – Leave your tools! THE FIELDS ARE WHITE UNTO HARVEST!') The larger question was which Christian group could survive longer under communist domination, the politicized, institutional United Church, or the individualized sects that could disappear underground, could 'die with Christ' to be reborn later.

The liberal missions, the ones that were willing to communicate with the new government, seemed to succeed at first. Many of the West China Canadians accepted the Christian Manifesto: 'Our people like the general tone of the ideas,' wrote H.J. Veals; 'what they say about imperialism is not the important thing. The important thing is that they remain true to Christ and His church.' Earl Willmott wrote enthusiastically of how he had been 'learning to participate in democratic processes' at the university, where he was attending 'innumerable meetings where everybody has full opportunity to say anything and all that he wants to say.' (Willmott wrote two articles in 1953 on 'The Church in New China,' and these created another controversy, because they, too, appeared out of a vacuum, prompting one woman to write to *The Observer*, 'I know nothing about Mr Willmott, and very little about China. However ... if he is sincere he has a right to express that opinion even in *The Observer*.')

The coming of the Korean War ended the co-operation between the missionaries in the field and the Chinese government. Nothing showed this more than the imprisonment of Dr Stewart Allen, who had reported favourably on the communist hospitals in 1946. He and his nurse, Constance Ward, were 'invited' to attend a meeting that turned out to be their own four-hour accusation ordeal. They had to kneel on the stage, their backs to the audience, facing a portrait of Chairman Mao – 'China's little Stalin,' Dr Allen called him – while hospital employees, mostly labourers, screamed prepared stories. The charges were not trumped up, but they were blown out of proportion: the most serious was that by not paying taxes amounting to one dollar on certain UNRRA drugs, he had denigrated the government. 'What shall we do with this devil in our midst?' the people were asked: 'and that meant going straight to jail.'

Dr Allen was under the erroneous impression that he could reason with his captors, that he could explain what had happened. The communist cadres, on the other hand, believed exactly the opposite; they would explain and he would listen and, moreover, he would learn self-criticism. There, in a tiny room in the Chungking hospital, night after night for eight months, the final deaf and dumb conversation was played out under a naked light bulb. Finally, after Dr Allen had signed his confession, he was held for a further two months in the common city jail until his exit permit was processed and he was escorted to Canton.

Three months later, in March 1952, the last six missionaries of the United Church cleared their books and left Chengtu. As they came across the border, two of them, Earl Willmott and William Small, son of 'Mission Builder' Walter Small and bursar of West China Union University, wore the blue cotton uniforms of the Chinese peasants and, when questioned by reporters, gave glowing reports of New China. 'There is no persecution of Christians that I knew anything about,' Willmott was quoted as saying, even though, as Catholic critics pointed out, he was accompanied on the train by a French priest who was still a prisoner. The picture of Willmott and Small holding their raised fists in the communist salute was widely broadcast throughout the world, even appearing in *The Illustrated London News*.

The third male in the party, Dr Leslie Kilborn, was not quoted as saying anything. Neither were the three wives. Privately, Dr Jean Millar Kilborn wrote, 'For me it was a relief to have the Willmotts off and on their way ... In Chengtu, we had to keep completely off politics ... We so often felt like hypocrites – accepting the hospitality of the W's and feeling about them as we did "inside."' To Ed and Gladys Cunningham, she wrote, 'Earl is spoken of "as a dangerous man." And his ruthless statements give me great fear ... How can anyone with experiences of Communism so fresh in mind delight to hear reports of its progress elsewhere?????!!!!!! It is regrettable that ugly politics has to come into our lives.'

On the very day that the Kilborns, the Willmotts, and the Smalls were crossing the bridge into Hong Kong, Jim Endicott was inspecting the battlefields of North Korea, where several Chinese scientists showed him canisters dropped by the American planes. These, the scientists explained, contained deadly viruses, infected rodents, and napalm. The Americans had admitted using napalm and, Endicott reasoned, to any country using such heinous weapons, 'germ warfare would seem merely a natural, logical, and in some ways more attractive, extension of existing weaponry.'

To those of us weaned on the Vietnam war, it does not seem beyond belief that the United States had already begun its descent into military hell – and, indeed, there is some indirect evidence for Endicott's assertions. But in the hysteria of 1952, American germ warfare was unthinkable. The Canadian government branded Dr Endicott 'Public Enemy Number One,' and considered arresting him for treason. *Maclean's* magazine splashed the headline: 'How Dr Endicott Fronts for the Reds.'

In rebuttal, Endicott and his supporters – he commanded a fair sector of Canadian public opinion by this time – organized a mammoth rally in Toronto's Maple Leaf Gardens that degenerated at times into violence and shouting. The rally was addressed by the senior Dr Endicott, brought out of retirement once more to defend his son. People still whisper that the old man – he was eighty-eight – was senile, but he certainly gave a lucid, inspiring connection between Jim's early upbringing, particularly between the lines from the children's song 'Dare to be a Daniel,/ Dare to stand alone' and Jim's present social conscience.

These two events were the last reprise of the Endicott controversy of four years before. Dr Arnup was quoted in the Canadian papers as saying that he had known for some time that Earl Willmott had pro-communist views, but it came as a surprise that William Small, one of the respected younger men of the mission, had joined him. The Toronto *Telegram*, a conservative newspaper, went further in quoting Arnup as saying that some sort of 'punishment' would be brought to bear on the two; but, he added, he hoped that they would take their time, so that he himself would have retired before their arrival in Canada. That was indeed what happened, but in one of his final acts as mission secretary, Arnup wrote a stiffly worded order 'not to talk about China,' which was delivered to Willmott personally, as he disembarked at Halifax, by three representatives of the church who had come from Toronto specifically for that purpose. Willmott wrote several letters to Dr Arnup and to his successor, David Gallagher, asking for help in finding employment within the church; but they did not help. Finally, he found a teaching position at Mount Royal College in Calgary on condition he never be seen with Jim Endicott in public.

Another voice fell silent.

There was only one voice left, and the United Church brought all its power to bear against it, denying Jim Endicott access to *The Observer* while sentencing him *in absentia*. His severest critic this time was Dr Allen, who wrote an emotional article for *Maclean's* magazine entitled, 'I Was a Prisoner of the Chinese Reds,' which was pointedly described as 'the first eyewitness report from China by a Canadian non-Communist.' *The Observer* called this a 'splendid article' and gave Dr Allen a wide hearing, publishing as many as four articles by or about him in a single issue.

When the Fifteenth General Council of the church met in September, the 'Endicott case' came up for discussion within the first hour of the sessions. One speaker, pointing to Endicott sitting in the balcony, said, 'If evil is there, let's name it.' Finally, after days of debate, the council voted unanimously to disassociate itself, 'with all Christian charity,' from Endicott and the peace congress. The following day, Dr Allen, who was a delegate, seconded a resolution to the effect that 'By all international standards our country should recognize forthwith this government save for one fact, namely, that it is supporting the opposition to the forces of the United Nations in Korea.' As soon as an armistice was signed, Canada should 'forthwith' extend recognition.

For the present, the United Church had joined the ranks of the silent. Like the Bishop of Shanghai, it ordered the faithful: 'Do not listen! Do not speak! Do not sign!'

Chou En-lai said, 'While China is putting its house in order, it is undesirable for guests to be present.' And so all the systems shut down.

In 1951, Dr Arnup warned returning missionaries that they were 'missing golden opportunities to keep their mouths shut ... In all public addresses we should especially avoid any attempt to interpret the relationship of Chinese Christians or missionaries to the Chinese government ... this should not be construed as to interfere with expressions on the part of individuals regarding American foreign policy.'

Mrs H.D. Taylor, secretary of the WMS, issued a sharper note to its women: 'Absolutely no public appearances should be made by anyone from China.'

'The last message from friends in China,' wrote Dr Jean Kilborn from Hong Kong, was 'Tell everyone NOT to write. When it is safe to write, we will write first.' According to Earl Willmott, the message to the Canadian churches was that the church in China was 'lost, gone, extinguished; there was no message.'

The last Canadian Catholic missionaries in China were three Jesuits from Suchow, who were expelled in 1955. When they 'took the train from Canton, a curtain of silence closed upon their work left to be done.'

The last Canadian Protestant was Miss Helen Willis, an independent Brethren missionary, who was allowed to operate a gospel bookstore in Shanghai until late in 1958. She was never arrested, unlike two British Jehovah's Witnesses and the American Bishop J.E. Walsh (Bishop Walsh was the last American missionary to leave China, because he had renounced his American citizenship and therefore could not be deported until 1970, after twelve years in prison), who were still in Shanghai. Miss Willis had been interrogated at length over five weeks, brought to trial on charges of 'counter-revolutionary sabotage activities,' and expelled on 27 April 1959. Her trial, she said, 'had produced no unpleasantness and that at all times she was treated courteously. Some 20 to 30 pastors attended her trial and she reports that the reason for this was that her case was to be the subject of the next Sunday's sermons in the remaining Shanghai churches.'

Actually two Canadian missionaries did remain in China: Father Paul

Sisters leaving Shanghai just before the arrival of the communists, 1949

Kam, the China-born pioneer missionary sent out by the Scarboro Foreign Mission Society, and Dr Victoria Cheung, Canadian-born head of the United Church hospital at Kongmoon. (A.C. Hoffman was wrong; one South China missionary *was* willing to work with the communists.) Dr Cheung died in 1962, with no further communication from Canada. Father Kam disappeared without a trace.

Epilogue:
The Lost Churches

'The China of the year 2000 will be very different from the China of 1900.'

Sir Robert Hart, on the Boxer Rebellion, 1901

'The missionaries have been building the scaffolding around this building of the church. Now the scaffolding is being taken away, and we will see what kind of a building we have erected.'

Rev. Arnold Lea, China Director of the CIM, 1950

'I can remember giving my story of leaving China,' said Dr Katharine Hockin, one of the 'sympathetic observers' who came out of West China in 1951, 'and so many people, they would look at me, and you felt the admiration ... I almost felt as though they thought I had God on a leash, like a little poodle, and He obediently came out of China with me.'

An odd metaphor, but many people at the time felt that Christianity had been left to die in China. It had never taken deep roots, had always been a small minority – about one-half of 1 per cent in 1949, three million Catholics and Protestants combined. Three times the Chinese government – Manchu, Republican, and Communist – had tried to evict it; the third time they succeeded. According to Marxist propaganda, the people would slough off all religion like a dead skin.

Now we see that the church did not die. It fell silent. The trials of Chinese Christians during those years would fill many books, but the history can be summarized briefly.

Last class of the Chefoo Schools, then located at Kuling, 1950

Christianity in China survived with comparative freedom until the late 1950s in three forms: the Three-Self or patriotic Catholic church, the Three-Self Protestant church, and small underground congregations, the so-called 'house churches.' Somewhere lost in the shuffle was a Roman Catholic church loyal to Rome, negligible because it was not recognized and because it had no clergy. (They either apostacized or were jailed.) The government guaranteed – in theory, if not always in practice – religious freedom. Though religion might be an opiate, as Marx had originally meant it, an opiate could be a comfort in difficult times. But first, the government expected – nay, demanded – patriotism. 'Minority groups with minority voices had no place in the China of the 1950s and '60s,' commented one historian. 'Recalcitrant, dissenting or stubbornly independent leaders were singled out, harassed, publicly denounced and removed from office. Ordinary believers found the limits on religious practice steadily tightened throughout this period.'

The plant (schools, hospitals, missionary residences) belonging to the foreign missions was confiscated – or, as in the case of the CIM headquarters, purchased. Significantly, the properties belonging to the Three-Self churches, the Christian Literature Society, and the YMCAS were not expropriated outright, although some of these organizations were forced to sell because of other pressures. Certain church buildings remained open for public worship, while others, especially those in outlying districts or ones that had been bombed during the war, remained boarded up for years. Still others were declared 'redundant' and converted into public halls, kindergartens, and warehouses. The evangelical 'house' churches, of course, owned no property and officially did not exist.

Mission schools and hospitals generally retained their functions and were incorporated into the state structure. Thus West China Union University was amalgamated with Szechuan University, across the city of Chengtu, so that today it specializes in teaching medicine and dentistry. The Marion Barclay Hospital in Kongmoon, another example, became the People's Number Eight Hospital.

In 1958 with the Great Leap Forward, and again in 1966 with the Cultural Revolution, Mao Tse-Tung loosed his little-red-book-waving masses to denounce heretics and revisionists. The Cultural Revolution is often seen in the West as anti-religious; it was more than that. It was anti-institutional. The government abolished its own Religious Affairs Bureau and banished the Three-Self churches. During this period, the Red Guards reduced the Kaifeng cathedral to rubble and carted its Jewish antiquities to the city museum. The Protestant Nanking seminary, the only one that had been allowed to continue – no Catholic ones were – was closed in 1966, along with all centres of worship, except for one mosque in Peking that served the foreign community.

The silence of the Chinese church deepened. But, when Christians – the 'recalcitrant, dissenting' ones – were sent away for re-education to camps, they made contact with other dissenters. They would start a cell for prayer and Bible study, thus spreading the witness faster than it might have had the believers remained isolated from each other.

Active persecution of the church ended with the death of Mao and the subsequent downfall of the Gang of Four in 1978. The Three-Self Protestant church was re-established in that year, and two years later the Nanking Seminary was reopened under the direction of Bishop K.H. Ting, a former student secretary with the Student Christian Movement of Canada in the late 1940s. Bishop Ting visited Toronto the following year, as part of his trip to the meeting of the World Council of Churches in New York, the first Chinese observer in thirty years. His visit culminated in a sermon at Timothy Eaton Memorial Church. The trip was more than symbolic (though it was that, too); it was the visible beginning of a new self-confidence of the church in China.

Since that time, the church has stepped forward, timidly at first, to take its place in Chinese society. The government has returned the church properties that were confiscated during the Cultural Revolution, and even paid for them to be refurbished. In some places, such as the former Alexander Sutherland Memorial Church in Chengtu, these churches now have Sunday services of a thousand or more. The Three-Self Protestant church has launched an ambitious program to publish Bibles and devotional works and has opened six regional seminaries to train younger ministers. Students have been sent abroad, some to the Toronto School of Theology, to study contemporary Western religious thought. The Three-Self church claims to speak for all Protestants and, indeed, it does include within its membership both religious conservatives, like the Little Flock and the charismatic pentecostals, and liberals, like the YMCA. As a result, all its official pronouncements have to be carefully worded so as not to offend either group.

Estimates of the numbers of Christians in China vary from the official twelve million in the Three-Self churches, Catholic and Protestant, up to thirty million claimed by evangelical churches in the West. Though these figures can be debated, they do indicate a resurgence of Christianity, more than merely the growth of family membership. This, too, can be seen to be part of a pattern; when the foreign missionaries returned to their stations after the Boxer rebellion in 1900, and again after the civil wars of the 1920s, they found that the church had continued to grow in spite of persecution – and despite the absence of foreign missionaries.

Partly because of Norman Bethune, and partly because of the influence of people like Bishop Ting and Jim Endicott, the Chinese church tends to react more favourably to the Canadian churches than to those in, say, the United States. Representatives of the Canadian Council of Churches, including Sister Theresa Chu, head of the Canada–China Program, and Dr Katharine Hockin, retired director of the Ecumenical Forum of Canada, were invited to tour China *at Chinese government expense* and to make contact with Christians of all kinds. In addition, hundreds of Canadian missionaries and their children have returned to China in sentimental journeys to places they knew thirty or forty years ago.

For many, there seems to be a sense of *déjà vu* when they attend these churches. The date might almost be 1935. Chinese Christians 'do things just the way we used to do it because that seems to be the only way Christians act, the way you worship, you sing the old hymns,' says Dr Hockin. The Catholic church still uses Latin in the mass and in its six seminaries, and the priests still face away from the congregations the way they did before Vatican II. The message coming out of these churches, both Catholic and Protestant, seems to be mainly evangelical rather than political, spiritual not social.

'If you judge by appearances, you throw up your arms and say the church in China hasn't moved at all,' says Sister Theresa Chu. 'But when you go deeper, when you talk to these priests and sisters and [ordinary] Catholics, you notice a kind of social consciousness which was not there when I was in China. They are no longer thinking in terms of they as individuals must save their souls regardless of what happens around them. They are now genuinely concerned with their neighbours. In other words, there is a process of humanization that took place through the experiences of the past thirty years. And that is not limited to the Catholics. On the contrary, it was the Catholics who participated in this process in the whole country.'

'The Church taught us to hate in those days,' said one of Sister Theresa's relatives in Shanghai of the 1950s period. 'It didn't teach us to love.' That, for her, was the lesson of the Chinese revolution.

The reopening of China has renewed the debate that has been

simmering in the churches of the West over the 'lessons to be learned' from the China experience. At first, pointing to the survival of the institutional church in China, the liberal Western churches claimed victory. The communist 'liberation' had proved that in order to change society one changes the structures of that society. They accepted the criticism that foreign missions had been allied with imperialism and tried to break those ties by 'deoccidentalization' and by 'contextualization.' The mission of the church is not primarily evangelistic, to convert non-Christians, but to make them better people within their own society and religion. This led during the 1970s to the development of the 'theology of liberation,' which sought to open a dialogue between Christianity and Marxism, and to place the church on the side of the 'people' in their struggle for justice.

The evangelicals, too, have seen the church in New China as a vindication of their own approach to individual salvation. Back in 1953, Olin Stockwell, an American Methodist who had been imprisoned with Dr Stewart Allen, prophesied that 'The only Church that will be in China is the one which Endicott and Willmott do not want – a pietistic one.' And that is what seems to have happened. The Western evangelicals still do not trust the Three-Self church, believing it to be an organization for state control, and claim millions of unregistered house Christians. David Michell of the Overseas Missionary Fellowship feels that the more information that comes out of China, 'we in the West are really in the position where we gain so much more from them than what we have to contribute to them. They are a church that has stood firm through suffering.'

The Roman Catholic church has to be more sensitive in dealing with the Chinese patriotic Catholic church because of the history of the past years. For the most part, Chinese Catholics consider that they have remained loyal to Rome in their hearts; it was Rome who deserted them. Eventually, it comes down to such legalities of canon law as: since excommunication is normally applied to individuals, was it in fact legally applied to the Chinese as a people?

'The terrific joy of the two trips I have had to China and visiting the church people,' concurs Dr Hockin, 'is the tremendous sense of dignity and respect they are given. Some people would say these are the servants of the government; I don't read it that way. I read it as a new sense of Christian self-confidence, self-respect, knowing they are Chinese and therefore being trusted. I think if you realize that they won their position and respect of the people, then you can see why they don't want to be seen again as the running dogs of the foreigners.'

I would like to end this book on a somewhat personal note. I would like to try to explain the mystique of the children of missionaries, 'mish kids' or 'M.K.s' as they were called in my youth. I do not intend this to be autobiographical – my only salient memory is crossing out of 'Red China' in 1951, at the age of six, in tears because the border guards had slit my teddy bear looking for smuggled gold. Rather, this is about a group of which I am proud to be a member.

There were byways I would have liked to explore in the course of this book. I would have paused, had I time to step back from the sweep of events, to talk with a little blond boy (Paul Jolliffe, but it could be almost anyone) poking his head through the lattice-gate of the mission compound, his eyes wide with mingled fear and curiosity, shouting to the soldiers – in Chinese – 'Protect us, we are foreigners.' I would have asked him – and his sister – how it felt to grow up behind walls, walls of language and culture, walls of Anglo-Saxon rectitude, physical walls of compound living. And, later, how would he feel when at the age of ten or fifteen he went 'home' to Canada for the first time? How did it feel to be an immigrant in one's homeland, a sojourner in the land of one's birth? How did Canada measure up to its mythology?

This sense of being in the world but not of it, is, I feel, the key to the understanding of the character of many missionaries' children. Pearl Buck, for example, spent her childhood watching people pass by the mission gate; from her vantage point, they were visible only from the knees down. Later she would contrast 'the small white clean Presbyterian American world of my parents and the big loving merry not-too-clean Chinese world, and there was no communication between them.'

Again and again, in trying to explain who they are, missionaries' children return to this feeling of differentness.

We were different, one anonymous respondent answered, 'not better but different ... For one, I'm not easily brainwashed by the pervasive advertising, nor ... do I regard the artifacts around me and the way of life as the exemplar of civilization.'

'I feel we were brought up in a privileged community,' recalled another, 'among friends, families, and playmates with much the same positive outlook on life, giving us a realization of the Brotherhood of Man and a meaning and a challenge to life and a responsibility.' 'We did a lot of talking about values – teachers to kids and we kids among ourselves,' a third continued. 'These values seem to be the ones I remembered and made my pattern.'

Though individual situations varied widely, certain common threads appear in almost every mish kid's story. Coddled by the Chinese amah, practically adopted by the water-carrier's family, they grew up in both worlds; indeed pictures of little Canadian children playing with little Chinese children, one blond head among the many black, were often published as examples of the brotherhood of children. But, as the realization grew which side they belonged to, these children learned to separate the world of gutter Chinese spoken with the water coolie from that of the King James English of family prayers. They learned not to dirty their pinafores and sailor suits, and not to lust after the scarlet cap with its tasselled Buddhas worn by the amah's children.

At the age of six or seven – with few exceptions, such as those whose mothers were teachers or who lived in a large centre – missionaries' children were sent away to boarding school. By nature, missionaries emphasized education; in far-off Tibet in the 1890s, for example, as soon as his son was born, Petrus Rijnhart vowed he 'must have the best training in English, French, and German, so that he may not feel that because he was a missionary's son he missed the joys that brighten other lives.' (This was the baby who died during the Rijnhart's ill-fated trip through Tibet.) Education of the children was a continuing problem in the early days, often leading to the separation of families when the mother would remain in Canada with the school-age children while the father would return to China. To resolve this, the China Inland Mission established a school for missionaries' children in Chefoo in 1881. The West China mission, once the number of its personnel reached one hundred, established its own school, called the Canadian School in West China.

The Chefoo schools were firmly in the British mould, divided into boys', girls', and preparatory. The teachers, male and female, often had degrees from British universities and emphasized high academic standards. In addition, the schools employed a large number of women – single, married, and widowed – as 'dorm aunties' and housekeepers.

A rumour was circulating recently in the Overseas Missionary Fellowship that a number of Chefoo students had grown up 'unbalanced and neurotic.' A written survey seemed to dispute this: even though 60 per cent responded that their school life was characterized by loneliness, homesickness, and institutional routine; only 30 per cent remembered it as fun. 'The only childhood I knew,' one replied, 'the

Students at the Canadian School in West China, Chengtu, dressed for a performance of *Alice in Wonderland*, 1932

only home I had for twelve long years – long, lonely, desperate years kept hidden behind my masked face. I kept step with the bells, the teachers, the religion and the social laws of my peers ... There was a strange man thousands of miles away – my father ...' 'We were sacrificed on the altar of our parents' missionary career,' echoed another. But most regarded this upbringing with mixed emotions, admitting that the 'astringent and ascetic' childhood had put 'that vein of Chefoo iron in their character.'

A very different survey was conducted among students of the Canadian School in West China. Located on the campus of West China Union University, the children were no more than 480 kilometres from their parents and could visit during the summer and winter holidays. The school was accredited in the Ontario school system and employed the standard Canadian curriculum. The principal, Lewis Walmsley, was not a distant headmaster but a wise and educated man who felt that the students should have at least some appreciation for Chinese culture. The Canadian School sounds like fun, with high-spirited performances of Gilbert and Sullivan, swimming in a tiled pool, excursions into the red-earth hills.

Both schools, like many boarding schools, exerted an influence on the students that outlasted their school days. Both still have annual reunions in Toronto, usually with more than one hundred people who had attended the school. (One woman who attended the 1983 Chefoo reunion had been at the school starting in 1897.)

'Missionaries went to China to do good,' the popular wisdom states; 'their children returned to Canada to do well.' And many of them have. 'We are at the top, in terms of occupations,' says Don Willmott, professor of sociology at York University, of his survey of his fellow students at the Canadian School. A few chose to follow the family profession, at least the religious side of it; we have already met some of them in this book: Jim Endicott and Katharine Hockin, Robert McClure, Leslie Kilborn, and Bill Service, William Mitchell and Norman Mackenzie. Many followed the secular side of their parents' work as educators, doctors, social workers, and diplomats. When the Department of External Affairs needed someone to conduct the sensitive negotiations leading to recognition of the People's Republic in 1970, it called upon Chester Ronning and Robert Edmonds; when it needed an ambassador, it called on, in turn, Ralph Collins, John Small, and Arthur Menzies. Dr Harold Johns, discoverer of the Cobalt-60 treatment, became a doctor, unlike his father. Others chose politics, usually of a left-wing nature: E.B. ('Ted') Jolliffe, leader of the Ontario CCF in the 1940s, and Norman Endicott, communist candidate in Toronto. The list could go on: Mary Jolliffe, E.B. Jolliffe's cousin, quite a theatrical lady herself, was the first 'theatrical press agent' for the Stratford Festival.

With the exception of Chester Ronning, who came out of the Lutheran missions, all of the above were raised in the Anglican and United Church missions. Because of its working-class origins, the CIM did not produce as many famous 'names,' but the Chefoo school, which took in children from non-CIM families, did produce two men who became quintessential symbols of Americanism: Henry Luce, founder of *Time* magazine, and the playwright Thornton Wilder. Two Canadians worthy of note were Senator Alistair Wishart and Kenneth Taylor, head of the Wartime Prices Board.

When questioned, most missionaries' children claim not to be interested in status and possessions. They rate themselves high in areas of internationalism ('more conscious of the world as a "global village"'), social concern, toleration ('I don't believe a C.S. student ever became a snob'), and anti-materialism. 'We were not poured into a mould, as it were, to come out bright and shiny, and fossilized.'

'There is a responsibility in being a product of a now extinct culture,' one missionary's daughter wrote in her autobiography. Another respondent to the Canadian school survey wrote, 'My first responsibility is to make of myself the best individual possible. That is my contribution to the Universe, just as a nearly perfect tree or a great symphony are unique parts of the Universe. But individuals cannot grow in a vacuum. They must relate to and receive from and give to others.'

'A thousand, thousand pages could not begin to tell it all,' concluded Muriel Beaton. 'All those memories, burning like candles: the beggar boy without an eye, the bloated corpses on the river, the mad dog in the field, the slave girl in the street behind the house, weeping, weeping, the skin and bones of the opium eater, the dying children on the street, the coughing tuberculous Bible woman ... Before I go, ask the Magician for me – Home is where?'

Bill Jolliffe was the son of Richard Orlando Jolliffe, founder of the West China dynasty of that name. Bill spent most of his life as Canadian trade commissioner in Hong Kong. When he died he asked that his ashes be scattered from the top of Mount Omei where he had spent his childhood summers. In 1980, when Szechuan was opened to foreign visitors, a group of his old school chums solemnly opened the small box and, with a prayer, emptied the contents onto the swirling clouds below. Bill Jolliffe had come home.

Notes and Sources

PREFACE

xiii   'Bringing in Chinese': Aimee Semple McPherson, *This Is That* (Los Angeles 1923) 63

xiv   'some Salvation Army missionaries': R. Gordon Moyles, *The Blood and Fire in Canada: A History of the Salvation Army in the Dominion, 1882–1976* (Toronto 1977) 165

xiv   'Handicapped by their foreignness': Jerome Ch'en, *China and the West: Society and Culture 1815–1937* (Bloomington, Ind. 1979) 149–50

xv   three million Protestants: *China Daily News*, 21 May 1984, cited in interview with Dr Katharine Hockin, CBC *Ideas*, June 1984

xv   'There are many good people': interview with Dwan Jin, CBC *Ideas*, 16 Jan. 1985

xvi   'regenerate': Ramsay Cook, *The Regenerators: Social Criticism in Late Victorian Canada* (Toronto 1985)

xviii   'What a lot of Giant-souled': D. Fuller McKinley, Chengtu, to A.R. Williams, Toronto, 24 Mar. 1911, in West China mission correspondence, WCM-19 / 200

xviii   'We are flotsam': Mrs John E. Williams, in James C. Thomson, Jr, *While China Faced West: American Reformers in Nationalist China 1928–1937* (Cambridge, Mass., 1969) x

PART 1: THE SAVING GOSPEL, 1888–1900

CHAPTER 1 Journeying Mercies: The China Inland Mission

The story of the first Canadian party of the China Inland Mission (CIM) has been told several times, particularly in the mission histories by Hudson Taylor's son and daughter-in-law: Geraldine Guiness (Mrs. Howard Taylor), *The Story of the China Inland Mission* (London 1894) in two volumes; Dr and Mrs Howard Taylor, *Hudson Taylor and the China Inland Mission: The Growth of a Work of God* (Toronto etc. 1918) and *'By Faith . . .': Henry W. Frost and the China Inland Mission* (Toronto etc. 1938); and Marshall Broomhall, *The Jubilee Story of the China Inland Mission* (Toronto 1915). There have been numerous biographies of Hudson Taylor, even in comic-book form; the latest official one is Benjamin Broomhall, *Hudson Taylor and China's Open Century* (London), the first five volumes, published 1980–5, cover his early life from 1832–67.

Unpublished sources for the Canadian CIM are almost non-existent. Instead, the most valuable published account of the mission's daily activities is its monthly *China's Millions*, published from 1875 in England and with a North American edition starting in 1893. (It is still published under the title *East Asia's Millions*.) These are all in the CIM Archives (CIMA), at the Overseas Missionary Fellowship, 1058 Avenue Road, Toronto.

There has been no comprehensive history of British missions to China, except the spirited account by Pat Barr, *To China with Love: The Lives and Times of Protestant Missionaries to China 1860–1900* (London 1972), which puts Taylor into the context of his contemporaries. Paul Varg, *Missionaries, Chinese and Diplomats: The American Protestant Missionary Movement in China, 1890–1952* (Princeton 1958) is an examination written shortly after the communist expulsion of the American movement.

1   'Enlighten China': Foster, *Imperialism*, 54
3   'I suppose, of course': Ruth Jenkins to her mother, Annie Lampman Jenkins, Ottawa, 16 Jan. 1921 (in possession of family)
4   'The Lord has given': Broomhall, *Jubilee Story* 184
5   'no American of his generation': Varg, *Missionaries* 52
6   'It seemed as if the only thing': Robert Wilder, in Varg, *Missionaries* 59
6   'Students . . . are apt': Taylor, *Hudson Taylor* 386–7
6   'China was the goal': Sherwood Eddy, in Varg, *Missionaries* 3
6   'The gospel must be preached': After Taylor's visit to Niagara-on-the-Lake, Niagara metaphors become frequent in his speeches. I have used the best-known example, given to the second SVM conference in 1894, his third visit to North America, quoted in Varg, *Missionaries* 68
7   'chimerical, and beyond': Hudson Taylor, *To Every Creature* (London 1889); see also *China's Millions* (Dec. 1889), 172, and Taylor, *Hudson Taylor* 479
7   'frightened': Taylor, *Hudson Taylor* 449
8   'chance providences': ibid. 451

9   'It must be a source': *Hamilton Spectator* (21 Sept. 1888) 4; also Toronto
     Globe (24 Sept. and 25 Sept. 1888)

10   'Should not the little things': *China's Millions* (Jan. 1889) 3

10   'I never knew anything': Taylor, *Hudson Taylor* 461

11   'the moan of China': *Missionary Outlook* (Methodist, Toronto, May 1906) 101

11   'There was scarcely': Taylor, *Hudson Taylor* 461

12   'the foreign dress and carriage': ibid. 90

12   'Things which are tolerated': ibid. 92

13   'we all meet': *China's Millions* (Mar. 1888) 33

14   'Have patience': J.F. Smith, *Life's Waking Part* (Toronto 1937) 79

14   'Fifteen millions of souls': *China's Millions* (Feb. 1889) 22

16   'was planned with a view': Taylor, *'By Faith . . .'* 170

17   'the missionary's fort': Varg, *Missionaries* 21

18   'quite sure': *China's Millions* (Jan. 1890) 10

18   'revealing his true character': ibid. (Dec. 1892) 160

19   'Hudson Taylor's wandering boy': interview with Mrs Marjorie Lugson,
     daughter of James Lawson

19   'like our barnyard': Smith, *Life's Waking* 84

20   'We are in our stations': *China's Millions* (Aug. 1891) 113-14

20   'We have many indications': ibid. (May 1891) 62

CHAPTER 2 The Old Homestead of China: The Presbyterians in North Honan

The primary sources for the Presbyterian missions are the correspondence files
in the Archives of the United Church of Canada (hereinafter cited as UCA): the
General Correspondence of the Presbyterian Church in Canada, Western Division, Foreign Mission Committee (FMC) to the Formosa mission (cited as FM),
and to the North Honan mission (NHM). Citations are by box and file. Margaret
Brown's manuscript *History of the Honan (North China) Mission of the United
Church of Canada, Originally a Mission of the Presbyterian Church in Canada, 1887–
1951* (written 1970), a documentary narrative in four volumes at the UCA, is the
best source for that mission; citations are by chapter and page.

Another primary source is the biographies: Islay Burns, *Memoir of the Reverend
William C. Burns, MA: Missionary to China from the English Presbyterian Church*
(London 1880); G.L. Mackay, *From Far Formosa: The Island, Its People and Missions*
(Toronto 1895); R.P. MacKay, *Life of George Leslie Mackay, DD, 1844–1901* (Toronto
1913); Rosalind Goforth, *Goforth of China* (Grand Rapids, Mich. 1937); J. Frazer
Smith, *Life's Waking Part: Being the Autobiography of . . .* (Toronto 1937); Margaret
Brown, *MacGillivray of Shanghai: The Life of Donald MacGillivray* (Toronto 1968);
W. Harvey Grant, *North of the Yellow River: Six Decades in Honan, 1888–1948*

(Toronto 1948); Rev. Murdoch Mackenzie, *Twenty-Five Years in Honan* (Toronto 1913). The biographical files in the UCA are also valuable.

23   'Brother, if you would enter' : Goforth, *Goforth* 80
23   'a waning relic': Valentin H. Rabe, 'Evangelical Logistics: Mission Support and Resources to 1920,' in John King Fairbank, *The Missionary Enterprise in China and America* (Cambridge, Mass. 1974) 60 This volume of essays, edited by Dr Fairbank, is the best scholarly examination of the missionary enterprise.
23   Erromanga Martyrs: for the effect of their story, see, for example, Smith, *Life's Waking* 16
24   'We have heathen': ibid. 62
24   'a rather unsystematic': John Foster, *Imperialism* 13
24   'one piece of denominational': ibid. 13
25   Dr Alexander Sutherland and Sutherland's boasting: Margaret Prang, *N.W. Rowell: Ontario Nationalist* (Toronto 1975)
25   'daring proposal': *Missionary Outlook* (May 1882) 65
26   Sutherland's caution: *Canadian Methodist Magazine* (Aug. 1896) 188
27   'a queer chap': Goforth, *Goforth* 32
27   'burning words': Brown, *History* II–8
27   'right condemning forefinger': Goforth, *Goforth* 63
27   'a God-intoxicated man': Rev. Adoniram Judson, in Varg, *Missionaries* 52
28   Mrs Virgil Hart: E.I. Hart, *Virgil C. Hart, Missionary Statesman* (Toronto 1917) 25
28   'like the rushing': Burns, *Memoir* 95
28   Dr Robert Morrison: Marshall Broomhall, *Robert Morrison: A Master Builder* (London and Toronto 1924) 62
28   The East India Company's policy: Sherwood Eddy, *Pathfinders of the World Missionary Crusade* (New York 1945) 24
29   'I think I can say': Burns, *Memoir* 394
29   'rewarded only by hopeful': ibid. 259
30   'of revival work and of persecution': Marshall Broomhall, *The Jubilee Story of the China Inland Mission* 15
30   'Born in humble though Christian': Rev. William Alexander MacKay, *Zorra Boys at Home and Abroad or Success Illustrated by Example* (Toronto 1901) 3
31   'reprove, rebuke, exhort': G.L. Mackay, *From Far Formosa* 24
31   'peripatetic school': R.P. MacKay, *Life of Mackay* 27
31   'Our usual custom in touring': G.L. Mackay, *From Far Formosa* 315–16
31   'the forceps and the Bible': R.P. MacKay, *Life of Mackay* 46
31   'Brother R. just sent': ibid. 33–4

32   'globes, drawings': G.L. Mackay, *From Far Formosa* 288–9

32   'two dozen fragile': G.L. Mackay to Dr Thomas Wardrope, Convenor of the FMC, Toronto, 5 Feb. 1886 FM-1 / 13

32   'missionary entrepreneur': the term was used in Irwin T. Hyatt, *Our Ordered Lives Confess: Three Nineteenth-Century American Missionaries in East Shantung* (Cambridge, Mass. 1976), to describe Calvin Mateer

33   'buying snakes': North Formosan Church at Tamsui (translated into English in Jamieson's handwriting) to Wardrope, 6 July 1886, FM-1 / 13

33   Mrs Jamieson's lament: Mrs Annie Jamieson to WMS, 13 May 1886, printed in pamphlet *Injustice to Rev. Dr. Mackay: Some Things that Should be Known to the Ladies of the Woman's Foreign Missionary Society in Canada* (Hong Kong 1889) FM-1 / 15 2

33   'so actively employed': Secretary of the WMS to Mrs Jamieson, 7 Oct. 1886, ibid. 4

33   'more and more the injustice': John Jamieson to Wardrope, 19 June 1888, FM-1 / 15

33   'I have been *misrepresented*': G.L. Mackay to FMC, 29 Aug. 1888, ibid.

33   'dreaming over the language': Jamieson to Wardrope, 25 Aug. 1888, ibid.

33   'Jamieson working now': G.L. Mackay to FMC, 2 Jan. 1889, FM-1 / 16

33   'all along *neighbourly*': Mackay to FMC, 19 Apr. 1889, ibid.

34   'Who counts the teeth': J. Somerville to Wardrope, 21 Jan. 1889, ibid.

34   'Some people say': S.D. McDonald to Wardrope, 7 Jan. 1889, ibid.; see also Brown, *History* II–11

34   'broke through the wall': R.P. MacKay, *Life of Mackay* 49

34   subversive doctrine: for the Japanese treatment of Christian 'Thought Offenders' in another colony, Korea, in 1936, involving Canadian missionaries, see Public Archives of Canada (PAC), External Affairs papers, RG 25 G 1, file 891

34   'It seems that no one': Goforth, *Goforth* 29

35   'a lone road': ibid. 32–3

35   'With subdued enthusiasm': *Queen's College Journal*, in Brown, *History* II–3

36   'free use': Smith, *Life's Waking* 229

36   'practise such care': *Proceedings of the General Assembly* (1887), in Brown, *History* III–2

36   'If the Lord wanted me': Goforth, *Goforth* 47

36   'his training of Rosalind': ibid. 66

36   'a terrible nightmare': ibid. 71

37   'We, with the intimate': Hudson Taylor to Wardrope, 18 July 1890, in Brown, *History* IX–5

39   'mixture of fear and self-love': Arthur H. Smith, *Chinese Characteristics* (London 1890) 184

39   'rather thrilling': J.F. Smith, *Life's Waking* 104; see also Brown, *History*, v

39   'when people are suffering': Smith, ibid. 104

39   'You see how many sick people': Smith, ibid. 106-7; Brown, *History* v-5

39   'It is a good land': *Canadian Presbyterian*, 9 Jan. 1889, in Brown, *History* v-5

40   'the old homestead': Donald MacGillivray, *Memoirs*, in Brown, *History* v-1

40   'almost as numerous': Smith, *Life's Waking* 94

41   'Believe in my Saviour': ibid. 142

41   'of the familiar type': Dr William McClure to FMC, 18 Apr. 1890, in Brown, *History* x-5

41   'in Abrahamic ignorance': *Knox College Monthly* (May 1890) in ibid. XII-2

41   'on the ragged edge': Goforth, *Goforth* 93

41   'We are not secret': *Knox Monthly* (May 1891) in Brown, *History* XIII-2

42   'a piece of meat': *Knox Monthly* (May 1890) in ibid. XIII-5

42   'a fine maroon-coloured': Smith, *Life's Waking* 148

42   'two and a half months': Brown, *History* XIII-7

43   'very seldom go outside': Dr Lucinda Graham to her brother, George, 19 Jan. 1892, in UCA bio. file

43   'They went to China': obituary, in ibid.

43   'Our Church is too small': MacGillivray to FMC, 15 May 1895, in Brown, *History* XXIV-26

43   'a true yoke-fellow': MacGillivray to FMC, 6 Dec. 1891, in ibid. XVI-5

43   '*There* he is ready': W. Harvey Grant to FMC, 3 Apr. 1893, in ibid. XVI-7

44   'one man may preach to a million': Timothy Richard to FMC, 4 Feb. 1899, in ibid. XXVI-12

44   'We consider Mr MacGillivray': Dr Percy Leslie to FMC, 14 Sept. 1899, in ibid. XXVI-18

44   'the unforgivable sin': Brown, *MacGillivray* 58; see also Brown, *History* XVI-6

44   'with his strong convictions': Goforth, *Goforth* 162

CHAPTER 3 'Our West China Mission': The Methodists in Szechuan

The primary source for the West China mission is the General Correspondence in the United Church Archives, between the Foreign Mission Board (FMB, later the Board of Foreign Missions [BFM]) in Toronto and the West China mission (cited as WCM), and between the Woman's Missionary Society and its missionaries (WCM/WMS). Citations are by box and file. The biographical files are also invaluable.

The Methodist Church of Canada was a prolific publisher with its own press, and published sources include: periodicals – *Canadian Methodist Magazine* (under various titles 1875–1906, cited as *Canadian Methodist*), the general *Missionary Outlook* (1881–1925), and the Young People's *Missionary Bulletin* (1903–22); and study books – *Our West China Mission: Being a Somewhat Extensive Summary by the Missionaries on the Field of the Work During the First Twenty-Five Years of the Canadian Methodist Mission in the Province of Szechwan, Western China* (Toronto 1920), Edward Wilson Wallace, *The Heart of Szechwan* (1906), Omar L. Kilborn, *Heal the Sick: An Appeal for Medical Missions* (1910), E.I. Hart, *Virgil C. Hart, Missionary Statesman* (1917), and George Hartwell, *Granary of Heaven* (1939).

The most valuable critical secondary source for all the denominational missions is John W. Foster, *The Imperialism of Righteousness: Canadian Protestant Missions and the Chinese Revolution, 1925–1928* (PHD Diss., York University 1977), which also has an excellent bibliography.

47 'Fire will spread': *Missionary Outlook* (Dec. 1888) 189
47 'a proof that God': *Canadian Methodist* (Dec. 1885) 561
48 'flowers forgot': Theodore H. White, *In Search of History: A Personal Adventure* (New York 1978) 67
48 'Last Best West': *Our West China Mission* 68
48 'virile, enterprising': ibid. 71
48 'Baltimore has 64': *Canadian Methodist* (Mar. 1893) 307. This statement is incredible. The only explanation is that the American figures are for full church members only, and that the Toronto one includes adherents as well. At the time the thirty Methodist churches of Toronto had a combined seating capacity of 27 600, the Presbyterians about 17 000. Ibid. (Oct. 1890) 380
48 'The Genius of Methodism': ibid. (Nov. 1886)
48 'the priesthood': ibid. (Jan. 1875) 19
49 'Methodism is a social': ibid. (July 1879)
49 'the Institutional Church': ibid. (Dec. 1894) 608–9
49 'soldiers of a new holy': ibid. (Dec. 1889) 562
49 'When the citadel': ibid. (July 1880) 92
49 'organizing the whole sisterhood': ibid. (Dec. 1891) 608
50 'young shoot': ibid. (Sept. 1890) 246
50 'but gleaners': ibid. (Dec. 1891) 609
50 'The women's missionary': Foster, *Imperialism* 29
50 'Who can estimate': *Canadian Methodist* (Apr. 1892) 269
50 'simply *work*': ibid. (Dec. 1894) 561

50   'to turn her eyes': *Annual Report of the Missionary Society of the Methodist Church* (1887–8) in Foster, *Imperialism* 20

50   Dr Leonora Howard: Wade Crawford Barclay, *History of Methodist Missions*, Part II, Vol. 3, *The Methodist Episcopal Church, 1845–1939: Widening Horizons 1845–95* (New York 1957) 415; *Canadian Methodist* (Jan. 1889) 90; obituary in *The New Outlook* (12 Aug. 1925) 25; after her marriage to Rev. Alexander King of the London Missionary Society, she lived 'a quiet, unostentatious life' in Peking and visited Canada only twice in forty-seven years.

51   'And for Canada': E.I. Hart, *Virgil Hart* 223; see also Barclay, *History* 396–406, for Dr Hart's previous work

52   'such as Christians': Mrs Howard Taylor, *Pastor Hsi, One of China's Christians* (London 1911) 198

52   'There was a sense of security': Susie Carson Rijnhart, *With the Tibetans in Tent and Temple* (Toronto 1901) 14

52   'clad in rags and sunshine': Rev. J.L. Stewart, *Missionary Bulletin* (June 1903) 200

53   'Remoteness is to be judged': 'James Endicott,' ms in UCA bio. file 1

53   'soaked in religion': Rev. Joseph Taylor, *West of the Yangtse Gorges* (ms typescript, Los Angeles 1936) 6; there were many descriptions of trips through the Yangtse gorges; see also *Missionary Outlook* (Aug. 1901), 174; *Canadian Methodist* (Feb. 1904) 99

54   'a city of steps and swear-words': *Our West* 224

54   'pulsating arteries': ibid. 89

54   'farmer's paradise': *Canadian Methodist* (Oct. 1894) 336

54   'something of the density': ibid. (Feb. 1904) 99

54   'the development of the modern': *Our West* 70–1

55   'As a colt champs': George Hartwell, 'Report of the Pearly Street Mission,' *Annual Report of the Missionary Society* (1893–4) 5–6, WCM-8 / 61

55   'at least a thousand': Hart, *Virgil Hart* 246

55   'The thought was': Kilborn, *Heal the Sick* 231

55   'one of the best chisels': *Canadian Methodist* (June 1891) 586

55   'worry along': Kilborn, 'Medical Mission Work in China,' ibid. (Mar. 1902) 250

56   'a very essential part': *Our West* 315

56   'We trust this': Hartwell, *Annual Report* (1893–4) 11

57   James Endicott: see particularly his UCA bio. file; concerning his 'prickliness,' the mission asked for him to be recalled – see Rev. Alexander Sutherland to Dr Virgil Hart, 5 Oct. 1899, Sutherland to Kilborn, 14 Dec. 1900 and 16 Mar. 1901, WCM-8 / 62

58 'the inhuman din': Hart, *Virgil Hart* 275; see also George E. Paulsen, 'The Chengtu Anti-Missionary Riot,' *Methodist History* (Lake Junaluska, NC, Apr. 1969) 24–32

58 'not in a vindictive spirit': Hart, *Virgil Hart* 290

58 'We will return': *Missionary Outlook* (Oct. 1905) 229

58 'greatest victory': *Annual Report of the Missionary Society* (1895–6) in Foster, *Imperialism* 57

58 'And so we were driven': *Our West* 43–4

59 Miss Crossthwaite: Sutherland to Hart, 30 Jan. 1897, WCM-8 / 61; see also CIM Archives.

59 'Our brethren are excellent': Sutherland to Hart, 29 Jan. 1897, WCM-8 / 61

60 'savoured of *downright*': Sutherland to Hart, 28 July 1898, WCM-8 / 62

60 'only twelve': *Our West* 31

CHAPTER 4 Foreign Devils

There are many accounts of the 'big history' of the Boxer rebellion. Primary sources for this chapter include: Sir Robert Hart, *These From the Land of Sinim* (London 1903); Marshall Broomhall, *Martyred Missionaries of the China Inland Mission, With a Record of the Perils and Sufferings of Some Who Escaped* (London and Toronto 1901); Alexander Saunders, *A God of Deliverances* (London *c*. 1901). Secondary sources include: Albert Feuerwerker, *The Foreign Establishment in China in the Early Twentieth Century* (Ann Arbor 1976); Paul A. Cohen, *China and Christianity: The Missionary Movement and the Growth of Chinese Antiforeignism 1860–1870* (Cambridge, Mass. 1963); Sidney A. Forsythe, *An American Missionary Community In China 1895–1905* (Cambridge, Mass. 1971).

The J.O.P. Bland diaries are in the Thomas A. Fisher Rare Book Library of the University of Toronto Library.

63 'At present the field': *Canadian Methodist* (July 1896) 42

63 'the year 1900 holds': Robert B. Ekvall et al., *After Fifty Years: A Record of God's Working Through the Christian and Missionary Alliance* (Harrisburg, Pa. 1939) 2

64 'a glittering life': Feuerwerker, *Foreign Establishment* 9

64 'blazed away': J.O.P. Bland, *Diary*, 27 Apr. 1884

64 'the vices of the scoundrel': *Canadian Methodist* (July 1890) 46

64 'We are placed in a country': Mrs J.H. Morrison, *Missionary Outlook* (July 1881) 2

64 'gentle-spirited Norwegian': Dr W.F. Adams, *Missionary Bulletin* (Mar. 1908) 8

65   'What other government': *Missionary Outlook* (Apr. 1900) 77

65   'The Society for the Diffusion': Varg, *Missionaries* 11

66   'loitering on the sombre': 'Nanking: American Jesuits in China' (pamph, nd) in Jesuit Archives (SJA), 'Jésuites Américains'

66   John Calvin Ferguson: There are biography files in UCA, the University of Toronto Archives (UTA) records of graduates, and in the Bishop W.C. White papers in the Royal Ontario Museum Archives (ROMA) SC 12 (Special Collections). He was granted an honorary DD by the University of Toronto in 1944 and died the following year.

67   Dr William Macklin: see William Macklin, *Under the Shadow of the Drum Tower* (Indianapolis, Ind. *c.* 1930); Reuben Butchard, *The Disciples of Christ in Canada Since 1830* (Toronto 1949) 262 Dr Macklin was joined by his sister, Daisy, also a doctor, and by several prominent Disciples missionaries, including Charles T. Paul, founder of the Hartford School of Missions.

67   Dr William Cassidy: Ekvall, *After Fifty Years* 150 See also a book by his daughter Bertha Cassidy, *China Adventure* (Brookline, Mass. 1962). His second daughter, Dr Mabel Cassidy, married W.J. Mortimore of West China.

67   Dr Susie Carson Rijnhart: Susie Rijnhart, *With the Tibetans in Tent and Temple* (Toronto 1901); see also Carlotta Hacker, *The Indomitable Lady Doctors* (Toronto 1974) 98; E.W. Wallace papers UCA, Wallace to family, 14 Apr. 1907, 2 / 15B

67   'summarily dismissed': *China's Millions* (Sept. 1893) 128

68   James Moyes' application to join the WCM: Dr Alexander Sutherland to Dr O.L. Kilborn, Chengtu, 28 Mar. 1908, WCM-9 / 70

69   'It would, in our judgement': *Canadian Methodist* (Apr. 1899) 383

69   'conversation of the deaf and dumb': at a conference on Canadian Missionaries sponsored by the York University–University of Toronto Joint Centre on Modern East Asia, 22 Apr. 1983

69   'Age of Contempt': Harold Isaacs, *Images of Asia: American Views of China and India* (revised title, New York 1962) 96

69   'over to a reprobate mind': Romans 1: 28–31

70   Mr Shen's conversion: Jonathan and Rosalind Goforth, *Miracle Lives of China* (Grand Rapids, Mich. 1931) 116–20

71   the convert's dream: *China's Millions* (May 1891) 58

71   Pastor Hsi: Mrs Howard Taylor, *Pastor Hsi: One of China's Christians* (London and Toronto 1903)

72   'I heard only yesterday': *Missionary Outlook* (Feb. 1899) 45

73   'We got so used to being pelted': Harlan P. Beach, in Varg, *Missionaries* 6

73   'the body of Christ': Alexander Williamson, ibid. 24

74 Death Blow to Corrupt Doctrines: Cohen, *China and Christianity* 47, and caption to illustration 2

75 'I have lain on brushwood': Marina Warner, *The Dragon Empress: Life and Times of Tz'u-Hsi, 1835–1908, Empress Dowager of China* (London 1972) 229

75 Misses Rutherford and Gowans: *Toronto Daily Star* (16 July 1900) 1 (2 Oct. 1900) 1

76 Sufferings of CIM missionaries: Broomhall, *Martyred Missionaries* 29, 30, 57, 128

76 Alexander Saunders: Alexander R. Saunders, *A God of Deliverances* 29

76 'state of great unrest': Dr William Malcolm, in Brown, *History* XXVII-5

76 'greatly increased our danger' and 'it was a miracle': Goforth, *Goforth* 132, 135

77 'falling rain': Brown, *History* XXVII-19

77 'shoulder to shoulder': Goforth, *Goforth* 140

77 'There is no use talking': *Toronto Daily Star* (2 Oct. 1900) 1

77 'You can't imagine': Mortimore Montgomery, ibid. (11 Oct. 1900) 7

78 'an act of more than justifiable reprisal': Arthur H. Smith, *Canadian Methodist* (Jan. 1901) 11

78 'casual exploitation': Capt. F. Brinkley, in Forsythe, *An American Missionary Community* 83

78 'gunpowder gospel': *Toronto Daily Star* (18 Aug. 1900); Varg, *Missionaries* 49

78 'set apart by the Legation': *Canadian Methodist* (Apr. 1902) 378

78 'inattentive right hand': Pat Barr, *To China with Love* 16

78 'The Church has been stirred': Varg, *Missionaries* 51

78 'those who say the least': *Missionary Outlook* (Dec. 1900) 266

79 'could think of nothing better': Brown, *History* XXVIII-7

79 'the ground that the terrible ocurrences': *Toronto Daily Star* (15 Oct. 1900) 4

PART 2: THE SOCIAL GOSPEL, 1901–1927

CHAPTER 5 Loved Ones in the Homeland

Manuscript sources for this chapter include, in addition to those mentioned in other chapters: the papers of the Laymen's Missionary Movement (LMM) and the Young People's Forward Movement for Missions (YPFMM), both in the UCA; and the Sir Joseph Flavelle Papers in the Queen's University Archives (QUA). Printed sources include the reports of the two Toronto conferences: *World-Wide Evangelization: The Urgent Business of the Church, Addresses Delivered Before the Fourth International Convention of the Student Volunteer Movement for Foreign Missions,*

Toronto, Canada, February 26–March 2, 1902 (New York 1902); and *Canada's Mission-ary Congress: Addresses Delivered at the Canadian National Missionary Congress, Held in Toronto, March 31 to April 4, 1909* (Toronto 1909).

The most relevant secondary sources are John Foster, *The Imperialism of Righ-teousness*; Margaret Prang, *N.W. Rowell: Ontario Nationalist*; Michael Bliss, *A Cana-dian Millionaire: The Life and Business Times of Sir Joseph Flavelle, Bart., 1858–1939* (Toronto 1978); Richard Allen, *The Social Passion: Religion and Social Reform in Can-ada 1914–1928* (Toronto 1971).

81   'Yes, China is awake': *Missionary Bulletin* (June 1907) 108

83   'Little Builders': *Missionary Outlook* (Aug. 1882) 126

84   'Yes, China is moving': George J. Bond, *Our Share in China and What We Are Doing with It* (Toronto 1909) 24–5

84   'The multimillion dollar': Valentin Rabe, 'Evangelical Logistics,' in J.K. Fairbank, *The Missionary Enterprise in China and America* 61

84   1905 and 1919 statistics: *The Christian Occupation of China* (Peking 1922) 346

85   'high mission': *Canadian Methodist* (Jan. 1899) 44

85   'looking at you': Bishop C.H. Fowler, ibid. (Oct. 1898) 370

85   'a large share': N.W. Rowell, 'Canada's Opportunity at Home and Abroad,' *Canada's Missionary Congress* 39, in Foster, *Imperialism* 63

86   'The attractiveness of mission work': James Shenstone, 'The Stewardship of Business Talents and Professions,' *Canada's Missionary Congress* 143, in ibid. 64

87   'the Church of Christ': *Missionary Outlook* (Oct. 1907) 231

87   'grim doctrine': Varg, *Missionaries* 68

87   'rested on the premise', 'the earthbound movements,' and 'the voice of prophecy': Allen, *The Social Passion* 4, 16–17

87   'Long live the Social': C.J.P. Jolliffe, West China, *Autobiographical Notes* (in possession of the family)

88   'calm, cheerful, kind': Karen Minden, *Missionaries, Medicine and Moderniza-tion: Canadian Medical Missionaries in Sichuan, 1925–1952* (PH D Diss., York University 1981) 76

88   David Yuile: his endowment of Wuan station, see Brown, *History* XLV; his support of his niece, Mrs Howard Taylor, *Margaret King's Vision* (Toronto 1934)

89   CIM statistics: gleaned from a comparison of a list of Canadian mission-aries with the annual directories, held in the CIMA

92   'living for God': Foster, *Imperialism* 14

92   'was the great cause': R. Pierce Beaver, *American Protestant Women in World Mission: History of the First Feminist Movement in North America* (Grand

Rapids, Mich. 1980); see also Jane Hunter, *The Gospel of Gentility: American Women Missionaries in Turn-of-the-Century China* (New Haven 1984)

93 'ordered freedom': Women's Auxiliary to the Missionary Society of the Church of England in Canada, *These Fifty Years, 1886-1936* (Toronto 1936) 10

93 'a most business-like manner': *Globe* (3 Oct. 1914), clipping in Metropolitan Toronto Reference Library (TRL) microfiche N5583, Vol. 209

93 'received a baptism of power': Helen B. Montgomery, in Beaver, *American Protestant* 89

93 'The Lord gave the word': This startling change was noted frequently in the late 1880s; see *Missionary Outlook* (May 1888) 72 Hudson Taylor used it as justification to station single women along 'the women's river.'

94 'in England women': Janie Thomas to Dr T.R. O'Meara, 5 Oct. 1908, and reply 17 Oct., Wycliffe College Archives (WYCA), O'Meara correspondence (Series 8-E) 'Gleaners' Union'

94 'once a month a band': Marilyn Linton, 'WMS: 100 Years of Woman Power,' *The United Church Observer* (June 1976) 16

94 'as their talent': *Missionary Outlook* (Feb. 1889) 25

94 'The figures in the WMS': *Globe* (3 Oct. 1914), clipping in TRL

95 'singing, readings, recitations': *Missionary Outlook* (Mar. 1889) 41

95 imaginary missionary trip: ibid. (Feb. 1907) 34-5

96 'Next to the Christian': Clifton J. Phillips, 'The Student Volunteer Movement,' Fairbank, *The Missionary Movement* 105

96 'enthusiasm is not': *Toronto Daily Star* (28 Feb. 1902)

96 'in to see God': John A. Mackay, in Varg, *Missionaries* 60

96 'We are young': *Toronto Daily Star* (27 Feb. 1902)

96 'The platform in Massey': ibid. (1 Mar. 1902)

97 'One million students': *Missionary Outlook* (Apr. 1902) 91

97 Dr Frederick Clarke Stephenson: see the Stephenson / YPFMM papers in the UCA

97 'specialized types of costumes': Margaret T. Applegarth, *Short Missionary Plays* (New York 1923) x

98 Broadway's exhibition: Toronto *Mail* (28 Feb. 1912), clipping in TRL

98 'for busy people': Bond, *Our Share* 5

98 'left too much to women': Prang, *N.W. Rowell* 64

98 'a matter of respectability': Varg, *Missionaries* 64

99 'Enlisting the whole': J. Campbell White, in ibid. 64

99 'put us on Easy Street': A.E. Armstrong, FMC Toronto, to Harvey Grant, Honan, 12 Mar. 1909, quoted in Foster, *Imperialism* 39

99 'One Society': Prang, *N.W. Rowell* 64

100   'the voice of the Church': obituary in *The Observer* (1 Apr. 1954); see also
       his UCA bio. file

100   Dr Jesse Arnup: see his UCA bio. file

100   'at the basis of Canadian finance': Henry James Morgan, *The Canadian Men
       and Women of the Time: A Handbook of Canadian Biography of Living Characters*
       (Toronto 1912), 'George Albertus Cox,' 270

101   'in a close alliance': Foster, *Imperialism* 66-7

101   'holding earnest discussions': Bliss, *A Canadian Millionaire* 121

101   'You are a trustee': ibid. 94

102   'trained to give': Fred Deacon to Joseph Flavelle, 1 Nov. 1922, in Foster,
       Imperialism 46

102   'to such an extent': Flavelle to Joseph Beech, Chengtu, 19 Feb. 1925, in
       ibid. 46

CHAPTER 6 Revival in North Honan, Mass Movement in West China

For an examination of educational policy and professionalism of the West China
mission, see Bruce R. Lawrie, *Educational Missionaries in China: A Case Study of the
Educational Enterprise of the Canadian Methodist Mission in Szechwan, West China
1891-1925* (PH D Diss., University of Toronto 1979).

105   'China, as she is now': *Missionary Outlook* (Nov. 1900) 250

106   Pink Pills: I am indebted to George T. Fulford and Dr Adrien Ten Cate of
       Brockville for this information. W.E. Smith, *A Canadian Doctor in West China*
       (Toronto 1937) 88, describes an attempt to recruit him as a drug-sales
       representative.

106   China Inland Mission: see for example, Mrs Howard Taylor, *'By Faith ...'*
       254

106   'in retrospect, the indemnity': *Chinese Recorder* (May 1923) in Brown, *His-
       tory* xxx-4

107   Herbert Hoover: Varg, *Missionaries* 49

107   'Are we now going to use': Dr Percy Leslie to FMC, 28 Oct. 1901, in Brown,
       History xxix-18

107   'triumphal procession': ibid. xxx-1

107   'giving her something of a military salute': *The Westminster* (22 Feb. 1902) in
       ibid. xxx-15

107   'declarations meant to convey': presbytery minutes (31 Oct. 1901) in ibid..
       xxx-5

107   'Amongst the Christians': James Slimmon to FMC, 22 Nov. 1901, in ibid.
       xxx-7

108   Three-Self Church: this phrase which is still applied to the official church in China was first used by Rev. Henry Venn, of the Church Missionary Society

108   'Cinderella': Brown, *History* LC-2

108   'trained educationalists': in Brown, *History* XXI-5

108   'a charge upon the finances': ibid. XXI-10

110   'We did not hear one unkind word': Miss Minnie Brimstin, *Missionary Outlook* (Jan. 1902) 22

110   'many a rascal': *Missionary Bulletin* (Mar. 1903) 10

110   'a man of rank': *Missionary Outlook* (Mar. 1902) 53

111   'Not a few attended': ibid. (Nov. 1902) 247

111   'as a result of necessary pruning': ibid. (Aug. 1902) 174

111   'Books of the Times': ibid. 174

111   'the missionary more trouble': *Missionary Bulletin* (June 1903) 193

111   'the loves-to-kill-men': Dr R.B. Ewan, ibid. (Mar. 1903) 13

111   gas lamps: *Canadian Methodist* (Sept. 1904) 282; straw hats: Dr W.F. Adams, *Missionary Bulletin* (Sept. 1903) 347

111   'Perhaps I cannot do better': *Missionary Outlook* (Oct. 1904) 221-2

112   'living in a foreign': Rev. W.J. Mortimore, *Missionary Bulletin* (Dec. 1909) 207

113   Edward Wilson Wallace: see the E.W. Wallace Personal Papers in the UCA; also Alvyn Austin, 'Edward Wilson Wallace,' paper presented at conference on Canadian missionaries sponsored by the Joint Centre on Modern East Asia, 2 May 1986 E.W. Wallace was the grandson of Dr Robert Wallace of the CIM board.

113   'a complete system of grading': *Our West China Mission* 322

113   'efficient and up to date': ibid. 331-2

114   'The only idea of discipline': *Missionary Bulletin* (Mar. 1909) 872

114   'securing an education': *Our West* 358

114   Dr William F. Adams: *Missionary Bulletin* (Dec. 1905) 296; (Sept. 1905) 135; he reapplied to the WCM – 'To this end was I born and for this cause came I into this world' – but the mission turned him down, Adams to General Board of Missions, 7 Oct. 1907, WCM-8 / 68; Rev. T.E.E. Shore, FMB, to Rev. A.B. Leonard, New York, 11 June 1908, WCM-9 / 70

115   'to the eyes of Chinese': Brown, *History* XLIX-1

115   Penghsien property: Dr Wallace Crawford, *Missionary Bulletin* (Mar. 1909) 852

115   'Has the heroic': Brown, *History* XLIX-11

115   'strange restlessness': Goforth, *Goforth* 177

115   'the spiritual laws': ibid. 179

115   'my heart went like lead': ibid. 156-7

116   'Jonathan Goforth went up to Manchuria': ibid. 187
116   'a level-headed Scot': ibid. 195
116   'But how explain': ibid. 199–200
116   'preaching fever': Gertrude Howe, *Missionary Outlook* (Jan. 1907) 2
116   'marked stillness': Goforth, *Goforth* 204
117   'I do not remember': R.P. MacKay to Donald MacGillivray, 24 Mar. 1910, in Brown, *History* XL–2
117   'continued to confess': Murdoch Mackenzie to FMC, 30 Nov. 1909, in ibid. XXXVII–4
117   John Bompas: ibid. L; W.H. Grant to FMC, 30 Mar. 1915; Bompas to FMC, 20 Oct. 1915; and W.H. Grant, 'Report of Presbytery,' 25 Jan. 1916; for the earlier 'heresy' of H.M. Clark, also an educational missionary, see ibid. XLI–7
117   'half-digested ideas': Rev. J.L. Stewart, *Missionary Bulletin* (Dec. 1907) 790
117   'for several years': presbytery minutes (Jan. 1911) in Brown, *History* XL–5
117   'to compel me': Goforth to FMC, 1 Dec. 1912, in ibid. XL–9
117   'can only be nominal': Grant to R.P. MacKay, 28 May 1912, in ibid. XL–11
118   'gospel nomads': Goforth, *Goforth* 232
118   'One thing is certain': Dr C.W. Service, Kiating, to T.E.E. Shore, 20 Sept. 1911, WCM–19 / 200
118   'Some newspapers': Dr Richard Wolfendale, Chungking, to F.C. Stephenson, 5 Dec. 1911, WCM–19 / 200
118   'I do not belong': C.R. Hensman, *Sun Yat-sen* (London 1971) 11
118   'Masses of undisciplined men': W.R. Brown, British Consul at Chungking, to Sir John Jordan, British Minister at Peking, No. 51644, in PAC, Governor-General's Files, RG 7 G 21, file 6278; there is also a copy in WCM–10 / 94; this PAC file contains diplomatic correspondence concerning the 1911 evacuation from West China
119   'with insistence': W.H. Wilkinson, British Consul-General at Chengtu, to Jordan, Circular letter No. 6211, 12 Dec. 1911, in PAC
119   John Jolliffe: see PAC; also WCM–11 / 99, 11 / 116
119   'You certainly have had': T.E.E. Shore to Dr Service, 12 Feb. 1912, WCM–19 / 200
120   craziest fashions: Dr Robert B. McClure, interview 30 Oct. 1970, York University Oral History Project, 'Missionaries in East Asia,' 16
120   'No one in this country': Shore to Service, 12 Feb. 1912, WCM–19 / 200
121   'the election of strong': Brown, *History* XLVI–14
121   'supervised democracy': Presbyterian Woman's Missionary Society, *The Story of Our Missions* (Toronto 1915) 62
121   Feng Yu-hsiang: Marshall Broomhall, *Marshal Feng: 'A Good Soldier of Christ Jesus'* (Toronto and Philadelphia 1924) 2; the authoritative biography of

Feng, 'the mystery man of China,' is James E. Sheridan, *Chinese Warlord: The Career of Feng Yu-hsiang* (Stanford 1966), but hagiographic works such as Broomhall's show the Christian preoccupation with him; see also Marcus Ch'eng, *Marshall Feng: The Man and His Works* (Shanghai c. 1926), and Jonathan and Rosalind Goforth, *Miracle Lives of China* 140–57

122 'If we would impress our Christianity': Broomhall, *Marshal Feng* 18

122 'The Republic has come': O.L. Kilborn, in Harry Priest, ed., *Canada's Share in World Tasks* (Toronto 1920) 44

122 'disillusionment and timidity': Brown, *History* LII–1

122 'Old orders are changing': Priest, *Canada's Share* 5

CHAPTER 7 New Labourers for the Vineyard

The primary source for the South China mission is the General Correspondence between the FMC in Toronto and the South China Mission (SOCM). The mission history is Hugh Angus Becking, *A History of the United Church of Canada's South China Mission 1902–1952* (BD Diss., University of Alberta 1955).

The most complete source for the Anglican Diocese of Honan is the papers of the Missionary Society of the Canadian Church (MSCC) in the Anglican Church Archives, 600 Jarvis Street, Toronto (ACA) GS 75–103, in particular box 67 (Series 3-2, Sydney Gould papers, China files), boxes 141–3 (series 8-1, Mission Dioceses, China), and boxes 84–8 (series 3-3, Leonard Dixon papers, China files). Bishop W.C. White's personal papers are in the Thomas A. Fisher Rare Book Library of the University of Toronto (UT / WCW). Further correspondence is in the Wycliffe College Archives (WYCA), especially the T.R. O'Meara papers, and in the Royal Ontario Museum Archives (ROMA).

The Ruth Jenkins Watts letters are in the possession of the family, except for three letters that have been deposited in the PAC, Frank and Annie Lampman Jenkins papers MG 30 (D 183).

125 'Then over the sea': *Letter Leaflet* (Anglican WA, Toronto, Mar. 1914) 165–6

125 Aimee Semple McPherson: Sister Aimee told her own story in at least three autobiographies, notably *This Is That* (Los Angeles 1923); see also Lately Thomas, *Storming Heaven* (New York 1970) and Alvyn Austin, *Aimee Semple McPherson* (Toronto 1980)

127 'We shall have to change': Miss Ethel Reid, Kongmoon, to R.P. MacKay, 27 Oct. 1913, SOCM-1 / 25

127 'the actual facts': Mrs Elliott Busteed to R.P. MacKay, 18 Jan. 1911, SOCM-1 / 13

127   'immediately ... set on foot': Mrs Busteed to R.P. MacKay, 14 May 1910, SOCM–1 / 10

127   'would not care to inscribe': A.E. Armstrong, Toronto, to Dr Jessie McBean, Kongmoon, 29 Sept. 1910, SOCM–1 / 11

128   'dead and cold': W.C. White, *Canon Cody of St. Paul's Church* (Toronto 1953) 66

128   'was able to say in a public': *Cap and Gown* (Wycliffe magazine, Apr. 1921) 3

128   Death of Robert Stewart: *Church Missionary Intelligencer* (CMS, London, Sept. 1895), 656*ff*

128   Rev. J.R.S. Boyd: see correspondence in O'Meara papers, 'Letters to Graduates' (Series 8–E–8) 1895–8, WYCA

128   Bishop W.C. White: He has been the subject of two recent biographies: Lewis C. Walmsley, *Bishop in Honan: Mission and Museum in the Life of William C. White* (Toronto 1974), and Charles Taylor, *Six Journeys: A Canadian Pattern* (Toronto 1977)

129   'public controversy': O'Meara to Henry Frost, North American Director CIM, Summitt, NJ, 1 June 1915, in WYCA O'Meara Personal Correspondence Letterbooks; this is among the only surviving correspondence between members of the Canadian CIM board

129   'Oh! Lord Jesus': Walmsley, *Bishop* 16

130   'their deformed limbs': Rev. William C. White, *Without the Gate, or Leper Work in Longuong, China* (Toronto *c.* 1904) 41

130   'to join in the extension': 'Memorandum on the Proposed Canadian Diocese in China' (1910) quoting resolution of Shanghai conference, 20 Apr. 1907, MSC–141 (bound volume) 8; see also George A. Andrew, *In Honan: 'So Built We the Wall'* (Toronto 1932) 44

130   'see its way': ibid. Board of Management meeting 24 Oct. 1907 9

130   'No scripture sellers': *China's Millions* (Oct. 1902) 101

130   Kaifeng Jews: W.C. White, *Chinese Jews: A Compilation of Matters Relating to the Jews of K'aifeng Fu* (Toronto 1942)

131   'afterwards confessed': Andrew, *In Honan* 43

131   'Thereupon the Hon.': 'Memorandum on the Proposed,' quoting resolution of the House of Bishops, 22 Apr. 1909, MSCC–141 24

131   'The landlord would not rent': W.C. White, 'Annual Report of the Honan Mission for the Year 1913,' in MSCC–141 33

131   'native helpers under': John Webster Grant, *Moon of Wintertime: Missionaries and the Indians of Canada in Encounter Since 1534* (Toronto 1984) 115

132   'complacent and inefficient': 'Memorandum on the Proposed,' quoting White's proposal, 6 July 1908, MSCC–141 10

132   'but a Chinese Church armed': Foster, *Imperialism* 257

132 Mrs Beatrice Jones: MSCC-67 / 'Women Missionaries – China'

132 'approached the building': Walmsley, *Bishop* 100

132 'no desk-bound administrator': Taylor, *Six Journeys* 58

132 'the Mission plant': White, 'Annual Report 1913,' MSCC-141 33

133 'Like many men': Walmsley, *Bishop* 102

133 'a candid and strictly': Rt Rev. S.P. Matheson to Honan missionaries, 7 May 1915, MSCC-86 / 'Constitutions and Canons'

133 'a strong man': Rev. A.J. Williams, Kaifeng, to Matheson, 21 June 1915, ibid.

133 'some of the missionaries': Nels A. Swenson, American Lutheran mission, Kaifeng, to Canon Sydney Gould, 24 May 1915, ibid.

133 'Juniors . . . dreadful': Dr Margaret Phillips, Kaifeng, to Matheson, 18 June 1915, ibid.

133 'a man who changed': Dr Paul V. Helliwell, Kweiteh, to Gould, 27 June 1915, ibid.

133 'rule his own house': Rev. George E. Simmons, Frankford, Ont., to Gould, 15 June 1915, ibid.

133 'neurotic': Phillips to Gould, 18 June 1915, ibid.

133 'willful': Simmons to Gould, 15 June 1915, ibid.

133 'Bishop White went': ibid.

134 'Our mission': Miss Bessie Benbow, Kaifeng, to Matheson, nd, ibid.

134 'Either I did not make myself clear': White to Rev. W.W. Lawton, American Baptist mission Chengchow, 30 July 1910, UT / WCW-4

134 'with electric light plant': White to Gould, 1 Apr. 1912, MSCC – 67, 'Extracts from Correspondence: Bishop White to General Secretary MSCC, Feb. 9th, 1911 – Feb. 21st, 1913'

135 'Day by day I am more' White to Gould, 22 Nov. 1912, ibid.

135 'Now the CIM': White to Gould, 2 Dec. 1912, ibid.

135 Dr Margaret Phillips: MSCC-67 / 'Women Missionaries – China'; 'frequent, uncontrolled' Benbow to Matheson, nd, in MSCC-86, 'Constitutions'

135 'responsibility for the hospital': Phillips to Gould, 15 Nov. 1914, MSCC-67

135 'hardly more than a *Dispensary*': White to Gould, 1 Apr. 1912, MSCC-67, 'Extracts from Correspondence'

135 'two large women's': Helliwell to Gould, 27 June 1915, MSCC-86, 'Constitutions'

136 'as unfit for the missionary': Swenson to Gould, 24 May 1915, ibid.

136 'must be kept clear': Gould to Primate C.L. Worrell, 9 Aug. 1933, MSCC-67, 'W.C. White 1930-34'

136 'An awfully nice bunch of girls': This and the following are from Ruth Jenkins to Annie Lampman Jenkins, Ottawa, 1 Nov. 1920; a brief biography of

Mrs Jenkins appears in Sandra Gwyn, *The Private Capital: Ambition and Love in the Age of Macdonald and Laurier* (Toronto 1984) 437–67

137   'a darling ... and is full': Jenkins 11 Sept. 1921

137   'the pet of the See House': Jenkins, 13 May 1923

137   'The Bishop, being the oldest': Jenkins, 28 Dec. 1923

137   'nurses to work as matrons': anonymous interview with the author

137   'Imagine me keeping accounts': Jenkins, 16 Sept. 1923

137   'I am to commence work': Jenkins, 18 Nov. 1923

138   'Darling, darling Mother': Jenkins, 19 Apr. 1925

138   'made no vow of celibacy': Alice Hageman, 'Women and Missions: The Cost of Liberation,' Alice Hageman, ed., *Sexist Religion and Women in the Church: No More Silence!* (New York 1974) 177

139   'The costume for the afternoon': Jenkins, 28 Aug. 1921

139   'escape from China in China': John Hersey, *The Call*, review in *New York Times Book Review* (20 Apr. 1985) 3

139   'and we set it going whenever': Jenkins, 16 July 1922

139   'We get crazy streaks out here': Jenkins, 11 June 1922

139   'Our life here': Jenkins, 21 Oct. 1923

139   'My bedroom walls are done now': Jenkins, 12 Mar. 1922

139   'Monday, school and tennis': Jenkins, 14 Sept. 1924

140   'The gorgeous moon seemed to shed': Jenkins, 14 May 1922

140   'This has been a very happy': Jenkins, 21 Mar. 1927 Mrs Watts was later a teacher of Chinese language under Bishop White at the University of Toronto.

CHAPTER 8   The Apostolic Vocation: Roman Catholic Missions

The primary sources for Canadian Roman Catholic missions are found in the archives of the various orders: Archives du Secrétariat des Missions jésuites, 3160, chemin Daulac, Montreal (SJA); Archives des Soeurs Missionnaires de l'Immaculée-Conception, 121 avenue Maplewood, Montreal (MICA); Archives des Prêtres des Missions-Etrangères, Pont-Viau, Ville de Lachine (PMEA). The mission magazines are especially valuable: *Le Brigand* (Jesuit, Montreal 1930–); *Le Precurseur* and its English companion *The Precursor* (MICA, Montreal, 1923–) and *Missions-Etrangères* (Pont-Viau 1940–).

   The best scholarly account of French-Canadian missions written since Chanoine Lionel Groulx, *Le Canada français missionnaire: une autre grand aventure* (Montreal 1962) is Jacques Langlais, *Les Jésuites du Québec en Chine (1918-1955)* (Quebec City 1979), which contains an extensive bibliography. See also La

Société Canadienne d'Histoire de l'Eglise Catholique, *Sessions d'Etude* 1971 (SCHEC) for the early history of the ME and MIC.

All French translations are by the author, aided by Maris Pavelson.

The Archives of the Scarboro Foreign Mission Society (SFMSA) are at the society, 2685 Kingston Road. In particular, see the magazine *China*, now called *Scarboro Missions* (1920–). The mission history is Grant Maxwell, *Assignment in Chekiang: 71 Canadians in China, 1902–1954* (Scarboro 1982).

A survey of Roman Catholic missions is contained in: Kenneth Scott Latourette, *A History of Christian Missions in China* (New York 1929). Thomas A. Breslin, *China, American Catholicism, and the Missionary* (University Park, Pa. 1980) is an unreliable source.

143   'Let us remember': *Le Brigand* (June 1937) in Langlais, *Les Jésuites* 20

143   Matteo Ricci: see Jonathan D. Spence, *The Memory Palace of Matteo Ricci* (New York 1984)

144   'What could be more absurd': Maxwell, *Assignment* 15

145   Sermon against Chinese Rites: Langlais, *Les Jésuites* 252

145   'reconcile himself': *Syllabus of Errors*, Article 80

146   Canadians registered with French embassy: Les Soeurs Adoratrices du Précieux-Sang (Sisters Adorers of the Precious Blood) working with the French Jesuits at Sienhsien, Hopei; see PAC External Affairs, RG 25 G 2, file 3050-AG-40 (access 1983–4 / 259)

146   'intrude himself': Latourette, *History* 218

147   'Not one descendant': Rosario Renaud SJ, *Süchow, Diocèse de Chine 1882–1931* 1 (Montreal 1955) 59

148   'Canadian soil': Langlais, *Les Jésuites* 20; see also Joseph-Louis Lavoie SJ, *Quand j'étais chinois* (Montreal 1961) 198

148   'We are nomads': Benoît Lacroix, 'Délia Tétreault: Femme de chez nous,' *Le Précurseur* (July 1985) 261

148   'it is hard to imagine': in Hilda Neatby, 'Servitude de l'Eglise Catholique,' in SCHEC (1971)

149   'in France they wrote': Lacroix, 'Délia Tétreault,' 262

149   *'Américain moi'*: in Langlais, *Les Jésuites* 8

150   'The inspiration came from Rome': Lacroix, 'Délia Tétreault,' 262

150   Jesuit statistics: Langlais, *Les Jésuites* 319ff; MIC statistics, MICA; for 1941 statistics of birthplaces of internees during the Second World War, see PAC External Affairs, RG 25 G 2, files 3050–40

151   'like going from St-Pierre-les-Becquets': interview with Michel Marcil SJ, CBC *Ideas*, 15 June 1984

151   'All the foreigners': Langlais, *Les Jésuites* 17

151 'majestic as Albion': Emile Gervais, *Un Mois en Chine avec les Soeurs Mission-naires N.-D. des Anges (en 1937)* (Sherbrooke 1940) 32, 18

152 'Down with England': 'Vacances 1939,' ms in SJA, 'Süchow sous les japon-nais'

152 'When I am an American': Marcil, interview

152 'The Canadian miracle': Gervais, *Un Mois* 91

152 Franciscans: *Les Franciscains du Canada et leurs missions* (Montreal 1927) 170

153 'a model of religious fervor': MICA, *Dreams of Soul Harvests Come True: Mother Mary of the Holy Spirit, Foundress of the First Canadian Missionary Order* (Montreal 1954) 9

153 'an added financial burden': ibid. 21; see also Mme Marie-Paule Rajotte La Brèque, 'Premières tentatives canadiennes d'établissement d'un Séminaire des Missions-Etrangères,' SCHEC (1971) 17

154 'Let the work': *Dreams* 38

154 'donated by their adepts': ibid. 53

154 'supported by a relatively small': Richard d'Auteil SJ, 'Les Jeunes et les Missions,' *L'Entraide* (MIC Montreal, Feb. 1934), in SJA, 'Ligue missionnaire des écoles'

155 'It would be truly wrong': *Rerum Ecclesiae*, in Langlais, *Les Jésuites* 13

155 Missionary Sisters of Notre-Dame des Anges: Emile Gervais, *Les Soeurs Missionnaires de Notre-Dame des Anges de Sherbrooke* (Sherbrooke 1962)

155 Missions-Etrangères and 'for the Canadian Church': *Dreams* 58; see also Jules Bernard, 'Les débuts de la Société des Missions-Etrangères de la province de Québec (1919–1931),' and Claude Guillet PME, 'Cinquante ans de réalisations: La Société des Missions-Etrangères,' in SCHEC (1971)

156 'carved rich populous': Francis A. Rouleau SJ, 'Bellarmine: Historical Retrospect,' *Mission Bulletin* (Oct. 1954) in SJA, 'Zikawei scolasticat SJ'

157 'essentially a directive': ibid. part 2 (Nov. 1954)

157 'one of the largest agglomerations': Armand Proulx SJ, *Mon Tang-li* (Montreal 1957) 12

157 'The House of Ten Thousand': Breslin, *China* 32

158 'awakened Catholic Canada': Maxwell, *Assignment* 78

158 'straight on like St Paul': ibid. 41

158 'like a dyed-in-the wool': ibid. 32

158 'flying but very fruitful': 'Father Fraser's Early History,' *China* (SFM, Feb. 1920) 38

158 'spared by God's mercy': 'China Mission College Meets with Universal Approval,' ibid. (Oct. 1919) 3

159 'Unknown to the Society's'; 'the discord'; 'pursuing'; and 'I'm always building': Maxwell, *Assignment* 70, 72, 102–3, 162

160   'to reach every Chinese': Latourette, in ibid. 18
160   'Chinese in China': P. Joy SJ, 'Ut Restitua Pace: Missiones Sinenses
       Floreant,' (1946) in SJA, 'Intentions missionnaires'
160   'more or less imprisoned': Maxwell, *Assignment* 92
160   'I saw a person committing' and 'the catechist knew': ibid. 42, 35
161   'The routine at each of the stations': Maxwell, *Assignment* 87
162   'medals of the Father': Alphonse Boileau, in Langlais, *Les Jésuites* 221
162   'Has baby': Maxwell, *Assignment* 87
162   'to send the most possible': Langlais, *Les Jésuites* 278
162   'near the end': Maxwell, *Assignment* 5
162   'It was well worth': ibid. 6
164   'Our crib is rich': *The Precursor* (Jan. 1924) 137-9
164   'forty dollars': ibid. (Nov. 1923) 103
164   'the vestibule of paradise': *Le Précurseur* (Nov. 1932) 715
164   'How happy they are': *The Precursor* (Jan. 1924) 139

CHAPTER 9 Clinical Christianity: Medical Missions

The primary sources for this chapter include the medical correspondence contained in the West China mission papers (WCM) and the North Honan mission
papers (NHM). Considerable medical information is also contained in the mis-
sionary magazines and in the mission study books, particularly: O.L. Kilborn,
Heal the Sick: An Appeal for Medical Missions (Toronto 1910) and George Bond, *Our
Share in China and What We Are Doing with It* (Toronto 1909). Also useful are med-
ical biographies such as: W.E. Smith, *A Canadian Doctor in West China: Forty Years
Under Three Flags* (Toronto 1939); Munroe Scott, *McClure: The China Years of Dr.
Bob McClure* (Toronto 1977). The biography files for the medical personnel in the
UCA are especially valuable.
    The main secondary sources are: Karen Minden, *Missionaries, Medicine, and
Modernization: Canadian Medical Missionaries in Sichuan 1925-1952* (PH D Diss., York
University 1981); Cheung Yuet-Wah, *The Social Organization of Missionary Medi-
cine: A Study of Two Canadian Protestant Missions in China Before 1937* (PH D Diss.,
University of Toronto 1982). Jessie Gregory Lutz, *China and the Christian Colleges
1850-1950* (Ithaca, NY 1971) discusses Christian medical education.
    Dr Leslie Kilborn's Chinese medical library has been deposited in the
Academy of Medicine, 282 Bloor Street West, Toronto.

167   'If the ancestral': *Report of the Special Committee on Policy for Medical Work*
       (1936) in Minden, *Missionaries* 69
167   'symbolized the new place': Brown, *History* LXVI-13

168   'The big problem': Dr R.B. McClure, 1970 York University interview, 5
168   'Unsanitary hospitals': *Spend Ten Minutes in China*, in Minden, *Missionaries* 68
169   'the multiplication of ourselves': in ibid. 316
169   Medical statistics: ibid. 64*ff*; Brown, *History*; MSCC papers; and the List of Canadian Missionaries of the CIM
170   'an inbred group': anonymous non-U. of T. West China missionary, in Minden, *Missionaries* 93
170   'like a roll-call': Dr P.H. Stevenson of the Rockefeller Foundation China Medical Board 1926, in ibid. 93
170   'all the leading features' and 'the suggestion': Dr Alexander Sutherland to O.L. Kilborn, Chengtu, 28 Dec. 1908, WCM-9 / 72
170   'hustlers': Dr Wallace Crawford, in *Our West China Mission* 392
170   Dr Ashley Lindsay: A.W. Lindsay, 'Dental Department,' in ibid. 401; UCA bio. file
170   Drs Edison and Gladys Cunningham: UCA bio. file Dr Gladys was also a regular correspondent of the WCM; see, for example, Cunningham to James Endicott, 28 Sept. 1931, WCM (United Church of Canada, UCC)-3 / 64.
170   Dr Irwin Hilliard: UCA bio. file; see also Mary Carol Wilson, *Marion Hilliard* (Toronto 1977)
171   Dr Leslie Kilborn: UCA bio. file; Bertha Hensman, 'The Kilborn Family: A Record of a Canadian Family's Service to Medical Work and Education in China and Hong Kong,' *Journal of the Canadian Medical Association* (26 Aug. 1967)
171   Dr Charles Winfield Service: UCA bio. file; Kenneth J. Beaton, *Great Living: Rev. Charles W. Service, MD, CM* (Toronto 1945)
171   Dr Davidson Black: Dora Hood, *Davidson Black: A Biography* (Toronto 1964)
171   Dr F.F. Carr-Harris and 'no place': Brown, *History* XLIV-11, XLV-15, LXIV-10
171   'My mother used to tell me': *Missionary Bulletin* (Sept. 1903), 355
172   Women doctors: Carlotta Hacker, *The Indomitable Lady Doctors* 93, 242*ff*; Minden, *Missionaries* 85
172   'If I were at home': Irwin T. Hyatt, *Our Ordered Lives Confess: Three Nineteenth-Century American Missionaries in East Shantung* 84
172   'not mere pretentious': ibid. 85
173   'cast-off snake skins': Kilborn, *Heal the Sick* 56
173   'an unending procession': J. Frazer Smith, *Life's Waking Part* 246
173   'really just giving the fellow a poke': McClure, 1970 York University interview 3, 28-9
174   'Jesus opium': Sterling Seagrave *The Soong Dynasty* (New York 1985) 334
174   'Every time you look': Beaton, *Great Living* 14

174   'shocked': Brown, *History* XLIV–1

174   'could hardly have had the status': *Our West* 405

174   'The aim of the medical': *Missionary Outlook* (Sept. 1903) 203

174   'but just across the street': Kilborn, *Heal the Sick* 24

175   'the patient who pays': Kilborn, 'Medical Missions,' *Canadian Methodist* (Mar. 1902) 252–3

175   'I was told I could do anything': Dr A. Stewart Allen, radio interview with the author, CBC *Ideas*, 7 July 1984

175   'the rich young men': Dr W.E. and Ada Speers Smith, 'Report of Medical Work 1932,' WCM–UCC-4 / 81

176   'with great éclat': *Our West* 251

176   'so far, the crowning manifestation': ibid. 209–10; Minden, *Missionaries* 173ff

176   Kiating hospital: *Our West* 380; Minden, *Missionaries* 207

177   Dr Jeannie Dow: UCA bio. file, obituary by Mrs John Griffith

177   'strongly emphasizes': *Our West* 388

177   'had no prospects': Brown, *History* XLIV–2

177   'not only physician': Kilborn, *Heal the Sick* 220

178   Peking Union Medical College: John Z. Bowers, *Western Medicine in a Chinese Palace: Peking Union Medical College 1917–1951* (New York 1972); see also Peter Kong-ming New and Yuet-Wah Cheung, 'Harvard Medical School of China: An Expanded Footnote in the History of Western Medical Education in China,' *Social Science and Medicine* (June 1982)

178   Cheeloo University prided itself that it was one of two Christian universities in China that used Chinese as the language of instruction.

178   'two miserable little rooms': Dr Retta Kilborn, *Missionary Bulletin* (Dec. 1914) 61; see also Lewis Walmsley, *West China Union University* (New York 1974)

178   'the habit of living': Sutherland to Kilborn, 31 Aug. 1908, WCM-9 / 72

178   'My Chinese colleagues': in Minden, *Missionaries* 284

179   'Our Chinese doctors': W.E. Smith to Endicott, 7 July 1932, WCM–UCC-4 / 76

179   Dr P.S. Tennant: Minden, *Missionaries* 232

180   'allowed the institution': Rev. Frederick Reed to Endicott, 19 June 1936, in ibid. 238

180   'While millions of people died': Pearl Buck, in Jerome Ch'en, *China and the West: Society and Culture 1815–1937* (Bloomington, Ind. 1979) 133

180   'mud-floored store-front': Minden, *Missionaries* 180

182   Dr Walter Clark: interview with his granddaughter, Patricia Kennedy

182   Dr Edward Fish: UTA bio. file; Mrs Howard Taylor, *'By Faith . . .'* 316–18; interview with his son Dr Edward Fish

182   Hwaiking Rural Medical System: McClure, 1970 York University inter-
       view, 4, 44–5; Scott, *McClure* 197

CHAPTER 10   Marching as to War

NOTE: On 10 June 1925, the United Church of Canada came into being, incorporating the three China missions of the former Presbyterian and Methodist
churches. Correspondence after that date is indicated by UCC.

There are three files of correspondence of the Presbyterian missionaries working with the Chinese Labour Corps in France (CLC) in the UCA. The PAC has official despatches concerning the CLC; these are listed in the bibliography of
Mitchell below.

   Two complementary papers presented to the Canadian Historical Associa-
tion on 10 June 1982 describe the CLC: Margo Gewurtz, 'For God or for King:
Canadian Missionaries and the Chinese Labour Corps in World War I,' and
Peter Mitchell, 'Canada and the Chinese Labour Corps, 1917–1920: The Official
Connection.' Stephen Endicott, *James G. Endicott: Rebel Out of China* (Toronto
1980) is an important account of the 'left-wing' tendencies within the West
China mission.

185   'I want you to sit': *Missionary Bulletin* (Dec. 1914) 55
185   'After 1911': Dr R.B. McClure, 1970 York University interview 12
186   'a fair idea'; 'verbatim copy'; and 'Now, there is a great battle': Dr Wallace
       Crawford, *Missionary Bulletin* (Dec. 1914) 108
186   'the fruits of Christianity': Brown, *History* LI–8
186   'godly German saints': *China's Millions* (Nov. 1914) 154
187   'We are not at war': R.P. MacKay to William R. McKay, Kongmoon, 19
       Sept. 1914, SOCM-1 / 31
187   'the people in many parts of Canada': Agnes Dickson, Kongmoon, to R.P.
       MacKay, 27 Sept. 1914, SOCM-1 / 31
187   'employ Japanese advisors': Joseph Taylor, *West of the Gorges*, 103; see also
       The Times History of the War Vol. 2 (London 1915) 397ff
188   'the critical element': Gewurtz, 'For King,' 17
188   'leaving their posts': *China's Millions* (Jan. 1918) 15
188   eight Canadian lads: interview with James Horne, grandson of W.S.
       Horne, whose father was one of the volunteers, Mar. 1983
189   'had listened': Murdoch Mackenzie, Changte, to R.P. MacKay, 25 Jan. 1917,
       NHM-5 / 69
189   'tragedy': Brown, *History* LIII–10

189   'He handled all the paperwork': Gewurtz, 'For King,' 19

190   'practically as freight': *New York Times*, 25 Feb. 1917

190   'absolutely cheerless': *Halifax Herald*, 16 Feb. 1920

190   'assiduously': Mitchell, 'Canada and the CLC,' 12; Colonel Ernest J. Chambers, Canadian Chief Press Censor, to Lieutenant Colonel A.W. Richardson, Corps of Guides, Kingston, 8 Aug. 1917, PAC–RG 6 E 1 Vol. 620, file 331

190   'a Company which has': 'Extract of letter from Lt. Col. G.D. Gray, Royal Army Medical Corps, 1918,' in CLC–1 / 2

190   'the backbone': Dr E.B. Struthers, France, to R.P. MacKay, 31 Jan. 1918, CLC–1 / 2

190   'These are testing days': Capt. Herbert A. Boyd, France, to R.P. MacKay, 20 Apr. 1918, CLC–1 / 2

190   'Lectures were delivered': Rev. Charles A. Leonard, American Baptist missionary, 'Confidential Report Letter No. 2 about the Chinese Labor Corps Service in France' (1919) CLC–1 / 3

191   'winning golden opinions': Dr Frederick M. Auld, France, to R.P. MacKay, 28 Dec. 1917, CLC–1 / 1

191   'the Chinaman': T.A. Arthurs, France, to R.P. MacKay, 6 Oct. 1918, CLC–1 / 2

191   'in the firm resolve': *Presbyterian Record* (Dec. 1919) 365

192   Death of Dr James R. Menzies: PAC, Governor General's Files RG 7 G 21, file 6278; Brown, *History* LIX

192   'like maggots': McClure, 1970 York University interview 20

192   'over-numerous and under-disciplined': Sir Miles Lampson, British chargé d'affaires Peking, to Wai Chiao Pu (Chinese Foreign Office) 5 Apr. 1920, in Brown, *History* LIX–12

192   'was the result': R.P. MacKay to W.H. Grant, Honan, 29 July 1920, in ibid. LX–8

192   'I know if the people': J.A. Paterson to R.P. MacKay, with copy to Honan mission, 19 Nov. 1920, in ibid. LX–11

193   North China famine relief and 'simply dried up': Brown, *History* LXI

193   'good advertising': Lewis Walmsley, *Bishop in Honan* 120

193   'all emotional charity': *Proceedings of the General Assembly* (PGA) 1895, Brown, *History* LXI–4

194   'a walking advertisement': PGA 1922, ibid. LXI–17

195   'People from a particular': *Honan Messenger* (July 1921) ibid. LXI–14

196   'It was commonplace': interview with Edward B. Jolliffe, CBC *Ideas*, Apr. 1984

196   McClure as Honorary CMO: Scott, *McClure* 118

197   'Mediation between Contesting Parties': W. Meyrick Hewlett, British
       Consul-General Chengtu, to R.H. Clive, British Minister Peking, 9 Sept.
       1920 PAC RG 7 21, file 6278

198   'First oust the extraprovincial': Hewlett to Sir Beelby Alston, British Min-
       ister Peking, 6 Sept. 1921, in ibid.

198   May Fourth Movement: Chow Tse-tung, *The May Fourth Movement: Intellec-
       tual Revolution in Modern China* (Cambridge, Mass. 1960)

198   'Gold and iron': in Jessie Gregory Lutz, *China and the Christian Colleges* 223

198   Babylonian wars: Rev. J.L. Stewart, 'An Anti-Christian Crusade in China,'
       The New Outlook (24 June 1925) 12

198   W.H. Leonard: Dr Kyle Simpson, Fowchow, to James Endicott, 9 June
       1924, WCM–15 / 156; W.H. Leonard to Endicott, 9 June 1924, ibid.; see also
       Alston to Lord Curzon, Foreign Office London, 28 Dec. 1921, PAC RG 7 G 21,
       file 6278

199   'crowds of coolies': Rev. Thomas A. Broadfoot, in *Forward with China: The
       Story of the Missions of the United Church of Canada in China* (Toronto 1928)
       212–13

200   'dumb, industrious': C.R. Hensman, *Sun Yat-sen* 105

200   'the Christians, including': W.R. McKay, Kongmoon, to A.E. Armstrong, 8
       July 1925, SOCM–UCC–1 / 3

200   'Harbours full of warships': Eleanor MacNeill, in Foster, *Imperialism* 117

200   'dreamers': 'The Province of Szechuan Storm Centre of China,' *Toronto
       Daily Star* (3 Mar. 1923)

200   Canadian government ban on KMT: PAC RG 24, Vol. 96, 'Chinese Activity in
       Canada'; Harry Con et al, *From China to Canada: A History of the Chinese
       Communities in Canada* (Toronto 1982)

201   'the combustible material': in Foster, *Imperialism* 122

201   'Give them a bit of lead': in Endicott, *J.G. Endicott* 88

201   'the effect is seen': Dr Kyle Simpson, Fowchow, to James Endicott, July
       1925, WCM–15 / 159

202   'Even those students': *The New Outlook* (1 July 1925) 9

202   'led by three hundred bolshevist': 'La Bataille de Shameen,' *Le Précurseur*
       (Jan. 1926) 369

202   'The Chinese newspapers': W.R. McKay to Armstrong, 8 July 1925, SOCM–
       UCC–1 / 3

203   '*masked* and on horseback': *Le Précurseur* (Jan. 1926) 369

203   'fortress of Britain': Harold Isaacs, *The Tragedy of the Chinese Revolution*
       (Stanford 1961) 70–1

203   'If the whole incident': Foster, *Imperialism* 185

203   'All true friends': *Forward with China* 211

203　'so wrapped up': Rev. Duncan McRae, Shekki, to A.E. Armstrong, 8 June 1925, SOCM-2 / 68

203　'The Cantonese-Russians': *Le Précurseur*, (Jan. 1926) 390

204　'We are afraid of a bombardment' and 'it was a real treat': *ibid.* 391, 395

204　'the better-thinking Chinese': W.R. McKay, Hong Kong, to Armstrong, 30 Sept. 1925, SOCM-UCC-1 / 3

204　'The relations between the Canadian': Foster, *Imperialism* 197

205　'a revolution is not': in Seagrave, *The Soong Dynasty* 215

205　'We are flotsam': Mrs John E. Williams, in James C. Thomson, Jr, *While China Faced West: American Reformers in Nationalist China 1928–1937* x

205　'Conditions in this part': Dr William Birks to Jesse H. Arnup, Secretary of the BFM, 27 Oct. 1926, WCM-UCC-1 / 9

205　'pressure from the Red': G.W. Sparling to Arnup, 'Re Agitation in the West China Union University Oct. 4–8/26,' WCM-UCC-1 / 5

205　Death of Mrs Edith Sibley: WCM-UCC-1 / 6; George Hartwell to James Endicott, 8 June 1926 ibid.; see also PAC RG 7 G 21, file 6278, S. O'Malley, British Legation Peking to Sir Austen Chamberlain, Foreign Office London, 8 July 1926

206　'the growing frequency': 'Confidential Conversation Between Consul and Mission Representatives, 11 June 1926,' WCM-UCC-1 / 6

206　Wanhsien incident: I have followed this incident as related by Endicott, *J.G. Endicott* 92ff, and Foster, *Imperialism* 357

206　'the neighbourly policeman': *Our West China Mission* 104

206　'this gunboat business': R.O. Jolliffe to James Endicott, 27 Sept. 1926, WCM-UCC-1 / 9

206　'Oh, yes, we believe in your': *Missionary Bulletin* (Mar. 1909) 798

206　*Chia-na-ta*: Simpson to Endicott, 8 July 1925, WCM-15 / 159

207　'I never read anything': Endicott, *Endicott* 79–80

207　'Every such crisis': Sparling to Endicott, 'Re Agitation,' WCM-UCC-1 / 5

208　'It is my personal duty': General Liu Tsen-ho, in Foster, *Imperialism* 370; for evacuation plans, see WCM-UCC-1 / 12, 14

208　'barb wire and sand bags': Rev. Kenneth J. Beaton, Shanghai, to Arnup, 11 Mar. 1927, WCM-UCC-1 / 13

208　'Across the barbed-wire': Isaacs, *The Tragedy* 146

208　'Whatinhell': Telegram received in Chengtu, 21 Feb. 1927, WCM-UCC-1 / 27

208　'So here we are': W.J. Mortimore to Arnup, 2 Apr. 1927, WCM-UCC-1 / 27

208　'the Great Man': Frank Dickinson to Arnup, 26 Sept. 1927, WCM-UCC-1 / 20

208　'that misguided agitator': Murdoch Mackenzie to FMC, 13 Nov. 1917, in Brown, *History* LXXII-2

209 'We, of course, wish': Harvey Grant to A.E. Armstrong, 22 Dec. 1926, NHM-UCC-1 / 16

209 'The first thought at home': Brown, *History* LXXVII-14

209 'My eyes once turned': Grant to Armstrong, 24 Aug. 1926, NHM-UCC-1 / 16

209 'soldiers of various armies': Brown, *History* LXXVII-6

210 'once more using the delaying': ibid. LXXIV-13

210 'a highly organized church system': Rev. Andrew Thomson, in *Forward with China* 152

210 'like serfs in the community': Varg, *Missionaries* 100

210 'church-wreckers': Harvey Grant, in Brown, *History* LXXIII-4

210 'We are proud to be British': Grant to Armstrong, 4 Apr. 1927, NHM-UCC-2 / 23

211 'the more *intelligent*': W.C.. White, 'Annual Report of the Honan Diocese for the Year 1925,' 20 Jan. 1926, MSCC-67, 'Canon Simmons 1920-28'

211 'is the greatest obstacle': White, 'Annual Report of the Honan Diocese for the Year 1924,' ibid.

211 'purely an auxiliary': Foster, *Imperialism* 281

211 'the first and only': White, 'Annual Report of the Honan Diocese for the Year 1929,' 26 Mar. 1930, MSCC-67, 'W.C. White 1928-30'

211 'There seem to be': Canon George Simmons, Chefoo, to R.A. Williams, Secretary of the MSCC, 30 Apr. 1927, MSCC-67, 'Canon Simmons 1920-28'

212 'You can imagine how hard': W.R. McKay, Hong Kong, to R.P. MacKay, 8 July 1925, SOCM-UCC-1 / 3

PART 3: THE POLITICAL GOSPEL 1927-1959

CHAPTER 11 New Life: The Nanking Decade

One indication of the decline in mission interest is the lack of mission surveys for this period.

The standard history of the Nanking decade is James C. Thomson, *While China Faced West: American Reformers in Nationalist China 1928-1937*

213 'It is regrettable': Dr Janet McClure Kilborn, Hong Kong, to Drs Edison and Gladys Cunningham, 1 Apr. 1952, WCM-UCC-14 / 362

215 'The Moderator': *The New Outlook* (3 Aug. 1927) 3

215 'Now that civil war': Harvey Grant, Changte, to A.E. Armstrong, 7 Nov. 1929, in Brown, *History* LXXXIV-1

216 Chiang's entry into Shanghai: Sterling Seagrave, *The Soong Dynasty* 223

216 'a grand puritan': Joyce Reason, *Chiang Kai-shek and the Unity of China* (London 1943) 21

217 Dr and Mrs Harrison Mullett: interview with Mrs Bea Mullett, CBC *Ideas*, Apr. 1984

217 'hostages to the necessities': Foster, *Imperialism* 371

217 'our merchants': ibid. 199

217 'It looks almost as if': W.R. McKay, Kongmoon, to A.E. Armstrong, 27 May 1927, SOCM–UCC-1 / 9

217 'I believe in God': 'Address of Dr James Endicott, at Dinner of West China Union University, Shanghai, Mar. 19, 1927,' WCM–UCC-1 / 23

218 'If you leave the impression': 'Address by the Moderator, Dr Endicott, to the Joint Councils, delivered Mar. 21, 1927,' WCM–UCC-1 / 24

218 'expressing their faith': Brown, *History* LXXVII-2

219 'We reëxamined ourselves': Taylor, *'By Faith . . .'* 327

219 'appeared to us to be': Dr R.B. McClure, 1970 York University interview 41

219 Statistics of 1927–30: 'List of West China Missionaries and their Relation to the Mission, 1928,' WCM–UCC-2 / 29; *West China Missionary News* (June 1931) 35 For an examination of this phenomenon in the American missions, see Shirley Stone Garrett, 'Why They Stayed: American Church Politics and Chinese Nationalism,' in Fairbank, *Missionary Enterprise* 283.

220 Rev. John D. MacRae: UCA bio. file; Brown, *History* LXXIII-3

220 'What shall I do': Goforth, *Goforth* 264

220 'realized almost at once': Harvey Grant to A.E. Armstrong, 23 Mar. 1927, NHM–UCC-2 / 23 This contradicts Goforth's continued propaganda; see 'Veteran Missionary of Presbyterian Church Tells of Chinese "Christian" Army,' Vancouver *Province* (18 July 1926)

221 'no place left': Goforth, *Goforth* 268-70; 'I think of today as being': ibid. 348

221 'transitional semi-stability': Thomson, *While China Faced* 6

221 'So much for': Dr I.E. Revelle, Luchow, to 'Dear Friends,' Nov. 1932, WCM–UCC-4 / 76

222 'All houses had been looted': Brown *History* LXXXI-2

222 'engage in any active': *Annual Report* (1928) in ibid. LXXXI-8

222 'the missionaries on the field': Board of Foreign Missions (BFM) to Synod of Honan, 29 Apr. 1930, ibid. LXXXIII-17

222 'it lays down certain rules': *Annual Report* (1928) in ibid. LXXXII-9

222 'After blowing up railway': W.C. White, 'Annual Report of the Honan Diocese for the Year 1929,' 10 Feb. 1930, MSCC-67, 'W.C. White 1928-9'

223 'official China seems': W.C. White, Kaifeng, to Canon Sydney Gould, 28 Feb. 1930, MSCC-67, 'W.C. White 1930'

223   'The outstanding event': 'Annual Report 1929,' MSCC–67, 'W.C. White 1928-9'

223   'Our Educational Work': White to Gould, 28 Feb. 1930, MSCC–67, 'W.C. White 1930'

223   'almost continuous physical': White to Primate C.L. Worrell, 12 July 1933, MSCC–67, 'W.C. White 1931-33'

223   'bishop emeritus': Gould to Worrell, 9 Aug. 1933 in ibid.

224   Royal Ontario Museum: Walmsley, *Bishop*; Charles T. Currelly, *I Brought the Ages Home* (Toronto 1956); see also ROMA For the current attitude of the Chinese to White's collecting, see Toronto *Globe and Mail* (25 Jan. 1983) 16.

225   'Secrecy played': Walmsley, *Bishop* 143

225   ' "treasure," the same': Gould to Primate S.P. Matheson, 23 June 1923, MSCC–54 (series 3-2, Bishops' Correspondence), 'Rupert's Land'

226   Museum of WCUU: Missionary donations to the museum are catalogued regularly in *West China Missionary News* during the 1930s The dinosaur was a gift from the ROM in return for four panda skins – see ROM of Zoology, *Annual Report*, Oct. 1934 to Apr. 1935.

227   continuing Presbyterian Church: Zander Dunn, 'The Great Divorce and What Happened to the Children,' *Canadian Society of Presbyterian History Papers* (1977)

227   Student Christian Movement: Margaret Beattie, *A Brief History of the Student Christian Movement of Canada 1921-1974* (Toronto 1975); Ernest A. Dale, *Twenty-One Years A-Building: A Short Account of the Student Christian Movement of Canada 1920-1941* (Toronto 1941); see also Richard Allen, *The Social Passion* The uncatalogued papers of the National Headquarters of the SCM are in the UCA.

227   'theology of radical reform': Allen, *The Social Passion* 302

227   'on a world-wide quest': *Varsity* (U. of T., 4 Oct. 1920) UTA Senate Clipping Files, box 24, 'Student Christian Association'

227   Henry Burton Sharman: H.B. Sharman, *Jesus in the Records* (Toronto c. 1917), as well as ten other Bible-study books; see also *This One Thing: A Tribute to Henry Burton Sharman* (Toronto 1959) Sharman was a professor at Yenching University in Peking, 1926-9.

228   'We got that method': Earl Willmott, interview with York University Oral History Project, 'Canadians in East Asia', 9 Dec. 1971 5

228   'are fed up with religious': 'A Conversation,' *West China Missionary News* (June 1925) 26 For Willmott's probable authorship, see Willmott, 'Report of Work 1924 – Jenshow,' WCM-18 / 186.

229   'Can a Missionary Be': Varg, *Missionaries* 172-4

229   'the high watermark': ibid. 167

229   'there were many': William Ernest Hocking et al., *Re-Thinking Missions: A Laymen's Inquiry After One Hundred Years* (New York 1932) 15

229   'is somewhat like asking': ibid. 4

230   'It is true that one member': Dr Wallace Crawford, Chengtu, to James Endicott, 8 Dec. 1932, WCM–UCC-4 / 76

230   West China contributions: Rev. Gerald S. Bell, Secretary WCM Chengtu, to Endicott, 10 Feb. 1931, WCM–UCC-3 / 58

230   Dr Robert Gordon Agnew: Endicott to Bell, 10 Dec. 1932, WCM–UCC-4 / 73; James Endicott, 'Well-Earned Recognition,' *The New Outlook*, 14 Dec. 1932; see also bio. files in UCA, UTA graduate records

231   'have given the Chinese people': Wilder Penfield, 'China Mission Accomplished,' *Journal of the Canadian Medical Association*, 26 Aug. 1967, 468; see also Minden, *Missionaries* 71

231   'humanism and relativism': Varg, *Missionaries* 179

231   Oxford Group Movement: the UCA has a useful clipping file; see also W.E. Taylor, 'The Oxford Group,' *Cap and Gown* (Wycliffe, Nov. 1934)

231   'The World-Spanning Christian': Weekly Supplement to *Witness and Canadian Homestead c.* 1934 in UCA file

232   Oxford Group in West China: Bell to Endicott, 3 Feb. 1933, WCM–UCC-4 / 86

232   John Sung: Leslie T. Lyall, *John Sung: Flame for God in the Far East* (Toronto 1954)

232   Andrew Gih: Andrew Gih, *Twice Born – And Then?* (London 1954)

232   'emotionalized individualistic': quoted in *China Missionary* (Roman Catholic, New York, 1950 in SJA

233   Pentecostals: see PAC, External Affairs RG 25 G 2, file 3050-H-40, 'Safety of Pentecostal Assemblies of Canada missionaries,' and 3050-J-40, 'Safety of Pacific Coast Missionary Society' (access 1983–84 / 259)

233   'gap men': Harold Watson Boon, *The Development of the Bible College or Institute in the United States and Canada Since 1880 and its Relationship to the Field of Theological Education in America* (D ED Diss., New York University 1950) 42; see also the archives of the Ontario Bible College (formerly the Toronto Bible College) 25 Ballyconnor Court, North York

234   'the Two Hundred': Frank Houghton, *The Two Hundred* (Toronto 1932); see also 'The Two Hundred: Something to Say to This Generation,' *East Asia's Millions* (Dec. 1981)

234   Miao written language: James Endicott, *Missionary Bulletin* (Dec. 1906) 614

235   'God's prairie-fire': Taylor, 'By Faith . . .' 227

235   'No one unfamiliar': ibid. 342

235   Morris Slichter: G.A. Combe, British Consul-General Yunnanfu, to Sir

Miles Lampson, British Minister Peking, 15 Apr. 1927, in PAC Governor General RG 7 G 21, file 6278

235   John and Betty Stam: Mrs Howard Taylor, *The Triumph of John and Betty Stam* (Toronto 1935)

235   Bishop Paul Yu-pin: obituary in *Saturday Examiner* (Hong Kong, 25 Aug. 1977) in SJA, 'Cardinal Yu-pin'

236   'Picture the scene': Bruce Collier, 'Hold the Fort,' 28 May 1936, WCM–UCC–6 / 127

237   'almost on the last lap': Frank Dickinson, Chengtu, to Endicott, 12 Oct. 1930, WCM–UCC–3 / 50; Dickinson was one of the mission's regular correspondents and also a regular contributor to *West China Missionary News*; see UCA bio. file

237   'cowology': Dickinson to Endicott, 26 Mar. 1932, WCM–UCC–4 / 77

237   'The clinic is not': Dr Gladys Cunningham, Chengtu, to Endicott, 28 Sept. 1931, WCM–UCC–3 / 64

238   'an even greater achievement': Brown, *History* LXVI-8

238   'To give a training': in ibid. LXVI-8

239   New Life Movement: See Thomson, *While China Faced* 163; Endicott, *Endicott* 141; Minden, *Missionaries* 220

240   'the one trusted': Thomson, *While China Faced* 76

240   'Military Discipline': ibid. 160

240   'His impression of the Kuomintang': Endicott, *Endicott* 151

240   'We must be loyal': ibid. 138

CHAPTER 12 The Days That Are Evil

Primary sources not mentioned above are PAC, External Affairs files RG 25 G 2, files 226/ 'Canadian Nationals in China 1935-39.' The 'secret' (now declassified) files of the Chungking and Nanking Embassy, series 50000, are in the Department of External Affairs (DEA).

243   'War, with all': R.E. Thompson, *Young China* (CIM Toronto, Jan. 1938) 484

244   'unnaturally fattened': Rhodes Farmer, *Shanghai Harvest: A Diary of Three Years in the China War* (London 1945) 97

244   Roman Catholic statistics: Joy, 'Ut Restitua Pace,' (1946) SJA, 'Intentions Missionnaires'

244   'Quite a lot of our newspapers': James Endicott to Harold Deeks Robertson, WCUU Chengtu, 8 Jan. 1932, WCM–UCC–3 / 64

245   'From the beginning': Robertson to Endicott, 23 Nov. 1931, ibid.

245 'but you know how the Chinese': Dr Gladys Cunningham, Chengtu, to Endicott, 28 Sept. 1931, ibid.

245 'avoid touching on things': Goforth, *Goforth* 306

246 'If personally we have nothing': *Le Précurseur* (Jan. 1932) 402

246 'perfect discipline': ibid. (Mar. 1932) 467

246 'as long as we didn't act': Bertha Crévier, '40 Ans Après: Souvenirs de Manchourie,' ibid. (July 1985) 276

247 R.A. Bosshardt: R.A. Bosshardt, *The Restraining Hand* (Toronto 1936)

247 'the deep waters': *China's Millions* (June 1937) 93

247 'There was tremendous excitement': Gerald S. Bell to Endicott, 26 Dec. 1936, WCM-UCC-6 / 123

247 'a patriotism new': *Chinese Millions* (July 1937) 109

247 'If our leader Chiang': 'Relation annuelle de la Mission de Süchow 1937–38,' in SJA, 'Süchow: Relations Annuelles'

248 'once the most populated': Farmer, *Shanghai Harvest* 93

249 'If there should be another': Rt Rev. William C. McGrath, *The Dragon at Close Range* (Shanghai and Scarborough Bluffs 1938) 93

250 'Day after day the refugees': Margaret Crossett, *Harvest at the Front* (Toronto 1946) 33–6

250 'a den of horrors': Scott, *McClure* 221

250 'the wounded soldiers': May Watts, Kaifeng, to L.A. Dixon, Secretary MSCC, 6 Apr. 1938, MSCC-65, 'May Watts'

251 'breathless': Scott, *McClure* 232

251 'no more compulsion': Dr Wallace Crawford, 'A Missionary Epistle from China,' *Missionary Review of the World* (Apr. 1939) 172

252 Dr Richard Brown: MSCC-98 (series 3–3. L. Dixon correspondence) 'Dr Richard Brown' See also bio. file in UTA graduate records; transcripts of *Bethune*, National Film Board 1964; Scott, *McClure*; Rod Stewart, *Bethune* (Toronto 1973), and interview with Brown's son, Peter Brown.

252 'Medical work under the J': Brown, Hankow, to Bishop W.C. White, Toronto, 19 Feb. 1938, MSCC-98, 'Brown'

252 'anti-God museums': Toronto *Telegram* (11 Feb. 1935) UTA

252 'psychopathic': *Bethune* transcript

252 'to the contrary': Brown to Dixon, 24 Nov. 1938, MSCC-98

252 'serious misgivings': Dixon to Bishop Lindel Tsen, 9 Apr. 1938, and Minutes of Executive Committee meeting, 17 May 1938, both in ibid.

253 'I am firmly of the opinion': Brown to Dixon, 24 Nov. 1938, ibid.

253 'Full marks': R.B. McClure, extracts of letter, 21 Nov. 1938, ibid.

253 'reasonable': G.A. Andrew to Dixon, 12 Dec. 1938, ibid.

253 'I myself longed': Bishop R.O. Hall to Tsen, 30 Nov. 1938, ibid.

254 'The Eighth Route Army': enclosed with McClure, 21 Nov. 1938; also quoted in *China Christian Year Book* (1938)

254 'merely waiting': Brown to Horace Watts, MSCC, 24 Dec. 1941, MSCC–98

255 'The faith was solidly': Rosario Renaud 1938, quoted in Langlais, *Les Jésuites* 65

255 'we went to them': Edouard Côté, *La Société Chrétienne* (c. 1946) in SJA, 'Süchow Pastorale'

255 'During these troubled years': Edouard LaFlèche, 'Histoire du diocèse de Süchow,' *Lettres du Bas Canada* (Jesuit, Montreal, Mar. 1953) in SJA, 'Agence Fides'

255 'I subject a city': LaFlèche, ibid.

256 'aggressive': 'Quelques impressions et constatations sur les tendances anti-étrangères et anti-religieuses dans nos régions,' in SJA, 'Süchow: Relations avec les japonnais'

256 'Providence was taking': LaFlèche, 'Histoire du diocèse,' SJA, 'Agence Fides'

256 'All the same': 'Quelques impressions,' SJA, 'Süchow: Relations ... japonnais'

257 'L'Ame Japonnaise': Albert Dupuis, 'Litterae Annuae: Mission de Süchow 1941–42,' in SJA, 'Süchow: Relations Annuelles'

257 'battery of Free-Masonry': Urbain M. Clouthier, *The Sino-Japanese Conflict* (Ottawa c. 1938), in SJA, 'Süchow: ... régime japonnais'

258 Gladys Aylward: Alan Burgess, *The Small Woman* (London 1957)

258 'From experience I knew': Greta M. Clark, Tsingtao, 'Annual Report, Nov. 25, 1939,' MSCC–86, 'Reports – Annual – Missionaries'

258 'I sold almost everything': Clark to May Watts, 24 Oct. 1943, MSCC–121 (Series 7, Publications Dept.), 'Honan correspondence 1940–48'

258 'everyone in our mission': Bell to A.E. Armstrong, 13 Nov. 1938, WCM–UCC–7 / 146

259 'The only way to get to Free China': 'Memorandum on Miss Margaret Brown, MA, B Paed.,' in UCA bio. file

259 'it packed its 8000 tons of machinery': Theodore H. White and Annalee Jacoby, *Thunder Out of China* (New York 1946) 57

260 'in a building that will ultimately': Rev. Ernest Hibbard, Treasurer WCM, to J.H. Arnup, 2 Jan. 1938, WCM–UCC–7 / 145

260 Chungking hospital: Minden, *Missionaries* 158; interview with Dr A. Stewart Allen, CBC *Ideas*, 1984

261 'to escape the stigma': Varg, *Missionaries* 265

261 'then, war or no war': Glenn Kittler, *The Maryknoll Fathers* (New York 1963) 216

261   'I have recently returned': James G. Endicott, radio broadcast, 23 Nov. 1941, CBC Archives, quoted in Alvyn Austin, 'Canadian Missionaries in China,' CBC *Ideas*, 25 Jan. 1985

262   'Made in U.S.A.': Rev. Albert Charles Hoffman to Endicott, 22 Nov. 1932, WCM–UCC–4 / 76

262   'We believe it is a moral duty': Varg, *Missionaries* 262

262   'I have been digging Canadian scrap': Scott, *McClure* 284-6

262   Jennie King Lay: see George Tradescant Lay papers in PAC MG 24 L 13

263   'is not only insulting': J.L. Granatstein, *A Man of Influence: Norman A. Robertson and Canadian Statecraft 1929-68* (Ottawa 1981) 99-101

264   'is one of those impetuous': Arnup to Bell, 22 Sept. 1941, WCM–UCC–8 / 175

CHAPTER 13   Redeeming the Time

Personal reminiscences of life in the wartime internment camps include: William G. Sewell, *Strange Harmony* (London 1946); J. MacAndrew, *Bondservants of the Japanese* (London 1946); *Through Toil and Tribulation: Missionary Experiences in China During the War of 1937-1945, Told by the Missionaries* (London 1947); Norman Cliff, *Courtyard of the Happy Way* (Evesham, Eng. 1977); Fay Angus, *The White Pagoda* (Wheaton, Ill. 1978).

External Affairs papers in the PAC dealing with the internment and repatriation include: RG 25 G 2, 3050-40 series (e.g., 3050-A-40, 'Safety of Franciscans') and 3051-40 series (e.g., 3051-A-40, 'Safety of Missionaries of the MSCC'), access 1983-4 / 259; 'Gripsholm' files 2864-40; 'Records of the Chungking Embassy,' 4558-40 series, access 259. The Victor Wentworth Odlum Papers MG 30 E 300 are also useful.

267   'By military necessity': Cliff, *Courtyard* 141

267   'So life changed': Mrs Dorothy Bell, *Nannie's Story* (Toronto 1982)

268   'We were always prepared': Rev. John A. Austin, interview with the author, CBC *Ideas*, July 1984

268   '"Busy" might describe': Rev. W.S. Simpson to 'Dad, Vivian and all,' 16 Oct. 1942, MSCC-121 (Series 7, Publications Dept.), 'Honan correspondence 1940-42'

269   'For years and years': Maxwell, *Assignment* 120-1

269   'on foot, by bicycle': ibid. 119

269   Friends' Ambulance Unit: Scott, *McClure* 291*ff*

270   'a feeling of remoteness': Gerald S. Bell, Chengtu, to J.H. Arnup, 24 Feb. 1942, WCM–UCC–9 / 196

270   'as morale officers': Religious News Service, *Press Release*, Chungking, 9 Feb. 1945, in MSCC–125

270   'China will win': Dr R.G. Agnew, *Toronto Daily Star* (23 Oct. 1943) in UTA bio. file

271   'the Yellow Chinese Cow': Frank Dickinson to Arnup, 11 Nov. 1941, WCM–UCC–8 / 192

271   'the worthless coin': Dr Irwin Hilliard to Arnup, 10 Jan. 1943, WCM–UCC–9 / 220

271   's.o.s.': Katherine Willmott to Arnup, 4 Oct. 1941, WCM–UCC–8 / 191

271   selling wedding presents: W.S. Taylor, Bloomfield, Ontario, to Arnup, 30 Jan. 1943, WCM–UCC–9 / 220

271   'It is hard to write': Bell to Arnup, 29 Jan. 1943, WCM–UCC–9 / 216

272   'Were I to go into': Dr A.E. Best to 'Friends of Centennial' (United Church), Toronto, 26 Dec. 1943, WCM–UCC–9 / 220

272   'I have been to London': Arnup to Bell, 23 June 1943, WCM–UCC–9 / 216

272   Chiang's 'marital relations': Armstrong to Bell, 30 Nov. 1944, WCM–UCC–10 / 239; see also Sterling Seagrave, *The Soong Dynasty* 379, 414

273   Odlum's mother: Victor Wentworth Odlum, Ankara, to Chester A. Ronning, 3 Dec. 1951, PAC Odlum MG 30 E 300, box 11, 'Ronning' Odlum's parents had been missionaries in Japan at the time.

273   'I am very direct': Odlum to Hugh Keenleyside, Department of External Affairs, 3 June 1943, PAC External RG 25 G 2, file 4558–P–40C

273   Odlum and the missionaries: PAC Odlum Papers has many letters from Canadian missionaries, see in particular J.G. Endicott, Leslie Kilborn files

273   'the Canadian flag': Odlum to H.H. Kung, Chinese Finance Minister, 17 Apr. 1944, PAC Odlum, box 33

273   'China can do for the Canada': Odlum to External Affairs, 2 Oct. 1945, quoted in Kim Richard Nossal, 'Business as Usual: Canadian Relations with China in the 1940's,' paper presented at the Canadian Historical Society annual meeting 1978 22

274   'The Americans now look upon': Odlum to W.L. Mackenzie King, 31 May 1943, PAC External RG 25 G 2, file 4558–P–40C

274   'analysis presupposes': Odlum to Norman Robertson, Secretary of State for External Affairs, 14 Apr. 1944, PAC Odlum, box 33

274   Odlum's private picnic: Odlum to External, 21 Aug. 1946 (No. 923, 925) DEA, file 50055–40, Vol. 3 (held in DEA Ottawa)

275   Ch'en Li-fu: Odlum to External, 21 Aug. 1946 (No. 928), in ibid.

276   'exercising their female': Arnup to Bell, 19 Mar. 1941, WCM–UCC–8 / 174

276   Dr Harrison Mullett: Arnup to Bell, 9 Dec. 1941, WCM–UCC–8 / 175; interview with Mrs Bea Mullett, CBC *Ideas*, Apr. 1984

276   Dr Richard Brown: Brown to Horace Watts, 24 Dec. 1941, MSCC-98, 'Dr Richard Brown'

276   Holy Cross missionaries: PAC External file 3050-U-40

276   'carried away in a Japanese': Venerable Bernard T.L. Tseng, Archdeacon of Eastern Honan, 'State of the Church in the Diocese of Honan, China, during and after the War,' received 14 Dec. 1946, MSCC-85, 'Ven. Bernard Ts'eng 1938-46'

277   'I still have a policeman': Susie Kelsey, Kweiteh, extracts of a letter 2 Aug. 1942, MSCC-121, 'Honan Correspondence 1940-48'

277   'educators, ex-marines': 'Report on Internment Conditions in the Far East compiled from Questionnaires answered by Canadian Nationals Repatriated in December 1943,' PAC External RG 25 G 2, file 4464-D-40 (access 1983-84/259): Part A-9, 'Internment of Allied Nationals at: Peking British Embassy Internment Camp'; Part A-1 'Manner of Internment: Hong Kong'; Part A-2 'Accommodation: Pootung, Stanley, Kobe'

278   Eric Liddell: David Michell, 'I Remember Eric Liddell' (pamphlet reprint from East Asia's Millions) 1984; interview with David Michell, CBC Ideas, June 1984; interview with Mrs Florence Liddell

278   Chefoo schools: Cliff, Courtyard; see also Sheila Miller, Pigtails, Petticoats and the Old School Tie (OMF press 1981) 137ff

279   'It was easy to stew': interview with S. Gordon Martin, Mar. 1979

279   'We had never seen people': 1984 Michell interview

280   's.o.s.': Angus, White Pagoda 117

280   'no more Christian': 1979 Martin interview

281   'the resilient young men': Sewell, Strange Harmony 102

281   'broad humanitarian directives': U.S. Department of State 'For the Press,' 12 Jan. 1944, in PAC External RG 25 G 2, file 3051-D-40 'Safety of CIM'

282   'these petitions': Rev. W.S. Simpson, Chengchow, to L. Dixon, 11 Dec. 1942, MSCC-121, 'Honan Correspondence 1940-48'

282   'the days of Arcadia': Sewell, Strange Harmony 105, 166-9, 182

283   'Historia concordatorium': Anthony Rhodes, The Vatican in the Age of the Dictators 1922-1945 (New York 1974) 39-40

283   'a greater degree of confinement': 'Report on Internment Conditions,' Part A-9 'Internment of Allied Nationals at: Peking British Embassy Internment Camp'

284   'You are probably asking': Le Précurseur (Mar. 1946) 480

284   Manchukuo: PAC External RG 25 G 2, file 3050-M-40 'Safety of Missions-Etrangères'; file 3050-J-40 'Safety of Frères des Ecoles Chrétiennes'; file 3050-K-40 'Safety of MIC'; 3050-L-40 'Safety of Clercs de St-Viateur'; 3050-

H–40 'Safety of Soeurs Antoniennes de Marie'; see also *Le Précurseur* (Jan. 1946) 415*ff*

285   'When captured': deposition of Br. Marie-Médéric, in PAC External RG 25 G 2, file 3050-J-40

285   'Nothing, absolutely nothing': Bertha Crévier, 'Après 40 Ans: Souvenirs de Manchourie,' *Le Précurseur* (July 1985) 274

285   'except those too distant': Edouard LaFlèche, 'Histoire du diocèse de Süchow,' *Lettres du Bas Canada* (Mar. 1953) in SJA, 'Agence Fides'

285   'encouraging enough': Albert Dupuis SJ, 'Litterae Annuae: Mission de Süchow, 1941-42,' in SJA, 'Süchow: Relations Annuelles'

286   Death of three Jesuits: 'Lettres Annuelles de la Mission de Süchow, 1942-43,' in ibid.; Morley Scott, for DEA, to Emile Papillon SJ, Montreal, 22 Apr. 1943, and Memorandum No. 52, 21 Jan. 1944, in PAC External RG 25 G 2, file 3050-P-40 'Safety of Jesuits'

286   'They will be escorted': 'Lettres Annuelles 1943-44'

286   'Twenty months of rest': Rosario Renaud SJ, *Süchow '48: Ad Usum Nostrorum Tantum* (Montreal 1949) 5, in SJA, 'Relations Annuelles'

286   'will give, it seems to me': 'Lettres Annuelles de la Mission de Süchow 1944-45,' in ibid.

287   'The end of the war': 'Lettres Annuelles de la Mission de Süchow 1945-46,' in ibid.

CHAPTER 14 The Last Days: Silence

289   'It should surely not be odd': Dr Gladys Story Cunningham, *The Observer* (15 Feb. 1949) 6

289   'haywire': Rev. Gerald S. Bell, Chengtu, to Dr Jesse Arnup, Toronto, 4 May 1943, in WCM-UCC-9 / 216

289   'too little and too late': Brown, *History* CIX-5

289   Planning conference: MSCC-87, 'Conference 1944'

290   'So long as we had': Bell to Arnup, 24 Feb. 1942, WCM-UCC-9 / 196

290   Canada's Mosquito airplanes: see Kim Richard Nossal, 'Business As Usual: Canadian Relations with China in the 1940s'; Liao Dong, *Chester A. Ronning and Canada-China Relations, 1945-1954* (MA Diss., University of Regina 1983)

291   'long time refused': Rev. Fred A. McGuire, 'Catholic Welfare Committee of China,' in *China Missionary* (Sept. 1950) 250

291   'scattered congregations': Brown, *History* CX-1

291   'spent hours in prayer': ibid. CXI-1

291   'For fourteen years': ibid. CIX-6

291 'an excellent job': ibid. CX-7

292 'some semblance of idealism': ibid. CXI-5-6

292 'With trained mechanics': ibid. CX-7

292 'the hospitals in China': ibid. CX-9-11

292 'beyond all words': ibid. CX-5

292 'acquiesced under severe pressure': ibid. CXIII-2

293 'enjoy the protection': Mao Tse-tung, 'On Coalition Government' (1945) in Donald E. MacInnis, *Religious Policy and Practice in Communist China: A Documentary History* (New York 1972) 14

293 'was a real revolution': Dr R.B. McClure, interview, CBC *Ideas*, June 1984

294 'Communism as carried out': G.K. King, 'Conditions in North Honan, June 1, 1947' This document received wide but secret distribution: Ambassador T.C. Davis sent it from Nanking to External Affairs, 16 June 1947, DEA file 50055, Vol. 4; meanwhile DEA had already received copies from missionary sources. The DEA passed it on to the U.S. Department of State.

294 'We expect Chinese Christians': Lu Ting-yi, Chairman of the Administrative Yuan's Committee on Culture and Education, 'Speech to 151 Protestant Leaders Meeting in Peking (Apr. 1951),' in MacInnis, *Religious Policy* 32-3

294 'Christianity consciously or unconsciously': 'The Christian Manifesto: Direction of Endeavor for Chinese Christianity in the Construction of New China,' ibid. 158-60; see also supplementary 'United Declaration of the Delegates of Chinese Christian Churches, Issued by a Conference of 151 Protestant Church Leaders Convened by Chou En-lai in Peking (Apr. 16-21, 1951),' ibid. 97-100

295 'help the People's Government': 'Chinese Christian Methodist Church Patriotic Covenant,' Apr. 1951, ibid. 101

295 'And so you just lost': Rev. John A. Austin, interview, CBC *Ideas*, June 1984

296 'Now we can join the angels': Bishop Lindel Tsen, Kaifeng, to L.A. Dixon, 25 Sept. 1945, in MSCC-85 'Bishop Tsen 1930-45'

296 'I am not in any way': Tsen to Bishop White, 6 Feb. 1946, ibid. 'Bishop Tsen 1946-47'

296 'There was no inkling': W.C. White, 'Service in the Diocese of Honan June 1, 1946 – July 14, 1947,' MSCC-87, 'Bishop White's Report'

296 'I don't like this China': W.C. White to Daisy Masters White, 28 Aug. 1946, in UT / WCW, box 35

297 'to investigate the social': Dixon to Department of Immigration, 13 May 1948, MSCC-85, 'Rev. C.Y. Cheng 1948-49'

297 'a study on his own': Dixon to Margaret Brown, Christian Literature Society in Hong Kong, 31 Jan. 1953, MSCC-86, 'News from China 1952-53'

297   'Is it not true that communism': Cheng to Dixon, 7 Apr. 1949, MSCC-85, 'Rev. C.Y. Cheng 1948-49'

297   'Long before the liberation': Memorandum 30 June 1954, MSCC-86, 'News from China 1952-53'

298   'no doubt there is some connection': Dixon to Brown, 31 Jan. 1953, ibid.

298   'We who are Christians': Brown to Dixon, enclosed clipping, 25 Jan. 1952, ibid.

298   'so ominous we shrink' White to Dixon, 20 June 1952, ibid.

298   'troubling the hearts': 'Lettres Annuelles de la Mission de Süchow, 1945-46,' SJA, 'Süchow: Relations Annuelles'

299   'Those schools were fundamental': R.P. Edouard Côté, Suchow, to T.C. Davis, Chungking, 28 Jan. 1948, PAC EA 3050-P-40 'Safety of Jesuits'

299   'Don't be afraid': Le Précurseur (Nov. 1946) 732

299   'the year of the martyrs': Gretta Palmer, God's Underground in Asia (New York 1953) 29

300   'courses in Marxist indoctrination': Father Antonio Bonin, Mon Témoinage (Montreal 1955) 31

300   'The fuse is still burning': Lionel Groulx, Le Canada Français Missionnaire 120

300   Albert L'Heureux: See Palmer, God's Underground 28-9; SJA, 'R.P. Albert L'Heureux'; clipping from Lettres du Bas-Canada (Jesuit, Mar. 1962)

301   'pagan rituals and correct them': Paul Serruys, 'Christian Adaptation of Wedding Ceremonials,' China Missionary 1 (1948), in SJA

301   'The persecution of the Church': Palmer, God's Underground 42

301   'shock troops': ibid. 64

301   'apparitions, revelations': Mgr Stanislas Lokuang, 'Le Culte de Notre-Dame en Chine,' Eglise Vivante (1949) in SJA, 'Notre-Dame en Chine'

301   'Rome of the first 300 years': Palmer, God's Underground 65

301   'Offer unto God': 'Lettre du Pape aux Chrétiens de Chine,' Prêtre et Missions (Montreal, Jan. 1953) in SJA, 's s Pie XII: Aux Chrétiens de Chine'

302   'Week by week the list': Palmer, God's Underground 136

302   'a simple talk between him': 'A Propos de Mgr. Riberi,' La Documentation Catholique (19 mai 1974) in SJA, 'Monseigneur Antonio Riberi'

302   Riberi's rumoured recognition: G.S. Patterson, Canadian Consul-General, Shanghai, to External, telegram No. 212, 5 Oct. 1949, and telegram No. 216, 17 Oct. 1949, PAC EA 50055-B-40, Vol. 1

302   'line: hold on': 'Directives pour la Situation Presente,' China Missionary (Dec. 1948) in SJA, 'Mgr Antonio Riberi'

302   Orphanage of the Holy Ghost: see scrapbook of clippings in MICA, 'Soeurs Prisonnières'; for possible Canadian government funding, G.S. Patterson,

Chungking, to External, 7 July 1943, and reply, 30 Aug. 1943, PAC EA 3050–K-40; see also Palmer, *God's Underground* 192-9; Jean Monsterleet, *Martyrs in China* (Chicago 1956) 223-7; for intervention by Indian Ambassador to China, see S. Panikkar, Peking, to C.A. Ronning, Nanking, 25 June 1951, PAC Odlum Papers, MG 30 E 300, Vol. 11, 'Ronning'

303   'sanitary conditions': *Hong Kong Standard* (5 Dec. 1951) in MICA scrapbook

303   Didace Arcand: Ferdinand Coiteux, *Père Didace Arcand, OFM,: Martyr du Communisme a Chéfoo le février 1952* (Montreal 1961) 41; see also Palmer, *God's Underground* 291

303   'miserable hovel': Groulx, *Le Canada Français* 122

303   'The ruins continued': ibid. 121; and 'The end of everything': ibid. 96

304   'According to Communist law': Cornelius Pineau, SJ, 'Süchow 1952-53,' *Lettres du Bas-Canada* (Mar. 1954) in SJA, 'Agence Fides'; see also 'Süchow sous régime communiste'

304   'Instituting the Legion of Mary': Maxwell, *Assignment* 150

304   'sitting by the window': ibid. 151

304   'the Church of Silence': Palmer, *God's Underground* 137

304   'You shall not go out': Isaiah 52: 12

305   'They did not want us to leave': Austin, CBC *Ideas* interview

306   Evacuation of CIM: Phyllis Thompson, *China: The Reluctant Exodus* (Sevenoaks, Eng. 1979); see also Miller, *Pigtails* 179-96

306   'At the end of April': *China's Millions* (June 1951) 88

307   'I don't hear anything': John and Ruth McRae, SCM Tokyo, 'Newsletter No. 6,' 25 Apr. 1953, MSCC-86, 'News from China 1952-53'

307   John Birch: A.T. Steele, *The American People and China* (New York 1966) 129

307   'On medieval maps': *The Reporter* (13 Nov. 1951) clipping in PAC Odlum papers MG 30 E 300, Vol. 11, 'Ronning'

307   'Here is a big hostile': Steele, *American* 60

308   'Did I tell you about my trip': J.H. Arnup to H.J. Veals, 21 Mar. 1950, WCM-UCC-13 / 329

308   Chester Ronning: see Chester A. Ronning, *A Memoir of China in Revolution* (New York 1974); Liao Dong, *Chester A. Ronning and Canada-China Relations, 1945-1954*

309   'Chinese Communism an evil': T.C. Davis to External, 16 June 1947, DEA 50055-40, Vol. 4

309   'almost a direct contradiction': V.O. Odlum, Ankara, to External, 13 Jan. 1948, DEA 50055-40, Vol. 4

309   'It must be the two of you': Odlum to Madam Chiang Kai-shek, Washington, 21 Dec. 1948, enclosed in Odlum to External, 24 Dec. 1948, DEA 50055-40, Vol. 4

310   'disjointed mass of inconsistencies': Davis to External, 27 Dec. 1948, DEA 50055–40, Vol. 4, and 7 Jan. 1949, ibid. Vol. 5

310   'who has had more faith': Davis to External, 28 Jan. 1949, DEA 50055–40, Vol. 5

310   'I am afraid that Uncle Sam': Davis to External, 27 Dec. 1948, ibid. Vol. 4

310   'such a hatred for Communism': Davis to External, 28 Jan. 1949, ibid. Vol. 5

310   'You speak Chinese or you don't talk': Davis to External, ibid., Vol. 5

311   'one-trick pony': Brian Evans, 'Ronning and Recognition: Years of Frustration,' paper presented at the conference on Canada–China Relations: Sources and Conduct of Canadian Policy, 8–10 May 1985, Montebello, Quebec

311   'When you stand for months': Ronning to External, telegram 23 Feb. 1950, DEA 50055–B–40, Vol. 5

311   'It is hard to see': Escott Reid, 'Memorandum for Mr. Arnold Heeney: Some Notes on Mr. Davis' talk on China,' 27 Oct. 1949, DEA 50055–B–40, Vol. 2

311   'equality, mutual benefit': Ronning to External, telegram 3 Oct. 1949, DEA 50055–B–40, Vol. 2

311   'in view of your long': External to Ronning, 2 Jan. 1951, PAC External 4558–Q–40, Vol. 2

312   'will soon be re-established': Dong, *Ronning* 271

312   'I am sure you appreciate': External to Ronning, 7 Mar. 1951, PAC External 4558–Q–40, Vol. 2

312   'Fatima or World Suicide': *Scarboro Missions* (May 1955); see copy also in DEA 6466–B–40, Vol. 4

313   'As a Catholic and as a Canadian': DEA file 6646–B–40 Vol. 6 has at least 150 copies of this petition, mostly from New Brunswick

313   'an atomic bomb or two dropped': Jacques Ferron, letter to the editor, 'Nos Savants,' *La Presse*, 14 Jan. 1960, clipping in SJA, 'Mgr Côté'

313   'The greatest mistake': letter to L.B. Pearson, 14 Feb. 1950, DEA 6466–B–40, Vol. 1

313   'We can inform ourselves': Lewis Walmsley, *University of the Air*, 18 Nov. 1958, CBC Archives 581118–1D

315   'active participation in political': Stephen Endicott, *J.G. Endicott, Rebel Out of China* 233; see also UCA bio. file

315   'jeopardizing the influence': Bell to Endicott, quoted in J.H. Arnup, 'Dr. J.G. Endicott and the Board of Overseas Missions,' *The Observer* (15 Mar. 1948)

315   'fellowship should be willing to lead': Joint Executive minutes, 2 Mar. 1946, Dr Leslie Kilborn to Arnup, 11 Mar. 1948, WCM–UCC–12 / 295

315   'boasting': J.G. Endicott, interview, CBC *Ideas*, Apr. 1984; see also Arnup, 'Dr J.G. Endicott'

316   'kicked out of the United': Arnup to Veals, 19 Mar. 1948, WCM–UCC-12 / 291

316   'He is suing the Toronto *Telegram*': Arnup to Dr Leslie Kilborn, 28 Apr. 1948, WCM–UCC-12 / 295

316   'I am a Christian': *The Observer* (15 June 1962) 17

316   'On Monday last his father': Arnup to H.J. Veals, 9 Jan. 1948, WCM–UCC-12 / 291

316   'a large part of the Church': Melville Buttars, *The Observer* (15 May 1948) 17

316   'wide and sympathetic': Arnup to Veals, 19 Mar. 1948, WCM–UCC-12 / 291

317   'I am not a reactionary': Arnup to L.E. Willmott, 10 Jan. 1948, WCM–UCC-12 / 292

317   'The crucial need for our Church': *The Observer* (1 July 1948) 4

317   'if possible they will visit': ibid. (1 Oct. 1947) 1

317   'Why cannot J.G. Endicott': ibid. (15 Aug. 1948) 17

317   'About 90 per cent': ibid. (1 Nov. 1948) 21

317   'I believe there is a very small': Dr Gladys Cunningham, 'A Missionary Looks at China,' *The Observer* (15 Feb. 1949) 6

318   Arnup's 'optimistic' interview: 'For Private Circulation – Not to be published,' 21 Nov. 1949, WCM–UCC-12 / 309

318   'a hoard of refugees': L.G. Kilborn to Arnup, 23 Sept. 1948, WCM–UCC-12 / 295

318   'Ministers – Leave your pulpits': *The Observer* (1 June 1947) 24

318   'Our people like the general tone': Veals to Arnup, 16 Aug. 1950, WCM–UCC-13 / 329

319   'learning to participate': 'Living Through It,' *The Observer* (1 July 1950) 4

319   'I know nothing about Mr Willmott': ibid., 1 Sept. 1953 21

319   Dr Stewart Allan: A.S. Allen, 'I Was a Prisoner of the Chinese Reds,' *Maclean's*, in UCA bio. file; *Reminiscences of a China Surgeon*, autobiographical ms in Dr Allen's possession; interview, CBC *Ideas*, 15 June 1984

319   Earl Willmott: see UCA bio. file, "Lesslie Earl Willmott'; UTA bio. file; L.E. Willmott, 1971 York University interview

320   'For me it was a relief': Dr Jean Kilborn to Mrs Margaret Outerbridge, Toronto, 11 Apr. 1952, WCM–UCC-14 / 362

320   'Earl is spoken of "as a dangerous': Jean Kilborn to Edwin and Gladys Cunningham, 1 Apr. 1952, Ibid.

320   'germ warfare': Endicott, *Endicott* 289–303; UCA bio. file

321   'punishment': clipping in UCA Willmott bio. file; see also 1971 York University interview

321   'splendid article': *The Observer* (1 June 1952) 8

321   'If evil is there': *Toronto Daily Star* (18 Sept. 1952); clipping in UCA bio. file; see also *Record of Proceedings of Fifteenth General Council, Hamilton, September, 1952* 61

322   'missing golden opportunities': Arnup, 'Memo to China Missionaries,' 24 Apr. 1951, WCM–UCC–12 / 341

322   'Absolutely no public appearances': Mrs H.D. Taylor, 'To WMS China Missionaries,' 11 July 1951, ibid.

322   'The last message from friends': Dr Jean Kilborn to the Cunninghams, 29 Mar. 1952, WCM–UCC–14 / 362

322   'lost, gone, extinguished': E.L. Willmott, 1971 York University interview

322   'took the train from Canton': Langlais, *Les Jésuites* 76

322   Helen Willis: C.J. Small, Canadian Trade Commissioner, Hong Kong, to External, 28 Apr. 1959, DEA 52–AE–1–40

323   Father Paul Kam: Maxwell, *Assignment* 151; Dr Victoria Cheung, see UCA bio. file

EPILOGUE The Lost Churches

325   'The China of the year 2000': Sir Robert Hart, *These from the Land of Sinim* 49

325   'The missionaries have been building': Arnold Lea, quoted by Mrs Emma Austin, interview with the author, CBC *Ideas*, 5 June 1984

325   'I can remember giving my story': Katharine Hockin, interview with the author, CBC *Ideas*, May 1984

326   'Minority groups with minority': Donald E. MacInnis, *Religious Policy and Practice in Communist China* 94

328   'do things just the way': Hockin, 1984 CBC *Ideas* interview

328   'If you judge by appearances': Sister Theresa Chu, interview with the author, CBC *Ideas*, 19 Apr. 1984

328   'The Church taught us to hate': Maxwell, *Assignment* 155

329   'The only Church that will be': *The Observer* (15 June 1953) 5

329   'we in the West': David Michell, interview with the author, CBC *Ideas*, June 1984

329   'The terrific joy of the two trips': Hockin, 1984 CBC *Ideas* interview

330   'Protect us, we are foreigners': Paul Jolliffe; many others recount similar stories

330   'the small white clean': Jerome Ch'en, *China and the West* 149; see also Theodore F. Harris, *Pearl Buck: A Biography* (New York 1969) 81

330   'not better but different': Brockman Brace, ed., *Canadian School in West China* (Toronto 1974) 132

330   'I feel we were brought up': ibid. 138

330   'We did a lot of talking': ibid. 139

331   'must have the best training': Rijnhart, *With the Tibetans* 165

331   'unbalanced and neurotic': Miller, *Pigtails* 116

331   'the only childhood I knew': ibid. 101

332   'We were sacrificed on the altars': ibid. 101

332   'astringent and ascetic': ibid. 113

333   'We are at the top': Brace, *Canadian School* 132

333   'We were not poured': ibid. 140

334   'There is a responsibility in being a product': Fay Angus, *The White Pagoda* (Wheaton, Ill. 1978) 9

334   'My first responsibility is to make myself': *Canadian School* 133

334   'A thousand, thousand pages': ibid. 308

Index

This book
was designed by
WILLIAM RUETER RCA
and was printed by
University of
Toronto
Press